P9-CLA-037

The Canadian West Saga

❖

The
Canadian West
Saga

by

Janette Oke

Inspirational Press
New York

First Inspirational Press edition published in 1995.

Inspirational Press
A division of Budget Book Service, Inc.
386 Park Avenue South
New York, NY 10016

Inspirational Press is a registered trademark of Budget Book Service, Inc.

Published by arrangement with Bethany House Publishers, a division of Bethany Fellowship, Inc.

Library of Congress Catalog Card Number: 95-75031

ISBN: 0-88486-112-0

Text designed by Hannah Lerner.

Printed in the United States of America.

CONTENTS

*When
Calls the
Heart*
1

*When
Comes the
Spring*
165

*When
Breaks the
Dawn*
359

*When
Hope Springs
New*
507

WHEN CALLS
THE HEART

To my oldest sister,
Elizabeth Margaret (Betty) Cox,
for having the patience
to let me "pull the needle,"
and for many other reasons.

CONTENTS

1   Elizabeth   7
2   The First Step   16
3   On the Way   19
4   Calgary   22
5   Family   27
6   Introductions   31
7   Mr. Higgins' Plan   40
8   The New School   46
9   The Wilderness   53
10   Lars   57
11   The Petersons   61
12   Trip to Town   64
13   Saturday   68
14   Sunday   70
15   School Begins   74
16   Joint Tenants   77
17   Sunday Service   82
18   Letters   84
19   The Living Mousetrap   87
20   A Visitor   90
21   Pupils   93
22   The School Stove   96
23   Plans   101
24   Napoleon   108
25   The Box Social   111
26   Andy   116
27   School Break   118
28   Dee   124
29   Return to School   128
30   The Christmas Program   134
31   Christmas Eve   138
32   Christmas Day   144

33 The Confession   148
34 Return to Pine Springs   152
35 Spring   154
36 School Ends   159

PREFACE

I would like to supply my readers with a few facts concerning the North West Mounted Police. The Force was founded in 1873 as an answer to the problem of illicit liquor trade and lawlessness in the West. It has been said that the Mountie was dressed in a red coat to readily set him apart from the U.S. Cavalry. The Mountie's job was to make peace with the Indians, not to defeat them; and many of the Indian tribes which he had to deal with had already had run-ins with the troops from south of the border. Whether for this reason, or some other, the scarlet tunic soon became distinctive, and set apart the man who was wearing it.

The uniform and the name both evolved. The title of *Royal* North West Mounted Police was granted by King Edward VII in 1904, in recognition of the Force's contribution to Canada. In 1920, the name was changed to Royal *Canadian* Mounted Police. Eventually, the red coat was adopted as the dress uniform of the Force, and a more practical brown coat was chosen for regular duty, because, said Superintendent Steele, it was "almost impossible for even a neat and tidy man to keep the red coat clean for three months on the trail." The hat also changed from the original pillbox, through various shapes and designs, to the Stetson that was approved in 1901.

It was the Yukon Gold Rush of 1895 that first brought the Mounties into the Far North. By 1898 there were twelve officers and 254 sergeants and constables in the Yukon. The Mounted Police by then were using a new form of transportation—the dog team. With the use of their huskies, they policed hundreds of square miles of snow-covered territory. Trappers, traders and Indian villages were scattered throughout their areas of patrol.

Although I try not to be *too* sentimental when I think of the Mounties and their part in the development of the Canadian West, to me, they are a living symbol of my Canadian homeland. To the people of the Lacombe area, may I assure you that among the names of Spruceville, Blackfalds, Brookfield, Turville and Iowalta; Woody Nook, Jones Valley, Canyon and Eclipse; Eureka, Spring Valley, Arbor Dale and Blindman; Central, West Branch, Birch Lake and Lincoln; Milton, Mt. Grove, Sunny Crest and Morningside; Gull Lake, Lakeside and Fairview; you will find no Pine Springs. Nor will you find a historic character that matches Pearlie's pa in the town of Lacombe itself. All of the characters in the story are fictional, with no intended likenesses to anyone either living or dead.

May I also assure you that having grown up in the Hoadley area and having spent my early school years in the little one-room school at Harmonien, I have a great deal of love for and many fond memories of rural Alberta community life.

1
Elizabeth

IT CAME AS a great surprise to me. Oh, not the letter itself. We were all used to the arrival of letters from brother Jonathan. They came quite regularly and always caused a small stir in our household. No, it wasn't the letter, but rather what it contained that caught me completely off guard. And Mother's response to it was even more astounding.

The day, April 12, 1910, had started out like every other day. I arose early, had a quiet prayer time in my room, cared for my grooming, breakfasted with the family, and left at 8:00 to walk the eleven blocks to the school where I taught. I had made it a habit to be there early so that I would have plenty of time to make my morning preparations before the students arrived. I was usually the first teacher to make an appearance, but I rather enjoyed the early morning quietness of the otherwise noisy building.

As I walked along on that delightful spring morning, the world appeared especially beautiful and alive. For some reason, the flower-scented air and the song of the birds caused me to take a rare look at my inner self.

And how are you this delightful spring morning? I asked myself.

Why, I am just fine, thank you, I silently answered, and then almost blushed as I quickly looked around for fear that someone might be able to read my thoughts. It wasn't like me to talk to myself—even inwardly, especially when walking along this public, maple-sheltered street. But no one shared the sidewalk with me at the moment so the self-dialogue continued.

Are you now? And what is it that makes your day so glorious—your step so feather-light?

The morning; life itself; the very fragrance of the air I breathe.

'Tis nice—but, then, you have always been a soul who took pleasure in just being alive. I do declare that you would be happy and contented anywhere on God's green earth.

No—not really Not really.

The sudden turn of the conversation and the switch of my emotion surprised me. There was a strange and unfamiliar stirring deep within me. A restlessness was there, begging me to give it proper notice. I tried to push it back into a recessed corner of my being, but it elbowed its way forward.

You're always doing that! it hotly declared. *Whenever I try to raise my head, you push me down, shove me back. Why are you so afraid to confront me?*

Afraid?

Yes, afraid.

I'm not afraid. It's just that I believe—I've been taught—that one ought to be content with what one has, especially if one has been as blessed as I. It is a shame—no, a sin—to feel discontented while enjoying all of the good things that life—and Papa—have showered upon me.

Aye, t'would be a sin to disregard one's blessings. I should never wish you to do so. But perhaps, just perhaps, it would quiet your soul if you'd look fairly and squarely at what makes the empty little longing tug at you now and then.

It was a challenge; and though I still felt fearful, and perhaps not a little guilty, I decided that I must take a look at this inner longing if the voice was ever to be stilled.

I was born Elizabeth Marie Thatcher on June 3, 1891, the third daughter to Ephraim and Elizabeth Thatcher. My father was a merchantman in the city of Toronto and had done very well for himself and his family. In fact, we were considered part of the upper class, and I was used to all of the material benefits that came with such a station. My father's marriage to my mother was the second one for her. She had first been married to a captain in the King's service. To this union had been born a son, my half brother, Jonathan. Mother's first husband had been killed when Jonathan was but three years old; Mother therefore had returned to her own father's house, bringing her small son with her.

My father met my mother at a Christmas dinner given by mutual friends. She had just officially come out of mourning, though she found it difficult to wrap up her grief and lay it aside with her mourning garments. I often wondered just what appealed most to my father, the beauty of the young widow or her obvious need for someone to love and care for her. At any rate, he wooed and won her, and they were married the following November.

The next year my oldest sister, Margaret, was born. Ruthie then followed two years later. Mother lost a baby boy between Ruthie and me, and it nearly broke her heart. I think now that she was disappointed that I wasn't a son, but for some reason I was the one whom she chose to bear her name. Julie arrived two years after me. Then, two and a half years later, much to Mother's delight, another son was born, our baby brother, Matthew. I can't blame Mother for spoiling Matthew, for I know full well that we shared in it equally. From the time that he arrived, we all pampered and fussed over him.

Our home lacked nothing. Papa provided well for us, and Mother spent hours making sure that her girls would grow into ladies. Together my parents assumed the responsibility for our spiritual nurturing and, within the proper boundaries, we were encouraged to be ourselves.

Margaret was the nesting one of the family. She married at eighteen and was perfectly content to give herself completely to making a happy home for her solicitor husband and their little family. Ruth was the musical one, and she was encouraged to develop her talent as a pianist under the tutorship of the finest teachers available. When she met a young and promising violinist in New York and decided that she would rather be his accompanist than a soloist, my parents gave her their blessing.

I was known as the practical one, the one who could always be counted on. It was I whom Mother called if ever there was a calamity or problem when Papa wasn't home, relying on what she referred to as my "cool head" and "quick thinking." Even at an early age I knew that she often depended upon me.

I guess it was my practical side that made me prepare for independence, and with that in mind I took my training to be a teacher. I knew Mother thought that a lady, attractive and pleasant as she had raised me to be, had no need for a career; after all, a suitable marriage was available by just nodding my pretty head at some suitor. But she held her tongue and even encouraged me in my pursuit.

I loved children and entered the classroom with confidence and pleasure. I enjoyed my third-graders immensely.

My sister Julie was our flighty one, the adventure-seeker, the romantic. I loved her dearly, but I often despaired of her silliness. She was dainty and pretty, so she had no trouble getting plenty of male attention; but somehow it never seemed to be enough for her. I prayed daily for Julie.

Matthew! I suppose that I was the only one in the family to feel, at least very often, concern for Matthew. I could see what we all had done to him with our spoiling, and I wondered if we had gone too far. Now a teenager, he was too dear to be made to suffer because of the over-attention of a careless family. He and I often had little private times together when I tried to explain to him the responsibilities of the adult world. At first I felt that my subtle approach was beyond his understanding, but then I began to see a consciousness of the meaning of my words breaking through. He became less demanding, and began to assert himself in the proper sense, to stand independently. I nurtured hope that we hadn't ruined him after all. He was showing a strength of character that manifested itself in love and concern for others. Our Matt was going to make something of himself in spite of us.

My morning reverie was interrupted by the particularly sweet song of a robin. He seemed so happy as he perched on a limb high over my head, and my heart broke away from its review of my family to sing its own little song to accompany him.

Well, I thought when our song had ended, *the restlessness does not come because I do not appreciate the benefits that God has given me, nor does it come because I do not love my family.* Some of the feeling of guilt began to drain away from me. I felt much better having honestly discovered these facts.

So . . . I went on, Why am I feeling restless? What is wrong with me?

Nothing is wrong, the inner me replied. *As you said, you are not unappreciative nor uncaring. Yet it is true that you are restless. That does not prove that you are lacking. It is just time to move on, that's all.*

To move on? I was as incredulous as if the answer had come from a total stranger.

Certainly. What do you think brings the robin back each spring? It is not that he no longer has his nest nor his food supply. He just knows that it is time to move on.

But to move on WHERE? How?

You'll know when the time comes.

But I'm not sure that I want—

Hush.

I had never even considered "moving on" before. I was very much a "home person." I wasn't even especially taken with the idea of marriage. Oh, I supposed that somewhere, someday, there would be someone, but I certainly had no intention of going out looking for him, nor had I been very impressed with any of the young men who had come looking for me. On more than one occasion I had excused myself and happily turned them over to Julie. She also seemed pleased with the arrangement; but the feelings of the young men involved, I must shamefully confess, concerned me very little.

And now I was to "move on"?

The uneasiness within me changed to a new feeling—fear. Being a practical person and knowing full well that I wasn't prepared to deal with these new attitudes at the present, I pushed them out of my mind, entered the sedate brick school building and my third-grade classroom, and deliberately set myself to concentrating on the spelling exercise for the first class of the morning. Robert Ackley was still having problems. I had tried everything that I knew to help him. What could I possibly try next?

I went through the entire day with a seriousness and intent unfamiliar even to me. Never before had I put myself so totally into my lessons, to make them interesting and understandable. At the end of the day I was exhausted, so I decided to clean the blackboards and go home. Usually I spent an hour or so in preparation for the next day's lessons, but I just didn't feel up to it this time. I hurriedly dusted off the erasers, shoved some lesson books into my bag, securely fastened the classroom door behind me, and left the three-story building.

The walk home refreshed me somewhat; I even saw the robin with whom I had sung a duet that morning! I felt more like myself as I climbed our front steps and let myself in. Mother was in the small sunroom pouring tea that Martha, our maid, had brought. She didn't even seem surprised to see me home early.

"Lay aside your hat and join me," she called. I detected excitement in her voice.

I placed my light shawl and hat on the hall table and took a chair opposite Mother. I felt I could use a cup of strong, hot tea.

"I got a letter from Jonathan," Mother announced as she handed me my cup.

I assumed then that her excitement was due to Jonathan's letter, or the news that it contained.

Jonathan was still special to Mother. Being her firstborn and only child from her first marriage, he was also her first love in many ways. Julie had on occasion suggested that Mother loved Jonathan more than the rest of us. I tried to convince Julie that Mother did not love him *more*—just differently.

I often thought how difficult it must have been for her to give him up, to let him go. Jonathan had been just nineteen when he decided that he must go west. I was only four years old at the time and too young to really understand it all, but I had been aware after he left that something was different about our home, about Mother, though she tried hard not to let it affect the rest of us. Three months after Jonathan had left, baby Matthew had arrived, and Mother's world had taken on new meaning. Yet not even Matt had taken Jonathan's place in her heart.

And now Mother sat opposite me, calmly serving tea, though I could tell that she felt anything but calm. Whatever the news in Jonathan's letter, I sensed that Mother was excited rather than concerned, so her tenseness did not frighten me.

"How is he?" I asked, choosing to let Mother pick her own time and words for revealing her excitement.

"Oh, just fine. The family is well. Mary is feeling fine. She is due soon now. Jonathan's lumber business is growing. He had to hire another clerk last month."

It all sounded good. I was happy for this older brother whom I barely remembered, yet somehow I felt that Mother's present mood did not stem from any of the facts that she had so hurriedly stated. I mumbled a polite response about being glad for Jonathan's good fortune and sipped my tea. I did wish that Mother would get to the point.

Mother didn't even lift her cup; instead, she reached into the bosom of her gown and removed Jonathan's recent letter. We were all used to her doing that. Whenever a letter from Jonathan arrived, she would read it through a number of times and then tuck it in the front of her dress. She carried it around with her for days and would pull it forth and reread it whenever time allowed.

She carefully unfolded it now. But rather than pass it to me as she normally did, she began to hurriedly read aloud. She passed quickly through Jonathan's greetings as though she was anxious to get to the real heart of the letter. As I continued to sip my tea, I could hear the excitement growing in her voice. She suddenly slowed down, and I knew that she intended for me to hear and understand every word.

"'There is no end to opportunities here in the West. I know several men who came out with nothing and who now have great homes and flourishing businesses. All that one needs is determination, stamina and a bit of horse sense.'"

Surely Mother isn't contemplating urging Papa to move West was the foolish thought that popped into my mind. Mother read on.

"'I have given a great deal of thought to my family lately. It would be so good to have one of my own here. I miss you all so much. Especially you, Mother, but you know that.

"'It's easy to think of the West as a man's land, and so it is; but there are plenty of opportunities here for women as well. And I might add that we in the West realize that if we are to grow strong, we need fine young women to make homes for our men and ensure proper families for our future.'"

I must have grimaced some as I thought, *What a cold, calculating way to look at marriage.* But Mother continued without interruption—I had missed a few words.

"'. . . so I thought of Elizabeth.'"

Confusing thoughts exploded in my mind. *Elizabeth? Me? Me WHAT? Is he suggesting that I go bargain-hunting for some western shopkeeper or backwoods rancher for a husband? Not me! Never! Never!* I felt that I would rather die first.

The blood had drained from my face as I started to rise from my chair. "Never," I whispered to myself. But Mother had paid no attention to my soft gasp and hurried on.

"'Teachers are sorely needed here. Many mothers in country areas still must tutor their children. But these women have little time and no training. We are anxious to change all of that. We want our next generations to be well educated, because in the future we hope to pick the leaders of our new province from among our own.

"'You say that Elizabeth is a fine teacher and a sensible young woman— and I am sure that she is. I talked today with a school superintendent whom I know. He is short of teachers, and some of those that he does have, he would replace if he could. He says that if Elizabeth is willing to come west, he would gratefully give her a position, and, as I said before, it would be so good to have someone from my family here.'"

Stunned, I watched Mother's eyes continue on down the page, but she was reading silently now. I got the impression that I was temporarily forgotten and that her thoughts were with her beloved son Jonathan somewhere out West.

I was glad for those few moments to compose myself before I had to meet her eyes again. Jonathan was actually proposing that I go west. For what? Before he had suggested the teaching opportunities, he had written that they needed young women to "ensure proper families." Well, I in no way intended to help them do that. Definitely not!

I hoped that Mother wouldn't be too hard on Jonathan when she replied to the letter. I knew that he had meant well, though he must have known that our mother would never agree to a daughter of hers, on the pretense of teaching, going off to the wilds to find herself a man. *Even if that isn't Jonathan's intent at all, I reasoned, and he is simply looking for more teachers, I have a perfectly good teaching position right where I am.*

Mother finished reading Jonathan's rather lengthy letter and again tucked it in her bosom. Her tea had grown cold, but she absently reached for her cup and sipped from it with a faraway look in her eyes. I was on the verge of, "Look, Mother, don't let it upset you. Jonathan meant well, but you needn't fear. I have no intention of taking it seriously, . . ." when she lifted her eyes from her cup and looked directly at me. I expected a mild reprimand of Jonathan, but instead she said simply, "Well?" She smiled at me, and I could easily detect eagerness in her voice.

I was startled and flustered.

"Well?" I questioned back, wondering just what she meant. I couldn't understand Mother's rather extraordinary reaction to Jonathan's preposterous proposal. *Is she actually thinking that I would even give the matter consideration? How CAN she? Surely she must see that it is totally . . .* And then in a flash it came to me. I was to be Mother's love-offering to Jonathan, his "piece-of-the-family" presented to him over the miles. Somehow my going west to be with him would bring comfort to my mother's heart.

I loved her. She was a dear mother. Never would I wish to hurt her. I didn't dare bluntly blurt out that the whole idea was outlandish and that Jonathan had been foolish even to suggest it. With Mother sitting there before me, the "well" still lingering in her gaze, I couldn't say no. But could I say yes? Definitely not. But I could say maybe, until I had taken time to think this whole thing through, to sort it out in my mind, and to plan some way I could get out of it without hurting my mother.

"Well—it's—it's such a surprise. I'd—I'd never thought of the possibility of leaving—of going . . ."

My mind fumbled about for words but found none to still the look of concern creeping into Mother's eyes. I willed my confused mind into control and hurried on.

"It sounds—interesting—very interesting." I tried to put some sparkle into my voice, but it was difficult when I could hardly get the words past my tight throat.

Mother relaxed some, and her eyes began to shine again. It was a moment before I realized that they were bright with unshed tears. I felt almost panicky. I *couldn't* disappoint her—at least not at the moment. I tried to swallow away the lump in my throat and forced a smile as I put down the fragile china cup.

"It's—well—I'll—I'll do some thinking about it and we'll—well, we'll see. . . ."

Mother reached out and touched my hand. The tears spilled a bit from her eyes, wetting her dark lashes and dropping onto her cheeks.

"Beth," she said, "there is no one whom I would rather send to Jonathan than you."

I was touched, but frightened. I swallowed hard again, attempted another smile and rose from my chair. After a light kiss on Mother's forehead, I excused myself. I had to get away, alone, where I could think. My whole world was spinning around, and I felt that if I didn't soon get control of things, I would end up hurling off somewhere into space.

I was willing to *consider* being Jonathan's love-package-from-home, for Mother's sake. Yes, I was even willing to consider teaching out West. But as for marrying some uncouth, unkempt man out of the frontier, *there* I drew a definite, solid line. Never!

Later that evening, Papa knocked quietly at my door. I had been trying to read in bed, a luxury that I normally enjoyed, but somehow Jane Austen's young women had failed to intrigue me.

He walked to my window and stood looking out at the quietness of the city. The street lamps flickered softly against the gathering darkness. I waited for him to speak; but when he said nothing, I laid aside my book, pushed myself up to a sitting position, and asked softly, "You've talked to Mother?"

He cleared his throat and turned from the window. He still didn't speak—just nodded his head.

"And what do you think?" I asked, secretly hoping that he would exclaim that the whole idea was outrageous and unthinkable. He didn't.

"Well—," he said, pulling up a chair beside my bed, "at first it was a bit of a shock. But after I thought it through for a while, I began to understand why your mother is rather excited about the whole thing. I guess it could be an adventure for you, Elizabeth, and, it would seem, not too risky a one."

"Then you think I should—"

"Consider it? Yes, consider it. Go? Not necessarily. Only you will be able to decide that. You know that you are loved and wanted here, but should you want this—this new experience, we will not hold you back."

"I don't know, Papa. It's all so—so new. I don't know what to think about it."

"Elizabeth, we trust you to make the right decision, *for you*. Your mother and I have agreed to abide by it. Whatever you decide, we want it to be what *you* feel you should do. Your mother, as much as she would love to see you go to Jonathan, does not want you to feel pressured to do so if it's not what you want. She asked me to tell you that, Elizabeth. She is afraid that your loyalty and desire to please her might lead you to go for her sake. That's not enough reason to make such a life-changing decision, Elizabeth."

"Oh, Papa! Right now I'm all butterflies. I never dreamed—"

"Don't hurry, my dear. Such a decision needs much careful thinking and praying. Your mother and I will be standing behind you."

"Thank you, Papa."

He kissed my forehead and squeezed my hand.

"Whatever you decide . . . ," he whispered as he left my room.

I didn't pick up Jane Austen's book again. I knew that now for certain I couldn't concentrate on the words. So I pulled the chain to put out the lamp and punched my pillows into what I hoped would be a sleep-inducing position. With the covers tucked carefully about me, I settled down for the night. It didn't work. It was a long time until I was able to fall asleep.

2

The First Step

THE NEXT FEW days were full of soul searching. I was so preoccupied that I sometimes wondered if I were actually teaching my students. They didn't seem to notice any difference in me, so I guess that I was at least going through the proper motions.

As she promised, Mother didn't press me; but I could sense that she was anxiously waiting for my decision. I knew that she was praying too. I did hope that she truly was leaving it to the Father's will and not merely pleading for Him to "send me forth."

I wavered—which was unusual for me. One moment I would think of all those that I loved: my family, my students, my church friends; and I would inwardly cry out, "I can't go, I just can't!" The next instant I would think of that part of my family in the West. Something invisible was drawing me to the older brother whom I had never really known. I also thought of all those children without a teacher, and I knew that they, too, wished to learn. I even considered the great adventure that this new opportunity held, and I would find myself reasoning, *Why not? Maybe this is the answer to the restlessness within me. Maybe I should go....*

Back and forth my feelings swung, like the pendulum on our grandfather clock.

After considerable debate and prayer and thought, I felt directed to Joshua 1:9: "Be strong and of a good courage; be not afraid, neither be thou dismayed: for the Lord thy God is with thee whithersoever thou goest."

I repeated the passage out loud and felt my anxieties relax into peace. I would go.

Mother was almost beside herself with joy and excitement when I told her. Julie begged to go with me. I loved Julie and I was sure that there would be many times in the future when I would wish for her company; but the thought of trying to watch over a girl like Julie, in a land filled with men looking for brides, fairly made me shiver. I was glad when Papa and Mother promptly told her no.

Another month, and the school year came to a close. I waved good-bye to the last pupil, packed up all my books and teaching aids, and closed the door of the classroom carefully behind me for the last time. Blinking back some tears, I said good-bye to my fellow teachers and walked away from the school without looking back.

I had let Mother tell Jonathan about my decision, and he seemed over-joyed that I actually was coming. He even wrote a letter to *me*, telling me so directly. His and Mother's excitement seemed to be contagious, and my desire to see my brother was growing daily.

Jonathan had passed the word to the school superintendent, and he, too, hurried a letter off to me. Mr. Higgins (the name somehow suited my mental image of him) assured me that he was pleased to hear that I would be coming west; and, his letter stated, he would give care and con-sideration in assigning me to the school that he felt was right for me, and he would be most anxious to meet me upon my arrival.

The days, filled with shopping, packing and finally shipping my be-longings, passed quickly.

Jonathan had said that anything I could spare should be shipped early. The freight cars had a tendency to get shuttled aside at times and often took longer for the trip than the passenger cars. I secretly wondered if Jonathan wasn't using this as a ploy, reasoning that the shipped-ahead trunks would be a measure of insurance against a girl who at the last moment might wish to change her mind.

It could have happened, too. When the day arrived that Papa and I took my trunks to the freight station and I presented my belongings to the man behind the counter, the realization fully hit me that I was taking a giant step into the unknown. Somewhat dazed, I watched my trunks being weighed and ticketed and finally carted away from the checking desk on a hand-pulled wagon. In those trunks were my books, bedding, personal effects, and almost my entire wardrobe. It seemed to me that a large part of my life was being routinely trundled away. For a moment fear again tightened my throat, and I had an impulse to dash out and gather those trunks back to myself and hurry back to the familiar comfort of my own home and room. Instead, I turned quickly and almost stumbled out of the building. Papa had to break into full stride in order to catch up to me.

"Well, that's cared for," I said in a whispery voice, trying to intimate that I was glad to scratch one more task from my awesome list. I think that Papa saw through my bluff. He answered me heartily but completely off the subject. "Saw a delightful little hat in that smart little shop beside Eatons. I thought at the time it was just made for you. Shall we go and take a look at it?"

Some men despise being seen in a lady's shop. My father was not one of them. Perhaps it had something to do with the fact that he had four daughters and an attractive wife. Papa loved to see his women dressed prettily and took pleasure in helping us to choose nice things. Besides, he was well aware of the fact that a new hat was often good medicine for feminine woes—especially when the difficulty was no more serious than a butterfly stomach.

I smiled at him, appreciative of his sensitivity. Who would pamper me when I was away from Papa? I took his arm and together we headed for the little shop.

Papa was right. The hat did suit me well; the emerald-green velvet looked just right with my dark gold hair and hazel eyes. I liked it immediately and was glad that he had spotted it. In fact, I decided right then and there that I would wear it upon my arrival in Calgary. It would give me a measure of confidence, and I had a feeling I would need all of it that I could get.

As we rumbled home in our motor car, I again thought of what a thoughtful man I had for a father. I reached over and placed my hand on the arm of his well-cut suit. I would miss him. I used my handkerchief to wipe some tears from my eyes, murmuring something about the wind in my face. There was still a week before I would board the train. I didn't need to get soft and sentimental yet.

3

On the Way

I FIDGETED ON the worn leather of the train seat, willing my nerves to quit jumping and my heart to quit its thunderous beating. I would soon be arriving in Calgary. The very name with its unfamiliar ring made my pulse race.

I would soon be seeing my brother Jonathan. My memories were vaguely outlined in the shadowy figure of a tall, gangly youth with a strong will of his own. I would also be meeting his wife, Mary, whom he declared to be the sweetest and most beautiful woman on the face of the earth. And I would be introduced to four little children—one nephew and three nieces. I was prepared for them, having purchased sweets at our last stop. Children were easy to win, but would my brother and my sister-in-law be pleased with me? Was I ready to step out of the relative safety of the train into a strange, new world?

My four slow-moving days on the Pacific Western, spent sitting stiffly in cramped train seats, and even slower-passing nights, had been gradually preparing me. I finally had been able to overcome my intense homesickness. The first three days I had missed my family to such an extent that I feared I might become ill. Gradually the ache had left, and in its place there now seemed to be only a hollow.

As the pain had left me, I had been able to find some interest in the landscape, which seemed amazingly different from what I was accustomed. Jonathan had tried to describe the land to me in his letters, but I had not visualized the emptiness, the barrenness, the vastness of it all. As I gazed out the train window, it seemed that we traveled on forever, seeing hardly any people. Occasionally we did pass small herds of animals—antelope, deer and even a few buffalo, roving slowly across the prairie, and delaying the train once in a while as they lazily crossed the iron tracks.

I had expected to see Indian teepees scattered all across the countryside. But in fact, I saw very few Indians at all, and they were almost all in the small towns that we passed through, looking very "civilized" indeed. I saw no braves painted for the warpath. Most Indian people moved quietly along the streets, concerned only with their own trading activities.

Now we were nearing the frontier town of Calgary, the home of my brother Jonathan and many other adventuresome persons. What would it be like? Would it be at all modern? After I had made my decision to go, Julie had read all she could find about the West. Where she discovered all of her information, I never did learn; but at any hour of the day or night that she could corner me, she would announce new "facts" she had gathered. According to her, the West was full of reckless, daring men, so eager for a wife that they often stole one. (I wasn't sure that she disapproved.) Julie painted word pictures of cowboys, voyageurs, miners and lumbermen—all roaming the dusty streets in their travel-stained leather and fur, looking for excitement, women, wealth and danger, though not necessarily in that order. And Indians—everywhere Indians. Though most were rather peaceable now, she was sure they still wouldn't hesitate to take a scalp if the opportunity existed. This irrepressible sister of mine had even dared to whisper that perhaps I should bob my hair so none of them would be overly tempted by my heavy mass of waves. She warned me that they might find my dark gold curls with their red highlights irresistible.

"My scalp, complete with its hair, is quite safe from the Indians," I had assured Julie, but I will admit that she made me shiver a few times. She had nodded solemnly and informed me that I was probably right and it was all due to the fortunate fact that the West now had the North West Mounted Police. According to Julie, they were the West's knights in red-serge armor, and Calgary abounded with them. Should the need ever arise, a lady had only to call, and Red Coats would come running. Judging from the sparkle in Julie's eye as she described this scene, I would have expected her to avail herself of their services quite regularly.

Julie had also claimed that Calgary was a land of perpetual blizzard. It stopped snowing only long enough to allow an occasional "chinook" to blow through, and then the cold and neck-deep snow would again take over.

Calgary was now only minutes away, according to the conductor, and on this August afternoon, with the hot sun beating down unmercifully upon the stuffy coach, I realized that Julie had been wrong at least on this one point—unless, of course, this was just one of those chinooks. Still, I couldn't help but wonder if Julie may have been mistaken about some other "facts" as well. I would soon see. In my impatience I stood up to pace the floor.

There really wasn't much room for walking, and I got the impression that my stalking back and forth in the narrow aisle was irritating to some of the other passengers. I smiled my sweetest smile at those nearest to me. "After sitting so long, I simply must work some of the knots out of my muscles before we reach Calgary," I explained. I hoped that they didn't realize it was in reality nerves rather than stiffness that drove me from my seat.

I walked to the end of the aisle and was nearly hit by the door when it swung open before the returning conductor. He looked at me with a startled expression and then got on with his job which was at this point to call out in a booming voice, "Calgary!—Calgary!" He passed through the car and into the next, still calling.

A bustle of activity followed in his wake as people gathered their belongings, said good-byes to new acquaintances, donned jackets or shawls, and put on bonnets or hats that had been laid aside. I used the reflection from the window glass to adjust my new green bonnet.

The train blew a long, low whistle. One could almost feel exhausted thinking of the amount of steam necessary to produce such a sound. Then the clickity-clack of the wheels began to slow down till I was sure that if one would choose to concentrate on the task, each revolution could be counted. We were now traveling past some buildings. They appeared rather new and were scattered some distance apart. Most were constructed of wood rather than the brick or masonry which I was used to back home. A few of the newest ones were made of sandstone. The streets were not cobblestoned, but dusty and busy. Men and, thankfully, some women too, hurried back and forth with great purpose. The train jerked to a stop with a big hiss from within its iron innards like a giant sigh that the long journey was finally over. I sighed too as I stood and gathered my things from the seat where I had piled them neatly together. Working my way toward the door, half-step by half-step in the slow-moving line of fellow passengers, I couldn't keep my eyes from the windows. It was all so new, so different. I was relieved to spot many men in business suits among the waiting crowd. It was a comfort of sorts to realize that the men of the West were not all rough-and-ready adventurers.

And then through the crowd, seeming head and shoulders above all others, I noticed two men in red tunics and broad-brimmed Stetsons. Julie's Mounties! I smiled to myself at the thought of her excitement if she were here! Even their walk seemed to denote purposefulness, and though people nodded greetings to them, the crowd seemed to automatically part before them out of respect. I bent down a bit so that I could get a better view of them through the window. I was immediately bumped from behind by a package tucked beneath the arm of a rough-looking man with a cigar in his mouth. I flushed and straightened quickly, not daring to meet his eyes.

When it was finally my turn, I carefully stepped down, grateful for the assistance of the conductor with all my parcels and a small suitcase. When I had negotiated the steps, I looked up into the smiling eyes of an almost stranger—yet somehow I knew instantly that it was Jonathan. Without a moment's hesitation I dropped what I was carrying and threw my arms around his neck.

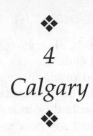

4
Calgary

❖

DESPITE MY PROPER upbringing, I was sorely tempted to stare at everything that our automobile passed on the way to Jonathan's house. Never in my life had I seen a town like Calgary! Cowboys on horseback maneuvered expertly between automobiles and pedestrians in the dusty street. Two ladies, their long skirts lifted daintily, crossed quickly in front of us. And there was a real Indian, in dark coat and formal hat with a long braid down his back! I tried desperately not to let my extreme fascination at the interesting activities around me show, but I guess I failed.

Jonathan chuckled, "Calgary is a show-off, isn't it, Elizabeth?" As the color moved slowly into my cheeks, he courteously turned his eyes back to the road so as not to embarrass me further. He had not lived so long in the West as to forget that it was improper for a lady to stare.

"Do you know that I've lived in this town for almost sixteen years, and I still can't believe what is happening here?" Jonathan continued matter-of-factly. "It seems that every time I drive through the streets another building has sprung up. It reminds me of when I was a child at Christmastime. I went to bed at night with the familiar parlor as usual; but in the morning, there was a bedecked tree, festooned with all manner of strings and baubles and glittering candles. The magic of it! No wonder children can easily accept fantasy. And this is almost like a fantasy, don't you think, Elizabeth?"

I could only nod my agreement, too spellbound to speak. I turned my head to glance back over the way that we had just come. We had climbed steadily as we left downtown Calgary. Jonathan's home must be up on a hill rather than in the valley beside the river.

As I looked back down the street, I could see the buildings of Calgary stretched out across the flatness of the valley. Water sparkled in many places, reflecting the afternoon sun. I looked in awe at the scene and finally found my voice.

"The river—it seems to twist and turn all around. Everywhere I look, there seems to be another part of the stream."

Jonathan laughed. "There are *two* rivers that merge down there. They're called the Bow and the Elbow."

"Unusual names."

"Yes, I guess they are. You'll find a number of strange names in the West."

I smiled. "Well," I conceded, "I will admit that we have our share of strange names in the East, too."

Jonathan nodded, a grin spreading over his face, and I could almost see names like Trois-Rivieres and Cap-de-la-Madelaine flitting across his mind.

"Tell me about Calgary." I just couldn't wait to learn something about this intriguing town.

Jonathan gave me an understanding smile.

"Where do I start?" he asked himself. "Calgary was founded as a fort for the North West Mounted Police in 1875—not so long ago, really. It was first named Fort Brisebois, but Macleod, the commander, didn't care much for that name, I guess. He renamed her Fort Calgary—this is a Gaelic word, meaning clear, running water—after his birthplace in Scotland."

"Clear, running water," I repeated. "I like it. It suits it well."

I looked again at the portions of the rivers that gleamed between the buildings and the thick tree growth of the valley.

Jonathan continued, "After the railroad was built in 1883, people began to take seriously the settling of the West. It was much easier to load one's belongings on a train than it had been to venture overland by wagon. And with the train, the women were even able to bring with them some of the finer things of life that previously had to remain behind.

"In the earlier days mostly adventurers or opportunists moved westward, and though a fair share of those still came, many dedicated men and women arrived each year hoping to make a home for themselves in this new land."

"It was still difficult, wasn't it?" I questioned.

"Fortunately for us, the Mounties got here before the bulk of the settlers. The new people at least had law to appeal to if the need arose— and the need often did. The Indians had already learned that the Red Coat could be trusted—that a lawbreaker, no matter the color of his skin, would be brought to justice. The Mounties helped to make Calgary, and the area around it, a safe place for women and children."

"That doesn't sound like the West which Julie told me about."

"Oh, we've had our skirmishes, to be sure, but they've been few and far between; and the North West Mounted Police have been able to restore control rather quickly."

"Have the Indians been *that* bothersome?" I asked, wondering if Julie had been right after all.

"Indians? Can't rightly blame the Indians. Most of the trouble comes from the makers of fire-water."

"Fire-water?"

"Whiskey. Well, I guess it can't really be called whiskey, either. It was known more often as—pardon me, please—as 'rot-gut.' It had an alcohol base, but the brewers threw in about everything they could find to give it taste and color-—pepper, chewing tobacco, almost anything. Don't know how anyone could drink the stuff, but some braves sold furs, their ponies—even at times a squaw—just to get hold of a few bottles."

"That's terrible!"

"It ruined many of the choicest young Indian men. Threatened whole tribes, at times. Some of the chiefs saw the danger and hated the rotten stuff, but they were hard put to control its evil. Wicked, horrible stuff! A real disgrace to the white men who peddled it at the expense of wasted, human lives." Jonathan shook his head, and I could tell that the previous trade of illegal liquor disturbed him greatly.

"Anyway," he continued, brightening, "the North West Mounted Police were organized, found their way west in spite of extreme hardship, and went right to work on the problem. Their first big job was to clean up Fort Whoop-Up."

"Whoop-Up," I chuckled. "That's even stranger than Elbow. Is that around here?"

"Doesn't even exist anymore. It was in Southern Alberta about six miles from where Lethbridge is now located. They say the things that went on there would make your hair curl. Old Johnny Healy operated the place, and his vile concoction could purchase about anything he wanted. One cup of his whiskey would buy him a choice buffalo robe. Old Johnny made himself rich. He gathered together a group of rascals with like leanings—rum-runners, wolvers, law-dodgers, and the like. He built himself a nice little fort for them all to flock together in. Nobody knows exactly how many were living there; in fact, the estimates seem to vary a lot, but, at any rate, it seems that there were *too* many. At times they went too far, drank their own whiskey and went on the rampage. It was some of the wolvers who eventually brought the whole thing to an end. They were led by a man who had, somewhere in his past, developed a real hatred for the Indians. He had already shown his hostility on more than one occasion. When a few bucks made off with his ponies, it wasn't enough for him to try to get his horses back. Instead, he used it as an excuse to start shooting. He and his men murdered several Indians at a place called Cypress Hills—they didn't seem to care that those Indians weren't even of the same tribe as the horse thieves."

"Was nothing done?"

"Word got back East, along with an urgent appeal to Prime Minister Sir John A. McDonald. He sped up the organization of the new police force for the West and sent them out as quickly as possible. That's why the North West Mounted Police were hurried westward."

"To bring justice, law and order to the West?"

"Right! From the start they had their work cut out for them. One of their jobs was to gain the confidence and respect of the Indians. After what had been happening between the Indians and the whites, you can believe that job wasn't any small task. But they managed it. The white offenders were brought to trial, and the Indians began to see that they had friends in the Force who wore red coats.

"The motto of the new Force was 'Maintien le Droit'——'Uphold the Right,' and they worked hard and long to accomplish just that."

"And the Indians did learn to accept them?" I asked.

"I guess Red Crow, the head chief of the Blackfoot Nation, sort of summed it up when he signed the treaty of 1877. This wise and cunning old man was speaking of Macleod at the time, but the same could have been said about the other commanders of the Force as well. Red Crow said, 'He has made many promises, and *kept* them all.'"

I had sat motionless, listening to Jonathan. What if Julie had been there to hear him? Thanks to all of the romantic notions with which she had filled her mind, she would be swooning at the very possibility of meeting one of the West's great heroes in red! Even with my more practical outlook, I was stirred by this background on the Mounties and their part in Canadian history. Certainly many men and women—not to mention a nation—owed them a great debt of gratitude. I added my thanks to the already lengthy list, then promptly shifted my thoughts to the present, content to place the North West Mounted Police back in history where I felt they belonged.

"How much farther?" I asked Jonathan.

"I must confess," he answered with a twinkle in his eye, "I have taken you on the scenic route. We could have been home several minutes ago, but I just couldn't wait to show you our—" He stopped in mid-sentence and looked at me with concern. "You must be tired, Elizabeth. I'm afraid my enthusiasm was ill-timed."

"Oh, no. I'm fine. I've truly enjoyed it," I quickly assured him. "It's all so new and so different, I'm—"

"Just one more thing, and I'll hurry you home—Mary will have my hide anyway. She's so anxious to meet you, and so are the children."

We topped a hill, and there before us was the most beautiful scene that I had ever beheld. I had seen glimpses of the mountains as the train rolled toward Calgary, but the panorama which lay before me now was indescribable. The mountains seemed near enough to smell the tang of the crisp air and feel the freshness of the winds. I didn't say anything. I couldn't. I sat and looked and loved every minute of it. Jonathan was pleased. He loved the mountains; I could sense that.

"That," he said at length, "is why I would never want to leave the West."

"It's beautiful beyond description," I finally managed to say, exhilaration springing up within like a fountain. To live and move and work in the shadow of those awe-inspiring mountains was more than I had ever dreamed of. A little prayer welled up within me, *Thank you, God, for the unexpected. Thank you for pushing me out of my secure nest.*

All too soon, it seemed, Jonathan turned the automobile around, and headed us down the hill and back into town.

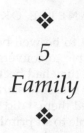

5

Family

MARY WAS WAITING at the door when we pulled up in front of the house and she ran to meet me as I stepped down from the auto. She pulled me into a warm embrace almost before my feet had a chance to properly settle on the ground. I was glad for the enthusiastic welcome and immediately felt I was with family.

I studied the woman who was Jonathan's wife, my sister-in-law. A wealth of reddish-brown hair was scooped rather casually in a pinned-up style. Curly wisps of it teased about her face and neck, giving her a girlish look. Her green eyes sparked with merriment and her full mouth produced the warmest of smiles. I smiled in return.

"Oh, Elizabeth," she exclaimed, "it is so good to meet you!"

"And you, Mary," I returned. "You are just as Jonathan described you."

She hurried me toward the house to meet the children while Jonathan busied himself in gathering up my belongings.

We passed right through the main hall and out a back door to a shaded yard that seemed to be filled with shouting, wiggling small bodies. These were my nieces and nephew. At once they made a dash for me; they were not at all reserved or inhibited. It did appear that they believed the coming of an aunt was a great event.

When Mary had restored order, I was able to meet each one of them in a quieter fashion.

At eight, William, the eldest, looked like Jonathan except that his hair had a reddish tinge which he had inherited from Mary. Sarah, six, was small and dainty; if any of the offspring could have been deemed retiring, Sarah would have been the one. Kathleen was next. This four-year-old looked like she should have been a boy; mischief sparkled out of her intensely blue eyes, and her pixie face was always fixed in a grin. Baby Elizabeth, named for my mother, had only recently joined the family and was much too young to take part in the present merry-making. She slept through the whole commotion.

After a quick tour of the house, the evening meal was served, and we gathered around the table. Jonathan believed that the family should share this special time of day, and so the children joined us at the table. As I watched them clamber into chairs, I wondered just what Mother would have thought of the whole event. In our home, children, even quiet, well-mannered ones, did not join the adults at the table until they had passed their twelfth, or at the earliest, tenth birthday.

Jonathan's children proved to be well-behaved in spite of their high spirits, and we adults were able to converse, uninterrupted by childish outbursts. It was obvious that they had been instructed well as to how to conduct themselves. *Maybe it is wise to start them young at the family dinner table*, I decided as I watched them. I did wonder as I studied Kathleen just how long she would be able to sit primly like a little lady. She looked like a miniature volcano about to erupt.

The meal, served by a maid named Stacy, was absolutely delicious. I was embarrassed at the amount of food I ate. Jonathan assured me that the crisp air affected one's appetite; I was glad to have something to blame it on.

"I'm so glad that you could come a few days early," Mary said. "Now we have opportunity to get to know you before you commence your teaching duties. We do want to show you around, and—" she added with a twinkle in her eye, "to show you off."

I smiled at her.

"Indeed," teased Jonathan, "I have a whole list of young men waiting to meet you. I finally gave up trying to keep track of who was to be first. I told them that they would just have to stand in line and wait their turn, but I'm afraid . . ."

My cheeks grew warm and I interrupted Jonathan before he could go on. "I'm quite happy to meet your friends," I announced firmly, "but I do want to make one thing clear: I came west to *teach*, not to *wed*. Had I been interested in matrimony, I could have stayed in the East and found an acceptable spouse. Julie, who by the way is our family expert on the subject, assures me that the men of the West are adventurers—undependable, rough and rowdy. I don't know if her research is totally reliable, but I've no intention of finding out. If you want a wife for one of your friends, you'd best bring out Julie. She'll be more than willing to consider the possibility. I? Never!"

It was a rather long speech under the circumstances, and the faces of the listeners changed from unbelief, to concern, to amusement. When I finished, I saw Jonathan steal a glance at Mary to see if she considered me serious. She gave him a barely visible nod, and he understood her to mean that I was. He cleared his throat, then waited a moment.

"I see," he said slowly, "that we shouldn't tease you so. Here we often forget the manners that our mothers tried so hard to instill in us. We tease and jest all the time. It helps the road to smooth out when it might otherwise be rough.

"Of course we have no intention of marrying you off." He then added with great sincerity, "But I could this night, personally, introduce you to a dozen good, clean, mannerly, well-bred gentlemen who would make your Eastern dandies look pale in comparison. But I won't do it," he hurried on, "lest my intentions be misconstrued."

I knew exactly what he was implying and realized with embarrassment that I deserved this mild rebuke for my tactlessness and bad manners. My face was suddenly drained of all color. I knew that I should apologize for my outburst, but somehow I couldn't get the words through my tight throat.

Jonathan chuckled, and the sound of his soft laugh eased the tension around the table. "I promise, little sister," he said with feigned seriousness, "to make no effort to see you married if you have no desire to be so. But, looking at you, I'd say you will have to get that message across yourself to more than one young man."

Mary seemed to agree. She didn't say anything—only smiled—but the warmth of that smile carried with it approval of her sister-in-law's appearance.

My cheeks flushed again, for a different reason this time. I was willing to assume the responsibility of getting that message across, if need be.

"I've had to do it before," I said calmly, "and I'm quite confident that I can again."

A small voice broke in. "When I grow up, I'm gonna marry Dee."

Everyone shared in the laughter; even I, who did not have the slightest notion who Dee was.

As Mary wiped the tears of laughter from her eyes she attempted to enlighten me. "Dee is a very dear friend. He's already close to thirty and as determined as you, my dear, to stay single."

"He's *my* friend," Kathleen insisted.

"Of course he is, sweetie. Now finish your dinner."

When we rose from the table, a wave of tiredness flooded over me. I wondered if I'd be able to hold out while Mary went to tuck in the children.

It was early yet, and I knew that it was unthinkable to ask to be shown to my room, and yet that was the very thing that I longed to do. Jonathan noticed it.

"You must be dead on your feet. Why don't you go and have a warm bath and get to bed early tonight? I never could get a proper night's sleep on one of those rumbling trains. The time change makes a difference too. According to Eastern time, it's now your bedtime."

I admitted that I was terribly weary.

"Go on, then," he insisted. "Your door is the first one on the right at the top of the stairs. The bath is in the room next to yours. After your long trip I'm sure you will enjoy relaxing in a tub again. I've already put your things in your room. I'm off to hear the children's prayers now, so I'll tell Mary. She will understand. There's plenty of time ahead for us to catch up on everything."

I thanked him and climbed the stairs. I could hardly wait to crawl into that tub. I sincerely hoped I would still have the energy to make it from the tub to the bed.

Soon I would need to write Mother and tell her all about Jonathan's lovely home and beautiful family. It was evident that the West had dealt very kindly with him. Mother would be proud. Jonathan himself had been very modest in his letters home, but I had no inhibitions about painting for Mother the complete picture.

Jonathan's home, a large three-story dwelling with many gables and bay windows, was a lovely structure of red brick; the elaborate wooden trim around the whole house was painted white.

The interior was spacious and cool, furnished with pieces shipped from the East. Colorful carpets covered the floors, and rich draperies softened the windows. Only Jonathan's study showed the unique influence of the West. Here was locally built furniture, massive and impressive. The wall bore mounted animal heads. A bear rug sprawled in front of the fireplace, while a buffalo robe covered the couch.

But the letter would have to wait. Tonight I was too tired to even consider writing. Tonight I wanted only a bed. Tomorrow—well, tomorrow I hoped to somehow have another look at those gorgeous mountains. I would attempt to tell my family back East about them as well, but already I knew that whatever I could say would never do the mountains justice.

6

Introductions

It DID APPEAR indeed that Jonathan and Mary were anxious to show me around, and to show me off. Never had I spent such a busy ten days as those that followed my arrival in Calgary. It seemed as though I was constantly changing my dress for the next occasion. But I will admit that it was all exciting, and I'm afraid it threatened to go to my head.

I had arrived on a Friday and Jon (I discovered that he favored being called Jon, so I complied, though it did seem a shame to go from a beautiful name like Jonathan to one as simple as Jon)—anyway, Jon and Mary decided that after my long train journey, I needed Saturday to rest. I didn't rest much, for I needed to unpack my clothes for my stay. I spent most of the day washing and pressing my things.

I was able to get to know my nephew and nieces, for everywhere I went, there they were at my elbow. It was delightful.

William had already finished two years in the classroom and was held in awe by his sisters. Sarah would shyly plead, "Show me, William—tell me—'splain it to me, William." William did, his self-esteem showing in those hazel eyes under his shock of reddish hair.

Kathleen was a dear. Her expressions sparkled with mischief as she chattered and watched everything that I did. It was apparent that Jon and Mary were parents who carefully guided and controlled their children, for even the energetic and outgoing Kathleen was not bold in her venturing, though her eyes showed that she found it difficult to restrain her bursts of enthusiasm.

As I unfolded an emerald-green velvet frock from the tissues that I had carefully wrapped it in, her eyes took on a special shine, and one hand reached out to touch the softness of the velvet. She quickly checked herself and tucked both hands behind her back where they would be safe from temptation. Her eyes sought mine, their message a plea for forgiveness for what she had almost done; but soon they were filled with a gentle question.

"Does it feel like baby chickies?" she asked in almost a whisper.

"You know," I answered honestly, "I have never, ever had the privilege of touching a baby chickie."

"You haven't?" Her eyes were big, and I knew that she could scarcely believe my ill fortune. A look of sympathy followed the wonder.

"I'll tell Papa," she said, very matter-of-factly, and I knew that she was confident Papa would care for my obvious need.

"Have you held baby chicks?" I asked her.

"Oh, yes."

"Then you touch the dress and tell me if it feels the same."

She looked at me, her big eyes wondering if I really meant it. I moved the dress nearer to her to assure her that I did. She slowly reached out one hand and then stopped herself, her eyes meeting mine with a twinkle as she said, "Oh—Oh." The hands were both turned palms up. "I'd better wash them first."

"They look fine to me."

She shrugged. "I'd better wash them anyway. Mama says some dirt don't see—don't look—" She struggled for the right word.

"Doesn't show?"

"Yah."

She ran hastily from the room and was soon back. She had splashed water on her dress in her hurry, and the hands that she had been so concerned about were still damp where the towel had not been given a chance to do its proper job. She finished drying them by wiping them up and down on the sides of her dress as she approached the velvet gown. She stood for a moment looking at its richness. Then she reached out slowly and touched a fold. Gently the little hand stroked the cloth, careful to brush it only in one direction.

"It does," she whispered, "and like a new kitten, too."

I reached down and pulled her to me.

"Baby chicks must feel nice; and I *have* stroked a new kitten, so I know *that* feels nice—but do you know what feels the nicest of all?"

She tipped back her head and studied my face.

"Little people," I said softly.

"Like boys and—and girls?"

"Boys and girls."

She giggled, and then threw her arms around my neck and hugged me. I swallowed hard. How wonderful to be able to hold a child, to love unreservedly and have the love returned.

Sarah called, and Kathleen released her hold.

"She's probl'y gonna say, 'Kathleen, wash for lunch,' and I've already washed!" She took great pleasure in the fact that she would be able to side-step the command. She started a lopsided skip as she left the room, not yet old enough to do it properly. At the door she stopped and turned back. "Thank you, Aunt Beth," she called. She threw me a kiss, which I returned, and was gone.

A few minutes later we were indeed gathered for lunch. William held us up because he was off climbing trees with a neighbor; it took Sarah several minutes to locate him. He was scolded gently and sent to wash and change his shirt, which had a ragged tear on one sleeve. He reappeared a few minutes later, fresh shirt properly buttoned but not so properly tucked in, and his face and hands scrubbed, though one could easily see the water line at his chin. Mary's rueful smile accepted him as he was, and the meal was served.

"After lunch I want you children to play outside—*in the yard*," said Mary, looking pointedly at William. "Aunt Beth may want to nap."

"Oh, no, "I hurried to explain, "I still haven't finished caring for my clothes."

Even as I said the words I realized just how much I would love to take time for a little rest.

"Baby Lis'beth still naps," Kathleen said seriously, and I could tell that she felt very proud about being allowed to go without an afternoon sleep.

"Baby Elizabeth is lucky," declared Mary. I guessed that there were many days when she gladly would have curled up for a nap herself if she had been given the opportunity.

Kathleen did not argue, though it was evident from the look in her eyes that she did not agree with her mother.

The next morning, Sunday, the house was filled with activity as we prepared to attend the church service. Kathleen tapped timidly on my door while I was fixing my hair. She came in to show me her dress and ribbons. She looked like she should have been on a calendar. Her pretty clothes and careful grooming accented her pixie-like quality. Her eyes sparkled as she caressed the lace on her pinafore.

"Do you like it?"

"It's lovely."

"Mama made it."

"She did?"

"She did," she nodded.

"It's beautiful. Your mama is a very fine seamstress."

"That's what Papa says."

She then studied me. "You look nice, too. Did you make your dress?" I shook my head, thinking of the shop in Toronto where the dress had been purchased.

"No," I said slowly, "Madame Tanier made it."

"She's good, too," Kathleen said solemnly.

I smiled, thinking of the madame and her prices. Yes, she was good, too.

The church building was new, though not as large as the one I had been used to attending. The people were friendly, and it was easy to feel at home, especially because I came as Jon's sister. It was plain to see that they regarded Jon and Mary with a great deal of respect.

I sat between William and Sarah. It was difficult for William not to squirm. He shifted this way, then that, swung this foot, then the other, made fists, then relaxed them. I couldn't help but feel sorry for him. Kathleen did not fare much better than William. Sarah, on the other hand, sat quietly. At one point, when we stood to sing a hymn, she slipped a little hand into mine. I gave it a squeeze and smiled at her. She cuddled up to me like a little puppy.

After the service was over I was introduced to a number of the people. The congregation was made up mostly of young couples, though I did see several men who seemed to be unattached. I appreciated the fact that Jon did not steer me in their direction. He left me with Mary and a few of her friends and went over to greet the men by himself.

The minister, his wife and four children were invited to join us at Jon and Mary's for Sunday dinner. The Reverend Dickson had come west three years ago. He wanted to talk of nothing but the West and was full of glowing accounts of the great things that were happening all around him. Mrs. Dickson was eager to discuss anything and everything about "back home." I felt much like a tennis ball during the conversation.

The next day Jon and Mary invited Mr. Higgins, the district's school superintendent, for dinner.

I was anxious to meet Mr. Higgins and to find out about my new school, but I was nervous about it too. What if he didn't feel that I could do a proper job? A man with his great responsibility, who was conscientiously searching for just the right teachers for his needy schools, could be extremely fussy about whom he chose to fill those needs.

I pictured Mr. Higgins as a rather reserved and learned man, balding, maybe a bit overweight, carefully clothed and austere. His bearing, his manner, his very look would speak the seriousness with which he regarded his responsibilities.

When Sarah announced that Mr. Higgins had arrived, I hastened to the parlor, pausing at the doorway to compose myself for this important meeting. I was not prepared for what I saw.

At first, I must confess, my eyes searched the room for a third party; I was certain that the gentleman laughing and joking with Jon was not, nor could *possibly* be, School Superintendent Higgins. But while my gaze traveled round the room, Jon turned and introduced his guest as Mr. Higgins.

The man was rather young—about thirty-five, I guessed. He was not carefully groomed, nor was he dignified or austere. His appearance and his conversation indicated to me that he was sloppy, loud, arrogant and bold. I didn't like any of those things in a man.

I felt an inner check, quickly reminding myself that one must never make snap judgments based on first impressions. Even so, it was difficult for me to smile politely and extend my hand, but I did. Higgins nearly broke my fingers as he pumped a generous, manly handshake. He boomed out, "How d'ya do? How d'ya do?"

He didn't say that he was pleased to meet me, but I got the feeling that he was, for his eyes carelessly passed over my face and form. He seemed to approve, for he kept right on staring at me. I felt the color creeping into my face. Brother Jon came to my rescue.

"Let's be seated," he said. "I'm sure that Miss Thatcher is anxious to find out all about our school district."

Mentally I thanked Jon for using my formal name. Perhaps that would keep the forward Mr. Higgins at bay.

I voiced agreement with Jon. "Yes, I'm most interested in everything concerning the schools of this area, in particular the one that I will be serving."

"Later!" thundered Higgins. "I never spoil a good dinner by discussing mundane things like work before I eat."

He laughed loudly at what he considered his wit and turned to ask my impression of the West. I could tell by his voice that he felt there was nothing, anywhere, that could in any way come near to equalling *his* West. I replied that I had been in the West such a very short time that I really hadn't had a proper chance for evaluation. I wasn't sure that he accepted my statement. I sensed that he felt one shouldn't need time to clearly see the West's superiority. But instead of contradicting me, he said something about "showing me around." Jonathan again rescued me by steering the conversation to other subjects, and it wasn't long until Mary announced that dinner was served.

The roast beef was delicious. I would have loved the opportunity to enjoy it, but Mr. Higgins spoiled it for me. His open stare followed my every move, and I felt so nervous that I could scarcely direct my fork properly. I had never met such a man before, and I mentally conceded that I had finally met my first bore. So puffed up was he with importance and his own opinions that he monopolized and manipulated the entire conversation. My first impression had been correct: I did not care for Mr. Higgins, School Superintendent. Hopefully, all of the men in the West were not like this man.

We never did discuss the school system, though it seemed like hours and hours before he finally had sense enough to excuse himself and go home. As he prepared to leave, he asked if he could call again.

"Well," I said, hoping that he would catch my meaning in the tone of my voice, "we do need to talk about the school that I am to teach, and I need to find out what I will require. We haven't found *time* for that yet."

He guffawed as if I was delightful and squeezed my hand as he shook it. I pulled away.

"I'll see you Wednesday," he said, and he winked. I was shocked at his brazen manner and a little gasp of surprise escaped me. He didn't notice it, and bawled a merry "good-night" that I was afraid might awaken the sleeping children, then went whistling down the walk.

"Someone should marry that man and polish him up a bit," Mary said softly.

I shook my head and said, "It will take more than polish. I would not impose such a task on *any* woman."

On Tuesday Jon decided that I should be introduced to Calgary's shops, so he drove me downtown and left me while he went to his office. Mary had planned to accompany us, but William had an earache so she stayed with him.

The shops were certainly different from what I had been used to. I didn't see any that would compare with Madame Tanier's, but I did find them all most interesting. How I wished that Julie were with me. What fun we could have had!

Jon had promised to meet me for lunch at a nearby hotel, and as twelve o'clock approached I felt hungry. I decided to make my way to the dining room he had pointed out earlier. As I moved down the sidewalk, I was aware of many stares that followed me. I felt a small nervous twisting in my stomach. Perhaps it was unacceptable for a lady to walk alone in Calgary. I would have to ask Jonathan. I hurried my steps.

The Calgary streets were alive with variety. Besides the dark-suited businessmen, there were ranchers, farmers, Indians, and just plain loafers. I caught my breath and hurried past a rough-cut foursome who slouched against a hardware store. I could hear remarks and laughs, but I did not try to untangle any of the comments. I had no desire to know if they concerned me.

When I reached the hotel dining room, Jon was already there, ten minutes ahead of the appointed time.

"I didn't want you to arrive before me and have to stand around alone and wait," he said. I deeply appreciated his thoughtfulness.

We were led to a table, and as we moved through the room Jon greeted many acquaintances. For some parties he stopped and introduced me, to others he only nodded his greeting and called them by name. I began to see the pattern. When Jon stopped and made an introduction, it was always to a couple or to a married man. Jon would then make reference to Mr. ——, who with his wife and family lived on such-and-such a street, or operated such-and-such a business. The gentlemen that he by-passed were obviously single. Jon was keeping his word and making no effort to pair me off. I smiled to myself at his obvious attempt to comply with my wishes.

As I sat down I could see and feel stares following me. I laid aside my gloves and purse and smiled at my brother. I hoped that pretending to be at ease would make me feel less edgy. It worked at least in part. Jon took over and soon I felt quite relaxed, even in my new surroundings. I was becoming quite attached to my brother. It was no wonder Mother idolized him. I wished that she could see him here, in this town with his lovely wife and well-behaved children, with his prestigious position in the community. She would be so proud. I also felt proud as I sat opposite him, and momentarily I was able to forget the stares.

"By the way," he said cautiously, "your clothes are lovely. Mary thinks so too. But Mary—well—even though she envies you, she—well—she has suggested that I hint, tactfully, that you should maybe have a few things a bit more practical for school teaching. Our classrooms are not all that fancy, and, well—, I'm not good at hinting so . . ."

I laughed. Jon looked relieved.

"Whew," he said, "I'm glad that you took it that way. I wasn't sure whether you'd be annoyed or hurt. I'm just no good at beating round-the-bush. But Mary *is* right; your high-fashion clothing looks marvelous, but it's not too practical for our way of living."

Jon's sincerity and sweetness took all sting out of his words. I realized that he and Mary were right; it was love that prompted them to suggest the change in wardrobe.

"I'll see what I can find," I promised, as our food arrived.

"By the way," I ventured, "is it improper for a lady to venture out without an escort on Calgary streets?"

"Why? Didn't you meet any ladies this morning?"

"Yes—yes, I did, come to think of it. Several. But—"

Jon frowned.

"Well, I just felt out-of-place. Wherever I went, people stared."

Jon grinned.

"People—or men?"

I flushed. There was no need to continue the conversation.

Jonathan suggested some shops where I might find the type of clothing suitable for a western schoolmarm, and promised that he would meet me at three o'clock to drive me home. At first I thought there would be no pleasure in shopping for things that I considered drab and unstylish, but the more I looked the more I liked what I found, and the more fun it became. Again I wished for Julie's company. She would have turned the shopping trip into a hilarious occasion.

I found some simple cotton gowns that would be easy to wash and iron, and some undergarments without much lace. I even purchased heavier stockings; though, I must admit, I didn't care much for the looks of them. I had the clerk bundle up my purchases and checked the time. It was already past three o'clock. I hurried from the store, concerned that Jon might be waiting.

He was there, just a few steps down the street, his broad back turned to me. I hurried toward him and then noticed that he was in conversation with another man. I hesitated. Should I make my presence known in case Jon was in a hurry to get home, or should I wait until he had finished his conversation?

They shifted their position somewhat. I now could see the gentleman to whom Jon was talking. He was a bit taller than Jon, which made him tall indeed. A broad-brimmed hat shaded his eyes, but I noticed a strong, though not stubborn, jaw, and a well-shaped nose. He had a clear, clean-cut look, though one would certainly never consider him a "parlor-gentleman." There was a certain masculine ruggedness about him that suggested confidence and capability. He smiled good-naturedly as he spoke with Jon, and I imagined an easy friendliness and an appreciation for a good joke.

My slight movement must have caught his eye, for his head lifted. This caused Jon to look around.

"Be right with you, Beth," he said, and they shook hands heartily. "Greet Phillip for us," Jon said as he placed a hand on the man's shoulder. In return Jon received a friendly slap on the back; then the man turned to me. He nodded slightly, raising his hat as he did so, allowing me a full look into his eyes. They were deep blue—and determined; but they gave a glint of humor now, even though his lips did not move. I found myself wishing to see him smile, truly smile, but before I could offer one to encourage him, he turned and strode away.

I could not understand the strange stirring within me. I suddenly wished that Jon had broken his rule and introduced us. Never before had I seen a man who interested me so much. I stood staring after him like a schoolgirl.

"A—a friend?" I stammered, and then blushed at my foolishness. Surely Jon would think me silly; it would have been apparent to anyone that they were friends.

"Yes."

That was all my brother said. No offering of the man's name or where he was from—nothing. I determined not to pursue the matter.

The next day Mr. Higgins showed up a bit after two o'clock. I was hoping that he was ready to get down to business. but he wanted to take me for a drive instead. I went, reluctantly. The whole thing was annoying, and I was very glad that I had a dinner engagement that evening and could insist that I must be home in plenty of time to prepare for it.

I pressed him about the school where I would be teaching, but he said that he was still undecided. I reminded him that I should know soon so that I could make adequate preparations. He continued to be evasive. I noted that there was only a week until classes would commence. He replied heartily that a lot could happen in a week, then exploded an uproarious laugh. I dropped the subject.

He left me at the door and remarked how quickly the afternoon had passed. He asked if he could see me on Friday. Helplessly, I replied that since it was imperative that I know my future plans, he could. He boldly put a hand on my arm as he shook my hand. "Oh, I do have plans, my dear," he said. "I do have plans for you."

The nerve of him, I thought, as I climbed the stairs to my room. Never had I met such an obnoxious man. And to think that I was in a position where he would be my employer! I did hope that our respective duties would rarely bring us into contact with one another.

Suddenly the face of Jon's friend came to mind. *What a shame that he didn't turn out to be Mr. Higgins*, I thought, but immediately scolded myself. How foolish to even think such ridiculous thoughts! But I was amazed at the intensity of my feelings. I had seen the man only once for just a moment. Why should he affect me so? I didn't know, but those blue smiling eyes stayed with me, to haunt me as I opened the door to my room. With a great deal of determination I pushed the image of the face from my mind and concentrated on choosing a gown for the evening ahead.

❖

7

Mr. Higgins' Plan

❖

MR. HIGGINS ARRIVED at eleven o'clock on Friday. I was reading to Sarah and Kathleen and was totally unprepared for such an early call. He rudely barged his way through the house and declared that we were going on a picnic. He carried a picnic basket as evidence that everything was prepared. I tried to stammer a refusal, but he cut me short with a laugh.

"You needn't bother your pretty little head about a thing. I know that I've surprised you—but folks will tell you that I'm full of surprises."

He seemed to consider people's comments regarding his surprises as great compliments.

He grabbed my hand and pulled me to my feet, not even letting me finish the final half of the last page.

"Come—come," he said. "Picnics don't like to be kept waiting."

"I like picnics," Kathleen announced hopefully.

"And someday your aunt and I will take you with us—but not today. Today is a picnic for just *two*." He turned to me with a wink. "Now run along, my dear, and put on something more suitable for a picnic." He glanced at my stylish slippers. "Especially on your feet," he added. "Those flimsy little things are hardly suitable for a walk in the country, and we must have peace and quiet to discuss your future."

I hurried upstairs and changed, muttering threats the whole time. I chose the plainest of the dresses that I had purchased in Calgary; but I wished with all of my heart that I had something made out of floursacking to wear instead. I searched through the closet for the walking shoes I had used for the classroom and put them on. *They're awfully plain—almost ugly*, I thought, but I was glad of it as I descended the stairs.

Mr. Higgins, I thought, *today you will tell me where I am to teach—or so help you . . .*

I stepped onto the front porch where my caller was waiting, gathered a light shawl from the porch swing, fastened my least becoming hat in place, and reluctantly turned to the impatient Mr. Higgins who sighed loudly with relief.

His gaze then swept over me, both complimenting and criticizing me.

"You won't need the hat. The sun will feel good—"

"A lady does not leave the house without her hat," I retorted.

"Here in the West—"

"*I* am of the East."

He howled as though I had made a hilarious joke. But he quickly forgot about the hat as his eyes fell to my shoes.

"Those shoes—" he said next, "how will you ever walk in them? They are much too—"

"Mr. Higgins," I cut in, "I am beginning to have doubts about accompanying you. If these shoes will not do, then I must question where you are about to take me."

He dropped the matter of my attire and offered me his arm. I pretended not to notice and proceeded down the walk on my own to a rather nice-looking buggy and horse.

Mr. Higgins made a great affair of pointing out to me the fall colors, and I would have enjoyed them had I been with any other company. I did miss the deep reds of the oak and maple I had known at home, but my spirit drank in the gold of the shivering poplar mixed with the green shades of pine and spruce in the river valley. It truly was breathtaking.

Mr. Higgins drove west out of the city. A hill rose directly ahead of us, and I knew that if we topped it, we'd see those glorious mountains. But I did not want to see the mountains with Mr. Higgins. I was deeply relieved when he stopped just short of the brow of the hill.

He leaped from the buggy and came around the horse to me, reaching a hand up to help me down. I could not refuse it without being dreadfully rude, but I pulled away from him as quickly as I was settled on the ground. He found a spot that suited him and spread out a rug and then the picnic things. Happily, the food was good. We talked about this and that; but remembering his comment about withholding business discussion until after one had eaten, I did not try to steer the conversation toward my teaching position. But I was determined that as soon as the meal was cleared away, I would broach the subject, if Mr. Higgins didn't bring it up himself.

As soon as he had finished eating, he stood up.

"Come, my dear," he said, holding out his hand.

I wished that he wouldn't use such a familiar term in addressing me. It unnerved me.

"Come," he said again. "I want to show you something."

I waved my hand toward the scattered remains of our lunch. "But the—"

"That'll keep. We'll pack it up when we come back," he said, unconcerned.

"By then the ants and flies—"

"My, my, you are a fussy thing, aren't you?" He sounded near exasperation, so I turned my back on the rug and its contents. After all, it was his basket, and if he didn't mind taking home a colony of ants, why should I?

We walked up the side of the grassy hill. I could see now why he had been concerned about my shoes. There was no path up the steep slope, and the walking was difficult. He offered his hand whenever I slowed a bit, so I hurried on ahead of him. By the time he called a halt, I was out of breath and glad to stop.

He reached out and turned me slowly so that I could look back upon the autumn-painted valley. The river and the town stretched out before us. From our vantage point the buildings of Calgary looked sheltered and protected. I tried to pick out Jon and Mary's house but couldn't find it.

"I've got something to say." There was excitement and a note of confidence in Mr. Higgins' voice.

"My school—you've decided . . . ?"

He laughed that hearty, grating laugh of his. I turned to look at him, uncharitably noticing the wrinkles in his suit.

"This property—right where we're standing—it's mine. I just bought it."

I blinked, unable to comprehend any connection between what Mr. Higgins had just said and any possible interest of mine. Then, remembering my manners, I offered, "Why, that's very nice. I'm happy for you. You certainly have picked a nice view. What do you plan—?"

"I'm going to build my house—right here—with a full, clear look at the valley."

I looked back down the valley. "Very nice," I commented rather absentmindedly.

"Do you really like it?"

"Why, yes. Yes, of course. It's lovely." I hoped that I hadn't tried to overdo it. It *was* lovely, but I really didn't feel that much enthusiasm.

"I knew that you would." The confidence was in his voice again. "We'll put the house right here," he said, waving his arm.

Noticing the "we," a sympathy for whoever the other member was swept through me, along with a slight thankfulness that even a man like Mr. Higgins could find someone with whom to share life.

"We'll face this way—the front entry, the living room . . ." he said, making grand gestures with his arm. "What do you think?"

I couldn't imagine why he was asking me, but I mumbled that I supposed that would be just fine.

"I think that we'll build of brick rather than lumber, though lumber is easier to get. Four or five bedrooms, do you think?"

"Mr. Higgins, I—"

"You don't need to call me Mr. Higgins, my dear Beth," he said ingratiatingly. I was shocked at his liberty in using my first name. "It's Thomas—Tom, if you like—" his eyes were filled with feeling as he looked at me, "or anything else you'd care to call me."

"Mr. Higgins," I stubbornly repeated his formal name. "I'm afraid that I don't understand. We came here to discuss my school, and instead—"

"Ah, my dear. I see that I haven't made myself clear. You won't need to take a teaching position. We can be married soon and I—"

"*Married?*" My reply sounded almost like a shriek. "Married? What are you speaking of?"

WHEN CALLS THE HEART

"Don't be coy, my dear. I see no need for waiting. Some may think it a bit hasty, but here in the West a man is given the privilege of deciding quickly. There is no need to wait just for convention's sake. The marriage—"

"But I came west to *teach*!"

"Of course," he said knowingly, "until such time as a suitable—"

"Mr. Higgins, I don't think that you understand." I took a deep breath to calm myself. "There were 'suitable' men back East. I have no intention of forsaking teaching to—to marry—to marry *you*!"

It was several minutes before I convinced Mr. Higgins that I meant what I said. He couldn't believe that any woman in her right mind would actually reject his offer—so you can readily see how he, henceforth, rated me. With disgust he abruptly turned to descend the slope ahead of me, and I was hard put to keep up with him. Without another word between us, he jammed leftovers, dishes, ants and all into his picnic basket, piled it all into the buggy, and we drove back to Jon's in awkward silence.

"Remember," he finally grated out as we neared my brother's place, "I am the school superintendent. I hire and I fire."

"Perhaps you would rather I returned to the East. I'll just tell Jonathan—"

"How absurd," he cut in. "We've plenty of schools where teachers are needed. I'm sure that I'll be able to find a spot suitable for you."

"Thank you," I said stiffly. "That *is* why I came."

The appointment came by letter. The note was short and formal. After careful consideration, it stated, I was to be given the Pine Springs school. Enclosed was a train ticket which I was to use the next Wednesday. The train would take me to Lacombe where I would be met by Mr. Laverly, the local school-board chairman. I would have the remaining days to get settled before classes commenced on the following Monday.

"Lacombe," I said aloud. "Where is Lacombe?"

"North," said Jon from behind his paper. "Why?"

"That's where I'm to go."

The paper went down and Jon's face appeared.

"Go? For what?"

"My school."

"That can't be."

"It's right here—even a train ticket."

"But it's—it's more than a hundred miles from here. That can't be."

"Over a hundred?"

"Right. There must be some mistake."

It hit me then. Mr. Higgins was seeing to it that I was a long way removed from Calgary. His revenge? Perhaps he was even hoping that I would refuse the placement and go whimpering back east. Well, I wouldn't.

"I'm sure that there's no mistake, Jon," I said evenly. "It sounds delightful."

"You mean you'd consider—"

"Of course."

"Lacombe, eh?"

"No, actually it's called Pine Springs."

"It's way out in the country!"

"Sounds delightful," I said again.

"It's backwoods, barely opened up. I'm sure there's been a mistake. I'll talk to Thomas."

"No, Jon, please," I said quickly. "I want to take it."

At the startled and hurt look in Jon's eyes I hurried to explain. "Oh, I'll hate to leave you, and Mary, and the children. I've learned to love you all so, but really, it'll be good for me. Can't you see? I've been so sheltered, so—so coddled. I'd like to find out if I can care for myself, if I can stand on my own two feet."

"You're sure?" Jon looked at my carefully groomed hair, my soft hands and manicured nails, at my stylish clothes.

I understood his look. "I'm sure," I said emphatically.

"Well, I don't know what Mother will think. You were supposed to be under my protective wing."

"Mother won't need to know—yet."

"But—"

"She'll know that I am on my own, certainly, but as to the distance between us, that would only worry her unnecessarily."

"I'm still not convinced, but if you think—"

"Oh, I do. I really want to try it, Jon."

Jon's newspaper went back up to indicate that he considered the issue closed. I sat very still and fingered the ticket to Lacombe.

"Say, I just thought of something," said Jon, coming out from behind his paper again. "Pine Springs—that's Wynn's country."

"Who?"

"Wynn, the fellow that you saw me talking to the other day when you did your shopping. Remember?"

Did I remember! I tried to sound very nonchalant. "Oh, yes, I believe I recall the one you mean. He's not from Calgary?"

"Not really. He comes and goes. He was in that day visiting his brother Phillip. Phillip's been in the hospital here."

"Oh, I see."

I could feel the excitement flowing through my veins, warming my cheeks. I was glad that Jon was behind his paper again.

I gathered up my short letter and my now-welcome train ticket and muttered something about beginning my packing, then headed for my room.

So Jon's friend Wynn was from Pine Springs. Perhaps when I reached Pine Springs I would have the pleasure of meeting him. Jon had not introduced me to him, even though he had been given the perfect opportunity. If I understood my brother's little code, this meant that Wynn was single. I smiled softly.

You silly goose! I scolded myself. *You're acting in a manner that even Julie would declare to be childish. Stop this nonsense this minute! I honestly don't know what has come over you.*

Still, I couldn't help but whisper as I fingered the train ticket, "Thank you, Mr. Thomas Higgins."

8

The New School

THE TIME DREW near for my trip to Lacombe, and I felt both excited and sad. I would miss my newly found family; Jon and Mary had become very dear to me, and the children were all so special. William hovered nearby to see how he might help, and Sarah looked ready to cry the entire time that she watched me pack. Kathleen insisted upon helping me fold the green emerald velvet as I returned it to its tissues; she expressed her sorrow that I hadn't even worn it during my stay.

I held Baby Elizabeth for the last time, and she gave me the most endearing smile. I kissed her soft dimpled cheeks and a tear or two trickled down my own.

Mary was forever reminding me that I would be welcome in their home at any time. "Please," she begged, "come whenever you can, even if it's only for overnight."

I promised that I would try.

"And should you find—"

"Everything will be fine, I'm sure." I knew that she was giving me an invitation to flee back to her if I found my situation unsuitable. I appreciated her concern, but I didn't want to be a baby. I suppose, too, that I wanted to show Mr. Higgins a thing or two!

"But you never know what kind of a family you will be boarding with," Mary suggested, her voice hesitant.

"I'm sure that they wouldn't place me in an objectional home," I said, trying to sound confident. In truth, I had little faith in Mr. Higgins' concern for my well-being. I did not know how far he might go in gaining revenge.

"But remember . . ." Mary said, and I assured her that I would.

Jon drove me to the train, and William, Sarah and Kathleen rode along. Kathleen, very serious, asked me, "Aunt Beth, will you 'member me if I grow up while you're gone?"

"Of course I will, sweetheart," I assured her. "But I'm not going to stay away nearly as long as that."

She seemed comforted by my reply.

"Wish you were gonna be *my* teacher," William pouted.

"Me, too," Sarah echoed with great feeling. She was to begin school the next Monday and, though she was looking forward to it, she had some fears also.

"So do I," I said, hugging them. "But I promise I'll write and tell you all about Pine Springs and my pupils there, and you can write me about your new teachers and friends."

They brightened at the thought of a letter.

After the final good-byes, I boarded the train and chose what I hoped would be a comfortable seat. A cigar-puffing man across the aisle made me realize that I had chosen unwisely, but I was reluctant to move for fear of appearing rude. His wife finally demanded that he put out his cigar; she couldn't stand the closeness of the "foul-smellin' stuff." I was delivered.

I thought that the train would never reach Lacombe. We limped along, stopping at any place with more than one building. The train hissed and coughed and shuttled and groaned, seemingly forever, at these tiny train stations before finally rolling on.

We spent an especially long time at a town called Red Deer. I watched with interest as dray wagon after dray wagon drove away with loads of freight—sacks of flour, unmarked crates, even a stove. At last, when I was sure that they must have removed even *my* luggage, we resumed our forward crawl.

The landscape had changed over the miles. We had left the prairies behind and now rolled through timbered land. Here and there were fields where settlers had cleared the land for the plow. Large piles of logs and stumps were scattered about, some of them surrounded by planted grain.

The crops that had been sown were now nearly ready for harvest, and much of the talk of my fellow passengers was centered on yield, quality and the weather. It was conversation unfamiliar to me, and I found myself listening intently.

It was well into the afternoon before the conductor came through calling, "Lacombe! Next stop, Lacombe."

I began to bundle together the items that I had brought with me. I carefully tucked away the wrappings of the lunch that Mary had insisted upon sending. I had been most reluctant to comply at the time she suggested it, but I was now glad that she hadn't allowed me to talk her out of it. I had eaten every morsel of the lunch and been thankful for it. I brushed at my lap for unseen crumbs and stood to my feet to smooth my skirt.

The train squealed to a jerky halt. I clutched my belongings and went forward to meet Mr. Laverly. Stiff and bedraggled after only these few hours on the train, I had difficulty imagining how I had endured the four days it had taken me to journey from Toronto.

As I descended the steps, my eyes searched hastily about for a man that looked like a Laverly. I easily spotted the one who had been sent to meet me; he was the *other* nervous person on the platform. I introduced myself, and he suggested that I might like a cup of coffee before we started out. He would stay and load my belongings. His daughter, Pearlie, was pushed forward with instructions to be my guide to the local hotel tea-room. I was glad to fall in step with Pearlie. The hotel was only a short distance, and she led me at a brisk pace.

We found a table in the corner, and after we had placed our orders and I had caught my breath, we began to chat. I was pleased to find that Pearlie was not shy and offered information freely. I was anxious to discover any information I could about Pine Springs.

"How do you like school?" I asked, thinking that this would be a normal question for a teacher to ask.

"Fine, but I didn't like my last teacher good as the one before. But," she hurried on, after a quick check of my response to that, "least he was better than the one 'fore that."

"Do you have a new teacher every year?"

"Most of the time. One I had for a year an' a half once."

She shrugged it off as of no consequence.

"How far is Pine Springs?"

"Pa says it'll take 'bout half an hour."

"What's it like?"

"Don't know. Never been there before."

My eyes must have opened wide at this reply.

"You don't live in Pine Springs?"

"Uh-uh. Live here in Lacombe."

"But I thought that it was your father who will be driving me to Pine Springs."

"'Tis. Nobody in Pine Springs has got an auto, so Mr. Laverly hired my pa to drive you on out. Team takes a long time an' Mr. Laverly said that by the time you got there by horse an' wagon, you might decide to pack right up an' head on back East. An' he sure didn't want that."

"I see." I smiled at Mr. Laverly's assessment of a lady from the East. "Then you aren't a Laverly."

"Nope. We're Ainsworths."

"You live and go to school here in Lacombe?"

"Yup."

"Do you have any idea how many children attend the Pine Springs school?"

"Never been any yet."

"Pardon me?"

"It's bran' new. They jest built it. They been tryin' to get a teacher, an' Mr. Higgins never had one for 'em. They built the school two years ago— an' no teacher. An' then last fall, no teacher. Now this year they get a teacher. Mr. Laverly sounded real excited. That's why he asked Pa to drive you out. My pa's 'bout the only one 'round here with a good auto," she added proudly.

"That's very nice. What does your father do?"

"He's an undertaker, an' business has been unusual good—I heard him tell Ma. Says that she can even have that new washing machine that she's been a'wantin'. Won't need to use the old scrub board no more."

I smiled and nodded. "That will be nice for your mother."

Pearlie watched me carefully. As soon as I had finished my tea, she rose from her chair.

"We best get back. Pa will be done loadin' your stuff."

"Are you going with us to Pine Springs?" I asked, hoping that she was.

"I gotta," she stated. "I gotta help Pa start the car."

"You help? What do you do?"

"I choke it an' things, whilst he cranks."

We walked back to the station and found Pearlie's pa pacing back and forth in an agitated fashion. Before him on the platform sat my trunks. I guessed by the look that the station master sent my way that he and Pearlie's pa had already had words. Without any preliminaries, Pearlie's father stated, "These'll have to stay. Got no place in my automobile for freight like thet."

"But I need them!" I protested. "They contain my clothing, my—"

"Can't do a thing 'bout thet. I can take the luggage thet you're a'carryin', but the trunks will have to stay here. Someone will jest have to come on in with a wagon an' pick 'em up."

I could see that his mind was made up. Besides, he appeared to be right. There was no room in the automobile for my trunks.

"I put yer other things on the backseat there. You can seat yerself there beside 'em."

I did as I was told. The station master was summoned with a wave and given instructions regarding my trunks. They were soon riding a cart into the small wooden building.

Pearlie took her place behind the steering wheel and expertly pulled and twisted knobs while her father began his cranking chore. It took a good deal of hard work before the automobile coughed into action. He came dashing from the front, through the door, and bumped Pearlie out of his way, his face red and sweaty from his exertion.

We began to chug our way carefully through the little town, avoiding potholes, pedestrians and teams. Dogs took pleasure in chasing this unusual conveyance, teasing and barking and snapping at the tires as they escorted us out of town. I held my breath lest we hit one of them, but Pearlie's pa drove as though they were not even there.

It was a long, dusty, bumpy ride. The road certainly wasn't built for speeding, and Pearlie's father couldn't have been accused of doing so. But lest I sound ungrateful, I was glad that I didn't have to make this trip by wagon.

I looked for my beloved mountains, but from this vantage-point saw only tree-covered hills.

We passed several fields that had been cleared from the timbered countryside, many of them holding a grain crop in various stages of ripening. Some fields grazed cattle or horses, and I even saw a few sheep. Most of the homes and outbuildings were of log construction; I found them fascinating.

I was about to tap Pearlie on the shoulder and ask how much farther when I remembered that she wouldn't know either, having never been to Pine Springs before. About ten minutes later, we turned into a driveway and there stood a log building that I realized must be my school.

We drove on past it, across the browning grass, and pulled up before a smaller building to the left and rear of the school itself.

"Here we are," Pearlie's father called above the roar of the motor. It came to me that he did not plan to turn it off—he did not wish the unpleasant exertion of starting it again. I didn't blame him.

I must have shown my bewilderment, for he boomed at me, "The teacherage—where you'll be stayin'."

Teacherage? I got my thoughts and my baggage gathered together and crawled from the car. My companions did not leave their positions in the auto.

"I don't have a key!" I wailed through the auto's window.

"A key?"

He acted as if he had never heard of such an object.

"Yes, a key—to let myself in the house."

"Won't need no key. Doesn't have a lock. Good-day, ma'am." And he tipped his hat, pushed the shift lever into gear, and the auto clattered and chugged its way out of the yard.

I watched them go. Pearlie waved wildly, and I lifted my hand in a limp salute. When they had disappeared from sight, I gathered up my parcels and tried the door. Pearlie's pa had been right; it opened readily to my touch, and I entered what was now my new home.

I had fully expected that I would be a boarder in some neighborhood home. A funny little fear rippled through me. But I told myself not to be silly, that living alone would be much more to my liking and that I would be so close to my classroom.

I learned later that the teacherage had been constructed over the last winter as an added incentive to Mr. Higgins to provide the community with a teacher. I was its first occupant.

I passed through an entry into a small room which was a combined kitchen and living room. A bit of a cupboard stood in one corner and next to it was a very used stove. A fire was burning in it, so someone must have recently been in the teacherage. A teakettle sat on the stove and sent forth a merry, soft purr with its column of wavering steam. Something about that kettle suddenly made me feel much more at home. I felt myself relax. My eyes quickly glanced around the room. It also contained a table and two chairs, mended and freshly painted a pale green. Two stuffed chairs, with homemade crazy-quilt throws carefully covering them and a small table sitting between them, made my living room. A chest of sorts stood against one wall.

I could see into a second room, and after making a hurried survey of the first, I quickly passed through the adjoining door to get a better look. This room contained a bed and a dresser. The furniture looked worn, but clean. The bed's mattress looked lumpy, but a new cover had been sewn for it of freshly laundered floursacking. A brand-new pillow graced the spot where my head would rest; I wondered if its soft downiness came from a neighbor's fowls. A colorful crazy quilt was folded neatly at the end.

Realizing I was still carrying my bags, I returned to the first room and tumbled them into one of the overstuffed chairs. In somewhat of a trance, I crossed to the stove and checked to see if it needed more wood. I had never taken care of a stove before and hadn't the slightest notion how to go about handling it, but it seemed fairly obvious as to where the wood should go.

I looked around me. There were some things set out on the table and I crossed over to them. A note caught my eye, and I stopped to read it.

Dear Miss
Thot that you'd be tired and hungry after yer trip so have left some things. We will call on you tomarra to see what you be needing. We hope you like it here. We are plenty glad to have you come.
                                                                Martha Laverly

On the table sat containers of tea, sugar, coffee and salt, as well as cheese, fresh bread and pound cake. I crossed to the cupboard and opened the doors. A collection of mismatched dishes and pots greeted me. I lifted out a brown teapot with a chipped lid, a blue cup with a rose on the side, placed it on a pale yellow saucer, and set about brewing myself a cup of tea.

While the tea steeped, I opened the other cupboard door and found staple items in small containers. Never having spent much time in a kitchen, I was thankful to see that they were carefully labeled.

On the cupboard sat a pan filled with water and in the water stood three jars. One contained cream, another milk, and a third, butter. *So this is how one keeps things sweet when there is no icebox.* I poked a finger into the water and was surprised at how cool it felt.

The chest standing near the door held a pail of water with a small dipper, a basin, and a tin container with a bar of soap. I poured a little of the water into the basin and washed my hands. Realizing that I had no towel on which to dry them until my trunks arrived, I went outside and shook the water from my hands and then walked back and forth, rubbing them lightly together until all the water had evaporated.

My tea was ready when I returned. I sliced a piece of the fresh bread and spread on the butter, then cut myself a generous portion of cheese.

Crossing to the stuffed chair that wasn't holding my belongings, I sat down with my repast. How good the hot tea and the fresh bread tasted! I couldn't remember ever having a more enjoyable meal.

My mind was beginning to clear of its fog, and I studied my new quarters more critically. The windows had white, rather stiff-looking curtains. The table was covered with a white cloth of the same material, but it was decorated with cross-stitching. The walls were bare except for a calendar. The rugs on the floor were small, bright rounds against the plainness of the bare wood. The furniture was definitely all secondhand. As I looked at it, I wondered about those folks who had given it up in order that the new teacherage might be furnished. Had it been a sacrifice for them? I set down my empty cup and again went to the bedroom.

The curtains that hung there were of the same coarse material. Two more quilts were neatly folded and stacked on a wall shelf. They were all homemade, obviously pieced together from the better parts of worn-out garments. Skillfully and artistically done, they were very attractive to look at. I admired the handiwork and appreciated the time which had gone into them. Three rugs were scattered on the floor, one in front of the bed, one in front of the dresser, and the third at the door. A mirror hung on the wall, a crack running jaggedly across one bottom corner.

So I won't be boarding, I again told myself. *I'll be living completely on my own, in this little pioneer log house.*

I returned to the lumpy chair and poured a fresh cup of tea. I looked around at my small, secondhand nest, feeling deep respect for the people who had worked so hard and sacrificed so much to bring me here. The sense of near-panic left me and a warm kinship with these pioneers began to seep into my mind and emotions. I felt almost happy as I thought about my still-unknown neighbors. *I will love your children, and I will teach them to the very best of my ability*, I decided then and there.

I smiled to myself and sipped the hot tea. I said aloud, "Thank you, Mr. Higgins. You couldn't have given me a more pleasant situation."

It wasn't until I went to find a basin and more hot water to wash up my few dishes that I discovered the covered pot of stew simmering on the back of the stove. It smelled delicious as I lifted the cover and stirred it, and even though my hunger had been completely satisfied with bread and cheese, I couldn't refrain from dishing myself a small serving. It *was* delicious. The rest would be my dinner for tomorrow.

9

The Wilderness

I SPENT THE remainder of the daylight in further exploration of my new domain. Besides the school (the door of which was firmly nailed shut) and the house, there was also a shed for the wood supply, a small barn and two outhouses, marked "Boys" and "Girls." A pump stood in the yard, and I realized that this was my water supply. Not being able to resist that handle, I tried it. It was a long time before the water made an appearance. When it finally did come and I pushed my hand under the stream of water, it was so cold that I shivered. I sat down on the small platform to catch my breath, touching my still-cold hand to my hot cheeks and forehead.

The yard that I surveyed certainly needed care, but then, of course, it had been unattended. The tall grass had recently been cut but had been left to lie, browning where it fell. It smelled musty and insects buzzed busily about it.

I peeked in one of the windows in the small school building and glimpsed some desks in various sizes and condition, a large, potbellied stove near the door, and a teacher's desk in front of a homemade blackboard.

I did not go back to the teacherage until the sun had retired for the night. The sunset was a splendid display. I wondered if it was showing off for my benefit or if it was often that spectacular. Rarely had I seen such a gorgeous scene; the riotous colors flamed out over the sky in shades that I had no words to describe. Birds sang their last songs of the day before tucking in for the night, and still the darkness hung back. *Now*, I thought, *I understand the word "twilight." It was created for just this time— in this land.*

The air began to cool, and the darkness did start its descent at last. I slowly began picking my way toward my small haven, wanting to sing aloud the song that reverberated in my heart, yet holding myself in check. This new world was so peaceful, so harmonious.

I was lingering by a window of the school building, taking one last fruitless peek into the dark interior, when a bloodcurdling, spine-chilling howl rent the stillness of the evening hour. It seemed to tear through my veins, leaving me terrified and shaking. The scream had hardly died away when another followed, to be joined by another.

I came to life then. A wolf pack! And right in my very yard! They had smelled new blood and were moving in for the kill.

I sprang forward and ran for the door of my cabin, praying that somehow God would hold them back until I was able to gain entrance. My feet tangled in the new-mown grass and I fell to my hands and knees. With a cry I scurried madly on, not even bothering to regain my feet. The sharp stubble of the grass and weeds bit into the palms of my hands, but I crawled on. Another howl pierced the night.

"Oh, dear God!" I cried, and tears ran down my cheeks.

Howls seemed to be all around me now. Starting as a solo, they would end up in a whole chorus. What were they saying to one another? I was certain that they were discussing my coming end.

Somehow I reached the door and scrambled inside. I struggled to my feet and stood with my back braced against the flimsy wooden barrier. I expected an attack to come at any moment. I heard no sound of rushing padded feet, only sporadic howling. But Julie had said that western wolves were like that—catlike and noiseless, silently stealing up on their victims.

My eyes lifted to the windows. The windows! Would they challenge the glass?

I forced myself to leave the door, checking first for some kind of lock. There was one, of sorts, but it was only a hook and eye. Totally inadequate against a half-ton wolf.

Julie had said that they were huge animals, with eyes that glared an angry red, jaws that were set in a grin of malice, and hackles that bulged a foot around their neck, making them look much like sinister men in heavy, broad-collared beaver coats.

With trembling fingers I fastened the hook on the door and rushed into the kitchen. What would deter them? Perhaps if I hung quilts over the windows, the smell of my warm blood would not reach them so readily. What had Julie said? Fire. That was it—fire. Fire was about the only thing that would hold them back.

I rushed to the stove. It was cold and flameless.

"I must get a fire started—I must!" I sobbed, and began to throw paper and kindling into the firebox. I knew that these supplies had been left for my use the next morning, but I needed them *now*.

My fingers fumbled with the match as a new burst of howls split the air. They didn't sound any closer, but perhaps that was their strategy, just to throw their victims off guard. Maybe some of them were sitting back and howling while others stole in quietly to make the kill.

The paper finally began to flame, and I thrust the kindling carelessly on top of it. The hungry, newborn flames consumed it greedily. I placed the lid on the stove. To my dismay there was then no evidence of fire except for the small amount of warmth that was beginning to radiate from the black metal of the stove top.

"I can't cover it—I can't, or it will be no protection at all," I told myself.

I removed the lid again. The flames were robust now, and I fed them more wood.

Smoke began to seep into the room, and as I huddled over the stove, as close to the flames as I dared, I began to cough. I pulled the handkerchief from my skirt pocket and covered my mouth. It was then I realized that my dress was ripped and hanging limply about my waist. I had nearly severed the skirt from the bodice. It must have happened during my frantic crawling.

I continued to feed the fire and huddle over it, coughing and crying into the woodsmoke. Suddenly I realized that it had been several minutes since I had heard a wolf howl. Was it a trick? Had they moved on, or were they just coaxing me away from the flames? I now wished that I had studied more about the habits of the wilderness creatures, like Julie had insisted. It had been foolish of me to venture into the wilds unprepared. Why, I didn't even have a gun or know how to use one.

My pounding heart sounded loud in the new stillness. I heard an owl hoot a few times, then it too seemed to move on. Still, I remained by the fire, not even daring to move to the window to look outside.

A harvest moon soon hung in the sky. I could tell by the brightness that it was full and orange like an autumn pumpkin. I stayed where I was and, between fits of coughing, stared at the shadows surrounding the trees at the far side of the yard. I could see plainly through the window as the moon rose higher and higher in the sky, but though I watched until my eyes ached with the strain, I saw nothing move. And then, to my amazement, two deer moved fearlessly out of the shadows and into the open yard. They began to feed, unconcerned, upon the scattered, mown grass. This was my first encouragement. Surely the deer wouldn't walk out boldly if the wolf pack was still around. But could the wolves so conceal themselves that even the deer couldn't detect them? Downwind—wasn't that it? The killer stalked his prey from downwind. Was there a wind blowing? Again I strained my eyes and my ears, but not a leaf shivered; I could not even hear a flutter in the stillness of the night.

I continued to feed my fire. The smoke in the room was almost unbearable now. I could not afford to leave the lid off the stove a minute longer or I would surely suffocate. Even with my handkerchief and the hem of my dress over my nose and mouth, I could scarcely stand to breathe the air of the room. My eyes watered until my handkerchief was soaked.

What could I do? To close the lid meant that my fire could not be seen, but to open the lid meant that I would soon be driven from the cabin. Perhaps that was what the wolves were waiting for. Maybe they knew that I could not endure the smoke-filled room much longer. Maybe they were gathered around my door at this very instant, waiting for me to stagger from the house and into their waiting jaws. I replenished the fire and closed the lid.

The minutes ticked slowly by. It was a long time until I was brave enough to step away from the stove. I was still struggling with some way to insure survival. *The lamp*, I thought suddenly. *The lamp might do as a fire substitute.*

I fumbled in the darkened room until I found the lamp and the matches. When the small flame flickered up, I beheld a room blue with smoke. No wonder I was having trouble breathing.

I looked around the room in dismay. There was nothing available for my defense, and it was very late. No one at this hour would be going by on the road that ran by my door. I guessed that, according to where the moon now hung, the night was half over. I ached with tiredness and fear, and my hands and knees stung from their scratches and bruises. What could I do?

It suddenly dawned on me that there was *nothing* that I could do, and that it was foolish to pretend to defend myself.

I placed more wood in the stove, set my lighted lamp on the table by the window, and went to my bedroom. Somewhere in my few belongings I had a nightgown, but I didn't bother searching for it. I closed the curtain and slipped my torn and soiled dress over my head. I left it lying where it fell and dropped on top of it one of my petticoats. Still wearing the other, I moved to the bed and spread the quilt over it. I had never slept without sheets before, and under different circumstances it might have bothered me to do so. It did not bother me now. I was about to lower myself onto the bed when I remembered the clean floursacking over the mattress. I stopped only long enough to gather up the skirt of my crumbled dress and carefully wipe my hands and feet on it. Then I lay down and pulled the quilt right over my head.

"Lord," I prayed, "I've done all that I know to do. You'll have to take over now."

The stuffiness under the quilt was no better than the smoke of the room. I was soon forced to uncover my nose so that I might get some air. Somehow I managed to cough myself to sleep.

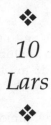

10

Lars

❖

WHEN I AWAKENED the next morning, the sun was already high in the sky. I woke up coughing, and it took me a few minutes to regain my bearings and realize what had happened. One glimpse of my garments lying in a heap on the floor, and it all came back to me.

The panic-stricken fear was gone. Julie had informed me also that wolves do not prowl around in broad daylight. I pushed back the quilt and moved my feet to leave my bed; stiffness and pain stopped me. I was instantly reminded of my bruised knees and realized that I should have properly cared for them before retiring. I slowly sat up and pulled up my petticoat to examine my wounds. The scratches were red and swollen but none appeared to be deep. A few days of healing would be all that was needed. I turned over my hands and looked at them, and found the same to be true. But I was shocked at their filthiness. Dirt-streaked and soot-smudged, I shuddered to think that I had actually gone to bed in such condition.

Crawling slowly and painfully out of bed, I limped around to open all of my windows in an effort to clear out the stubbornly clinging smoke. Then I washed myself as thoroughly as I could in cold water and dried myself on the cleanest portion of my soiled dress.

My scratches stung as I soaked the dirt out of them with the bar of soap and patted them dry. I wished that I had been sensible enough to bring some kind of ointment with me. Having none, I decided to try a small amount of cream from that jar that had been provided for my table. It did soothe the cuts some. I dressed rather stiffly and did the best I could with my hair. It was badly in need of a good washing after my dusty trip in the Ainsworths' automobile and the smoke of the previous night.

I had barely put things in order, built my fire and put on the coffeepot when there came a knock on my door. I had just prepared myself for a trip to the woodshed to replenish my wood supply. I had burned almost all of it from the big wooden box by my kitchen stove in my efforts to keep the wolves from my door. *My, it must take a lot of wood to get the folks around here through the winter—with the wolves and the constant blizzards and all,* I was thinking when the knock came.

I opened the door, and there stood a young boy whom I judged to be eight or nine. He was dressed in patched denim trousers and a freshly pressed cotton shirt. His blond hair was rather unruly, but his freckled face shone from its early morning washing.

"Hello," he said, a shy grin trying to get past his wary eyes.

"Hello," I answered, so glad to see him that I could have hugged him. He must have read the pleasure in my face, for his grin broke forth.

"Come in," I welcomed him with a smile of my own. "I'm Miss Thatcher."

He stepped forward awkwardly, timidly looked around for a moment, and then decided that he'd better get down to business.

"Ma sent me over to see if I could help ya none." His words were thick with a Scandinavian accent.

Some, my teacher's mind corrected, but I let it pass.

"That's very kind," I said.

"I can carry yer vood an' vater an' t'ings," the boy continued. Then he stopped and sniffed. "Smoky," he stated simply. "Havin' trouble vid yer fire?"

"It'll clear soon," I assured him, not wanting to blame the dependable old stove, but not knowing just how to bring up the matter of the wolves, either.

The aroma of the coffee made my stomach gurgle.

"Before you start on the wood and water, would you like to join me for breakfast?"

"T'ank ya, but I already haf my breakfast."

"Then make this a lunch," I suggested, and the boy laughed.

"Just sit down," I pointed toward the pale green chairs. "Take your pick."

He stepped to the nearest one and sat down. I spread four slices of bread with butter and strawberry preserves, poured milk for him and coffee for me, and joined him at the table. I bowed my head and said a short grace; his eyes showed no surprise. The bread and jam were delicious, and he seemed to enjoy them as much as I did.

"Yer lamp is still burnin'," he said suddenly. In the light of day I had failed to notice it. The wick had burned down so that only a tiny flame showed. I felt my cheeks flush in embarrassment, but without further comment the boy leaned over and blew out the struggling flame.

I wondered just how to start our conversation so that we might get to know one another. But he took care of that problem.

"I live on da farm yust over dere," he began, pointing a finger toward the northeast. "Vasn't fer da trees, you could see our house an' barn real plain."

This was good news. I had no idea that I had neighbors so near.

"Will you be one of my new pupils?"

"Ya mean, vill I go to school?"

"That's right."

"Me an' my sisters, Else an' Olga, an' my broder, Peter."

"That's nice," I said and really meant it. "And what is your name?"

"Lars—Lars Peterson. I vas named after my grandfader."

I could tell by the way he said it that he was proud of the fact.

"And your father's name?"

"Henry Peterson. An' Ma is Anna."

"And what class will you be in, Lars?"

"Don't know yet. Never been to school, but Pa has tried to teach us some letters an' some vords. Ma doesn't know da English vords too good yet. Pa studied a little bit in English ven he first came over. Ma came six mont's later vid us younguns, an' she didn't haf time to study. But she knows numbers real good. Numbers ain't much different in any country, I guess."

I nodded and smiled, but I was thinking about the shame of a child nearing ten without ever having been in a classroom.

"I vas pretty little yet ven ve came from da old country." Lars continued. "Olga vas not t'ree yet and da tvins yust babies."

"How old are they now?"

"Olga is seven and a half, an' Else an' Peter are yust turned six."

"And you?"

"I'm nine."

He wiped the last crumbs from his cheeks and arose from the chair.

"I best be carryin' dat vood," he said, "yer almost out." I was relieved that he made no comment on the extraordinary amount I had used. "T'ank ya fer da good break—lunch," he finished with a grin. "I'll git ya some fresh vater first."

I moved to get him my water pail, pouring what still remained into the reservoir on the stove.

"Lars," I said slowly. I had to know, yet hardly knew how to ask, "What do people around here do about the wolves?"

"Volves?" He looked surprised and confused. Then he answered confidently, "Ve don't got no volves."

"But last night I heard them. And if your farm is so near, you should have heard them, too."

"Oh, dem. Dem's coyotes."

"Coyotes?"

"Yah, yust silly ole coyotes. Pa says dat coyotes are yella-livered. Scared of der own shadows, dey are. Von't even take on anyt'ing bigger dan a hen or a mouse."

"But they sounded—"

"Don't dey make a racket!" His eyes sparkled. "I like to listen to 'em. Dey sound so close-like, an' dey all howl togeder an—"

"Yes, they do sound close," I put in, shivering at my recollection. "And they never attack people?"

"Naw, not coyotes. Dey're scared silly of everyt'ing—especially people. Dey run vid der tails 'tveen der legs. I tried to sneak up on 'em a coupla times to get a good look at 'em, but soon as you git a little close, dey turn tail an' run off, slinkin' avay as fast as dey can go."

I felt relieved and embarrassed as I thought of my terror during the night I had just endured. Coyotes—harmless, noisy coyotes! Humiliation flushed my cheeks.

Lars suddenly turned to me, the empty water pail still in his hand.

"Miss T'atcher, ya know vat? Ven I vas little, I vas scared of 'em. I used to lay in bed vid my head under da covers, sveatin' and cryin'." He blushed slightly. "Den my pa told me 'bout dem bein' sissies. Dey'd be more scared dan me if ve met up sudden. Pa says he's gonna git a coupla good dogs, yust to keep da coyotes away from da chickens—chickens be 'bout da only t'ings dat need fear coyotes." He turned to go, then turned back. "Ya von't tell, vill ya—dat I used to be scared of silly coyotes?"

"No, I won't tell. No one will know—you can be sure," I promised him. He left the room with relief showing in his eyes.

I won't tell, I said to myself, *about hiding under the covers, or fear, or fires, or burning lamps—anything. I'll never tell.*

11
The Petersons

AFTER LARS HAD returned with the pail of fresh water, he began to haul wood. He did not stop until I insisted that I would be unable to get out of my house if he brought in any more. He grinned, then proceeded to chop a fine supply of kindling. I wanted to offer him a quarter, but somehow I felt that it wouldn't be right in the eyes of his mother who had sent him over; so, instead, I fixed him a few more slices of bread and jam. He sat on my step and ate them, while I sat beside him.

"How many students do you think I'll have?"

"'Bout eighteen or nineteen, or more maybe if da bigger boys come."

Perhaps twenty students, of all ages and abilities. It seems like an awesome task.

"Ve only haf desks fer sixteen, so da ot'ers vill haf to haf tables an' benches," Lars continued.

"And who will look after getting tables and benches?" I asked him, knowing that he was right about the desks. I had counted them the night before but had seen no evidence of tables or benches.

"Mr. Laverly asked Mr. Yohnson to build 'em. He's a car—car—builder."

I smiled. "I see. Will they be ready for Monday, do you think?"

"S'pose to be."

Lars finished his last bit of bread, "I'd better go. Mama vill need me. T'anks fer da bread and yam. Oh, yah. Ma says, 'come to supper tonight.' Six o'clock. Right over dat vay——cross da field. Can ya come?"

"I'd be delighted."

He frowned slightly, "Does dat mean ya vill?"

"I will."

"Good." And with a grin, he was gone.

"Thank you for the wood and water," I called after him.

I spent the rest of the day sorting through my little house, making a list of the items I would need to purchase and wishing desperately that I had my trunks. Mr. Laverly did not come by as I had hoped, and I had no way of knowing where or how to contact him.

At twenty minutes to six I straightened my hair, brushed off my dress, and set out to find the Petersons. Lars was right. As soon as I passed through the growth of trees behind the school grounds, I could see their farm sitting on the side of the next hill. At times I lost sight of it as I passed through other groves of trees, but my bearings seemed to hold true; it was always there, just where I expected it to be, whenever I emerged from the woods.

Anna Peterson greeted me with a warm smile. Her English was broken, and she spoke with a heavy accent, but her eyes danced with humor as she laughed at her own mistakes.

"Ve are so glad ya come. Ve need school bad—so chil'ren don't talk none like me."

Mr. Peterson "velcomed" me too, and the warmth of their friendliness made it easy for me to respond. Olga and Peter were very shy. Else was a bit more outgoing, though still quick to drop her gaze and step back if I spoke directly to her.

Anna was a good cook. The simple ingredients in her big kitchen produced mouth-watering food. It was awfully nice to enjoy a meal with a family again.

The evening went quickly, and before I knew it, I could see the sun sinking slowly toward the treetops. Dusk was stealing over the land, making me feel like curling up and purring with contentment.

"I must go," I announced. "I hadn't realized—it will soon be dark and I'm not very sure of my way."

"Lars vill go vid. He knows da vay gud."

I accepted Lars' company with gratitude.

Mrs. Peterson insisted on giving me a basket of food—milk, cream, butter, eggs, bread and fresh vegetables from her garden. I tried to explain that I still had milk and cream on hand.

"T'row out milk. Vill be no gud," she insisted. "Save cream for baking, maybe. Make lots gud t'ings vid sour cream. Ve vill send more t'ings vid Lars to school for you."

"I will be happy to buy . . ."

"Buy not'ing. I gif. I glad you here. Now my boys an' girls learn—learn to speak, to read. I don't teach—I don't know. Now dey teach me."

"I'll show you, Mama," Else spoke up. "I'll show you all I learn."

"Yah, little vun teach big vun," Mrs. Peterson smiled, placing a loving hand on Else's head. "'Tis gud."

Lars and I walked slowly through the twilight. I allowed him, at his insistence, to carry the basket. Already I loved him and his family and could hardly wait for Monday, to meet the other children of the community.

We were about halfway home when a now-familiar but nonetheless heart-stopping howl rent the stillness. My first impulse was to lift my skirts and dash for home, but I restrained myself. I'm sure my face must have lost all of its color, and my hands fluttered to my breast, but Lars didn't seem to notice. He was telling me about his Holstein heifer calf and didn't even break his sentence.

The howl came again and was joined by many others. Lars merely raised his voice to speak above the din. I fought hard to keep from panicking. Eventually Lars probably noticed my reaction and commented,

"Silly ole coyotes. Sure make a racket. Sound like yust behind next clump, yet dey vay over in da field."

Then he went on with his story.

Lars' easy dismissal of the animals reassured me, and my heart slowly returned to its normal beat.

When we reached the teacherage, Lars went in with me. He found the matches and lit the lamp, then unloaded the basket of food onto my small cupboard.

"Ya be needin' a fire?"

"Not tonight. It's plenty warm, and I won't be staying up long."

I was beginning to feel weary from the lack of sleep the night before.

"Guess I go now," said Lars. He walked toward the door, basket in hand.

"Thank you so much, Lars, for seeing me home—and for carrying the basket."

He would never realize the difference that his calm presence had made when the coyotes had begun to howl.

"Yer velcome," he grinned.

"I wish I had some books to send home with you so that you and your sisters might practice reading, but I have none here. All my things are in my trunks, and I need to see Mr. Laverly before I can get them."

"Ya need Mr. Laverly? Vere yer trunks?"

"Still in Lacombe. There wasn't any room to bring them in the automobile."

"Ya need 'em?"

"I certainly do," I said emphatically.

He nodded, then with a wave and grin pushed open the door. "'Night, Miss T'atcher."

"Good-night, Lars."

I watched him move away in the soft darkness. Soon the moon would rise to give light to the world, but for now his way was still dark—yet he moved forward without uncertainty or fear. The coyotes howled again, but Lars paid no attention to them as he hurried off toward home.

I turned toward the coyotes now. They still made little tingles scurry up and down my spine each time I heard their mournful cry, but I refused to allow panic to seize me.

"Oh, no, you don't," I spoke aloud to them. "You made a cringing, frightened coward of me last night, but never again—never again!"

Still, I was glad to hook my door behind me as I entered the little teacherage I now called home.

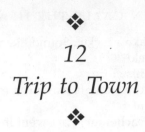

12
Trip to Town

❖

THE NEXT MORNING before I had even finished my breakfast, a team and wagon turned into my lane. The driver approached my house and knocked on the door, hat in hand. He introduced himself as Mr. Laverly. Lars, my special helper, had already ridden over on horseback to his farm that morning and informed him that I needed my trunks.

"Sorry, ma'am," the man apologized. "Wanted to be over to greet you yesterday right off, but my wagon busted a wheel an' it took nigh all day to fix it. 'Course I had me no idee that you was without yer belongin's, or I'd a borrowed an outfit from a neighbor an' been right over." His round face mirrored his sincere apology.

"I sure feel terrible that yer things didn't get here the same time that you did," he hurried on, wiping his hands and face with a bright square from a pocket. "I was 'opin' to spare ya a trip by wagon over those long, dusty roads. I'd be happy to jest go on in an' pick up yer things fer ya, an' ya can jest wait here."

"Oh, I'd love to go along, Mr. Laverly," I interjected quickly. "The weather is lovely, and the trees are so beautiful—I'm sure that the trip to town will be an enjoyable one in spite of the dust."

He relaxed some—even smiled.

"Would you care for a cup of coffee while I get my hat?" I asked, and he nodded that he would.

I motioned him toward one of the green chairs and poured coffee into the cup with the fewest chips, then cleared the table. When I had things tidied I went to the bedroom.

I did wish that I had another dress. The one that I had been wearing when I arrived hung, dejected and torn, from a peg in my bedroom. I had no sewing supplies with me to repair it. The dress that I now wore was the only other one I had with me. Besides appearing somewhat wrinkled and soiled, it was not the gown that I would have chosen to wear on my first day in a new town and did not go well with my hat.

Looking in some dismay at my reflection in the small cracked mirror, I placed my hat on carefully and pinned it in place. I smoothed out my skirt the best I could and picked up my handbag, then went to inform Mr. Laverly that I was ready when he was. He drained the last of the coffee from the cup and rose to go.

Mr. Laverly was not an eloquent man, I discovered, yet he did tell me of the parents' desire to provide education for the children of Pine Springs. I admired these people for working so hard and long to get someone who would teach, and I felt honored to be that "someone."

At Lacombe, Mr. Laverly dropped me off at the general store and went on to the train station to collect my trunks. I did not dally but set to work filling my long shopping list as quickly as I could. There seemed to be so many things that I needed, but I held myself in check and purchased only essentials—with the exception of one extravagance. I had determined that I would drink my tea like a lady, even in a log house; so I purchased a teapot and two cups and saucers of fine china. I felt somehow Mama's mind would be much more at ease about me if she knew that I was having my tea in the proper fashion. After all, civilization could not be *too* far away from Pine Springs if I had such amenities!

I had not finished my shopping when Mr. Laverly returned. He kindly assured me that I needn't rush. He suggested that we meet at one o'clock and perhaps I would like to get myself some lunch at the hotel before we started our long journey back. I agreed, and he went off on some business of his own. I finally rounded up all the items that I needed in order to keep house. I then bought a further supply of staple groceries and set out for the hotel.

While waiting for my meal to arrive, I wrote a short letter to my family and also a note to Jon and his family. I assured them that I would write more later, but I did want them to know that I had arrived safely and was very pleased and excited about my living arrangements and my school. I omitted telling Mama just exactly where my school was. She had sent me west to Jonathan and expected me to stay within the shelter of his protection. I shuddered to think how she would feel if she knew that I was about one hundred and fifty long, slow miles away from him.

My food arrived, and I placed my brief notes in the addressed envelopes. The waitress said I could post them right there at the hotel.

Mr. Laverly, true to his word, appeared at one o'clock. We returned to the store, and he and the clerk loaded my purchases. I looked longingly at the inviting little town, wishing that I had time to explore it, but Mr. Laverly was now in a hurry to be on his way.

The September afternoon sun rode hot and high in the sky. The horses sauntered along, and the wagon bumped and jostled. With each mile, I came to realize more why Mr. Laverly had been concerned about saving me this trip. My excitement and the loveliness of the weather and scenery had gotten me to town without too much discomfort, but I began to feel that the trip home would never end.

By the time we arrived at the teacherage, I was hot, tired, dirty and sore. Nothing would interest me more than a long soak in a hot tub; and then I remembered—I had no such thing, except for the round metal washtub I had just purchased that day for my laundry. Well, it would have to do.

Mr. Laverly unloaded all of my belongings. The trunks were heavy for one person, and I insisted upon giving him a hand. It was a difficult task to get all the things from the wagon into the teacherage, and my help, though freely offered, was barely adequate.

When finally everything was in my house, and Mr. Laverly had graciously refused my offer of a cup of tea, I remembered to ask him about the schoolhouse door. He had the nails out in a jiffy, and then his wagon rumbled out of the yard.

Gone were the thoughts of a bath in my excitement at getting settled. With a feverish eagerness I attacked the trunks and the purchases and began to make myself a home in the "wilderness." Dusk was approaching and I still had not stopped for breath. I was weary, dusty, and hungry, and if I didn't stop, I would be exhausted. Though tired, I gazed around me with pleasure. It did look and feel much more like home now, but darkness would come soon and if I wanted a bath, I needed to haul the water for it.

I placed my new boiler on the stove and poured the water from the pail into it. Then I ran for more water, pumping in near panic. If the coyotes were to begin their howling right now, I wasn't sure that I, as yet, would be strong enough to face them alone. Fortunately, I was just entering the house with my second pail of water when the first howl broke over me. *I really don't need more water anyway*, I assured myself and fastened the door behind me.

I started the fire in the stove beneath the boiler and also made room on the stove top to put on the kettle for tea. I fixed a simple meal, which I practically wolfed down in my hunger, and then I drank my tea slowly from my new teacup, staring at the other teacup as I drank. Would there ever be a second person in my little teacherage to share my teatime? Suddenly a wave of loneliness overtook me. I was happy here, but I was alone. I longed for Julie, and then realized that even she would not properly fill the void I was feeling. Julie would be bubbly and chatty and light. I needed someone with serenity, strength, purposefulness to share my thoughts and my days. Someone like—and my mind involuntarily began to review the men that I had known. Each face that appeared in my mind's eye was readily dismissed. Then suddenly, without warning, I saw again the face of Jon's friend. The intense eyes, the slight smile, and the strength of character that was evident was attractive and yet made me stir uneasily. In spite of the fact that not another soul was anywhere near, I found myself blushing in embarrassment at my foolishness. Changing my thoughts to safer things, I stood quickly, teacup in hand, and proceeded to add wood to the fire. Oh, how I was anticipating that hot bath!

While I waited for the water to heat, I carried my small washtub to my bedroom and placed it on the rug. Then I began the slow procedure of dipping and transporting the warm water to fill it. By the time I had finally finished my preparations, the water had cooled considerably. *Next time*, I informed myself, *I must begin with the water on the hot side.*

I stepped into the small tub and experimented with ways to curl myself into it. *Why didn't I buy the larger one?* I chided myself. I twisted and turned and curled and uncurled, but there was no way that I could get all of me into the tub at one time. Finally I hung my legs out over the edge in hopes of getting the warm water onto the aching parts of my body. It wasn't very satisfactory. Still sore from the wagon's jostling, I finally gave up the effort. Drying myself thoroughly, I slipped into my warmest nightgown and snuggled under the quilts. I would empty the tub of water in the morning.

Safe in bed, I listened to an occasional coyote howl. It didn't sound so spine-chilling now. In fact, I imagined that, with a little time, a person might even be able to get used to it.

13
Saturday

WHEN I AWOKE the next morning, I felt stiff all over. I was tempted to stay under the covers, but my body would not allow me the privilege. I thought of the small structure marked "Girls" way across the clearing and wondered if my legs would be able to walk the distance. I did wish that they had thought to build it nearer the teacherage.

I dressed clumsily and started walking slowly. The sun was up and shining down on a picture-pretty world. By the time I had traveled across to the building and back, some of the kinks were loosening, and I decided that I would be able to face the day after all, even emptying the tub of cold bath water!

While I waited for the water to heat for my morning coffee, I took my Bible and turned to the passage in Nehemiah where I had been reading. Though Nehemiah was leading a whole nation and rebuilding a city, I found some exciting parallels between his story and my new life way out here in the Canadian frontier. The day suddenly seemed to hold great promise. The kettle was singing merrily before I finished my prayer, and I proceeded to fix my breakfast.

I spent the morning carrying books and classroom aids to the little schoolhouse, then made a quick lunch and spent the afternoon organizing things. The classroom soon looked inhabited and inviting. I even wrote a few simple adding exercises on the blackboard. I hung the alphabet and number charts, put up some study pictures and maps, and the room began to come alive.

Around five o'clock while I was still lingering in the classroom, choosing the Psalms that I would read for the opening on Monday morning, I heard the jingle of harness. It was Mr. Johnson delivering the tables and benches. He had a near-grown son with him who took one look at me and went red to the very roots of his hair. I pretended not to notice, to save him further embarrassment, and showed them where to place the furniture. Mr. Johnson gazed around the now-furnished classroom, and tears began to gather in his eyes and trickle down his creased cheeks.

"Da Lord be praised!" he exclaimed. "It really be so. Ve do haf school. Yah?"

His deep feelings touched me.

After they had gone, I surveyed the schoolroom again, my feelings swinging between pride and apprehension. Walking back and forth, touching each article, changing this or that, rearranging something here or there, I was only too aware that I had very few aids to assist me in teaching these children. How I wished that I had more—but that was foolishness. I would just have to do what I could with what I had.

After writing "My name is Miss Thatcher" in block letters on the blackboard, I reluctantly turned to go home to prepare my evening meal.

Monday, I thought, *please come quickly—lest I burst.*

As I walked toward the door, I noticed a printed list posted beside it. I had not spotted it before, and I now stopped to read it. It was captioned, "Rules for the Teacher," and my eyes ran quickly down the page. They read as follows:

1. A teacher may not marry during the school year.
2. Lady teachers are not to keep company with men.
3. Lady teachers must be home between the hours of 8:00 p.m. and 6:00 a.m., unless attending a school function.
4. Man teachers must not chew tobacco.
5. There must be no loitering, by male or female, in downtown stores or ice-cream parlors.
6. A teacher may not travel outside the district limits without permission from the school-board chairman.
7. Neither male nor female may smoke.
8. Bright colors are not to be worn, either in or out of school.
9. Under no circumstances may a lady teacher dye her hair.
10. A lady teacher must wear at least two petticoats.
11. Dresses must not be shorter than touching the ankle.
12. To keep the schoolroom neat and tidy, the teacher must sweep the floor and clean the chalkboard every day.
13. The schoolroom floor must be scrubbed with hot, soapy water at least once a week.
14. The teacher must start the fire, when needed, by 8:00 a.m. so that the room will be warm for the pupils by 9:00 a.m.

I didn't expect to have any trouble obeying the lengthy list; still, it bothered me some to be dictated to in such a fashion. At first I was going to blame the whole thing on Mr. Higgins; but then I remembered other such lists that I had read and realized this one wasn't so different after all. I decided to pretend that I hadn't seen it. I would have observed all of its mandates anyway.

14
Sunday

THERE WASN'T ANY reason for my early rising on Sunday except perhaps habit. After I had carefully dressed and groomed my hair, I fussed about my small kitchen, fixing myself a *special* breakfast, as had been our tradition at home on Sunday mornings. It really didn't turn out to be very special, for I had gained very little experience in cooking. I determined that I would put time and effort into learning how to prepare tasty dishes. *No matter one's education or other abilities, a woman should be able to hold her head up proudly in her own kitchen,* I decided.

After I had cleared away the mess I had managed to make, I went outside for a walk. The sunshine felt good on my shoulders and back where the stiffness from my wagon ride still made me feel old and creaky. I wanted to lie down in the grass and let the warm rays do for me what my inadequate tub had not been able to do.

The morning hours seemed to lag. Eventually I returned to the house, hoping that my clock would tell me it was now time for me to prepare my noon meal. It was still plenty early, but I started the preparations anyway.

Again I ate, cleared away and cleaned up, all without using up very many minutes out of the lengthy day.

In the afternoon I read more about Nehemiah and spent time in prayer. I missed, more than I had ever thought possible, our church back home. I thought, too, of Jon and Mary and the family in Calgary and the Sundays that I had enjoyed worshiping with them in their small church. I should have thought to ask the Petersons if there was a church nearby where I might meet on Sundays with other believers. I couldn't imagine living, Sunday after Sunday, without an opportunity for worship and fellowship. How dry the endless days would become with no Sunday service to revive and refresh one's spirit!

I was sorely tempted to find some excuse to journey over to the Petersons', but my Eastern reserve and mother-taught manners held me in check. I had not been invited; one did not impose upon others.

I tried to read; I took short, unsatisfactory walks; I fixed afternoon tea; and all the time I ached with loneliness, and the day dragged on.

About six-thirty I heard voices. It was Lars and Else. I don't recall ever being happier about seeing visitors. I fairly ran to meet them! They must have seen my eagerness, but Else held back as Lars walked with me to my door.

"Lars," she whispered, "'member."

"Yah," he answered, but kept on walking.

"But Mama said," Else persisted.

"It's okay," Lars said, seeming a little exasperated.

"What is it?" I asked.

"Mama said not to bot'er you."

"She said, 'if Miss T'atcher vas busy or didn't vant company,'" Lars informed Else. "She's not busy." He turned to me quickly, "Are ya?"

"Oh, no." I hurried to assure them, lest they get away from me. "And I'd really like some company."

I sat down on my step, and they joined me. It had been such a lonely day.

"I'm not used to a Sunday all alone, nor am I used to a Sunday without going to church. Is there any church around here?"

"Nope—not yet," said Lars. "Mama vould sure like vun, but dere are only two Lut'ran families—not 'nough fer a church."

"Ve have church," Else corrected her brother in great astonishment.

"Not *in* a church," Lars replied.

"Still, church," she insisted.

"Where?" I asked, excited about any kind of service.

"In the school," Else said.

I was confused.

"But I've been here all day—no one came."

"I know," Lars said. "Mr. Laverly said dat ve vouldn't haf it today. He said dat da new teacher might not be happy vid us all meetin' here, messin' up t'ings. Ve'd yust haf to vait an' see."

"So that's it," I said, thankful that I wouldn't have to put in another Sunday like this one. "I will speak to Mr. Laverly, and we'll have church as usual next Sunday."

Else's eyes lit up, and I could tell that she, too, had missed church that day. Lars didn't appear to care too much one way or the other.

"Ma says, 'Ya need anyt'ing?'"

"No—no—nothing. You hauled such a good wood supply that I still have plenty. The days are nice and warm, and I let the fire go out as soon as I have finished cooking my food."

"An' vater?"

"It's good for me to haul my own water. I just finished getting a bucket."

I glanced down at my hands. My scratches were healing nicely, but already my hands had lost their well-cared-for look. I wasn't unduly upset by it, but I wasn't especially pleased with the new look either. Julie would laugh, or cry out in alarm, if she could see my hands now. I smiled.

Looking back at Lars, I suddenly thought of Matthew. How good it would be to have him here with me! For some reason, which I couldn't put my finger on, I decided that this land would be good for my young brother Matthew also.

Else's quiet question brought my mind back to my visitors.

"Did ya get da books?" she asked in a soft voice.

"Yes—yes, I did. Mr. Laverly came right over after you saw him on Friday, Lars. I must thank you for going over so promptly."

Lars flushed slightly at my thanks, so I hurried on. "We went to Lacombe in the wagon and got all of my things. I've unpacked everything and organized both the schoolroom and my house. Do you want to see them?"

I could tell by Else's eyes that she did, so I led the way.

The house was certainly nothing fancy. I had brought very little with me in the way of furnishings—a few pictures of my family, a spread for my bed, a soft rug, a few favorite ornaments, some dresser scarves and small pillows; but they managed to give my little home a feeling of warmth. It was plain to see that Else was impressed. Even Lars seemed to notice the difference.

"It's nice," he said.

I saw Else's eyes skim over everything, then rest on my china teapot and cups and saucers. I knew at once who would be the first person that I would invite for a cup of tea—though she was but six years old. She could drink milk from the cup if she preferred.

Even as Else's eyes assured me that she appreciated my little house, they also declared that something was missing. At length she gave voice to her concern.

"Is dat all da books?" She pointed at my Bible and the book of poetry with which I had attempted to fill my day.

"Oh, no. I have no bookshelves you see, so I had to leave my books in the trunk."

I raised the lid of one of my trunks to show her the volumes that had become my good friends over the years. Her eyes caressed them.

"Maybe you'd like to see the school. I took the books for classroom use over there."

They both flashed excited glances at each other, so together we walked to the school.

If I had been in doubt about teaching in a one-room classroom with students who had never had any formal learning, I would have lost all such doubts after seeing their response to their first look at the school.

First they stopped and stared, their eyes traveling over everything. Lars began to softly name the letters on the alphabet chart, while Else migrated toward the meager stacks of primers and books on the two small shelves at the front of the room. I went with her and lifted a book from the others.

"Here, try this one," I encouraged her. "You may look at the pictures if you'd like."

She took the book, crossed to a desk and sat down. She gently turned each page, missing nothing as her eyes eagerly drank in the pictures and her mind sought for the words on the printed pages.

Time passed quickly. Before we had realized it, the sun was crawling into bed. Lars, who had also chosen a book and retreated to a desk, looked up in unbelief.

"Ve gotta go," he said quickly. "Mama vill vorry. Come, Else."

Reluctantly Else handed me the book.

"Why don't you take it home with you and show it to Olga and Peter? I'm sure that they would like to see it, too. You may bring it back in the morning."

She hesitated, wondering if she was worthy of being entrusted with such a treasure.

"Go ahead," I said. "Lars may take his, too."

They ran off then, now eager to get home for more than one reason. I walked slowly back to the teacherage.

I felt contented now. I was sure that in the evening hours I would be able to enjoy Wordsworth, Longfellow, or Keats. Perhaps my heart wouldn't even skip a beat tonight at the howling of the coyotes. I sat warm and comfortable in my lumpy chair and sipped tea from my china cup. I knew that tomorrow held great promise.

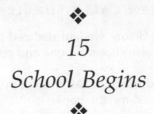

15
School Begins

❖

I WAS UP with the birds on Monday morning. I was far too excited to sleep. I had always enjoyed teaching, but never before had it affected me in quite this way; the eagerness of the people in the area had rubbed off on me.

The bell was to be rung at nine o'clock. I felt that I had already lived two full days that morning before nine o'clock arrived.

Dressing carefully, I did my hair in the most becoming way that I knew. It really was too fussy for the classroom, but I couldn't reason myself out of it. I tried to eat my breakfast but didn't feel at all hungry, so I finally gave up and cleaned up my kitchen area.

I left early for the classroom and dusted and polished, rearranged and prepared, and still the hands on the clock had hardly moved.

The first students arrived at twenty to nine. Cindy and Sally Blake were accompanied by their mother and father. Mr. Blake was a quiet man— but every family can use *one* quiet member, I decided. Mrs. Blake was chattering before she even climbed down from the wagon, and didn't actually cease until the schoolroom door closed upon her departing figure.

The Clarks came together—seven of them. It took me a few moments to sort them all out, and the harder I tried the more confused I became. It helped when I learned that there were two families involved, cousins— three from one family and four from the other.

Mrs. Dickerson brought her small son in by the hand. I think she had hoped he would be shy and reluctant to leave her side, but his face brightened at the first glimpse of his school.

Others came too quickly for me to learn each name as they entered. I would have to wait until the bell rang and the students had taken their places—and their parents had returned home.

I smiled at the Peterson children. Else and Lars presented me with carefully wrapped packages. Their mother wanted the precious books to be returned safely without soil, so she had wrapped them in brown paper and tied them securely with string.

The morning was spent in organizing a roll call and trying to determine the grade level of each student. Even the older ones had previously had very little opportunity to learn, so it was going to be "back to basics" for the first few weeks of my teaching. I prayed that I would be able to present the simple lessons in a manner that would not offend the older students. It was difficult to include a girl of fourteen with a row of six-year-olds for a lesson on the alphabet or the phonic sounds without making her feel embarrassed, but I'd need to devise a way to do it.

Not all of the students were eager to attend school. I picked out three who, for one reason or another, seemed to prefer going their own way on this lovely fall morning.

Sally Clark seemed rather absent-minded and uncaring. She was fifteen and probably reasoned that if she had managed thus far without school, why bother now? Besides, she would likely marry in a few years, and she could already bake bread, make quilts and care for babies. Time spent in a classroom with a lot of little children seemed like a total waste of time.

Eight-year-old Andy Pastachuck may have wanted to learn, but it was clear that he wasn't capable of learning very much. I was told that Andy had been kicked by a horse when he was three years old. The side of his head bore a rugged, vicious scar, and I concluded that Andy's little mind bore a scar as well. I determined that I would do all that I could for him. With his older sister, Teresa, I longed to find some way to protect him from the cruel, angry world.

David Dickerson had no problem with ability. He was wiry, witty, and had a constant, seemingly uncontrollable energy. He wished to be at all places and involved in all things at once, and found it most difficult to sit still long enough for a *fact* to catch up to him. This six-year-old thrived on ideas rather than information and jumped quickly from one to another. *If I can ever corral all that energy and steer it in the right direction,* I thought, *I'll have an exceptionally capable student.* In the meantime, David seemed to wish to be in the wheatfield, the playground, on his pony, up a pine tree—anywhere but quietly seated at a desk in the classroom. Still, he did have a hunger for knowledge, and I was sure that if I could only get him to sit still long enough, he would learn quickly.

By the end of our first day spent together, I had been able to introduce my pupils to the open door of learning; but I knew that many difficult days lay ahead before I would be able to sort them into legitimate classes. Certainly I couldn't divide them by age. I would have to wait and discover their learning abilities.

I went home from my first day in the classroom excited and exhausted. Every student I had—and there were nineteen—needed individual tutoring. Would I be able to handle it? Where would the time come from? How long before some of them could work on their own?

It seemed that my only recourse was to prepare individual assignments, both after school at night and before school each morning. Then each member of the class would have something to work on as I took time with the individual lessons.

I sighed deeply at the awesome task that lay ahead of me. Reminding myself that it was a challenge but not an impossibility, I squared my shoulders as I entered the teacherage door.

I brewed some tea and carried the teapot and my china cup to my chair and sat down. Poking at some of the chair stuffing to make it fit me better, I decided I should get some sort of footstool so that I could put my feet up for a few minutes at the end of the day. I recalled seeing a small wooden crate in the storage shed. Surely I could find enough pieces of material in my sewing basket to cover it. I planned that it would be my next Saturday's project.

As I relaxed in my big chair and sipped the hot tea, I thought about each student and how best I could teach him. As soon as I had drained my cup, I began preparing some simple assignments. I worked well into the late evening by the wavering light of the lamp. Tonight even the howling of the coyotes failed to distract me.

The week was a busy one. I arose early each morning to write assignments on the blackboard and to add last-minute ideas to the lessons that I had prepared on paper. The day was given entirely to the students. Already some of them were beginning to show abilities in one area or another. A small group was slowly emerging who would be able to take a forward step in arithmetic. Another group was ready to go on in the second primer. Two students showed real promise in art and three had musical ability.

Daily I felt frustrated by my lack of materials for teaching. *If only I had . . .* , I often started thinking. But I didn't have, so I tried to make up for the lack with creativity.

At the end of the classroom time, I lingered for a few moments to correct work and plan the next day, then rushed home, made my cup of tea and rested for a few moments in my overstuffed chair. All the time that I sipped, my mind refused to relax. It leaped from one idea to another, from plan to plan. As soon as my cup was empty I returned to work in the classroom, trying to put my ideas to work.

By the end of the week I was physically weary, but I was perhaps the happiest I had ever been in my life. I had planned to work on the footstool on Saturday, but instead I asked my students if they knew of anyone with whom I could ride into town. The growing list of items that I might find to assist me in the classroom prompted this request. I dreaded another long trip to town in a bumpy wagon, but I couldn't very well hand the list over to someone else and expect him to do the shopping for me.

To my delight, Sally Clark brought word on Friday that her folks were going to town on Saturday and would be happy to pick me up at eight o'clock the next morning.

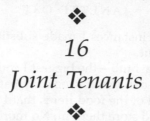

16
Joint Tenants

TRUE TO THEIR word, the Clarks arrived at ten to eight. My list and I were ready to go. I did not plan to make a weekly trip to Lacombe, so I had tried to think of all that I might be needing in the near future.

One of the needs came to my attention when I discovered that I was not living alone. How many other occupants the house held was still unknown to me, but it was easy to tell by the evidence that I found on several mornings that I was sharing my home with a family of mice.

I guess the mice felt that *I* was the intruder; it was apparent that they assumed the entire place belonged to them.

The first morning that I saw the evidence, I was frightened. I had never lived with mice before. What if they were to climb into my bed and nibble my fingers or, horrors of horrors, become tangled in my hair? What could I do about them? How did one go about getting rid of mice? I added mousetraps to my list, but I wasn't sure what I was to look for. I had never seen a mousetrap.

The next morning I had found a corner nibbled from my fresh loaf of bread. Now I was angry—the nerve of the little beasts! There was no way that I was going to share my home *and* my food with rodents. I boldly underlined mousetraps on my list.

Before I went to bed the next night, I placed all my food stuffs in the cupboards, out of the rodents' reach. On the fourth morning of my busy teaching week, I found evidence of the mice having romped over my dishes—right in my cupboards! I was furious and repelled. I took all of the dishes from my cupboards, washed them in hot, soapy water and scalded them with boiling water from the teakettle, all the while breathing vengeance against those nasty creatures. Indeed, something had to be done. I thought of sending a note to Mr. Laverly with one of the students who passed by his farm, but I stubbornly rejected the idea. Surely I could handle a little problem like mice.

So, as I traveled to town on that overcast Saturday morning, sitting on a makeshift seat in the Clarks' wagon, I thought about my unwelcome tenants. After today I would be rid of them, for I planned to leave traps throughout the house. I felt no pity whatever for the creatures who would be caught in those traps.

As soon as the Clarks dropped me off at the general store, I set to work on my list. I could find only a portion of the items that I had desired for the classroom. In a few instances I made substitutions. In many cases I was forced to do without.

I purchased a large washtub—the biggest I could find, determined that I would have a decent soak when I took my bath.

I carefully selected all of the food items that I felt I needed and added a few metal containers to store them in. No more would mice be sharing my loaf of bread while I waited for my traps to do their job.

"Now," I said to the long-nosed clerk, "I need mousetraps—the best that you have."

I don't know what I expected him to show me, but certainly not that little bit of wood and wire.

"This is a mousetrap?"

"Yes, ma'am."

"Is that all you have?"

"What did you have in mind, ma'am?"

"Well—I'm—I'm not sure. I've never needed—but I thought . . . How does that catch them—what holds them in? There's no cage."

"No, ma'am." I think that he smiled, though he turned too quickly for me to be sure.

"Why don't they run off?" I persisted.

"They don't run off, ma'am—'cause they're *dead*," he answered me, his face solemn but his eyes twinkling.

"Dead?"

"Yes, ma'am."

"What kills them?"

"The trap, ma'am."

I looked at the small thing, bewildered.

He finally picked up a trap and, as though speaking to a small child, proceeded to show me.

"You place the bait here, ma'am—just a touch. Then you pull this back and hook it, gently, like this. You place it carefully in the path you think the mouse will follow. He comes to steal the bait"—he reached out with the pencil from behind his ear—"and—."

There was a sharp bang, and the trap sprang forward—and I backward. The pencil was snapped in the firm grip of the trap. I staggered over bails of twine that were stacked behind me on the floor and nearly lost my balance while color flooded my cheeks. The clerk bent his head down as he freed his pencil from the trap—and, I imagine, composed his face.

"I'll take ten of them," I said with all of the dignity that I could muster.

"Ten?" He cleared his throat and blinked. "So many?"

"I have no idea how many mice there are."

"One trap is usable over and over, ma'am."

This was further news to me.

"You just lift the wire," the clerk explained patiently, "release the dead mouse and reset."

It sounded easy enough.

"Fine," I said. "I'll take one."

He put the trap with my other purchases.

By the time the Clarks returned to pick me up, I and my new belongings were ready for the long trip home.

There was still daylight left when we arrived home, so I started to work on the footstool. Rather than piecing material from the bits and scraps in my sewing basket, I had decided to purchase some sturdy material in town. I had even bought some batting so that the footstool would be padded.

Humming as I sewed and tacked, I found this project challenging and gratifying. I was pleased with my first attempt as furniture-maker. I even had enough material left to make a small pillow to match the stool.

By the time I had sorted my purchases, placing those in the schoolroom that belonged there and the others in my house, it was late and I was weary.

I dragged my large tub into my bedroom, poured the water that I had heated and enjoyed my bath. It wasn't like our fine tub at home, but I could at least sit in it and splash the water over the rest of me.

It had been a good week, I decided, as I crawled into bed. I felt that I had made progress in the classroom. The children were learning. I had a tub big enough for bathing, and I—I hadn't set the mousetrap! I climbed out of my warm bed and re-lit the lamp, burning my fingers on the still-hot chimney.

It looked so easy when the man in the store had demonstrated it. It wasn't easy at all. I rubbed a small portion of butter on the metal bait piece, and then stretched the wire back—back. I was trying to fasten it down when—"ping"—it snapped together and flew from my hand across the floor. Shaken, I went after it, feeling as if it were capable of attacking me. Again I tried and again it snapped. The sixth attempt got my finger, and I cried out in anger and frustration. I wasn't sure what I was the most angry at--the homesteading mice or the offensive trap.

Finally, on about the tenth try, I managed to secure the wire, and I gingerly placed the unruly bit of wood and metal on the floor by the cupboard. Eyeing its location, I decided to move it over just a bit with my foot when--"ping"--it sprang into the air. I jumped and struck my hip against the stove.

Almost in tears, I again went through the procedure. Eventually the trap was set and placed on the ideal spot. As I inspected it now, I couldn't see any butter left on the little projection intended for the bait, but I refused to touch the thing again.

I blew out the lamp and crawled back into bed. My finger was still smarting and my hip throbbed from its encounter with the hard iron of the stove. I snuggled under the warm quilt and tried to think of things more pleasant than mousetraps and unwelcome guests.

* * *

I suppose that it was about one o'clock when the sharp "ping" of the trap brought me upright in my bed, staring toward the open door of my bedroom. In my drowsy state, I did not understand where the sound had come from, but I then remembered what had taken so much of my time the night before. Well, at least it had worked. Maybe now my problems with unwanted roommates would be over.

I snuggled back down but I couldn't go to sleep. The thought of an animal out there in my kitchen, all tangled up in the metal of that trap, disturbed me. What should I do about it? Should I go and release it at once? Was it already too late? But I couldn't bring myself to face the situation by the flickering light of my lamp.

The dawn was approaching when I finally was able to doze off.

When I awakened again it was full daylight. At first I felt alarmed, realizing that I had slept long past my usual waking hour. Then I remembered it was Sunday and settled back to enjoy the comfort of my bed for a few more minutes. I planned a leisurely day, thankful indeed that today there would be a church service in the schoolroom. I had sent the message home with all of the pupils that I would be only too happy to share the community school with a Sunday congregation, and the service had been set for two o'clock.

I wasn't used to an afternoon service, and it seemed a long time to wait, but at least it was something to look forward to. Surely I would be able to somehow fill the long morning hours with productive activities while I waited. I began to take a mental inventory of what I had on hand to read.

I crawled out of bed, stretching and flexing my muscles. If I didn't lie just right on my mattress, I could wake up with some stubborn kinks. This morning I seemed to have several. I wasn't concerned. I had all morning to gradually work them out.

I slipped on my robe and slippers and headed for my stove. I'd make the fire and start the coffee.

In my early morning reverie, I very nearly failed to notice a small object on my floor. I was just about to lower my right foot on it when I jerked back with a gasp. My mousetrap had jumped halfway across the floor from its original position. There it lay, and securely clamped to the wood base was a limp, dead mouse.

I shall not describe further the sight that met my eyes or my revulsion as I looked at it. My first thought was to run, but I soon stifled my panic and convinced myself that the trap and its victim could do me very little bodily harm.

My next thought was not a welcome one—it was up to *me* to care for the furry corpse in my pathway. Somehow I must remove the mouse from the trap if I were to have the trap for future use, as the clerk in the store had indicated. The thought of touching it made me shudder. I couldn't. I knew I couldn't. At length I took the broom and dustpan and swept the whole thing up. Holding the dustpan at arm's length, I marched outside and across the clearing. The helpful clerk had said to simply release the dead mouse and reset the trap. How clever—and how impossible.

I walked resolutely on, trying to keep my eyes from the contents of the dustpan. I neared the two small buildings at the far side of the clearing. Glancing furtively about to make sure that no one was watching, I headed for the one marked "Boys." I did not want to share even my outhouse with the dead mouse.

As quickly as I could, I stepped into the building and dumped the mouse, trap and all, down the hole. I then hurried out, again glancing about as one committing a crime, and headed back to the house.

I took a scrub pail and washed the floor where the mouse had lain, my dustpan, and even my broom; and then I began to scrub my hands. I never did succeed that morning in making them feel really clean, so I didn't bother fixing any breakfast. Instead, I poured a cup of coffee (I didn't have to actually touch that), picked up my Bible and headed for the classroom. I would calm myself, read and pray, and wait for the afternoon service.

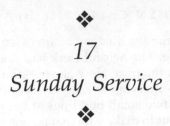

17
Sunday Service

NOT TOO MANY had arrived at the school by two o'clock. The Petersons were the first to appear. Because the day was cloudy and cool, Lars was allowed to build a fire in the big stove.

The Dickersons came and then the Blakes, the Johnsons and a family by the name of Thebeau. They had two teenage sons who would not be in school until after the harvest—if at all.

Mr. Dickerson was in charge of the service. We sang several songs and read scripture. Mrs. Thebeau gave a Bible lesson for the children, then Mr. Dickerson gave some thoughts on a passage of scripture. It was *not* a sermon, he clarified, because he was *not* a preacher. He voiced some worthwhile insights, and I appreciated his direct approach. I even found myself thinking that it was a shame he was *not* a preacher.

As we stood around visiting after the short service, other teams began pulling into the schoolyard. My first thought was that they had misunderstood the time for the afternoon meeting and were arriving late. What a shame!

I glanced about me. To my surprise there was activity going on all around me in the schoolroom. The fire had been built up and a large kettle of water placed on to heat. Tables were being pushed together, items laid out upon them, and men were busy rearranging the desks. Seeing my puzzled look, Anna Peterson crossed over to me.

"Da folks wanta meet da new teacher. Dis be gud vay, yah?"

I was astounded. But as the afternoon went on I agreed with Anna. Yes, this was a good way. All of my students and their parents were there— except for Phillip Delaney and his parents; they, I was informed, were very sorry to miss the gathering but they were, of necessity, in Calgary for the weekend. Others from the community, though they did not have children of school age, took advantage of the opportunity to get together with the neighbors and perhaps to satisfy curiosity about the new schoolmarm. They all welcomed me heartily.

There were a few men whom I presumed to be unmarried. Two of them were in their twenties, I would have guessed, and the others were older. Three of them in particular made me uncomfortable—I wasn't used to such open stares. One was especially bold. I was afraid that he might approach me, but he never left his companions. I hoped that I wouldn't be thrown into his company at some future date.

Unconsciously, I found myself watching for a possible glimpse of Wynn, but I did not see him. It was obvious that he was not concerned about meeting the new schoolteacher. A foolish disappointment trailed me about the room as I made the acquaintance of my new neighbors. I forced the ridiculous thought from my mind.

I liked my new neighbors. In comparison to my upbringing, they lacked refinement and polish; but they were open and friendly, and I respected their spirit of venture and their sense of humor. They were hearty people, these pioneers. They knew how to laugh and, obviously, they knew how to work.

When the last of the group had returned to their homes, I walked slowly to my teacherage, my heart singing. I already felt that I was a part of this community, and I liked the feeling. I was completely happy here; then I thought of my still-present mice companions, and my song left me. What would I do with them? Live with them, I guessed. . . .

18
Letters

I WAS BUSY chalking an assignment on the blackboard the following afternoon when I heard a firm rap. Before I could respond, the door began to open, so I continued on with my writing, thinking that it was a student who had forgotten some item.

"Be right with you," I said without turning around, and set out to finish the sentence that I was writing.

"That's fine, Miss Thatcher," came a very grown-up, male voice. I swung around leaving a "g" with a very odd, long tail. I'm sure my face must have betrayed my surprise. There was Jon's Calgary friend, Wynn. My breath caught in a gasp and I stood staring for what seemed like eons. My voice would not cooperate in saying the greeting I knew I should extend.

"I'm sorry if I startled you," he began.

"Oh, no—it's fine. It's just—I thought—"

"I've frightened you." His voice held apology.

I shook my head and tried to laugh. It sounded ridiculous, high-pitched and nervous. I decided not to laugh any further.

"I was expecting a student to be standing . . ." My voice sounded nervous also.

"I might have a lot to learn." He smiled and his eyes hinted at teasing. "But I'm afraid that I would look a little out of place in your classroom."

I swallowed, then rubbed at the chalk dust on my hands.

"I'm afraid that I had to miss your party, Miss Thatcher. I hear that it was a success."

"Yes—yes, it was—very nice," I said lamely.

His eyes took in my white-dusted hands that were rubbing together nervously, then lifted to meet my eyes. Afraid that he was about to make some silly statement about my students being lucky to have such an attractive teacher, I squared my shoulders. He didn't. His eyes shifted to the assignment on the board and then glanced around the room. He stepped away from me and went on a brief tour, carefully taking in all that there was to see. I stood watching him, noticing that even in this small room, he moved with confidence and purpose. Keenly aware of the chalk dust on my frock and the strands of hair that had loosened themselves and wisped about my face, my thoughts tumbled over each other. *What a sight I must be. I probably even have a shiny nose.*

He finished his tour, seeming to approve of what he found.

"I'm so glad that we finally have a school," he said with sincerity, his voice deep and convincing.

"Yes," I almost whispered, "I'm glad too. They are so eager . . ."

Love for my pupils and his unsettling presence made my voice waver, and I was forced to turn from my visitor. I slowly erased the last "g" I had put on the board and rewrote it properly. Finishing the sentence carefully, I put away the chalk I was holding and wiped my hands on a cloth that I kept for the purpose.

"Now, Mr.—Mr.—?" I faltered.

"Forgive me," he said. "I was so fascinated with your room I forgot to introduce myself. I'm Wynn Delaney—long-time friend of your brother Jonathan."

I did not bother to explain that I was quite aware of that last fact.

"How do you do, Mr. Delaney?" I even managed to smile slightly. I admired myself for my control—now that I felt it slowly returning. "Won't you sit down, Mr. Delaney?"

"Thank you, but no. I must go. I apologize for bursting in on you unannounced and unknown, but I admit to having a feeling of already knowing you. As I said, I've known Jon and Mary for a number of years, and I have seen you—though I was not granted an introduction."

And, I mentally supplied for him, *"I never forget a pretty face"*—right, Mr. Delaney?

He did not say that, nor anything like it, however. He continued, "I spent the weekend in Calgary and was asked to deliver to you this packet of letters. Mary seemed to feel that it was quite urgent that you receive them to stave off your great loneliness." His eyes twinkled again. "They asked how you were, but I had to confess that I knew nothing, except that school was in session."

He smiled and handed me a bulging envelope.

"Thank you. It was kind of you to act as messenger-boy." I hoped that he recognized and appreciated my attempt at humor.

"No problem—since I was going right by. Should I see your family again soon, may I relay that you look to be in good health and spirits?"

"By all means, Mr. Delaney. I am quite enjoying the community and my school."

He nodded his own dismissal with a slight smile, replaced the hat he carried in his hand, and left the schoolroom.

I stood and gazed toward the closed door. I could hear the jingle of harness and the creaking of wheels in the yard, but I did not allow myself the privilege of running to a window.

He had not said that he hoped to see me again. He had not made any mention of finding another excuse to call. He had not even offered any of the light flattery that I was rather accustomed to expect.

A long sigh escaped me, and I turned back to my chalkboard. It was no use. I couldn't concentrate on what I had been doing. I looked down at my hand that held the packet of letters. The letters! Of course, it was the letters from Jon and the family that had disrupted my thoughts. I would hurry home, have my tea and read my letters. After that I would be myself again and able to gather my thoughts back to my lesson preparation.

I hurried home, built my fire and put on the kettle. I immediately began digging into my parcel of mail. There was a short note from William telling me about his new schoolteacher, and a copied, carefully penned note from Sarah—my name filled most of one sheet. She also wrote I MISS YOU in big block letters, and squeezed her name in at the bottom. There was a sheet with hugs and kisses from Kathleen, and in one corner was a little hug and kiss marked from Elizabeth; Mary had written an explanation that Kathleen insisted Baby Elizabeth have opportunity to send her love as well.

Jon's letter was brief and brotherly, expressing concern for my well-being and happiness, and imploring me to come to Calgary whenever I had opportunity. Mary's letter, a lengthy epistle, included a recitation of everything that had happened in the brief time I had been gone. She added anecdotes and cute sayings from the children. I devoured it all hungrily. I was so glad to hear from them. I wished they were nearer so that I might more readily share my happiness with them.

My tea water had boiled and then cooled because I had neglected to fuel the fire beneath it. I coaxed a flame back to life and nourished it with more kindling and then larger pieces. While the fire took hold again and began to reheat the kettle, I prepared some bread and cheese.

As I sipped my tea and nibbled the bread, my feet resting on my new footstool (which wasn't very ladylike, according to Mother), I again scanned through my letters. I laughed at Mary's comments concerning Mr. Higgins. She had met him at a downtown store, and he had awkwardly asked about me. Mary had replied that she assumed I was just fine, although she had not heard from me since just after I had arrived. He had replied with astonishment, "You mean she stayed?" "Of course she stayed," Mary said. "Isn't that what she was supposed to do?" "Oh, yes—yes, of course," Higgins mumbled and walked off with a red face.

My thoughts kept turning from the letters to their courier, but I refused to let my mind dwell on him. Even though I deliberately tried to keep my mind from straying to Wynn Delaney, I found that the name and the face kept taunting my fancies. Finally I laid aside my teacup, changed my dress and went out to split wood for my fire. Perhaps some vigorous activity would settle my imagination, I reasoned, and I attacked my woodpile with a vengeance.

19

The Living Mousetrap

THE FOLLOWING MORNING I got up to find that the furry squatters had been prancing around on my cupboard top. I *had* to do something! There simply was no living with them. I could not bear sharing my cozy home with the mice.

I again washed and boiled all of my dishes and scrubbed and rubbed everything that I imagined they might have touched. With a great deal of difficulty, I moved two empty metal trunks from my bedroom and placed all of the dishes from the cupboard in one and all of the foodstuffs that I could fit into the other. *Surely the mice will not be able to get in there,* I determined as I closed the lids with a bang and marched over to my school, too upset to bother about breakfast.

By the time the students began to arrive, I had calmed down a bit and was able to welcome them with a smile.

The next two days went well, though it was a nuisance to be digging around in the trunks every time I fixed a meal.

On Wednesday, Lars brought me a fresh supply of produce and stared in amazement as I placed bread, cheese and eggs in my large trunk.

"I have mice," I informed him as I went to place the milk, cream and butter in the metal pail with a lid in the dugout on the north end of the house.

"Ya need a cat?" he asked, and I wondered why I hadn't thought of that.

"Do you have one that I could borrow?"

"Ve have lots. More all da time."

"I'll think about it."

We went to the classroom together.

On Thursday morning I awoke to find a drowned mouse in my slop bucket. I was horrified as I stared at the soggy lump of lifeless fur.

Well, at least it wasn't my water pail, I thought as I carried my slop bucket to the farthest corner of the school grounds and dumped it. I half expected the dead mouse to jump up and dash for my house but, fortunately, it stayed put. I turned and ran for the house myself.

I wanted to scrub out the slop bucket with soapy water, but that seemed foolish, so I just rinsed it a bit and set it a little farther away from my eating area. Again I skipped breakfast and went right to school.

That night I laid aside all of my reserve and headed over to the Petersons' to beg, borrow, or steal a cat.

The one that Lars offered me was rather mangy looking, a big, yellow thing.

"She be a good mouser," he maintained, and I didn't doubt him for a moment.

He carried her home for me—an act that I appreciated very much. I would rather have had one of the many cute little kittens, but Lars talked me out of that. "No good fer mice," he said. I took his word for it.

Lars deposited the large, hungry-looking cat in my kitchen and turned to go. "Vatch da door," he cautioned. "If she get out, she run home."

I watched the door. Lars left and the cat stayed.

Later I almost wished that she had gone. She prowled and yowled until I thought I wouldn't be able to stand another minute of it. Still, if she cleared my house of mice, the noise and commotion would be worth it.

At bedtime I shut my door against her nervous activity. I could hear her prowling and climbing, jumping and mewing, and I mentally followed her about the room—my chair, my table, my cupboard, my trunk. That cat didn't respect a single piece of furniture.

And then I heard a dreadful crash. *If that was my teapot!* was my first thought as I reached for a match to light the lamp. Fortunately, it was only a chipped cup that I had neglected to remove from the table. I swept up the broken pieces and dumped them into the stove. I took my teapot into the bedroom and carefully placed it in the trunk with my books. Then I blew out the lamp and crawled back into bed. I tried to force my thoughts away from the restless cat as it prowled about my house. *No mice will show tonight,* I thought, *with all of that racket going on.* I was wrong. About four in the morning I was awakened by a commotion in my kitchen, and then a sharp, sickening squeak of fright or pain. The cat had pounced.

The dreadful sound reverberated through my brain long after the cat had decided to call it a night. What an awful thing to be a small mouse caught by a mammoth cat!

In the morning my revulsion toward the incident hung over me like a cloud. I delayed getting up for as long as I dared. I was sure that I would find my kitchen strewn with dead mice. I didn't. Puss was still there, looking hungry and lean. There was no evidence of her nocturnal hunting.

I was nearing the conclusion that I must have imagined the sounds in the night when my tidying brought me to my favorite chair. At first I supposed that a small twig had somehow found its way onto the seat. I reached down and picked it up. It was in my hand before I recognized it—the tail of a mouse! The cat had dared to have her dinner right where I did my evening relaxing!

That did it. I went to my door, and feeling a little foolish, opened it slightly and called the cat. As she slinked out and started running for home, I asked forgiveness of the mice. Surely there was a more civilized way of getting rid of them. One thing I knew for sure: there must be a quieter way.

20
A Visitor

BEFORE LONG, I was reminded again that I was still not rid of mice. I had no idea how many remained, but I judged it to be more than enough.

My cupboard stood empty while my trunks fairly bulged with what should have been on the shelves. Just making a cup of tea required extra effort. Those things that I couldn't fit into my trunks I covered. I covered my water pail. I even covered the spout of my teakettle. No matter what job I did, I checked first for the evidence of a mouse having been there before me. It was an awkward way to live, but I forced myself to adjust to it.

My pupils were progressing favorably. I had been assured that after the field work was finished, I would have three or four more students.

I was having a problem with Phillip Delaney. He tended to occupy himself with things other than what he was assigned to do. When, for three days running, his copy work was not completed by dismissal time, I asked him to stay for a chat after the pupils had been dismissed. I explained very carefully that should it happen again, I would require him to remain behind to finish his work.

The next day, to my dismay, his work was not completed.

"Phillip, I am disappointed," I said. "You had plenty of time to do your work."

He didn't seem concerned. "Shall I stay and do it like Tommy does?"

"Thomas needs special help with his lessons. He doesn't understand them on his own. That's why he stays, so that I can help him."

"But you said if I didn't finish, I'd have to stay."

"That's right."

He made no comment but reached fur his pencil and began to work.

He finished his work quickly and then lingered until I insisted that he run home.

The next day his work went unfinished again.

"You'll have to stay until it's done," I declared. "Maybe this will help you to learn to work more quickly." I knew that Phillip's problem was not difficulty in understanding, for Phillip, unlike Thomas, was a bright child.

He did not protest. Again the work was done in good time, and again Phillip hung around chatting. I finally sent him home.

A short while later, I had an unexpected visitor. I was just putting away the last of the books that had been used in the day's lessons and was tidying up, when there was a rap on the door. Wynn Delaney walked in.

As usual, his presence unnerved me, and I expect that I flushed slightly.

"Am I interrupting?" he asked.

"Not at all. I was just leaving. Please come in."

He stepped to the front and took a seat near my desk. It looked odd to see such a tall man curled up in the small desk. He had to stretch his long legs out before him to make room for them. Somehow his relaxed attitude put me more at ease.

"More letters?" I asked mischievously.

He smiled and shook his head.

"No, this time it's school business. I came to see you about Phillip. He's had to stay after school a couple of times."

I thought, *What do you have to do with Phillip?* But I pushed it aside as the issue of my discipline being questioned seemed more important.

"You object to my method of discipline?"

"Not at all," he responded, almost as quickly. "I merely wonder if it's the best way to handle Phillip."

"Meaning?"

"Tell me, Miss Thatcher, how did Phillip respond to staying late? Did it upset him—annoy him?"

"Not at all." I was becoming defensive.

He smiled—a slow, deliberate smile, and in spite of myself I noticed what a pleasant smile he had. Yet his smile also told me that he had somehow just proved a point. He didn't even say anything; he just waited for me to understand what he had just said.

"You mean . . . ?" I began slowly.

"Exactly. Phillip likes nothing better than the extra time and attention, Miss Thatcher."

"I see," I said, looking away from him, realizing as I reviewed the past few days that he was quite right. I turned slowly back to him.

"So—" I began, reaching out for advice, "what do you suggest?"

"Well, his mother and I—"

His mother and I. The words hit me like a pail of cold water and I could feel the air leaving my lungs and the blood draining out of my head. For a moment I felt dizzy, and I lowered myself into my chair, not even checking first to make sure that it was really where it was supposed to be. *His mother and I—Delaney . . . of course, Phillip Delaney—Wynn Delaney.* This was Phillip's father. *What a fool I've been,* I upbraided myself, *to be nursing illusions about a married man.*

I recovered quickly as I realized that Mr. Delaney was waiting for my response to his suggestion, which I had missed in my dismay.

"I'm sorry—" I stumbled along awkwardly, "I'm afraid my thoughts . . . I—I was off somewhere and I didn't—"

I left it dangling and he repeated, "His mother and I thought that if you could send uncompleted work home with him, we would see that it was finished and returned."

"Of course." I felt embarrassed that he had to explain again.

It seemed like a good enough plan. And right now I was willing to agree with almost anything that would speed this man's departure from my schoolroom.

I stood up and hurried on, "That sounds like a good approach. I will tell Phillip of the new arrangement. And now if—if you'll excuse me, Mr. Delaney, I do have things—a lot of things to attend to."

He arose with a questioning look in his eyes; I then remembered I had told him when he entered that I was finished and ready to leave. He did not mention the fact, however, and excused himself in a gentlemanly fashion.

Odd feelings were quivering within me as I watched him go. What a silly goose I had been to blithely assume that he was unmarried. The fact that he was the most attractive man I had ever met I could not deny— but had I known he was married, I never would have allowed him another thought. *Well, I know now—so that is that,* I thought, mentally giving myself a shake. I firmly pushed all thoughts of the man from me and walked briskly from the classroom. I decided to run over to Anna's for a cup of her good, strong coffee. She was always coaxing me to come, and I too often pleaded busyness. Well, tonight I would take time. I was in no mood to sit by myself and calmly sip tea. *I might even stay for supper if she insists,* I told myself, knowing full well that she would. *It will save me standing on my head to dig something from my trunks,* and thus keeping my thoughts in control, I resolutely shut the door behind me.

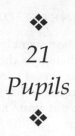

21
Pupils

O NLY ONCE DID Phillip need to have work sent home with him. He gave it to me the next morning, carefully completed. From then on, Phillip finished his work easily in the allotted time.

He was a little charmer. I suppose that, try as I might not to, I must have shown a slight amount of favoritism. He found little ways to spend time with me, and I'm sure that I enjoyed it every bit as much as he did.

Else Peterson was also one of my "special" students. She was quick to learn and eager to please. I did have opportunity to have her for Saturday "tea." That day she had run across the field between us with some warm coffeecake fresh from her mother's oven. It was delicious, and we called it "tea" cake instead, eating it right away with our tea served in my china cups. Else's tea, diluted with milk, was a marvelous treat for her, and her eyes sparkled through her shyness as she looked at the cups and the dainty teapot.

"Miss T'atcher," she told me solemnly, "it is like having a fairy picnic." I loved little Else. She was a precious, gentle child.

Sally Clark also found a warm place in my heart. She was rather pathetic, this girl-turning-woman. She wanted so much to enter into the adult world, yet she clung to her childish world as well. I noticed, as the days went by, her shy watching of me and her awkward attempts to copy me. I took it as a sincere compliment, and I often wished that I could take her home with me and put her in one of my pretty dresses, arrange her hair, and then let her see the attractive girl in the mirror. She was a pretty girl in her own way, and I often had the impression that someday we might waken and find this shy little butterfly free of her cocoon. I realized that I would be unwise to try and rush nature's own slow, yet certain, process. To show Sally through my wardrobe and tempt her with pretty things that I had always taken for granted would only make her worn and simple clothing look all the more drab in her eyes. So, rather, I made simple suggestions and spoke words of encouragement when I could: "Blue is one of your best colors"; "That type of collar suits you well"; "Your hair looks very pretty that way—you have such pretty hair." I tried to build up each one of my pupils with sincere praise, but with Sally my smiles and words had extra meaning. She flushed slightly when I did this, but I knew that my approval was important to her.

Then there was Andy. Even to look at him made my heart ache. He seemed to grow worse as the days went by. At times I saw him reach up and grasp his head with both hands as though he were in pain, a look of confusion and misery filling his eyes. I tried not to draw attention to him, but as soon as I was able I'd come to his side and kneel beside him.

"Andy, why don't you just put your head down on your arms for a few minutes," I would whisper.

What I truly longed to do was gather him into my own arms and shelter him there, though I seldom had the appropriate opportunity. Usually he would look at me with thankfulness in his eyes, and then he would do as I suggested, sometimes rocking himself gently back and forth. I was concerned that his inability to cope with the schoolwork might be causing him physical problems. I did not push him, but I did so want to offer him all that he was capable of retaining. I was on the verge of trying to find out where he lived so that I could call on his folks when, one school morning, Andy did not arrive with his sister Teresa.

"Mamma think he need rest," she said, and I nodded my head in sympathetic agreement.

All the students missed Andy. He was a favorite with everyone, for even though he could not fully participate in classroom learning or outside games, he vigorously cheered on all who could. In the classroom his eyes would shine whenever anyone read or recited well, and occasionally he spontaneously clapped his hands in jolly appreciation. I never reproached him for his exuberance, and the students watched Andy as they recited, hoping to win his favor. On the playground he watched the games with intent, and shouted and jumped wildly for any accomplishment. Andy did not pick favorites. He cheered everyone on with the same enthusiasm. His clapping hands and fervent exclamation of, "You did good! You did good!" was something that each student worked for.

Carl Clark, just entering his teens, was a problem for me. He was Sally's cousin and made it known that he didn't need this "dumb ol' school"— he was going to be a cowboy and work on a ranch in southern Alberta. He spent far more time practicing with his lariat than poring over his reader. He spent every recess roping fence posts.

He had started out roping fellow students until I had firmly put a stop to it.

One day I gave Harvey Mattoch, one of my younger children, permission to leave the room; and, as I did with all of my children, I kept an eye out for his return. The minutes ticked by, and still no Harvey. I went on with the spelling lesson, but my mind kept wondering about Harvey. When I dismissed the class for recess, I immediately went to look for him. I found him cowering behind the woodpile in tears.

"Harvey," I coaxed, "come on out and let's talk about it."

He shook his head, and a fresh torrent of tears began to fall.

"What happened?"

He cried harder.

I sat down on a block of wood and waited for his outburst to subside. As soon as he seemed to have control, I passed him my handkerchief, let him mop up and blow his nose, then asked him again.

"The—the door to—to the boys' place is all tied up," he managed between sobs.

Sure enough, it was—with Carl Clark's lariat. Harvey had tried to get the rope untied and the door free, but not in time to avert an "accident." I gave him permission to run home for dry clothes.

"You stay right here out of sight," I told him, "until I call the children in from recess. No one else has missed you yet."

I wrote a quick note to his mother in the hope that the boy wouldn't be scolded or shamed at home, smuggled it to him, and then rang the bell. A few minutes later I saw the bobbing of his head as he ran down the road in his hurry to get home unnoticed.

At the end of the day I asked Carl to remain behind. I told him how disappointed I was that he would use his rope to tie up a *needed* building and that for the next week his recesses would be occupied in hauling wood for the school stove. I also told him that his lariat was not to be seen at school again. He sulked as he left the room, but I had no further problem with the rope. Eventually Carl even joined the other boys in their games. I did have to revise my recess punishment, however. The weather had been too mild to use the big iron stove, and Carl hauled enough wood in two days to completely fill the wood storage bin in the schoolhouse and stack more by the door.

Considering the fact that my students had never had any formal education prior to this year; considering the fact that I had very few educational aids to use on their behalf; considering the fact that I had all of them under one roof and on all grade levels; considering the fact that they came from various ethnic backgrounds, and some of them did not even speak English well; considering the fact that I was young with only two previous years of teaching experience, I was rather proud of everyone—well, almost everyone.

During the weeks that followed I had the pleasant experience of being invited to several neighborhood homes for Sunday dinner or a weekday supper. Some of the homes I visited were even more simply furnished than my little teacherage. A few were surprisingly comfortable and charmingly decorated and arranged. But wherever I went, the people were anxious to share with me the best they could offer. I loved them for it.

It was difficult for me to accept their hospitality when I was not in a position to return it. They seemed to sense how I felt and were quick to assure me that this was their small way of saying thanks to me for coming to teach their children. It made me more determined than ever to do the best that I could.

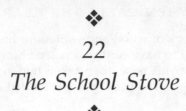

22
The School Stove

❖

V ERY SUDDENLY THE warm weather turned cold and rainy. One morning I awoke to a cloudy, dark sky, a cold wind and rain like ice water. Even in my snug little house I shivered as I dressed. I could hardly believe that a day could be so drastically different from the one just preceding it. I decided that my schoolroom must have a fire—the first one yet needed. At least we were well stocked for wood, thanks to Carl.

As I looked at the sky, I was glad that it was Friday. Maybe by Monday we'd have our sunshine back again.

I built my own fire and put on my coffeepot. The hungry flames began to lick at the wood quickly, and the warmth was soon spilling out into the room. As I looked at the dismal day, I wondered how many of my students would venture forth. I wouldn't have blamed them if they'd stayed home.

I decided to do everything that was necessary before leaving the house so that once I had crossed to the schoolhouse in the rain I could stay there.

With this in mind, I cared for my daily grooming, almost gasping for breath as I washed in the cold water; I breakfasted, had my morning Bible reading, and tidied my two small rooms. Before I left I banked my fire the way that Lars had shown me and then bundled myself up tightly in my coat, tied a scarf on my head, and dashed for the school.

It was cold in the room, all right, but I still had plenty of time to take the chill from the air before my students arrived.

I threw aside my coat and went to work on laying the firewood. My hands were already numb with the cold and dampness. I got the paper and kindling ready to light but, though I searched everywhere that a matchbox might be, I found none. I buttoned on my coat, donned my damp scarf, and dashed back through the rain to the teacherage for some matches. In my haste as I returned to the school, I stepped into a big puddle and splashed muddy water up my leg. Undaunted, I ran on and, once inside, threw off my coat and dripping scarf and went to work on the fire again. I had no problem getting the kindling to accept the flame and soon a brisk fire was begging greedily for more fuel; also, soon the room was beginning to fill with blue woodsmoke. I opened the door of the stove and peered in. Smoke puffed out and stung my eyes. I slammed the door shut. *Maybe it will take just a few moments to begin to draw,* I thought, thinking of my father's words concerning our fireplace at home.

The minutes passed by, and the stove did *not* draw; it only seemed to *blow*—billows of choking smoke filled the classroom.

I poked and fussed with the fire, but it only increased my coughing and watering eyes and got soot and ashes all over my hands and clothing. Determining that the only way to save my room from total disaster was to drench the fire, I picked up the pail of water. I was about to heave it into the stove when the school door opened and there stood Wynn Delaney. I gasped, choked, and began another fit of coughing.

Without speaking he crossed to me, took the pail from my hands and set it back on its shelf. Then he moved on to the stove.

"These country school stoves can be contrary things," he stated matter-of-factly as he flipped some metal lever on the stove pipe and another on the stove itself. Then he walked purposefully to the windows and began to open them one by one. After the last one had been flung wide, he returned and picked up my coat.

"I have a few minutes," he offered. "Why don't I stay and tend the fire while you go on home and freshen up. It'll be a good forty minutes before any students appear."

He held my coat for me, and I shrugged into it without speaking. I fled from the building in embarrassment at being discovered in such a predicament. What a mess I was! I had soot streaks up my arms and even across my cheek. My legs and dress were splattered with mud, my shoes were soggy, and my hair was tumbling down. I eyed the clock as I scrubbed and changed but I did not hurry. I even had a second cup of coffee, feeling a bit like a child stealing from the cookie jar. I then slowly and deliberately picked my way across the yard to the schoolhouse, skirting all of the deeper puddles. By the time I reached the school, most of the smoke had cleared, and the room was beginning to warm with the cheerily burning—and smokeless—fire. My benefactor was still there.

In spite of my embarrassment, my sense of humor held me in good stead, at least in measure.

"I want to thank you," I began, "for rescuing the schoolhouse. We nearly went up in smoke."

When he saw that I could laugh at myself, his eyes began to twinkle, but he was too kind to tease me.

"Someone," he said, placing all the blame on an unknown and unseen "someone," "left the damper completely closed." He stepped over to the stove and turned the damper lever slightly. "When the fire gets going well, you can turn it—like this—to slow it down some; but to start with, it should always be turned upright, like this."

I nodded, berating myself for not thinking of dampers. He didn't remark about my folly, though, but went on, "I must warn you, though, don't *ever* use a full pail of water to douse a fire in a stove like this. It can be very dangerous—and at best, very messy. The water forces the ashes, some of them carrying live sparks, to blow out through the stove door."

A mental image of the forcefully splashing water, the flying ashes and soot made me thankful that he had come in when he did.

"If you must quench a fire," he continued, "*gently* pour on water, a dipperful at a time, working your way over the flames. Remember, too, it doesn't take long for an iron stove to heat; a sudden change in temperature might even split the metal."

I nodded meekly, feeling that I had just been given a fatherly lecture on fires.

"Never did hold to this business of a young woman teacher having to care for her own fire," he remarked, as though to himself. I cringed inwardly as I imagined him at some future meeting of the parents in the community, taking his stand to argue that young women teachers had no business caring for the fire in the classroom.

I quickly assured him, "It'll be fine, now that I know how it operates."

He threw two more good-sized chunks of wood on the flames, closed the door of the stove and straightened to his full height. I saw his eyes fall to my hands, and I became more self-conscious and nervous. Was he noticing that my hands showed I was not used to manual work of any kind? Was he checking to see if they were losing their cared-for look under the rigors of work in a country school?

I moved to a window.

"Do you suppose we can close them now?" I asked in an effort to direct his attention elsewhere.

"Certainly," and he moved to the nearest one.

I looked around my room and as soon as the last window had been closed, I turned to him.

"I do want to thank you—and I will remember to check the damper. Now, if you'll excuse me, I have lessons to prepare."

He smiled slightly and reached for his hat. It was strange, this feeling I had. I knew instinctively that he was the kind of man who would be worthy of anyone's friendship, especially since he was a long-time friend of Jonathan's; yet I felt that I dared not encourage a friendship of any kind. I had never felt such a barrier, or rather the need for such a barrier, with a man before. Perhaps I feared lest he somehow was aware of my attraction to him before I had realized that he was a married man. Perhaps if I met his wife I would be able to feel differently. But for now I held myself stiffly at a distance.

"I stopped to let you know that Phillip won't be attending class today. He has a cold, and his mother has decided not to send him out in the rain."

At the words "his mother," I backed away a step farther from the man who spoke to me.

"I'm—I'm sorry," I managed. "I do hope that it will not be serious."

"I'm sure that it won't. You know children. They can be back racing about in an hour's time. Mothers take a little longer to recuperate from a child's illness." He grinned.

"Yes," I answered. "I guess so."

"I'll be coming back this way sometime between three and four. Lydia would like me to pick up Phillip's work so that he won't fall behind his classmates. She'll go over the lesson with him at home—if that's not too much trouble for you."

"No—no, of course not. I'll have it ready for you when you come by."

He smiled again, nodded slightly and left, his hat still in his hand. I turned to my blackboard, trying hard to concentrate on the lessons that I had to prepare. I dreaded the day ahead, for I knew that at its end I must see him again. I wished that I could keep Lars with me, to send him out to meet this man and hand him the required lessons. Of course I knew that I couldn't do that. Lars was needed at home and, anyway, I would not hold any student for such a foolish and personal reason. With time and effort I would get over my silly feelings and accept the man as Jon's married male friend—nothing more. He had never behaved as other than a perfect gentleman in my presence.

To my amazement, all of my students except Phillip and Andy appeared for class. In fact, the total number that day was swelled, for the three older boys who had been working in the harvest fields were released because of the rain and attended classes for the first time.

It soon became apparent, much to my consternation and embarrassment, that it was the young schoolmarm, rather than the lessons, who had brought them; they were not much younger than I and took every opportunity to tease and flirt a bit. I felt my cheeks flush several times during the day and was thankful when this awkward school day was finally over.

Immediately, I set to work in preparing the material for Phillip's home lessons. I did not want Mr. Delaney to be required to stand around waiting for them.

The students had not been gone long and I had just finished my hurried preparations when his knock sounded on the schoolroom door.

I gave him the packet, which he tucked inside his jacket to protect it from the rain, and then I dismissed him—rather curtly, I'm afraid.

"I must get home and tend to my fire," I told him, and hurried into my coat as I said the words. I made sure that I stood far enough away from him that he couldn't offer assistance.

He looked at me, then out the window, then at my flimsy shoes.

"I could take you across on my horse," he offered as I moved toward the door.

I stopped in mid-stride. What a perfectly ridiculous idea! *And how does he propose to do that?* He must have read my shock.

"It's knee-deep out there in places."

Anger took hold of me now. I forgot to think of him as Jon's friend and thought of him only as some woman's husband.

I inwardly fumed. *Here he is, wanting to transport me home on his horse. How would he do that—fling me across its back, or carry me in his arms?*

"I'll manage," I declared, and he didn't argue further. He left with Phillip's homework, and in frustration I stamped about the classroom, putting away books, erasing the blackboard and shoving desks into line.

At length I calmed down and went out to face the storm, careful to close the classroom door tightly behind me.

As the cold rain whipped into my face, I became more clear-headed. I reminded myself that Mr. Delaney was a longtime friend of my brother Jonathan. His offer to deliver me home on his horse was a simple courtesy—out of a desire to care for the helpless young sister of a man whom he considered almost a brother; his thoughtful offer was nothing more than that. I felt better having sorted it out in my thinking. Perhaps Lydia Delaney's husband merely was overly helpful, and she need have no worries after all. I put the whole thing from mind and began to plan a comfortable and restful evening.

Mr. Delaney had been right—the water was deep. By the time I reached my door my shoes were ruined, my skirts were covered with muddy water, and my spirits were as soggy as my wet-to-the-knees hose.

But I refused to mope about for the evening. My little ritual with teacup, familiar chair, and a favorite Dickens story went a long way toward improving my outlook.

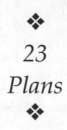

23
Plans

SATURDAY WAS ALSO cold and rainy. I hand-washed my laundry and strung lines around my house to dry it. In the afternoon I had to haul more wood. It was a wet, muddy job, and I didn't enjoy it.

Sunday, too, was wet and miserable. Few people turned out for the afternoon service. Lars came over early to start the fire in the school stove. It did not smoke. Those who gathered were glad for its warmth and cheeriness. As previously arranged with Mr. Dickerson, I welcomed the children into the teacherage where we had a special Bible story, so I did not have much opportunity to visit with the other worshipers. Mr. Delaney was there with his mother, a very sweet-looking person, and when I met her I realized from whom Mr. Delaney had inherited his warm, friendly smile. Phillip was still homebound with his cold, so his mother had stayed at home with him.

After the service and my class was over, I escorted the children to the school, bid farewell to the worshipers, checked the stove in the classroom and sloshed home through the puddles. The rain had now stopped, and the sun was reappearing. Soon the earth was steaming from the heat. Fortunately, it looked as if our present spell of bad weather would be short-lived.

By midweek the yard and roads were dry again. On Wednesday our other "sun" returned; Andy was back. The whole class cheered for him as he entered the schoolyard. I was just going out to ring the bell when he appeared, and I must admit that I, too, wished to cheer when I saw his sparkling eyes. His joy at being back lit his whole face.

By midmorning I could tell that something was very wrong, but Andy shook his head when I asked him if he'd like to rest his head on his arms. By afternoon the pain dulled his eyes, and even resting his head didn't help. I called Teresa aside and suggested that she take him home.

"He shouldn't come," she said anxiously, "but he been so sad, an' he coax an' coax."

We bundled him up. They didn't live far from the school, but I was anxious as I let him go, praying that he would be able to make it home.

Just as Andy and Teresa moved out the door, Carl Clark's hand shot up. He didn't even wait to be recognized, something that I usually insisted upon. "Teacher," he said quickly, "how 'bout I go along? Andy might need some carryin'."

There was real concern in Carl's eyes, and my appreciation and relief must have shown on my face. Silently I nodded my permission.

The entire class watched the three of them leave. The silence was broken by Else's whisper, "He's real sick, ain't he, Teacher?"

Swallowing over the lump in my throat, I could only nod. I even ignored the "ain't."

"His folks should've taken him to the doctor again," Mindy Blake commented.

"They ain't got no money." This from Lars, my star grammar student, his frustration apparent in his voice and choice of words.

"Then we should help them," offered the shy Olga. She rarely spoke out in class.

"Us? How?" replied many voices.

Olga withdrew in embarrassment. Her seat mate, Maudie Clark, put a protective hand on her arm and then spoke boldly. "It wasn't a dumb idea. We could, you know. We could bring our nickels and dimes or pennies even—an' do special things at home so our pa's might give us more money. An' then we could put it together an'—"

"Nickels an' pennies don't pay a doctor none," this from Mike Clark.

"They'd help." Maudie wasn't going to back down. I decided to get things back under control.

"I'm glad that in your concern for Andy, you're willing to do something to help him, and I think that it's a good idea—and a workable one. I'm sure that there is some way that we can find . . ." My words hung for a moment. It did sound possible. I just wasn't sure yet how to go about it.

"I want you to think about this tonight—all of you. What might we be able to do? Ask your parents for ideas. And tomorrow when we come, we'll discuss our ideas and see what we can do."

All of the faces before me brightened. We settled back to our studies, but I often caught pensive looks and muffled whispers; I knew that thoughts were still on Andy and a possible way that we might help in getting him the medical attention he needed.

I still had not solved my mice problem; my declaration of war daily seemed more impossible. The mice were not content with peaceful coexistence or with taking over my entire cupboard, having driven me to my trunks; but they wanted the rest of my house as well. Every time I cleaned up after them, my anger increased.

On Friday morning it was apparent that they had enjoyed a good night's romp. For the first time I found evidence that they had joined me in my bedroom. This was too much. Already in a foul mood after seeing where they had been, I went to the top drawer of my chest to get a fresh handkerchief. I hadn't noticed it before, but the drawer had been open slightly because of a glove that had caught. Meticulous about closing drawers, I wondered how this one had missed my attention.

I laid the glove properly in its section of the drawer and reached in the handkerchief box. Before my hand touched one of them, my eyes flashed me a message. Something was wrong—seriously wrong, and then I realized what had happened. The mice had been at my handkerchiefs! With a cry I pulled them out and stared at them. Pretty lace and embroidery had been reduced to chewed fragments. My favorite handkerchief, with the daintiest lace that I had ever seen, had suffered the worst. It was beyond repair, and frustrated tears gathered in my eyes and rolled down my cheeks as I looked at it. Angrily I returned the box to the drawer, slammed the drawer shut and marched off to the classroom. This time the mice had gone too far!

After class I planned to call on the school-board chairman, Mr. Laverly, and insist that someone, somehow, dispose of those despicable rodents. I would refuse to live in the teacherage until something was done.

By the time the students had arrived, I had managed to quiet my anger. We began our day by saluting our flag and reading some verses of scripture. I realized as the class took their seats that it would not do to go directly to our lessons. Their excited faces told me that first we must discuss what we as a school could do to help Andy.

Many suggestions were presented, some to cheers and others to groans. I listed them all carefully on the board. I wrote in large letters, realizing that Tim Mattoch had an eye problem and could hardly see the board. His parents could not afford to get him glasses, so Tim struggled on, squinting and squirming, often having to approach the board so that he might make out a letter or a number.

There were many good suggestions. I decided to let the students discuss them for a few minutes before we commenced our lessons. After a fair amount of discussion, Mindy suggested that we take a vote. It seemed reasonable. The voters decided that we would have a penny circus and a box social on October 25 at the school; all money raised through the event would go to help Andy Pastachuck. Everyone was happy and excited, but once the matter was decided, they were better able to settle down to their lessons. I was proud of them for their concern, and I was also eager to help Andy in any way that we could.

At the end of the day I asked for the directions to the Laverlys' farm. The place would not be hard to find but required a three-mile walk. Undaunted, I put on my hat, buttoned my coat, and set off. For the first two miles I walked with the Clark girls. The boys had hurried on ahead, for they had chores awaiting them. Also, they didn't care to be seen with a bunch of girls. The Blake girls had also walked with us for the first mile.

It was a pleasant day, and I found the little expedition enjoyable. Only a few mudholes remained in the road from the recent heavy rain, and those we were easily able to skirt.

After I left my students, I walked more briskly. I missed their chatter, but on the other hand I was glad for the solitude after a busy school day. At last the Laverly farm came into view.

The Laverly sons were no longer of school age, and I thought that it was very commendable of Mr. Laverly to have worked so hard to get a school when none of his family would directly benefit from it.

Mrs. Laverly was a bustling, energetic woman with a great deal of curiosity. She pumped me with questions, not only about my work in the classroom but about my family and background as well. She insisted that I have coffee and sandwiches. After she had set the pot on to boil, she went to the back porch and pounded with a metal rod on a large iron plate. I jumped at the first loud, harsh sound.

"Thet'll call in the menfolk," she explained. "They're in the field out back."

I apologized for interrupting Mr. Laverly from his work. I hadn't even considered that he might be busy, so anxious was I to be rid of my free-loading tenants.

"Thet's a'right. Thet's a'right," she assured me. "They'll be wantin' somethin' to eat anyway. An' b'sides, it's time for one of 'em to start chorin'."

Mrs. Laverly set to work on a huge plate of man-sized sandwiches. Thick slices of homemade bread, generously—though not particularly carefully—spread with fresh butter and covered with large portions of cheese or cold roast beef were quickly assembled, while her tongue moved as fast as her hands. I wondered if I'd be able to get such thick sandwiches into my mouth. I offered to help her, but she waved me off with the butcher knife which she was using on the beef.

"No need to be a helpin'. Me, I'm not used to another woman under-foot. Had to do it alone all my life. Jest raised boys, ya know—five of 'em. Lost one, but still got four. One of 'em's married an' lives near Edmonton. Other three lives right here an' helps with the farm. Don't know what their pa would do without 'em. Middle one's kinda got 'im a girl, an' the youngest one's been a'lookin'. Oldest one don't seem much interested. S'pose I'll end up havin' to find someone for 'im an' draggin' 'im off to the preacher myself."

She rambled on as if it were one continuous sentence with hardly a pause for breath.

The sandwiches were placed on the table, and tin cups for coffee were set out. We could hear the menfolk tramping toward the house. They stopped on the back porch to slosh water over their faces and arms, squabbled some over the rights to the coarse towel, brushed the worst of the straw from themselves, and came in.

It was apparent from their faces that they hadn't expected to see me. Three grown men suddenly turned shy. One of them flushed beet red, while another fiddled nervously with his hair, his collar, his suspenders.

The third one seemed to regain his composure almost immediately and decided to make the most of the situation, appearing to take pleasure in the discomfort of his brothers. He turned out to be George, the middle one, the one with a girl. The red-faced one was Bill, the youngest; the nervous one was the eldest son, Henry. I recognized them as three of the men who had huddled near the door during my welcoming party.

We sat up to the table together, and the men reached for the sandwiches, the enormous size giving them no pause. I managed, too, in spite of the fact that the portions were anything but dainty; they were delicious, especially after my nice, long walk.

Mr. Laverly was cordial and warm. He was even allowed to ask me a question or two in between the ones peppered at me by Mrs. Laverly. The three sons were at first too busy with eating to pay any attention to the conversation—or so I thought. By the time the supper was over, George was joking and teasing, and Bill was openly staring. But Henry kept his eye on his plate and cup, unwilling—or unable—to participate in the talk around the table.

I waited until after the meal—for it was a complete meal by my standards—before I asked to talk to Mr. Laverly concerning my mice problem. He was such a nice man that I approached the subject very calmly, making sure I didn't insinuate that the mice were inhabiting the teacherage with his permission. I hurriedly poured out my whole tale. He stuffed his pipe and lit it, inhaled a few times, but all of the time that I talked, he offered no comment. I told him of the mice dwelling in my cupboards, entering into my bedroom, and taking over my dresser drawers. However, I did not tell him about my lace handkerchiefs. I was afraid that if I went into those details I would lose my temper, or cry—or maybe both.

He listened patiently, but eventually I gathered that he felt that a few mice in the house were really nothing to get so worked up about. When I finally stopped for breath, he removed the pipe from his mouth.

"We'll git ya some traps."

"I tried that."

He looked surprised.

"Well, a cat might—"

"I tried that, too," I said in frustration. I avoided explaining *why* they hadn't worked.

"Me an' the boys'll go over an' see what we can find. Must be comin' in somewhere. We'll take some tin an' nail up the holes."

This sounded good, but I was not completely satisfied.

"What about those that are already in?" I asked.

"We'll care fer 'em."

I was more content then.

"Hope ya don't mind us stirrin' round in yer quarters none. We'll git at it this next week."

I thought of the silent Henry, the teasing George and the flirting Bill.

"Perhaps it would be best if I moved out for the week."

"Moved out?" He looked alarmed, as though if I left the teacherage, he might never see me again.

"To the Petersons. Anna has already told me that should I ever need a room, she could spare one."

He looked relieved.

"Good idea," he said and removed his pipe. He shook the ashes into the coal bucket and laid the pipe back on the shelf, as though to indicate that the matter was closed.

I went back to the kitchen to thank Mrs. Laverly for the supper. She was busy wrapping a portion of the cold meat and a jar of her pickles for me to take home.

"The boys have gone fer the team," she said.

At my questioning look, she explained, "Too late fer ya to start out a'walkin'. One of 'em will drive ya." She began to chuckle. "Saw 'em a'flippin' fer it."

I wondered who would be taking me—the winner or the loser of the toss. I found myself trying to decide which one I hoped it would be.

The lucky—or unlucky—one was Bill. He came in grinning from ear to ear, announcing that he was ready any time I was. Bill—the one who was "a'lookin'." I smiled rather weakly, I'm afraid, and followed him out. He didn't offer to help me up, so I scrambled over the wagon wheel on my own, dragging my skirts and clutching my food parcels. Then we were off.

The team was spirited and Bill liked speed, which didn't enhance the comfort of the rough wagon. Bill muttered over and over about "havin' to talk to Pa 'bout a light buggy." Jostling along, trying to cling to my precarious perch, I felt sure that the sweating team, and all of Bill's future passengers, would approve of a lighter vehicle for traveling at such a pace.

My main concern was staying on the wagon seat. I had to hold onto the brown paper bag containing my cold beef and pickles, so I clutched the edge, white-knuckled, with the other hand. By the time we reached the teacherage, my bones felt like I had been trampled. I clambered slowly down over the wheel, wondering if my legs would still hold me when my feet reached the ground.

Bill, removing neither himself from his seat nor his hat from his head, seemed rather pleased with himself, as though he had perhaps made the run in record time. I felt sure that he had. He grinned at me, and I knew that he expected me to appreciate his feat.

"Thank you for bringing me home," I said shakily. "It—it was very kind of you."

Bill's grin widened.

"Next time, maybe I'll have me a buggy. Then we won't be held back by this ol' lumber wagon."

I hoped there would be no "next time," but I said nothing. Bill wheeled the horses around and left the yard at a near gallop. I shook my head, waved the dust away from my face, and turned to go into my house.

Tonight I would pack for my move to the Petersons and tuck everything else away, safe from the mice. I would go over right after my evening meal the next day, if this worked out for Anna.

"You'd better enjoy yourselves tonight," I warned the little varmints. "It might be your last chance."

From the evidence I found the next morning, it appeared they had.

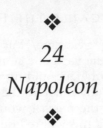

24
Napoleon

M Y WEEK AT the Petersons' went by quickly. I enjoyed the company of Anna and the cheerful chatter of the children. Even Olga warmed up to me somewhat when the two of us were alone.

On Friday, Bill Laverly stopped by the schoolhouse, grinning his wide grin, and assured me that the teacherage was now mouse-proof and mouse-free.

I decided that I would move back on Saturday morning so that I could spend the day scrubbing and cleaning and putting the things back into my cupboard.

Bill offered to drive me over to the Petersons' for my things. I was quick to assure him that I had taken very little with me and would have no problem carrying it home. I thanked him for his kindness and returned to my classroom.

Moving back home posed no difficulty. Olga and Else came with me, insisting on helping me carry my belongings. After they had left, I changed into an old skirt and shirtwaist and set to work with hot, soapy water. It gave me great satisfaction to see gleaming clean cupboards restored to their proper order.

I was tired at day's end but deeply pleased with my labors. It was good to be home and have my little house all to myself.

The area harvest was nearing completion. Some of the farmers were already finished. The older boys had now come back to the classroom, making my days more difficult. They longed to be adults and yet they did not have the skills of even the youngest children in the room. My heart ached for them, but they did try my patience to the limit. Their attempts to flirt annoyed me, and at times I had to suppress a strong desire to express my displeasure. I knew that they were immature and unsure of themselves, so I tried very hard never to embarrass or humiliate them. But I did wish that they wouldn't act so silly.

We were all busily involved in planning for the coming box social and penny circus. Assignments had been given to the students, and they were working hard to prepare for the big event. The parents were wonderful in their support. Almost daily, some note of encouragement or offer of help was brought to school by a student. I was pleased and thankful for the community backing.

On the home front, I felt rather smug: There had been no evidence whatever of mice in my kitchen. The tin patches in my cupboard and around the walls seemed to have done the trick. I did not know—nor ask—how the men had taken care of the unwelcome inhabitants. I was simply glad that they had been removed.

I was weary by Friday night. The older boys had been particularly trying, and the week had been filled with many extra duties for the upcoming fund-raiser. After I had cleared away my supper dishes, I retired to my large chair (the lumps were now fitting nicely around me) with a cup of tea and a book. I slipped off my shoes and put my feet up on my footstool. How my mother would have gasped to see her daughter sitting in such an unladylike position, but it felt *so* good. I sighed contentedly, sipped hot tea and opened my book.

A tiny movement near the stove caught my eye. The bit of shadow turned into a live thing—a tiny mouse poked out his head. His black, shiny eyes sought out any danger and his nose twitched sensitively. My first angry impulse was to pick up my shoe and throw it at him, but I froze where I was. Venturing out a little farther, he sat up and began to clean himself, rubbing his tiny moistened paws over his head, his back and his chest. He did look comical. He also looked small and helpless and hungry. I had never actually seen one of my house guests before—alive, that is. *He IS rather cute,* I reasoned, though there had been nothing much to commend them when they were dead.

I must have stirred slightly, for he darted back under the stove and was lost in the shadows.

He appeared a few more times that evening, each time carefully grooming himself. I wondered if this were just an attempt to keep himself busy and his thoughts off his empty tummy.

Before I went to bed, I scattered a few crumbs by the leg of the stove. I told myself that I was doing it to provide what he needed so he wouldn't have to climb into my cupboard looking for it. In the morning the crumbs were gone.

In the next few days, very busy days, I saw the small mouse on several occasions. I named him Napoleon because he was so tiny, yet so bold. Each night I put a small amount of food out for him, each time reasoning that if he had food easily accessible he wouldn't snoop in my cupboards for it.

I found myself actually watching for him. He was entertaining, and I even had the ridiculous thought that I no longer bore the loneliness of living by myself.

During school on Friday, a knock on the classroom door drew my attention. I excused myself and went to answer it. Bill Laverly had been to town and picked up some articles that I had requested for the penny circus. I told him to set them inside the door of the teacherage, then went back to my class, anxious for the school hours to end so that I could get busy on my projects.

Bill was soon back at the classroom door.

"Ma'am," he said, "there was another mouse in yer place there. Don't know how we ever missed 'im."

At the sight of my chalk-white face he hurried on, "It's okay, ma'am—I killed 'im."

My gratitude expected, I mumbled something that I hoped made sense, and Bill left, his eternal grin firmly in place.

It was a few moments before I could go back to my class. I knew that it was right—that it was better—that it was what I *should* have wanted. But I'd miss Napoleon. He had been so little, and so clever—and so cute.

25

The Box Social

WHEN THE DAY of the Box Social arrived, my students were all so excited that they could scarcely think of another thing. They spent the morning attempting to finish their lessons, and devoted the entire afternoon to getting ready for the big event.

The older boys strung wire across the room, and the girls pinned old blankets and sheets on the wires, thus forming small booths. Within each booth a game, contest or entertainment was set up by each of the students who had been put in charge. Excitement ran high, and it was hard for me to hold them all in check. At last we had done all that we could do in preparation, and they were dismissed to go home.

I circled the room, checking and rearranging. The students had done a fine job on their projects. It looked as if the night would be great fun as well as a help to the Pastachucks. There was a ring-toss, a fish pond, pin-the-tail-on-the-donkey, a mock camera, some pins to knock over, a pail-and-candy-toss game, and a bean-sack toss. Each game would cost the player a penny.

Our main source of income was to be our box social. I had spent two evenings decorating my box and had sent to town for special food items to prepare for the lunch to fill it. Each woman and older girl would have a decorated box filled with enough lunch for two people—although the lunch stuffed into some boxes would feed many more.

Mr. Dickerson had agreed to be our auctioneer. The men would bid on the boxes, and the highest bidder would share the food with the lady whose box he had purchased. I wondered who would end up being my partner for the evening's lunch. It was harmless enough to sit in a roomful of people, eating together. I was not concerned about the evening—only curious.

"Mama showed Pa *her* box," Mindy Blake had declared.

"She shouldn't've," said Maudie Clark.

"Well, she did," said Mindy in a huff. "She had to make 'nough for all us kids, ya know, an' she wouldn't want any ol' man gettin' all that."

"All you're worried 'bout, Mindy, is the food," Carl Clark accused.

"Boy, I should git me thet box," cut in Tim Mattoch, and everyone laughed. Tim was more than a little on the heavy side, and all of the students knew that he dearly loved to eat.

"He'll buy the biggest box there," said Mike Clark.

"He better not," Else interrupted, "'cause it'll be my ma's. She had to pack for all of us kids, too, and she put it all togeder in a great big box, dis big." She indicated how big the box was and then immediately clamped her hand over her mouth, realizing that she had divulged a secret.

As I prepared my lunch, I was glad I didn't need to fix one for a whole family; but I also knew that some of those hardworking single males of our community were hearty eaters. It would not do to short-change them.

The wagons, buggies and saddle horses began to arrive shortly before eight o'clock. I was already in the classroom and had a big pot of water heating for making the coffee. Coffee tonight would be free, as was the milk for the children. All else would be paid for and the money would go into the Pastachuck fund.

The schoolroom began to fill with excited children and chattering grown-ups. The attendance was going to be good and the little schoolroom was going to be crowded. Already some of the men were opening windows. *How good of these people to care and do something about the need of a family in their community. Bless our efforts, Lord,* I prayed silently.

I had prepared carefully for the evening, putting on one of my favorite gowns. I knew that I was a bit overdressed for this informal occasion, but somehow I thought that folks would expect it of me. I had arranged my hair with fastidious curls, which I heaped mostly on the top of my head, carefully letting one or two hang down on one side. My appearance was not unnoticed by the cluster of single fellows near the door, who were ogling, guffawing and slapping one another on the back.

The Delaneys arrived. Mr. Delaney found his mother a chair and took the coats of his womenfolk to pile on a corner table with those of their neighbors; we had long ago run out of coat hooks. The younger Mrs. Delaney reached a hand up to her hair, then smoothed her already smooth skirt. Her back was to me, so I couldn't see her face. I wanted to look at her—and I didn't, both at the same time. She stood chatting with neighbors, a slim, dark-haired young woman, attractively attired. I found myself noting that her dress was not nearly as pretty as mine and immediately rebuked myself for my cattiness.

When Mr. Delaney had gotten the womenfolk settled, he moved off to chat with some of the neighborhood men. The crowd around Mrs. Delaney thinned somewhat and she took a chair. I saw her clearly then. Dark eyes sparkled under long, dark lashes. She had a straight, rather small nose. Her cheeks were flushed with excitement and full rosy lips parted slightly as she smiled easily at those she greeted. She was more than just attractive.

I turned back to my duties but had hardly organized my thoughts before I felt a tug on my hand.

"Miss Thatcher, my mom wants to meet you." It was Phillip.

For a moment near panic seized me, but I knew that I was being foolish. It was inevitable that I meet this woman, and it may as well be now. I prepared my nicest smile and let Phillip lead me toward her.

As we approached, her eyes lit up, and she stood to her feet.

"Miss Thatcher," she said warmly, extending her hand, "I'm so happy to meet you at last. I'm Lydia Delaney. I've heard so many nice things about you."

She was so sincere, so open and friendly that I responded to her immediately.

"Thank you," I said; "it's nice to meet Phillip's mother." I meant those words.

She looked me over appreciatively. "No wonder Phillip was happy to stay after school."

I smiled. Phillip still held my hand, and he beamed up at me. I put my arm around his shoulders and gave him a squeeze. I'm sure that she could see how I felt about Phillip. I spoke then to the elder Mrs. Delaney; she took my hand in both of hers and greeted me.

"I'm so sorry," said Lydia, "that we haven't yet had you over, but things have been so unsettled at our house. We have been off to Calgary most weekends and, well, we hope that things will soon change so we can return to normal living."

Called away by one of my students, I had to excuse myself. I walked away with the feeling of Lydia Delaney's warm, brown eyes upon me.

The evening progressed well. I was kept busy circulating among the students and helping them in any way that I could with their booths. Every now and then a whispered report was given to me of how many pennies had been collected at a certain station. The students were excited about their achievements.

Activity at the booths began slowing down as the people started to think of the lunch boxes. We cleared some more room for chairs and benches by putting aside the games from the booths and taking down some of the dividers strung on the wires. Then Mr. Dickerson took his place at the front.

Anna Peterson and Mrs. Blake were not the only women who had packed for extra mouths. Many of the boxes were enormous. As the bidding began, it became apparent that Mrs. Blake was not the only woman who had informed her spouse what to look for. Without exception, husband and wife got together and spread out their goodies for themselves and their offspring.

I watched with interest and amusement as Mr. Delaney prompted Phillip in the bidding for his mother's basket. Phillip felt very grown-up as he shouted his bid, and when he had finally been successful in his purchase, Mr. Delaney counted out the money for him to pay the auctioneer's clerk himself.

The older girls had their own baskets, and the older boys, with dimes, quarters, red faces and much teasing, lined up to make their bids.

My basket was the last one to be held up. I scolded myself for my flushed cheeks and wished with all of my heart that I had begged off from participating. It was apparently common knowledge about whose basket was being offered, for the young men moved in from beside the door, and the bidding opened vigorously. The color in my cheeks deepened with each bid; I kept my eyes averted and pretended to be very busy serving coffee. The teasing and joking did not escape me; but it was a few moments before I realized that Mr. Delaney was among the bidders. This knowledge upset me so that I could not stop my hand from shaking as I poured coffee.

Why would he do that? *Why?* There sat his wife and his mother—right before his eyes, and here he was . . . I choked on the humiliation for us all. A new thought struck me. Perhaps his mother had fixed a box, and he supposed this to be it. I glanced around the room and could see that such wasn't the case, for there sat the two Mrs. Delaneys and Phillip sharing a chat with the Blakes as they ate their respective lunches. Lydia Delaney chatted gaily with Mrs. Blake, stopping occasionally to smile at the antics of the bidders.

How can she? I thought. *How can she? She must be humiliated nearly to death. How can she endure it so calmly? Is she used to such behavior? Doesn't it bother her when her husband publicly deserts her?*

She certainly appeared unperturbed by it all. In fact, one could even have accused her of enjoying it. Was it just a cover-up? My anger boiled hotter with each bid placed by Mr. Delaney.

There was much laughter, shouted comments and jockeying for position as the bids climbed. Finally only Bill Laverly and Mr. Delaney remained as bidders. I had never expected to find myself championing the grinning Bill Laverly, but I did so now, hoping with all my heart that he would outbid the other man. At a bid from Mr. Delaney, Bill went down on both knees and began to empty all of his pockets, spreading out all of his bills and change, even offering the auctioneer chewing tobacco and a pocket knife. There was much knee-slapping, joking and clapping by the appreciative crowd. It was obvious that Bill could go no higher. He implored some of his buddies for a loan, and the bidding continued. But it was Mr. Delaney who was finally handed the basket as he paid the clerk.

I was furious, not just for my sake—but for *hers.*

I knew that I was expected to leave my coffee-pouring and go share lunch with the man who had purchased my basket, but I couldn't—and I wouldn't.

I turned and said in a loud, though somewhat unsteady, voice, hoping that the smile I was trying so hard to produce actually showed on my face, "Mr. Delaney has just purchased a bigger bargain than he realizes. Because my duties will be keeping me busy, he gets to eat all of the lunch himself."

Laughter followed my announcement, along with hoots from the young men who had lost out in the bidding. I turned back to the pot of coffee, not daring to look at Mr. Delaney again. *And I hope he chokes on it*, I thought angrily. Three women rushed with offers to take over my job so that I could sit down and enjoy my lunch. I turned them all aside—firmly, and I hoped, courteously. I later noticed Mr. Delaney sharing his lunch with some good-natured chatter with Andy Pastachuck.

As the evening drew to a close, the money was gathered and counted. We placed it all in a big tin can and had Mr. Laverly, our school-board chairman, present it to the Pastachucks. They accepted it with broken English and tear-filled eyes. They planned to leave soon for Calgary and a doctor, and would send word back as soon as they had a report. Teresa was to stay with the Blakes during their absence, and the Thebeaus had volunteered to care for their farm chores.

It didn't seem quite fitting to simply pass them the money and send them on their way, so I stepped forward hesitantly. First I thanked all of those who had come and participated so wholeheartedly. Our total earnings, including donations from neighbors, came to $195.64. A cheer went up when the sum was announced.

"We all have learned to love Andy," I continued. "Our thoughts and prayers will be with him and his parents, and as a token of our prayers and concern, I would like to ask Mr. Dickerson, our auctioneer of the evening, to lead us in prayer on Andy's behalf."

A silence fell over the room. Eyes filled with tears, heads bowed and calloused hands reached up to sweep hats aside.

Mr. Dickerson stepped to the center of the room and cleared his throat. His simple and sincere prayer was followed by many whispered "Amens."

Our evening together had ended. Folks crowded around me shaking my hand, saying kind words and thanking me for my efforts toward the success of the evening. I felt very much at one with these gentle, warm-hearted people.

The Pastachucks were the last to go. Mr. Pastachuck offered his hand and shook mine firmly. His wife could only smile through tears, unable to speak. But Andy looked at me with shining eyes, as though to herald a personal triumph on my behalf. "It was fun," he enthused. "You did good, Teacher, real good!"

I reached down and pulled him close, holding him for a long time; his thin little arms were wrapped tightly about my neck. When I released him, I was crying. Andy reached up and, without a word, brushed the tears from my cheek. Then he turned and walked out into the night.

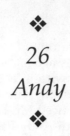

26
Andy

MIDWEEK, WORD CAME from Calgary. As we had feared, Andy's condition was serious. The old injury had flared up. A tumor had formed, causing pressure on the brain. The doctor suspected that bone chips were responsible, and he decided that surgery was imperative as soon as possible.

The whole class wrote notes to Andy to send with Mrs. Blake and Teresa to the hospital. The outcome of the pending surgery was sufficiently doubtful that Teresa was being taken to Calgary to see her brother before his operation.

I wrote a note, too. It was short and simply worded so that Andy would have no trouble understanding it when it was read to him. I said that we were all very busy at school; that we thought of him and prayed for him daily in our opening prayer; that we missed him and would be so glad when he would be well and able to be back with us.

But Andy did not return. He died during surgery in the Calgary hospital. We were told that even the nurses who attended him wept when the small boy lost his battle for life.

It was a Wednesday afternoon when we all gathered at the schoolhouse for Andy's short funeral service. Mr. Dickerson read the scripture, and a visiting priest gave the last rites. We then left for the little cemetery on the hill.

Many of my pupils were crying as we filed from the schoolroom. Else Peterson and Mindy Blake clung to each of my hands. My eyes were overflowing, but I was able to keep the sobs from shaking me.

It was a short distance to the cemetery so we walked to it, the little procession, with the small pine casket at its head, stirring up little pillowy swirls of dust. The day was bright, the autumn sun glistening in a tranquil sky. A few clouds skittered across the blueness. The leaves still clinging to the trees were in full dress, but many others lay scattered on the ground, rustling at each stirring of the breeze.

Else broke our silence.

"Andy would have liked this day," she whispered, looking up at its brightness; and I knew that she was right. I could imagine the gentle little boy with his shining eyes cheering this day on.

"You did good," he would exclaim to the beautiful morning. "You did good."

I cried then, the great sobs shaking my whole body. I remembered the last time that I had wept, and how the little boy in my embrace had reached up awkwardly, and yet tenderly, to brush away my tears. "You did good, Teacher," he had whispered. And now that small boy had passed beyond—so young to journey on alone. But then I remembered that he hadn't traveled alone—not one step of the way, for as soon as the loving hands had released him here, another Hand had reached out to gently take him. I tried to visualize him entering that new Land, the excitement and eagerness shining forth on his face, the cheers raising from the shrill little voice. There would be no pain twisting his face now, no need to hold his head and rock back and forth. Joy and happiness would surround him. I could almost hear his words as he looked at the glories of heaven and gave the Father his jubilant ovation—"You did good, God; You did real good!"

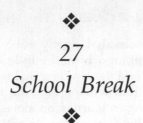

27
School Break

WE DECIDED TO close school for the rest of that week. All of the students were deeply affected by the loss of Andy, and Mr. Laverly thought that it would do us all good to have a few days of rest. I agreed. I suddenly felt very tired. I would go to visit Jon and his family.

That afternoon, I packed a few things in a small suitcase and asked for a ride to town. Mr. Mattoch, who had a light buggy with spring seats, was my driver. The trip was much more comfortable and took considerably less time than had the previous wagon transportation.

The train did not leave for Calgary until the next morning, so I took a room in the hotel and spent a miserable, lonely night there. The next morning I spent some time shopping until the train came. I didn't see anything which attracted me, but perhaps it was my mood rather than the lack of merchandise.

Finally I was Calgary bound; but the train did not seem to be nearly as eager to reach Calgary as I was. The first thing I did upon my arrival was to telephone Jon's home. Mary answered, and her excitement at hearing my voice went a long way toward cheering me. Jon arrived to pick me up at the station before I had time to properly get myself in order. He had just purchased a new Buick and was anxious to show it off. Not many autos had as yet made their way onto the Calgary streets, and those who did use the new means of conveyance seemed to consider it a daily challenge to try and outdo one another both in model and speed.

When we pulled up in front of Jon's house, the entire family was waiting to welcome me. Even little William gave his aunt a big hug. I'm afraid that I clung to the children longer than I should have, my sorrow still very fresh in my mind and heart.

One could not nurse sadness for long in Jonathan's home. The children's shouts of excitement gave me little time to think about the loss of Andy. They promptly showed me everything that they had attained or obtained since I had left them. William presented a new bow and arrow, and Sarah read to me from her first primer; but Kathleen wouldn't even leave my side long enough to produce her new dress or her doll.

They all shared in presenting to me the much-grown Elizabeth and her latest accomplishments. She could smile, she could coo, and once she even giggled. The little sweetheart warmed up to me immediately and allowed me to hold and cuddle her.

I did not need to return to Pine Springs until the following Monday. The train ran north on Monday, Wednesday and Friday; and south on Tuesday, Thursday and Saturday; so the days that Mr. Laverly had set aside for this school break were planned accordingly. The long weekend that stretched before me seemed nicely adequate for my visit, but I knew that the days would go all too quickly.

On Saturday, Kathleen danced into my room before my eyes were even properly open. "Dee is coming! Dee is coming!" she cried with glee.

I smiled at her sleepily, thinking, *Who is Dee?* Then I recalled her long-ago declaration of, "When I grow up, I'm gonna marry Dee." I yawned and rolled over to look at her. My thoughts changed to, *So, I am to meet Kathleen's marvelous Dee, the thirtyish bachelor who is a dear—and determined to stay single.*

He sounded harmless enough to me.

"When is Dee coming?" I asked as Kathleen twirled about my room.

"Tonight—for dinner. Did you meet him yet?"

"No, not yet," I answered rather casually.

"Did you know that I'm gonna marry him when I grow up?" she asked, not a bit put off by my nonchalance.

"I remember that you told me," I answered her.

She was soon gone again, off to share her good news with her baby sister—who would be even less impressed than I had been.

As the day wore on, the anticipation for the evening dinner party grew. It was obvious that the whole family regarded Dee highly and were pleased that he was coming.

I dressed carefully for dinner that night, not because of the unknown Dee but simply because it felt good to soak in a warm bath and then spend a little more time and effort than usual on how I looked. It seemed to be such a long time since our box social and I had reason to dress up. Kathleen came in to offer suggestions and coaxed me to wear the green velvet. It was still hanging in the guest room closet, a last-minute decision when I had left for Pine Springs. "I will never need a fussy thing like that in a country school," I had impulsively declared. "Mary, do you mind if I just leave it hanging here?" Mary agreed, so I had unwrapped it from its tissues and left it hanging in the spare bedroom. Now it shimmered in the light and caught Kathleen's eye. I gave in to her pleading. She helped me with my buttons, and I retied her hair ribbon so that we could state that we had helped one another to prepare for dinner.

She skipped out as I put the finishing touches on my hair, but she was soon back.

"Dee is here!" she exclaimed excitedly. "Hurry—hurry!"

"I'm coming, dear," I laughed. She grabbed my hand, eager to drag me off to meet her Dee. I did hope that he wasn't another Mr. Higgins, but I quickly discarded that idea. I gave Kathleen credit for better judgment than that.

"Nanna is here, too," she informed me as she led me through the hallway and down the stairs.

"Nanna?"

"Yes, Nanna. Mamma's grannie. Nanna Smith."

"Oh," I said in surprise. "I didn't know that Nanna was coming."

"Mamma didn't know, either," Kathleen laughed. "Mamma never knows. Nanna just comes—she likes surprises."

"Oh, I see—like your Aunt Beth did, I guess. She just popped in."

Kathleen laughed merrily at that.

"You *couldn't* tell us," she said, having heard the explanation I gave to Mary, "but Nanna could. She lives just over by the river. She could have telephoned or anything—but she doesn't. She just comes. She likes surprises. We like it, too. It's fun."

A few minutes later I was meeting Nanna, an older woman with a sparkle in her eyes. I could easily imagine that she indeed liked surprises. I had always felt that I liked surprises myself—until the one I received in the next few minutes.

Kathleen had left me with Nanna and had run to find her Dee so that I might have the pleasure of making his acquaintance. I stood chatting, my back to the door, until Kathleen called out merrily, "Here's Dee, Aunt Beth."

I turned slowly around and found myself looking into the face of Mr. Wynn Delaney.

My face must have blanched.

I could not find my voice; I could only stare. My mind groped for an answer; how could this dreadful mix-up ever have taken place? For a moment I thought that I read concern in his eyes, and I wondered if he feared that I might divulge something he would rather have left secret.

The color seemed to be returning to my face—in overabundance, I feared; but I felt that perhaps I could move again.

I saw Mr. Delaney advance a step and place an arm around Kathleen's shoulder. The flash of concern had left his eyes, and a teasing smile replaced it.

"Your Aunt Beth and I have already met, Moppet."

I remained dumb. "You're—?

"Dee—" he finished for me. "William's two-year-old version of 'Delaney'! All of these children have called me that."

"I see . . ."

I didn't really. The pieces of this strange puzzle didn't fit together at all. Something was all wrong here.

"Mr.—De—Delaney," I stammered, knowing even as I spoke that what I was asking was foolish indeed, "do you happen to have a twin?"

He seemed about to laugh at that, and then realized that my question had been an honest one. He shook his head, then looked at me with renewed concern. My bewildered eyes and flushed face must have made him think that something was wrong with me, for he gently took my arm and led me to a nearby chair.

"Are you all right?" he asked in a low voice.

I assured him shakily that I was just fine.

His inbred courtesy prompted him to turn then to speak with Nanna, whom he seemed to know very well.

I sat numbly, listening to the hum of voices about me. Mr. Delaney and Nanna chatted like old friends. Suddenly Kathleen, who had been left out of the conversation for what she felt was too long, announced, "Did you know I'm gonna marry Dee, Nanna?"

The conversation stopped. Dee reached for Kathleen and seated her beside him on the lounge where he sat.

"What's this, Moppet?"

"I'm gonna *marry* you," she said, pointing a finger at his broad chest. "I'm gonna marry you when I grow up. Right?"

"I don't suppose so." He spoke very slowly, carefully. "You see, just because one likes someone very much doesn't always mean that they will get married. People can still be very special to one another—the best friends in the whole world—and not marry."

Kathleen's face began to cloud.

"Take you now," Mr. Delaney hurried on, "you love your daddy—very much—but you don't need to marry him to share that love, do you?"

Kathleen slowly shook her head.

"And you love your mamma, and Nanna, and Baby Elizabeth, and your Aunt Beth and your Teddy—but you aren't going to marry *them* either, are you?"

Kathleen brightened at the twinkle in his eyes, seeing the fun that he was having.

He continued, "Well, that's like us. We are very special to one another, but we don't need to marry each other to stay special."

Kathleen nodded. Dee had been quite convincing.

Mary called, and Kathleen bounced down from the lounge, her recently troubled eyes again shining, and ran from the room.

"You could have humored her a bit," scolded Nanna.

"How?"

"Well, you could have said, 'Someday—sure, someday.'"

"But it won't be 'someday.'"

"Yes, *we* know that—and Kathleen would know it too, as she grew older."

"But if she didn't?"

"She's only a child."

"A child who will grow up. Yet she will still be a child for many years to come. What would happen, Nanna, if I found someone else to marry before she discovered the truth on her own?"

"*You*—marry?" Nanna laughed.

Mr. Delaney smiled slowly as though enjoying his own joke.

"Or, what if she didn't discover the truth on her own and went into womanhood expecting this *old* man to marry her?"

Nanna shrugged and said teasingly, "Maybe the day will come when you'll be glad to accept her proposal."

Mr. Delaney became serious then. "If ever anyone deserves the truth, Nanna," he said, "a child does. They can accept things, even hurtful things, if they are dealt with honestly, in love. I hope that I'm never guilty of telling a falsehood to a trusting child."

His words hung about my head, making me angry. How could he say these things—he who was living a horrible lie. I excused myself from the room and headed for my bedroom. I feared that I was going to be sick.

Mary found me a few minutes later.

"Dee was worried about you, Beth. Is something wrong?"

Everything is wrong, I wanted to scream—*Everything*. Instead I said, "Mary, didn't you tell me that Wynn Delaney—Dee—whoever, is unmarried?"

"Yes."

"And didn't you say that he—he wanted to *stay* that way?"

She nodded.

"Well, maybe—" I said, blanching white again, "maybe, the reason that he hasn't taken a Calgary wife is that *he already has one*."

"Wynn?" Mary used his given name.

"Yes, Wynn."

"That's impossible. We've known Wynn—"

"Well, apparently you don't know him very well."

"Elizabeth, we know—"

"He *has* a wife—and a son. I've met them."

"You've what?"

"His son, Phillip, is my student."

"Phillip?"

"Yes, Phillip, and I've—"

"Elizabeth, Phillip is Lydia and Phillip's child."

"Whose?"

"Lydia and—"

"Is she divorced?"

"Lydia?" Mary's voice was incredulous.

"She lives with *Wynn*," I insisted.

"Wynn is the senior Phillip's brother."

"And where is this—this other Phillip?"

"Here—in the hospital. That's why Wynn is in Calgary so often. Lydia and Phillip, Jr. are here now too, staying with her parents."

My knees felt weak. I groped behind me for the bed and sat down.

"Beth—are you all right?" Mary asked anxiously.

I honestly didn't know. My head was whirling and my stomach was in knots.

After a long silence, I whispered, "Mary, are you *sure*?"

"I'm sure—*very* sure."

Parts of the crazy puzzle began to slip into place. Lydia—her friendliness—her statement that "everything has been so upset"—her ability to laugh and enjoy the spectacle of the battle for my box at the social.

"Oh, Mary," I moaned, but I could say no more. I buried my face in my hands and thought of the times when I had been rude—inexcusably so, I was now discovering—to Wynn Delaney. How could I ever make him understand? How could I ever make things right?

"They have good news," Mary continued brightly. "Phillip can go home on Monday. I talked to Lydia today, and she is wild with excitement."

"I'm—I'm sure—I'm sure she is," I stammered.

"I must go, Beth. Are you sure you're okay?"

I managed a weak smile. "Sure—I'm fine—just fine. Just give me a minute or two and I'll be right down. I guess things just caught up with me all of a sudden. Don't worry. I'm all right."

Mary left, and I tried hard to find some composure. My heart thumped so hard I could almost hear it.

Wynn Delaney was not a married man. He was not Lydia's husband. He was not *anyone's* husband. And so many times, when he had made some small gesture of kindness, I had coldly rebuffed him. How would I ever explain my foolishness? What must he think of me? Now I *knew* that I was going to be sick.

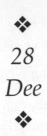

28
Dee

❖

I DID APPEAR for dinner. I must have still been pale, and I felt that my smile looked a little weak; but in the midst of the chatter and laughter around the table, I hoped that it wasn't noticed. I was quiet during the meal, but I never had done a lot of talking, and I was able to respond when I was spoken to.

Kathleen had requested that she sit between *her* Dee and *her* Aunt Beth, and on this occasion her mother saw no harm in humoring her; after all, she had just been "jilted" by the man whom she had planned to marry. Dee fussed over her, perhaps in an effort to show her that he still cared about her even though the wedding was "off." Kathleen did not act as one forsaken and forgotten. Her little tongue was constantly going, telling Dee of her new doll—"show ya right after dinner"; her new green dress—"almost the color of Aunt Beth's"; what she did while Sarah was at school—"helped Mamma"; and how much Baby Elizabeth liked her.

Occasionally Kathleen would say, "Isn't that right, Aunt Beth?" And I would be obliged to enter into their conversation.

I was glad for the seating arrangement. At least I did not have to sit opposite Wynn Delaney—Kathleen's Dee—where I would have to look at him once in a while throughout the meal. Those sensitive eyes might look right through me and see my tumbled emotions.

When Jonathan decided that there had been enough children's chatter, he excused them from the table to go to their rooms for a bit of play before bedtime.

The grown-ups then had a quieter conversation over second cups of coffee. I had preferred the din of the children, for with their leaving attention suddenly focused uncomfortably on me. Jon and Mary plied me with questions about my school, my pupils, my neighbors and my little teacherage. Because I loved them all so much, I imagine that love showed in my eyes and voice, in spite of the way I was feeling.

"Elizabeth must be very tired," Wynn interjected after a time, and I looked at him in surprise. For one thing, I had never heard him call me "Elizabeth" before.

"She's been working very hard with her students," he elaborated, "and then she took on the extra load of organizing a money-raising social for a local family in need."

I had already told Jon and Mary about Andy, and the eyes around the table softened at the mention of the fund-raising effort.

I swallowed hard. I still found my heart hurting at the mention of the dear little fellow.

"The work wasn't too much," I hurried to explain. "If things had turned out differently—"

Wynn reached across the empty chair that separated us and gave my hand a sympathetic squeeze. Shocked, I looked up quickly to catch the expression in the eyes around the table. But no one looked surprised. I presumed they understood such gestures better than I did—and they also knew the man better than I. Mary quickly took charge of the situation. I think that she was a little afraid that talking of Andy would have me weeping again.

"I have four children to care for," she announced with a smile. "Jon, dear, why don't you move our guests to a more comfortable setting, and I'll join you in a few minutes."

"I must go, my dear," Nanna said, rising. "This has been lovely, and I so much enjoy sharing dinner with you and your children. It's much better than sitting up to a table alone." She gave a mock shiver. Mary stopped to kiss her on the cheek.

"We love to have you. You just come over whenever you wish."

"Oh, I do—I do," she said with a twinkle.

Jon took Nanna home. We all said appropriate things as we bid her good-bye, and then Mary hurried upstairs to put the children to bed.

The moment that I had dreaded had come. I knew that Wynn deserved an explanation for my rudeness in days past, but I didn't know quite how to approach the subject.

Wynn and I were sent to the front parlor and each given another cup of coffee—which I neither wanted nor needed, but at least the cup gave me something to do with my nervous hands. I knew that Jon would soon be back to join us, so I decided I dared not fill in the time with small talk.

"I'm afraid that I owe you an explanation," I began in a rather quavering voice as soon as we were seated before the fire.

He had been watching the flames, but he turned to look at me. I didn't know if it was my words or my voice that gave away the fact that what I had to say was important.

His eyes held a question but he did not speak, so I went on.

"You see, I thought—that is, I understood, that—that you were Phillip's father."

His jaw dropped with astonishment.

"You thought that I—that I—that my brother's wife was raising my child?"

"I didn't know that you had a brother."

"You thought that—that *what*?"

"I thought that Lydia was *your* wife."

"But how . . . ?" He shook his head in disbelief, then held up a hand as though to stop me from proceeding too quickly. Finally he spoke again.

"Lydia is a sweet, lovely woman—but my brother Phillip is the fortunate man."

"I know that *now*. Mary told me."

He stood up and paced a few steps, then stood gazing into the fire. When he swiveled to face me, his face was still filled with puzzlement.

"You thought that I—was a married man?"

"Yes."

He again shook his head, then stood thoughtfully looking into the fire. Finally he turned toward me.

"Where did you ever get such an idea?" His tone was not accusing, merely baffled. But I was on the defensive now. Surely it wasn't all stupidity on my part. Tears were stinging my eyelids. I stood to my feet.

"I got the idea," I said, with deliberate emphasis, "because *you* were living in the same house as Lydia, *you* came to school to see me about young Phillip, *you* asked me for his homework, *you* spoke of 'his mother and I,' and *you* shared the same last name—and *nobody* ever mentioned to me that there was such a person as Phillip, Sr."

My voice had become quite loud by the time I had finished my speech. The astonished look left his face as he followed my reasoning; a look of frustration took its place.

"I see . . . ," he said a little lamely when I had finished, and he turned to the flames again.

I sat back down. My hands were trembling. Carefully I set my cup and saucer on the small table beside my chair.

"I see," he said again, and turned back to me. "So, figuratively speaking, you tossed your box lunch back in my face?" Again, his openness and honesty took the sting out of the words.

I couldn't speak. I couldn't even look up. I just sat there twisting my handkerchief slowly around a finger and feeling the color rising into my face. Suddenly I heard a soft chuckle. I looked up quickly then, wondering why his sudden change of mood.

"It's rather funny, isn't it?" His eyes held their usual good humor, and he chuckled again. "Here I spend ten dollars and sixty-five cents so that I can sit with the pretty schoolteacher; and, instead, I eat alone because she thinks—"

"You paid *ten dollars and sixty-five cents*? For a box lunch?"

He laughed as he nodded sheepishly, like a schoolboy.

"But that's—that's ridiculous! All of the baskets were going for one or two—"

"Not that one."

Now my face was hot with embarrassment. That evening I had not paid attention to the price that my basket had brought.

"It was a good cause," he assured me seriously, "so I do not begrudge the ten-sixty-five."

I remembered little Andy again. It *had* been a good cause. . . .

"And," he said, this time in false lament, "it could have been a good *buy* as well."

"I'm—I'm sorry. Truly, I—I—"

"So am I, Miss Thatcher." His eyes fixed on mine for an instant, then he turned back to the fire.

The few seconds of awkward silence that followed seemed far longer.

"Actually," he ventured, "perhaps it was all for the best." He stepped back from the fire and took the seat opposite me, putting down his now-empty cup.

"The *best*?" I questioned, not understanding him.

"I'm afraid I was beginning to think like a farmer."

"And there is something *wrong* with thinking like a farmer?"

He smiled. "Not for a farmer."

"And—you're not a farmer?"

"I?"

I nodded.

"No, not I."

"But you—"

"I was given a special leave so that I could give Phillip a hand—to take off his crop. I was raised on the farm, so at least I know what to do and when to do it. I even enjoyed it—for a change. Once or twice, I even wished that I had stayed on the farm myself. A farmer is, after all, his own boss—to the extent that the elements will allow him, while . . ." He paused and shrugged. "But Phillip will soon be back to again take charge of his farm—and his son—*and* his wife."

He was teasing, and I once more felt my face flush.

I wanted to ask what he now would do, where his work would take him, but I didn't. Instead, I went to the window and looked out on the quiet evening. I was just in time to see Jon return from taking Nanna home.

"I think that I will go say good-night to the children," I said and gathered up the coffee cups to take them to the kitchen.

I felt his eyes upon me as I left the room. It was rather impolite of me to desert him, but Jon would soon be in to keep him company.

29

Return to School

WE SAW WYNN, Lydia and Phillip, Jr. at church the next morning, but we had little opportunity to chat. I was glad about that. I still had some sorting out to do.

That afternoon, Mary and I had some time alone; she directed the conversation to Wynn.

"So," she said directly, "what do you think of our Dee—now that you've allowed him his rightful single status?" She laughed as she said it, and I tried to laugh with her, but I flushed too.

"He's—he's a very nice man." The words sounded silly, but I couldn't think of anything else that I felt was appropriate to say.

"He's more than nice," Mary said with enthusiasm. "He's—very special. I had even dared to hope—" She restrained herself, and looked at me quickly as though to see if I had caught on to what she had been about to say. Changing her mind, she said, "Just wish he weren't so stubborn."

"Stubborn?"

"Well, not about everything, but he's got this crazy notion that marriage and his work do not go together."

"Oh?" I was hoping she would understand that as a question.

"He's determined—absolutely determined—that he will *never* ask a woman to share his life with him. He says that other men can run their lives in this order: God, wife, work; but his has to be God, work, wife, and he won't ask a woman to take the lesser position."

"My, my," I said, trying to sound casual and even a bit sarcastic, "he must be a *very* special man."

"No, no. *He* doesn't think he's special. He just thinks that his *job* is. He's totally dedicated to it—but then, of course, it does take him into some rather primitive settings. He has already spent time up north, and I'm sure he will again. And he says that he won't ask a woman to share that. I guess it's rather tough—"

"But if a woman really loved a man," I interrupted, "surely she wouldn't mind . . . Doesn't he know there is such a thing as love—real love—and if a woman—"

"Little Beth," Mary said, her eyes twinkling, "maybe you'll have to show him."

"Now wait a minute . . ." I started, blushing to my roots. Mary laughed outright.

"I really don't think that he would be such a difficult pupil; and I have heard that you're a *good* teacher," she teased.

Though blushing and tongue-tied, I still refused to be baited.

"So—" I began, trying to gain control of the conversation—and myself, "what is this special, oh-so-important, impossible-to-live-with job?"

Mary became serious.

"You don't know what Wynn does?"

"No. Why should I know?"

"He's a Mountie."

"What?"

"A North West Mounted Policeman."

"I know what a Mountie is. I'm just surprised. I never thought . . ."

Then, as if I finally had found the lever to release the nervous tension of the previous twenty-four hours, I burst out in laughter. "Julie would swoon," I gasped out.

"What?"

"Oh, nothing." I was starting to recover from my laughing.

Baby Elizabeth cried, and Mary rushed off to look after her. I was left alone with my churning thoughts and emotions.

I remembered the words, ". . . I was beginning to think like a farmer," and I thought that I now understood what Wynn had meant—at least a bit. A farmer certainly didn't need to worry about his work conflicting with the taking of a wife.

On Monday morning I wanted to spend time in the local library to search out some information I needed in my teaching; I asked Jon if he would drive me downtown well before train time. So he delivered me to the station where we purchased my ticket and left my suitcase with the clerk. I bid Jon good-bye, trying hard to explain just how much the weekend had meant to me. I now felt ready to return to my classroom.

I walked the short distance to the library and began to browse through the titles. It was a small library so I had not bothered asking for help but went looking on my own. My eyes caught a rather unusual title, *The Origin and Meaning of Names*. I pulled it from the shelf and flipped through the pages. I found "Elizabeth." It was Hebrew, the book said, and meant "consecrated to God." The meaning pleased me. It was nice to belong to Him.

I cast a quick look around to see if anyone was near, then turned quickly to the W's. I didn't expect to find Wynn, but I did. "Old Welsh," it said— "fair one." I closed the book quickly and tucked the small bit of information away. I agreed with the book. I then thought of Mary's teasing—that *I* should try to change Wynn's mind about marriage. Against my will, the idea popped into my mind, *I'd like to—I'd really LIKE to.* With a smile I thought that I should have taken lessons in winsomeness from Julie. I had no idea how to go about changing a man's mind—especially regarding marriage. I jolted myself from my reverie and set about searching for the information I needed for teaching.

Boarding the train in plenty of time, I selected my seat. It appeared that the coach would not be very full. I settled myself for a long, tedious journey as we pulled away from the depot. This time I was prepared—I had brought along a book to read. Perhaps the stopping and unloading, loading and shuffling, would not bother me quite so much if I kept my mind occupied.

I couldn't concentrate on my book. I found myself staring out of the window watching the slowly passing landscape and the bustle of activity in the small towns where we stopped to exchange passengers and cargo. As we pulled out of Red Deer, I decided to take a walk through the coach and stretch my legs.

When I stood up and looked down the car, I discovered that I had been sharing the car with the Delaneys. I attempted to quietly sit back down before I was spotted, but Lydia noticed me. She waved and I returned her greeting, and then she beckoned me to come and join them. I didn't see how I could politely refuse. Wynn rose to his feet as I approached them, and he motioned for me to take his seat beside Phillip, Jr., facing Lydia and Phillip, Sr. I had not met the elder Phillip before. It would have been easy to tell that he and Wynn were brothers, even though Phillip was pale from his hospital stay and was shorter and fairer than Wynn. Lydia was beside herself with joy; it was plain to see that she had missed her husband terribly, and I imagined the strain it must have been on her. No wonder there had been so many weekend trips to Calgary. It seemed strange to me that Phillip had never mentioned his father, but perhaps that was the way the small boy had determined to handle his anxiety. In fact, I had never heard him refer to his Uncle Wynn either, though he certainly seemed to think highly of him.

"Mother is waiting at home," Lydia confided. "She can hardly wait for Phil to get home so that she can fatten him up! I can imagine that she's been cooking for two days straight."

"I'm willing," her husband said. "I am so weary of hospital cooking that I'll be happy to have Mother fuss for a while. I see that she's managed to put a few pounds on Wynn—though I'm sure that it wasn't as many as she would have liked."

"That was a difficult assignment," Lydia jested. "Wynn worked it off as quickly as Mother cooked it on."

Young Phillip decided to take his new *Animals of the World* picture book to the seat across the aisle. I then moved over so that Wynn might sit down again.

Although Phil seemed to have the same sense of humor as his brother, he didn't possess quite the same unruffled confidence. *Perhaps it is because Phillip has been ill,* I reasoned. But even beyond that, there was something about Wynn that set him apart. *Maybe being a member of the Mounted Po-*

lice has given him assurance, I further told myself—but that didn't seem to be the whole answer either. I finally decided that it was just "Wynn." That was why he took his work so seriously and why he was capable of such dedication to his difficult job. I was convinced that he must be a very efficient member of the Force.

I said that I was so glad Phil was now able to rejoin his family.

"I'm sure that Wynn, also, is glad to see me finally make it," said Phil. "I think that he may be a bit tired of riding the binder and milking the cows."

"Soft touch!" was Wynn's rejoinder.

"Now he's going to tell me that he'll be glad to get back to some *real* work," Phil predicted.

"Right," teased Wynn, "I was getting—"

"Don't say it." Phil held up his hand. "Soft or not, we couldn't have made it without you."

"You'll need a few months to regain your strength, but I guess you'll get it back during the winter. It'll be five months before you'll need to put your hand to the plow."

"I'm afraid that I'm going to have a tough job holding him down," said Lydia.

"Young Thebeau is good with stock. There's no excuse for Phil to get out there," Wynn assured her.

The Delaneys continued discussing future plans, and I realized that Wynn had no thought of staying on at the farm once Phil was home again. I wondered where he was going and if I'd ever see him again. But I was afraid to ask.

I noticed Lydia holding Phil's hand tightly. She looked as if she were afraid to let go, lest he leave her again. I could imagine how many things they had to talk about. I stood up.

"I must get back to my seat," I said. "I need to gather my things together."

Wynn stood and moved aside so that I could pass him. The train gave a sudden lurch, and I nearly lost my balance. His arm was quick to steady me. I hurriedly righted myself by grabbing the back of a seat and withdrew from him. This contact, however short and unplanned, had unnerved me.

I had gathered my few belongings together in short order and knew by the landmarks that we still had some minutes left before arrival. I picked up my book and stared at the pages, but I didn't read. I heard a stirring and looked up in time to see Wynn lower himself in the seat opposite me.

"May I?"

"Certainly."

"I wondered if you had arranged for a way home."

"I—not really. I guess when I left I wasn't thinking that far ahead."

"Fine. Then you can ride with us."

"I—thank you."

"You don't mind?"

"No, of course not. That is, if *you* don't mind."

"Then it's settled."

He was about to go but I detained him. "Mr. Delaney," I said. I had never called him by his first name, though I thought of him as "Wynn." "I know that I tried to explain about the box social, but I didn't say how—how sorry I am for publicly embarrassing you."

"Embarrassing me?"

"Yes. Even though I thought that you were married, your neighbors—they knew that you weren't, and they had no idea that I thought—what I did—and—"

"Would it have made a difference?" His tone was forthright. "Would you have *found* time to share your lunch if you had known the truth?"

"Of course."

He considered that for a moment.

I started, "Why else would I—"

"Miss Thatcher," he said and he grinned at me—that slow, teasing grin, "I am not so conceited as to believe that a young lady such as yourself, cultured and refined, would jump at the chance of sharing a lunch with the likes of me—untamed and unpolished—under any circumstances. You were quite within your rights to turn me down—for whatever your reason—no questions asked."

I gasped.

"But—but I *wouldn't* have."

"And if Bill Laverly had been the lucky purchaser, as he wanted to be, would you have had lunch with him?"

I was cornered, but I had to be honest. I struggled for words. There didn't seem to be any truly appropriate ones—just truthful ones.

"Yes—yes, of course. That was the whole idea."

He lifted his hat to me with the same smile shining out of his eyes.

"You're a good sport, Elizabeth," he said. "See you in Lacombe." He replaced his hat and was gone.

A hired auto was waiting for us in Lacombe. It had been arranged for Phil so that the trip would not be too tiring. Because the family still clung together, I shared the front seat with Wynn who was driving. I'm sure that he noticed my silence, but he said nothing about it. Instead, he gave me a short Alberta biology lesson about the local flora and fauna. I found it all very interesting; in fact, he was providing some of the very information for which I had unsuccessfully searched in the Calgary library.

"Could you—would you mind coming to the school and telling some of this to the students?" I blurted out without thinking. "It's exactly what I've wanted to teach them, but I know so little—and I couldn't find any books."

"I'd love to," he said, and I was certain that he meant it, "but I'm leaving tomorrow. It's back to work for me on Wednesday."

"I see."

I sat silently. He spoke, "You can go ahead and use the little that I've told you; and the next time that I see you, I'll give you an additional lesson—how's that?"

My heart skipped—then made up for the lost beat in double time. I would be seeing him again.

"You come home often?"

"No—sometimes not for months, or even years. It depends on where I'm posted."

"And where will you be posted?"

"I don't know that yet."

"You don't know? You go back to work in two days, and you don't even know where?"

"I'll know in time to get to the place they want to send me."

"Then there may not be another lesson," I said dully. *I may not ever see him again,* my heart mourned.

"True," his voice as serious as mine, "there may not."

We drove in silence for a while. Suddenly he turned to me in excitement.

"Will Blake!" he exclaimed. "He's a real woodsman. If anyone knows about our area, Will does. He would be glad to come and speak to your pupils. Want me to talk to him?"

Disappointment seeped all through me. Couldn't he see that it was more than knowledge that I was interested in? Still, I appreciated the fact that he had bothered to consider the needs of my pupils. I forced a smile.

"That's fine," I said. "You'll be very busy. I'll talk to him. Thank you."

30

The Christmas Program

M Y STUDENTS AND I settled back into classroom routines. The air was colder now, so each morning I shivered my way through starting my own fire; and then, just when the teacherage was beginning to get comfortable, I had to leave the warmth of it and hurry across to the school to get the fire going there. It certainly helped to know how to handle the dampers properly. Even so, on some days I seemed to get more smoke than flame.

The students, for the most part, were working hard and making steady progress. Even the older boys were beginning to study seriously. Andy was still talked about in loving terms. We missed our cheering section.

In mid-November we began work in earnest on our Christmas program. The students were so eager to make a good showing that they coaxed me daily for a chance to practice. I thought that part of their enthusiasm might be due to the fact that rehearsal kept them from studying spelling and geography, so I vetoed the idea of spending too much time away from the books and encouraged them to learn their lines at home.

As the time for the performance drew near, we were all caught up in the excitement. First there would be the program. All of the students were involved in presentations. After that portion was over, Santa would make an appearance, and hand out eagerly awaited candy bags. Mr. Laverly had a committee in charge of the bags—and of arranging for Santa, and I was glad that they were not my responsibilities. I was sure that I would have all I could do to get the program and the school in order. After the arrival and departure of the jolly red elf, we would all enjoy a lunch together. It sounded simple enough, but it actually took hours and hours to prepare.

Whispers began to circulate among the girls as to what each would be wearing. Many even spoke of *new* dresses that their mammas were going to be making out of "Jane's old one" or "Sally's full skirt" and, in some cases, even brand-new material, purchased just for that purpose. It was easy to catch their excitement. If ever they felt in need of and entitled to a new dress, now was the time.

The boys said nothing about what they would be wearing. Instead, they talked of the new bells for the team harness or the fact that their pa had said that they could do the driving. It seemed that Christmas was an important time for beginning drivers.

We all hoped for good weather, for snow on the ground to make things pretty, and temperature not too cold for the teams. The people could bundle up, but the poor horses had to stand in the cold while they waited for the proceedings of the evening to end.

The night finally arrived, crisp and cold but clear. The wind was not blowing, and I felt thankful for that fact as I trudged through the snow on my various errands between the teacherage and schoolhouse. Each step squeaked and crunched in the dry snow.

I built the fire early so that the room would be comfortably warm, and put on two big kettles of water to heat. The pump handle was so cold that even through my woolen mittens, my hands complained.

I carried the pails of water carefully, knowing that water splashed on my skirt or shoes would be ice by the time I had finished my chore and would make for a most uncomfortable evening.

My breath preceded me in little wisps of silvery smoke curling around my head as I moved forward. Overhead the stars shone so brightly that I felt I had only to reach out my hand to feel the warmth of them. As I walked toward the schoolhouse, one glittering star was shaken from its celestial bed and streaked earthward, leaving a long silver streamer trailing behind it.

In the distance I heard the wail of a coyote. They were not very close tonight. I waited for the answer of the pack, but it did not come. Perhaps the rest were snuggled closely together in an underground den.

By the time I heard the jingling of harness bells and the squealing of sleigh runners, the schoolroom was comfortably warm and the final preparations were complete. I straightened my hair, smoothed out the skirt of my green velvet dress that I had decided to bring with me from Calgary for this very night, and prepared to meet the first arrivals.

The women and children bustled into the schoolroom to be unbundled from their many wraps, while the men remained outside for a moment to care for the horses. Blankets that had been used to tuck in children were now thrown over animals, and hay was placed within the teams' reach. There was not enough room in our small barn, so many of the horses were tied to fence posts around the schoolyard.

The Christmas program went very well, all things considered. There were a few minor calamities: Mindy Blake forgot her lines and fled the make-shift stage in tears; Tim Mattoch, with his poor eyesight, tripped his way onto the platform, but he bounced back up and led the people in the laughter; Maudie Clark became confused in the drill and misled Olga Peterson and Ruthie Clark—soon the whole group was in a snarl, so I had to stop the whole thing and have them start over. Their second attempt was nearly flawless. Sally Clark did a wonderful job reciting "The Night Before Christmas," and little Else sang "Away in a Manger" in such a sweet, clear voice that it brought tears to more than a few eyes. Our playlet went well, too, and we had a most responsive audience. I'm sure that with the evening's performance each of the students felt like a star, and there were no parents there who would have argued with them.

When the program had ended, each of the students found a seat. It was now time for Santa to make an appearance. We waited, every ear straining, and then we heard a distant jingling of my hand-held school bell and a "Ho-ho-ho." A cheer went up from all of the children in the group—I think that even some of the adults joined them.

Santa entered—red suit, whiskers, and all—with his hoho-ho ringing out merrily. He said a few muffled words to the children, asking if they had been good, to which they replied in chorus, "Yes!" He then went right to work calling out names and passing out the candy bags. At the sound of each name, a child bounded forward, eyes shining and hands reaching out eagerly. As the last child returned to her seat, I gave Mr. Laverly a nod—he was to thank our unknown Santa. But to my surprise, Santa produced another bag, this one from within his jacket. He called loudly, "Miss Elizabeth Thatcher."

I stood dumb-struck.

My students cheered and clapped.

"Miss Elizabeth Thatcher," Santa called again.

"C'mon, Teacher. C'mon," the students coaxed.

I could feel my face flushing, but I finally got to my feet and began moving toward Santa.

"C'mon now, Miss Thatcher," Santa echoed the children in a hearty, disguised voice. "Step right up here on the platform. Don't be shy, now."

With the help of several hands I found myself on the platform. I reached timidly for the brown bag in Santa's hand, but he pulled it back with another ho-ho-ho.

"Not so fast now, Miss Thatcher. Have you been a good girl?"

The children howled, and I blushed.

"I—I've tried to be," I answered.

"Has she, children?" Santa asked my little group. A big cheer went up, along with some shrill whistles. Santa ho-ho'ed again.

"Well, then I guess you can have it. But first give Santa a little kiss." He tapped his whiskered cheek with a gloved hand.

I'm not sure if my face was red or white at that point.

"C'mon now," he said, "give Santa a little kiss." He continued to point at his cheek. Cheers and howls filled the room.

I looked at the whiskered cheek, shrugged my shoulders slightly, and standing on tiptoe, planted a kiss on dear old Santa amid shouts, cheers, whistles and clapping.

My face still red, I left the platform clutching the small brown bag. By the time I had regained my composure and my post by the brewing pot of coffee, Santa's ho-ho-ho's were fading in the distance.

We proceeded to serve the lunch. I poured coffee and hot chocolate. When I finally ran out of customers, I decided to have a cup of hot chocolate myself. Lydia Delaney motioned me over to her family. It was good to see Phil with more color in his cheeks, and he had gained a few pounds since I had last seen him. They made room for me between the two Mrs. Delaneys. They were anxious to know about my Christmas plans, and I told them that I intended to spend the holiday recess with Jon's family in Calgary.

I wanted to ask them about Wynn—where he had been posted and if they expected him home, but I didn't trust my voice to be casual enough, so I held my tongue.

A small stirring drew our attention to the far side of the room and I noticed Phillip, Sr. watching it with interest. Henry Laverly seemed to be circulating among the young men, prompting a number of them to dig disgustedly into their pockets. Phil stood up and sauntered toward them, greeting and talking with neighbors as he worked his way across the room.

It wasn't until after nearly all of the crowd had bundled up and headed for home, sleighbells ringing and harnesses crackling, that word reached me. It seemed that some of the neighborhood young men had made bets as to who would be the first to get a kiss from the new, young schoolteacher; and bashful, reserved Henry Laverly, with his sneaky Santa routine, had just collected the bets.

31
Christmas Eve

I DIDN'T REALIZE just how much I was looking forward to Christmas break until I climbed aboard the train in Lacombe and was finally bound for Calgary. A lonesomeness for my family back East swept over me in an almost overwhelming wave, and for a moment I considered buying a ticket for Toronto and heading home. My sense of reason, and my love for my students, held me steady, so instead I began to plan the days that I would spend with Jon and his family.

The train ride was, as usual, long and slow; and by the time we arrived in Calgary the short winter's day was almost spent, and darkness was creeping upon us.

Jon met me at the station. He had brought the three older children with him, and they all took turns trying to dislodge my hat with their wild bear hugs. My enthusiasm may have been more controlled but nonetheless sincere.

The family was preparing for Christmas. Festive decorations greeted us at the front door, and delicious odors reached us as soon as we stepped inside. It was like coming home, and my homesickness began to leave me.

The first days I spent in shopping and being entertained by the children. Sarah had to bring me up-to-date on her reading skills, and William demonstrated his ability on the violin, while Kathleen, chattering constantly, followed me about.

There was to be a special Christmas Eve service in the church, and the children talked about it constantly, probably as much from the opportunity to "stay up late" as anything else. By the time the day arrived, I, too, had caught their excitement.

We traveled the short distance by sleigh, for the cold weather made unpredictable the starting of automobiles left out in the elements. Besides, Mary maintained, the sleigh was much more in keeping with Christmas. The rest of us agreed. We burrowed together under furry buffalo robes and enjoyed the twinkling of the stars in the clear sky overhead and the crisp sound of the snow under the runners.

The team, a pair of magnificent bays, snorted and tossed their heads, sending out small clouds of frosty breath. I had the feeling that the two would have enjoyed a good run, so I was glad that Jon was well able to handle them.

* * *

Jon seated us quite near the front of the church. I sat nestled between Sarah on my left and Kathleen on my right. The room was glowing with candlelight; shadows danced across the faces of the two playing the parts of Mary and Joseph and looking down on the Christ Child lying in the manger bed. The green wreaths made of spruce not only looked Christmasy, but they brought a lovely Christmasy smell to the sanctuary as well.

The service was delightful. We sensed again the awe of the first Christmas so long ago when God sent His most precious gift, His Son Jesus, into the world to be born of a woman so that someday, as a sacrifice, He could provide salvation for the whole human race.

The familiar Christmas carols had never meant as much to me as they did on that night. As I recited the words, I pictured the young Mary, her hour having come, with no one to care for her—no warm bed, no private room, no skilled midwife—only straw, a stable, and an anxious husband nearby. She herself cared for the newborn Son of God, the baby Jesus.

I thought of my Lord, the Maker of Heaven and Earth, now reduced to a helpless child, not even able to express His needs and wants, far less demand the honor due Him; and I thought of the Father who must have watched anxiously from His throne as the new Babe made His appearance in the world that He had fashioned. God himself lay snuggled against the breast of a young peasant girl in a dimly lit stable in Bethlehem. How God must have loved mankind, to allow Him to come.

I left the service that night with a full heart and overflowing eyes. I brushed away tears with my handkerchief as I smiled at Kathleen and Sarah.

"Baby 'Liz'beth wasn't born with the cows," Kathleen whispered.

I nodded my head and gave her a squeeze to let her know that I knew how she felt.

"I'm glad," she insisted. She thought silently for a few minutes, then continued, "If she would have been, would she have been a Jesus?"

I smiled. "No, dear, she still would have been an Elizabeth. And Jesus would have still been Jesus, the Son of God, if He had been born in a hospital room or a King's chamber. Where one is born doesn't change who one is. But God knew where Jesus would be born, so He told us through His prophet, many years before it actually happened."

"God's pretty smart, huh?"

"Yes, Kathleen. God knows all things."

We followed the others down the aisle. The candle flames flickered and wavered, sending light and shadow to play on smiling faces while friends greeted one another as they moved toward the door.

"Hello, Elizabeth."

At the sound of the familiar voice, I turned quickly around and found myself looking up into the face of Wynn. It was the first time I had seen him in uniform. If I had found it difficult before to imagine him as a Mountie, as I looked at him now I could not imagine him as anything else. His strength was more than physical. There was a strength of character and purpose about him that made the red tunic look deserving of the man.

My breath had caught in a little gasp and it was a moment before I could answer him.

"I wasn't expecting to see you," I said shyly, and his widening smile brought a flush to my cheeks.

By then Kathleen had realized who was beside us and had claimed his attention. Jerking his sleeve, she was demanding, "Are you coming to our house, Dee? Are you coming to see our tree?"

"Hey," he said, "slow down, Moppet. As a matter of fact, your mother has invited me to your house, and I think—" he teased lightly, "I think *maybe* I'll come."

She ignored his teasing and clapped her hands. "He's coming, Aunt Beth! Isn't that good?"

I was busy trying to understand the strange fluttering of my heart. Was it the aura of the red jacket, or the fact that he had spoken my name? I hoped that Kathleen could keep his attention until I was able to get myself well under control.

Mary called Kathleen and the girl went to join her family. I was left, heart thumping, standing very close in the crowded aisle to this awesome man in the red coat.

"Jon has suggested," he began, and then his eyes began to twinkle, "—no, that's not true. Jon has agreed to *my* suggestion that, since I am to spend the evening at his house, you could ride over with me so that I might catch up on the Pine Springs news." He laughed then—a soft, good-natured chuckle. "Maybe that's not entirely true either, but I do want a chance for a bit of a talk, because once we get to Jon's and in the company of his chattering offspring, there will be little chance to even ask how you've been."

I smiled, knowing that he was right.

"Would you, Elizabeth?"

My smile seemed to wobble a little. "I'd like that."

He took my arm and steered me through the crowd and out to his waiting team. As the team stomped impatiently, the bells on their harness jingled clearly through the night air and seemed to echo again and again from the nearby buildings.

Wynn helped me into the sleigh and tucked the robes closely about me. As soon as we were on our way, he opened the conversation.

"So how is my big brother?"

"He's fine. I saw him and the family just a few nights ago at the Christmas program. He looks much better—has gained weight and picked up some color—and he looks absolutely happy."

"Good," was all he answered, but he spoke the single word with great feeling.

We were silent for several moments. I held my tongue, and my breath, until I feared that I would burst. I gave up. I had to know.

"And are you posted here in Calgary?"

"For now, but I'm not sure for how long. I expect that another posting will come soon, though I don't know where. I'm enjoying Calgary. The city is growing so fast that there's always something going on, but I'm rather anxious to get back—"

"Back to where?"

"I've spent six years at various posts in the North. I like it there."

"What do you do? I didn't think that there were many settlers in the North."

"Settlers, no—not too many. Trappers mostly. But the North is full of people. We are far more than law enforcement to the people there; Mounties are the only dentists, doctors, coroners, arbitrators, advisors—and clergymen, that many of the people have. They depend upon us, Elizabeth, not just to bring justice but to bring hope and help."

I thought about his words, and I thought about Julie. I wondered if her impression of the scarlet-coated Mountie was so accurate after all. Rather than adventure and excitement, their job sounded like a great deal of responsibility and hard work to me. And it sounded noble, though I didn't think that Wynn Delaney would care for that word, so I kept it to myself.

"Are there many women there?" The words were out before I could stop them.

"White women? No. Very few. Oh, a few of the North West Mounted Police have taken brides—unwisely."

"Unwisely?"

"It's a very difficult life. No modern homes, no shops, no entertainment. Often there are no white friends, unless it's a trapper's wife. It's not the place for a lady."

"But don't they need schools?"

"There are some mission schools, often taught by men. But for the most part, no—they don't think much about needing schools. The men know how to hunt and fish and care for their traps, and the women know how to tan the hides, dry the meat, haul the wood, tote the water. What more do they need to know? Those are the things necessary for surviving in their land."

I could tell by his voice that he was smiling as he said the words, yet I knew he was speaking from firsthand knowledge; he had worked among the people of the North. I did not try to argue.

He suddenly turned to me. "Here we are almost to Jon's, and you were to have given me all the news from Pine Springs. You'd better fill me in quickly," he prompted.

I laughed, and in as few words as possible I told him of some of the happenings of the community.

We pulled up to the front door and he stopped the team and helped me out of the sleigh. I had taken his offered arm to ease myself to the snow-packed ground when my foot caught in the buffalo robe. I tumbled forward, grabbing frantically for something solid. His reactions were quicker than mine, and before I could right myself I was held firmly in two strong arms.

"Are you all right?" he asked anxiously against my hair. I quickly steadied myself and gently pushed myself away from him.

"Just clumsy," I said in embarrassment. I released my hold on his coat sleeves and stepped back. I was thankful that he could not clearly see my face.

"It's slippery under foot," he cautioned.

"I'll *try* to be careful." I even managed a slight laugh.

"As soon as I care for the team, I'll be in."

I went quietly up the stairs to my room. In front of a mirror I removed my hat that had been jarred askew by my fall against Wynn. Straightening my hair with a trembling hand, I gave myself a few moments to regain my composure. By the time I arrived downstairs to join the family, Wynn was already there. Our eyes met briefly but neither of us made any comment.

Mary was serving cocoa and popcorn, and the children were jostling for a position close to the fire. As soon as they had finished their refreshments, Mary led them off to bed.

We spent the rest of the evening chatting and playing dominoes. It was nearly ten o'clock when Mary brought the coffee and Christmas baking. Jon threw more wood on the fire, and we pulled up close to the crackling flames and comfortably visited. At length, Mary asked Wynn, "Are you going to the wedding?"

He nodded.

"You don't seem very enthusiastic," she teased.

He still said nothing.

"So, why not?" Mary persisted.

"It's none of my business, I suppose," Wynn said slowly, "but I think that it's a mistake."

"Whose mistake?" Jon asked.

"Withers'."

"Is Withers the young Mountie?"

Wynn nodded.

"Mistake—how?" Mary asked, puzzled.

"You are a pest," Wynn teased. He stood up and moved closer to the fire. "Okay—I've said it before; here it is for you again. Withers is posted at Peace River—his young bride comes from Montreal. She is used to plays and concerts and dinner parties. She's trading that for blizzards and sickness, wild animals and loneliness. Do you think that she'll be able to appreciate the exchange? Come on, Mary—even *love* can't stand a test like that."

"Some women have done it, you know. Wynn, you might be short-selling love."

He turned back to the fire. "Yes," he said slowly, "some have. But I'd never want to ask it of the woman I loved."

I could tell that he truly meant those words, and something deep down inside of me began to weep. But Mary didn't let Wynn have the last word.

"Then you would also be short-selling the woman you loved," she said softly, "*if* she really loved you."

Wynn shook his head slightly, but his eyes did not turn from the fire.

32
Christmas Day

CHRISTMAS DAY DAWNED bright and glistening. During the night there had been a fresh fall of snow, and the cleaned-up-world shimmered in the rays of the winter sun.

The day began early with the glad shrieks of the children as they discovered the gifts that were in their stockings and under the tree. We enjoyed a leisurely morning of games, nut roasting and chatter. Dinner was to be served at one o'clock. Wynn joined us for dinner and he presented each of the children with a package. Jon, Mary and I were each given fur mittens made by Wynn's northern Indian friends; I looked forward to using mine.

In the afternoon the children begged for a chance to try their new Christmas sleds. So, following Mary's suggestion, Wynn and I accompanied Jon when he took them to the hill. We all bundled up—I was glad for this opportunity to wear my new mittens—until we could barely waddle and headed out, laughing and jostling, for the hillside.

At the hill we all rode on the sleds. I was soon exhausted after the breathless rides and long return climbs. I decided to sit down on a fallen log partway up the hill and rest while the others enjoyed another ride.

I could hear the shrieks and laughter as they sped downward, Jon and Sarah on one sleigh, Wynn and Kathleen on another, and William on his own.

A few birds fluttered in a nearby tree and two squirrels fought over winter provisions. I leaned back against a tree and enjoyed the sparkling freshness of the winter air.

I could hear the children's chatter at the foot of the hill when Wynn suddenly swung into sight.

"Jon said that I should take you up to the top of the ridge and give you a look at the mountains."

"Oh," I cried, springing up eagerly, "can you see them from here?"

"From right up there," he answered, pointing above and beyond us.

"Then lead the way—I'd love to see them."

The loose snow made climbing difficult. Wynn stopped often to let me catch my breath, and a couple of times he held out his hand to me to help me over a fallen tree or up a particularly steep place.

At the top I discovered that the climb had been worth every step. Stretched out before us, their snow-capped peaks glistening in the winter sun, were the magnificent Rockies. I caught my breath in awe.

"Someday," I said softly, "I'm going to visit those mountains—and have a picnic lunch right up there at the timberline."

Wynn laughed.

"That's quite a hike up to the timberline, Elizabeth," he cautioned.

"Well, I don't care. It'll be worth it."

"How about settling for a picnic lunch beside a mountain stream instead—or at the base of Bow Falls or maybe among the rocks of Johnson Canyon?"

"You've been there—to all of those places?"

"Several times."

"Is it as beautiful as I imagine?"

"Unless you have a very exceptional imagination, it's even more beautiful."

"Oh, I'd love to see it!"

"Then you must. I wish that I could promise to take you but . . ."

Reluctantly I turned from the scene of the mountains to make my way back down the slope to Jon and the children. My thoughts were more on Wynn's unfinished sentence than on where I was placing my feet. He was so determined, so definite. He left no room at all for feelings, for caring. Somehow I felt that there should be something I could say or do to make him at least re-think his position, but I couldn't think of what it might be—at least not while I was scrambling down a steep hillside behind a man used to walking in such terrain.

Suddenly my foot slipped on a snow-covered log and my ankle twisted beneath me. I sat down to catch my breath and test the extent of the injury. To my relief, nothing much seemed wrong. I knew that nothing was broken, and I was sure that there was not even a serious sprain—just a bit of a twist. I was rising to my feet to hurry after Wynn when he looked back to check on my progress.

"What's the matter?" he called, his voice concerned.

I tried to respond lightly, "I'm fine—just twisted my ankle a bit."

I took a step but he stopped me.

"Stay where you are, Elizabeth, until I check out that ankle."

"But it's fine—"

"Let's be sure."

He was hurrying back up the hill toward me when a strange idea entered my head. Maybe this was a way to delay him for a few moments until I had fully considered what I could say. I sat back down on the tree stump and stared at my foot.

Wynn had been only a few steps ahead of me, breaking trail, so he was soon down on a knee before me. "Which one?" he asked, and I pointed to the left ankle.

He lifted it with gentle firmness and removed my boot. Carefully he began to feel the injured ankle, his fingers sensitive and gentle.

"Nothing broken." He squeezed. "Does this hurt?"

It did—slightly, though not enough to make me wince as hard as I did. I said nothing—just nodded my head in the affirmative. After all, he hadn't asked how *much* it hurt.

Wynn surveyed the trail ahead.

"It's only a few more steps until we are on the level. Can you make it?"

I knew that I could, but I didn't say so. Instead, I murmured, "If you could help me just a bit . . ."

He replaced my boot, leaving the laces loose.

"Too much pressure?" he asked.

"No—no—that's fine."

"Good. We wouldn't want to take a chance on frostbite as well. Are you ready?"

I had visions of limping down the trail with Wynn's arm supporting me. *Surely*, I thought, *under such conditions it should be easy to think of the right thing to say to this man.* But instead of offering his assistance, Wynn swept me up into his arms in one quick, gentle movement. The suddenness of it startled me, and I threw my arms around his neck.

"It's all right," he reassured me. "It's only a few steps down this bit of a bank, and we'll be on the level."

"But I—"

"I could throw you over my shoulder and carry you dead-man style," he teased.

"I think I would prefer—" I was going to say, "to walk," but that wasn't true, so I lamely stopped.

"So would I, Elizabeth," he said with his slow smile and looked deeply into my eyes.

That was when I should have made my little speech, but my brain was hazy and my lips dumb. I could think only of this moment—nothing more—and I rested my cheek against his coat and allowed myself this bliss that would in the future be a beautiful memory.

All too soon we were at the slope where Jon and the children were still sledding. Wynn put me down, cautious that I would not put my weight on my left foot. For one confused moment I could not remember which foot was supposed to be injured and had to look at my boot to see which one had the untied laces.

We had not spoken to one another for several minutes. As he lowered me to a seat on a log, his cheek brushed lightly against mine, and I feared that he would surely hear the throbbing of my heart.

"How is it?" he asked. "I hope I didn't jar it."

"Oh, no. You were most careful. I don't see how you were able to come down there so—" I couldn't finish.

"We'll get you home as quickly as possible," he promised, and he waved to William who came trudging up the slope with his sled.

Wynn insisted that I ride home on the sleigh, and I could hardly refuse.

To insist upon walking would have given my ruse away, so I rode the sled, feeling foolish and deceptive.

When we arrived at the house, Wynn carried me in and deposited me on the couch. He suggested that ice packs might make my ankle more comfortable. Soon to be on duty, he couldn't stay for the evening. After promising to stop by to check on me at his first opportunity, he left.

I feigned a limp whenever I moved around for the rest of the day. It was hard to keep Jon and Mary from calling a doctor. I would have been mortified if one had been summoned on Christmas Day to look at my "injury." When bedtime finally arrived, I was relieved to take my perfectly fine ankle, and my guilty conscience, to the privacy of my own room.

I went to bed troubled. I could feel again the roughness of Wynn's wool coat against my cheek, and the strength of his arms supporting me as he carried me. I realized that I unwillingly had fallen in love with the man; and I might have missed my only opportunity to plead my case. Still, if a man was determined not to care for a woman, what could she possibly say to change his mind? I had no idea, having never been in such a position till now. For a moment I wished that I had learned a few of the feminine ploys that Julie used to such advantage, then checked myself. I had already used more trickery than I could feel comfortable with. What in the world had ever possessed me to make me promote such a falsehood? Shame flushed my cheeks. Never would I resort to such devious tactics again.

33
The Confession

THE NEXT MORNING I lightly brushed aside the inquiries concerning my ankle and assured everyone that it was just fine. I was embarrassed over the whole affair and was not anxious to discuss it. Mary insisted that I stay off my feet; so to appease her and to escape from everyone's sympathy, I retreated to Jon's library where I buried myself in a good book.

About noon, Jon entered with William reluctantly in tow. One look at their faces, and I could see that it was to be a serious discussion. I rose to excuse myself but Jon stopped me.

"Sit still, Beth. We'll only be a few moments. No need for you to bother that ankle of yours."

There it was again—my poor ankle. I flushed and was glad that the book hid my face. My guilt must certainly have shown.

Jon sat down and pulled William to him.

"Now, Son, what explanation do you have? Do you realize that what you've done is wrong?"

"Yes."

"Do you realize that what you've done is *sin*?"

"It's not *that* wrong."

"Oh, yes, it is. God has said, 'Thou shalt not,' but you did. Now, doesn't that make it sin?"

"Well, it wasn't a very *big* sin," William argued.

"There are no 'big' or 'little' sins, Son. God hasn't divided them up that way. Sin is—sin. Do you know how God feels about sin?"

William nodded his head in the affirmative, but the stubborn look lingered in his eyes.

"He don't like it."

"Right—He doesn't like it. Do you know *why* He hates it so much?"

"'Cause He's God?" William asked.

"Yes, He's God, and He's righteous and pure and good. There is nothing false or wrong or hurtful in the character of God. But I think there is an even *bigger* reason why God hates sin so much."

William's eyes were wide as they studied his father's face.

"It's because sin cost Him the life of His Son, Jesus. God decreed that those who sin must die. Man sinned—but God still loved him. God didn't want man to die for his sin, so God provided a substitute. If man accepted the fact that another had died in his place, and was truly sorry for his sin, then he wouldn't have to die."

"I know that," William said, his lip trembling. Jon's arm went around his son's waist.

"Many times," Jon continued, "folks get the idea that it was only the big sins, like murder and idol worship, that made it necessary for Jesus to die. But it wasn't, Son. It was, and is, any and *all* sin. If there had been any other way, if our holy God could have ignored sin, or blinked at it, or turned His head, or pretended that it just hadn't happened or didn't matter, then He would never, never have sent Jesus to die. God loved His Son—yet the death of His Son was the only way for God to spare us from the penalty of death that we deserve. He *loves* us. So that's why God hates sin—all sin, because it meant death for His Son. And if we still hang on to our sin, it means that we don't value what Jesus did for us."

"But I do," William protested. "I didn't mean to hurt Jesus—honest." A tear coursed down each cheek. Jon pulled the boy close.

"I know you didn't, Son. We often hurt God without meaning to. Now I want you to tell God that you didn't mean it, and that you are sorry, and that with His help you will not do it again. After that, we will go and have a talk with Stacy."

"Do I have to?" William pleaded. "Do I have to go to Stacy? I'll talk to God, Pa—but can't *you* tell Stacy?"

"No, Son. Part of being forgiven is making things right. God asks that of us—always. It's called 'restitution.' If Jesus was willing to pay the death penalty for us, to make things right between us and God, then it's not too much for God to ask that we make things right between ourselves and whomever we have wronged."

They knelt together by Jon's big chair, and a tearful William asked God's forgiveness. Then hand-in-hand, they left the room to go speak with Stacy, the kitchen helper.

I never did discover what William's wrong was. It did not seem important—for pricking at my own conscience was my dishonesty of the day before. I looked down at my ankle, feeling a hatred for the offending member; then I reminded myself that it wasn't the ankle that was at fault.

I was called for lunch. William appeared at the table, all traces of tears gone. In fact, he looked happier than usual, and when Stacy served the dessert, I noticed that William received a larger-than-usual serving. William noticed it, and he gave Stacy a grin. She winked—ever so quickly and slyly. Repentance, confession and restitution. William knew all about the benefits, while I still sat miserable and squirming in my chair.

After lunch I went to my room. It seemed that my battle lasted most of the afternoon. I was like William. I didn't mind telling my wrongdoing to God, but to speak to Wynn? The very thought of it made my cheeks burn. Yet, plead as I would for God's forgiveness, I had no peace of heart.

Confession—confession—kept ringing in my mind. Finally I threw myself upon my bed in desperation.

"God, it was such a foolish little thing," I pleaded.

"It was a *wrong* thing," my conscience answered.

"Yes, it was wrong—"

"It was sin. You *chose* to make someone believe an untruth."

"But the untruth will hurt no one."

"How can you speak of *hurt*? It cost Jesus His life."

"But—please don't make me talk to Wynn—not Wynn. Do you know what he'll think of me?"

"Do you care what God thinks of you?"

"Of course, but . . ."

I wept, I pleaded, I argued, but at length I gave in.

"Okay, if that's what must be, I will confess to Wynn at my first opportunity."

Peace came, but my dread of the encounter with Wynn did not go away.

I did not need to be in misery for long, for Wynn dropped by that evening to check on my "injured" ankle. He was only passing by, he said, so couldn't stay. After exchanging a few words with Jon and Mary, he picked up his fur winter hat and prepared to leave. I swallowed hard and stood up. My face felt hot and my throat dry.

"I must see you for a moment—please."

There was just a flicker of surprise—or concern—on his face.

"Of course."

I led the way to Jon's library, making sure that I, in no way, favored my "injured" ankle. Once inside, I closed the door and faced him. I wanted to run away, to hide my face, to lie again—anything but to face this man with the truth. Before I could change my mind and do any one of those things, I plunged in.

"I have a confession—about my ankle. I didn't injure it. I pretended. It's fine—I—" I dropped my gaze. No longer could I look into those honest, blue eyes. I turned slightly from him.

"I didn't think you would carry me. I just wanted—a little—a little more time . . ." I knew that I had to be honest, as much as it humbled me. "I acted like a silly child," I said, making myself look straight into his eyes. "I guess—I guess—I—I wanted your attention—and I—I didn't know how else to get it. I know it was foolish—and I'm—I'm sorry."

Wynn was looking directly at me. His eyes did not scorn or mock me, nor did he look shocked or disgusted. There was an understanding—and, yes, a softness that I had not expected to see. I turned from him lest I would do something very foolish—such as cry, or throw myself into his arms.

"I have confessed my dishonesty to God—and asked for His forgiveness. He has graciously granted it. Now—" My voice was almost a whisper, "now I would like to ask *your* forgiveness, also."

I felt Wynn's hands on my shoulders and he turned me gently to face him.

"Elizabeth," he said softly, "I can't tell you how much I respect you for what you've just done. Few people—" he hesitated a moment. "You've asked for my forgiveness. I give it—willingly, and now I, in turn, must ask yours."

I know that surprise must have shown on my face.

"Elizabeth, I examined your ankle—remember?"

I nodded.

"It was my choice to carry you—right?"

I just looked at him, not able to follow his thinking.

"Elizabeth, I am trained in first aid—to recognize breaks, and injuries, and sprains—"

I understood then.

"You *knew* . . . ?"

He nodded, his eyes not leaving mine. I turned from him, confused. What was he saying? He knew that my ankle was not injured when he examined it, yet he had carried me and held me close against his chest. Was it to shame me? To see how far I would let the charade go?

"Why?"

As I spoke, my back was still toward him. He paced to the window where he stood looking out on the darkness.

"Why?" he echoed. "I should think it rather obvious."

He stood for a moment, and then, his somber mood changed. He crossed back to me, his Mountie's hat in his hand ready to be placed on his head. I knew that he was leaving. The twinkle of humor had returned to his eyes and made the corner of his lips twitch slightly.

"And frankly, Elizabeth," he said through that controlled smile, "I've never enjoyed anything more." And with a slight nod he departed, and the door closed softly behind him.

34

Return to Pine Springs

I SAW WYNN a number of times that week. Neither of us ever mentioned my ankle. Nor were we ever alone. All of our time together was shared with Jon or Mary or one of the children.

But I learned much about him; that he loved people, young and old alike; that he was respected—by White and Indian; that he was knowledgeable, seeming to know something about almost everything; that he read widely and was able to converse about science as easily as he could recite poetry; that he had a deep and solid faith in God; and that he sensed a mission to help those whom many believed to be second-rate citizens. The more I knew of him the more I admired him, and what had previously been an infatuation was daily turning into a feeling much more deep and permanent.

He was kind to me, even solicitous. He even seemed to enjoy my company, but never once did he give me reason to believe that he had changed his mind concerning his conviction that marriage was unwise for a Mountie.

I couldn't understand how a man could be so stubborn, and if I hadn't already learned to love him so much, I would angrily and painfully have dismissed him from my thoughts.

Reluctantly I packed my bags and prepared for my trip back to Pine Springs. Mr. Laverly had promised to have someone meet my train at Lacombe.

I spent the entire long journey trying to make some sense out of my feelings for Wynn. It was not the least bit difficult for me to understand why a woman would fall for such a man—but why she should persist against such an obvious stone wall of stubborn determination to remain single was beyond me. Perhaps, I reasoned, I preferred his polite, enjoyable company to the alternative of not being with him at all.

Bill Laverly stood on the platform, his smile stretched from ear to ear, when I descended from the train. He was the last person I wanted to see, but what could I do? He loaded my suitcases and tucked me in with a bearskin rug, taking far too much time in the process, I thought.

He had talked his father into buying a light cutter and I knew, before we even moved out of the town, that I was in for the ride of my life. Bill cracked a whip over the team, and we jerked away in a swirl of snow, bells jingling and horses snorting. My only consolation was that the faster we went, the sooner I would be home and away from the company of this grinning, speed-mad man.

He seemed to be continually looking at me and adjusting the bearskins, but when he dared to put his arm across the back of the seat behind me, I drew the line. Drawing myself away from him, I informed him that I would be much more comfortable if he used *both* hands to guide the racing team.

As we entered the lane to the teacherage, I noticed smoke coming from the chimney. *Surely Bill hadn't lit the fire before he left*, was my first thought. Bill might like a pretty face, but thoughtful he was not.

After he had pulled the team to a snow-swirling stop, he drew out my suitcases, handed them to me and then with a scraping swish, he spun the cutter around and headed his galloping team for home. "See ya!" he yelled over his shoulder, his wide grin still spread across his face.

When I entered the little house it was easy to tell who had been there. The fire was burning cheerily, foodstuffs were arranged neatly on the cupboard, and my table was adorned with fresh coffeecake—Anna's specialty. A small pot of stew simmered near the back of the stove and the teakettle hummed merrily. How nice to be welcomed home, and how cold and miserable it would have been to enter the house that had seen no occupant or fire for two weeks.

While I ate the hot stew and fresh bread, my mind did a complete shift. I was anxious to get back to my students and the classroom. Faces flashed before me, and I thought of the achievements and the needs of each one. I was proud of my students. They had already accomplished so much in the short time that we had been together. I promised that I would do my very best for them in the months that lay ahead.

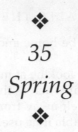

35
Spring

THE PUPILS SEEMED to share my enthusiasm. The next few months went very quickly, with our total concentration being given to our teaching and learning.

In March we had a visit from the district inspector. I don't know who was more nervous—my students or I.

Mr. Matthews, a tall, thin man with a pinched face, quick, dark eyes, and a high-pitched voice, spoke loudly, as though that would give him added authority. All the while that I taught that day, I could feel those sharp eyes on me, boring, probing, and even daring me. By lunch hour I was already exhausted, but he pulled a bench up close to my desk and began questioning me.

In the afternoon he shifted his attention to my pupils, quizzing them and calling on them to work sums or read a passage. I watched the poor, frightened children squirm and sweat, and I wished, for their sakes as well as my own, that the man would go away. Eventually he did, and all of us sighed and then laughed together in an effort to shake off our tension. I dismissed the class early for home.

The next day I had another visitor. Wynn had come to see Phil and Lydia, so he stopped by the school to deliver a note from Mary. I wished that I could invite him to the teacherage for supper, or at least tea, but I knew that such was forbidden and perhaps unwise, as well. We chatted of general things, and he waited while I wrote a quick note for him to take back to Mary. He had not yet received another posting. Just as my heart sang at the news, he stilled the song by informing me that it was bound to come, though he knew not when. One of the other fellows had just left for Lac La Biche, he said, and another Mountie who had been in Calgary for three years had just received a posting to Grouard, on Lesser Slave Lake.

"Did they have families?" I asked—not "wives," but "families"—hoping that Wynn would not guess my thoughts.

"McKenzie did—a wife and a young son."

"Did they mind going?"

"She didn't seem to, but she's been north before."

One point for me, I thought. He had had to admit that there was at least one woman who didn't mind going north with her husband. But Wynn went on.

"Aitcheson had a girl. When his posting came in, she called off the wedding."

My heart sank.

I wanted to say, "Well, some women can handle it—others can't." But I said nothing.

When Wynn left, he surprised me by giving me a compliment, at least it seemed like one to me.

"I think that this country life must agree with you, Elizabeth. You look more healthy and pretty every time I see you."

Healthy and pretty! It wasn't exactly as if he had declared me beautiful, but it was close—and coming from Wynn, who wasn't given to flattery, I decided to regard it as special.

I hummed happily after he had left.

Easter's arrival nearly caught me unawares, in the midst of my busyness. I packed for a trip to Jon and Mary's, anticipating a wonderful time in the city. I did enjoy the change and being with my family, but the fact that Wynn was spending time at Regina took much of the pleasure out of my holiday.

Mary delighted in letting slip frequent references to Wynn and his obvious high regard for me. I couldn't see how Mary could come to such conclusions, and I did wish that she would stop her nonsense. She seemed to be of the opinion that if I'd just show Wynn that I truly cared for him, he would shelve all his previous opinions regarding marriage and declare his undying love. I wasn't about to throw myself at any man, Wynn Delaney included; and besides, I was convinced that to do so would accomplish nothing, other than making a complete fool of myself.

I spent the week shopping, reading, loafing, playing with the children and snuggling Baby Elizabeth. At the end of the week I was eager to return to the classroom. I had not asked Mr. Laverly for a ride from the Lacombe station, nor even informed him of the train on which I would arrive. My plan was to hire Pearlie's father to drive me out in his automobile. When I alighted from the train I discovered that the Clarks were in town. They kindly offered me a ride, which I gladly accepted.

Upon arriving at my teacherage, I built my own fire, fixed a simple supper and then went to the schoolhouse. I wanted to get an early start on lesson preparations for the last few weeks of the school term.

Wynn mailed me a book—or rather, a manual, which I imagined was used by the North West Mounted Police. It contained many facts about Alberta, including its vegetation, animals and their behavior, the peoples and their way of life and industry. I found it fascinating—especially since it had come from Wynn. His short note had stated that he thought I might find the information interesting and helpful. I did. I used much of the book in my classes. The students and I took advantage of the early spring weather to go on a nature hike and identify the growth according to the manual.

April passed into May, and May into June. The wild roses began to appear, first as scattered blooms and then as walls of blossoms beside the roadway. The children hunted strawberries, which they shared with me, delivering them in sticky, dirty palms. It was a delightful time of year, and I gloried in each sun-splashed new day, hearing, seeing and breathing the newborn summer.

The families of the school children began another round of have-the-teacher-in-for-supper. I loved this time. I loved the people. I loved my visits in their homes. I loved the walks in the pleasant sunshine, to and from their farms. I loved the family chatter around the table. It was much nicer than living and eating alone.

It was a Friday evening and I had been invited to the Blakes'. We enjoyed a pleasant meal together. Mrs. Blake had fixed roast chicken, and the girls had found enough strawberries to supply a somewhat skimpy shortcake. I lingered awhile over a cup of coffee and then reluctantly started for home.

After walking down the road for about a quarter of a mile, I came to the shortcut through the trees which the Blake children used to reach the school. I decided that nothing would be more delightful than a stroll through the woods on a warm, pleasant evening, so I left the road and started down the path. I had not gone far when I heard a commotion on the trail ahead of me. I cautiously took a few more steps; right before my eyes was a *bear*, busily rolling over a dead log. I knew that it was a bear—there was no doubting that—though what he was doing in these woods I could not for the life of me imagine. No bears that I had heard of had ever been seen here. I tried to remember what Wynn's book had said about bears, and I tried to determine what kind of a bear this one was, but my mind would not work.

The bear spied me at about the same instant that I spied him. We were only a short distance from one another. I wasn't sure who had startled whom the most. The bear suddenly gave a grunt and rose up on his hind legs. He looked mammoth. I wanted to run but my legs had turned to jelly. I wanted to scream but my mouth would not open, and my throat closed up on the sound.

The bear stood there, swinging his big head back and forth, sniffing and growling, his front paws held in readiness before him. Then he took a step toward me, snorting as he did so—and I felt my world going black. I crumpled to the earth in total darkness.

When I began to revive I sensed that I was moving, being carried in strong arms. For one terrifying minute I thought that it might be the bear toting me off. I fought to regain consciousness. My eyes slowly focused. It was Wynn.

"Steady, Elizabeth. It's all right." His arm tightened about me. I turned my face against him and began to cry.

He carried me out to the roadway and then lowered me to my feet, but he did not let me go. He pulled me close and let me shiver and weep until I began to regain some sense. All this time he had held me and stroked my hair or patted my shoulder, saying, "It's all right now, Elizabeth—you're fine—you're with me—it's gone—it's gone."

Finally I had control of myself enough to stand on my own feet and speak.

"A bear—"

"I know," he said, "I saw him."

"I was going to take the shortcut," I babbled on.

"I saw you."

"Where'd you come from?"

"I was driving to your house when I saw you leave the road. I left the automobile and ran after you, so that I could give you a ride home. Just as I caught up with you I saw—"

"The bear."

"Yes, the bear. I was going to call out to you, but I was afraid that you might run—running is the worst thing that one can do."

"I couldn't run—I couldn't . . ." and I started to sob again. The world was whirling and my knees were getting weak. I clung to Wynn, my thoughts back with that reared-up bear slowly advancing toward me.

Wynn's arms tightened about me and then I was being kissed—a kiss that drove all thought of the bear far from my mind. Slowly my arm stole up and around the back of Wynn's neck. I floated in a world where only Wynn and I existed, a world that I never wanted to end. But it did. Wynn stopped kissing me and swung me into his arms and carried me to the auto that was waiting on the roadway.

"Your mother sent a parcel to Jon and Mary," he said matter-of-factly as he walked. "She included a number of things for you, so, as I had a couple of days off, Jon suggested that I borrow his vehicle, visit my brother and deliver the packages to you."

"I see," I murmured against Wynn's shirt front as he lifted me to the seat of the car, then went around to climb in beside me—but I didn't see. I was still far too busy remembering Wynn's kiss. I expected him to start the automobile, but he didn't. Instead, he hesitated, and I dared to hope that he might kiss me again. Instead, he cleared his throat to speak, reaching for my hand and holding it.

"Elizabeth, I owe you an apology."

Startled, I came back to full consciousness.

"I had no right to kiss you like that—I know that. And I didn't mean by it—" He stopped and gazed at me. "I could see that you were thinking again of that bear—your face was going white and your eyes looked terrified, and I thought that you might faint again. I had to make you think of something else, to get your mind off the bear; and the only thing that I could think to do—well—I—I kissed you."

Slowly the words sank in. At first they had made no sense, but the sting of them began to reach through my numbed senses. Wynn had kissed me just for the medical benefit of snapping me out of shock. But that wasn't how I had kissed him. Surely he had been aware of my response, my eagerness. Oh, yes, he would have been aware all right, and now he was apologizing for having kissed me at all! He wanted to be sure that I knew that he meant nothing personal by the kiss and to point out that the response on my part had been ridiculous and unfounded. He was still Mr. Mountie, married to his profession, and a mere, hapless schoolteacher was not about to turn his head.

With one quick motion I jerked back my hand.

"No man ever *has* to kiss me—not for *any* reason," I threw at him. "I would rather have been mauled by that bear than to be so—so indebted to you, Mr. Delaney!" I jumped from the auto and ran blindly across the ditch and down the pathway from which I had just been rescued.

I did remember the bear, but in my anger I was convinced that he would be no match for me. I heard Wynn call my name, but the sound only made me more angry and my tears fall more freely. The nerve of the man to get me to throw my love at his feet and then turn his back upon me with a trite apology! I would never, never, never look at him again.

Phillip, Jr. brought the gifts from my mother to school the next day. The package only helped to heighten my new resolve to return home. The East was where I belonged.

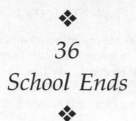

36

School Ends

MY DETERMINATION TO put Wynn from my mind did not make it any easier to accomplish the fact. I thought of him constantly. I loved him, hated him, forgave him, scorned him, and pined for him by turn.

By the time the last week of school had arrived, I had thoroughly made up my mind. I was going home—back to Toronto. Maybe there my broken heart would have a chance to mend. In the evenings I packed my trunks; in went my books, my clothing, the china teapot, the knick-knacks, and the simple masterpieces presented to me by the children—"to teacher with love." I even packed my footstool, though why I kept it I couldn't be sure. I was certain that Mother wouldn't welcome the thing in the house.

Each item that I packed brought back memories, and when I came to the fur mittens, my gift from Wynn, I could endure no more. I threw myself on my lumpy bed and gave way to the luxury of tears. I loved this country—its bright, cloudless, blue, blue sky; the scent of roses in the air; the long, lingering twilight; even the wail of the cowardly coyotes. I loved the people—Anna with her hands that always held out some gift; Else with her shy eagerness; Mr. Dickerson with his desire that the community people be led in worship; Mr. Laverly who fought for a school even though his own sons were past school age; the Clarks, the Mattochs, Delaneys, Pastachucks, Thebeaus and Blakes. They had become my neighbors, my people. Then I thought of dear, loving Andy and his honest praise for the efforts of his fellowman—"You did real good." The sobs shook my whole body.

I could have been so happy here, I mourned inwardly.

Then why run away? asked the other me.

I must—I must, was my only answer.

I went through the motions of teaching that last week. Each accomplishment of a student, each act of kindness raised a lump in my throat.

On the final day we had a picnic. Everyone from the community was there. I was flooded by kind and sincere compliments. It could have gone to my head had I been able to think clearly. Over and over again I heard the question, "Will you be back next fall, Miss Thatcher? Will you be our teacher again?" I could only reply in my dazed condition, "I don't know— I'm not sure."

Everyone seemed to enjoy the picnic, and as long as I kept busy I enjoyed it too. In the back of my mind the words kept hammering, *My last day—my last day.* I had to force my mind to other things so that I wouldn't succumb to the temptation to cry, right in front of them all.

It was time for them all to leave. My hand was shaken so often and so vigorously that it went numb—*as numb as my heart,* I thought, and then realized that my heart wasn't numb after all, for a sharp pain was twisting it.

I hugged my younger students and the older girls. Many of them cried, and I longed to cry with them. The boys stiffly shook hands in an embarrassed way, and even that touched me. At last the final wagon pulled away from the schoolyard, its occupants still waving and calling good-bye, and I turned back to the schoolroom. There really wasn't much that needed to be done, but I wanted to leave everything in good order. I swept, dusted, arranged, cleaned the blackboards, and scrubbed the floor. When everything was as clean as I could possibly make it, I took one last look around and, with tears in my eyes, went out and closed the door tightly behind me.

I spent the evening gathering and packing the last of my belongings and giving the teacherage a thorough cleaning as well. I was glad for every job that I found to do, for it kept my hands busy, if not my thoughts.

Just before retiring I went to my trunk and unpacked the china teapot and the two cups and saucers, wrapped them carefully and placed them in a small box. Then I also pulled out the footstool. I looked at it long and lovingly, and then set it beside the door with the box.

The coyotes began their evening chorus. Their cries no longer frightened me; instead, they filled me with such a loneliness that I cried with them. *I may never hear them again,* I thought, and I knew that I would miss even them.

The next morning the whole Peterson family drove me to the station. I was so busy taking a good look at everything for the last time that I wasn't very good company. In fact, we were all rather quiet on that trip to Lacombe.

When we arrived at the station, Lars and Mr. Peterson checked my trunks while I purchased my ticket. We chatted in a rather empty fashion for a few minutes, and then it was time for me to go.

I hugged Anna warmly.

"I can never tell you how much your friendship and thoughtfulness have meant to me, and I have left something in the teacherage that I want you to have. You have given me so much and I've never given much in return." Anna protested, but I went on. "I want you to have my teapot, and I'd like Else and Olga to each have one of the cups and saucers to remember me by. And for Lars, for hauling wood and water and being such a good help to a green city girl, I have left my footstool—and for each of the children, one of my books. Lars always sat on the footstool when he read my books, so when he reads again, perhaps he can use the footstool and remember just how much this schoolteacher thought of him."

Then we all hugged some more and the whistle of the train announced that it would soon be leaving. I had to go. The train pulled away from the station with all of us still waving to one another.

I didn't cry *all* the way to Calgary. It was much too long a trip for that, but I did soak several lace handkerchiefs with my tears.

My day spent at Jon and Mary's was no better. They tried to convince me to stay, but I reminded them that my trunks were likely already on the way to Toronto. I was half-afraid that had I not taken the action of booking them to Toronto from Lacombe, I might have decided to stay. I couldn't do that. I just couldn't.

As Jon, Mary and the children took me to the station the next day, we were all red-eyed. Kathleen clung to my hand.

"I wanted you to be my Aunt Beth for *always*," she declared sadly.

"But I *am* your Aunt Beth for always."

"But I wanted you to be my Aunt Beth here."

I looked back at the hill where we had gone sledding. From the high rise above the hillside, one could look out over the Rockie Mountains. I had not made my promised trip to the mountain streams or steep slopes.

I'm coming back—someday, I silently promised. *I'm going to keep that promise if it's at all possible.*

Again there were tearful good-byes. I held each one of the family: the big brother that I had come to love and respect; Mary, my bright-haired new sister; William, the boy who would soon be a man; Sarah, with her shy, winning ways; Kathleen, the chattery, lovable bundle of energy; and Baby Elizabeth, a small bit of warmth and love who bore my name.

"I will miss you all so very much," I said through my tears.

Kathleen needed one last hug. "Come back, Aunt Beth—please come back soon." I promised to try, and then was making my way to the boarding platform, struggling with my tears.

"Elizabeth."

A hand was placed on my shoulder, and through the mist in my eyes I saw a red-coated chest and I looked up into the face of Wynn Delaney. His eyes looked troubled as they gazed deeply into mine.

"Elizabeth, I must see you."

"But my train—"

"I promise not to be long. There are still a few minutes."

His eyes seemed to plead and I could no longer bear to look at him. I lowered my gaze and nodded an agreement. He took my arm and steered me through the crowd and back into the station, while a confused red-cap followed with my luggage.

"Dick," Wynn said to a man wearing a station man's uniform, "I need to borrow your office for a minute."

The man nodded. I was ushered into an office and the door closed behind me. Wynn turned me around to face him.

"Elizabeth," he said slowly, "I couldn't let you go this way. I've been miserable."

"Look, Wynn," I cut in rather hastily, "we were both wrong. It shouldn't have happened like that—but it did. You don't need to apologize."

I went to turn away from him and escape back to the train, but he held me firmly.

"Elizabeth, look at me."

Reluctantly I raised my eyes. My tears spilled over and ran down my cheeks.

"Elizabeth, I must confess that I kissed you because I *wanted* to—not merely to save you from fainting again. But I didn't come here just to apologize."

My eyes must have asked my question.

"I came here to ask you to forgive me, yes—but I also came to—to ask you not to go. I know it's selfish, and I know that I have no right, but I must at least tell you before you go—before you decide—that—I love you, Elizabeth. I want you to stay. I want you to consider being my wife. I know that I have nothing to offer—that I—"

I don't know what other nonsense Wynn might have gone on declaring had I not stopped him. I was still mulling over the words, "I love you, I want you to be my wife." And with a glad little cry I threw myself into his arms.

"Oh, Wynn!" I sobbed, and my tears spilled freely on his red tunic until he lifted my face upward and began to kiss me.

When he stopped and looked at me, I was breathless and flushed with happiness.

"I still don't know where I'll be posted—"

"It doesn't matter. Can't you see? It really doesn't matter."

"I believe you. Somehow I believe you." And he kissed me again.

The next question that he asked me made my eyes shine even more.

"How would you like a honeymoon in those Rockies—by a mountain stream?"

"Oh, Wynn, I'd love it. I'd just love it! Could we?"

Then a sharp train whistle reached my ears and even as I listened I could tell that it was getting farther away.

"Oh, dear," I said and looked at Wynn in dismay.

"What is it?"

"I do believe that my train has just left without me."

Wynn smiled his slow, deliberate smile. "Isn't that a shame," he said with exaggerated alarm.

Then I began to laugh—a soft, merry, tremendously happy laugh.

"Do you know," I said, "that my poor old trunks have gone on east without me?"

He pulled me close and laughed with me, kissing the top of my head.
"I do hope that you have *some* belongings, Elizabeth."

"Just my two suitcases."

"We'll wire ahead and have your trunks sent back—because I'm not
letting you go after them. Trunks or no trunks, you're staying here—
where you belong."

I had no objections.

WHEN COMES
THE SPRING

Dedicated with love to
my patient and peace-loving
fourth sister,
Margie L. Wiens,
and to her equally easygoing
husband, Wilf.
I love you both.

CONTENTS

1   Days of Preparation   169
2   Good News and Bad News   173
3   Stepped-Up Plans   180
4   Preparing   186
5   The Wedding Day   192
6   Marriage   195
7   Banff   201
8   Mountain Lake   209
9   Back to Calgary   214
10   The Journey Begins   219
11   Onward   232
12   By Wagon   237
13   The Last Day on the Trail   245
14   Home   249
15   Making a Home   253
16   Neighbors   258
17   Adjustments   265
18   Teas and Such   272
19   Friends   277
20   Change of Direction   284
21   The Storyteller   288
22   Studies   293
23   Winter   297
24   Settling In   305
25   The Storm   311
26   Aftermath   318
27   Village Life   323
28   March   327
29   Nimmie   332
30   Making Do   342
31   A Watchful Eye   346
32   Traps   350
33   Spring   355

1

Days of Preparation

"IS IT DONE yet?"

It must have been at least the tenth time that my young niece, Kathleen, had asked the question in the last few days.

"No," I answered patiently, "not yet."

She stood silently beside me, her favorite doll dangling lopsidedly from her arms.

"How come it takes so many times to make a wedding dress?" she asked again.

Much time, the schoolteacher in me silently corrected her. Aloud I said without lifting my eyes from the needle moving smoothly in and out of the creamy white satin, "Because a wedding dress must be perfect."

"Per-fect?" queried Kathleen.

"Um-hum. That means 'just right'—for the man I'm going to marry."

"Dee's not gonna wear it." Her voice boded no argument.

I lifted my head and chuckled softly at Kathleen's perplexed look. It sounded as if Wynn's nickname was still firmly in place.

"No, *he* won't wear it. But he is going to see *me* wear it, and I want it to be just right."

Kathleen stood there stubbornly, now a look of frustration on her pixie face.

"He won't care," she said with feeling. "Daddy said that Mama would'a looked beau'ful in an old 'tata sack."

I laughed and drew Kathleen to me. "Maybe you're right," I said, pushing back a soft curl from her forehead. Her eyes told me that something else was troubling her. I decided the dress could wait for a few minutes. Checking to see that I had left the sewing machine foot in proper position and the precious folds of satin material carefully placed on the tissue paper spread beneath them, I rose from the chair. My back ached and my shoulders felt cramped. I needed a break. Perhaps I should have done as Mother had suggested and arranged for Madam Tanier to sew my dress after all. I had wanted to sew my wedding gown myself, but I had had no idea what a big job it was going to be. I took Kathleen's tiny, somewhat sticky, hand in mine and led her to the door.

"Why don't we take a little walk around the garden?" I asked her.

The shine in her eyes was her answer. She wedged her flopping doll under one arm and skipped along beside me.

We walked through the garden together. The early flowers were already in bloom. As I looked at them, I found my mind rushing ahead to the wedding planned for the first part of September, and I wondered what flowers would be available. That was another decision that had to be made. Oh, my! Was there no end to them? It seemed that ever since Wynn had asked me to become his wife, I had been making one decision after the other—some big and some not-so-big. As my thoughts turned to Wynn, I smiled to myself. How fortunate I was to be engaged to marry such a man. He was everything a girl could ever desire—his height, his bearing, his smile, his quiet self-assurance, his caring. And he loved *me*! I would have gone on and on daydreaming but Kathleen interrupted me.

"Mama's gonna make my dress."

I nodded.

"Have you seen the color?"

I nodded again, remembering the hours Mary and I had spent poring over materials and styles, debating and deciding. Both Kathleen and Sarah were to be in my wedding party.

"*It's* gonna be perfect, too," insisted Kathleen.

"Yes," I agreed. "With your mama doing the sewing, it's going to be perfect, too."

"Mama is already done Sarah's dress."

There was silence while I studied the soft shades of a garden rose. *These colors would be just right*, I was thinking, *but will they still be blooming in September? I must ask Mary.* But again Kathleen interrupted my thoughts.

"How come I'm last?"

"Pardon?" My busy mind had not followed Kathleen's line of wondering.

"How come I'm last? Sarah's dress is already made, but Mama has just started mine."

I looked at her anxious face. It was an honest question but, for such a small girl, a troubling one.

"Well," I stammered, reaching for some satisfactory explanation. "Well . . . your dress will be ready in no time. Your mama is a very good seamstress and a very efficient one. It doesn't take her long at all to sew a dress—even a fancy dress like she will be making for you. Your dress will be ready long, long before September gets here. In fact, your dress will be ready long before mine will, I'm sure. So yours won't be last . . . mine will."

Kathleen's eyes had not left my face as I spoke. She seemed to relax with my final words. Her breath escaped in a soft little sigh.

"You're slow, all right," she agreed solemnly. "I'm glad Mama's fast."

Then her thoughts turned in another direction.

"Why is Mama making the dresses so quick?"

"So soon? Because your mama has so many things that she wants to do, and the dresses are one thing that she can do now."

"What things?"

"Well, she is planning the reception dinner. And she wants lots of time to get ready for Grandma and Grandpa. And she has some redecorating she wants to do. And she plans to give the house a thorough cleaning . . ."

I continued thinking of poor Mary and all of the work that my coming wedding was causing her. How I loved her! It wasn't one bit necessary for her to fuss so, but she insisted. After all, it would be the first time her in-laws would be in her home and she, too, wanted everything to be perfect.

"Is Grandma fuzzy?" asked Kathleen seriously.

"Fussy?" I smiled but did not let Kathleen know her word had come out wrong. "Well, yes and no. Grandma likes nice things, and when she is in charge she tries very hard to see that everything is just right. But she does not judge other people by the same rules she uses on herself."

"What's that mean?"

"It means that Grandma loves people as they are. She doesn't ask for everyone to be perfect or to live in perfect houses."

"It's gonna be fun to see Grandma," Kathleen enthused.

My eyes misted and I swallowed the lump in my throat. "Yes, it will," I said softly. "It will be just wonderful."

But it still seemed such a long way off. The folks would not be arriving in Calgary until just before our September tenth wedding, and this was only the middle of July.

"Would you like to swing for a minute?" I asked the now quiet Kathleen, to get my thoughts back to safer ground.

She grinned at me, and I took that for her answer. Kathleen loved the swing.

"The tree swing or the porch swing?" I asked her.

"The porch swing," she quickly decided. "Then you can sit by me."

We settled on the porch swing and set it in motion with the rhythm of our bodies. Kathleen cuddled up closely against me and rearranged the dangling doll into a more baby-like position. I realized then that she had been missing personal attention. With my thoughts all concentrated on the upcoming wedding, and even Mary wildly involved in the preparations, we had both subconsciously pushed the youngsters aside. I determined that in the days ahead I would be more sensitive and considerate. I pulled Kathleen closer to me and held her—such a precious little thing. We swung in silence for many minutes. My mind went to the other children. Were they feeling the strain of the busy household as well?

"Where is Sarah?" I asked Kathleen.

"She went to Molly's house. Molly's mama is letting them make doll dresses out of the scraps from Sarah's new dress."

Good for Molly's mama, I thought, *but no wonder Kathleen has been wandering around feeling left out.*

"And where's William?"

"Daddy took him down to the store. He's gonna help pile things. He even gets money for it." Kathleen squirmed to look at me, her envy showing on her face. "William thinks he's *big*," she said with some disgust. "He's gonna save the money and buy a gun that shoots little roun' things."

Kathleen curled up her short fingers to demonstrate the little round things. Then she ventured some more information. "An' Baby 'Lisbeth is sleepin'. She sleeps most all the time. An' Mama is sewing. Not for me— for Baby 'Lisbeth. An' Stacy said that the cookie jar is already full, so we can't bake any more cookies."

My arm tightened about her. *Poor little dear*, I thought, but I didn't say it. Instead I said, "How would you like to take the streetcar uptown and stop at the ice cream parlor?"

The shine was back. "Could we?" she cried. "Could we, Aunt Beth?"

"I'll ask your mama."

Kathleen clapped her hands in her excitement and then threw her arms around my neck. I felt the combs holding my hair in place being pushed all askew.

"Let's go check," I said. Kathleen jumped down and quickly ran ahead of me to find Mary.

By the time I had entered Mary's sewing room, Kathleen was already there and had excitedly posed the question. Could she go with Aunt Beth uptown for ice cream? Mary looked at me with a question in her eyes.

"Have you finished your dress?" she asked pointedly.

"No. I have quite a ways to go yet," I answered honestly, "but a rest will do me good." I didn't add that I thought Kathleen needed some special attention, too.

Mary nodded. "A little break would do me good, too," she said, pushing back from the machine. "Come, Kathleen, I will clean you up." Mary rubbed her tired neck and led Kathleen from the room.

I went back to my own room to change my dress and repair my hair. My eyes wandered to the pile of lustrous satin. Part of me ached to be there at the machine. I was so anxious to see the final product of all my labors. But I pushed the dress from my mind. Kathleen was more important. Besides, I had been so busy with details of the wedding that I had felt myself becoming tense and edgy. I had not even been able to relax and enjoy Wynn's company, and he would be coming to call in the evening. An afternoon in the pleasant company of Kathleen might be just the thing to put me in a more relaxed frame of mind. I picked up my small brocaded purse and left the room, shutting my door on all the satin and lace. I took a deep breath and smiled as I went to meet my excited niece.

2

Good News and Bad News

WYNN ARRIVED A little earlier than I had expected. I was still in my room making last-minute preparations, so it was Sarah who let him in. All afternoon she had been looking for people who would admire her doll all dressed up in the finery of her new hand-stitched dress, a shimmery pale blue. Wynn gave it a proper inspection and complimented the young seamstress on her fine work. Sarah beamed and deserted Wynn to wait on the steps for the return home of her father. She was most anxious to show him the new dress as well.

Kathleen took over entertaining Wynn, regaling him with all our afternoon adventures. I'm sure Wynn must have been surprised that I had found *time* in my rushed schedule to spend a rather leisurely afternoon with my niece. All he had heard from me recently was about the plans and work and preparation and diligence I was giving to every detail of the coming wedding. Kathleen had succeeded in bringing me up short. *People are more important than fussing over preparations. Why, I haven't even been good company for Wynn,* I realized, looking back in humiliation over some of our last evenings spent together. Well, I would change that. After all, a *marriage* was of far more importance than a *wedding*.

I hummed to myself as I walked slowly to the parlor. I had intended to be in the parlor waiting for Wynn when he arrived, instead of entering rushed and harried after he had already come . . . like I had done on so many previous evenings.

Wynn was listening attentively to the chattering Kathleen, and I couldn't help but smile at the homey picture they made.

"An' after that, we went an' looked in the store windows—just for fun," explained Kathleen. "An' then we took a ride on the streetcar just as far as it would go—just to see where it went—an' then we took it back *all the way home again!*" Kathleen waved her small hand to show Wynn just how far all the way home really was.

Wynn smiled at the little girl. Clearly he was enjoying their conversation.

"Was it fun?" he asked, not because he needed the answer but because he sensed Kathleen needed to be able to express it.

"It was *lots* of fun!" exclaimed Kathleen. "We ate *two* kinds of ice cream. Even Aunt Beth ate two kinds. An' we brought home lemon drops for Sarah and William.—Baby 'Lisbeth might choke on lemon drops," she explained seriously, so Wynn would understand why Baby 'Lisbeth had been left out. "Then we walked all the way up the hill, right from the bottom, 'stead of ridin' the streetcar—'cause Aunt Beth said she needed the ex'cise." She giggled. "To work off the ice cream," she added. "And we sang songs when we walked."

It *had* been a fun day. I realized it even more as I listened to Kathleen share it with Wynn.

"Next time will you take me, too?" Wynn asked seriously and Kathleen nodded, suddenly feeling sorry that Wynn had missed out on so much.

"Maybe we can go again tamora," she said thoughtfully. "I'll go ask Aunt Beth."

Kathleen bounded from the couch to run to my room and then noticed me standing by the door. Wynn's eyes looked up, too. Surprise, then pleasure, showed on his face as he stood to his feet and held out a hand to me. Neither of us spoke, but I could read questions coming my way.

"We had a wonderful day," I confirmed Kathleen's story.

"You *look* like you've had a wonderful day," Wynn said, taking my hand and drawing me closer to him. "Your cheeks are glowing and your eyes are shining—even more beautifully than usual."

I pulled back a little as Wynn tried to draw me close, thinking of the curious eyes of young Kathleen. Wynn must have read my thoughts.

"Kathleen," he said, turning to the wee girl, "why don't you go out on the step and wait with Sarah for your daddy and William to come home. They'll want to hear all about your big day, too."

Kathleen ran from the room, and Wynn smiled at me and pulled me close. I did not resist him. The strength of his arms about me and his gentle kiss reminded me again of how much I had missed really spending time with him during the previous distracting days. I would be so glad when the long weeks ahead had finally passed by and I would be *Mrs. Wynn Delaney*. Right now it seemed forever. I forgot about all I had to do in the next few weeks and thought instead of this man I loved.

When he stopped kissing me, he whispered against my hair, "I love you, Elizabeth. Have I told you that?"

I looked up at his face. His eyes were teasing, but his voice was serious.

"Not often enough, or recently enough," I teased back.

"I must remedy that," he said. "How about a walk in the moonlight tonight?"

I laughed, thinking of how late the Alberta night would be before the moon was shining.

"Well," I said, "I'd kind of like to hear it before that. You know it doesn't even start to get dark until after ten o'clock. That's an awful long time to wait."

Wynn laughed too. "Let's not wait for the moon then," he agreed. "I'd still like to go for a walk."

"We'll walk," I promised, "and just talk. We have so much to talk about, Wynn."

"More wedding decisions?" He sounded almost apprehensive.

"Not tonight. That can wait. Tonight we will talk—just about us. There is still much I want to know about the man I'm going to marry, you know."

Wynn kissed me again.

The sound of the front door told us that Jonathan had arrived home. He entered the house to encounter his two young daughters talking excitedly. Jonathan tried to listen to them both, attempting to share in the excitement and the enthusiasm they felt. And William had tales of his own he was bursting to tell. He had worked just like a man at his father's business and was making great plans for all the money he was sure to make over the summer.

Mary joined the happy commotion in the hall and was greeted by her husband with a warm hug and a kiss. Jonathan did not agree with the tradition of parents hiding their affection from their children's seeing eyes.

"Who needs to know more than they, that I love you?" he often told Mary; and the children grew up in a household where loving was an accepted and expected part of life.

At the sound of the family moving our way, I drew back reluctantly from Wynn. Perhaps now wasn't quite the time for me to openly show my feeling for Wynn in front of Jonathan's children, though I knew it was not in the least hidden. How could I hide it, feeling as I did?

The pleasant supper hour seemed to pass very quickly. All around the table was shared laughter and chatter. The children were allowed and even encouraged to be a part of it. Baby Elizabeth, who now insisted on feeding herself, was the reason for much of the merriment. Her intentions were good, but not all of the food got to its intended location. She ended up adorned with almost as much as she devoured. The children laughed, and Elizabeth put on even more of a show.

Wynn enthusiastically entered into the gaiety of the evening. Now and then he reached beneath the damask white tablecloth to give my hand a gentle squeeze. From all outward appearances, he was his usual amenable self; but, for some reason, the meal had not progressed very far until I sensed that something about him was different. There seemed to be an underlying tension about him. I looked around the table to see if any of the others had noticed it. Jonathan and Wynn were talking about some of the new businesses that had recently been established in our very young city. They were pleased for the growth and what it meant to the residents of the town. Jonathan seemed to sense no difference in Wynn. My eyes passed on to Mary. Though busy with the struggling Elizabeth who was refusing her proffered help, Mary seemed to be her usual relaxed self. I decided that maybe I had imagined the undercurrent and concentrated on what was being said.

But, no. I was sure it was there. The way Wynn looked at me, the way he pressed my hand at every given opportunity, the way he leaned slightly my way so his arm brushed against my shoulder—all sent unspoken little messages to me. I found myself anxious for the meal to end so I might be alone with this man I was to marry.

I had no appetite for dessert. I begged off with the excuse that I had already eaten two cones of town ice cream with Kathleen. I sat there, impatiently twisting my coffee cup back and forth in my hands as I waited for the rest of the family to finish the meal. I had determined to be completely relaxed tonight—completely relaxed and a pleasant companion for Wynn. I had determined to push aside all of the plans and decisions concerning the coming wedding so I might concentrate only on him—and here I was, tensing up inside again. And for no reason I could explain.

"Why don't we take that walk?" I asked Wynn when the meal was finally over. I was rewarded with a broad smile.

"Why, there is nothing I would rather do, Miss Thatcher," he teased. But I saw a certain seriousness in his eyes, and a funny little chill of fear went tingling through my body.

We left the house and strolled up the familiar street. We had not gone far when I turned impulsively to him and asked, "Would you mind very much if, instead of walking, we went for a drive? I'd love to drive up to where we could see the mountains."

He smiled. "That's a wonderful idea," he agreed. "Perhaps we can stay and watch the sunset."

The sun would not be setting for several hours. I smiled back at Wynn. It sounded good to me—all of that time to sit and talk.

We walked back to the house and were about to enter Wynn's car, when he suggested, "Perhaps you should have a shawl or coat, Elizabeth. It may be cool before we get back. Can I get you one?"

"I left a light coat in the back hall. It will do."

Wynn helped me into the car and went for the coat. I imagined that while inside he also told Jon and Mary of our change of plans. When we were on our way, Wynn chatted easily. We left the city and drove up the familiar hill to the place we could look out at the mountains to the west. Still I could sense something, though I did not question him.

When we reached the summit, we left the car and walked to a fallen log. It was a perfect spot from which to look out at the mountain grandeur before us. I sighed as I settled myself. In just about seven weeks' time, I would be visiting those mountains—visiting them as Mrs. Wynn Delaney. I wished instead that our wedding would be next week—no, I wished that it were tomorrow!

Wynn sat down beside me and his arm pulled me close. He kissed me and then we fell into silence, both of us gazing out toward the mountains. His arm tightened. He must have been thinking of the coming honeymoon, too, for he broke into my thoughts with a question.

"You aren't going to change your mind, are you, Elizabeth?"

"Me?" I said, astonished.

"Well, I wondered with all the work and preparations if you might decide that it wasn't worth it after all."

I sighed again, but this time for a different reason. "I've been a bore, haven't I? All the talk and all the fretting and all the frustrations showing. I'm afraid I haven't been much fun to be with recently, but I—"

Wynn stopped me with a gentle kiss. "I haven't been very supportive, have I?" he confessed. "The truth is, I would like to be, but I just don't know how. I had no idea that along with a wedding came so much planning and . . . and . . . frustration," he ended weakly. "I'm sometimes afraid it will all be too much for you and for Mary. You both look tired and pale."

"Oh, Wynn," I almost wailed. "It's awfully silly. Today I saw just how silly. I'm going to talk to Mary tomorrow. We can do things much more simply. There is no need to wear oneself out before beginning life together. Why, if I put half as much effort into making a marriage work as I have put into trying to prepare for a wedding—"

I left the sentence dangling. Wynn's arm tightened about me again.

"Is that what is bothering you?" I finally asked.

I felt the tension in Wynn's arm.

"Did I say something was bothering me?" he asked.

"No. You didn't say it," I said slowly, "but I could sense it somehow. I'm not sure just how, but—"

Wynn stood up, drawing me with him. He looked deeply into my eyes.

"I love you, Elizabeth," he said quietly. "I love you so very much. How foolish I was to ever think I could live without you."

He pressed my head against his chest, and I could hear the low, steady beating of his heart.

"There is something, isn't there?" I asked, without looking up, afraid of what I might find in Wynn's eyes.

Wynn took a deep breath and lifted my chin so he might look into my eyes.

"My posting came today."

His posting! My mind raced. It must be a terrible place to make Wynn look so serious. Well, it didn't matter. I could take it. I could take anything as long as we were together.

"It doesn't matter," I said evenly, willing him to believe me. "It doesn't matter, Wynn. Really. I don't mind where we go. I've told you that, and I really mean it. I can do it—really I can."

He pulled me against him again and pressed his lips against my hair.

"Oh, Elizabeth," he said, and his words were a soft moan. "It's not *where*, it's *when*," he continued.

"When?" I pulled back and searched his face. "When? What do you mean?"

"I'm to be at my new post by the first of August."

My head refused to put everything into focus. I tried hard to get it all to make sense, but for some reason nothing seemed to fit.

"But you can't," I stammered. "Our wedding isn't until September the tenth."

"But I must. When one is sent, one goes."

"But did you tell them?"

"Certainly."

"Can't they change it? I mean—"

"No, Elizabeth, they expect *me* to do the changing."

"But where are you posted? Is it up north as you had hoped?"

"Yes, it's up north."

"But that's such a long way to travel to come back for the wedding. It really doesn't make sense to . . . It would be such a long trip back and forth and would waste so much of your time—"

"Elizabeth," said Wynn gently. "The Police Force does not allow men to come out of the North until their tour of duty is finished."

"What do you mean?"

"I mean that once I go to my posting, I will be there—probably for three or four years without returning. It depends on—"

But I cut in, my eyes wide and questioning. "What are you saying?"

"I'm saying that there can't be a September wedding."

I felt the strength leave my body. I was glad Wynn was holding me— I'm afraid I could not have stood on my own. For a moment I was dazed, and then my foggy brain began to work again. No September wedding. The Police Force would not let Wynn travel back from the north country once he had set up residence there. Wynn was to be at his posting in only two short weeks. That didn't leave much time.

I willed the strength back into my legs and lifted my head to look at Wynn again. I had never seen his face so full of anguish.

"How long does it take to get there?"

He looked confused at my question, but he answered, "They said to allow six days for travel."

"Six days," I mused. "That leaves us only nine."

Wynn looked puzzled. "Nine?"

"My folks can be here in three or four days," I hurried on. "By then I should have my dress ready. That will make it about right for a Saturday wedding. That leaves us four days in the mountains and one day to pack to get ready to go. Can we do it, Wynn?"

Wynn was dumbstruck.

"Can we do it?" I repeated. "Can we pack in a day?"

"Oh, Elizabeth," Wynn said, crushing me against him. "Would you— would you—?"

I moved back and looked deeply into Wynn's eyes. The tears were burning my own.

"I couldn't let you go without me, Wynn. I couldn't," I stammered. "The wedding might not be just as we planned, but it's the marriage that counts. And we will have our family and friends there. It will still be beautiful."

There were tears in Wynn's eyes as he kissed me. I finally pulled away and looked out at the mountains. So it wouldn't be seven weeks before I would be visiting there as Mrs. Wynn Delaney. It would be less than a week. It seemed unreal, almost heady. Wynn must have thought so, too. "Bless the Police Force," he murmured in almost a whisper.

"Bless the Police Force?" I repeated, wondering at his sudden change of emotion.

He grinned at me.

"September always seemed such a long, long ways off."

I gave him a playful push, though the color rose in my cheeks. I could feel the glow. "Well, September might have been an awful long ways off," I agreed, "but this Saturday is awfully close. We have so much to do, Wynn, that it's absolutely frightening."

I suddenly realized the full impact of the statement I had just made. "We'd better get back to Mary. My, she will be just frantic."

"Hold it," said Wynn, not letting me go. "Didn't you promise me this whole evening?"

"But that was before I knew that—"

Wynn stopped me. "Okay," he said, "I won't hold you to your original promise. I will admit that things have changed somewhat in the last five minutes. However, I am going to insist on at least half an hour of your undivided attention. Then we will go to the house and Mary."

I smiled at him and settled back into his arms.

"I think I'd like that," I answered shyly.

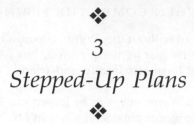

3

Stepped-Up Plans

❖

THE HOUSE WAS full of commotion in the next few days. Mary seemed to be running in every direction at once. Surprisingly, it was I, Elizabeth, who took things rather calmly—I who had always dreamed of the perfect wedding. I who had pictured myself many times coming down the aisle of a large stained-glass cathedral on the arms of my father, the altar banded with delicate bouquets of orange blossoms or gardenias, my exquisite arrangement of orchids trailing from my satin-covered arm. I had envisioned masses of attendants with shimmering gowns designed by the best seamstress in England or Paris. I had listened wistfully to strains from the magnificent pipes of the organ, as the wedding march was played.

And now I was to be married in a very simple, tiny, rough-constructed church. There would be no stained-glass windows to let in the summer light. There would be no magnificent sounds from the throat of a pipe organ. There would be few attendants, and their gowns would be unnoteworthy by the fashion world's standards. And yet it would be sheer heaven, for I would be standing at the altar with the man I loved. That was all that mattered, I suddenly realized. And so it was I who slowed Mary down and calmed her with words of assurance that everything would be just lovely. Everything would be just right.

The telegram was sent home, and Mother and Father and Julie and Matthew would be arriving on Friday's train. My one regret was that I wouldn't have more time to see them before the Saturday wedding. Well, it was far more important that I be ready to go north with Wynn.

I hurriedly finished my wedding dress, and it was ready on time—in fact, I had a whole day to spare; so I turned my attention to other things. I went quickly through my wardrobe, selecting the few things that would be suitable for life in the North. I packed all the clothing I had used in the classroom and then took the streetcar uptown to make some more purchases. Wynn had assumed all the responsibility for purchasing and arranging the household items we would need. I felt a bit of misgiving but realized that Wynn—having lived in the North—would have a much better understanding of what would be needed than I would. Still, I found it difficult not to be involved. My womanly instincts told me that Wynn might be a little short on home comforts and concentrate instead on survival. I tried to push the anxious thoughts from me whenever they invaded my mind and told myself that I could trust Wynn completely.

Thursday fled all too quickly. I lengthened the day by staying up half the night. I continued to sort and pack and try to think ahead of what a woman would need to survive the rigors of the north country for three or four years without a return to civilization. My mind seemed to go blank. How would I know? I had never been farther than a few short miles from the city shops.

Wynn had been every bit as busy as I—sorting, crating, and labeling the items and supplies we would need for our household. It would not be fancy, he kept reminding me; and I kept assuring him that I did not care. I gave him the few items I had purchased last year for my housekeeping chores in the teacherage, hoping they would help curtail our expenses. He seemed pleased with them and told me that with all I had, plus the few essential items which would already be in stock in our northern cabin, there were few things further he would need to add.

I thought much about our home in the wilderness. I did want to make it a home, not just a bare and functional place that Wynn came to at the end of a long, hard day. But how did one go about converting log walls and wooden floors into a cozy homelike place? Curtains and cushions and rugs seemed to be the answer. I had no time for such things now. I had all I could do just to get packed and ready. I decided to purchase some materials for these things to take with me. So, early Friday morning, I boarded the streetcar for uptown. I did not buy thin, flimsy muslins. Instead, I spent my time poring over heavier, more masculine materials. They seemed far more suited to a northern cabin than the lighter, frillier furnishings would be. In the heavier materials I chose bolder, brighter prints than I normally would have purchased and then added a few finer fabrics just in case I should be sewing for a new member of the family before we got back from the North. My cheeks flushed slightly at that thought, and I hoped no one I knew was observing my shopping for pastel flannels. I had almost neglected to even think of such a possibility in my lastest rush, but three or four years was a long time.

With all my purchases weighing me down, I took the streetcar back to Jon's and tried to rearrange my trunks to crowd in the additional items. I had to leave behind a few dresses, but I decided I would do very well without them. The sewing material was much more important. After pushing and straining and shoving things as tightly into place as I could, I did manage to get the lid of the trunk down and latched.

I sat back on the floor, perspiration dampening my forehead. *I must look a mess,* I mused. I could feel my coppery curls beginning to slip from their combs. My face felt flushed and warm, my dress was crumpled, and my hands . . . I looked at my hands. They were trembling—trembling as though I had had an awful fright or just plain overexerted myself. Well, it mattered not. I had done it. I was packed and ready. Ready to go with

Wynn to his north country. All that remained to be done were the final preparations for our wedding; then we would be off for a very brief honeymoon. And then, after a hurried day of final preparations, we would be on our way to the little cabin we would call home.

I pushed the hair off my forehead with my shaky hand and, with the help of my nearby bed, pulled myself to a standing position. It was twenty minutes until the noon meal would be served. I still had time for a quick bath and a hair repair job. I mustn't stand around brooding. I must hurry. Friday morning was gone and there was still much to be done for my wedding. And my family would be arriving on the four o'clock train.

"Beth!"

Julie's cry made many heads turn in time to see the pretty, well-dressed Easterner drop whatever was in her arms and rush headlong for me.

I wanted to cry her name and run just as headlong to her, but I checked myself. I did run to meet her though, and the two of us fell into each other's arms. I had not known until that very minute just how intensely I had missed her. We both wept as we held one another. It was several minutes before we could speak.

"Let me look at you," Julie said, pushing herself back from me.

I just wanted to cling to her. I knew how short our time together would be.

She had changed. She was still just as attractive. She was still just as bubbly. But there was a certain maturity about her. How I loved her! I had missed her more than I could describe.

She threw her arms wildly about me again, dislodging my hat. "Oh, I've missed you so!" she cried. "How could you, Beth? How could you come out here and decide to marry some man who will take you off from me forever?" But there was teasing in Julie's voice.

"You just wait until you *see* the man," I teased back.

"Ah," said Julie, pushing back again and reaching up one hand to help my wayward hat. It didn't seem any more secure after Julie was done with it. "Ah," she said again. "Beth, the practical one, has met her match."

We laughed together, and then I was claimed by other arms. Mother arrived not in a whirlwind as had Julie but in her usual, quiet, dignified way.

"Elizabeth," she said very softly. "How are you, dear?"

My tears came again, rushing down my cheeks and threatening to soak everyone near me. Mother was weeping, too, but softly—like gently falling rain, not in wild torrents.

We held each other close for a long time. "You look beautiful, dear," she whispered in my ear. "Methinks that love becomes you."

"Oh, Mother!" I exclaimed, "just wait until you meet him. I can hardly wait—"

"Nor can I, dear." Wynn, on duty till 5:30, could not be with us to meet the train.

Jon claimed Mother then. It was touching to see mother and son greet one another after the many years they had been separated. After Jon had held her and allowed her to again regain her composure, he proudly introduced his Mary. The two of them seemed to fall in love immediately. The children crowded around. I could hear them as they took their turns being hugged by their grandma and Aunt Julie. But I was busy getting some hugs of my own. Father held me. I had often been held in my father's arms, but this time it was different. I think we both sensed it. For this time, I was no longer his little girl. I was now about to leave his care and be turned over to the arms of another man. He brushed a kiss against my hair just above my ear and whispered to me. "I'm happy for you, Elizabeth. Happy—and sad—all at one time. Can you understand that?"

I nodded my head against his shoulder. Yes, I understood, for that was the way I felt. I hated to leave my family. It would be so wonderful if I could have just packed them all up too—like I had done my simple dresses and the yards of material—and taken them along with me into the northland. But, no. I honestly wouldn't have wanted that. I didn't even need that. Not really. Wynn was all I really needed now. Things had changed. And, though I still loved my family, I was not dependent on them anymore. I was cutting the ties. I was binding myself to another. The solemn words would be spoken on the morrow, but my heart knew it had already made its commitment. Already, in thinking and feeling, I was Wynn's—his alone for all time and eternity. He would be my family, my protector, my spiritual head, my lover, my friend.

"I love you, Daddy," I said softly. "Thank you for everything. Thank you for raising me to be ready for a home of my own. I didn't realize it until—until—now. But you did. You prepared me for this—for Wynn— and I thank you."

Suddenly I felt calm. Very calm and sure of myself. I had been too busy to even think of just what a difference the morrow would make in my life. I had been too in love to even consider that there might be problems to face and adjustments to be made, but I saw it now. The arms of the man who held me made me think clearly of all that was ahead, and I suddenly realized that I was indeed ready for it. This was not just a whim, not just a schoolgirl romance. This was a love. A love deep and lasting, and I would be a wife and a helpmeet for the man I loved. My father had showed me how. Unconsciously, in all of those years of my growing up, he had been showing me the way to a good marriage relationship— with his kindness, consideration, and strong loyalty to those he loved. I held him more tightly. I loved him very much.

When Father released me, I was facing a tall young man with gangly arms and a lopsided grin. At first I just stared at him, unable to believe my eyes. But it was, it really was, my dear Matthew. He wasn't quite sure of himself, nor of just how he should handle all this emotional greeting of his family members; so he stood back a pace somewhat as an onlooker. I blinked away tears and looked at him again. How he had grown in the short year I had been away. I wasn't quite sure how to greet him either.

"Matthew," I said, barely above a whisper. "Matthew, my—you've—you've grown up—so tall."

He took one step toward me as I moved to him, and then I was hugging him just as I had done so often when he was a little boy. His arms tightened around me, holding me tightly.

"Oh, Matt, I can't believe it! You're taller than Father." I tried not to weep, but it was impossible to stop all the tears from falling.

Matthew swallowed hard. He was almost a man, and weeping was not to be considered. Instead, he rather awkwardly patted my back, much as one would greet an old school chum. Jonathan was there then. It was the first time my younger brother had met my older brother, and they sized each other up man to man. They must have liked what they saw; for, moving almost as one, they changed from the handshake to a warm embrace. I could see Matthew's eyes, for he was facing me. They shone with admiration. I knew then that this trip west was going to have a lifelong effect on young Matt.

We finally collected ourselves and all of our belongings, piling into the two cars waiting for us. Jonathan had engaged the services of a friend to help transport us all back to the house. Wynn was invited to join the family for supper. I could hardly wait to show him off to my family and to introduce my family to him. I was so proud of them all. I loved them all so very much!

It was a noisy group that arrived at Jonathan's. We had so much catching up to do. And then there were the children. Each one of them was in a terrible hurry to make up for lost time and get to know their grandma and grandfather and this new aunt and uncle as quickly as possible. As usual, we all seemed to talk at once.

Jon and Mary showed each of the family members to their respective rooms, Mary apologizing that the intended cleaning and redecorating had not been done because of the earlier wedding date. Mother declared that everything was just lovely as it was; and I think Mary felt that Mother meant every word of it.

Julie, as exuberant as ever, exclaimed over everything. She and Baby Elizabeth, who was now taking a few shaky steps on her own, seemed to be kindred spirits. The other children all loved Julie immediately, too, but I noticed that Kathleen still clung to me.

Matthew soon found an admirer in the young William. He looked up to Matthew with the same devotion showing in his eyes that Matthew had for Jonathan.

Julie was going to share my room with me, so with both of us loaded down with her suitcases and hat boxes, we climbed the stairs.

"Oh, that old train," lamented Julie. "It was so stuffy and so warm! And there was this fat little man with foul cigars who sat right in front of me. And there was this party of four who sat down the aisle and kept talking and laughing in such a crude manner that—"

Julie would have gone on, but I stopped her with a laugh. She looked at me, bewildered, but I reached over and gave her another hug.

"You've changed," I told her. "A few years ago, you would have been seeing each one of those men as a possible suitor."

Julie's eyes twinkled. "Oh, I did that too," she admitted. "The only difference is that I'm a bit more selective now. There were some very fine-looking specimens on that train. I just haven't gotten to that yet."

"Oh, Julie. You little goose," I teased.

"I still can't believe it. My big, cautious sister marrying a frontiersman!"

"He's not a frontiersman. He's a Royal North West Mounted Policeman," I corrected her.

She shrugged and threw her hat on my bed. A few years back, I would have reminded her that was not where it was to go. Instead, I picked it up myself and laid it carefully on the closet shelf.

"You wait until you see him," I reminded Julie. "You'll be jealous of me."

Julie laughed. "Well, I sort of figured that where there is one good catch, there should be more of the same. Right, Beth? How about introducing me to a few of Wynn's friends on the Police Force? There are other unmarried ones, I expect."

"Certainly. A number of them. But don't expect to find another one like Wynn."

"He's that special, is he?" Julie's eyes shone. "Perhaps, Elizabeth Marie Thatcher, you're a wee bit prejudiced."

"We'll see," I told her, willing away the minutes until Wynn would arrive and Julie could see for herself.

"I must go help Mary," I finally told Julie, reluctant to leave her even for a minute. "You make yourself at home. The bath is just down the hall and the laundry room is down the steps to the right if you need to press anything."

It is so good to have them all here, my heart sang as I went down the stairs. *I just wish I had more time to visit with them.* But tomorrow was our wedding day, and after that Wynn and I would be leaving. And yet I did not wish, for one moment, that I could push my wedding into the future—not even for the chance to visit with my family. I started to hum as I entered the kitchen. The tune sounded something like "Here Comes the Bride."

4
Preparing

"Is EVERYTHING READY?" Wynn asked as we took a little walk alone later that night. We needed this solitude. Inside, the house was still buzzing. My family had taken an immediate liking to the man I was to marry, and it seemed to me that each one of them enjoyed monopolizing his time. Julie especially was awestruck. I could see it in her eyes. It was difficult for her to believe that her big sister, who had so many times expressed her disgust with the male side of the species, was so fortunate to be blessed with a union to one as marvelous as this.

How did you do it, Beth? her expression seemed to ask across the room. *Where did you ever find him?*

To which my eyes silently answered, *I told you so.*

But now Wynn and I were finally alone, and things were quiet enough so we could actually have a decent conversation.

I was momentarily checked by Wynn's question. Not sure that it had registered properly, I repeated it. "Is everything ready? I—I honestly don't know. My thoughts are all in a whirl. But does it matter? I mean, does it *really* matter? You have the license and the ring; I have my dress; the family is here. We're ready enough to go ahead with the wedding. So what if some of the details—"

Wynn laughed and reached for me. "You are unbelievable, Elizabeth," he said. "Who would ever have expected my stylish Eastern miss to be making such statements!"

He kissed me. It was still light and we were walking on a Calgary sidewalk with many homes nearby. Someone was bound to see us. His "stylish Eastern miss" pushed back from him without really wanting to.

Wynn laughed again. "I'm sorry, Elizabeth," he said. "I just couldn't resist. But I'll be good, I promise. Until tomorrow." His eyes twinkled.

I flushed slightly and resumed walking.

"Your family is wonderful," Wynn said, suddenly changing the subject and our moods.

"And they all love you!" I exclaimed. "I knew they would. Oh, Wynn, I'm so happy."

Wynn reached for my hand and squeezed it. I did not try to withdraw it. Let the neighbors watch and frown if they cared. This was the eve of my wedding day, to the man I loved.

"Are *you* all ready?" I asked.

"Everything's all set and crated. I had an awful time finding enough of the medical supplies I need. Had to have some sent down from Edmonton, but I finally got it all together."

"Medical supplies?" I queried, surprised.

"We need to take everything, Elizabeth," he reminded me. "Not just for ourselves but for the whole settlement."

I had forgotten Wynn had such a big task. "They have a Hudson's Bay Post there," he went on, "and shipments of supplies coming in. But one never counts on them for such important things as medicine. Blankets, flour, salt, traps—now, those things we will be able to get there with no problem."

Traps. I thought of this strange world to which I was going. It fascinated me. There was so much to learn. I was eager to get there, to get involved in Wynn's life.

"I'm all packed, too," I proudly informed him. "I got everything shoved into the one trunk. Mind you, it took some doing! I had to leave behind those books I had wanted, and that one hat I was going to take, and two pairs of shoes and two dresses, but I got all the rest in. I won't really need all those things anyway."

"You should have some of your books, Elizabeth. They might be a—"

But I cut in, "Oh, I did take a few of my favorites. The ones I left were mostly those I thought I might use if the Indian children would like to have a school."

"You still haven't given up on that idea, have you?"

"Well—" I hesitated. "No."

He pressed my hand again. "I'm glad," he said. "It would be wonderful if you could teach some of them to read." I smiled, appreciative of Wynn's understanding and encouragement.

"I think I might be able to find some little corner to stick more of your books in if you'd like, Elizabeth."

I wanted to throw my arms about his neck and hug him, but we were still on the Calgary streets and it was still daylight; instead, I squeezed his hand and gave him another smile. "Oh, thank you. I would so much like to take them. There really aren't very many and they don't make a very big stack, but I just couldn't get one more thing into my trunk."

We walked on, talking of our new life together and many other things. There was something very special about this night before we would become husband and wife. We hated to see it end.

When we did return to the house, the western sun had just dipped behind the distant hills. A soft light glowed from each of the windows along the lazy sidewalk. The air was becoming cooler but was still pleasant. Wynn slowed his steps as we went up the walk.

"I don't think I will come in, Elizabeth. You need this last evening with your family. I'm going to have you for the rest of our lives."

Wynn stepped from the walk to the warm shadows of the big elm tree. I knew I would not protest this time when he took me in his arms.

"I won't see you until tomorrow at the church," he whispered. "Now don't you go and change your mind."

"There's not a chance," I assured him, my arms locked tightly about his neck.

"I still can't believe it—tomorrow! And tomorrow is finally almost here. You'll never know what a fright it gave me when I got that early posting."

"Fright?"

"I thought I would have to leave you behind. I knew it would be unfair to ask you to wait for three or four or even five years. I was almost beside myself. I thought of quitting the Force, but I didn't have the money to start out some place else."

"Oh, Wynn."

"I never dreamed you would ever be able, and willing, to rush into a wedding like this. I hope you never feel that you've been 'cheated,' Elizabeth."

"Cheated?"

"Cheated out of the kind of wedding you've always dreamed of."

I laughed. "The fact is, Wynn," I said, "I spent very little time dreaming about weddings until I met you. *Then* I dreamed—I dreamed a lot. But the wedding wouldn't be much without you there by my side, now would it? So, if there's a choice between the trimmings or you—then it's easy to leave out the trimmings."

Wynn kissed me again.

"I must go," he said after several moments. "My bride must be fresh and glowing on her wedding day; and if I don't let you get your beauty sleep, it will be my fault if you aren't."

He saw me to the door and left. I went in to join the family. Father and Mother were ready to retire for the night. It had been a long, hard day for them. At Father's suggestion, we gathered in the living room for a time of Scripture reading and prayer. Tears squeezed out from under our eyelids as we prayed together. Even Matthew, somewhat shyly, prayed aloud. I was touched at his earnest petition that God would bless his big sister Beth and her Wynn as they started out life together. It was a time I shall always remember. Never had I felt closer to my family than when we sat, hands intertwined, praying together as our tears flowed unheeded.

I did not really get the rest Wynn had suggested, for Julie and I could not refrain from catching up on a whole year in the next few short hours. We talked on and on. Each time the downstairs cuckoo sounded out the hour, I would determine that I must stop talking and get some sleep; but each time one or the other of us would think of something we just had to share or had to ask the other.

Julie insisted on knowing all about Wynn—where I had met him, how I had won him. She would have loved to hear each detail of our romance;

and, if I had been like Julie, I might have wished to share it all. I was not like Julie and therefore kept many of the details to myself. They were treasured things and not to be shared with any other than Wynn himself.

"When did he first tell you he loved you?" asked nosey Julie.

"Hey," I said sleepily, "isn't that a bit personal?"

"Oh, come on, Beth. It must have taken your breath away. Tell me about it."

"Not a chance," I countered. "It took my breath away, yes. But it is for me alone."

I thought back to the scene at the railway station when I was all set to head back east. That was the first time Wynn had confessed that he loved me. I still tingled as I thought of it.

"How long did it take before he proposed?" Julie persisted.

"Forever," I said with meaning, and Julie laughed.

"Oh, Beth. Get serious."

"I'm serious."

"Did you love him first?"

"I thought I did. I thought so for a long time. Wynn has told me since that he did love me. He was just so sure it wouldn't work that he wouldn't admit he loved me."

"'Wouldn't work'?"

"Because of his job. He didn't think I was the kind of woman who could endure the North."

"Oh, pshaw!" exploded Julie, then covered her mouth guiltily in case she had disturbed the sleeping household.

"My feelings exactly," I returned in a loud whisper; and we both giggled, bringing the blankets up to our faces to muffle the sound like we used to when we were kids and had been told to go to sleep but talked instead.

"How did you finally convince him?" Julie asked.

"Well, I—I—I'm not sure," I stammered. "I left."

"Left?"

"On the train—for home."

"But you're still here."

"Well, yes. I never really went. But I was going to leave. I was all set to go. I had even shipped my trunks. I was all ready to board the train."

Julie, sensing an exciting romantic adventure, squealed and then jerked up the cover to smother it.

"Look, Julie," I said firmly. "That's all that I'm going to tell you. I was leaving; Wynn came to get me. He asked me to stay; he asked me to marry him. I stayed. Now, let's talk about something else."

"We really should go to sleep." Julie tried to hide the disappointment in her voice.

"Well, we have only tonight to talk. Or do you want to go to sleep? You must be tired after all that time on the train."

"Oh, no. I'm not tired. Not at all. I want to talk. I haven't even told you yet—"

For several hours, I lay and listened to Julie recount her romances of the last several months. There were thrills and there were heartbreaks. There were fantastic fellows and there were bores. There were ups and there were downs. I wondered whom Julie would have to share all her secrets with once I was gone.

"Is there anyone special?" I finally asked.

Julie thought deeply. "You know, that's a funny thing, Bethie. Even as I lie here and think of them all, not a one of them is really what I want. Isn't that silly?"

"I don't think so."

"Then why do I pay any attention to them?"

"You just haven't found the right one yet," I assured her. I could have also added, *and you just haven't matured enough to know what it is that you do want*, but I didn't.

"You know what I think?" said Julie slowly, deliberately, as though a new and astonishing truth had suddenly been revealed to her. "I think I've been going at this whole thing all wrong. I've been out looking for the fellow—oh, not particularly the right one, just anyone—and I should have been like you and let him come looking for me."

"But Wynn wasn't looking for me, either," I confessed.

"Well, it happened, didn't it? You did get together. Somebody *must* have been looking for *someone!*"

We lay quietly for a few minutes.

"Beth," Julie whispered. "Did you ever pray about the man you were to marry?"

"Sometimes. I prayed that God would keep me from making a wrong decision."

"And Mother prayed. I know that. She prays all the time. She doesn't say much about it, but I'm always finding her praying. And Father prays. In our family prayer time, he always prays that God will guide each of his children in every decision of life."

"What are you getting at?" I had to ask her.

"Maybe it wasn't you—and maybe it wasn't Wynn. Maybe it was God who saw to it that you got together."

"I've always felt that," I answered simply.

"Well, I've never seen it that way before. Guess I sort of thought if I left it to God, He would pick out some sour-faced, serious older man with a kind, fatherly attitude—and poor looks. I'm not sure I was willing to trust Him to choose my future husband."

I laughed in spite of myself, but Julie was very serious.

"No, Beth, I mean it," she continued. "God didn't pick that kind of man for you. Wynn is just—is just—"

She hesitated. I wasn't sure if she couldn't come up with the right word or was afraid I would object to her "swooning" over my husband-to-be.

"Perfect." I finished for her.

"Perfect," she repeated. "Tall, muscular, strong—yet gentle, understanding, and so very *good-looking*!" she finished with an exaggerated sigh.

I laughed again.

"Do you think God could really find me one like that?"

"Oh, Julie. There is only one just like Wynn."

"I s'pose," Julie sighed again. "Well, what about second best?"

"Look, Julie, when God finds you the right one, you won't think he is second best—not to anyone in the world."

"Really? Do you truly think God could direct in *this*, too, Beth?" Julie was serious again.

"Why don't you leave it with Him and see?" I prompted her.

"Why is it so much easier to trust God for some things than for others?" she wondered.

"I really don't know. We should be wise enough to know we can trust Him with everything, but it seems as if He is forever needing to remind us—one thing at a time. Maybe it's because we just hang onto some things too tightly, wanting our own way too much."

"It's hard to let go of some things."

"I know."

"I wasn't going to tell you this, Beth; but, after you left home, I cried. I cried every night for two weeks, and then I finally realized I had to let go. I prayed about it—and really meant what I prayed—and God took away the sorrow from my heart and gave me a new love and respect for my older sister. I can be happy with you now, Beth, even though it means I really am going to lose you."

I reached out a hand in the darkness and placed it on Julie's cheek. It was damp with tears, but her voice did not break.

"I missed you, too," I said honestly. "I missed you, too; and, Julie, my deepest desire for you is that someday God truly might bring someone into your life—oh, not another Wynn, but someone you can love just as much, be just as proud of. I'm sure that somewhere there is someone— just for you. Be ready for him, Julie. Be ready to be the kind of wife he needs, the kind of woman he can love deeply, can be proud of—not just of her outer beauty but of her inner beauty as well. I love you, Julie."

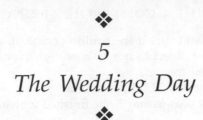

5
The Wedding Day

❖

In SPITE OF the fact I had not slept much the night before, I awoke the next morning with excitement bringing me quickly and easily from my bed. Julie still slept, one hand tucked beneath her pretty face. She looked more like a beautiful child than an attractive young woman, still oblivious to the world and all the duties of this important day.

I tiptoed about as I dressed and left the room. The wedding ceremony had been set for eleven o'clock. Following that would be the reception dinner with family and close friends. Mary, bless her heart, had insisted she would be responsible for that and had engaged some caterers to help her with the preparations and serving.

After the reception, we would open the wedding gifts and spend some time with family and friends before boarding the four o'clock train for Banff.

Our honeymoon would not be nearly as long as we had once planned it. Four days in the beautiful mountains did not seem nearly enough. We would not travel leisurely. We would not be taking a cabin in some remote area where we could hike and climb and just rest and relax in the grandeur of those magnificent mountains. Instead, we would take the train; Wynn had booked a room at the hotel, and from there we would make our little excursions into privacy.

The day we would be returning from Banff would be the day before we headed north, so all of our time then would be taken with last-minute preparations and final packing.

My friends from Pine Springs had been so disappointed we would not have time to visit them before leaving. They had planned a community shower to follow our wedding, if it had occurred in September as originally planned.

"Ve can't let you yust go off—like dat," wailed Anna. "Ve need to gif you our vishes, too!"

"Can't you come to the wedding?" I pleaded over the sputtering lines of the telephone system.

"Ve'll try. Ve'll try so hard. Da little ones vould hurt so to miss," said Anna. "Dey haf talked 'bout not'ing else for veeks."

"Perhaps Phillip would have room to bring you," I suggested. But I was afraid Phillip's car might be full.

"Ve'll see," promised Anna. "Ve'll see."

But I shoved all of that from my mind and tried to concentrate instead on what needed to be done in the few brief hours before my wedding.

Mary, already in the kitchen, motioned me to a chair beside her and nodded her head toward the coffeepot on the back of the stove.

"Pour yourself a cup, Beth, and join me. Always best to organize one's thoughts before plowing on ahead. Saves time that way."

I agreed and went for a cup. The next several minutes were spent "organizing."

Mary held a pencil in her slim fingers and jotted down as we discussed.

"The flowers!" she squealed suddenly. "Beth, did you order the flowers?"

My hand shot to my forehead. I had not. I had thought of it a number of times but never did get it done.

Mary looked nervous. "What ever will we do?" she asked me, not nearly as composed as when we began.

For a moment I was stunned; then suddenly I remembered those beautiful roses growing in Mary's backyard.

"Do you mind sharing your roses?"

"My roses?"

"The ones out back. They are beautiful. I noticed them a few days ago. They would work—"

"But we have no one to arrange them," Mary interrupted me.

"You can arrange them. You do a beautiful job. I'd like two bouquets—one on each side of the altar."

"But your bridal bouquet—"

"I'll carry roses, too."

"But—" Mary was going to protest again.

"I'll just carry a loose bouquet. Just a few long-stemmed flowers. They'll be beautiful."

"They are all thorns," Mary argued.

"We'll cut the thorns off. Matthew or William will be glad to do that."

Mary smiled. Then she nodded her head and took another swallow of coffee.

"So we have the flowers settled. Where do we go from here?"

We went over everything again. My dress was ready. Julie was to stand beside me. Her dress would need pressing after its long train ride, but Julie would take care of that. The dresses were all ready for Sarah and Kathleen. The cake had been done by a lady friend of Mary's. It was simpler than it would have been had she been given more time; but I was finding more and more beauty in simplicity. Phillip, Wynn's brother, was to stand up with Wynn; and Phillip, Jr., was to bear the rings.

"We have no pillow for the rings!" I cried suddenly when we came to that item.

"That's no problem," a soft voice said behind me. "I've been feeling bad that I have had nothing to do with getting ready for my daughter's wedding. Just give me some pretty scraps and I'll have a pillow in no time."

It was Mother. I jumped from my chair to hug her. She held me for a moment.

"Do you have any suitable pieces?" she asked at last.

"I have some nice bits left from my wedding dress."

"That will do just fine. And lace?"

"I've some of that, too, though I'm not sure it's enough."

Mary had been pouring another cup of coffee. She set it on the table and pulled up another chair for Mother.

"I've lots of ribbon and lace," she assured us. "I sew most of the girls' things, and they always insist upon 'fancies' on all of their dresses."

We drank our coffee and continued to cover all the details of the coming wedding. Here and there we had to improvise and make other arrangements. For some reason, it did not panic me. The "organized Elizabeth" of old would have been horrified to do up a wedding so—so *haphazardly*. Instead, I went through the activities of the morning in a comfortable daze. In just a few short hours, all the fussing would be behind me; and I would be Mrs. Wynn Delaney.

6
Marriage

OUR WEDDING DAY was gloriously sunshiny. I had not even thought to check the weather until I was actually in Jonathan's car and on my way to the church. It could have been pouring and I would never have noticed in my state of excitement. I stopped long enough to breathe a very short prayer of thanks to God for arranging such a beautiful day and then turned my thoughts back to my wedding again.

There had been some moments when I thought I would never make the eleven o'clock date with Wynn. In spite of our "organizing," there was much last-minute commotion, and the whole house seemed to be in a frenzy. Even Jonathan and Father were enlisted for tying little girls' bows and putting on slippers.

After I had slipped into the soft, creamy folds of my satin gown, I began to work on my hair. The locks that normally fell into place with little coaxing refused to go right. I tried again with similar results. I noticed then that my hands were shaking in my excitement. Julie came to my rescue and, with a few deft turns and skillful motions, she had my hair smartly and firmly in place, ready for the veil. I thanked her and went to slip into my wedding shoes.

By the time Julie and I came downstairs, one carload had already left for the church. Mother and Father waited in the hall looking serene and composed in spite of the last-minute flurries of the household. Mother's eyes misted slightly as she looked at me.

"You look beautiful, my dear," she whispered. "Your dress is lovely."

Father remarked, "It's a shame to spend so much time on something that will scarcely be noticed."

I looked at him, puzzled.

"With your cheeks glowing and your eyes shining so, Elizabeth, no one will be able to take their eyes from your face."

Understanding, I smiled at Father as he stepped closer, and I reached up to kiss him on the cheek.

We formed a close circle, the four of us—Father, Mother, Julie and I— our arms intertwined as we stood together for one last time in the hallway of brother Jon's lovely Calgary home. Father led in prayer, asking that the Lord would make my home, wherever it might be, a place of love. "Might there always be harmony and commitment, love and happiness. Might there be strength for the hard times, humor to ease the tense times, and shoulders always available for the times of tears," he prayed. I found it difficult to keep the tears from falling now, but I did not want to reach the church with swollen eyes and a smudged face, so I refused to allow myself to cry. Mother blew her nose softly and wiped at her eyes, and then we hastened to the car.

As I stood waiting at the entrance of the church, my eyes on the back of the man whom I would soon be joining at the altar, my heart pounded wildly. Father must have sensed it, for he reached a reassuring hand out to me and held my hand tightly. I watched Julie slowly make her way down the aisle with proper and graceful steps, her soft skirts swirling out gently as she went. For a moment it had a dizzying effect on me, and I closed my eyes. It was my turn next, and I must be ready.

I was still standing with my eyes tightly closed when Father took his first step. Startled, my eyes quickly opened and Father hesitated, to let me get in step with him. It was time—time for me to walk down the aisle to meet Wynn.

I was completely oblivious to all the people in the pews. I don't even remember seeing the preacher who stood directly at the end of the aisle. All I remember is Wynn's face as he turned to watch me make that long, long, short walk to him. In a few minutes, I would be his wife! *My husband, Wynn,* was the refrain in my thoughts as I moved toward him. *Lord, make me a worthy wife to this man.*

With a gentle pressure on my arm, my father stopped me. Had he not checked me, I'm sure, I would have kept right on walking until I could take Wynn's hand. My thoughts began to sort themselves out, and I hurriedly went over the ceremony in my mind. I was to wait here with my father until he responded to "Who giveth this woman to be married to this man?" Then I could step forward to be at Wynn's side.

From then on, I concentrated very hard on the ceremony and was able to make the right responses at the right times. I was very, very conscious of Wynn by my side, of the significance of the words we were saying. As the soloist sang "The Wedding Prayer," we looked deeply into one another's eyes, secret messages passing between us. Wynn was saying, *Are you absolutely sure?* And I answered without a moment's hesitation, *I've never been so sure of anything in my life.* We had time for each to add, *I love you so very, very much,* and Wynn gently squeezed my hand.

The ceremony was over, and we walked back down the aisle together. Husband and wife. From now on, I would be with Wynn always. There would be no separation. Nothing would ever come between us.

The entry of the church was packed with well-wishers. Anna and her entire family were there. I did not even have opportunity to ask them how they had come. We hugged one another and she kissed my cheek, telling me how beautiful I looked. I greeted the children. Lars had grown noticeably, even since I had last seen him. Olga grinned and whispered a few well-rehearsed phrases about my future happiness, but Else stopped and cautiously reached out a small hand to caress my dress.

"It's beautiful. Did you make it?"

"Yes, I did," I answered her.

"It's beautiful," she said again. "So soft and smooth. You're a good sewer, Miss Thatcher."

I did not notice the familiar title, but Wynn did. "Whoa now, Else," he laughed. "It's not 'Miss Thatcher' anymore."

Else flushed slightly but laughed with Wynn. She put a small hand to her mouth and giggled, "I mean 'Mrs. Wynn,'" she corrected herself.

We let that go. Mrs. Wynn. It sounded rather homey. I wouldn't mind being called Mrs. Wynn at all.

After we had been greeted by those who had shared our day, we returned to Jon and Mary's house for the reception. I don't remember much about the reception. I guess I was just too excited. I'm sure the lunch was delicious, but only because I heard other people say so.

The meal was cleared away and we opened our gifts. We received so many lovely things, it kept me busy imagining how much they would add to our little wilderness home. There would be no problem in making it cozy and homelike. I also reminded myself of the last busy day we would have when we returned from our honeymoon—all of these additional things would have to be carefully packed. I was too excited to give it further thought now. I must take one thing at a time.

It was finally time for us to change for our train trip to Banff. I went to the room I had shared the night before with Julie and eased the satin gown carefully over my head to keep from disarranging my hair. I stepped out of the brand-new shoes that pinched slightly and kicked them from me. It would be nice to wear something more comfortable.

I decided to take a quick bath before dressing for the train. It would take only a few minutes and would help me to be relaxed and fresh.

Afterward I donned a summery-looking suit of teal blue that Mother had brought with her from Madame Tanier's shop. I loved being so stylish way out here in the West! Father had chosen the hat, they said; I carefully put it in place, pleased at how well it suited me. I then picked up my bag and, with one last glance in the mirror, went to join Wynn.

Jon was driving us to the station, so it would mean saying goodbye to my family before we left. I would have hated leaving them had not the future held so much promise. To enter the new life meant to say goodbye to the old. There was no way to hang onto both. Even I knew that.

But it was hard to leave all those I loved. Our goodbyes were rather long and tearful, and repeated a number of times. Yet I was eager to be off, and finally we were able to pull ourselves away. Jon's car left the drive at a bit faster pace than normal. It would never do for the Banff train to leave without us.

We reached the station just in time and, with a flurry of bags, managed to board the train.

At first I was still in a whirl. Though my body had ceased to rush about, my mind still raced back and forth. Part of it was back with my family;

part of it was reliving the wonderful, the harried, the tense, the busy moments of the wedding. Part of it was busy imagining my new life with Wynn. I tried to ease myself into the cushiony seat of the Pullman; but neither my body nor my mind would cooperate.

Wynn seemed perfectly relaxed. He stretched out his long legs and smiled contentedly. He looked at me, and his eyes told me he would like to sweep me into his arms. Respecting my reserve in front of an "audience," he refrained because of the many other passengers on the train. Instead, he gave me a wink that made my heart leap. He reached for my hand and I clung to him. He must have felt the tenseness in me, for he began to stroke my fingers, talking softly as he did so.

"It was a lovely wedding, Elizabeth. I don't see how it could have been nicer even if you had had all the time in the world."

My whirling thoughts went over a few things I had overlooked or mixed up or that were not as I would have planned them.

"Your gown was beautiful; did I tell you that?"

I managed a little smile. "Father said no one would notice," I murmured.

"I almost didn't," Wynn admitted. "Then I remembered a note of advice from brother Phillip. 'Be sure to take a good look at the dress,' he told me. 'She will expect you to know every detail, each row of lace, and the number of buttons.' Well, I will admit, Elizabeth, I didn't count the buttons, nor even the rows of lace, but I did take a good look at the lovely silk dress."

"Satin," I corrected.

"Satin," Wynn repeated, still rubbing a big finger softly up and down the back of my hand. "How would I know silk from satin? All I know for sure is that it wasn't serge or denim."

In spite of my preoccupation, I laughed. It eased my tenseness some. I thought of Father's prayer about humor for the tense times! I hadn't realized before how important a bit of laughter could be. Wynn's pressure on my hand increased.

"What will you remember about today, Elizabeth?" I knew he was trying to help me relax, and I appreciated it. I tried again to let my body snuggle against the back of the seat, but it was still stiff and resistant. I turned slightly to Wynn, making my voice even and light.

"The rush. The last-minute flurry. The fear that I would never make it on time and that you would be waiting at the church, furious with me for being so late—and maybe even change your mind about getting married," I teased.

Wynn smiled. "Oh, I wouldn't have changed my mind. There were at least three other single ladies there—I checked, just in case."

I pulled my hand away in a mock pout. Wynn retrieved it.

"What else?" he prompted.

I became more serious then. "Father's prayer. He always prays with us before any big event in our lives. I remember when Margaret was married. I was her bridesmaid, so I was there for Father's prayer. It was so beautiful. I remember thinking, 'If I don't ever get married, I'll miss that.' Still, I wasn't convinced that the prayer was sufficient reason to risk a marriage."

"You're serious?"

"At the time I was. Honest! I didn't really think I would ever feel inclined to marry."

"Here I was taught to believe that every young girl is just waiting for the chance to lead some man—any man—to the altar."

"I guess some are."

"Then why not you?"

"I don't know, really. I guess it wasn't because I was so against marriage. I just didn't like the insinuation that it was all a sensible girl thought about—that women were just for the marrying, that if I didn't marry, I was nothing. I didn't like that—that *bigotry*."

I wasn't exactly calming down as Wynn had intended. The thoughts from my past and the ridiculous beliefs of some of the people I had known were stirring me up instead. I pulled slightly away from Wynn and was about to expound further on the subject.

"Women are quite capable—" I began but was interrupted.

"Hey, take it easy, Mrs. Delaney. You don't need to convince me. I believe you. I watched you in the teacherage, remember; and I'm sure that you, as a single woman, could handle anything. But I'm glad you didn't decide you must prove your point for an entire lifetime. *You* might not need a man—but I need you. That's why women marry, Elizabeth—to give their inner strength to some weak man."

His face was serious, but I knew there was a certain amount of teasing there, too. I slumped back against him and let the intensity die quickly from my eyes.

Wynn reached over and lifted my chin, tipping my face slightly so he could look into my eyes.

"Your inner strength—and your outer beauty, Elizabeth—I need both."

I wanted to lean over and kiss him, but my upbringing forbade it. Instead, I looked back at him with my love in my eyes and then leaned against him, my body finally relaxed enough to comfortably fit the seat. After a few moments of silence, I took up Wynn's little game.

"What will *you* remember about today, Wynn?"

There was no hesitation. "The look on your face when we said our vows. The way your eyes said that you meant every word of them."

"I did," I whispered. "I do."

"The dimple in your cheek when you smiled at me."

Self-consciously, I put a hand up to my cheek.

"The way your hair glistened when the sun came through the window."

I waited for more.

"The softness of your hand when I held it." He caressed the hand now, looking down at it as he did so.

"The beautiful color of your eyes, so deep and glowing."

I looked at him teasingly and added one for him. "And my 'silk' dress."

He laughed. We were both completely relaxed now. The long, beautiful, tiring, tense day was over. Our wedding had been lovely, but it now was in the past. Our whole future lay before us. Our marriage. I think that at that moment, as never before, I determined in my heart to make my marriage a thing even more beautiful than my wedding had been.

Perhaps Wynn felt it too, for he whispered softly against my hair, "This is just the beginning, Elizabeth. We have today as a memory, but we have all of the tomorrows as exciting possibilities. We can shape them with hands of love to fulfill our fondest dreams. I wasn't much for marrying either, Elizabeth, but I am so glad you came into my life to change my mind. I've never been happier—and with God's help, I plan to make you happy, too."

7

Banff

BANFF WAS BEAUTIFUL. There are no words to adequately describe the beauty of those mountains. I wanted to look and look at them—to carry them always in my heart.

The next morning we arose to another glorious day of sunshine. We enjoyed a leisurely breakfast in the hotel's terraced dining room and watched the sun turn the valley rose and gold as its fingers reached into the depths. After some inquiring, Wynn discovered a church, and we took hotel transportation into the sleepy little town of Banff to attend the morning services. Afterward, we found an inconspicuous little cafe where we enjoyed our lunch of mountain trout and then spent a lazy afternoon walking through the town, enjoying the sights and feel of the mountains and the enjoyable companionship of one another.

"Tell me about Banff," I said rather dreamily as we walked along in the sunshine.

"As far as the white man is concerned, this is a very young town," responded Wynn. "Of course, the Indian people have known the area for many years. Explorers came through the area first. They came and went and didn't pay too much attention, except to admire the beauty, until in the 1880s when the railroad arrived and the small town of Banff was born."

"And people loved it and just couldn't stay away," I ventured.

"Well, what really brought the visitors was the discovery of the mineral hot springs in 1883. And then, those who knew people and knew investment built and opened the Banff Springs Hotel to care for the trade. The hotel was billed as 'The Finest on the North American Continent' and was visited by tourists from all over the world."

"And here I get to spend my honeymoon in this famous hotel," I interrupted, excited by the thought.

"People have always been fascinated with mountains; and all the unclimbed, unconquered, and uncharted mountains have brought many climbers to see if they could be the first ones to the summits. They brought in experienced Swiss guides to help attract mountaineers, and the area was soon famous."

"I think it's still rather—" I paused for the right word. "Rustic," I finally decided.

Wynn smiled at my choice. "Yes," he agreed. "I guess that's part of its charm. The ruggedness, the trail guides, the fur traders—they all mingle on the streets with the wealthy from around the world. While we've walked, have you noticed all the different languages around us?"

I had noticed. It was rather exhilarating, like being in a foreign country.

I sighed deeply. "There are so many things I would like to see that I don't know where to begin," I told Wynn. "We have such a short time."

"We'll plan carefully," he assured me. "Right now, let's start with some place to eat."

As we ate our evening meal in the luxurious hotel restaurant, I heard the people at the table next to ours discussing a hike they had taken that day and the sights they had seen.

"Could we?—" I asked Wynn. "Could we go? Please? I would so love to really see the mountains, not just the town."

"Why not?" Wynn smiled. "It's a bit of a climb, but I'm sure we could do it. It will be very exhausting, especially at these heights, but worth it."

"When?"

"Let's do it tomorrow."

I clapped like an eager child, then quickly checked myself; it was too undignified for a married woman.

For the rest of the meal, we discussed our plans for the next morning. I planned to be up bright and early so we would get a good start.

When we went back to our room, Wynn said he had a few arrangements to make. He had mentioned having the kitchen prepare us a lunch to be taken along on the trail, so I nodded and set about looking over my long skirts to decide what I would be able to wear the next day. In spite of the rigors of the trail, I did want to look good for Wynn. No man wants a plain or shabby bride. I found a skirt I thought would do. It was stylish enough to be becoming but not too full to inhibit my walking. Then I selected my shoes. None of them were really made for a long hike, but I did have one pair with me that wasn't too uncomfortable or flimsy.

After I had made my selections, I ran a nice warm bath, humming to myself. I would take a leisurely bath while Wynn was gone. My thoughts were filled with anticipation for the coming day and the glorious climb we would have together. I prayed for good weather. I wanted to look out from some lofty peak at the beautiful, tree-covered valleys beneath me.

I soon heard Wynn return and stir about our room. I hurried then. I remembered I had left my clothes for the hike spread out on the room's most comfortable chair, the one Wynn might be wishing to use. Wrapped snuggly in my new white robe, I hurried out, intending to move the skirt and other articles of clothing. They were gone. Wynn now occupied the chair. One glance told me that Wynn had hung the clothing carefully back in the closet.

"Oh, thank you," I managed, but I was a bit embarrassed that he might think I was messy and careless. "I wasn't planning to leave it there," I hastened to explain. "I was just trying to smooth out some of the wrinkles for tomorrow."

"Tomorrow?" He looked questioningly at me. "I'm afraid by the time we have our hike tomorrow, there won't be time for anything else."

"That's what I mean. For the hike."

Wynn looked surprised.

"*That* outfit—for the *hike*?"

I was a bit taken aback, but stammered, "It's all I brought that was suitable, really. I thought the other dresses too fancy to be walking in."

"You're right. So is that one," he said, with a nod toward the skirt still visible through the open closet door.

"But it's all I've got," I argued.

"I got you something." Wynn sounded quite confident.

"You got me a dress?"

"Not a dress."

"Well—skirt, then?"

"No skirt. You can't climb a mountain with a skirt swishing about your legs, Elizabeth."

"Then—" I was puzzled and a bit apprehensive by this time.

"Pants."

"Pants?"

"That's right."

"I've never worn *pants* in my life," I blurted out, emphasizing the word with some disfavor.

"Then this will be a first," said Wynn, completely unflustered, nodding his head toward the bed.

I followed his gaze. There, tossed on our bed in a rather awkward and haphazard fashion, was a pair of men's pants. They were an ugly color and very wrinkled, and I almost collapsed in shock as I looked at them.

"Those?" I gasped.

Wynn was now catching on. He stood to his feet. His eyes sought my face. He must have read my honest horror, for his voice became soft.

"I'm sorry, Elizabeth," he apologized sincerely. "I guess I didn't think how they would look to you. They are rather a mess, aren't they?" I caught a glimpse of disappointment in his eyes as he crossed to the bed and picked up the pants he had just purchased. He awkwardly began to smooth out the wrinkles with his man-sized hands. I felt repentant. I reached to take them from him. "It's all right," I said, not wanting to hurt Wynn. "I could press the wrinkles out. It's not that. It's just that—that I couldn't go out—I couldn't be seen wearing something like that—in public and all—I—" I stammered to a stop.

Wynn said nothing but continued to stroke his hands across the coarse fabric of the pants. The wrinkles refused to give up possession.

"My skirt will be fine, Wynn; but thank you for thinking about—"

Wynn looked at me evenly and didn't allow me to go on. "You cannot climb a mountain in a skirt, Elizabeth. Those are not just hiking trails. They are steep. They are dangerous. You cannot possibly go without proper clothing."

Sudden anger flared within me. "And you call *that* 'proper clothing'?" I responded, jerking a thumb at the disgusting pants.

"For what we intend to do, yes."

"Well, I won't wear them," I said, a bit too quickly.

Wynn tossed them into a chair. "Very well," he said, and his voice was calm.

I had won. I wasn't sure if I should be happy or sad. It was our first little tiff and I had won. Now, as a wife, how was I to win graciously? I sought for words, for ways to show Wynn that I would not expect to win *every* battle. I didn't know what to say, so I crossed the room and began to take down my hair and brush it with long, easy strokes. The tension remained within me, even though Wynn seemed untroubled.

I stole a glance at him. He was reading a paper. He must have bought it, too, when he had gone out for the pants. I noticed a pair of brown boots sitting on the floor by the bed. I started to ask Wynn about them and then realized how small they were. They would never fit Wynn. What were they doing in our room? Then it dawned on me: Wynn had purchased them, not for himself but for me—*for me* to wear on my hike up the mountain! Not just the unsightly pants, but the mannish boots as well. How could he even have considered being seen with a woman in such outlandish attire?

I was stroking so hard with the hairbrush that I winced with the pain of it. I couldn't imagine a man even thinking such a ridiculous thing. Well, my skirt and shoes would be just fine. I wouldn't be caught traipsing around on my honeymoon looking so utterly unkempt and ridiculous.

Someone had to break the silence of the room.

"What time do we leave?" I asked innocently. We had already established a time, but I had to say something.

"Where?" said Wynn, lowering his paper.

"Up the mountain," I replied with some impatience.

Wynn was slow in answering. "Elizabeth, I'm afraid I'm guilty of not fully explaining our trip up the mountain." He laid the paper aside and rose to his full height. I felt dwarfed beside him.

"Parts of the trail are very steep. It's tough climbing. One doesn't need ropes, but one does need to be very careful. A fall could mean serious injury."

"You told me that. I'll be careful. I promise."

"Coming back down, there are parts of the trail where it is wise to sit down and ease yourself down over some of the steeper spots."

He looked at me to be sure I was understanding what he was saying. I nodded that I understood.

"There are places so steep that you need to use the branches of the nearby trees and the handgrips of the rocks to help boost yourself up."

I remembered that Wynn had told me that before, as well. I nodded again.

"It's a long way up to the mountain lake. It's a long, hard climb."

"Just what are you trying to say, Wynn?" I demanded. "Do you think I don't have the endurance to make the climb?"

"No," he said evenly. "I think you could make it. We wouldn't need to hurry. I could help you whenever you needed it—if you needed it. It would be my pleasure."

I thought of our much-talked-about trip up the mountainside. I thought of Wynn's description of the beautiful mountain lake. I thought of sharing the sack lunch way up there in the isolation of the mountains. The thoughts stirred my emotions. I was more anxious than ever to go.

"So when should we leave?" I asked again.

Wynn took a deep breath and looked squarely at me. "I'm afraid we won't be going, Elizabeth."

My hand stopped midstroke. I stared at him incredulously. What was he doing? Punishing me for winning? But Wynn didn't seem the type to retaliate. Yet Mother had always said you don't know a person until you live with him. So this was Wynn? I couldn't believe it.

"Not going?" I finally choked out. "Why?"

"You can't climb a mountain in a dress, Elizabeth; and you have refused to wear the pants," he stated calmly and finally.

So I hadn't won. Wynn had agreed to the "no pants," but he hadn't agreed to the "no pants" *and* the mountain hike.

"That's silly," I almost hissed. "I've been in a dress all my life, and I've never been a casualty yet."

"You've never climbed a mountain yet," was his matter-of-fact response.

"And I guess I'm not about to now," I threw back at him. Even I was surprised at the intensity of my words.

"I'm sorry," was all he said. He turned and went back to his paper. I continued to briskly brush my hair. It didn't need it. I had brushed it quite enough already, but I didn't know what else to do with myself.

My thoughts whirled in a confused state. I had heard of first quarrels. I knew that Wynn was not one to be pushed around. But this was such a silly little thing to be fighting over. *Surely he doesn't expect me to give in and wear those ridiculous and unsightly pants!* No man who loved his wife would ask such a thing. I bristled even more. *Why, Mother would be ashamed to own me were she to see me in such an outfit!* Wynn understood nothing about women's dress and propriety.

Finally Wynn laid aside the paper. I knew he really hadn't been concentrating on it—just hiding behind it.

"You're angry with me, aren't you, Elizabeth?" His voice sounded so contrite that I prepared myself for his change of mind. I did not answer. I didn't yet trust my voice.

"Do you realize that we have been married for one whole day and we have already had a disagreement?" asked Wynn softly.

I still did not answer.

"I really wasn't prepared for this," stated Wynn. "Not yet, at any rate. I'm sorry, Elizabeth. I do love you—you know that. I love you very much and I do wish this hadn't happened." He spoke so sincerely that I laid aside the brush. Maybe he wasn't so stubborn after all. I was quite ready to make up and forgive and forget. Men didn't understand about women's concern for how they looked, that was all. Now that Wynn knew, there wouldn't be any future fusses on that score.

I crossed to him and put my arms around his neck. He pulled me down on his lap and held me close. I returned his kiss and ran my fingers through his thick, dark hair. I loved him. He was my husband and I loved him.

"I'm sorry," I whispered. "Truly I am. I acted like a spoiled child and I'm—I don't usually act so silly. I guess I was just terribly disappointed."

He kissed me again, holding me very close. I could scarcely breathe, but I didn't mind.

I traced the outline of his firm jaw with a finger. "What time would you like me to be ready?" I whispered.

"You won't be too embarrassed at being seen in men's pants?"

I started, then stood up, pushing away his arms.

"Wynn," I said firmly. "I am *not* wearing those pants!"

He stood up, too, and said just as firmly, "Elizabeth, if you are not wearing the pants, then we are not going up that mountain. Do I make myself clear? I will not take you over those dangerous trails, sweeping along a skirt behind you. You could fall and kill yourself. It's the pants, or not at all, Elizabeth. You decide."

I whirled from him. *How can he be so stubborn?* I couldn't believe the man.

"Then I guess we will have to find something else to do," I said defiantly. "I will not wear those pants. *Do I make myself clear?*" I stressed every one of the words. "I wouldn't be caught dead wearing those ugly men's pants or—those—those equally ugly heavy boots. Not even to climb a mountain on my honeymoon with the man I love."

I whirled again to leave him, but Wynn caught my arm.

"Don't fight dirty, Elizabeth," he said softly, but there was steel in his voice and a soft sadness, too.

The words jarred some sense into me. I couldn't believe how I was acting. This was not the way I had been raised. In our household, the man was always the one in charge; Mother had carefully schooled each one of her daughters to believe that was the right way for a Christian household to be run, and here I was—one day married—and fighting back like a bantam hen.

I bit my lip to stop its trembling and turned away from Wynn. He did not release me.

"We need to talk, Elizabeth," he said gently. "I don't think that either of us is quite ready for it now. I'm going to take a walk—get some air. I won't be long—and when I get back—if you are ready—" He left the sentence unfinished and let go of my arm. I heard the door close quietly behind him.

I really don't know how long Wynn was gone. I only know that I spent the time in tears and, finally, in prayer. Wynn was the head of the home—my home. Even though I did not agree with him, I still needed to submit to his authority if ours was to be a truly Christian home—a happy home. He had not been wrong. I had been wrong. Deep within myself I knew I would have been disappointed in Wynn if he had allowed me to be the victor when he felt so strongly about my safety. I needed to be able to lean on him, to know for sure that he was in charge. So then, why had I tried to take over? Why was mere fashion so important to me? I didn't know. I only know that by the time Wynn's footsteps sounded in the hall, I had worked it all out with prayer and tears of repentance.

I met him at the door. Considering my concern for how I looked, I must have looked a mess, but Wynn made no mention of it. He took me in his arms and began to kiss my tear-washed face. "I'm sorry," I sobbed. "I'm truly sorry. Not for hating pants—I don't expect that I'll ever like them, Wynn; but I'm sorry for getting angry with you for doing what you thought was right for me."

Wynn smoothed back my hair. "And I'm sorry, Elizabeth. Sorry to hurt you when I love you so. Sorry there isn't some other way I could show you that mountain lake. Sorry I had to insist on the pants if—"

"*Have* to insist," I corrected him.

He frowned slightly.

"Have to insist on the pants," I repeated. "I still want to see that lake, Wynn; and, if you will still take me, I'll wear the pants. Just pray that we won't meet anyone on the trail," I added quickly. "I wouldn't even want to meet a bear wearing those things."

Wynn looked surprised, then pleased, then amused. He hugged me closer and laughed. "Believe me, Elizabeth, if there was any other way—"

"It's all right," I assured him.

"I love you, Elizabeth. I love you. Trust me?"

I nodded my head up against his broad chest.

"There will be times, Elizabeth, when we won't agree about things. Times when I will need to make decisions in our future."

I knew that Wynn was thinking ahead to our life in the North.

"I might have to ask you to do things you will find difficult, things you can't understand or don't agree with. Do you understand that?"

I nodded again. I had just been through all that in my talk with my God.

"I love you, Elizabeth. I will try to never make decisions to satisfy my ego or to show my manly authority, but I must do what I think is right for you—to care for you and protect you. Can you understand that?"

I searched his face and nodded again.

"This time—the pants—it would be too dangerous on the trail in a skirt. I know the trail, Elizabeth. I would never expose you to the possibilities of a bad fall. I—"

I stopped him then by laying a finger gently on his lips. "It's all right. I understand now. I'm glad you love me enough to fight my foolish pride. I mean it, Wynn. Thanks for standing firm—for being strong. I needed that. I'm ready to let you be the head of the home. And I want you to remind me of that as often as necessary—until I really learn it well."

I had tears in my eyes. But then, so did Wynn. I reached up to brush one of them from his cheek. "I love you, Mrs. Delaney," he whispered.

"And I love you, Mr. Delaney," I countered.

His arms tightened about me. "I'm truly sorry this happened," he said.

I looked at him, deep into his eyes. "I'm not," I said slowly, sincerely. "I'm ready now—ready to be your real wife. Ready to go with you to the North—to the ends of the earth if need be. I need you, Wynn. I need you and love you."

8

Mountain Lake

WE WERE UP early the next morning. We had a quick breakfast and then went to prepare ourselves for the trip up the mountain. Wynn had gone to the kitchen to pick up our lunch, which he put in a backpack along with a good supply of water. I dressed while he was gone, not wanting even my husband to see me in the ugly pants.

I wasn't going to look at myself in the mirror. I didn't want to know what I looked like. I walked to the dresser to pick up a scarf and accidentally got a full look at myself. Later I was glad I did. The sight stopped me short and resulted in my doubling over with laughter. Wynn found me like this. He wasn't sure at first if I was really amused or just hysterical.

"Look at me!" I howled. "I look like an unsightly bag of lumpy potatoes." When Wynn discovered that I really was amused at how I looked, he laughed with me. The bulky pants bagged out at unlikely points, hiding my waist and any hint of a feminine shape. I had looped a belt around my waist and gathered the pants as tightly about myself as I could. This only made them bulge more.

"They are a bit big," Wynn confessed. "I guess I should have asked you about the size."

"I wouldn't have been able to tell you anyway, never having worn pants before. Oh, well, they'll do."

I stopped to roll up the legs and exposed the awkward boots on my feet.

"Are you about ready?" asked Wynn when we both stopped laughing at the spectacle I made.

"Ready," I answered, standing to my full height and saluting. We laughed again and headed for the door.

Wynn was kind enough to take me out the back way to avoid meeting other hotel guests. We circled around and followed the path to the mountain trail and began our long climb upward. We hadn't gone far when I realized what Wynn had meant. I had to grab for branches and roots in order to pull myself upward. Time after time, Wynn reached to assist me. We climbed slowly with frequent rests. I knew Wynn was setting an easy pace for me and I appreciated it. Every now and then, I would stop to gaze back over the trail we had just climbed. It was incredibly steep. I could catch a glimpse of one valley or another through the thickness of the trees. I could hardly wait to be above the timberline to view the lonely world beneath us.

By noon we had reached our goal. Sheer rock stretched up and up beyond us. Below us lay the valley with the little town of Banff nestled safely within its arms. It truly took my breath away. Here and there I could see the winding path we had just climbed, as it twisted in and out of the undergrowth beneath us.

"It's breathtaking," I whispered, still panting slightly from the climb. "Oh, Wynn, I'm so glad we came."

Wynn stepped over to wrap an arm securely about me. "Me, too," was all he said.

We found a place to have our lunch. By then I was ravenous. Wynn tossed his coat onto a slice of rock and motioned for me to be seated. I did, drinking in the sight before me.

"Where's the lake?" I asked him.

"See that ragged outcropping of rock there?" he pointed.

I nodded.

"It's just on the other side of that."

"Does it take long to get there?"

"Only about half an hour."

"Let's hurry," I prompted.

Wynn laughed at my impatience. "We have lots of time," he assured me. "It's faster going down than coming up."

He took my hand and we bowed together to thank God for the food provided. Wynn's prayer also included thanks for the sight that stretched out before us and our opportunity to share it together. I tightened my grip on his hand, thinking back on how close we had come to not making the climb. I looked down at the funny pants I was wearing. They no longer shocked me. They only brought a bubble of laughter.

We were almost finished with our lunch when we heard voices. Another group had also made the climb. They were getting very close, and I was looking about for a place to hide. I recognized one of the voices. It belonged to a very fashionable lady I had seen in the hotel lobby the day before. Oh, my goodness! Whatever would she think of me when she spied me in the insufferable pants? I could see no place to shield myself, and then I braced myself and began to chuckle. So what! I'd likely never see the woman again in my life. The pants had provided me with a very pleasant day with my new husband. They were nothing that I needed to be ashamed of. I took another bite of sandwich and flashed Wynn a grin. He had been watching me to see which way I would choose to run.

A man appeared. He was tall and dark, with very thin shoulders and a sallow face. He looked like he was more used to trolley cars and taxis than his own legs, and I wondered how he had managed to make the climb. He did seem to be enjoying it and turned to give his hand to the person who followed him. I was right. It was the attractive young woman. I wondered how she had managed to climb a mountain with her hair so perfectly in place. Her body came slowly up over the sharp rise and into view. I gasped. She, too, was dressed in ugly men's pants. Wynn and I looked at one another, trying hard to smother our laughter.

At that moment, she spotted us and called out from where she was hoisting herself up, "Isn't it absolutely glorious?" She had an accent of some kind. I couldn't place it at the moment. Around my bit of sandwich, I called back, "Yes, isn't it?"

They came over to where we were seated and flopped down on the rock perch beside us, both breathing heavily.

"I've never done anything like this before in my life," said the young man.

"I had a hard time talking him into it at first," informed the woman to my surprise.

"You've done it before?" I asked her.

"With my father—many times. He loved to climb." She looked perfectly at home in her pants and stretched out her legs to rest them from the climb.

"This your first time?" she asked me, sensing that it must be.

"For me it is," I answered. "My husband has been here before."

She gave Wynn a fleeting smile. "Once you've been," she stated simply, "you want to come back and back and back. Me, I never tire of it."

"It's a sight all right," Wynn agreed.

I suddenly remembered my manners. I looked at our packed lunch. There were still some sandwiches left. "Here," I said, passing the package to them. "Won't you join us?"

"We brought our own," she quickly responded, and he lifted the pack from his back. "We just needed to catch our breath a bit."

We sat together enjoying the view and our lunch. We learned that they, too, were honeymooners. From Boston. She had pleaded for a mountain honeymoon and he had consented, rather reluctantly, he admitted; but he was so thankful now that he had. He was an accountant with a business firm, and she was the pampered daughter of a wealthy lawyer. Her father was now deceased and she was anxious to have another climbing mate. Her new husband hardly looked hardy enough to fill the bill, but he seemed to have more pluck than one would imagine. They were planning to take on another mountain or two before returning to Boston.

After chatting for some time, Wynn stated that we'd best be going if we wanted to see the lake before returning, and the young woman agreed. It was a steep climb back down the mountain, she stated, one that must be taken in good light.

We went on, bidding them farewell and wishing them the best in their new marriage, which they returned. I got to my feet, unembarrassed by my men's pants. If a wealthy girl from Boston could appear so clad, then I supposed that a fashion-conscious gal from Toronto could do likewise.

The trail around the mountain to the little lake was actually perilous in spots. I wondered how in the world any woman would ever have been able to make it in a skirt. She wouldn't. It was just that simple. I was glad for my unattractive pants that gave me easy movement. I was also glad for Wynn's hand which often supported me.

The lake was truly worth the trip. The blue was as deep as the cloudless sky above us, and the surface of the lake was as smooth as glass. It looked as though one should surely be able to step out and walk on it, so unrippled it was. Yet, when we got close and I leaned over carefully to get a good look into its depths, I was astonished to discover just how deep it was. Because of the clearness of the water, one could see every rock and every shadow. I stood up and carefully stepped back, feeling a bit dizzy with it all.

We did not linger long. The climb back down the mountain was a long one, so we knew we had to get on the trail. We met the other young couple. They still talked excitedly as they walked carefully over the sharp rocks and slippery places. I expected that their future would hold many such climbs. In a way, I envied them. The North held no such mountains—at least not in the place where Wynn had been presently stationed. Wynn had said the mountains did stretch way up to the north country as well; but they were for the most part uninhabited, so very few men were assigned to serve there. I was sorry for that. I would have liked to live in the mountains.

We felt our way slowly back down the trail. In a way, I found the climb down more difficult than the climb up had been. It seemed that one was forever having to put on the brakes, and it wasn't always easy to be sure just where one's brakes were. On more than one occasion, I started sliding forward much faster than I intended to. Wynn was right. One did need to sit down and attempt to ease down the steepest parts in a most undecorous fashion. *What if Mother could see me now?* I thought unruefully. I grasped for roots, branches, rocks—anything I could get my hands on to slow my descent. By the end of the day, my hands were scratched in spite of borrowing Wynn's leather gloves for the worst places; my men's pants were a sorry mess of mountain earth and forest clutter; and my hair was completely disheveled.

However, I still wore a happy smile. It had been some day, a memory I would always treasure.

We stopped at a gushing mountain stream. I knelt down and bent forward for a drink of the cold, clear water. It had come directly from an avalanche above, Wynn informed me; and I was willing to believe him. The water was so cold it made my fingers tingle and hurt my teeth as I drank it. We didn't really need the drink. Our backpack still held water we had carried with us, but Wynn felt that to make the day complete I must taste the mountain water. I agreed. I wiped the drips from my face and shook my hands free of the coldness and told Wynn how good it tasted. Wynn drank, too, as a reminder to himself that he had been right. No other water on earth tastes quite like that of a mountain stream.

9

Back to Calgary

THE NEXT DAY I ached all over. I wouldn't have believed that one had so many body parts to hurt. Wynn suggested a soak in a hot tub. It helped some, as long as I stayed there and sat very still. The minute I moved, I hurt again.

"I had no idea I had so many muscles," I complained.

Wynn offered to give me a rubdown, and I accepted it.

"I wonder how *he* feels," I mumbled into my pillow, as Wynn worked at sore muscles in my back.

"He? He who?"

"Her husband. That young couple yesterday. He didn't look exactly like he was built for climbing mountains."

Wynn chuckled at my comment. "Guess he didn't," he agreed.

"Come to think of it," I went on, "I wouldn't have picked her out as a climber either."

"Well," Wynn said seriously, "when I first saw a certain, beautiful young schoolteacher I know, I wouldn't have picked her out as a climber either."

I laughed in spite of my aches, and then I made a decision. "That's enough," I said to Wynn. "We have only one more day here in the mountains and I want to see as much as I can. Maybe my muscles will ease up some as I walk. Where can we go today?"

"You're sure?" Wynn asked, a bit doubtful.

"Positive," I answered.

"Climbing or walking?" asked Wynn.

"Just walking. Those old pants aren't fit to be worn anywhere till they are washed."

"Do you have proper shoes?" inquired my practical husband.

I pointed to the pair I had chosen for the day before. Wynn shook his head.

"Not good enough," he stated, and this time I didn't even argue.

"Okay," I said, "I'll wear the boots." I went for them, hoping with all my heart that my long skirt would hide them.

It almost did. I smiled to myself and announced to Wynn that I was ready to go.

We wasted no time. In the morning we went to Bow Falls. They were not high falls but were nevertheless lovely to watch. The water ran wildly between two uprisings of mountain rock which confined it on either side. As it pounded and boiled down the drop of several feet, the water turned from clear, bright translucent to a foaming milky white. One could hear the roar long before rounding the turn where one could look upstream and view the spectacle. It nearly took my breath away. I would have sat and watched the falls, mesmerized for the rest of the morning, had not Wynn roused me. "I hate to prod, but if we are going to fit in the Cave and Basin, we must be going. It's rather a long walk."

It *was* a long walk, and already my feet were tired from lifting the heavy boots step by step; so, as soon as we reached the area where public transportation was available, I agreed it would be wise to ride rather than try to hike all the way.

The guide at the Cave and Basin was a jolly Scot who seemed to be having the time of his life escorting visitors through what he treated as his private domain. When he saw Wynn, his face spread with a grin.

"Aye, an' how be ya, Delaney?" he cried, wringing Wynn's hand vigorously.

He didn't allow Wynn a chance for an answer. "An' shur now," he went on, "an' don't be a-tellin' me thet ye've found yerself a lass—an' a bonnie one she's bein'."

Wynn proudly introduced me. I hoped with all my heart that the jovial man would not look down and see my mannish boots peeking out from under my sweeping skirt. He didn't look down. Instead, he grabbed a lantern and hurried us off on our tour of *his* Cave and Basin.

"A sight like this ye'll never be seein', not anywhere in this world," he informed me, rolling his r's delightfully.

I shivered some as we followed the man into the cave and along rocky uneven steps to deep within the earth. It got cooler and more mysterious as we advanced; and the old man talked in a spooky, confiding tone, pointing out strange shapes and shadows as he whispered eerie suspicions about what they might have been in some long ago yesteryear. I shivered more noticeably now, and Wynn reached to place a protective arm around me. "Don't pay any attention to his stories," he whispered in my ear. "He makes them up as he goes along."

"An' look there now," went on the Scot, leaning close and lowering his voice as though someone from the dead past might hear him and take offense. "See there by yonder wall—that there mysterious shape." His finger pointed it out, and the lantern swung back and forth, making the strange shadows dance.

"Right there," the man leaned even closer to me to make sure that my eyes were following his pointing finger. "Thet there is a skeleton. Thet of an Indian warrior caught here in the cave. He must have been wounded in battle—or else waitin' out a thunderstorm—and somehow he got caught and held here an' never did leave." He paused. "'Course, I just tell thet to the young lasses thet I don't want to spook none," he added confidentially. "What really happened, I'm a-wagerin', is thet he was murdered right here." The r's rolled round and round on his tongue.

I shivered again and we moved on, the lantern bobbing and shivering, too. Again and again, we had things pointed out to us and then we descended a ladder to an underground pool steaming with heat.

"Kneel down careful like and put yer hand in."

I wasn't very brave and clung to Wynn's hand as I knelt to feel the water. It was, indeed, nice and warm.

"What heats it?" I asked in surprise.

"Aye," laughed the Scotsman. "Only the good Lord knows. He keeps a few secrets of His own. I'm a-guessin' we'll never know unless He decides to be tellin'."

We retraced our steps. I was looking forward to being back out in the warm sun again, though I wouldn't have missed the experience for anything. I was unprepared for the brightness as I stepped out from the cave. My eyes protested and I closed them tightly and turned away in the opposite direction so I might open them at my own choosing.

My eyes soon adjusted and I was able to turn back to the cheery guide with a smile of approval for his Cave and Basin. He seemed to feel it was very important that we had enjoyed our venture. I put out my hand.

"Thank you so much," I said, meaning every word of it. "I enjoyed that ever so much."

His eyes twinkled. He took the proffered hand and shook it heartily and then turned to Wynn.

"I always wondered why ye kept on a-waitin' and a-waitin' instead of takin' ye a wife, an' now I know. Ye were just a-waitin' fer the finest thet there be."

Wynn grinned.

"Well, the best to ye both now," said the Scot, and he gave Wynn a hearty slap on the back and turned to care for more of his tourists.

We were almost back to Calgary when my honeymoon reverie was broken and my thoughts went instead to all that needed to be done in one short day. I stirred rather uncomfortably and Wynn sensed my restlessness.

"Something wrong?" he asked, very sensitive to my changing moods.

"I was just thinking of all that needs to be done tomorrow," I admitted.

"It shouldn't be too bad," he tried to assure me. "Your trunk is all ready to go and most of the other things are all packed and waiting. There will just be a few last-minute things to be gathered together."

"But all those wedding gifts?"

"Julie and Mary volunteered, didn't I tell you?"

"I don't recall—"

"I'm sorry. I meant to tell you, so your mind would be at ease."

"That's fine," I said, feeling better about it. "I do hope they are careful and use lots of packing. Some of those porcelain things are very delicate."

"Packing?" echoed Wynn. "They won't need much packing. Mary has volunteered to store them in her attic. They will be careful, I'm sure."

"Store them?"

Now it was Wynn's turn to show surprise. "Elizabeth, you weren't thinking we would be taking all these things with us, were you?"

"Well—yes—I—"

"We couldn't possibly. The Police Force allows so many pounds of baggage per person. We have already stretched our limit. Besides, such things would serve no purpose—have no function—in the North."

For a moment I wanted to argue. Their function would be to make a home—to make me feel more like a homemaker. Wasn't that function enough? I didn't argue though. I remembered well my prayer of three days before and my promise to my God to let Wynn be the head of the household. I waited for a moment until I was sure I had complete control and then I looked at Wynn and gave him one of my nicest smiles.

"I guess that is all taken care of then."

Wynn put an arm around me and drew me close, even though we were on a crowded train.

"Thank you, Elizabeth," he whispered against my hair, and I knew I had gained far more than I had lost in the exchange.

As expected, the next day was a busy one. My family was still with Jon and Mary. They would be staying for a few more days before heading back east. I was glad I still had this one brief day with them before I would be heading north.

However, there would be no more late-night chats with my sister Julie. Her things had been moved from the room I had used for so long at Jon's, and the room was now set up for Wynn's and my use. It seemed rather strange at first, but I quickly got used to the idea. Already, I didn't know how I had ever managed without Wynn, and I had been a married woman only four short days.

Wynn was gone a good share of the day, running here and there making final preparations. He had an appointment at the Royal North West Police Headquarters for last-minute instructions and took our last trunks and crates down to be weighed and checked in. We would be starting our journey by train, then switching to boat, and ending by ox cart or wagon. Had it been the winter months, we would have also used dog teams.

We did not retire early. There was no need to conserve our energy. We had all the next day to sleep on the train if we wished. It seemed far more important now to sit and chat with the family. Reluctantly, we finally went to bed.

I climbed the stairs to my room for one last time. Who knew when I might sleep here again? I had grown to love this room. I had always felt welcomed and loved in Jon's home. I would miss it. I would miss them. I would miss each one of the children. They might be nearly grown before I saw them again. And what of my dear mother and father? Would they still be in their Toronto home when I returned from the north country? What about Julie? Would she marry while I was gone? And Matthew? He would be a man.

I did not dread my future with Wynn in his North. The only thing that bothered me was that I would miss so much of what went on here. If only I could freeze everything in place until I came back again so I wouldn't need to miss so much. But that was impossible. One could only be at one place at one time. The world in Toronto and here in Calgary would continue to go on without Elizabeth Delaney, and I must accept the fact.

I felt a bit teary inside as I turned my face into my pillow. For a moment, I was afraid I was going to cry; and then Wynn reached for me and rubbed his cheek against mine.

"Are you ready for adventure, Elizabeth?" he whispered to me, and I could detect excitement in his voice.

"Um-hum," I murmured, reaching up my hand to feel the strength of his jawline. I smiled into the darkness, and Wynn could feel the pull of my facial muscles as they formed the smile. He kissed me on the temple.

"I've never been so excited about heading north, Elizabeth," he confided. "Always before, I've known how much I was really leaving behind. This time I can only think of what I am taking with me."

I stirred in his arms.

"I hope I never disappoint you, Wynn."

"I'm not worried about that." His voice was very serious now. "I only hope and pray that you are never disappointed. The North can be cruel, Elizabeth. It's beautiful, but it can be cruel, too. The people—they are simple, needy people—like children in many ways. I guess it's the people who draw me there. I love them in some mysterious way. They trust you, lean on you, so simply, so completely. You sort of feel you have to be worthy of their trust."

"And I'm sure you are."

"I don't know. It seems as if I've never been able to do enough. What they really need are doctors, schools, and most of all missions. Missions where they can really learn the truth about God and His plan for man. They have it all so mixed up in their thinking."

A new desire stirred within me, a desire not just to teach Wynn's people how to read and write, but how to find and worship God as well. Funny. I had never met them—not any of them—yet I felt as if I already loved them.

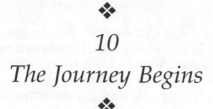

10
The Journey Begins

AFTER A TEARY last farewell, we were on our way. I felt sad and excited all at the same time. I couldn't really understand or sort out what was going on inside of me. Wynn sensed my feeling and allowed me some quiet thoughts. On occasion he did point out things of interest, but he didn't push me for enthusiasm. The first several miles of the trip I had seen many times, as it took us through Red Deer and Lacombe. As the train stopped in Lacombe, I looked closely for someone on the street whom I might know; I was about to conclude that there was no one when Phillip, Lydia, and young Phillip—Wynn's brother, sister-in-law, and nephew—came aboard, ushering Wynn's mother down the aisle.

"The conductor says they will be here for a few minutes, so he will give us warning when they are about to leave," Phillip informed us.

We soon became busily engaged in conversation, catching up on all of the area news. It was no time until the conductor came to tell us that the train would be ready to leave again in about five minutes. We hated to see them go but were so glad for the time we were able to spend together. It was the first I had been able to call Mrs. Delaney, Sr., *Mother*, and I took pleasure in doing so.

"God bless you, Elizabeth," she said. "It isn't as hard for me to let Wynn go this time, knowing he will be well looked after. You take care, though. From what Wynn has said in the past, the North can be a lonely place for a woman."

I tried to assure Mother Delaney that I would be fine and was quite prepared for all that lay ahead. I wasn't quite as sure of myself as I tried to sound. With every mile of the whirling train wheels, my stomach tied into a little tighter knot. Had it not been for Wynn beside me, I'm sure I would have panicked and bolted long before we had reached even Lacombe.

I tried to concentrate on the small settlements through which we passed. It was not easy. My mind was on other things. Even when Wynn spoke cheerily, pointing out this or that, I still couldn't get enthused—though I did try.

I finally decided I must be tired and what I needed was sleep, so I curled up beside Wynn with my head against his shoulder and tried to do just that. It didn't work. My mind was far too busy. Sleep would not come. I heard soft breathing coming from my husband and realized he had been successful. I was glad for him. He was even more tired than I, I was sure. I hoped he would rest well. I tried to sit very still so as not to disturb him. *I* might have been still, but the train was not. We made another jerky stop and then, with a hiss and a chug, we began shifting this way and that in an effort to disengage some of the cars.

Wynn quickly awoke and stirred slightly. I knew by the way he moved that he was afraid of waking me, so I sat up and smiled at him.

"It's all right," I assured him. "I'm already awake."

"Did you get any rest?" he inquired, concern in his voice.

"Rest, yes. Sleep, no," I answered.

"I'm sorry. Guess I dozed off there for a while."

"Not for long," I informed him. "You might have if the train didn't keep stopping at every little house and teepee."

Wynn chuckled. "That's the way it seems, doesn't it? Well, it isn't too much farther to Edmonton now."

"What happens at Edmonton?"

"We spend the night. I have a short meeting in the morning with some officials before we move on. You can sleep late if you like."

"When do we leave?"

"Not until about eleven."

"When do I need to be up?"

"I wouldn't think until about nine—unless you want to see a bit of the city."

"I think I'll pass," I said, smiling tiredly. "Even nine sounds way too early."

When I awoke the next morning, Wynn, as promised, had left me sleeping. I looked at the clock on the wall. It was already after nine, so I climbed quickly from my bed. I would need to hurry if I was to be ready when Wynn came back for me.

I had just finished doing my hair when Wynn's key turned in the lock.

"You're up," he greeted me. "I was afraid you might oversleep."

"I did. A little," I admitted. "I really had to hurry to make up for lost time."

"I don't think your sleeping time was lost time," he assured me. "You needed that."

He crossed to kiss me. "You look more rested," he stated. "How do you feel?"

I smiled. "Fine," I returned, trying to hide any anxiety I might feel. "Ready to start the trip to your wilderness."

He gave me a big bear hug. "Then let's get going," he said. "You still need some breakfast before we start out."

We continued our trip by river barge, a new experience for me. At first I was rather apprehensive. The day was cloudy and overcast and I didn't feel too safe on the free-floating contraption. It was guided along the river with only the help of long poles held in the hands of the men in our crew.

Wynn said that in the earlier days we would have been able to make the same trip on the North Saskatchewan in the comfort of a sternwheeler cabin, but with the advent of the railroads the boats had lost business and had been retired. There was no railroad to take us where we wanted to go, and so now we traveled on the flat barge, allowing the river to carry us along as it flowed northeast. The men who owned and operated the boat did not believe in wasting fuel on the downriver trip. Coming back up-river, they would put a simple motor to work.

The sky looked like it might pour down rain. I wasn't sure how this odd boat would function if the waters started coming down from above. Would it still stay afloat?

The seats provided weren't all that comfortable, and I soon was aching for a chance to stand up and walk around a bit. There didn't seem to be any opportunity, as nearly every square foot of the barge was piled high with something. I couldn't believe the amount of cargo it had heaped within its bulging sides. I looked around for our trunks and crates and almost panicked when I didn't see them. Wynn must have read my thoughts.

"They're over there under the canvas," he stated simply, putting my mind at ease.

"Want to stretch?" he asked after many minutes had passed by.

"I'd love to," I responded quickly, "but where?"

"Come," he said, holding out a hand to me. "I think we can manage a few minutes of it."

It was difficult. We had to step over things, around things, duck under things, and hang on for dear life. The wind was up, and at times the river was rough. I tied my scarf more tightly under my chin and told Wynn that I would be fine for the time being. We returned to our uncomfortable seats.

In the early afternoon the rains came. There wasn't any place to go to avoid them. Wynn found some kind of slicker and wrapped it tightly around me. The wind kept whipping and tearing at it, making it difficult to keep all sides of me under it at any given moment. I could feel patches of wet spots grow bigger and bigger. I tried not to think about them, but it wasn't easy. The rainwater was cold and the increasing wind made it even colder. In a few hours' time, I was really miserable but I tried hard not to show it.

Wynn kept fussing over me—shifting the makeshift shelter this way and that, tightening it here, and tucking it in there. In the meantime, he, too, was getting wet. Those operating the barge seemed to take the storm for granted. They had likely been wet many times before while making this run.

As the day passed, the sky was getting darker and the rains heavier. I wondered if we would travel all night long. How far would we go on this river anyway? I had heard the word *Athabasca*, but I didn't think that was our destination.

Wynn came to tell me, "We're going to pull in early tonight. We'll try to dry out a bit. There's a little trading post ahead where we can take shelter. We should have gone farther tonight, but we'll wait for morning."

I shivered and nodded my head thankfully. It was good news to me.

It wasn't long until the shouting and straining of the barge crew told me that we were going ashore. There was a jolt and a thump as we hit some kind of dock in the darkness. Then Wynn was there to help me to solid ground. The wind and rain loosened my scarf, and soon my hair was tumbling crazily about my face. I tried to tuck it back again but I really didn't have a free hand. I gave up and decided to just let it blow.

We headed for a dark shape in the gathering gloom. Then I spotted a light in a misty window. Though faint, the light did signal humanity; and I breathed a prayer of thankfulness as I tried, with Wynn's help, to hurry toward it.

The smell of wood smoke reached my nose, and I thought of the wonderful warmth that would go with it. I hurried faster. In my eagerness to get to the house, I did not see the tree stump in my pathway.

"Watch out!" Wynn cried when he saw what was about to happen, but it was too late. I banged my shin hard against the tough wood, and let out a sharp little cry at the stinging pain.

Wynn kept me from falling, but from there to the house I stumbled along, limping painfully. Wynn asked to carry me but I stubbornly shook my head.

When we reached what I had thought to be a house and stumbled through the door, I was disappointed to see that it was no house at all. It was a shed—a shed for trade. Boxes and crates and heaps and piles were stacked all around the single room in a haphazard fashion. One dim lamp sat upon a makeshift counter, throwing out an anemic light. The single window was so stained and dirty I wondered how I had been able to see the light from outside at all.

In the corner of the room was what looked like a stack of furs. Upon closer observation, I discovered that it was, instead, a bed—of sorts. I shuddered to think of sleeping there.

"Howdy," a voice said, and I whirled to see an ill-kempt man sitting beside the potbellied stove in the middle of the crowded room. He let fly with a line of dark spit that missed an open can, spattering against the side of the stove, causing a sizzling sound. He had not risen to meet us and he did not move now.

Wynn jerked his head at the man. "Howdy, Charlie," he said. "Mind if we borrow your chair for a minute? My wife just gave her leg an awful whack on that tree stump you've got out front."

It was the room's only chair, and Charlie rose reluctantly with a grunt of disgust.

Wynn sat me down and lifted my skirt to get a good look at my injury.

"Bring your lamp, would you, Charlie?"

From the tone of Wynn's voice, I knew that, though it was Charlie's lodging, Wynn was in charge here. Everyone knew it.

Charlie brought the lamp. My leg was bleeding, seeping through my torn stocking, making a sticky dark patch.

"You've got to get out of those stockings," Wynn said to me.

I looked helplessly about the room. There was no place to go.

"But I can't," I insisted, casting a nervous glance at Charlie.

"Turn your back, Charlie," Wynn ordered, and the grumbling Charlie obeyed. The light of the lamp turned with him. I felt a bit more comfortable in the semi-darkness and hastened to raise my skirt and unfasten the garters that held up my ruined stocking. I slipped it down as quickly as I could and let my skirt drop back in place. Charlie shifted from one foot to the other and spit again. I don't know where that one landed. Weakly I sat back down.

"Okay," said Wynn, "let's have the lamp, Charlie."

Charlie turned around. For one awful moment, I feared he might spit in my direction. He didn't. He stood holding the lamp nervously, trying not to look at the leg that Wynn was studying.

"I don't think it's too deep," Wynn was saying. "Nothing broken that—"

"Except my stocking," I interrupted. Wynn's eyebrows went up.

"Legs heal," I said, to inform him. "Stockings don't—and I was able to bring only a limited number with me."

In spite of himself, Wynn smiled but made no reply.

"Charlie, do you have any first-aid supplies around here?" he asked.

Charlie grumbled and then muttered, "A few things."

"Set the lamp down and get them, please," said Wynn. "I don't want to have to unload the barge to get at my supply."

Wynn stood up to check the kettle sitting on the stove. It held water and that seemed to please him.

While Wynn cleansed and bandaged my swelling leg, the other men entered. Apparently they were satisfied that they had secured the barge against the storm, and now wanted to be in where it was warm and dry.

They greeted Charlie boisterously. In return, he greeted them with an oath, a spit, and a slap on the back.

I felt very much out of place. It was apparent that these men didn't spend much time in the presence of a lady. They joked and swore and jabbed at one another with harmless fists. One man soon produced a rum bottle, which they seemed to think was just the thing needed to take the chill out of their bones.

Wynn took charge because no one else seemed to have any mind to do so. He put on the coffeepot and asked Charlie for some tins of food for an evening meal. Charlie seemed reluctant to share until Wynn reminded him that he would be paid for anything that the Police Force used. Charlie then produced a couple of tins, and Wynn set about making some supper.

I offered to help him but he declined my offer. "I think you should rest that leg all you can. Here, let me help you."

Before I knew what had happened, Wynn lifted me from my spot on the chair by the stove to the pile of foul-smelling skins in the corner. I wanted to protest but the words caught in my throat.

"I'm sorry, Elizabeth," whispered Wynn, "but I guess this will be your bed for tonight."

I closed my mouth against the protest and the odor that came from the pile of furs as Wynn settled me gently on the bed.

"You mean this is all there is here?" I asked incredulously.

"This is it," answered Wynn.

"But what about you—and them?"

"We'll stay here, too. At least it's dry, and the fire will have our clothes dried out by morning."

I looked quickly at the tiny, crowded, overstocked room. Suddenly it seemed terribly stuffy and suffocating. I wished for the out-of-doors so I could breathe freely again. But when I heard the howl of the wind and the lashing of the rain, I closed my eyes and tried to be thankful for the warmth of the smelly little cabin. Wynn patted my shoulder in sympathy.

When supper was ready, a makeshift arrangement of a table was dragged up close to the stove. Wynn came to help me to it. I told him I really wasn't hungry and would gladly settle for just a hot cup of tea or coffee. He realized then that I was still in my wet clothes and shivering with the cold.

"I'm sorry, Elizabeth," he said. "I was so anxious to get some hot food in you that I forgot about your wet things. I didn't realize you got as wet as you did. I guess the slicker didn't keep out much of the rain, eh?"

"Oh, it did," I insisted bravely, comparing his soaked appearance to mine. "I only have a spot here and there, that's all."

Wynn reached out to feel my clothing. "You're wet," he argued, "through and through. We'll get you out of them as soon as you get some hot soup down you."

I wanted to protest further, but Wynn would have none of it. I allowed myself to be helped to the chair, and Wynn poured me a cup of the soup he had made. I sipped it slowly. It wasn't the best meal I had ever eaten, but it was hot, even tasty in a "canned" sort of way. My clothing on the side closest to the stove began to steam. I shifted around some to direct the heat on another section. I didn't really warm up, although a few spots of me were actually hot. It was a strange sensation to feel so hot in places and yet chilled at the same time. I finished my cup of soup and motioned to Wynn that I was ready to return to the heap called a bed.

"Got a couple of blankets, Charlie?"

Charlie lumbered up from the barrel on which he was sitting and spit at the stove as he reached up to a shelf.

"Hudson's Bay," he grumbled. "Hardly used."

"They'll still be hardly used come morning," Wynn answered, not to be intimidated by Charlie's growling. Wynn moved to where he could screen me from view with the blanket. "Now," he said, "get out of those wet things."

I looked at him, wondering if he really meant what he said. The room was full of men.

He meant it. I shrugged, unfastened my wet skirt and let it fall. I then removed my shirt and my petticoats, casting apprehensive glances at the blanket Wynn held for me.

I could tell by the noises on the other side of the make-shift wall that the four men were now enjoying Wynn's supper soup. There were slurps and smacking, and I was glad I wouldn't need to see as well as hear them eat. I wondered if Charlie could eat and chew tobacco at the same time, or if he actually disposed of his wad while he was dining.

"Now climb up there and lie down," Wynn spoke softly, "and I'll tuck you in."

He did as promised, using both of the blankets Charlie had provided. I lay there shivering. Wynn went back to the stove, took the cup I had used, and poured soup for himself. He then got a cup of coffee and came back to my bed. "Are you warming any?" I thought I was, though my teeth hadn't really stopped chattering.

Now that Wynn no longer claimed the stove for his meal preparation and I no longer occupied the one chair in the room, the men moved in closer to the heat. Their clothing began to steam and smell, not improving the odor in the room. I was glad I had already eaten. I couldn't have swallowed with that strong, offensive smell in the room.

I tried to move over to give Wynn room to sit down on the bed beside me, but this was truly a one-man bed. Wynn crouched beside me and sipped his coffee. I could see the clothes hugging tightly to him.

"You're still wet," I stated. "You'll get sick."

"I'll dry soon. I'll be okay. Why don't you try to get some sleep?"

I wanted to retort, "Here?" But I knew that "here" was the best he could offer, so I simply nodded.

Wynn moved back to the stove where the men were busy eating and joking.

"Hey, Sarge," quipped one of the boatmen. "Not bad soup for a law-man."

The other men joined in his guffaw at his tremendously funny joke. Wynn just nodded his head.

"Much obliged for your home and your bed tonight, Charlie," said Wynn sincerely.

Charlie looked over to the corner where I huddled. He had finished eating, so he was free to chew and spit again, which he now did. It landed on one of the boatmen's boots. The fellow did not even glance down.

"No problem," Charlie assured Wynn. "Me, I ain't aimin' on usin' the bed tonight nohow."

The other men laughed and I wondered why. I didn't need to wonder for long. The makeshift table was quickly cleared of the few cups and a pack of cards was produced.

"Ain't got nothin' 'gainst cards, have ya, Sarge?" asked the chubby boatman.

"Not as long as they're fair and don't cause any fights," answered Wynn.

"Then I guess thet this here's gotta be a fair game, gents," the man said to his comrades; and they all laughed uproariously again, slapping their thighs and one another's backs.

Crates or barrels served as seats, and a couple of bottles soon joined the cards on the table.

"You wantin' to join us, Sarge?" invited the little dark man with the French accent and long mustache.

Wynn shook his head.

The four men hunched over the table, and the long night began. There wasn't much place for Wynn to go. Attempting to dry out his wet clothes, he pulled a block of wood close to the stove and sat down, leaning against a pile of crates.

The lamp flickered now and then, and an unwashed hand would reach out to turn the wick up a bit. The jesting got louder and more coarse. Wynn reminded them a lady was present, and then for a few minutes it was quieter in the cabin. As the night progressed and the bottles were emptied, the commotion grew. Wynn eventually watched it without comment, seeming to pay little attention to the whole thing; but I knew he was well aware of every movement in the room.

From my bed in the corner, I watched too. I was no longer shivering— the scratchy Hudson's Bay blankets were doing their job well. I nearly dozed once or twice, and then laughter or a stream of obscenity would jerk me awake again.

Wynn rose from his place by the fire to check on me. When I saw him coming, I closed my eyes lightly. I knew it might be considered deceitful, but I did not want Wynn to worry about me. He already had enough on his mind. I did not fool him, however.

"Are you all right?" he asked softly.

I didn't answer immediately. The truth was, I felt very strange, very out of place, in the room with the cursing, gambling men. I had never been in such a situation before. It was the kind of thing I had avoided all my life. If it hadn't been for the presence of my husband, I would have been stiff with fright. I glanced quickly at the four men in the room. The big one was taking another long drink from the bottle; and the dark, little one was impatiently waiting his turn, hand outstretched. I looked quickly back to Wynn. Concern showed in his face.

"I'm fine," I managed weakly; but then I repeated it more firmly, willing myself to realize I spoke the truth. "I'm fine."

"Your leg?"

"It doesn't hurt too badly at all."

"Are you warm?"

I merely nodded my head for this one.

He knelt beside me and shifted my blankets some, tucking them in tightly around me. "I'm sorry, Elizabeth. I planned the trip so you would have better accommodations than this. If this storm—"

"It's all right," I hurried to assure him. "You're here—that's what matters."

He leaned over and kissed me, the love showing in his eyes, but the worried look did not leave his face. "Try to get some sleep," he whispered.

I smiled at him and he kissed me again, and then went back to his place by the stove.

It was getting very late and the men were still playing cards, drinking, and cursing. Charlie rose from his crate and went to bring another bottle. When he placed it on the table, Wynn, hardly moving, stood slowly, leaned over and removed it. Four pairs of eyes turned to look at him.

"We've got a long trip ahead of us tomorrow. I want some sober bargemen. Charlie, you can drink if you want to. It's your liquor, but don't pass your bottle around."

There was authority in Wynn's voice; and, though there were some grumbles around the table, no one challenged him.

The card game went on, but it was clear that much of the "fun" had gone out of it.

At length, the men decided they'd had enough. They pushed back their makeshift seats, cleared a little space around the stove, and stretched out on the floor to sleep. For a few moments, it was blessedly silent. Then, one by one, they filled the room with a chorus of snores.

The snoring seemed even louder and more vulgar than the conversation had been. Resigned, I turned my face to the wall and tried to get some sleep in the little time that was left.

Once or twice I heard stirring as the fire in the stove was replenished. I knew without even looking that it was Wynn.

When morning came, I was still bone-weary. But at least the effort of trying to sleep was over. The rain was still falling, but the wind seemed to have died down. I was thankful for small mercies.

At my first stirring, Wynn was beside me.

"How do you feel, Elizabeth?" he whispered.

I ached all over, and my sore leg throbbed with each beat of my heart. I managed a faltering smile. "Okay," I answered. "Can you help me up?"

Wynn's strong arms helped me to my feet and shielded me with the blanket while I fumblingly got into my clothes. They were thoroughly dry now and felt much softer than the blankets had.

The men were still scattered around on the floor, sleeping off their binge of the night before.

"I need to go out, Wynn," I whispered. "Where do I go?"

Wynn nodded toward the one door.

"Anyplace in the woods," he answered me.

At my troubled look, he glanced back to the men. "Don't worry about any of them. They wouldn't wake up until next week if they were left alone. I'll watch them."

I was relieved but still apprehensive about the whole outdoors as a facility.

"Do you need help walking?" Wynn asked.

I tried my weight on my poor leg to be sure before I answered, "I'll be all right."

"Are you sure?"

I took an unsteady step. "I'll hang onto the cabin if I need support," I told him.

He helped me over to the door and opened it for me. Then he reached for his jacket. "Here," he said, "you'd better use this. It's still raining."

I wrapped the jacket tightly about me and stepped out into the misty morning. The nearby river was almost hidden by the fog that clung to it. Water from the trees dripped on the soggy ground beneath. Every step I took was in water. I was glad the wind was not blowing.

I took no longer out-of-doors than was necessary. Even then, by the time I hobbled back into the little, smelly, over-crowded cabin, my shoes were soaked through and the hem of my dress wet for several inches. I longed for the stove's warmth, but I hesitated to step over the sleeping men. Wynn helped me around them, and I took my place in the one chair and stretched my feet out toward the glow.

"Not very nice out there, is it?" Wynn commented.

"It's wet and cool, but the wind isn't blowing like yesterday."

Wynn seemed to approve of my healthy attitude. He gave me a smile and placed a hand on my shoulder as he handed me a cup of hot coffee.

"Now that you've seen the day, what do you think? Would you like to get back on the journey or wait out the storm here in the cabin?"

I looked at the four sodden men on the floor. The liquor from the night before mingled with the other smells. Snores still came forth from half-open mouths, sometimes catching in their throats in a rugged growl which snorted to a finish.

I glanced back at the makeshift bed in the corner. It was so narrow one could scarcely turn over and so lumpy I wondered how Charlie ever managed to get any sleep at all.

"Where will we be tonight?"

"There's a small post downriver."

"Are there—are there—?" I hesitated to say "houses," for I wasn't sure if there were any *houses* as such in the North. "Are there accommodations there?" I finally managed.

"Quite comfortable," Wynn replied.

"Then I vote to move on," I said without hesitation.

Wynn smiled and moved forward to stir the sleeping barge captain. The man didn't even open an eye, just shifted his position and started to snore again in a different key.

"Blackjack," Wynn called loudly. "Time to hit the trail!"

The man just stirred again. Wynn knelt beside him and shook his shoulder. "Time to get up. Get this crew of yours off the floor," Wynn commanded the man.

Blackjack scowled up at him as if about to argue the point, but Wynn would take no argument.

"You're being paid to get us to River's Bend, remember? If you want the pay, then deliver the goods."

The man cursed and propped himself on an elbow.

"Coffee's hot," Wynn prodded him. "Get some in you and let's get going."

It was rather amusing to watch the revelers of the night before. They didn't look so lively now. Grumbling, holding their heads and muttering oaths, they tried to get their bodies to obey.

Wynn had little sympathy. "Let's get moving," he ordered again. "The fog's about to lift, and we have some time to make up."

They were finally on their feet and stirring. Wynn poured each a cup of coffee, except for Charlie. In spite of the commotion all about him, Charlie had slept on, only stirring now and then to reposition himself.

"Finished with the bed, Elizabeth?" Wynn inquired. When I gladly nodded that I was, Wynn unceremoniously lifted Charlie up and carried him to his bed. Wynn straightened out the unconscious body to what looked like a comfortable position and threw a blanket over him. Charlie slept on.

Two of the men went out to prepare the barge for departure while the other fellow mumbled and complained about the lousy day for traveling.

Wynn looked at his pocketwatch.

"Gotta be out of here in ten minutes, Wally," he stated flatly. "Ten minutes, no more."

Wally, still grumbling, went to join the others.

Wynn left money on the shelf by the coffeepot to cover our expenses for the night's lodging and the food. Charlie was still snoring as we closed the door behind us.

Back in the boat with the slicker arranged around me, I discovered it was not raining hard. Without the wind, I was sure I would fare just fine.

In spite of the constant peppering with fine raindrops, I found myself enjoying the scenery on the riverbanks moving swiftly from view on either side. There was very little habitation, but occasionally I did spy the smoke of a woodstove and a cabin, half-hidden by the trees.

By midmorning the rain had stopped, the wind had died down to a light breeze, and early in the afternoon the sun actually came out. The slicker laid aside, I let the warm sun fall on my shoulders. We had not stopped except to eat a hurried noon meal consisting of a few tins of canned food heated over an open fire.

The country through which we passed was fresh and clean. No factory smells tainted the air with civilization. I appreciated the crispness of the air even more after having spent the night at Charlie's.

We passed through a marshy area, and Wynn moved close to me to point out two large moose. They put their heads completely under water for what seemed ever so long. When they finally lifted their heads, their mouths dripping with long marsh grass, they looked toward us almost with disdain, seeming to indicate that this was their territory and we were trespassers.

"Look at them," I said to Wynn in astonishment. "You'd think they didn't even have to breathe, they are under so long!"

"Oh, they breathe all right," Wynn assured me, "though they are unusual. They can even dive to get their food—some say as deep as thirty feet if need be. They scoop up the grasses on the bottom and then come back up again."

"Do they need to go back to land to eat it?"

"Oh, no. They just tread water. Moose are wonderful swimmers. Don't suppose there are many animals any better."

"Aren't they ugly, though? They look like—like leftover pieces of this and that."

Wynn laughed. "Well, there's a saying," he mused, "that a moose is a horse made by a committee."

We chuckled together at Wynn's joke.

Since the barge hands had started the day in bad spirits, I tried to stay as far away from them as I could. Now and then one of them would hold his head and weave back and forth. I wondered if they were in any condition to steer the barge, especially when we hit some white water; but they seemed to be alert enough when they had to be. Wynn did not seem worried, so I relaxed, too. Eventually their dispositions improved. In the later afternoon, I even heard Blackjack singing.

With the passing of the day, I guess my disposition improved as well. Wynn had often been by my side to point out interesting items in the water or on the riverbanks. The sun was swinging to the west, the men were no longer cursing with every breath, and the country all around me seemed mysterious and exciting. Yes, things were definitely improved over yesterday.

Lying in that little cabin, I had wondered if I'd ever make it as a Mountie's wife. How could anyone endure such conditions? Today I was confident I could. My leg wasn't even bothering me anymore. We would soon be at the post, and Wynn had said we would have good accommodations there. I wasn't sure how many nights it would take us to make the trip, but I was now certain I could endure. I had gotten through the first night, and it surely couldn't be any worse. From here on I would have no problem.

11
Onward

THE CABIN WAS simple but seemed very adequate, and the best thing was that I didn't need to share it with four drinking men. Another nice thing was that I could share it in privacy with Wynn.

After we had gone to bed I heard a strange sound. It seemed to grow louder and louder until it was humming steadily in my ears. I was puzzled and wished I could ask Wynn about it, but I could tell by his breathing that he was already asleep.

In the darkness something stung me. I jumped and slapped at it. Another sting. I swatted again.

"Put your head under the covers if they are bothering you," said Wynn softly.

"What is it?"

"Mosquitoes."

Now I had seen mosquitoes before. I had even been bitten by a few; but this—this *din* was something new to me.

"Are you sure?" I asked Wynn.

"I'm sure," he answered. "This cabin doesn't have any screens on the windows."

"How do you ever sleep?"

"You get used to it."

Wynn turned over to pull me close and shelter my face with the blankets.

"Try to sleep, Elizabeth," he encouraged me. "You didn't get much last night."

I lay quietly in Wynn's arms, not stirring for fear I would keep him awake. The hum was a rising and falling crescendo. I wondered how many million mosquitoes it took to make such a sound.

In spite of the protection of Wynn's arms and the blanket, the mosquitoes still found me. I could hear their hum get closer and then I would feel the sharp sting as they sucked out my blood.

One thing is sure, I promised myself. *Our cabin in the North will have coverings over the windows even if I have to tear up my petticoats!*

In the morning I rose tired and grumpy. I would be so glad to get back on the barge and away from the mosquitoes.

My triumph was short lived; though we were soon back on the river, the dreaded mosquitoes swarmed around us, following us down the stream.

"Wynn," I said crossly, "they are coming with us."

"There are lots of mosquitoes in the North," Wynn informed me. "They are one of the area's worst pests."

"What are the others?" I muttered sarcastically, but Wynn didn't catch the tone of my question.

"Blackflies," he replied. "Blackflies are another real plague to man and beast alike."

Wynn was right. The mosquitoes were joined that day by the black-flies. I thought I would be bitten and chewed to pieces. Right before my eyes, new welts would rise on my arms. I hated to think what my face must look like. I was almost frantic with the intensity of the itching.

Wynn was sympathetic. "I might have something that will help," he offered and went to dig around in his medical supplies.

He came back with an ointment. It had a vile smell and looked awful, but I allowed him to rub it on anyway. It did help some, though it didn't seem to discourage the dreadful insects from taking further bites out of me.

"Why didn't they bother us yesterday?" I asked Wynn.

"The wind and the rain kept them away."

"Really?"

"They can't fly well in strong wind. They are too light, and they don't care for the rain either." I was ready to pray for more wind and rain. Anything to be rid of the miserable pests.

I guess I eventually got used to them. I was able to think about other things after a while and even to again enjoy, in a sense, my trip.

In the late afternoon, Wynn pointed out a mother bear and her two cubs. She was foraging at a bend in the river. Perhaps she was fishing, because she was staring intently at the water, seeming to ignore the barge completely as we went by.

The cute cubs took my mind off the mosquitoes and flies for a few minutes while I considered having a cub for a pet.

It was already getting dusk before we pulled into River's Bend, the place where we were to spend the night. Wynn lifted me ashore as there was no dock. This didn't make sense to me.

"Why is it," I asked, "that there's no dock and yet this is the place where all our things need to be unloaded? Isn't it going to be an awful job carrying all those heavy trunks and crates ashore?"

Wynn rewarded me with a broad smile. Apparently he liked a wife who was observant.

"The dock is around the bend in the river. Our things will be unloaded there. There are also a couple of temporary buildings and a Hudson's Bay Post, but I thought you might prefer to use this trapper's cabin. It is more private, though I'm afraid not luxurious. I've made arrangements with Pierre to use it for the night."

"Who's Pierre?"

"He runs the post."

"Is he married?"

"Nope. He batches. And his quarters are even worse than Charlie's."

I couldn't even imagine what that would be like.

"I don't want you to have to stay in those kinds of conditions again," Wynn stated firmly. "I know it must have been extremely offensive to you."

I thought back to Charlie's. The smelly, crowded cabin. The cursing, drinking, card-playing men. No, I wasn't particularly interested in that again either. I was pleased Wynn had made other arrangements.

Wynn opened the creaky, complaining cabin door; there was some quick scampering as some former resident took immediate cover. I stepped closer to Wynn. He put a reassuring arm around me. "Nothing that small could harm you," he smiled.

Wynn found and lit the lamp, and I placed my small case on the newspaper-covered table.

"Is this Pierre's cabin?" I asked, looking around me at the bare little room.

"No, it belongs to some trapper."

"Then why did Pierre—?"

"It's customary. Trappers always leave their cabins available for others to use. Pierre likely asked the trapper about using his lodgings for travelers like us; but even if he didn't, we still won't be considered trespassers."

Wynn moved about, swishing the heavy dust from the few pieces of furniture and checking what was available for making a fire. There was a good supply of dry wood in one corner, and Wynn soon had a fire going. "Remember your first experience with a wood stove at Pine River?" His eyes twinkled at me, and I had the grace to blush. It's a wonder I hadn't burned down the building! I wrinkled my nose at him and we laughed together at the memory.

Wynn went outside to the river, dipped the kettle full of water and placed it on to boil. Then he checked the bed. It was a very narrow one, and I secretly wondered how it would sleep two. Wynn flung back the Hudson's Bay blankets; they had seen a good deal of wear and very few washings. A heavy piece of denim material was spread across a mattress of spruce branches crisscrossing one another topped with moss. I winced and hoped Wynn hadn't noticed.

Our meal was a simple one of dried biscuits and canned police rations. Tasty it was not, but I was very hungry and ate heartily.

I insisted on washing the dishes. Wynn had been our wilderness cook all along our journey, and I was glad I could finally do something helpful.

It didn't take me long to wash the few things and place them back on the unknown trapper's shelf.

Wynn spread one of the worn blankets on the wooden floor in front of the fire and we settled down before it to talk. I looked about the simple, quaint little cabin and wondered if my own would look like this. I decided to ask.

"Do you know what our cabin will be like?"

"Not really. I haven't been to Beaver River before."

"But you have a pretty good idea?"

"Pretty good."

"Will it have just one room?"

"Not likely. A Mountie's home usually serves a double function—office as well as home. So it likely has at least two rooms."

I was pleased to hear that. I did want the privacy of a bedroom.

"It will be log?"

"I'm sure it will."

"With wooden floors?"

"With wooden floors."

We were silent for a few moments. Wynn broke the silence, his arm tightening about me as he spoke, "That must seem awfully crude to you, Elizabeth."

I turned so I could look into his eyes.

"In a way, yes—but really—I don't mind the thought of it at all. Look at this cabin now. True, it isn't much—but with a little fixing here and there—" I hesitated, wondering even as I spoke just what "fixing" one could do to make this very bare cabin look homey.

Wynn brushed a kiss against my cheek.

A strange, mournful, bloodcurdling sound interrupted us. I felt the hair on my scalp rise and my spine tingle. I had gotten used to the coyote's cry, but this—this was something entirely different. I pressed closer to Wynn.

"A timber wolf," he commented. I shivered as the cry came again and was answered from the other direction.

I had heard of timber wolves. Most of the tales had come from imaginative Julie. Wolves traveled in murderous packs, had menacing red eyes, and crept up stealthily on those whom they would devour.

"Are they all around us?" I whispered nervously, my eyes big with fright.

Wynn hugged me, sheltering me in the circle of his two strong arms.

"I doubt it," he said, without any trace of concern whatever. "But if they are, there is nothing whatever to be worried about. I suggest you just lie here in front of the fire and listen carefully, Elizabeth. You can almost count how many there are in the pack by the difference in their cries. They are a part of our world here in the North—a part that needs to be respected but not feared. Accept them—maybe even enjoy them if you can."

I doubted I would ever live to enjoy the cry of a timber wolf, but I did try to be calm. Another cry tore through the night air.

"Hear that?" noted Wynn close to my ear. "I'm guessing that was the leader of the pack. Did you hear the authority in his voice?"

I tried to shake my head, but Wynn was holding me too close. Authority? Not particularly.

Another cry reached us. This one was shorter and farther away.

"That one now, he's answering the boss. Checking in. Could you hear the difference?"

This time I could. It was unbelievable.

There was another cry. It came from very near our cabin, yet it wasn't as spooky and bloodcurdling for some reason.

"A female," commented Wynn. "Probably the leader's mate."

"Are the females tamer than the males?" I asked, thinking that this one sounded so much gentler than others.

"Oh, no," laughed Wynn. "In fact, the female can be even more aggressive and more deadly than the males—especially if she has pups. The hunting pack always consists of some females. I'm not sure how the males would fare without them. The pack depends on their skill and aggressiveness for the kill. The female must have food not just for herself but to feed her young—and she will do anything to get what she's after."

The wolves were a part of Wynn's wilderness. I wasn't sure I would ever be able to listen to their howl without shivering, but Wynn's calm and easy acceptance of these wild creatures had certainly helped me to see them in another light.

Another howl. Another shiver. Another explanation from Wynn. He seemed to paint a picture of the pack around us, locating and identifying each member. He did not describe them with sparkling red eyes and drooling tongues. I was seeing them as needy, hungry creatures, depending on nature and their skills to feed themselves and their families.

"Contrary to what you may have heard," Wynn told me, "the wolves only hunt to survive. In the wilderness, survival is not always easy."

I listened to the echoing calls of the wolves as they moved on, away from the cabin. My heart quit thumping. I found myself even wishing them good hunting.

12

By Wagon

WE TOOK THE trail the next morning to the small, hastily constructed buildings that formed the small outpost. Before we had left the little cabin, I had remade the bed and washed the dishes. Wynn had brought in a fresh wood supply, making sure he left more stacked against the wall than we had found the night before.

The trail through the woods crossed a stream on steppingstones, and Wynn pointed east to where the beavers had dammed the water and made themselves a small lake. The morning sun was already promising a fair day, and the birds sang and winged overhead among the trees. The walk would have been perfect had it not been for the miserable insects. Even Wynn walked with a screen of cloth draped from his hat at the back.

When we reached the fort, I looked about at the sorry arrangement of small buildings. Even from the outside, I was sure I wouldn't have wanted to stay overnight in any of them. I was so glad Wynn had arranged for the cabin.

"I think you should wait out here," Wynn said to me. I wondered why, but did not question him. I found a nearby tree stump and sat down. No one seemed to be around, so I lifted my skirt to inspect my leg. It was no longer covered with a bandage; Wynn had decided the air would do it good.

Ugly scabs of various density and color covered the shin. I moved my foot back and forth. Almost all the pain was gone. Wynn had said that it was most important to have bodies capable of healing themselves when one was miles away from medical help. He seemed very pleased he had picked a woman with this quality.

Wynn was not in the cabin for long. He returned with a look of frustration on his face.

"What's wrong? Are they drunk?"

"Drunk isn't the word for it. They are *out*! Every last one of them. I couldn't even raise them."

"You're angry with them for drinking, aren't you? I don't blame—"

But Wynn didn't let me finish my intended consolation.

"Yes, I'm angry. With their drinking? I don't like it, but I can't stop it. That's their business, I guess—their way of life. That's the way they ease through the difficulties of life in the North. When men don't have God, they need substitutes. To my way of thinking, whiskey is a poor substitute—but many men depend upon it. But what I am angry about is that they didn't obey my orders."

I looked up in surprise.

"They were supposed to unload the barge last night before they started their drinking. I knew very well they wouldn't be any good for anything this morning. There sits the wagon, nothing on it; and in there, sprawled out on the floor, are the men who were to load it and the man who was supposed to drive it."

"What do we do now?" I finally asked in a small voice.

Wynn roused and reached over to cup my chin. He smiled then for the first time since emerging from the house.

"We do it ourselves, my love," he answered, strength and confidence back in his voice.

It was a long, hard job. The morning sun was high in the sky before we finished. I really wasn't much help. The crates and trunks were all too heavy for a woman's shoulders, and Wynn would not even let me try. Wynn had driven the wagon down as close to the dock as possible in order to save unnecessary steps. I volunteered to hold the team, as there was no hitching post. Wynn seemed pleased that I was willing to help, but the job I had did not go well.

The horses were skitterish. The mosquitoes and flies were plaguing them, and they kept tossing their heads and stamping around. Wynn watched my efforts warily for a while and them decided to unhitch the horses, take them up the bank and tie them securely to a tree. Now I had nothing to do.

I tried to give a hand now and then but soon found I was more in the way than anything else. At length I gave up and found a tree stump in the shade.

As I sat there, I angrily thought about the men in the nearby cabin. There they slept in a drunken stupor while my husband labored to do the work they had been hired to do!

Finally the loading was completed and the horses rehitched to the wagon.

Wynn made one more visit to the cabin to check on our hired driver.

"Any luck?" I asked when he returned, his lips set in a thin line.

"None." It was a crisp, blunt reply.

"What do we do now?" I asked. "Do we have to wait here until he wakes up?"

"No, we don't wait. We are late enough getting away now. We'll never make it as far as we should today. We *drive*. When he wakes up he *walks*."

The horses were not made for speed and the wagon was clumsy and heavy. It had been much faster traveling on the river. The sun grew hot on my back and the insects buzzed persistently.

We didn't talk much. Wynn concentrated on his driving, and I tried to keep my mind busy with things other than my discomfort. The river barge seemed like a pleasure boat compared to this lumbering wagon.

We stopped at noon for a quick meal. Wynn ate with one eye on the sky, for clouds were gathering. I knew he feared a storm before we reached our destination. Neither of us voiced the concern, but I noticed that Wynn pushed the horses a little faster.

The track could, at best, be referred to as a trail. It wound up and down, around and through, following the path of least resistance, much like a river would do. At times there was no way but to challenge the terrain head-on. The horses strained up steep hills, then slid their way to the bottom again, the wagon jolting behind. Fortunately, Wynn was an expert teamster, and I breathed a prayer of thanks whenever we reached fairly level ground again.

At one point, even Wynn feared for the safety of the horses and wagon. He asked me to climb out and walk down the incline. It seemed to be almost straight down. On further thought, Wynn crawled down from the wagon, rustled through some of his belongings, and came up with the horrid men's pants. They had been washed since I had seen them last, which I assumed Wynn had done himself.

"You'd best put these on," he said. "You might spend part of the descent in a sitting position."

Without question I quickly obeyed and stuffed my simple skirt and petticoat into the overnight bag lying on top of the load.

Wynn went first. I didn't really want to watch, but I couldn't tear my eyes away. A good brake system on the wagon kept the wheels skidding downhill, always on the heels of the sliding horses.

I stood there with bated breath, now and then gasping and covering my eyes, then quickly uncovering them again to make sure Wynn was still all right.

I forgot to follow. When Wynn finally rolled the wagon to a halt on comparatively even ground, I still stood, with my mouth open, at the top of the hill.

I blushed and hurried down to join him. His call, "Slow down," came too late. Already I had picked up more speed than I could control on the steep slope. I tried to brace myself against the momentum, but soon my body was moving far too fast for my clumsy feet, and I felt myself falling and rolling end over end. The next thing I was aware of was Wynn's white face bending over me.

"Elizabeth," he pleaded, panting for air, "Elizabeth, are you all right?"

I moaned and tried to roll over into a more dignified position. I wasn't sure if I was all right or half dead. I did have enough presence of mind to be glad for the horrible pants.

Wynn began to feel my bones. I roused somewhat, my dizzy head beginning to clear.

"I think I'm okay," I told him, struggling to sit up.

"Lie still." he ordered. "Don't move until we are sure."

He continued to check. By now my head was clear.

"I'm okay," I insisted, feeling only a few places on my body smarting. "Just embarrassed to death, that's all."

Wynn satisfied himself that nothing was broken and sighed with relief. He then turned his attention to the scratches and bruises.

"Let me up," I implored him and he carefully assisted me to my feet.

He brushed the dirt from my clothing and the leaves from my hair, showing both relief and concern on his face.

"I wanted you to walk down to keep you from injury," he said softly, shaking his head in dismay.

I began to laugh. Wynn looked at me with more concern in his eyes and then he smiled slowly.

"That's some record for coming down that hill," I said between gasps of laughter.

"I think," he remarked, "I might have set a record for coming back up—Hey!" His shout made me turn to follow his gaze. The deserted team had decided to plod on without us. They were not far ahead, but they were still traveling; and if we didn't hurry or if something spooked them, we might be walking for a long way. Wynn ran down the remainder of the hill, chasing after them. I followed, but at a much slower pace. I didn't want a repeat performance. I was already smarting and aching quite enough.

Wynn caught the team about a quarter of a mile down the road. They had not exactly followed the trail though, and Wynn was hard put to back them out of the dead end they had led themselves into among the trees.

Finally back on the trail again, we noticed the clouds had gathered more darkly overhead. It had cooled off noticeably and the wind was picking up.

"Is there anyone living nearby?" I asked him, sensing his uneasiness.

"Not that I'm aware of," he answered.

Even the horses seemed to sense the coming storm and tossed their heads and complained at the load.

They balked when we came to a stretch of marshy land where they were required to cross on corduroy (wooden logs placed side by side). Wynn coaxed and then forced them to take the first steps. The logs rolled and sucked, squeezing up oozy marsh soil as we passed over. I felt as reluctant as the horses. I wished I could walk but then rethought the matter. In places the logs lay beneath the surface of the water.

The horses clomped and slipped, snorting and plunging their way ahead. One horse would balk and refuse to take another step while its teammate was still traveling on. Then the horse would give a nervous jump and scramble on, slipping on the logs as he did so. By then, his teammate would have decided to balk. We jerked our way across the precarious floating bridge, and I breathed a sigh of relief when the wagon wheels finally touched solid ground again.

The horses, sweating more from nerves than from exerted energy, were even more skittery now, so when the first loud crack of thunder greeted us, they jumped and would have bolted had Wynn not been prepared and held tightly to the reins.

I moved uneasily on the seat, my eyes on the clouds overhead. It would pour any minute and there was no place to go for shelter.

Wynn urged the team on. It was impossible to expect them to run. The wagon was much too heavy and the track too poor, but he did ask of them a brisker walk. They obliged, seeming as reluctant as we were to be caught in the storm.

Just as the rain began to spatter about us, we rounded a corner and there before us was a shed! It was not in good repair and we weren't sure what its use had been in the past; but it was shelter, and Wynn turned off the rutted track, heading the team quickly for it.

"Run in before you get soaked, Elizabeth," he urged, helping me down from the wagon seat. I did not stop to argue.

Wynn hastened to unhitch the team and then he was there, bringing the horses right in with him. He moved them to the far end of the shed and tied them to a peg in the wall. A loud crack of thunder made me jump and the horses whinney in fright. Now the rain came in sheets. I had never seen it rain so hard.

The shelter we had found was in no way waterproof. We had to watch where we stood in order to prevent the rain from running down our necks.

There was one spot along the south wall where it seemed to be quite dry. Wynn pointed to it and suggested we sit there to wait out the storm. The building had a dirt floor and again I was glad that I still wore the pants. We sat on the floor and leaned against the wall of the building. Outside the angry storm continued to sweep about us, flashing and booming as it passed over our heads.

It did not last long. In less than a half hour or so it was over. The dark clouds moved on, the thunder continuing to rumble in the distance.

The storm had not improved our road any. Where we had, a few minutes before, been traveling in dust, we now were in muck. Wynn said we were lucky—such a hard rain had a tendency to run off rather than to soak like gentler rain would have done. But I wondered how the trail could possibly have gotten any muddier.

I felt sorry for the horses as they labored through the mud which made the already heavy load even heavier. We both walked whenever we could find halfway decent footing to save them the extra weight. Wynn stopped frequently to let them catch their breath. Their sides heaved and their backs began to steam; but they seemed impatient to get on with it and were soon chomping at the bit at every stop.

The storm brought one blessing. For a few merciful minutes, the mosquitoes stayed away. I was just about to share my joy with Wynn when the pests began to buzz around us again.

"I've been told that there are some trappers who live along this route," Wynn informed me as we trudged on. "I had hoped to make it to their cabin tonight."

I was glad to hear there were people living along the trail. Then I remembered Charlie.

"Just men?" I asked.

"No, they have womenfolk—and children, I believe."

That was even better news.

"How far?"

"I'm not sure. I've never been up this way before."

"Do you think we'll make it by dark?"

"I'm hoping so—but, if not, we'll be fine camping out if we need to. Remember, you had wanted the experience of sleeping under the stars on our Banff honeymoon."

I nodded. I remembered well. And then our honeymoon had been cut so short there wasn't time.

"It might be fun," I answered Wynn. "Do you think it will rain some more?"

Wynn checked the sky. "I don't think so. Not tonight. Maybe a little tomorrow."

"Oh, dear," I fairly groaned at the news. "Will we get held up again tomorrow?"

"I hope it won't be stormy enough to stop us—but it might be rather miserable traveling for a spell."

The long summer day of sunlight allowed us to continue traveling till after ten o'clock. We had not even stopped to eat, munching instead on hard, dry sandwiches and sipping water from the flask Wynn had filled that morning.

"Well," Wynn said, just as I was beginning to realize how very weary I was, "I'm afraid we are going to have to give up on that cabin. We need to stop. You must be exhausted, Elizabeth, and the horses need a chance to rest and feed."

I looked around at the scraggly evergreens. We had passed through much prettier spots earlier in the day.

"It looks like there might be a clearing just up ahead. The grass should be better there. Let's have a look."

Wynn was right. Much to our surprise, at the opposite side of the clearing stood a small log cabin.

"Well, look at that," said Wynn, relieved. "The trappers. And right when we need them."

The cabin appeared to be very small. I looked around for another one.

Wynn had mentioned more than one family. I couldn't see another cabin. It must be hidden in the trees.

"Do you think one of the families might have room for us?" I asked Wynn.

Wynn smiled. "Oh, they'll have room all right. Even if we all have to stand still to manage it, there'll be room."

I looked perplexed and Wynn explained. "Hospitality in the North is as much a part of life as eating and sleeping. They might not have much, but whatever they have is yours."

As we approached the cabin, I looked down at myself in embarrassment. Wynn had said there were women here, and I would be turning up at their door in my male attire looking like a pincushion—bites and scratches and bruises indicating a much-used pincushion at that. I didn't have the time or the opportunity to make any repairs on my appearance. We had already been spotted.

We were met in the yard by four small children—three boys and a girl. I had never seen such chewed-up hands and faces in my life. I was a mess, but they were even more so. They seemed to take it all for granted, chatting with us and swatting insects as though it was the most natural thing in the world.

The children ushered us into the house and, to my surprise, we found that it was home to two families. The men saw no reason to furnish and supply wood for more than one cabin. It was one long, open room shared by four adults and four children. Another baby was on the way, probably due any day.

The woman who met us at the door and welcomed us in was just as mosquito-bitten as the children, as was the one who turned from the stove and smiled a shy welcome. I relaxed about how I looked, but at the same time I winced. Would I look like this the entire time I lived in the north country? *Surely not, God*, I whispered in dismay.

With great ceremony we were immediately seated at a crude table, while the woman at the stove brought huge bowls of steaming stew and set them before us. They had been about to have their evening meal; and upon our arrival, the women had given us their places at the table. I wanted to protest, but Wynn nudged me forward and I understood that to decline their invitation as welcomed guests might offend them. With mixed feelings I sat down and smiled at them appreciatively. I was hungry and the food smelled delicious.

I recognized none of the vegetables I saw in my dish. Wynn informed me that the women were experts at combing the forest for edible plants. I smiled at them again, thanking them for sharing their supper.

"We be so glad to see ya, yer doin' *us* the favor," declared the older one with simple courtesy.

No grace was said before we began, so I offered, unobtrusively, my own short prayer of thanks. I blessed Wynn's food as well, as the men did not give him any time for such an observance. Immediately they began plying him with questions about the outside world.

The children ate noisily. It was plain that manners were not considered necessary around this table. A common cup passed from person to person with the hot drink that went with the meal. I smiled and passed it on. To my chagrin, Wynn lifted it without hesitation and drank deeply. I fervently prayed again—that God would keep him from getting some dreadful disease.

"That was very good," I said to the cook when we had finished. "I wish we had time to let you show me how to make it."

She dipped her head shyly.

"Wasn't nothin'," she stated. "It's the bear that gives it the flavor."

"Bear?" I echoed, feeling my stomach contract.

"Bear meat's 'bout the best there is," observed her cabin-sister.

For a moment, I thought I would bolt from the table; but then I saw Wynn's amused eyes on my face and I swallowed hard and smiled.

"Well, it certainly is," I answered her evenly. "That was very tasty."

I saw the look of unbelief cross Wynn's face, and I smiled again—directly into his eyes. "Maybe when we get settled, you can shoot a bear," I challenged him, "and *I* can make *you* some stew like this."

He laughed outright. I'm sure no one else at the table understood our little joke.

We did spend the night with the trappers and their families. There were two beds in the room. We were given one of them. The two women took the other; and the two men, without comment or protest, took robes and blankets from a stack in the corner and spread out on the floor with the children, everyone sleeping fully clothed.

13

The Last Day on the Trail

AFTER WYNN HAD dressed my injured leg the next morning and expressed again his pleasure at how nicely it was healing, we were on our way. With luck, this would be our last day on the trail.

I followed Wynn's advice and draped a scarf over my head and down around my neck, but the pesky little mosquitoes and flies still got at me. The hairline at the back of my neck seemed to be their special delight.

"How do the people stand it?" I asked Wynn as I scratched at the swelling lumps.

"It's one of the things they learn to live with," he shrugged.

I didn't like the answer. Mostly because I knew that it implied I must learn to live with it as well.

It was a beautiful July day; and, though clouds passed by overhead, it did not rain. The warm sun soon had dried the rain of the day before from the track. Only in spots did we still plow through messy, gooey, wet places, the horses throwing themselves against their collars and straining to pull the heavy wagon. Wynn would always stop them for a breather and soon they were chomping and straining to be on the way again.

Occasionally, we traveled along the banks of a stream or beside a still lake. The fish would jump to feed on the swarming insects that got too near the water's surface. I wished them good hunting—each fish's dinner was one less to bother me!

We stopped around noon in an area covered with tall fir trees. I recognized several different varieties, but I didn't know enough to be able to separate them by name. Wynn was much too busy unhitching the horses and getting the fire going to answer questions, so I walked off alone, observing as I walked and storing questions for later. I kept Wynn in sight so I wouldn't get lost.

By the time the fire was burning briskly, I was back to help with our meal.

We did not stop for long.

In a swampy area I spotted a mother moose and her young one, even without Wynn pointing them out to me. I was pleased with myself.

"Look!" I cried. "A moose—two mooses."

Wynn smiled and nodded his head as he followed my pointing finger. He turned to me and said simply, "I must correct you, Elizabeth, so you won't be laughed at. —Moose is both singular and plural."

I guess I had known that; but, in my excitement, I had forgotten. I nodded in appreciation of Wynn's concern for me. I also appreciated the fact that he had not laughed.

I watched the moose until they were lost from sight and then I turned to Wynn. "What else?" I asked.

"What else, what?" he puzzled.

"What other animal names are both singular and plural?"

"Deer. Elk. Caribou." Wynn stopped.

"Bear?" I asked him.

"Bear? No, it's quite all right to refer to 'The Three Bears.'"

"Any other?"

"Likely."

"Likely? You mean you don't know?"

"They don't come to mind right now."

"How will I know what to say if—?"

He smiled at me and reached to push back a lock of unruly hair that insisted upon curling around my cheek. "You'll learn. You're very quick."

I flushed slightly under his smile and the compliment. It was good to know Wynn was not afraid that he might be embarrassed by his city-bred wife.

"Are we almost there?" I asked Wynn like a child for the tenth time. We had stopped for our evening meal.

He smiled at me and spread out his map. He carefully studied our surroundings, looking for some identifying signs. I couldn't make head nor tail of Wynn's map. After a moment of study, he pointed to a spot on the map. "We are about here," he said. "That should leave us about nine or ten miles to go. No, not quite," he corrected himself. "More like seven to eight."

"Will we make it tonight?"

"I certainly hope so—but it won't be early. It's a good thing we have lots of daylight for traveling. I'm afraid we're going to need it."

I loaded our supper things back in the wagon while Wynn hitched the horses, and we were on our way again. Perhaps we had made our last stop—I certainly hoped so. Excitement took hold of me as I thought of how close I was getting to my *new home*.

The horses seemed to sense they were getting close to home, too; and Wynn had to hold them back in spite of their tiredness and the heavy wagon they pulled.

I felt too excited and tense to even talk, so the last leg of our journey was a quiet one. But my mind was full of questions—some that even Wynn would not have been able to answer, not having lived at Beaver River himself. *What will our little cabin be like? What will our neighbors be like? Will there be any white women at the Post? Will the Indians like me and accept me? Will I ever be able to converse with them?* The thoughts whirled about in my head, making me almost dizzy.

The sun dropped into the west, closer and closer to the horizon. Still we had not reached Beaver River, and I was beginning to wonder if Wynn had made an error in his estimation—easily forgiven considering the little information he had been given. I was about to wonder aloud when Wynn spoke.

"Would you spread out that map on your lap, please? I want to take another look at it while it's still light enough to see well."

I spread out the map and, without comment, Wynn began to refigure.

"If I've got it worked out right, the settlement should be right over this next hill."

I wanted to shout for joy. In my excitement I reached over and gave Wynn a quick and unexpected hug which sent his Stetson tumbling into the dust of the roadway. By the time Wynn got my arms untangled and the team stopped, his Royal North West Mounted Police hat had been run over by the steel rim of the heavy wagon wheel. Horrified, I watched Wynn walk back to retrieve the poor thing from the dirt. It was now quite flat where it should have been nicely arched. I covered my remorseful face with my hands but Wynn returned to the wagon smiling; and, after a bit of pummeling and a punch here and there, he settled the hat back on his head—a few unsightly lumps, but it was in better shape than I had dared to hope.

Wynn was right. As we rounded the brow of the hill before us, there lay the little settlement at our feet. I refrained myself from hugging Wynn again. Instead, it was Wynn who hugged me.

"There it is, Elizabeth," he whispered against my cheek. "There's home."

"Home," I repeated. It was a magic word and brought tears to my eyes. I tucked my arm within Wynn's, even though he did need both hands on the reins. To think of it! We were almost home.

In the gathering dusk, it looked like a friendly little village to me. We could see the flag flying high over the Hudson's Bay Company Store. Scattered all around that central building were others of various sizes. At our approach, dogs began to set up a howl. People appeared in doorways and looked our way. A few of them even waved an arm to the approaching team. I suppose everyone in the settlement knew well who was in the coming wagon. They would be waiting to size up the new lawman and his wife. I held Wynn's arm more tightly.

"Tell me again," I asked, "what did you say the name of the Hudson's Bay man was?"

"McLain," said Wynn. "Ian McLain."

"And he's not married?"

"I couldn't find anyone who knew. I asked, but no one had heard of a Mrs. McLain."

"I suppose that means there isn't one," I said in resignation.

"Not necessarily. There really isn't much reason for the records to show if there is a wife or not. The agent is listed, not his family."

I took this as a spark of hope, but I wasn't going to count too strongly on another white woman in the village.

Darkness was closing in quickly now that we had passed down the hill. Windows were beginning to light up with lamps. The noise of the dogs increased as more people gathered around. I looked over the crowd of white men and several Indians. My eyes searched on. Who was Mr. McLain? Was he alone?

Wynn pulled the team to a halt before the large Hudson's Bay building and called out a friendly greeting to the men gathered there. A tall, square man with a heavy beard stepped forward. "Welcome to Beaver River, Sarge," he said. "Name here is Ian McLain."

He was alone.

14
Home

W YNN SHOOK HANDS with many of the men who had gathered around and nodded his head to others as he moved about. For a moment I felt forgotten. I didn't know whether to climb down from the wagon or to stay where I was until someone noticed me. Eventually I could feel eyes turning my way. Wynn invited the Hudson's Bay Post employee closer to the wagon and smiled up at me. "My wife, Elizabeth. Elizabeth, Mr. McLain."

McLain reached up and gave my hand a hearty shake.

"Come in. Come in," boomed Mr. McLain, but Wynn cut in rather quickly.

"We've had a long six days, and Elizabeth is anxious to get settled. If you could just point out the cabin for our use, we'd be grateful."

Mr. McLain nodded in understanding. He pointed west toward a stand of trees. The outline of a cabin showed faintly against the last glimmer of daylight.

"Right on over there," he informed us.

"Is there a place there to keep the horses?"

Mr. McLain took a look at the team and suddenly remembered something.

"Where's Canoue?" he asked.

"Sleeping when I last saw him. He got to sharing whiskey with the boys and I wasn't able to rouse him. I couldn't wait, so we left him behind."

The Hudson's Bay man shook his head. "He has his problems with the bottle. I warned him. 'Canoue,' I said, 'don't you go messin' this one up. I can't keep findin' you work if ya ain't able to stay with it.' Needed that money." McLain shrugged his shoulders. "There ain't no place for horses over to 'the law'; you can bring 'em back on over here. I got a corral out back," the man continued.

All the time this conversation was taking place, I could feel eyes studying me. Mostly we were surrounded by men, but now I saw a few Indian women and some young people and children. I smiled at them, though I must admit I felt as out of place and uncomfortable as I ever had in my life. I was anxious for Wynn to end his conversation and get us out of there and home.

At last he climbed back up into the wagon, turned the team around and headed for the little cabin which was to be our first home.

I felt tingles go all through me. What would it be like? Would it be in good repair? Would it have that private bedroom I wanted so badly? I fought the temptation to close my eyes until I actually got there. I was anxious and afraid—all at one time.

When Wynn said "whoa" to the team, I knew the moment was at hand. He turned to me and drew me close. "Well," he murmured softly, "are you ready?"

I couldn't get my lips to move, so I just nodded my head against him. "What will you need tonight?"

I really didn't know. I had no idea what I might find in the cabin.

Then we heard voices behind us and turned to see a group approaching. It was McLain's voice that called out to us.

"Thought we might as well unload that there wagon tonight and save ya the trouble in the mornin'. Then ya won't need to fuss with the team ag'in."

It was a thoughtful offer, and I was sure Wynn appreciated it. I should have appreciated it, too, but I had wanted to enter our new home in privacy—just the two of us. Now we were to be ushered in by the Hudson's Bay trader and a host of local trappers. I felt disappointment wash over me. If only Wynn would quickly send them all away and tell them the load could wait until morning. He didn't. He withdrew his arm, climbed down from the wagon, and turned to help me down. "Appreciate that," he responded. "Shouldn't take long at all with the good help you've brought along." I blinked away tears in the semidarkness and knew instinctively that Wynn would not understand how I, as a woman, felt about the intrusion. He would consider the practical fact that the wagon loaded with heavy trunks and crates needed unloading. I sentimentally thought that a man and his wife deserved to walk into their first home alone and together. Perhaps foolishly, I realized now, I had had visions of being carried over the threshold.

By the time my feet were firmly planted on the ground, the men were already bustling about the wagon.

"Perhaps you'd like to go in and show them where you would like things put," Wynn suggested.

I wanted to sputter that I would prefer things left right where they were, but I knew that was foolish and would be misunderstood; so I walked numbly to the door as Mr. McLain, who had taken the first crate forward, stood aside to let me get the door for him. How romantic!

The door was stuck, and I had to put both hands on the knob and pull hard. It finally gave and, in the process, skinned my knuckles. The injured hand stung smartly, and the tears in my eyes multiplied and spilled down my cheeks before I could stop them.

The house was dark. I had no idea where to find light. It was quite dark outside by now and the few small windows let in very little light. I hesitated. McLain shuffled his feet. He was waiting for me to make up my mind so he could rid himself of the heavy load he carried.

"Just set it down against that wall," I told him.

I guess he realized I was a little at a loss, for he volunteered, "I'll see if I can find the lamp." He soon had it lit and placed where it could bring the most benefit to the men who were unloading our belongings.

In and out they went. Men I had never seen before were clumping in and out of my new home, never stopping to wipe their feet. One of them even spit on *my* floor. Wynn did not enter himself. He was far too busy overseeing the unloading. I stood dumbly in the middle of the room, wondering what I should do; and then I remembered I did indeed have a responsibility: I was to tell the men where to put things. How did I know where to put things? I still didn't even know what rooms we had to furnish. So I just pointed a finger, which they probably couldn't see anyway from behind their big loads, and said, "Over there," until one wall was stacked high with our belongings.

Finally the stream of groaning, heaving men stopped. There was only the sound of their voices from the yard. Wynn was talking to the men before they returned to their own homes. I tapped my foot impatiently. Why did he take so long? Why didn't he just thank them and send them away?

I noticed a soft hum, which was soon a whine. Then another and another, and I realized we had given the mosquitoes a wonderful welcome. The open door, with the lamp burning in the room to light their way in, had not been ignored. Already our cabin must be filled with hundreds of them. With an angry little cry, I rushed over and slammed the door shut.

Wynn was still talking to the men. I turned dejectedly to the stack of our belongings and wondered just where I might find some blankets to make a bed. Picking up the lamp, I went over and began to check the pile. Labels of contents didn't help me much. All the crates on the top seemed to be things for Wynn's use as northern-law-enforcer and area-medical-supplier.

How would I ever make a bed? The past few nights on the trail I had promised myself that I would need to endure sleeping in such makeshift ways only for a few nights, and then I would be in my own home and sleeping in my own clean and fresh-smelling bed. And now I couldn't find my bedding. As a matter of fact, I didn't even know if there was a bed. Just as I was leaving the room, lamp held high, to find out if there was a bed in the cabin, Wynn poked his head in the door. I sighed with relief until I heard his words, "I'm going to take the team over, Elizabeth. I shouldn't be long. You make yourself at home."

I don't suppose he could have chosen any words that would have upset me more. *Make yourself at home.* This was home? Piled boxes. No husband. No blankets for my bed. And me, bone-weary. All I wanted was a warm bath to remove the messy trail dirt and a clean bed to crawl into. *Then* I might have been able to make myself at home. And Wynn. I wanted Wynn—my husband. After all, it was because of him that I had come to this strange, faraway land.

I let the tears flow freely then. Wiping my eyes and sniffing dejectedly, I stumbled into another room with the lamp held before me. There was a table, a stove, some rough shelves, and a cot—but no bed, at least not one that would hold two people.

I did not stop to look further but went on through another door. This room had pegs along one wall, a dilapidated stand with drawers and, yes, a double bed. It even had a mattress rather than spruce boughs—at least it was a mattress of sorts. It wasn't very clean, and it was rather lumpy; but it was a mattress. There was no bedding. I looked around for a shelf and found one, but there was no bedding on it either.

Going back to the other room again, I looked all around but still found nothing that would provide bedding for the night. There were three chairs I had missed before. Two of them were wooden and the third an overstuffed chair sitting in front of a fireplace. I was pleased with the fireplace, and then I realized it was probably more functional than anything else. It was likely the only source of heat in the cabin. I flashed the lamp around the room once more. It was quite bare—and not too clean. And then I spotted something I had missed in my first perusal. Over the fireplace hung a large fur that had been tanned and used as decoration or heat-retainer—I wasn't sure which. I put my lamp down and walked over to it. I gave it a pull. The fur was firmly attached. I pulled again. It still stayed in place. I grasped it in both my hands and put all my strength into the pull. With a tearing sound and a billow of dust, it came tumbling down from the wall and I went tumbling down to the floor.

I pushed the heavy fur off and got to my feet. It felt rather unyielding and bristly, not soft like the furs I was used to seeing. I pulled it to the bedroom and worked it through the door. I then went back for the lamp. I did finally manage to get the fur up on the bed and spread out in some way.

I looked around me. This was my new home! It was bare and dirty and had a lumpy bed, with no sheets, no blankets, and a smelly fur hide. There were no curtains, no soft rugs, no shiny windows—nothing. Even the chimney of the sputtering lamp was dirty with soot. But, worst of all, I was alone! That thought brought the tears streaming down my face again. I carried the lamp back out to the other room and set it on the table—I'm afraid it was more to coax the mosquitoes out of the bedroom than to provide a safe and welcome light for Wynn. Then I walked back to the bedroom, kicked off my shoes, crawled under the awkward animal skin, and began to cry in earnest. I didn't even have my evening talk with God. I was so miserable I thought He'd rather not hear from me. And in my present state, I really didn't want to hear from Him. I was very weary, so I did not cry for long. Sleep mercifully claimed me.

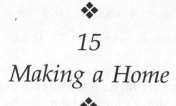

15
Making a Home

WHEN I AWOKE the next morning, it took me several minutes to sort out where I was. With the knowledge came some of the hurt of the night before, but it wasn't as painful as it had been then. I looked down at myself. I was now covered with blankets. The fur I had struggled with was spread out on the floor by the bed, looking soft and even inviting. I was still in my clothes, my skirt and blouse now wrinkled as well as travel-stained. I knew my hair must be a sight—I had not even removed the pins the night before. They had worked loose in the night, so now part of my hair hung wildly about my face while part of it was still caught up with one pin or another. I removed the last pins and let my hair all tumble about my shoulders, combing my fingers through it to make some order out of the mess.

At my faintest stirring, Wynn was there, concern and pain in his face. "Are you—?" But he didn't finish. Instead, he pulled me into his arms and held me so tightly I had to fight for air. "I'm so sorry, Elizabeth," he whispered, and there was a tremble in his voice.

I looked up at him then and saw his eyes were misted with unshed tears. It brought my tears again. I clung to Wynn and cried away all the feelings I had bottled up the night before. He let me cry.

When the tears finally stopped, Wynn tipped my head and looked deeply into my eyes. Perhaps he was looking for answers to some unspoken questions. I wasn't quite ready to smile yet, but I was ready to carry on. I avoided his eyes by shutting mine. He kissed me softly and then let me go.

"Are you hungry?" he asked. It wasn't until then that I smelled coffee. Surprisingly, I realized I *was* hungry. I looked again at my clothes and my hands.

"I'm not sure what I need the most," I said, "food or a bath."

"How about the food first? Then we'll look after that bath."

I slipped into my shoes and futiley smoothed my skirt. Then I looked at Wynn. "Where do I go here?" I asked him.

He understood my question. "Out," he answered.

"Just—out?"

He nodded.

"You mean they don't even have any—any—outbuilding here in the village?"

"We're a quarter of a mile from the village."

"Still—"

"I'll make arrangements as soon as possible," Wynn stated and turned away to return to whatever he had been doing before I awakened. The pain was in his eyes again. I thought he might be thinking that he had been right—a girl like me didn't belong in the north country. I blinked back some new tears that stung my eyes and went *out*.

The day was filled with sunshine. A large flock of birds chattered in the nearby trees where they were already gathering, making their plans to return to lands where winter snow would not blow. In the village, a quarter of a mile away, I heard distant voices and barking dogs. I breathed deeply of the morning air. The hillsides were covered with evergreens and scattered with poplar and birch trees.

It was beautiful country. I would make it. I would! I would fix the house and—and—clean myself up, and I'd prove to Wynn that I could be happy here—as long as he was with me. A nagging fear gripped me then. What about all the times Wynn's duties would take him elsewhere? Like last night? He had to care for the borrowed team. He couldn't just turn them over to the Hudson's Bay trader. That man had his own responsibilities. Wynn had done only what needed to be done, and yet . . . It was going to take a lot of resolve on my part to create a home, a happy home, in Wynn's wilderness. I couldn't crumble like I had last night every time I faced difficulties, every time modern conveniences were not at my disposal. I wanted to be happy here. Most of all, I wanted to make Wynn happy. I was going to need help. I knew of only one true source readily available to me. I stopped for a few moments of prayer.

By the time I returned to the cabin, I had myself in hand again. Wynn was busy with the crates. He had carried my trunk to the bedroom and placed it beside the wall under the one lone window. I opened the lid, hoping to find a more suitable skirt and blouse in which to be seen at breakfast; but the ones I lifted from the trunk were just as wrinkled as those I wore. I gave up and went to see if I could find a basin to wash my hands. Wynn had already set one out, and a towel was hanging on a peg beside it.

I washed and moved on to the stove. The coffeepot was sending out a delightful aroma and Wynn had made a batch of pancakes that needed only to be poured on the griddle. It was hot and ready, so I began to spoon out the batter. The sizzle and the good smell made my stomach beg for a taste.

Wynn was soon in the kitchen beside me. "Smells good," he said, his hands on my shoulder behind me. "I had a tough time waiting."

"Why didn't you go ahead—or waken me?"

"I thought you needed the rest. And I didn't want to start my first day without you."

I swallowed hard and willed away the tears. That was all over now. I needed to put it firmly behind me.

"So what do you think?" I said, in order to initiate conversation.

"Think?" asked Wynn.

"About the cabin," I went on.

"It's bigger than I had dared to hope." Wynn sounded pleased, and I realized for the first time that he was right. I had seen three rooms in the darkness. I had been hoping for at least two. I had not even thought till now to be thankful.

I smiled at Wynn now. "That's right. I had hoped for a private bedroom, and it has a private living area as well." I looked around me. It wasn't much, this living area, but it had possibilities. There was the fireplace, with one small chunk of the fur I had yanked down the night before still dangling over it. There was a window looking out to the east and the village. There was the cot with the hard-looking covering, the, well—the *easy* chair. Nearer at hand were the stove, some makeshift cupboards, the table and two chairs, and a stand where the basin and two large pails of water rested.

"Where'd they come from?" I asked Wynn. I had not noticed the pails the night before, and they weren't the ones from the teacherage that I had given Wynn to pack for our use.

"I borrowed them," he answered simply. "I thought you'd be aching for a bath last night so I asked McLain for them. It took us awhile to heat that much water—I guess I would have been wiser to have hurried back instead of waiting on it."

I looked at the heavy pails. They were filled almost to the brim. Wynn had carried them full of hot water the night before—for a quarter of a mile—hurrying and stumbling through the dark so I might have a bath. And what had he found? A childish woman who had cried herself to sleep under a musty old hide.

I crossed to Wynn, the pancake turner still in my hand. I reached my arms up and tightened them around his neck. "I'm sorry," I whispered.

He held me and kissed me. We didn't speak. I guess we were both busy sorting out thoughts. The smell of burning pancakes pulled me back to reality. Fortunately, they weren't so burned we couldn't eat them. In fact, after the dried and canned trail fare, they tasted good.

Wynn helped unpack our crates and trunks. It took us all morning to sort through our things and get them into the rooms where they would be used. After a light lunch, Wynn had some things to attend to at the store. I assured him I would be just fine. I was going to be very busy with a scrub brush and hot, soapy water.

I was scrubbing out the shelves which would be our kitchen cupboards when I heard men's voices. I expected a knock on our door, but after several minutes when none came I went to the window and cautiously looked out. Two men, with a team of horses and a dilapidated old wagon piled with rough lumber, were busily studying a large sheet of paper and arguing over the right way to go about their assigned task. They must have figured something out, for soon shovels, hammers and saws were industriously put to work. I was puzzled at first; and then as the small building began to take shape in the late afternoon, I realized Wynn had lost no time in keeping his promise. There was to be a private outbuilding—and soon. I felt a pang at having caused Wynn this additional problem, but at the same time I was greatly relieved. I couldn't imagine living for very long without some kind of accommodation.

I kept scrubbing and cleaning, and the men outside continued pounding. My back began to ache and my arms cramp. Still I kept on. I was determined to have a clean house by nightfall.

I did the cupboards, the windows, the floors. I wiped off the mattress of the bed and managed to drag it outside for a bit of air and sunshine. I pulled the hard seat covering of the cot out into the sun, too. Then I washed all our dishes and pots and pans and put them on the newly scrubbed shelves. I arranged tins and cans of food on the remainder of the shelves, stacking some things on the floor. There just wasn't room for everything to be put away. Certain items, like the dishpan, the frying pan, and some of the utensils, I hung on the pegs on the wall.

It didn't make a particularly tidy-looking kitchen, but it was clean, and I was pleased. I put away the thought of asking Wynn for doors on my cupboards to conceal all the clutter. It was enough that I was getting the little outbuilding and, as I considered it the far more important of the two, I would just do without the cupboard doors—or I would think of some way to conceal the shelves myself.

It was getting late in the afternoon when I went out to retrieve the mattress from the stumps where I had propped it in the sun. It was even harder to drag back in than it had been to get it out; but after much tugging and yanking, I finally managed to get it back in on the bed. I made up the bed then with clean sheets and blankets. How good it would be to have our own clean bed to sleep in again. I took my clothes from the trunk and hung them on the pegs in the wall. They were still wrinkled, but I would have to wait to get to that. I couldn't do everything in one day.

By the time Wynn arrived home, the house was in quite good order—that is, the two rooms which we considered our house. The large room that was to be Wynn's office still needed to be arranged, but Wynn had told me to leave that to him. We had been delighted and surprised at the discovery of a storage room off the bedroom. Our crates, boxes, and supplies could all be kept there, out of our living accommodations. Wynn had placed the crates in the little room as we had emptied them that morning.

Our supper that night came from tins of North West Mounted Police rations. I had no other meat and no vegetables of any kind. It was a simple meal, but we ate with a deep feeling of satisfaction. We were where we belonged, doing what we felt called to do. We had a home, and we had one another. True, there was much more that needed to be done before we were *settled*, but we had made a good start. I forgot my tired arms and back and chatted with Wynn about all the possibilities the little cabin held. I looked out of my window to the rough little shanty with its crooked door and crude shingles and felt more thankful for it than for the fanciest bathroom. "Thanks, Wynn," I said, "for having that little building built so soon. I appreciate your thoughtfulness."

"I want to make you happy and as comfortable as possible," he said with a smile.

This was our start in our new life. After a good, hot soak in the tub I had found hanging on the outside wall, I was sure that I would feel content with my world.

16
Neighbors

WYNN WAS VERY busy taking on his Mountie responsibilities in the next few days, and I managed to keep just as busy. I was trying so hard to turn our little cabin into a real home. The material I had purchased in Calgary came out of the trunk, and I set to work in earnest with needle and thread. It was not an easy task. The material was heavy and, as I had no access to a sewing machine, I had to do all the sewing by hand. There were no frills. I made things as simple as I could. Soon the windows had curtains and the cot resembled a couch with its new spread over the hard foundation. I hand-stitched some cushions to toss on the cot, and it took on a homey look. Wynn surprised me with some fur rugs he purchased from an old trapper who tanned his own. They were much nicer than the old one I had pulled from the wall. Wynn moved that one onto his office floor. I placed the two new ones on the floor in front of the fireplace and beside our bed. They added a nice touch to the rooms, though I still couldn't get used to the odd smell lingering around them.

I had found the irons Wynn had packed for us and constructed a makeshift ironing board on which I was able to remove some of the wrinkles from our clothing. I wasn't satisfied with the job, however, but I shrugged it off as the best that could be done under the circumstances. We came to our first Sunday in the North. It was strange not having a church to attend. I asked Wynn what we would do in the place of a Sunday service. I suggested we might have our own and invite the people from the village to join us, but he felt it would be wise to take our time with any such plans. Then he proposed that, if I liked, we could take our lunch and go for a hike along the river. I was pleased with his idea and at once went to see what would be suitable for a picnic.

The countryside was beautiful. A few of the trees were already beginning to show their fall colors. It seemed awfully early to me, but I was reminded that we were now much farther north than I had been used to.

We didn't walk far. Everything was so new to me that I kept stopping for a good look and questions. Wynn answered them patiently. We saw a couple of cabins back in the bush, not far from the stream, and I asked Wynn if he knew who lived there.

"Not yet," he answered. "This next week I expect to find out more about our neighbors. I'll be gone a good deal of the weekdays, Elizabeth. Some nights I won't get home until quite late."

I nodded my head but said nothing.

"Does that bother you?"

I was slow to answer. I wouldn't look forward to long days without Wynn. But I had spent some time in prayer my first morning in the settlement, and some of my praying had been about that very issue.

I was able to say honestly now, "I'll miss you, certainly. But I'll be all right. I had a—a long talk with God about it and—I understand. I know that you can't stay in your office all the time. Or even around the settlement. I'll be fine. I still have so many things to do that I'll keep busy."

I managed a smile.

Wynn reached for my hand. "I know you've been very busy. Our little house looks much different since you've fixed it up, and I'm proud of you." His smile of appreciation filled me with a warm glow. "I've been wondering, though, if you might find some time now to get acquainted with some of our neighbors," he went on. "We will be living among them; it would be nice if you could soon find some friends."

"I've been meaning to," I told him. "Every day I've been telling myself, 'Today I will walk over to the store and meet some of the people.' But each time I find something more that needs to be done, so I put it off again."

Wynn nodded in understanding.

"I'll take some time this week. Tomorrow I need to do the washing, but maybe Tuesday I can go to the store."

"I'd like that. I'd like you to get to know some of the women so you might have company on the days I'm away."

I was quiet for a few moments. Wynn noticed.

"Something's bothering you," he commented, more as a statement than a question.

"Not 'bothering' really. It's just—well, I worry some about how I'll ever—" I didn't know just how to express that strange little fear twisting inside of me. Finally I just blurted out, "How do you get to know people when you can't talk to them?"

"You'll be able to talk to them. Oh, I know it will be hard and there will be times when you'll have problems expressing yourself. But you will pick up a few of their words quickly—many of the Indians already know a number of English words. Then there are always signs. The Indians are very good at making one understand them by using their limited English and their hands. They point out all kinds of messages. You'll catch on quickly—but you can't learn about them if you are not with them."

I knew Wynn was right, and I determined I would no longer hide behind my work but would venture forth and meet my new neighbors. It would be so much easier for me if Wynn could be along, but I knew his duties did not allow time for him to escort me around.

The sky was beginning to cloud over, so I picked up our picnic remains and we hurried to our cabin. The day suddenly went from sunshine to overcast to a thunderstorm. Wynn made a fire in the fireplace and we stretched out before it on the bear rug and talked about the people we had left behind and the folks who were our new neighbors here.

Thus far, my contact with the villagers was only on the night we had arrived. I had seen and been seen by a circle of friendly looking faces. Thinking back on it, though, I would have called them more curious than friendly. I could not remember even one smile except from the big man, Ian McLain. From my window I had watched as the two workmen had constructed our little shanty out back, and I had seen a few Indian women and children at a distance as they walked one or another of the paths that passed by our place. They always looked toward our cabin with a great deal of interest. But none of them had stopped and, as I hadn't known what to say to them, I had not called a greeting or invited them in.

Well, all of that must change. Even if it did mean learning a difficult new language, I must somehow break down the barriers and get to know my northern neighbors. *If only,* I mourned to myself, *one of them were a white woman.* There would be a common ground, a common bond, with her.

"You haven't even been in the Hudson's Bay Store, have you?" Wynn was asking.

"Not yet."

"I think you'll be surprised at the number of things available there. Of course, they are quite expensive. The shipping charges added to the cost make it far wiser to bring all you can with you rather than pay the extra price."

I remembered the heavy wagon loaded with all the crates, barrels, and boxes that brought our belongings to the settlement.

"Did that driver ever turn up?" I asked suddenly, my thoughts going back to our experience on the trail.

"Driver?"

"The one who should have driven us here but who was sleeping—?"

"Oh, him. Yes, he came walking in a couple of days ago—with all kinds of excuses and stories. Ian gave him a good scolding—like one would scold a child. Then Mrs. McLain filled the fellow up with roast duck and baking powder biscuits."

"Mrs. McLain?"

"Didn't I tell you? There is a Mrs. McLain after all."

My face must have beamed. I could hardly wait now for the opportunity to go into the settlement for my first visit. It would be so nice to have a chat with another woman. Perhaps I would even be able to invite her for tea on one of the afternoons when Wynn was away. It would help to fill in a long day.

"What is she like?"

"I haven't met her. I just overheard McLain telling about the wayward team driver and the lecture and then her feeding him."

Attempting to picture Mrs. McLain, I began by imagining a woman my age, then quickly amended that. If she were married to McLain, she must be a good deal older than I.

"Do they have a family?" I queried.

"I haven't heard."

"Well, I'll find out all about them when I go to the store," I said, quite satisfied with the thought of my new venture.

Over our breakfast the next morning, I shared with Wynn my revised plans of going to the store that afternoon. He seemed pleased that I was making the venture to get acquainted.

"What can I say?" I asked him.

He looked puzzled. "What do you mean, what can you say?"

"Well, I can't just march in there and announce that I came to meet his wife."

Wynn smiled. "I'm not sure that would be so bad. People would be pleased to think that you are anxious to meet them. But—if you are hesitant to do that, do your purchasing first; and then, if you have a chance for a little chat with McLain, you shouldn't feel enbarrassed to mention the fact that you are most anxious to meet his wife."

"Purchases? I hadn't thought of purchasing anything."

"There must be something there you could use. Look around a bit."

I hesitated. Wynn looked at me questioningly.

I went on, slowly, picking out the words to voice my concern.

"You said it's a trading post, right? Well, I've never been—I've never bought anything at a trading post. I don't know how to . . . I've never *traded* for things before. What do I trade? I don't have any furs or—"

Wynn began to laugh. He reached out and lifted my chin and kissed me on the nose, but the laughter was still in his eyes. I knew I had just showed my city breeding. I either could get angry with Wynn for laughing at me or choose to laugh with him. For a moment I was very tempted to be angry. Then I remembered my father's prayer—the part about humor for the difficult times—and I began to laugh with Wynn. Well, not laugh really, but at least I smiled. "I take it I'm off-track?"

He smiled and kissed my nose again. "A little. It's true that it's a trading post and that the trappers bring their furs there. But Mr. McLain is very happy to accept good hard cash as well. However, for you that won't even be necessary. We have a charge account there with Mr. McLain. You pick what you need and he will enter it in his little book under my name. I also would like you to keep an account of what you spend, so I can enter it in my little book. That way, when Mr. McLain and I settle up each month, hopefully our accounts will agree."

I nodded. It all seemed simple enough.

After Wynn was gone, I hurried with the laundry. Wynn had already filled every available pail and the boiler that sat heating on our wood-burning stove.

The clothes were all hand-scrubbed on a galvanized board we had brought with us from Calgary. On any other laundry day I would have taken my time, but today I was so excited about the prospects of meeting Mrs. McLain that I rushed through everything. I was hoping to finish the wash around noon. Then I would have time to walk down to the store while the clothes dried on the outside lines.

Wynn did not come home for the noon meal, so I had a simple lunch and then hurried to tidy myself for my trip to the store. I was still a bit concerned as to exactly how to approach the subject of meeting Mr. McLain's wife. Maybe if I was really lucky, she would be in the store as well.

The afternoon was a bit breezy and my carefully groomed hair threatened to be undone from its pinning. I had chosen one of the best dresses I had brought along. It swished in the loose dirt of the trail into the settlement. I held my hat with one hand and my skirt up with the other.

Many small, sometimes shabby, shacks lined the sides of the clearing as I neared the store. They were not placed in any regular pattern but rather built wherever a man had a mind to build. Some had smoke streaming forth through small chimney pipes. Some of them had no chimney pipe, and the smoke billowed instead out of unglassed windows. Children of various sizes and states of dress played in the dusty areas surrounding them, stopping to stare at me out of dark eyes in round brown faces. Dogs seemed to be everywhere. Some of them looked ferocious, and I was glad a few of the meaner looking ones were tied up. I dared not imagine what might happen if they were given their freedom. Once or twice I took a brief detour in order to stay a little farther away from a dog that didn't seem to be friendly.

The little children weren't too friendly either. I smiled at many of them, but the expression on the small faces did not change. I could not blame them. To them I must have looked strange indeed with my piled-up, reddish-gold hair and my long, full skirt swishing at the ground as I walked. I decided that the next time I ventured forth I would wear something less conspicuous, but this time I had so wanted to make a favorable impression on the settlement's only other white woman.

When I reached the Hudson's Bay Store, Mr. McLain was busy with another customer. The man did not look totally white nor did he look totally Indian. I assumed this was one of the mixed race people who Wynn had said were common in the North. He spoke English, even though rather brokenly, and there were some words mixed in with it that I did not understand. Mr. McLain seemed to have no difficulty. The two got along just fine. In fact, Mr. McLain himself also interchanged his English with words I had never heard before.

Mr. McLain spoke to the man and then moved my way. "Good-day to ya, ma'am," he said with a big smile, "an' may I be helpin' ya with something?"

"I'll need a while to look," I assured him. "You go right ahead with your customer. I'm in no hurry."

He nodded to me and went back to the other man.

I looked around the store. Wynn had been right. I was surprised at the amount and variety of merchandise carried. I was also shocked at the prices. Three times I selected something from the shelf, and three times my frugal nature made me put it back. I was about ready to give up and leave the place in embarrassment when I spotted some tacks. Now I did need some tacks. They, too, were expensive; but as I truly did need them and as I couldn't possibly get them from anywhere else, I decided to buy them.

I had just made my selection when the other customer left the store and Mr. McLain came my way.

"Have ya found what you're needin'?" he boomed.

"Yes. Yes, I think these will be just fine," I fairly stammered.

Mr. McLain led the way to the counter. I laid the box of tacks on the wooden square by the cash box. They looked very small and insignificant.

"And will this be all?" asked Mr. McLain.

I guessed he was used to his customers coming in and buying supplies to last them for many weeks. Here I was buying only a box of tacks. It must seem to him very much like a wasted trip. I flushed.

"I'm still not settled enough to know my needs," I tried to explain, "and we brought most of our supplies with us." Then I wondered if that was good news to a man who ran the only local store. I flushed more deeply. "I—I mean—we'll certainly be needing many things as the winter sets in and all—"

Mr. McLain seemed not to notice my discomfiture.

"Everything in good shape at the cabin?" he asked.

"Fine," I answered, not too sure just what he meant. "Just fine."

"The man before you wasn't much of a housekeeper," he commented. "I had to send one of the trappers' wives over to sorta sweep out the place after he left. The fella before him—now, he was some fussy. Made the men take their boots off when they went to his office—finally got so many complaints, the department said he had to stop it." Mr. McLain shook his head. "He was some fussy all right, that one."

I appreciated his consideration in sending over a woman to clean our cabin. I had thought it dirty when I arrived—I couldn't imagine what it might have been before.

As Mr. McLain talked, he got out a big black book and flipped to a page marked "Delaney, R.N.W.P." and began to make an entry. There were already several items listed on the page. In my brief glance I noticed some of them were to do with lumber—probably the building the two men constructed for us.

I took one more glance around the room and then let my mind go back to Mrs. McLain. How did I broach the subject of meeting the trader's wife? Mr. McLain solved the problem for me.

"My wife's out back in the garden. She's right anxious to meet ya. Got a minute to step around with me and say howdy?"

A smile flashed across my face. "I'd love to," I stated as I tucked the small box of tacks in my handbag and prepared to follow Mr. McLain.

The garden was weed-free and very productive. I wished with all my heart that I had one just like it. Next year I must try. It would be so nice to have some fresh vegetables. Some of them here were unfamiliar to me, though there wasn't much variety. I knew the frosts came much earlier this far north. I had also been told that, because of the long summer days, some vegetables did very well, with the added hours of sunshine to make them grow rapidly.

I took my eyes from the plants and looked about for a woman. She was at the far end of the garden patch, her dark head bent over a row of beets to which she was giving her total attention.

"Nimmie!" Mr. McLain hollered. "Got Mrs. Delaney here."

The dark head lifted; then, in one graceful movement, the woman was standing and facing me. A quiet smile spread over her face. She moved to meet me, extending a hand as she came.

"I am so pleased to meet you," she said softly.

She was Indian.

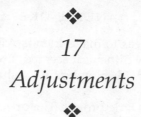

17

Adjustments

I WALKED HOME slowly, paying little attention to the staring children or the barking dogs. I had not stayed long to chat with Mrs. McLain. After my initial shock, there really didn't seem to be much to say. I hoped with all my heart that my shock hadn't shown on my face. Why hadn't Wynn warned me? Or had he known? And why hadn't I expected it? Wynn had told me that often the men in the North married Indian women. They were used to the lifestyle, the hardships, the work and weather, and weren't always fussing for their husbands to take them back to civilization. So why hadn't I prepared myself for that possibility?

I guess it was simply because I had so much wanted to have one white woman in the area, and it seemed that the Hudson's Bay man was the only candidate. In spite of telling myself that I was being foolish, I felt an intense disappointment. There wouldn't be a woman in the area after all with whom I could share intimacies. No one for little tête-à-têtes over an afternoon cup of tea. No one to understand women's fashions and women's fears. It was going to be a lonely time, the years ahead. They would be sure to get me down if I didn't take some serious steps to avoid allowing myself to be caught in the trap of self-pity.

I wasn't quite prepared at the moment to take those steps or to make future plans. For now it was enough just to sort out my thoughts and to spend some time in prayer concerning my feelings.

I did pray as soon as I got home, and I was feeling much better by the time I went to bring in the clothes and apply the irons to the garments.

As I ironed, I thought, *What might I have to offer these Indian people? What things do we as wives have in common?* What could I do to improve their living conditions? I knew Wynn didn't want me rushing in trying to change their way of life, but weren't there little things we might enjoy doing together?

Perhaps a sewing class? I was a good seamstress, though I did admit difficulty in adjusting from machine to hand work. It seemed so clumsy and slow to me, and my poor fingers always seemed to be pricked full of holes in spite of a thimble.

Sewing might be a good idea. Then we could have tea. Maybe Indian ladies enjoyed tea every bit as much as white ladies did. I began to feel excited about the prospects. By the time the ironing was completed, my plans had begun to take shape.

The first thing to do was to make friends with them. At the first opportunity, no matter how difficult it seemed, I was going to speak to the Indian women. Even if I made blunders, it would be a start. I would never learn unless I tried.

But first I had another little project. The open cupboard shelves bothered me. I had lots of material I had brought along; and now, with the help of the tacks obtained from Mr. McLain, I would do something about covering them.

As soon as my ironing was done, I put away the laundry and the makeshift board and went to Wynn's office in search of a hammer. I found one hanging on a nail with the rest of his few tools and went to work. With material, scissors, hammer and tacks, I soon had the open-cupboard area nicely draped with curtains. They hung in attractive folds and I was quite pleased. They certainly were an improvement on the exposed dishes, pots and pans, and food stuffs. I cut matching place mats for the table, hemming them up as I hummed to myself.

I was finished just in time to get busy with the supper preparations. I could hardly wait for Wynn to get home and see how much nicer the kitchen looked. Again I wished for a white woman to share with. She would have understood my satisfaction and pleasure with the accomplishments of the day. Wynn, being a man and troubled with the duties of a law officer, might not be able to fully appreciate just how important this little addition was to me. A woman would, I was sure.

Wynn did notice my kitchen, complimenting me on how nice it looked. I beamed with pleasure.

As we had our evening meal together, he asked me if I had met Mrs. McLain as planned. I did not want Wynn to know about my great disappointment in not finding a white woman, so I tried to make no comments that would give away my true feelings.

"She seems to be somewhat younger than Mr. McLain," I began.

"I understand that he was married before," commented Wynn.

"She has a garden," I said with some enthusiasm. "I would love to have one like it next year. It would be so nice to have fresh things."

Wynn agreed. "You shall have your garden next year," he smiled. "I'll even see that the ground is broken for you. I think fresh vegetables would be a treat, too. That's one thing, I must confess, I miss about Calgary."

"I didn't recognize all her vegetables," I confided, "but she had lots of carrots, beets, potatoes, and onions."

"What's she look like?" Wynn asked, remembering that looks might be considered important to a woman.

I hesitated. I hadn't really looked at Mrs. McLain too closely. I drew from my memory in the brief glances I had afforded her.

"She's dark, not too tall, rather slim."

It wasn't much of a picture; but I couldn't really remember much more.

"Was she pleasant?"

"Oh, yes. Most pleasant," I hurried with my reply.

"That's nice," said Wynn. "I'm glad you have a white woman to—"

So he hadn't known. "Oh," I interrupted him, hoping my remark sounded very offhand and matter of fact, "she isn't white. She's Indian."

I turned from Wynn to get the teapot, so I didn't see if his surprise equaled mine or not. When I turned back to him, his face told me nothing.

"I'm sure she'll be good company," he encouraged. "I hope you'll be good friends."

The next morning I heard some women's voices approaching our cabin on the trail to the west; and, true to my resolve, I went outside so I could greet them. Three Indian women approached me, talking rapidly as they came.

They were dressed in a combination of Indian buckskin and calico purchased at the trading post. Lovely beadwork made a splash of color against the natural tan of the soft deerskins.

At my appearance, things were suddenly very quiet.

I knew no Indian words. I had to take the chance that they might know a few English ones.

"Good morning," I said with a smile.

There was no response.

I tried again. "Hello."

They understood this. "Hello," they all responded in unison.

"I'm Elizabeth," I said, pointing a finger at myself. That seemed like such a long name to expect anyone to learn. I changed it. "Beth," I said, jerking my finger at my chest.

The youngest woman smiled and nodded to the others.

"Beth," I said again.

She giggled, hiding her face behind her hand.

I didn't know what to try next. I wanted to invite them in but didn't know what words to use. Well, since I only had English, I would use English.

"Would you like to come in?" I asked, waving my hand toward the cabin.

They looked puzzled.

"Come in?" I repeated.

The middle one seemed to get my meaning. She held up a basket she was carrying and said distinctly, "Berries."

I understood then that they were on their way to pick berries and didn't feel they had time to stop. At least, my logic came up with this information.

I nodded, to assure them I understood. The other two women lifted their containers to show me that they were berry-pickers as well.

I nodded again. How did one tell them that she wished them great success in their picking. I scrambled around in my mind for some words;

but before I could come up with something, the young woman surprised me by pointing a finger at me, lifting her basket in the air, waving a hand at the trail ahead, and saying, "Come?"

It caught me off-guard, but I was quick to respond.

"Yes," I smiled. "Yes, I'd love to come. Just wait until I get a pail."

I ran into the house, hoping they wouldn't misunderstand and go off without me. I quickly scribbled a note for Wynn in case he should come in while I was out, grabbed a small pail, my big floppy hat and a scarf to ward off mosquitoes, and dashed back out the door.

They were still waiting for me.

They took one look at my hat, pointed at it, and began to laugh loudly. There was no embarrassment, no discourtesy. They thought it looked funny and enjoyed the joke.

I laughed with them, even making the hat bounce up and down more than was necessary to give them a good show. They laughed harder, and then we moved on together down the path to the berry patch.

I had no idea where we were going. I decided to watch closely for landmarks in case I had to find my own way home. I wasn't much of a woodsman, and I would have hated to require Wynn's leaving his other duties to come looking for me.

We followed the path to the stream and the stream to the river and then followed the trail that paralleled the twists and turns of the river. I was sure I could find my way home so far.

We had gone maybe a mile and a half when the women cut away from the river and headed through the bush. There was no path now and I began to get worried. I could never find my way home without the aid of a path. I sincerely hoped the other women could. We might all be lost!

We walked for about another mile before we came to the berry patch. The bushes were thick with them, and they were delicious-looking. The women talked excitedly as they pointed here and there. Then they set right to work.

I couldn't begin to keep up with them. Their hands seemed to flash as they whipped berries into their containers. I tried to follow their examples but ended up spilling more berries than I got to my pail, so I decided it was wiser for me to take my own time and get the berries safely where they belonged.

While the women chatted, I listened intently. I tried so hard to formulate some pattern in their speaking, to pick out a word that was repeated and sort out its meaning; but it was hopeless. As they chatted, they often stopped to double over in joyful, childlike laughter. It was clear they were a people who knew how to enjoy themselves. I wished I could share in their jokes. Then I wondered if I might indeed be the butt of their jokes; but, no, they didn't seem to be laughing at me.

It was almost noon when the youngest one came over to where I was picking. She looked in my pail and seemed to be showing approval on my good job. Then she showed me her basket. She had picked twice as many. She knelt beside me and quickly picked a few handfuls which she threw in my pail. The others came with their full containers. They gathered around me and they, too, began to pick berries and deposit them in my pail. I was the only one who still had room in my container. With four of us picking, the pail was full in no time. I thanked them with a smile, and we all got up and stretched to ease the ache in our backs.

"Ouch," said the oldest lady, and everyone laughed.

We started home then, full containers of berries carefully guarded. It was well after noon when we arrived at my house, and none of us had had anything to eat. I was starving. I wondered if they were, too.

"Would you like to come in?" I asked them, motioning toward the door.

They shook their heads and nodded toward their baskets, informing me that they had to go home to care for the berries. I lifted my pail then. "Some of these are yours," I reminded them, pointing to the berries and then at their baskets.

I began to scoop out berries to add to their already full containers, but they shook their heads and pulled the baskets away.

"Keep," one of them said, the others echoing, "Keep."

I thanked them then and they went on their way, while I went to find something to eat and then to care for my own bountiful supply of berries. Such a delightful surprise! The berries were sweet and juicy and would be such a welcome addition to our simple meals. And the contact with the Indian women had been just as pleasant a surprise.

I wondered where they lived and if I would see them again.

I told Wynn I had a surprise for supper that night.

"Where did you get these?" he asked in astonishment when I brought out the pie.

"I picked them myself—well, at least most of them."

"How did you find them?"

"You'll never believe this," I began enthusiastically. "Some Indian women came by today; and when I greeted them, they said they were going berry picking and they invited me to go along . . . so I did. I didn't quite fill my pail on my own. They helped me."

"So you found some women who could speak English?"

"No. Not really."

"Then how—?"

"Oh, they said 'hello' and 'berries' and 'come.'"

Wynn smiled.

"We sort of filled in the rest with gestures. Oh, Wynn, I wish I could understand them! They had so much fun."

"Give yourself a little time. You'll soon be joining in. Who were they?"

"That's part of the problem. I don't even know their names. I couldn't ask them where they live or anything."

Wynn reached out and gently stroked my hair. "It's hard, isn't it?" he said.

"I might have found some friends—and lost them—in the very same day," I mourned.

I was working about my kitchen the next morning, wondering how I was going to fill my long day, when a loud call—almost in my ear—spun me around. There stood the youngest member of the trio who had shared the berry patch the day before. After my initial fright, I was able to smile at her and indicate a chair for her. She shook her head and held up her basket. She was going to pick berries again.

"Yes, I'll go," I nodded to her. "Thank you for stopping for me. It will take me just a minute to get my things."

I thought as I bustled about finding my hat and my pail that she probably hadn't understood one word of what I had just said.

We went out into the sunshiny day and there, waiting at the end of our path, were four more women. Two of them had been with us the day before and the other two were new to me. I smiled at all of them, pointed to myself and said, "Beth," which they repeated with many giggles and varying degrees of success, and we started off. This time we went in a different direction when we came to the river. All along the way, the women chattered and laughed. I could only smile.

We picked berries until noon again. As before, they filled their containers before me and helped me to finish.

We walked home single file, the women laughing and talking as they went. How I wished I could join in. I wanted to at least ask them their names and where they lived. I might as well be mute for all the good my tongue did me.

When we got to our cabin, I again motioned for them to come in. They showed me their brimming pails and pointed to the settlement. I wouldn't let them go without *some* information. I would try it again. So I pointed at myself and said, "Beth." Then I pointed at the youngest woman who had been the one to walk right into our home. The women looked at one another and smiled.

"Evening Star," the young woman said carefully, and then she went around the little circle pointing her finger at each of the ladies and saying their names. It was a strange mixture. The middle-aged woman was Kinawaki, the older woman Mrs. Sam, and the two new ones who had gone with us were Little Deer and Anna. I reviewed each of the names one more time to make sure that I had them right. The ladies nodded. I turned back to Evening Star, aching to communicate.

"Where do you live?" I tried.

She shook her head, not understanding. I looked at the other women grouped around her. They all looked blank.

"Your house? Where is your house?" I pointed at my house.

Evening Star's face lit up. "Law," she said. She must have thought that I was asking something about my own home.

I pointed toward the settlement. "Do you live over there?" I asked again.

"McLain," said the woman. At least she knew the name of the Hudson's Bay trader.

I knew I couldn't hold them any longer. I smiled and stepped back, nodding them a good-day. They smiled in return and started one by one down the path. Anna, the small, thin woman with the missing tooth, was the last to turn and go. Just as she passed by me, she stopped and leaned forward ever so slightly. "She doesn't understand English talk," she whispered, and then followed the others down the path. I stared after her with my mouth open.

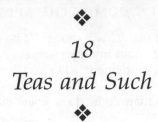

18
Teas and Such

WE WENT FOR berries the following day, too. Anna was there, and I directed my inquiries to her. I would not be cheated again out of conversation. I found out that the five women all lived in the settlement. Two of them, Mrs. Sam and Anna, were married to white trappers. Mrs. Sam had wished to be called as white women are called, by their husband's names. She did not understand quite how the system worked. Sam was her husband's first name; his last name was Lavoie.

Anna spoke English well because she had attended a mission school in another area. Beaver River had had no school. Anna did not consider herself superior, just different from the others. I found out later that she had had more schooling than her trapper husband, even though it was only the equivalent of about grade four. She was the one who did the figuring when she and her husband went to the trading post.

I also asked Anna about the families of the women. Anna didn't offer much on her own, but she did answer my direct questions. Evening Star was married to Tall One and had four children. She had had two others who had been lost at a young age to *dark blood*. I wondered what *dark blood* meant to the Indian. I tucked it away to ask Wynn. Kinawaki had been married—twice. Both her husbands had died. I decided that it would be improper and insensitive to probe for details. Kinawaki had borne nine children, five of them still living. Mrs. Sam had never had children. She had much time to do nothing, according to Anna. Little Deer, the short, round woman, had two boy-children who were always in the way; and she, Anna, had five—two in Indian graves and three at home.

The mortality rate appalled me. The resigned way in which they seemed to accept it bothered me even more. Was it expected that one would raise only half of one's family?

I was learning how to fill my pail more quickly than I had previously, but the women still gave me a hand before we left for home. On our way home, I walked along beside Anna. The path was not made for walking two abreast—now and then we would come to thick growth where I would have to step back, allowing her to go on without me, and then hurry to catch up to her again. I wanted to be sure to let her know that I would welcome any of the women into my home at any time.

"Not today," said Anna. "Today we have much work. We must dry berries for cold. Takes much work."

I agreed.

"Berries almost gone now," she went on. "Bears and birds get rest. Not pick anymore."

"When the women are finished with their berries, then will they have time to come?"

"I'll ask." She spoke rapidly to the other ladies, who were trudging on single file down the trail. No one stopped and no one turned to enter the conversation; they just called back and forth. After a few minutes of exchanges, Anna turned to me.

"Why you want us come?" she asked forthrightly.

I was a bit taken aback. "Well, just to—to—to get to know you better. To make friends—to maybe have some tea—"

She interrupted me then. "Tea," she said. "That's good."

She talked again to her companions. I heard the word "tea," which seemed to be a drawing card. There was a general nodding of heads.

"We come—sometime," said Anna.

"Good!" I exclaimed. "How about tomorrow?"

Anna looked puzzled. "Why?" she said. "Why tomorrow?"

"Well, I—I'd like you to come as soon as possible."

"Come when ready," responded Anna, and I nodded my head.

"Come when ready," I agreed.

Two days later I looked up from my sewing to see Little Deer standing in my doorway. I had not heard her knock. She came in smiling and took the seat I offered her. I got out the teapot and made the tea. We couldn't talk, so we just sat smiling and nodding at one another. She had watched with great interest as I lifted china cups from my cupboard. I didn't have any cake or cookies, so I cut slices of fresh bread and spread it with the jam I had made with some of my berries.

We had just taken our first sip from the cups when Evening Star walked in. She had not knocked either. I got another cup and we continued our tea party. When we finished I decided to show the two ladies around our house. They carefully looked at everything, their faces showing little emotion. I couldn't tell if they were pleased, puzzled, or provoked at what they saw. Nothing seemed to move them in the least.

I came to my kitchen and proudly demonstrated how I could sweep aside my curtains and reveal the dishes and food stacked on the shelves. Evening Star reached out a hand and tried it herself. She lifted the curtain, peered in behind it and let it fall back in place. Then she did it again. She turned to Little Deer and spoke a word in her native dialect. Not only did she say it once, but she repeated it, and Little Deer said it after her. At last, I had found something that impressed them! I said the word over and over to myself so I would remember it. I wanted to ask Wynn about it when he got home.

It wasn't long after our tea party until Wynn was home for supper. I still had the Indian word on the tip of my tongue. I wanted to be sure to ask him before I lost it.

Almost as soon as he entered the door, I asked him. It was a difficult word for my tongue to twist around, and I wasn't sure I could say it correctly.

"What is *winniewishy*?" I asked him.

Wynn puzzled for a moment and then corrected my pronunciation.

"That's it. What does it mean?"

"Where'd you hear that?" asked Wynn.

"Two of the ladies were here today for tea," I informed him excitedly. "What does it mean?"

"Well, in English, I guess we'd say *nuisance*. Why?"

Nuisance! They had viewed and touched my curtains and pronounced them *nuisance*? For a moment I was puzzled and hurt, and then it struck me as funny and I began to laugh.

"What's so funny?" asked Wynn.

"Oh, nothing, really. That was just the opinion of the ladies about the pretty, unpractical curtains over my cupboards."

It was Sunday again, though I had a hard time really convincing myself of that fact. It seemed so strange not to be preparing for church. I missed the worship. I missed the contact with friends. I missed being with my own family. But, most of all, I missed the feeling of refreshing that came from spending time with other believers in praise and prayer.

We set aside some time, just the two of us, in a manner that would become our practice for the years ahead in the North; and, with Bible in hand, we had our own brief Sunday worship service.

The next day, my washday, I was busy with ironing when a call from within my doorway announced another visitor. It was Evening Star. Right behind her came Mrs. Sam and Little Deer. I put aside my ironing and fixed the tea. The women seemed to enjoy it, smacking their lips appreciatively as they drank. We had just finished when Anna appeared. I made another pot and we started all over again.

With the coming of Anna, I was able to talk to the women. "I thought you might like to do some sewing," I said to them. "I have things all ready."

I went to my bedroom trunk and brought out material that I had already prepared to make pillows. I also brought needles and thread and proceeded to show the ladies how to go about stitching up the pillows. They started somewhat clumsily with the lightweight material, but seemed to catch on quickly enough. When they had finished, they handed the pillows back to me.

"Oh, no," I told them. "You may keep them. Take them home with you." I pointed to the many pillows I had on the cot. "You can use them in your own homes," I said, and Anna passed on the information. The women still looked a bit hesitant, but they all left with their pillows.

The next day the women came again, all walking right in as they arrived. I decided I would talk to Anna about it—explain that one did not just walk into another's house without knocking first. She would be able to inform the other ladies. It was uncomfortable for me, not knowing when someone might suddenly appear at my elbow.

Again we had our tea. I began to wonder just what I had started. Did the ladies think they needed to come to my house every day of the week for a tea party? I was glad they liked to come, but I wasn't sure how to put a stop to this as a daily event.

After tea I was all prepared to go and get some more sewing. They seemed to easily have mastered the simple cushion; now perhaps they would like to try something a little more difficult. I excused myself and went to my bedroom. While I was gone, there was a shuffling in the kitchen. Little Deer left the room and went to the outside step. I had returned to the kitchen-living room when she came back with some baskets on her arm. The ladies had each brought her own sewing. I stood dumbstruck as I watched the deft fingers move rapidly in and out of the material. Intricate designs in thread and bead-work were quickly forming under skilled hands. I could feel embarrassment flooding my face with deep color. To think that I, Elizabeth Delaney, had had the foolish notion that I could teach these women how to sew! Why, their work would put mine to shame any day. I didn't even know the right words to apologize.

Well, Elizabeth, I said to myself, *you certainly have a lot to learn.*

I did speak to Anna about my desire for the women to knock before entering. She looked puzzled. It seemed that even at the mission school knocking was not a custom. However, she nodded her head and passed the word on to the other women. They, too, seemed at a loss for the reason behind this, but they also nodded. I was relieved that the matter had been well taken care of.

The next day I was in the yard shaking a rug when Anna arrived. She was alone, but I expected that a number of the others would soon follow. I led her into the house, opening the door for her and letting her pass on ahead.

She hesitated. Neither of us moved for a moment, and finally Anna said, "You not knock."

"Oh, no," I tried to explain. "That's fine. Go ahead. It's only at your house that I would knock. Not at my house."

She looked at me like I had really lost my senses, but she went in.

That day we were joined for tea by Mrs. Sam and Kinawaki, both of whom knocked before entering even though they arrived together. Evening Star and Little Deer did not come.

When Wynn got home that night, he took off his heavy boots and stretched out his long legs to rest his tired muscles. I knew he had been working very hard during these first few weeks on the post. He wanted to know his area thoroughly before the bad weather set in, so he might be well-prepared for trouble spots. I was bustling around with last-minute supper preparations.

"You know," he said to me, "I saw the strangest thing when I came through the village tonight. There was Anna, knocking on her own door. They never have a lock on their doors, so she couldn't have been locked out. I couldn't imagine what in the world she was doing. I asked McLain. He said that somewhere she had picked up the notion to knock, to chase out any evil spirits that were in the house before she entered."

I gasped. How could she have misunderstood me so? I certainly had no wish to be fostering false ideas about the spirit world. I explained it all to Wynn and he smiled at my dilemma. I was horrified.

The next time Anna came to see me, I informed her that I had been wrong, that it wasn't necessary to knock after all. She could enter at any time and call as she had always done.

Anna nodded impassively, but I was sure she was wondering about those crazy white people who couldn't make up their minds! From then on I never knew for sure if I had company until I had checked over both shoulders, and I made a habit of doing that frequently.

19
Friends

"DID YOU KNOW that Ian McLain's sister lives here?" Wynn asked one morning at the breakfast table.

I looked up in astonishment. I certainly didn't know that. I wondered where she had been hiding. Then I checked myself—that wasn't fair. I hadn't been to the settlement more than two or three times myself.

"No," I said now. "Have you seen her?"

"Just at a distance."

"What's she like?"

"She's rather tall, like Ian. Not broad though. She walks very erect and briskly—that's all I know. All I saw was her retreating back."

"Where does she live?" I asked next, thinking eagerly about visiting her.

"I think she has one of the rooms at the back of the store, but I'm not sure even about that."

Well, I would find out. When I tracked her down, I would invite her for tea. Perhaps some morning. The Indian ladies still came often in the afternoon.

I switched my thoughts back to Wynn. "Have you heard her name?"

"She's a Miss McLain. I don't know her given name."

"She's never married? Is she quite a bit younger than her brother?"

"I don't know that, but I wouldn't expect so."

Wynn rose from the table and reached for his Stetson. The poor thing still had the telltale wagon-wheel marks.

"I won't be home until late tonight," he said. "I have a lot of ground to cover today."

I dreaded having him gone from morning to dusk. It made the day so long. I said nothing but stepped over to him and put my arms around his neck for my goodbye kiss. "Be careful," I whispered. "Come home safely."

He held me for some minutes before he gently put me from him; and then he was gone, walking out our door and down the footpath in long, even strides.

I watched him until he had disappeared. With a sigh I turned and began clearing the table. Then I remembered Miss McLain.

So there *was* another white woman in the settlement! I couldn't wait to meet her. I wondered what she would be like. She would be older than I, certainly. Perhaps even twice my age. Had she been raised in the North? Or had she come up from the city, like I had?

I needed a few items from the store anyway, so I would just take a walk after I had done the morning household chores and see what I could find out.

I wasn't too eager to walk into the village. I didn't quite trust some of the dogs with their snapping teeth and snarling jaws. I was fine if they were kept tied; but the trappers and their families were sometimes a little careless about that, being so used to the dogs themselves. I had seen some of the Indian women carrying a heavy, thick stick as they walked through the village. When I asked Wynn about it, he nonchalantly remarked that it was needed against the dogs.

This morning, I was so enthused about meeting the white woman that I decided to even dare the dogs. As soon as I had finished up the dishes, tidied up the two rooms that composed our home, and swept the step, I freshened myself and started for the store. This time I had a respectably long list of needed items.

Fortunately, the dogs did not give me too much cause for concern. The more ferocious ones were all securely tied. Children played in the dirt of the roadway. Since we were now into September, I was very conscious—as a schoolteacher—that they really should have been in school. Again I longed to start some classes, but I realized I had none of the words of their dialect—well, just "nuisance"—and they had only a few of mine.

Mr. McLain was busy waiting on some Indian women. One of them was Mrs. Sam. I greeted her as an old friend, but we were still unable to say more than hello to one another.

I purchased my items, even adding a couple of things I hadn't thought about but spotted on the stacked shelves. Mr. McLain listed the items under our account, and I carefully itemized each one in my little book to give Wynn an accurate account for his records.

"Care for some coffee?" offered Mr. McLain in a neighborly fashion, jerking his thumb at the pot which ever stood ready on the back of his big airtight heater. A stack of cups was scattered around on a nearby stand. Some of them were clean, but most of them were dirty, having been used by former customers that morning. At first reluctant, I changed my mind.

"A cup of coffee would be nice," I said and walked over to the stove to help myself. I still wanted a chance to talk some with Mr. McLain, and a cup of coffee might prolong my stay enough to be able to do so.

"My husband was telling me that you have a sister living here," I ventured, after taking a deep breath. To make the statement seem less important, I then took a swallow of coffee. It was awful. It was so weak it hardly tasted like coffee at all—and so stale that what little flavor was there was almost completely eclipsed. It was hot though—I had to give Mr. McLain credit for that. I burned my tongue.

Mr. McLain kept figuring. Finally he lifted his head. "Katherine. Yeah, she lives here. Has lived here now for almost twenty years."

I wasn't sure what to say next. Katherine was such a pretty name. I tried to visualize the lady to whom it belonged.

"Where was she from, before that?" I asked rather timidly. Maybe the answer would tell me something about her.

"From St. John."

"St. John? My, she has come a long way from home, hasn't she?"

"Guess you could say that," agreed McLain. "She was a schoolmar'm back there."

"Really?"

Already I was warming up to this unknown lady. She had been a school-teacher, educated, cultivated. I was confident we would have much in common.

"I was a schoolteacher, too," I went on. "I'd love to meet your sister. I'm sure we'd have much to talk about."

McLain looked at me in a strange, quizzical way. He didn't answer for many moments and then he said simply, "Yeah," very abruptly and curtly.

I waited, hoping to discover how I could go about making the acquaintance of this woman. Mr. McLain said nothing.

Finally I ventured, "Is she—does she live around here?"

It was a stupid question. "Around here" was the only place there was to live—that is, if she was considered a part of this settlement.

"Out back," said McLain shortly. "She has the room with the left door."

I stammered on, "Do you—do you suppose she would mind if I called?"

McLain looked at me for what seemed like a long time and then jerked his big head at the door. "I don't know why she'd mind. Go ahead. Leave your things right here 'til you're ready to go off home."

I thanked him and went out the door and around to the back of the building to look for the door on the left.

Mrs. McLain was in the backyard hanging out some laundry. I felt embarrassed. What if she saw me? But, then, what did it matter? She had her back to me, anyway, as she sang softly to herself.

I rapped gently. There was no response. I knocked louder. Still no response. I hesitated. Clearly Miss McLain was not in. I decided to try one more time. To this knock there was a loud call of "Come," and I opened the door timidly and went in.

The room was dark, so it took me a few minutes to get accustomed to the lack of light and locate the room's occupant.

She was seated in a corner, her hands idly folded in her lap, staring at the blank wall in front of her. I wondered if she might be ill and was about to excuse myself and depart for a more convenient time, but she spoke. "You're the lawman's wife."

Her voice was hard and raspy.

"Yes," I almost whispered, wondering if her statement was recognition or condemnation.

"What do you want?"

"Well, I—I just—heard that—that a white woman lived here, and I wanted to meet you."

"White woman?" The words were full of contempt. "This is no place for a white woman. One might as well realize that anyone who lives here is neither white nor a woman."

I couldn't believe the words, and I certainly could not understand the meaning behind them. I turned and would have gone, but she stopped me.

"Where are you from?" she demanded.

"Calgary. I was a schoolteacher near Lacombe before coming here. I was born and raised in Toronto."

"Toronto? Nothing wrong with Toronto. Why'd you come here?"

"Well, I—I—married a member of the Royal North West Police. I—"

She turned from me and spit with contempt into the corner.

When she turned back, her eyes sparked fire. "That's the poorest reason that I ever heard for coming to this god-forsaken country," she said. "Some people come because they have to. My brother came for the money. Nothing else, just the money. Buried his first wife here, and still he stayed. But you—"

She did not finish her sentence but left me to know that I had done something incredibly wrong or stupid, perhaps both.

I felt condemned. I also felt challenged. Suddenly I drew myself up to my full five feet, three inches. "Why did *you* come here?" I asked her.

Again her eyes flashed. I was afraid for a moment that she might throw something at me, her anger was so evident. But she would have needed to leave her chair in order to do that—she had nothing near at hand.

"I came," she said deliberately, hissing out each word, "I came because there was nothing else that I could do—nowhere else where I could go. That's why I came."

I was shaken. "I'm—I'm sorry," I murmured through stiff lips. I stood rooted to the spot for a moment and then I said softly, "I think I'd better go."

She did not comment, only nodded her head angrily at the door, indicating that I was quite free to do so, and the sooner the better in her estimation.

I was glad to step out into the warm sunshine and close the door behind me on the angry woman inside. I stood trembling. I had never seen anyone behave in such a way. *My, what deep bitterness is driving this woman?* I wondered. It could completely destroy her if something wasn't done. But what could one do? Personally, I hoped I would never need to encounter her again.

A soft song caught my ears and I remembered Mrs. McLain. She was still there hanging up her laundry. I didn't want to make contact with the woman, especially not in my present shaky condition. I hastily headed down the path in hopes of dodging around the building, but she saw me.

"Good morning, Mrs. Delaney," she called pleasantly.

I had to stop and respond. I managed a wobbly smile. "Good morning, Mrs. McLain," I returned. "It's a lovely morning, isn't it?"

"It is. And I am just finishing my washing and stopping for a cup of tea. Could you join me?"

I thought to wonder then about her excellent grammar. She had only the trace of an accent.

I still wanted to head for the security of my little home, but that would be very rude; so I smiled instead and said, "That is most kind. Thank you."

She pegged the last dish towel to the line, picked up her basket and led the way through the right-hand door.

The room was very pleasant and homey, a combination of white and Indian worlds. I noticed what a pleasant atmosphere the blending gave the room.

She seated me and went out to her small kitchen. Soon she was back with a teapot of china and some china cups. She also brought some slices of a loaf cake made with the local blueberries. It was delicious.

"So, are you feeling settled in Beaver River?" she asked me.

"Oh, yes. Quite settled."

We went on with small talk for many moments, and then she became more personal. Eventually it dawned on me that this was the kind of conversation I had been aching to have with a woman. The kind for which I had been seeking white companionship.

"Does it bother you, being left alone so much?" she asked sympathetically.

"I guess it does some. I miss Wynn, and the days are so long when he is gone for such a long time. I don't know how to make them pass more quickly. I have sewed up almost all the material I brought along, and there is really nothing else I can cover, or drape, or pad, anyway," I said in truth and desperation.

"When you have a family, you won't have so much free time," she observed. "In fact, when winter comes, you will be busier. It takes so much more of one's time even to do the simple tasks in the winter," she went on to explain. I hadn't thought about that, but I was sure she was right.

I switched back to her earlier comment. "Do you have a family?" I asked.

"No," was her simple answer, but I thought I saw pain in her eyes.

"Have you always lived here?" I said, partly to get on to another subject.

I expected her to say she had come to Beaver River from another area, so I was surprised when she said, "Yes. I have never lived more than a

few miles away. My father used to have a cabin about five miles up river.
I was born there."

I know that my surprise must have shown on my face.

She smiled.

"You are wondering why I speak English?"

I nodded.

"I'm married to an Englishman." She laughed then. "Not an Englishman, really. He is a Scotsman. He was raised from childhood by a Swedish family. At one time he went to a French school, he was apprenticed
under a German, and he speaks three Indian dialects—but his mother
tongue is English."

"My," I said, thinking about McLain with new respect. I had wondered
why he didn't speak with a Scottish accent. His sister did not have one
either, come to think of it. "My," I said again. "Does he speak all of those
languages?"

"Some French, some Swedish, some German, and much Indian." She
said it with pride.

"But that still doesn't explain your English."

She looked at me as though she thought I should have understood, and
perhaps I should have. "If my husband can speak seven languages," she
said, "it seemed that at least I should be able to learn his."

I nodded. What spirit the young woman had.

"And how did you learn?" I persisted, feeling very at ease with her.

"Books. When he saw that I was really interested, he got me books; and
he helped me. In the long winter evenings, we would read to one another
and he would correct my pronunciation and help me with the new words.
I love English. I love reading books. I wish my people had all these wonderful stories to read to their children."

Excitement filled me. "Have you ever thought of writing the stories for
them? You know, putting the Indian stories down on paper for the children to read."

"None of them can read," she said very sadly.

"But we could teach them," I was quick to cut in.

She smiled, and her smile looked resigned and pitiful.

"They do not wish to learn. It takes work. They would rather play."

"Are you sure?" I asked incredulously.

"I'm sure. I have tried." She looked older then. Older and a bit tired.

"I'll help you. We can try again."

A new spark came to her eyes. "Would you? Would you care enough
to really try?"

"Oh, yes. I've just been aching to get going, but Wynn said that I should
wait. That I shouldn't go rushing in. I even brought some books along so
that I might—"

I stopped. I was getting carried quite away with it all.

She reached out and took my hand. "I thank you," she said sincerely. "I thank you for feeling that way. For caring. Maybe we *can* do something."

"I'll show you my books and the things I have and—"

She stopped me. "Your husband is quite right, Mrs. Delaney. We mustn't rush into this unprepared. The Indian people have waited for many generations for the chance to read and write. A few more weeks or months will make little difference."

I supposed she was right. I swallowed my disappointment and glanced at the clock on the wall. It was almost noon, I discovered with surprise.

"Oh, my," I said, "look at the time. I had no idea. I must go."

I stood quickly, placing my empty cup on the nearby small table.

"Thank you so much for the tea—and the visit. I enjoyed it so much."

"I've enjoyed it, too. I do hope that you will come back again soon, Mrs. Delaney."

"My name is Elizabeth," I told her. "Elizabeth, or Beth—you can take your pick. I'd be pleased if you'd call me by my given name rather than Mrs. Delaney."

She smiled. "And my name, Elizabeth," she said, "is Nemelaneka. When I married Ian, I thought he would like a wife with an English name, so I spent days poring over books and finally found the name Martha. 'Martha,' I told him, 'will be my name now.' 'Why Martha?' he asked me. And I said, 'Because I think that Martha sounds nice. Is there another name that you like better?' 'Yes,' he said, 'I like Nemelaneka, your Indian name.' So I stayed Nemelaneka, though Ian calls me Nimmie."

"Ne-me-la-ne-ka," I repeated, one syllable at a time. "Nemelaneka, that's a pretty name."

"And a very long and difficult one," laughed the woman. "Martha would have been much easier to say and spell."

Just as I was taking my leave, Nemelaneka spoke softly. "Don't judge poor Katherine too quickly," she said. "There is much sorrow and hurt in her past. Maybe with love and understanding—" She stopped and sighed. "And time," she added. "It takes so much time, but maybe with time she will overcome it."

I looked at her with wonder in my eyes but asked no questions. I nodded, thanked her again, and hurried home after retrieving my shopping from the store.

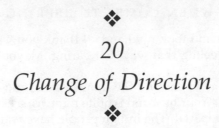

20

Change of Direction

❖

NO LADIES CAME for tea that day. I had thought I would welcome a day to myself, wondering at times how I was ever going to put a stop to the daily visits; but now, with none of them coming, I found that I really missed them. I fidgeted the entire afternoon away, not knowing what to do with myself. Eventually, I laid aside the book I was trying to read and decided to take a walk along the river.

I did not go far and I did not leave the riverbank since I was still unsure of my directions.

It was a very pleasant day. The leaves had turned color and, mingled among the dark green of the evergreens, they made a lovely picture of the neighboring hillsides.

The river rippled and sang as it hurried along. Occasionally I saw a fish jump, and as I rounded one bend in the trail I saw a startled deer leap for cover. I was enjoying this wilderness land. But Nimmie had been right. I was lonesome at times as well.

I thought now about all the family I had left in Calgary and Toronto. I thought, too, about my friends and school children at Pine Springs. *I wonder if the school has a new teacher?* I certainly hoped so. The children who had finally been able to start their education needed the opportunity to continue.

I wished there was some way to learn what was going on back home. I seemed so far removed from them all, so isolated. *Why, something terrible could happen to one of them and I would never know!* The thought frightened me, and I had to put it aside with great effort or it would surely have overwhelmed me with depression.

I firmly chose to think of other things instead. It was easy to go back to my visit with Nimmie. I was so glad to have found a kindred spirit. One who was just as concerned—no, *more* concerned—about the need of schooling for the village children. I could hardly wait to get something started, but I knew Nimmie and Wynn were right. One must go slowly and do things properly.

Reluctantly, I turned my steps homeward again. I earnestly hoped Wynn wouldn't be too late. I had so many feelings whirling around inside, and I needed so much to be able to share them with someone—someone who would listen and understand.

The day passed slowly. Dusk was falling and still Wynn had not returned. I walked around the two rooms we called home, looking for something to do but finding nothing that interested me.

I paced the outside path, back and forth, and tried to formulate in my mind just where I would plant my next year's garden.

I stirred the supper stew and rearranged the plates on the table and stirred the stew again.

I sat with a book near the flickering lamp and pretended to myself that I was interested in the story.

Still I was restless and edgy. My agitation began to turn to anger. Why did he have to be so late? Was the job really that important? Did his work matter more than his wife? Was this dedication to his job really necessary, or was he just putting in time, choosing to be late every day?

My angry thoughts began to pile up, one on top of the other. *Wynn could have been home long ago had he chosen to be!* I finally concluded.

It was now quite dark. Even Wynn had not expected to be *that* late. My thoughts took a sudden turn. What if something had happened? What if he were lost? Or had had an accident? What if some deranged trapper had shot him? Mounties were warned of this possibility. Suddenly I was worried—not just a little worried, but sick-worried. I was sure something terrible had happened to my husband and here I sat not knowing how or where to get help. What if he were lying out there somewhere, wounded and dying, and I sat idly in my chair fumbling with the pages of a book and fuming because he was late?

What could I do? I couldn't go looking for him. I'd never find my way in the darkness. Why, I could barely find my way in the broad daylight! Besides, I had no idea where Wynn had gone. What should I do?

Indians! They were good at tracking. Didn't they have some sort of sixth sense about such things? I didn't know any of the Indian men, but I knew their wives. I would go to them for help.

I ran for my light shawl. I would go to the village and knock on doors until I found someone.

Then I remembered the dogs. They were often untied at night because the owners were not expecting anyone after dark. Out in the darkness of the woods by our pathway, I searched the ground for a heavy stick.

Footsteps on the path startled me. I swung around, my breath caught in my throat, not sure what I would be facing.

"Elizabeth!" Wynn said in surprise. "Did you lose something?"

I wanted to run and throw myself into his arms but my embarrassment and my remembered anger stopped me. I wanted to cry that I had been worried sick, but I feared that Wynn would think me silly. I wanted to run to my bedroom and throw myself down on the bed and cry away all my fear and frustration, but I did not want to be accused of being a hysterical woman. I did *not* want to explain what I was doing out in the tangled bush by the path in the darkness, and I would not; so I simply said, rather sharply, "What took you so long? Supper is a mess," and brushed past him into the kitchen.

Wynn said nothing more at the time. He ate the nearly ruined supper and I pushed mine back and forth across my plate with my fork.

Supper was a long and silent meal.

I had had so much to tell him, so much to talk about; and here we sat in silence, neither of us saying anything. It was foolish, and well I knew it.

I stole a glance at Wynn. He looked tired, more than I had ever seen him before. It occurred to me that he might have things to talk about, too. What had happened in his day? Were there things that *he* wished to talk about?

Taking a deep breath, I decided I should lay aside my hurt pride and ask him.

"You were very late," I began. "In fact, I was worried. Did something unexpected happen?"

Wynn looked up, relief in his eyes.

"A number of things," he answered. "Our boat got a leak, we were charged by an angry bull moose, the trapper we went to see chose not to be home and we had to search for him and we ended up bringing him in handcuffs; and the Indian that I had taken along to act as my guide took a nasty fall and had to practically be carried the last two miles on my back."

I stared at Wynn in unbelief. Surely he was joking. But the look on his face told me he was not.

"Oh, my," was all that I could say. "Oh, my."

Wynn smiled then. "Well, it's over," he said. "That's the only good thing I can say about this day."

But it wasn't over.

We hadn't even finished our poor meal when there was a call from outside our window. A man in the village had accidentally shot himself in the leg while cleaning his gun and Wynn was needed to care for the wound.

Wordlessly, he put on his hat and followed the excited boy.

It was very late when Wynn returned home. I was still waiting up for him. He crossed to me and kissed me. "I'm sorry, Elizabeth," he said; "you should have gone to bed."

"I couldn't sleep anyway," I said honestly.

The truth was that while Wynn had been gone, I had been doing a lot of thinking. I really had no idea how Wynn filled his days. When he came home at night, after a long day being—well, somewhere—we talked about what I had done with *my* day. I had never really asked Wynn about his before. What were Wynn's days like? Surely they weren't all as difficult as this one had been.

I had been anxious to tell him about my tea with Nimmie and about meeting Miss Katherine McLain. He had faced grave problems and possible death and likely would have made no comment about either if I hadn't made an opportunity just to make idle conversation. I felt ashamed. *From now on,* I determined, *I'm going to pay more attention to my husband and be less concerned with my silly little doings.*

By the time Wynn had returned from dressing the wound, I was feeling quite meek. Hadn't I come north with him to be his companion and support? I had been living as though I had come merely for his decoration.

I tipped my face now to receive Wynn's kiss, then asked, "How is the man?"

"He'll be okay, though he does have a nasty flesh wound. Barring infection, he should have no problem."

I shivered thinking about it.

"You're cold," said Wynn. "You should be in bed."

"No, I'm not cold, just squeamish," I answered. "Would you like a cup of something hot to drink? Coffee? Tea?"

"Tea sounds good. Is the water still hot?"

"I kept the fire banked. It will just take a minute."

"It's very late, Elizabeth. I know you're tired. I don't need—"

"It's no trouble," I assured him as I moved to the kitchen area.

Wynn sat down in the one easy chair and I could hear him removing his high-topped boots. *He must be nearly dead of exhaustion,* I thought.

I brought Wynn's tea and he gulped more than sipped it.

"You wanted to talk?" he said, lifting tired eyes to me.

"It can wait for morning."

"It doesn't need to wait," maintained Wynn.

"It's not that important. I just met Miss McLain today and had tea with Mrs. McLain. I'll tell you all about them at the breakfast table."

I took Wynn's empty cup from him and carried it to the table. Then I turned to him. "Come," I said. "This day has been long enough already."

21

The Storyteller

THE NEXT FEW weeks were rather uneventful. Wynn still was busy; but now that he had carefully patrolled all the area to which he was assigned, he was able to do more of his work from his one-room office. I liked having him around more, and it also helped me to become more familiar with what he did.

He was police, doctor, lawyer, advisor, handyman, and often spiritual counselor—and so much more. The people came to him for any number of reasons. He was always patient and just, though sometimes I wondered if he wasn't a little too frank. They seemed to expect it. If he said, "No, Cunning Fox, that is not your territory for trapping; and, if you insist upon using it, I will need to lock you up," the Indian did not blink. At least he knew exactly what to expect.

The Indian women came often for tea, though not nearly as regularly as they had at first. Mrs. McLain, my friend Nimmie, called, too: and I always enjoyed her visits. Miss McLain did not come, though I had bolstered up my courage to invite her on more than one occasion.

We still did not have a school. Nimmie and I had spent hours poring over books, both hers and mine. I was so anxious to get started; but she felt it was far more likely to succeed if we could convince the chief, or at least some of the elders, that it would be good for the children. This would take time, she assured me. As the chief of the band did not live in our village, but in a village farther west, we had no way to hurry our negotiations.

One Wednesday morning, a swollen-faced Indian came to see Wynn. After a brief examination, Wynn came into the kitchen.

"Got any hot water?" he asked me.

I indicated the kettle on the stove, and Wynn pulled out a pan and put some simple instruments in it, then poured the water over them and set the whole thing over the heat.

"What are you doing?" I asked, curious.

"Reneau has a bad tooth. It's going to need to come out."

"You're going to pull it?" I asked in astonishment.

"There isn't anyone else," Wynn answered. Then he turned teasingly to me. "Unless, of course, you want the job?"

"Count me out," I was quick to reply.

Wynn became more serious.

"In fact, Elizabeth, I was about to do just that," he said, turning the instruments over in the pan. "How would you like a little walk, for half-hour or so?"

I must have looked puzzled.

"I have no anesthesia. This man is going to hurt."

I realized then that Wynn was giving me opportunity to get away from the house before he began his procedure.

"I'll go to the store," I said quickly.

It didn't take me long to be ready to leave the house. Wynn was still with the shaking Reneau. I wondered who was dreading the ordeal ahead more—Reneau or Wynn.

There really wasn't anything I needed from the store, so I decided to drop in on Nimmie. She didn't answer my knock on her door. I turned to look around me, and then I spotted her in a little grove of poplar trees just beyond her garden. She had gathered about her a group of the village children. I hoped I wasn't interrupting things and approached quietly. Nimmie was telling a story, and all eyes were raptly focused on her face. *She must be a good storyteller—not a child is moving!* I marveled.

I stopped and listened.

". . . the man was big, bigger than a black bear, bigger even than a grizzly. He carried a long hunting spear and a huge bow and arrow with tips dipped in the poison potion. Everyone feared him. They feared his anger, for he roared like the mighty thunder; they feared his spear, for it flashed as swiftly as the lightning. They feared his poison arrows, for they were as deadly as the jaws of a cornered wolverine. They all shook with fear. No one would go out to meet the enemy. They would all be his slaves. Each time they came from the trapline they would have to give to him their choicest furs. Each time they pulled in the nets, he would demand their fish. Each time they shot a bull elk, they would have to give him the meat. They hated him and the slavery, but they were all afraid to go out to fight him.

"And then a young boy stepped forward. 'I will go,' he said. 'You cannot go,' the chiefs told him. 'You do not have the magic headdress. You do not have the secret medicine. You are not prepared for battle.' 'I can go,' said this young boy named David, because I take my God with me. He will fight for me.'"

I stood in awe as the story went on. I had never heard the story of David and Goliath told in this fashion before. I was surprised to hear Nimmie telling it now. Where had she heard it? She had not attended a mission school. And why was she telling it to the children in English? Few of them could understand all of the English words.

I was puzzled but I was also intrigued. How often did Nimmie tell the local children stories, and how often were they taken from the Bible? Did she always interpret the stories with Indian concepts and customs?

"'See,' said David, 'I have here my own small bow and five tried arrows. God will direct the arrow. I am not afraid of the bearlike Goliath. He has spoken against my God and now He must be avenged.'

"And so David picked up his small bow and his five true arrows and he marched out across the valley to the wicked enemy. Goliath laughed in scorn at David. 'What are you doing,' he cried, 'sending out a child instead of a brave? You have shamed me. I turn my head from you. I shall feed this little bit of meat to the ravens and foxes.'

"But David called out to the man as tall as the pine tree, 'I come not as a child, nor yet as a brave; but I come in the name of my God, whom you have insulted,' and he thrust one of the tried arrows in his bow, whispered a prayer that God would guide its flight on the wings of the wind, and pulled the bow with all of his strength.

"The arrow found its mark. With a cry, the big warrior fell to the ground."

If I for one moment had doubted that the children were able to follow the story, the shout that went up at the moment of Goliath's defeat would have convinced me otherwise. They cheered wildly for the victorious David.

When the noise subsided, Nimmie went on, "And so David rushed forward and struck the warrior's head from his body and lifted his huge headdress onto his own head. He picked up the long spear and his big bow and arrows and carried them back to his own tribe. They would never be the slaves of the wicked man again. David had won the battle because he had gone to fight in the name of his God."

Again there was a cheer.

"And now you must go," said Nimmie, shooing them all away with her slim hands.

"Just one more. Another one. Only one," pleaded a dozen voices.

"You said that last time," laughed Nimmie, "and I gave you one more and you say it again. Off you go now."

Reluctantly the children began to leave, and Nimmie turned. She had not been aware that I was standing there. A look of surprise crossed her face, but she did not appear to be disturbed or embarrassed.

"What a bunch," she stated. "They would have one sitting all day telling stories. —Come in, Elizabeth. We will have some tea. Have you been waiting long?"

"Not long, no. And I enjoyed it. Do you tell the children stories often?"

"Often? Yes, I suppose so—though not often enough. I don't know who enjoys it more, the children or I. Though I try to make it sound like they are a nuisance."

She laughed again and led the way to the house.

"But you told it in English," I remarked. "Do they understand?"

"They understand far more than you would think. Oh, they don't catch all the words, to be sure; but as they hear the stories again and again, they pick up more and more."

"And you told a Bible story," I continued, still dumbfounded.

"Yes, they like the Bible stories."

I wanted to ask where she had learned the Bible stories but I didn't.

"I love the Bible stories, too," she explained without being asked. "When I was learning to read English, the Bible was one of the books I read. At first it was one of the few books my new husband had on hand, so he taught me from it. I enjoyed the stories so much that, even now that I have many books, I still read from the Bible. They are such good stories."

She opened the door and let me pass into her home.

"I like the stories about Jesus best," she continued. "The children like them, too. I tell them often. The story about the little boy and his fish and bread; the story about the canoe that nearly was lost in the raging storm; the story about the blindman who could see when Jesus put the good medicine on his eyes. Ah, they are good stories," she concluded.

"You know, Nimmie," I pointed out, "those aren't merely stories. Those are true reports of historical events. All those things really happened."

She looked so surprised and bewildered that I said, "Didn't—didn't Ian tell you that—that the Bible is a true book, that those events, those happenings—?"

"Are they *all* true?" asked Nimmie incredulously.

"Yes, all of them."

"The ones about Jesus?"

"Every one."

"And those wicked people really did put Him to death—for no reason?"

I nodded. "They did."

There was silence. Nimmie looked from me to the Bible that lay on the little table, her eyes filled with wonder and then anger. "That's hateful!" she protested, her voice full of emotion. "How could they? Only a white man could do such a thing—destroy and slay one of his own! An Indian would never do such a shameful thing. I would spit on their graves. I would feed their carcasses to the dogs." Her dark eyes flashed and her nose flared.

"It was terrible," I admitted, shocked at her intensity. "But it wasn't as simple as you think. The reason for Jesus' dying is far more complicated than that. We could read it together if you'd like. I'd be glad to study the story with you, right from the beginning, and show you why Jesus had to die."

She began to calm herself.

"He didn't stay dead, you know," I went on.

"Is that true, too?" she asked in disbelief.

"Yes, that's true, too."

She was silent for a moment. "I might like to study that."

I smiled. "Fine. Why don't we start tomorrow morning? At my house?"

She nodded and rose to prepare the tea. She turned slightly. "Elizabeth, I'm sorry—sorry about what I said concerning the white man. It's only—only that sometimes—sometimes I cannot understand the things men do. The way they gnash and tear at one another—it's worse than wolves or foxes." This time she did not say *white* man, though I wondered if she still thought it.

"I know," I agreed shamefacedly. "Sometimes I cannot understand it either. It isn't the way it was meant to be. It isn't the way *Jesus* wants it to be. It isn't the right way. The Bible tells us that God abhors it, too. He wants us to love and care for one another."

"Does the white man know that?"

"Some of them do."

"Hasn't the white man had the Bible for many years?"

"Yes, for many years."

"Then why doesn't he read it and do what it says?"

I shook my head. It was a troubling question. "I don't know," I finally admitted. "I really don't know."

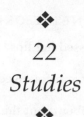

22
Studies

❖

OUR BIBLE STUDIES together started the next day as planned. We did not meet together every day, but we did meet regularly. Ian did not seem to object, and Wynn was most encouraging.

Nimmie was a good student; and as we began to piece together the whole plan of God for His creation, she became excited about it.

"Katherine should be here! She needs to hear this," she insisted.

I wondered about Katherine. I doubted that she would come out of her bitterness long enough to even listen, but Nimmie kept insisting.

"Do you mind if I bring her?" she continued.

"Well, no. I don't mind. I'm not sure—I'm not sure she'd come that's all. I've asked her to my house many times, and I've never been able to get her to come."

"For Bible study?"

"Well, no, not for Bible study necessarily. Just for tea. But if she won't come even for tea, I surely don't think she'll want to come for study."

"She might," persisted Nimmie. "I'll ask her."

When Nimmie arrived for the next study, she had Katherine with her. I never will know how she effected the miracle. I tried to keep the shock out of my face as I welcomed them both in.

Katherine scowled as we opened our Bibles and began to read. She had brought a Bible of her own, but it didn't look as though it had received much use. She said nothing all morning long, even though Nimmie often stopped in the reading to comment or ask for an explanation. She was eager to know not just the words but the *meaning* of the words, now that she knew each of the stories was true.

When the two ladies left that morning, I told them I would be looking forward to our next time together. Katherine frowned and informed me in unmistakable tones, "Don't expect me back. I came just to get this here woman off my back. There's nothing in this book that I don't already know. I'm not a heathen, you know—I was raised in church."

"Then you must miss it," I said softly.

She wheeled to look at me.

"I was raised in church, too," I continued, "and if there is one thing about the North that I miss more than any other, it is not being able to go to church on Sunday."

She snorted her disgust, pressed her lips together and marched out the door.

Nimmie looked at me sadly and followed the other woman.

I don't know how it came about; but the next time Nimmie came for her study, Katherine was reluctantly trudging along behind her, her Bible tucked under one arm.

I made no comment except to welcome them both, and we proceeded with our reading and discussion.

The weather was getting colder. Daily, large flocks of ducks and geese passed overhead as the birds sought warmer climates. Almost all the leaves were dancing on the ground rather than clinging to the now-bare branches. The animals' coats began to thicken; and men talked about a long, hard winter.

Wynn hired some men to haul a good supply of wood for the fire, and we prepared ourselves as well as possible for the winter weather ahead.

The inevitable day came. The north winds howled in, carrying sub-zero temperatures and swirling snow. We were in the midst of our first winter blizzard. I was so thankful that Wynn was home, safe and sound, instead of out someplace checking on a far-off trapper.

In spite of the fire in the stove, the temperature in the cabin dropped steadily. Wynn lit the fireplace and hung some blankets over the windows to shut out the cold. Still the chill did not leave the air. We piled on the clothing to keep our body heat in.

That night we banked our fires and retired early, hoping that the next day might bring a break in the storm. During the night, Wynn was up more than once to be sure the fire was still stoked with wood.

"I do hope there are no casualties," Wynn said. "This is unusually severe for this time of year. Some folks might not have been prepared for it."

I hoped, too, that there were no casualties. It would be terrible to be caught out in such a storm.

When we awoke the next morning, we were disappointed to find the fury of the storm had not slackened. Still it raged about us.

"Look," I said to Wynn when I found the water in the washstand basin frozen, "it *really is* cold in here!"

I was about to empty the chunk of ice into the slop bucket when Wynn stopped me. "Don't throw it out," he instructed. "Heat it and reuse it."

"Use *this*?"

"Who knows when we might be able to get more water. We only have three quarters of a pail, and we will need that for drinking and cooking. We'll make the wash water last as long as possible."

When I had finished the breakfast dishes, I did not throw out that water either. Instead, I left it in the dishpan at the back of the stove. It would

have to serve for washing the dinner dishes and perhaps even the supper dishes as well.

I was all set to enjoy a lovely day with Wynn in spite of what the
weather was doing outside; but he came from the bedroom drawing on
a heavy fur jacket.

"Where are you going?" I questioned in alarm.

"I need to go down to the Hudson's Bay Store and make sure there
are no reports of trouble. I shouldn't be gone too long; but if something
comes up and I don't get back right away, you're not to worry. There is
plenty of wood. You shouldn't have any problem keeping warm and dry."

He stopped to kiss me. "Don't go out, Elizabeth," he cautioned, "not
for any reason. If something happens so I can't get back to you by nightfall, I'll send someone else."

By nightfall? What a dreadful thought!

Wynn slipped out into the swirling snow, and I was left standing at
the window watching his form disappear all too quickly.

I don't remember any day that was longer. There was nothing to do
but to tend to the fires. Even with both burning, the cabin was cold. I
borrowed a pair of Wynn's heavy socks and put on my boots. Still my
feet were cold.

I walked around and around the small room, swinging my arms in an
effort to keep warm and to prevent total boredom. The storm did not
slacken. It was getting dark again. Not that it had ever been really light
on this day, but at least one had realized it was day and not night.

I fixed some tea. I had quite forgotten to eat anything all day. I was
sorry I had not thought of it. It could have helped to fill in a few of my
minutes.

It was well after I had lit the lamp and set it in the window that I heard
approaching footsteps. I rushed to the door. It was Wynn. He was back
safe and sound. I could have cried for joy.

"Is everything all right?" I asked, hugging him, snowy jacket and all.

"As far as we know," he replied, stamping the snow from his boots.
"We had to go and get Mary. She had no fuel for a fire and wouldn't
have made it through the storm, I'm sure."

"Who's Mary?"

"She's a woman who lives alone since she lost her husband and family three or four years ago. They call her Crazy Mary—maybe she is;
maybe she isn't, I don't know. But she refuses to move into the settlement, and she has a tendency to rant and rave about things. She was mad
at me tonight for bodily removing her from her cabin and bringing her
to town."

"Bodily?"

He nodded. "She absolutely refused to go on her own."

"What did she do? Did she fight?"

"Oh, no. She didn't fight; she just wouldn't move, that's all. I carried her out and put her on the sled, and she rode into town like a good girl. But I had to pick her up and carry her into Lavoies' cabin as well."

I smiled, thinking of this determined Indian lady. She certainly had gotten her point across.

"Well, she should be all right now," said Wynn. "Mrs. Sam is sure she will stay put as long as the storm continues."

I was glad Crazy Mary was safe. *What is the real story behind her name?* I wondered.

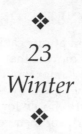

23
Winter

WITH THE COMING of the winter, many of the men had to leave their warm cabins to go out to their traplines. The furs they trapped in winter were the most profitable because of their thickness, and each trapper had a designated area that was considered his. When I asked Wynn how they made the arrangements, he said it seemed to be by some kind of gentleman's agreement rather than by any legal contract. I did learn that trapping another's territory was considered a major offense.

There was the problem of stealing, as well. There wasn't much common thievery in the North. No one felt over-concerned about locking up what he owned. Houses were left open and belongings left about the yard. The cabins that were constructed by the trappers for protection while working the traplines were free to be used by others who were passing through. Most trappers even made sure there was an adequate wood supply and blankets, matches and rations for any guests who might drop in during their absence. Of course, they knew the other trappers would extend the same courtesy.

So in an area where usual theft was not much of a problem, a very serious temptation and offense was stealing from another's trapline. Such a criminal was considered to be the lowest of the low, not only a thief of valuable animal pelts, but of a family's livelihood as well. Vengeance was often immediate and deadly, and few felt that the wronged man could be blamed for taking the law into his own hands. The Royal North West Policeman must be on guard all the time for this. Any suspected thieves must be spotted and the guilty party apprehended immediately before a brutal beating or even a murder might occur. Wynn watched the lines and kept his eyes and ears open for any complaints of offenses.

Mostly it was the men who worked the traplines, but Crazy Mary also claimed a small territory as her own. So, once the storm had blown itself out, she refused to stay at the Lavoies' and headed back, poorly clothed, to protect her interests. She hinted rather loudly that there might have been someone messing with some of her traps.

Most people shrugged off the story as one of Crazy Mary's fancies, but Wynn could not dismiss it so easily. It must be checked and proven false to put everyone's mind at ease. When the storm ended, Wynn took snowshoes and dog team out to investigate.

Wynn did not keep his team at our cabin but in an enclosure by the Hudson's Bay Store. One reason was that the food supply for the dogs was over there, and also their clamor would not keep us awake at night.

Each dog had been carefully picked by the men of the Force who had preceded Wynn. The dogs were chosen for their endurance, dependability, and strength, not particularly for their good disposition. Many of them were scrappers and, for that reason, they had to be tied well out of range of one another. Some of them had ragged ears or ugly scars from past fights. I didn't care much for Wynn's sled dogs. Harnessing them to the sleigh was a tough job. Things could be going well; and suddenly one of the dogs would get mad at something another dog did, and a fight would break out. Before long the whole team would be in a scrap, tangling the harness and making a general mess of things. Yet the dog team was very necessary. Wynn used his dogs almost every day during the winter.

He had been talking about choosing his own team and training them himself for harness. With different training, he thought the dogs might be better-tempered and make less problems on the trail. It sounded like a good idea to me. It was going to take time and work, but Wynn was watching for promising pups.

When he went out after the storm to check on Crazy Mary's story, he informed me he also planned to swing around and see a litter of pups which a trapper by the name of Smith had for sale near the west branch of the river. I found myself wishing I could go with him, but I didn't even mention the thought to Wynn. It was still very cold and the snow was deep. The sled dogs were enough trouble on the trail. He certainly didn't need me along to complicate matters.

Wynn didn't return until late that night. He had talked with Mary and gone over her trapline with her. She had shown him "signs" and ranted on about her suspicions. This was the trapline her late husband had managed, and Mary was steadfast in her belief that it now was her exclusive property. But someone was moving in, she maintained, infringing on her area. She hadn't found any evidence yet of stolen pelts, but the new traps were getting in too close. They found no traps that belonged to another trapper, but Mary was sure one or two had been there. She could see the marks on the ground; she dug around in the snow to prove her point. But Wynn could not accept her "evidence" as valid. He left her, promising to keep a sharp lookout and asking her to get in touch with him if she still suspected anything.

Then, as planned, Wynn pulled his team around and went to see Smith. Smith was away from his cabin when Wynn arrived, so Wynn went in, started up a fire and made himself a cup of tea. The pups were in a corner of the cabin, so he had a good chance to look them over well for potential sled dogs. There were some possibilities. Wynn watched them play and tussle, liking what he saw.

It was getting late in the day and Smith had still not arrived at the cabin; so Wynn banked the fire to try to keep the cabin warm for the trapper's return, carried in a further wood supply, and turned his team back on the trail for home.

Wynn had learned to appreciate one thing about his sled dogs. While on the trail they usually laid aside all grudges and pulled together. They were considered to be one of the fastest teams in the area. Speed could, at times, be important to a policeman. A few minutes might mean the difference between life or death.

The team was in a hurry to get back to the settlement, so Wynn was hard pushed to keep up with his dogs. On the smoother terrain, he rode the runners; when the way was rough, he snowshoed behind it, guiding it over the crusted snow.

When Wynn told me about his day as we sat in front of our fireplace that night, I found myself almost envying him. It sounded exciting and almost fun to be swinging along the snow-crisp trail behind the sled dogs. Wynn must have seen the wistful look in my eyes, for he surprised me a few days later.

"Want to take a little ride?"

I looked out the window. The day was filled with sunshine, the wind was no longer blowing, and the snow lying across the countryside made a Currier and Ives Christmas card of the scene.

"I'm going back out to check on Crazy Mary."

"Do we have to call her Crazy Mary?" I objected.

Wynn smiled. "There are four Marys in the area—Little Mary, Old Mary, Joe's Mary, and Crazy Mary. All the people refer to them in this way."

"Well, I don't like it. It's—it's degrading."

"You're right. But, from what I've been hearing, her neighbors are probably right. I think she does have mental problems. It sounds like it started when she lost her children in a smallpox epidemic. Her husband was away at the time and Mary was all alone. She watched all five of them die, one at a time. She hasn't been quite the same since. If she were in one of our civilized areas, she would have been institutionalized and cared for. Here, she is still on her own. She doesn't care about people and won't take help when it is offered. Now and then, if the weather really gets bad, one or another of the men leaves a quarter of meat on her doorstep. They have never been thanked for it, but it does disappear; so they assume she does make use of it."

I felt sorry for Mary. *What an awful way to live! What an awful way to be known,* I mourned. I had never seen her, but I was sure that if people really tried, *something* could be done.

"You haven't answered my question," Wynn's voice broke into my thoughts.

"The ride? I'd love to, though I have no idea what you have in mind."

"I want to keep a close eye on Mary and her problem. I also plan to stop and see if Smith is home. I'd like to get two or three of those pups."

My face lit up then. "I'd love to go," I said again.

"I'll go get the team. Wear the warmest clothes you have. Those old pants are a must."

I hurried to get ready. I didn't want to keep Wynn waiting. I borrowed a pair of Wynn's long drawers and pulled the old pants over them. The combination of the two meant I could hardly move. I also borrowed Wynn's wool socks and pulled on my own heavy sweater. The footwear had me concerned. All I had were the old hiking boots, and common sense told me they would not keep my feet warm.

Wynn soon returned, leaving the team lying fan-style on the ground when he came in for me. I was still trying to struggle into the heavy boots.

"Here," he said, "I think these will be much warmer."

He handed me a pair of beautiful, fur-lined Indian moccasins. They had elaborate designs in bead and quill work, and I exclaimed as I reached for them.

"They are wonderful! Where did you get them?"

"I had Mrs. Sam make them. I knew you would be needing something warmer for your feet. Fortunately, they were ready this morning."

"They are so pretty," I continued.

"They are pretty," agreed Wynn. "They are also warm."

I caught his hint that they were for wearing rather than for admiring, and I hastened to put them on. Then, donning my heavy mittens, I followed Wynn out to the sleigh.

Since I could not maneuver showshoes, I was privileged to ride. Wynn ran along beside or behind me, calling out orders to the dogs. They obeyed immediately. Maybe Wynn's "secondhand" team wasn't so bad after all. They certainly behaved themselves better in harness than out. I was gaining respect for them as we glided over the crisp winter snow.

"This is fun!" I shouted to Wynn as the sled flew over a slight rise in the trail. He laughed at my little-girl exuberance.

We came to an area where the wind had swept across the path, leaving the snow only a few inches deep.

"Would you like to walk for a while?" Wynn asked me. I did, so I scrambled from the sleigh and set out to follow him and the team.

The team would have left me far behind if I had just walked along behind. I had to run. I could tell Wynn was holding the team back with his commands. Still they seemed to gain ground. I hurried faster, but it was hard to keep at it with all the clothing I was wearing. Wynn soon stopped the team, and I laughingly tumbled back onto the sled. I was out of breath and panting, but it had been good for me.

Wynn found Crazy Mary out working her traps. She was a little woman.

Too small to be handling this man-sized job, I reasoned, and my concern for her deepened.

She had straight, black hair which had been chopped off at the jawline. In the morning sunshine, she wore her parka hood back, and her hair kept flopping forward, covering her face. She peeped out from between strands of it, her eyes black and flashing. There were some scars on her face, and I realized that somehow she alone had survived the smallpox epidemic. Over her back she wore a skin sack of some kind, and I could see fur pieces sticking out of it. Apparently, Crazy Mary skinned the animals just where she found them, then threw aside the carcasses and stuffed the fur into her sack. Wynn had told me that as soon as the trapper got back to his cabin, he cleaned and stretched the pelts onto a wooden frame for drying. Crazy Mary would still have work to do when she got home at the end of the day.

I stayed near the sleigh while Wynn talked to her. I could not hear their conversation. But I could tell she was still agitated. She waved her arms and pounded her fists together and then gave little shrieks like a wounded animal. I didn't know if she was giving Wynn a demonstration of something that had happened or just expressing her feelings.

After some minutes Wynn came back to the sled.

"Well?" I asked.

"She still says someone is pushing back her boundary lines."

"Do you think they are?"

"I don't know. It's hard to tell when there really aren't any actual, visible lines in the first place."

I waved to Crazy Mary as we moved away. There she stood, one little woman alone fighting against the elements and an unseen, unknown enemy. I felt very sorry for her. I refused to refer to her as "crazy." If she had to be identified, they could call her *Brave Mary* or *Trapline Mary.* There was no need to call her Crazy Mary at all.

At Smith's cabin, his dog team was tethered in the yard and began howling and barking as our team swung around to the front. Smith himself came to the door. Seeing Wynn's uniform under his parka, he waved an arm to us, beckoning us to come in. I didn't suppose that he got many visitors.

He wasn't much for conversation, but he grinned and went about making up a tin pot of very strong, hot tea.

We sipped slowly. I was given the honor of the only chair in the room, the men half crouched, supported by the wall of the cabin.

They talked about lines, furs, and the economy. I didn't join in. I was too busy watching the litter of puppies that ignored us and went about their play. What fluffy round balls they were, with sparkling eyes and curly tails. It was hard to believe they could grow up into snarling, fighting, mean-spirited dogs. They were good-sized already, and I knew that they were well past the weaning stage.

After a few minutes, Smith seemed to feel there had been enough small talk.

"So what brings you out this way, Sarge?" he asked Wynn.

Part of Wynn's job was to gather information where he could, and another part of his job was to scatter a little information, too.

"Mary has reported that someone is getting a little too close with their traps," Wynn said, carefully studying the man's reaction.

"That crazy woman! She's the one broadening *her* boundary. She's been mismanaging her traps for years; and now that she can't find the animals, she's moving her lines. Did you see where she's got her traps?"

Wynn agreed that he had.

The trapper pulled a hand-drawn map from the shelf in the corner and spread it out on the table.

"Looky here," he said, agitated. "This here is my trapline. I've had it for years. Goes right along the river here, swings to the north by that stand of jackpine, follows up the draw, dips down to that little beaver dam, turns around west here, and comes back along this chain of hills. Every trapper in the territory knows those are my boundaries. So what does she do? She's sneaking traps in here and a few over in here." His finger stabbed at the map, punctuating each statement. "And the last time I was out, she even had a couple in here."

It was clear that Smith was upset.

"If she wasn't a woman," the man exploded, "an' a crazy one at that, I'd—" But he didn't finish the statement.

Wynn continued to study the map. "I'll do some checking," he said quietly. "It's clear that we've got to find out who's crowding who."

Then Wynn turned his attention to the pups snapping and fighting playfully on the dirt floor.

"I'm looking for some new sled dogs," he said. "Hear that you raise good animals. They look pretty good to me. Planning to sell these, are you?"

It was the first time Smith smiled. He reached down and scooped up a fluffy pup. It rewarded him by chewing on his thumb. He roughed its woolly back and clipped its ears playfully.

"Hate to, but I gotta. Got all of the team dogs now that I need. Another litter due in a couple of weeks. Which one you got your eye on?"

I knew which one I had *my* eye on. It was a little fellow with a full fluffy tail that curled over his back. He was a silver grey in color with shining black eyes and a sticky red tongue. He had been licking the snow off my boots.

I waited breathlessly for Wynn to name his dog.

"What do you think, Elizabeth?" he surprised me. "Which ones would you pick?"

"How many do you need?"

"I thought I'd start with two."

"For sled dogs?"

"What else would we need them for?"

I reached down and picked up the cute pup. He turned from licking at my boots and began to lick at my hands. *I think he likes me,* I exulted.

"Well, I was just thinking that it wouldn't be a bad idea to have a dog at the house. I mean, it would be company and—"

"You want a *dog*?"

I did not hesitate but answered him with the same intensity with which he had asked his incredulous question.

"Yes."

He laughed then, softly. "I thought you were afraid of dogs."

"The ones in the village, yes. They snarl and growl and snap when you go by. But I like dogs, generally. Really. A dog of my own, there at the cabin, might make me feel—well, less lonely—and more secure when you are away."

Wynn could see that I really wanted the pup.

"Okay," he smiled. "You go first."

"Go first?"

"You take your pick first."

That was no problem for me. I held up the pup already in my arms. "This one," I said without a moment's hesitation.

Smith and Wynn were both grinning at me when I looked up.

"What do you think, Smith?" asked Wynn in a teasing way.

"I think the little lady got you," grinned Smith.

I must have looked puzzled.

"I think she did, too. Picked the best one in the bunch. I had my eye on that one for lead dog." Wynn reached over and tussled the pup's fur. It growled playfully and pawed at his hand.

I felt very happy with myself. I had picked a winner. Still, if Wynn had wanted this one for the lead dog, perhaps I should— "You can have him if you like," I said, offering the pup. "You need him. I just want him."

Wynn lifted his hand from the pup and touched my cheek. "You keep him. I think he'll be just right for you. There are plenty of others for me to choose from. They look like the makings of good sled dogs, too."

Wynn made his two selections. They were pretty little dogs as well, but I was glad I'd had first choice. Wynn paid Smith and we bundled up our armload of pups and headed for home.

The pups were not easy to transport. Wynn fared better with his. He put them in a knapsack with only their furry heads protruding and secured them on his back. They watched, wide-eyed, as we hurried over the trail.

My little fellow was more difficult. I insisted on carrying him on my lap. He didn't like being confined, and wiggled and squirmed and whined and yapped. I was about to give up on him when he decided that he had had enough, curled up and went to sleep.

I kept my hand on him, gently stroking the soft fur. I was so happy to finally have a dog of my very own. Being raised in the city, my folks thought our house and yard were too confining for pets. I guess I had secretly always wanted one. Maybe that was why I had enjoyed the small mouse, Napoleon, for the short while he had been with me in the teacherage. And now I had a dog! And a beautiful dog it would be. I would name it myself. I began to go over names in my mind. *A dog like this should have a name that is rather majestic, like King or Prince or Duke.* But I rejected each of those as too common.

Suddenly I thought of something. I turned slightly in the sleigh.

"Wynn," I hollered against the swishing of the sled runners and the yipping of the dogs. "Do I need a boy-name or a girl-name?"

There was laughter in Wynn's voice as he called back, "A boy-name, Elizabeth."

24
Settling In

I NAMED MY dog Kip. If someone had asked, I really wouldn't have been able to explain why. It just seemed to suit him somehow. He was a smart little thing, and Wynn said that it was never too early to begin his training. So I started in. I didn't know much about training dogs. Wynn told me obedience was of primary importance. A dog, to be useful and enjoyable, must be obedient. Wynn gave me pointers, and in the evenings, if duties did not call him out, he even worked with me and the young dog.

It was amazing how quickly Kip grew. One day he was a fluffy pup, and the next day it seemed he was a gangly, growing dog. He turned from cute into beautiful. His tail curled above his silver-tipped, glistening dark fur. He was curious and sensitive and a quick learner. I loved him immediately and he did so help to fill my days. Aware of his needs, physical and emotional, my own life was enriched.

Kip needed exercise, so I took him out for walks, bundling myself up against the cold. It was a good way to get my exercise as well. When the snow got deeper and more difficult to navigate, I asked for snowshoes so that I might still keep up the daily exercise program. Wynn brought some home and took me out to introduce me to the use of them. They were much more difficult to manage than it seemed when watching Wynn maneuver in them. I took many tumbles in the snow in the process of learning. Kip thought it was a game; every time I went down, he was there to lick my face and scatter snow down my neck.

Eventually I did get the feel of snowshoes. The cold or the snow no longer kept me confined. I walked along the river trails, along the treeline to the west, and to the settlement. Whenever I went to the store with Kip, I picked him up and carried him. He was getting heavy and he was also getting impatient with me. He hated to be carried; he wanted to run. But I was fearful about all the dog fights I had seen on my trips to the village. I did not want Kip to be attacked. And so, as the weeks went by, each time our outings included the store, or Nimmie's for Bible study, I picked up my growing, complaining dog. I wondered just how much longer I could manage it. I hated to be stuck in the house, and I hated to leave Kip at home alone. I guessed that eventually all our walks would have to take us away from the dogs and the village and into the woods instead.

* * *

As the weeks went by, more snow piled up around us. The people began to be concerned about food and wood supplies. It took all their time and attention to provide a meal or two for the day and to keep their homes reasonably warm.

Christmas seemed unreal to me. There was no village celebration, no setting aside of this important day. Wynn and I celebrated quietly in our home. We read the Christmas story, and I shed a few tears of loneliness. I tried not to let Wynn see them, but I think he was suspicious. We did not have a turkey dinner with all of the trimmings. We had, instead, a venison roast and blueberry pie made from the berries I had gathered and canned. The Indian women had dried theirs, but I knew nothing about the drying process. Besides, I thought I preferred the canned fruit; to my way of thinking, they did taste awfully good in that Christmas dinner pie.

In the afternoon, Wynn suggested we take Kip for a run. It was fun to be out together, but the weather was bitterly cold, so we did not stay out for long. I think even Kip was glad to be back inside by our warm fire.

We were soon beginning a new year. Repeatedly, Wynn had to dig us out from a new snowfall in the mornings. If it had not been for Kip, I'm sure I would never have left my kitchen. He would whine and scamper about at the door, coaxing for a run.

The trappers now and then brought home meat for their families. The women supplemented this with some ice fishing in the nearby river. It was cold, miserable work; and I ached in my bones for them. Children and women alike were often out gathering wood from the nearby forest. I wondered why more of them did not prepare for the winter by stacking up a good fuel supply. Most of the Indians gathered as they needed it, and that was a big task when the fires had to be kept burning day and night.

I still met for studies with Nimmie and Miss McLain, though she still had not thawed out much. She seemed so deeply bitter and troubled. Little by little I learned her story. She had been orphaned at the age of three; Ian was five at the time. A fine Swedish family in the East had taken pity on the two children and raised them along with their own six. They had been treated kindly enough, but the family was poor and frugal, and all the children were required to work at an early age.

Schooling was one thing the family had felt was important, so each one of the children had been allowed to attend the local school as high as the grades went. When they reached their teen years, they were soon on their own. When Ian left the family, he apprenticed to a merchant in a nearby town as a bookkeeper and stock-checker. The man was German, and Ian lived in his home and learned German. Katherine had her heart set on being a schoolteacher, and so she found employment in the home of a doctor as housemaid and took classes whenever she could crowd them in.

The woman of the house was impossible to please, and young Katherine often found herself the victim of fits of fury. She would have left if she had had any place to go. At length her schooling was completed and she was able to obtain a position at a local school. The doctor's wife suddenly realized that she was losing good help, and she tried to bar Miss McLain from getting the job. It didn't work. Miss McLain was hired and moved out of the home and into a boarding house. There was a young man staying at the boarding house as well; and, after some months, they became attracted to one another and eventually engaged. Miss McLain was now a happy girl. For the first time that she remembered, she had a job she loved, a salary on which she could live, and—most importantly—someone who loved her.

The young man seemed happy, too, and he was anxious for the wedding to take place. Miss McLain told him she had to wait until she could afford her dress and all the other things she needed. The man declared that he hated to wait longer and then came up with a lovely plan. He had a sister in town. He was sure she would be ever so glad to help them.

They boarded a streetcar and went to see the sister. Miss McLain was excited. If her John was correct in assuming his sister would help, she would soon be a married woman with a husband and home of her own.

When the streetcar stopped and they walked the short distance to the sister's home, Miss McLain could only stand in frozen bewilderment. There must be some mistake. They were at the home of her former employer.

She did go in, but things did not go well. Not only did the angry woman refuse to help her, but she raged and ranted about her dishonesty, her ill temper, her laziness, and even her bad name. John only stood there like a statue, not even defending his Katherine.

In the end, the rift between them was so great that it could not be repaired, and John called off the engagement. Miss McLain left behind her school and her dreams and headed for her brother, who was by now living in the North.

She had never buried her bitterness. In her twenty years in the North, she had nursed it and fostered it and held it to her until now it was a terrible, deep festering wound in her soul. She was miserable; she deserved to be miserable; I think she even enjoyed being miserable; and she did a wonderful job of making those around her miserable, too.

In spite of her bitterness and her anger with life, I began to like Miss McLain. I felt both sorry for her and angry with her. Other people had suffered; others had been treated unfairly. They had lived through it. There was no reason why Miss McLain could not pull herself out of her misery if she had a mind to.

Nimmie was always patient and loving with her. Miss McLain, in turn, was spiteful and cutting with Nimmie. She didn't bother much with me. Perhaps she didn't think I was worth the trouble, or perhaps she thought I would not be intimidated by her; I do not know.

In spite of the difficulty, we were able to proceed with our Bible study. As we went through the lessons together, I was sensing a real change in Nimmie.

There was an eagerness, a softness, an openness that really thrilled me. She was so disappointed if a storm kept us from meeting. After a morning of study, she would share with Ian at night the things that she had learned. I was surprised and delighted that Ian seemed interested in what Nimmie told him. He, too, seemed eager to hear truth from God's Word.

In the middle of January, a bad storm hit. In all of my life I had never seen so much snow fall in so short a time. I was worried about Wynn; he was somewhere out in that whiteness with the dog team. I knew that dogs had an unusual sense of direction even in a storm, but I paced and prayed all day that the animals wouldn't let us down now.

The temperature dipped and the water in the basin again glazed over with ice. I worked hard to keep the cabin warm, adding fuel to the fire regularly. Kip whined at the door to go for a run, but I put him off. He was so insistent that eventually I sent him out for a few minutes on his own. I had never let him out alone before and I was afraid he might not come back. But he was soon crying at the door to be admitted to the warmth.

I fed Kip and made myself tea. Still Wynn did not come.

It was dark outside when there was a thumping at the door. I ran to it with my heart in my throat. Who could it be? Wynn did not knock at his own door. Who else would be coming and why? *Has something happened to Wynn?*

But it *was* Wynn, and in his arms he had a bundle. I opened the door wide for him.

"It's Crazy Mary," he said. "She was alone in her cabin with no heat and no food."

I hurried ahead of Wynn and tossed the cushions from the cot to make a place for her.

He opened the blankets, and she lay shivering. For a moment, I wondered if she was conscious, and then her eyelids fluttered and she looked at us. I smiled, but it was not returned.

"Do you have any food ready?" asked Wynn.

"There's soup in the pot, and I just made tea."

"A little soup. Not too much. I'll have to feed her."

While I went for the soup, Wynn finished unbundling the blankets from Mary, and now he removed the moccasins and wrappings of hide from her feet. He was working over her feet when I came with the soup. He went to take the bowl from me, but I indicated her feet. "I'll feed her," I said. "You do whatever is necessary there."

At first she refused the soup on the spoon; but when I was able to trickle a little of it into her mouth, she opened it ever so slightly and I was able to give her more. She swallowed several spoonfuls before I decided it was enough for the time.

"Should I give her some tea?" I asked Wynn.

"A little," he replied, and I got a cup of tea and spooned some of it into the woman's mouth.

She still shivered. I had never seen anyone who looked so cold. I went for more blankets.

We fixed a bed for Mary on the cot and looked after her throughout the night. Several times I awoke to find Wynn absent from bed and bent over the old woman, spooning hot soup or massaging her frostbitten feet.

The next few days were taken up with nursing Mary. Her toes swelled to a disturbing size. There didn't seem to be much more we could do for them. About once an hour I would spoon-feed her. She ate more heartily now, though she still was unable to feed herself.

I knew she could talk, but she did not speak to me. I had heard her talking to Wynn the day we had visited her on her trapline. She had been quite vocal then. I knew her silence now was not because she couldn't speak but because she chose not to. For whatever reason, I decided to respect it. Oh, I talked to her. I talked to her as I fed her and as I cared for her feet. I talked to her about the weather as I moved about the house doing the dishes or feeding the fire. I talked to her much like I talked to Kip—including her in my activities but not expecting an answer.

She lay on the cot, her black eyes watching every move I made; but she said nothing.

When the worst of the storm was over, Mrs. Sam and Evening Star came for tea. It had been some weeks since I had had their company and I was so glad to see them. I suspected they had come to see Mary. They may have, but if so they certainly kept it well hidden. After one glance in the woman's direction, they completely ignored her. They crossed to my kitchen table where they knew they would be served, and seated themselves.

They talked about the storm, the need for wood for the fire, the difficulty in catching fish—mostly communicating with waving, expressive hands, though they did add a word here and there. Evening Star played with Kip, seeming to like my dog. The Indians were not accustomed to having a dog in the home, and it must have seemed strange to her.

When they rose to leave, I followed them to the door.

"Mary is getting much better," I said quietly, to introduce the subject of her stay with us into the conversation. "In a few days, we hope she will be able to sit up some."

There was no response.

"As soon as she is able to sit, we think she will be able to feed herself, and then before too long she will be able to get around again. It's going to take awhile, but she is getting better."

I wasn't sure how many of my English words the two women understood, so I used hand gestures to accompany them.

Mrs. Sam was shaking her head. She turned at the door and looked at me.

"Not stay," she said clearly.

"Oh, she must stay," I persisted. "She needs lots of care yet. She couldn't possibly care for herself for many days."

But Mrs. Sam still shook her head. "Not stay," she insisted. "She go— soon."

Mrs. Sam was right. When we got up the next morning, Mary was not there. How she ever managed to drag herself from our home and back to her cabin I'll never know. She had been so weak and her feet so swollen, and yet she was gone. Wynn immediately went after her. She was already home—sitting in her cold cabin, her scanty blankets wrapped around her. She refused to move.

He gathered wood and built her a fire and made her a cup of tea from the supplies he always carried with him. Then he spent the morning gathering a wood supply for her.

He went out with his rifle and was rewarded in his hunt with a buck deer which he cleaned and hung in a tree close to Mary's cabin. Preserved by the cold, it would supply meat for many weeks for the lone woman.

He gave her instructions about caring for her feet, unloaded all of the food supplies he had with him, and left her.

I cried when Wynn told me. I felt so sorry for the little woman all alone there.

"There is nothing more we can do," Wynn comforted me. "If we brought her back here, she would only run away again; and next time she might not make it."

I knew he was right. He had done the best he knew how for Mary. We hoped it was enough to keep her alive.

25

The Storm

STORM AFTER STORM hit the little settlement. We lived from one day to the next, accepting the weather as it came. On the good days, when the wind calmed down, I went out with Kip. On the days of snow and wind, I shivered and stayed in. I came to hate wind. Not only was it cold and miserable, but it was confining and, I was soon to learn, deadly.

One brisk, windy morning, Wynn returned from the Hudson's Bay Store where he had gone for a few needed supplies and reported that he had to take a trip south.

"Today?" I asked incredulously. It was bitterly cold. The windchill must have lowered the temperature to -50ºF or worse.

"Now," he answered, "I'm on my way as soon as I get the team."

Wynn came into the cabin long enough to add some extra clothing to what he was already wearing and to pack his supply sack with more food and medical equipment. I felt panic seizing me as I noticed his precautions. It looked as though he expected delays.

"I may not make it back home tonight, Elizabeth," he said, straightening up and drawing me into his arms. "Don't worry about me. There are several trappers' shacks along the trail, and if the storm gets any worse I can take cover. Do you have everything you need?"

Me? I was all right. He was the one going out into the storm. Wynn checked the wood supply.

"There is plenty more wood stacked right outside the door if you should run out," he informed me. "Don't leave the cabin until you are sure the storm is over. And then if you do go out, be sure to take Kip."

I nodded. It sounded as if he was planning to be gone *forever*! Tears welled up in my eyes.

"I'll be fine," he said, brushing the tears away tenderly. "I love you."

I tried to tell him that I loved him too; but it was difficult to get the words out. My throat felt tight and dry.

"Where—where are you going?" I finally managed to ask.

"Word just came in that a trapper out near Beaver Falls hasn't been seen for a couple of weeks. His friend says he always shows up at his place for a Friday night card game, but he hasn't been there for two Fridays now. He's worried about him."

"Doesn't he have a cabin?"

"They checked it out. He's not there."

"If he's been gone for two weeks," I said, annoyed, "why didn't some-one report it before—when the weather was decent?"

"I can't answer that; but it's been reported now, and I have to go."

I was angry with the careless trapper. I was disgusted with his friend who had let it go for so long without reporting it. I was even a little put out with Wynn for taking his duty so seriously. Surely it would be wiser to wait until the weather improved.

I kissed him goodbye and let him go, because there was nothing else I could do.

Even Kip wasn't much help in filling in the long day. I talked to him and fed him and petted him, but my heart was with Wynn. *I hope he makes it home before dark*, I anguished inwardly.

Night came and Wynn did not come. I sat up, curled in a blanket and tucked between pillows, on our cot. Kip snuggled at my feet, now and then lifting his head to listen intently to the sounds of the night. I heard the howl of a wolf above the wind, and Kip heard it too. He stirred rest-lessly but did not answer the cry.

I watched the fire closely. If Wynn returned—no, *when* Wynn returned—he would be chilled and would need the warmth.

I dozed off now and then; each time I awakened, I strained to hear footsteps approaching the cabin. They did not come. Toward morning I finally gave in and fell asleep.

I awoke to find the cabin fairly shaking with the wind. The fire was nearly out, and I quickly went for more fuel to build it up. The wind seemed to scream through every crack and crevice of our little home. The temperature dropped further and the snow swirled all around the cabin. Even Kip seemed to be uneasy.

All day I kept the fires burning. I knew I would soon be drawing on the supply from outside. I wondered about the Indian families. They weren't as well stocked for wood as I had been. Surely by now they would have exhausted their supplies. I wished there was some way of bring-ing them to the warmth and protection of our cabin. With my fingers, I scratched a spot in the frost on the window and looked out. I could not see the buildings of the settlement. I could not even see the birch tree that grew about fifteen feet from the door. All I could see was angry, swirl-ing snow.

I tried to drink a cup of tea, but my hands shook when I lifted the cup to my mouth. I was on the verge of tears, but I knew that tears would do no good.

I fed the fire, I prayed, I walked the floor, I prayed, I read my Bible, I prayed; and somehow this even longer second day of storm passed by, hour by hour.

Another night, and still Wynn had not come. Again I did not go to bed. Kip whined uneasily and pressed his nose against my hand. I stroked his rich, fluffy fur and spoke to him in caressing tones, but I could not keep my tears from falling as I did so.

Somehow we made it through another night. We awoke to another day of snow and wind. I thought I couldn't stand it any longer. The wind was driving me mad with its incessant howling. I clung to my Bible and prayed until I felt utterly exhausted. Mid-morning, after reading, weeping, and praying for what seemed like hours, I fell asleep. The long days and sleepless nights had taken their toll, and my body demanded some rest even if my mind fought against it.

When I awoke, I could scarcely believe my eyes. Sunshine! The wind had stopped. The snow was no longer falling. The storm had passed. I wanted to shout; I wanted to run. I wanted to break out of my confining cabin and find human companionship. How had they all fared through the storm? And I wondered about Wynn. Now that the storm was over, he would soon be home. I must have a hot meal ready for him.

It was then that I realized the fires were no longer burning. I must get them started again quickly. I had only a few more pieces of wood that I had brought in from outside, but there was plenty more by the door. I rushed to get some. But I could not budge the door. I pushed again, not understanding; but it would not give. *The snow!* It had drifted us in. I tried again. Surely we wouldn't be shut in here for long. Surely, with enough strength, I could get it open. I tried again and again, but the door would not move.

I let the fire in the kitchen stove go out and just kept the fireplace burning in order to conserve the little fuel I had. Wynn would soon be here. Surely the fuel would last until then. When he came, he would dig us out and all would be well again.

But the day wore on and Wynn did not come.

I walked to my window and scratched a spot to look down at the settlement. I could see smoke rising from cabins. There was stirring about as people and dogs moved among the buildings. I tried to wave, but I knew that was foolish. There was no way anyone could detect a hand waving in my small, frosted window. I put the last stick of wood on my fire and waited again. *Surely Wynn will soon be here,* I told Kip silently.

The fire burned out. I wrapped myself in blankets and huddled on the cot. Even that was cold. I began to fear for my hands and feet. I picked up the heavy fur rug from the floor and wrapped myself in that, too. It was bulky, but it did offer some protection. Kip whined to go out, but there was no way I could let him. I thought of trying to push him through the window, hoping that he might run down to the settlement and attract someone's attention concerning my plight. But the window was too small for Kip's nearly full-sized body.

Night was coming again. I bundled myself up as best I could and tried to go to sleep. I fell asleep praying.

I vaguely remember stirring once or twice during the night and feeling terribly cold. In my benumbed state, I couldn't sort out the reason for the cold. Kip stirred, too, and I pulled the blankets more tightly around myself and dozed off again, Kipp curled up on my feet. He felt heavy, but I did not make him move.

"Hallo. Hallo in there," a voice finally brought me to consciousness. I struggled out of my blanket covering and hurried to the door. It still would not open. "I can't open the door," I called as loudly as I could. I heard shovels then. Someone was digging us out. It was McLain and a couple of the Indian men. I was glad to see them, but I was disappointed that Wynn wasn't with them. When the door was finally cleared enough for them to enter the house, my first question was, "Have you heard from my husband?"

McLain paused for a moment and looked around. "Have you heard from Wynn?" I asked again.

"No, not yet, ma'am; but he'll be all right."

I took what comfort I could from his words. I wondered if McLain knew what he was talking about or if he was simply trying to put my mind at ease.

"How are you?" he asked me.

"I'm fine—I think," I answered, trying my arms and legs to make sure they still moved properly. "I was never so glad to see anyone in my life! Thank you."

"How long have you been without heat?"

"Just overnight."

"That's too long," the big man said, reaching for my hand. "How are your fingers?"

"Fine."

"Your feet?"

"Okay."

"Let's see them."

I started to protest, but he would have none of it. "Let's see your feet, Mrs. Delaney."

I went to my bedroom to remove my long stockings and padded out again in my bare feet. The cabin floor was ice cold. Mr. McLain sat me in a chair and looked at each foot in turn.

"You're a mighty lucky lady," he said at last. "I don't know how you kept them from freezing."

"Kip slept on them," I said, suddenly remembering.

"What?"

"Kip. My dog. He slept on them. I remember waking up in the night and I could feel the heaviness from his body on my feet."

"Well, I'll be," Mr. McLain said, and then he began to laugh. "Well, boy," he said, running a hand through Kip's fine fur, "I guess you're more'n just pretty."

One of the Indian men had been working on a fire in the fireplace. It was burning briskly now.

"We've gotta thaw this here place out," said McLain and crossed to the kitchen stove. "This here water in the pail is frozen solid."

It was. So was the basin, and so was, I discovered to my dismay, my china teapot. It had split right down the side from the force of the freezing tea. All of those days of enjoying tea with friends were behind me. I wanted to sit right down and cry, but the men were bustling all about, and I didn't want them to see my hurt. Besides, I was still worried about Wynn.

"Better get your feet dressed again," said Mr. McLain, and I realized I was still puttering about in my bare feet.

I obeyed, slipping into my nice warm moccasins and then I went to my kitchen to see what other damage had been done. A few tins of food were split from frost as well. The pail was okay. I guess the dipper sitting in it had given the ice an upward, rather than outward, thrust. The kettle I wasn't sure about. I would have to wait until it thawed before I would know if it would still hold water without leaking.

The basin was okay, too. It had slanted sides and the ice just seemed to move up them. There really hadn't been too much damage. And, thankfully, I still had all my fingers and toes.

"We didn't see any smoke from your chimney this morning. Gave us quite a scare," Mr. McLain was saying.

"I was scared, too," I admitted. "I didn't know when someone might come."

"The storm was tough on everyone. Nimmie has a whole Fort full of people that she's trying to get hot food into. A number of the families ran out of wood."

"Was anyone—?" I started to ask if any lives had been taken by the storm, but I couldn't finish the question. I was half-sick with worry about Wynn.

Mr. McLain surmised the question and hesitated for a moment, then answered slowly.

"We lost a few—mostly older ones. A little girl died, too. She was always sickly, and this cold was just too much for her. It's been hard on Nimmie. The girl was one of her special pets."

Poor Nimmie.

The fires were burning brightly now, and the room was losing some of its chill. It would be some time until it was really warm again. The two Indian men left. Mr. McLain brought in a good supply of wood from beside the door, and then he, too, turned to go.

"You should be just fine now," he assured me. "We'll keep a better lookout from now on. I don't think it's gonna blow tonight. Sky looks clear."

"Can I come with you?" I asked quickly. I knew that Nimmie needed my help. I was torn between going to her and waiting in the cabin in case

Wynn came home. My conscience finally won over my heart and I reached for my heavy coat.

Kip moved to follow me, but I pushed him back.

"You wait here," I said to him. "I won't be long."

"I don't mind if you bring him, if you like," said Mr. McLain.

"He might get in a fight with a dog in town," I objected.

"He might."

"Well, I wouldn't want him hurt."

"Is that why you used to carry him?"

We had shut the door on the whining Kip and were making our way across the drifts of snow to the settlement.

My breath was blowing out before me in puffy white clouds. I didn't answer McLain; he was walking too briskly for me to maneuver my snowshoes, keep up, and talk all at the same time. I just nodded my head in assent.

"So you planning on shutting him in all the time now?"

I shook my head.

"What will you do then?"

"I'll walk him out there," I said, waving my arm at the vast emptiness in the opposite direction of the village.

"You won't be able to keep him away from dogs forever, you know."

I had thought about that.

"Appears to me," said the husky man, "that Kip would likely hold his own pretty good in a fight. You've been feeding him well, and he has several pounds on some of the village dogs that just forage for their food. He's had good exercise, so he's developed strong bones and muscles. He's right smart. I think he'd handle himself just fine up against another dog."

I wasn't sure just what the man was trying to tell me.

"Are you saying—?" I began, but Mr. McLain cut in, "I'm saying that, with a child or a dog, you've got to give them a chance to grow up— natural like. You can't pamper them forever, or you spoil them. They can never be what they were meant to be. Kip's a Husky. Sure, they are a scrappy bunch when the need arises. And the need will arise someday. Here in the North, it's bound to. I think you oughta give Kip the chance to prove himself before he gets up against an animal where his life depends upon his fighting skill."

I wanted to argue with this man—to tell him that Kip would never need to fight, that I would keep him away from such circumstances. But I knew Mr. McLain was probably right. Kip was a northern dog. He would have to be prepared to live in the North. I hated the thought, but it was true.

I walked on in silence, slowly turning over in my mind the words of the man beside me. I would have to let Kip grow up. I would have to expose him to the rigors of the village and the fangs of the other dogs.

First, I would talk to Wynn about it and see if he agreed with this man. Oh, if only Wynn would get home! He had been gone for three days. Surely his mission shouldn't have taken him this long.

I blinked back tears that made little icicles on my cheeks and hurried after Mr. McLain. Nimmie needed me.

26
Aftermath

THE SITUATION AT the Hudson's Bay Store was even worse than I had expected. People were crowded in everywhere. Nimmie, busy filling bowls from a steaming pot of thin soup, gave me a welcoming smile. Mrs. Sam was the only one in the group whom I recognized. A few of the children I had seen gathered around Nimmie for her storytelling.

Some of the people had bandages on hands or feet, and I assumed they were being treated for frostbite.

I crossed to Mrs. Sam. "Where's your husband?" I asked her. When she looked at me blankly, I said, "Sam? Where's Sam?"

"Trap," she answered, making a motion like a trap snapping shut with her hands.

"What about the others? Evening Star and Little Deer and Anna? Have you seen them?"

She shook her head.

We stared at each other, recognizing the questions and concern in the other's eyes. I didn't know if their husbands had been out on the traplines or not, not sure how much difference it would make to have them home or away.

Nimmie was relieved to see me. "I'm so glad you're all right," she said when she had finished serving the last bowl. "That was the worst storm I ever remember. I was afraid you wouldn't have enough wood."

Apparently Mr. McLain had not told Nimmie about the smokeless chimney, not wanting to alarm her until he had checked further. "Oh, I had plenty of wood," was all I said now. "What can I do to help?" I asked her.

"Those people over there—they still haven't had anything to eat. I've run out of bowls or cups. I don't know—"

"What about Miss McLain?" I asked. "Would she have some bowls we could use?"

"I hadn't thought of that—"

"I'll go see." I hurried out the door and around to the back of the building.

A call gave me permission to enter. I found Miss McLain in a warm room sitting before her fireplace, her feet on a block of wood to soak up the heat, and her hands folded in her lap.

I stood looking at her in bewilderment, wondering if she was totally oblivious to all that was going on just next door. I finally found my voice.

"I came because of Nimmie," I began. "She has two or three dozen people to feed and she has run out of dishes. We were wondering if we could borrow some."

She didn't even look at me. "Guess you can," she said flatly with no interest.

Her attitude made me cross, but I held my tongue.

I swallowed and then said evenly, "Where are they?"

"Now where do you suppose dishes would be?" she returned with exaggerated sarcasm.

"May I help myself?" I asked, still in check.

"I don't know who will if you don't," was her biting reply.

I took a deep breath, crossed to her cupboards and began to lift out dishes. I piled them in a dishpan sitting on a nearby shelf. When I had all I could find, I turned to go.

"Just make sure they're boiled when you're done with them," stated Miss McLain, her eyes not leaving the fire.

I swung around to face her. "Do you realize," I flung at her, "there are people just beyond that wall who are fighting for their lives? Do you know that some of them may well lose their fingers or their toes? Do you know that Nimmie has been up half the night taking care of them? And here you sit, all—all bundled up in your great self-pity—thinking only about yourself and your lost love! Well, do you want to know what I think? I think you were well rid of the man. If he thought no more of you than to—to desert you because of a whining, accusing sister, then he wasn't much of a man.

"And do you know what else I think?" I was pretty sure Miss McLain wasn't one bit interested in what I thought, but I went on anyway. "I think that if after twenty years, you are still sitting by your fire and tending your little hurt while people out there are suffering with cold and hunger, then you're not much of a woman either. And maybe—maybe the doctor's wife was right. Maybe poor little John is better off without you."

I left the room, slamming the door behind me. I was halfway back to the store before what I had just done fully hit me. I bit my lip and the tears started to flow. I had been praying so diligently for this woman. I had been trying so hard to show her real love and compassion. Nimmie had been trying to break down the barriers for so many years—and I had just wiped out any faint possibilities of progress in a moment of anger. I would have to apologize. I didn't expect her to accept my apology. I would never be able to repair the damage I had done.

"Oh, God, forgive me," I wailed in remorse. "I should never have said that."

The apology would have to wait. Nimmie needed me and needed me now.

We worked all forenoon. The people were fed and looked after to the best of our ability. Mr. McLain and some of the men made an inspection tour to all the village houses. It was even worse than we had thought. Besides the little girl, the storm had claimed five other victims: an older man and his equally old wife living in a cabin alone at the edge of the village; a grandmother in the household of our erstwhile driver on the trip to the settlement, and an elderly gentleman who had been very sick before the storm struck. The general opinion was that he would have died regardless because of his weakened condition. Also dead was a middle-aged woman who had attempted to gather more wood and lost her way in the storm. Because of the heavy snow and the cold weather, digging of graves was impossible, so the bodies were all to be bundled up in blankets and tied up in the branches of the trees to await springtime. The Indian people had a special stand of trees which served that purpose—the "burying trees," Mr. McLain called them. But before the bodies could be prepared for the burying trees, they had to be examined by the Royal North West Police and permission given. So they were lined up in a vacant cabin to await Wynn's return.

Caring for the needs of the people in the village helped to some extent to take my mind off Wynn, though I wasn't able to ignore his absence completely. Throughout the day Nimmie and I had our hands full taking care of all those who needed our help. By early afternoon the store was beginning to empty. Many had now gathered fuel for their fires and returned to their own cabins. Those who remained behind needed to be fed again; and so I worked over the stew pot, getting another all-too-scanty meal ready for them.

Nimmie had just finished checking a swollen hand when I heard her exclamation, "Katherine! Are you all right?"

I swung around and, sure enough, there stood Miss McLain. I knew my apology was overdue and that it shouldn't be put off, but this hardly seemed the time or the place. I wasn't sure what to do.

Miss McLain said nothing, so Nimmie went on, "Did you want something?"

"Yes," said Miss McLain matter-of-factly. "I want to help."

I don't know who was more astounded—Nimmie or I. We both looked at Miss McLain with our mouths open. Her eyes were red and swollen, and I could tell she had been weeping.

"I want to help," she repeated. "Would you tell me what I can do?"

"Well, uh, well—we are fixing something to eat again. Some of these people have just come in and they haven't had anything to eat for a couple of days. Elizabeth is making stew."

"What can I do?" asked Miss McLain one more time.

"Well, we'll—we'll need the dishes. We haven't had time to wash the dishes yet." Nimmie motioned toward the dishpan filled with dirty dishes still sitting on the back of the big stove. Without a word, Miss McLain moved to the dishpan, rolled up her sleeves, and set to work.

Nimmie looked at me and I just shrugged my shoulders helplessly. I had no idea what had brought about the change. And I wasn't about to ask—here.

By mid-afternoon we had done all we could for the village people. All had now returned to their homes. Smoke rose from the cabins circling the town clearing. Nimmie suggested we sit down and have a cup of tea, but I said I would rather get back home. Kip was still in and unattended, and I was sure Wynn would soon be home. And by now the fire would have burned out, leaving the cabin cold again. With all these reasons, Nimmie let me go.

Kip was glad to see me, fairly knocking me over with his enthusiasm. I let him out for a run while I rebuilt the fires. It took awhile for the rooms to warm up and for the teakettle to begin to sing. It leaked a bit around the spout, but was still usable. I lamented again over the loss of my teapot. I wanted a cup of hot tea now. I finally dug out a small pot and made the tea in that. Maybe I imagined it, but for some reason, it didn't taste quite the same.

When darkness came, the cabin was quite warm and cozy, but I still felt chills pass through me. Where was Wynn? How long did it take to find a lost trapper? I sat before my fire, reading and praying. Finally I laid aside my Bible and began to pace the floor, letting the tears stream unchecked down my face.

Finally I banked the fire, bundled up in blankets and curled up on the cot again. Kip climbed up to lie on my feet. This time I didn't scold him for being on the cot. I remembered the night before and the fact that Kip might have saved my toes.

There was a full moon and the rays of it streamed through the little frosted window. It seemed ever so bright, reflecting off the freshly blown snow. I was trying to pray again when there was a commotion at the door; and, before I could even worm my way out of the blankets, Wynn was there.

I didn't even jump up and run to him; I just buried my face in my hands and began to sob until my whole being shook. I was so relieved, so thankful, to see him safely home. He walked over and took me in his arms. As I clung to him, he held me for a long time, stroking my hair and patting my back. "There, there, Elizabeth," he murmured as to a small child.

We didn't try to talk. We really didn't need to. Later we would hear from one another all the details of the four miserable days of separation. For now it was enough just to be together again.

Wynn had a busy and rather unpleasant day following his return. Besides the bodies awaiting his investigation, he had also brought one back with him on the dog sled. He had found the man in question, but not in time to prevent his death.

It looked as if the fellow had accidentally stepped into one of his own traps. He had managed to free himself; but, with the mangled leg, he was unable to get to his cabin or to find help. Wynn had discovered the body beside the trail.

I asked if he had a wife and family. "No," Wynn said, "his wife died in childbirth three years ago."

It was a sad time for all of us. After the bodies had been inspected and Wynn had filed the necessary reports, the Indian people were given permission to bury their dead.

It was a solemn assembly that filed, single form, out of the village that afternoon and made their way to the burying trees. Wynn and I joined the somber procession. The sound of mourning sent chills up and down my spine. I had never heard anything like it before. Not the sound of weeping, it was a cry, a whine, a deep guttural lament that rose and fell as the column moved along. It tore at my soul, and I wept quietly with the mourners.

At home again as twilight came, the drums took up their steady beat. As they echoed through the settlement, thumping out their message of death, even Kip stirred and whined.

"Will they keep on all night?" I asked Wynn, feeling restless and edgy with the intensity of the beating.

"Oh, no. They should be stopping any time now."

Out the window, I could see in the settlement below us open bonfires in the central area. Around the fires, Indians moved in a dance pattern. The drummers sat in the firelight beating the drums with their hands and chanting a monotone tune that rose and fell on the night air.

Wynn was right. The drumming stopped as abruptly as it had begun. I looked out the window again and saw the silhouettes of figures disappearing into the shadows of the buildings. The fires had died down to a dim glow. The dead had had a proper and respectable burial.

27

Village Life

❖

J ANUARY PASSED INTO February. We had more storms but none with the violence of the mid-January blizzard. For the most part, life seemed to slip into some sort of a daily routine. We still continued our Bible studies, and Miss McLain never missed a study. Though she was still difficult at times, her attitude had changed from the inside out. I never did apologize for my outburst—not that I wasn't willing to do so. It just didn't seem like the appropriate thing to do under the circumstances. *Thank you, Lord,* I prayed, *for turning something bad into something good.*

When new babies were added to the village families, the Indian mid-wives did the delivering. Four were born between the first of October and mid-January. And so far, in spite of the cold winter, we had lost no children except for the one little girl. It was a shock to me when I first heard Nimmie and Miss McLain gratefully discussing this fact.

You mean you expect to lose children? I wanted to ask. But their conversation told me very plainly that in the North death was nearly as accepted as life. Because of the severe weather, the lack of medical care and the poor nutrition, they did indeed lose children regularly. I was appalled. Especially when I knew that medicines and doctors could have saved a good number of them.

Wynn kept a close eye on the Mary-versus-Smith situation. He had been out to see Mary many times. She was again working her traplines. How she managed it, Wynn did not know. The stamina of that little lady was remarkable. She had lost some toes from her severe frostbite, but she hobbled along, checking and resetting her traps and skinning out her furs. She was getting quite a pile, Wynn said. He also said that all the evidence supported Smith's assessment: Mary was crowding his territory.

"There must be some mistake," I argued. "If she is cutting into someone else's territory, she must not realize it. I'm sure she wouldn't do that on purpose."

Wynn just smiled.

Kip was a beautiful dog. I discussed with Wynn what Mr. McLain had said, that I had to allow Kip to find his own place in the dog community of our settlement.

"Do you think he's right?" I asked reluctantly, fearing that Wynn might agree with Mr. McLain.

"I'm afraid so, Elizabeth," he said. "It will come sooner or later, whether you want it to or not. Kip will be challenged, and he will either need to meet the challenge or run."

I couldn't imagine Kip running. I wasn't sure I even wanted him to run. But to fight? I didn't want that either.

"Do you think he's ready now?" I asked, a tremble in my voice.

I looked at Kip's beautiful, silver-tipped fur and the lovely curve of his tail. I shuddered to think of him with torn bleeding ears and ragged scars.

"Don't rush things," said Wynn and squeezed my hand. "There's plenty of time."

Wynn spent many hours training his new dogs. They were getting big like their brother Kip, but Wynn did not want to put them in harness for several months, waiting for their bones and muscles to be fully developed. He had chosen another two pups from the second litter Smith had spoken about at the time of our visit. Wynn was very pleased with the new dogs. They were smart and strong and learned very quickly. So far there was no evidence of a mean streak. Wynn had trained them with firmness and kindness rather than harshness. They responded to him with respect and devotion.

My friends from the village were much too busy keeping the fires going and their families fed to have much time for tea. Occasionally, one or two did appear for a few minutes. The women I had joined in the berry patch sometimes brought new neighbors for me to meet. We still couldn't speak much to one another. Many of the ladies knew some English words, but most often they were words needed for trading at the post, not words that might be used for a chat over a cup of tea. With all of us combining our knowledge, and by using our hands extensively, we did manage to converse some; but often we sat for a period of time without saying anything, just enjoying companionship. It was a new experience for me. I had been used to chatter. To sit quietly did not come easy. However, with time and patience, I was learning.

Evening Star was expecting another baby. I had been waiting daily for the good news, praying that all would go well and that she, too, would deliver a healthy child.

She was a bit vague about the expected time of arrival. When I asked her about it, she just shrugged off my question. I thought she must not understand me, so I put the question another way. Again she shrugged, answering only, "Come when ready," which was Anna's translation.

We were awakened in the dead of night by someone opening our door and calling Wynn's name. Both of us sat bolt upright in bed, and then Wynn reached in the darkness for his clothes and hurried into them.

My heart was in my throat as I listened to the anxious voices coming from the other room. Soon Wynn was back to the bedside, lamp in hand.

"It's Evening Star," he said. "She's having trouble delivering."

Wynn completed his dressing and then turned to place a kiss on my forehead.

"Try not to worry," he said. "I'll be back as soon as I can."

I tried not to worry but I wasn't doing very well at it. If the experienced midwives were unable to help Evening Star, what could Wynn do?

I finally got out of bed and went out to put more wood on the fire. I placed the lamp on the little table, wrapped myself in a blanket, and picked up my Bible. I paged through the Psalms, snatching underlined verses here and there of promise and assurance. It was one of those times when I couldn't really concentrate on my reading. Finally I closed my eyes and began to pray. For Evening Star and the unborn little one. For Wynn, that he would have wisdom and guidance. For myself, that God would still my trembling spirit enough for me to be able to concentrate on His Word.

After some minutes, I went back to the Bible. Again my eyes skimmed the pages. My spirit was calm now. My trembling had ceased. I read passage after passage until I came to Psalm 27:14. I stopped and read it through again. "Wait on the Lord: be of good courage, and he shall strengthen thine heart; wait, I say, on the Lord."

Yes, Lord, I prayed. *All I can do is wait.* I picked up the knitted sweater I had nearly completed for the new baby and worked while I waited.

It was almost daylight when Wynn returned. He was weary but his eyes smiled at me the moment he came in the door, and I knew he brought good news.

"She's all right?" I said.

"And so is her boy," Wynn answered me.

I shut my eyes for a moment of thanks, the tears squeezing out under my eyelids. Then I looked back up at Wynn, smiling.

"You must be very tired," I commented. "Would you like a cup of coffee before you go back to bed?"

"Back to bed?" laughed Wynn. "My darling, I do not intend to go back to bed. It's time to start another day."

So I fixed breakfast while Wynn shaved; and then, after eating and having our time of family prayer together, he did indeed go out to start another day—or continue the one he'd already started.

When chopping frozen logs for firewood, one of the children had an accident with an axe. They brought him to Wynn who, fortunately, was at home at the time. One look at the injured leg, and I felt as if I would lose my dinner. We removed the pillows from our cot, and Wynn stretched the boy out on the thin mattress.

His pantleg was ragged and torn and covered with blood. The first thing Wynn had to do was to clean up the area so he could see how bad the wound was. He asked for my scissors to cut off the ragged pantleg and then for hot water in the basin and his medical supply kit.

The Indian youths who had brought the boy stood around helplessly. They understood very little English and they didn't look much less queezy than I.

Somehow I managed to follow all of Wynn's orders—bringing the water and the sponge cloths, boiling the instruments in a pan on the stove, and handing Wynn whatever it was he needed.

Wynn cleaned the wound thoroughly, managing to stop the bleeding, and then put in several sutures. The boy's only indication of the pain he must have been suffering was a pale face and clenched jaw. I looked only when I had to. Most of the time, I was able to keep my eyes off the leg and look at my hands or the floor or Wynn's face. It seemed to take forever but, in actuality, it was all taken care of rather promptly. I sighed when Wynn said, "That's it." Now I could collapse.

But I didn't. Somehow I managed to stay on my feet. The two Indians moved forward to pick up the brave boy; he was pale and exhausted from the ordeal. I stepped forward, too.

"Perhaps he should stay here for a while," I suggested to Wynn. "He's too weak to move now, and I'll care for him."

Wynn, surprised, turned and spoke to the Indian boys who had carried in their friend. After a brief exchange, they nodded and left. Wynn made sure the young lad was comfortable and then picked up his hat.

"I'd better go see his mother," he said. "I want her to know exactly what's happening."

In about fifteen minutes Wynn was back with a worried-looking woman.

She crossed to her son and spoke some words softly to him. His eyes fluttered open and he answered her. She spoke again, nodded her head to us, and left the room.

The young boy's name was Nanook. He stayed with us for five days before he hobbled home on two clumsy sticks. I had enjoyed having him. He could not speak to me, but he could laugh. And he could eat—my, how that boy could eat! His leg didn't become infected, for which we were thankful. Wynn watched it very carefully, dressing it morning and night. By the time Nanook left us, it was beginning to heal nicely.

Before he left, I gave him a loaf of fresh bread to take with him. He tucked it inside his coat, his eyes twinkling. Then he patted Kip, whom he had grown to love, and hobbled out the door.

28
March

WHEN MARCH CAME, I began to think *spring*, but Wynn warned me that this was much too premature. No one else in the whole village was looking for spring at this early date. I chafed. Winter had been upon us for—for *years*, it seemed to me.

I was restless and I was lonely. My Indian friends had been too busy to come for tea for quite a while. Nimmie had been down with the flu, so our Bible study together had been missed. I still didn't feel very much at ease with Miss McLain, though I had now been given permission to call her Katherine. I could have talked myself into visiting her, but she was busy nursing Nimmie. I would have liked to have been Nimmie's nurse myself, but I knew it was important to Katherine to be able to do this. So I stayed home.

There was no sewing to be done, my mending was all caught up. I had read all my books over and over. It seemed that the extent of my day's requirements was to get three meals and do the dishes.

I was tired of the meals as well. It seemed as if I just fixed the same things over and over—from tins. Tinned this and tinned that. We did have fresh fish and fresh wild meat. But I was tired of them also. I really didn't enjoy the wild meat and craved even one taste of beefsteak or baked ham.

I longed for spring. But in the North, spring is slow in coming.

I decided to take a walk to the store. Maybe I would find some food item on the shelves that wouldn't be too expensive and would be a delightful change for our daily menu.

I bundled up and pulled on my mittens. Kip was already waiting by the door, his tail wagging in anticipation.

"You want to go for a walk?" I asked him, an unnecessary question. I struggled into my snowshoes and started out. It was a bright sunny day and I dared to hope that maybe this once Wynn was wrong. Maybe spring really was coming.

We walked through the morning sunshine, Kip frolicking ahead or running off to the side to check out something that only dogs knew or cared about. I was feeling good about the world again.

I had not given even fleeting thought to the village dogs, so intent was I in getting out for a walk again. Had I thought about it, I might not have proceeded any differently. I had finally made up my mind that Mr. McLain and Wynn were right: I could not go on protecting Kip against real life.

Mr. McLain greeted me heartily about halfway into the village. I asked how Nimmie was, and he seemed relieved and said she was coming along very well now.

We were walking toward the trading post together when there was a rush and a blur at my side as a dog ran past me. I jumped slightly with the suddenness of it; then a yip to my left whirled me around.

Kip had been busy poking his nose into a rabbit burrow, and this dog from the village was heading right for him. I gasped, my hand at my throat.

Surprisingly, the dog stopped a few feet from Kip and braced himself. From where we stood, we could hear the angry growl coming from his throat. Kip stood rooted, unsure as to what this was all about. Mr. McLain reached out a hand and placed it on my arm.

"They're going to fight, aren't they?" I said in a tight voice.

"We'll see," said McLain. "Kip might be wise enough not to take the challenge."

"Wise enough? But you said he'd *have* to fight."

"Not this one. Not Lavoie's Buck."

I swung around to look at McLain. "What do you mean?" I threw at him in alarm.

"He's boss here, Miz Delaney. He's licked every dog in the settlement."

I looked wildly about me in search of a club or a rock or anything that might stop the fight. There was nothing. "We've got to stop them!" I cried. "Kip might be killed!" I took a step forward, but McLain stopped me.

"You can't go in there. If there's a fight, you could get all chewed up."

The Lavoie dog was circling Kip now, fangs bared, his throat rumbling. Round and round he went, and I think he must have said some very nasty words in dog language. Kip looked insulted—angry. I expected at any moment the dogs to be at each other's throats.

And then a very strange thing happened. Kip's tail lowered and began to swish mildly back and forth. He whined gently as though to apologize for being on the other dog's territory. The big dog still bristled. He moved forward and gave Kip a sharp nip. Kip did not retaliate. The Lavoie dog gave Kip one last look of contempt, circled him once more, and—still bristling and snarling—loped back toward the village houses.

I didn't know whether to be relieved or ashamed.

Mr. McLain just grinned. "One smart dog," he said. "But ol' Buck better watch out in a month or two."

I didn't know what Mr. McLain meant, but I started to breathe again and hurried on to the village. The day didn't look nearly as sunshiny as it had previously, and I was rather anxious to make my purchases and go home.

Finally Anna and Mrs. Sam came for tea. I was especially glad to have Anna, because it meant that I could catch up on some of the village news.

We talked now of the families and how they were faring. The life in the village seemed to be made up getting through the winter and coasting through the summer; and the summers were all too short.

Evening Star and her baby were both doing fine. I had not seen them since I had taken over the new sweater and a container of soup soon after the baby had safely arrived. He was a nice little fellow and Evening Star was justifiably proud.

We had had another death. An Indian woman in her forties had died from the flu. She had not been well for some years. She had given birth to fifteen children, and each time another child was born she seemed to weaken further. Of her fifteen, only seven were now living. Her body, also, had been blanketed and left in the burying trees. The ritual drums had thumped out the message, and the open fires had gleamed in the night.

Another baby had been born, too. This time the midwives did not need help from Wynn.

There had been some sickness, but no major epidemics. Everyone seemed to hold his breath and speak softly when the possibility of an epidemic was mentioned. The people lived in fear of a dreadful disease sweeping through the camp while they sat helplessly by, with no doctors, hospitals, and very little medications.

Our conversation turned to brighter things. I talked about my longing for springtime. Of learning from the women about finding edible herbs and plants in the forests. Of planting my own garden. Of finding the berry patches. We all looked forward to the days of sunshine and rainshowers. Even the dreaded mosquitoes would be endured when spring came.

"How is Nanook doing?" I asked.

"He runs," said Anna, her eyes lighting up.

"That's wonderful. Good. That's good."

"I often wonder about poor Mary," I went on. "I don't know how she ever manages to care for her trapline with some of her toes missing."

"She crazy," muttered Anna, slurping her tea.

I wanted to argue but instead I said, "I feel sorry for her. First she lost all her children, and then her husband died. Poor thing."

But Anna only said, very calmly, "Husband not die."

I looked at her. Surely she knew better. She lived right here and had for years.

"Are you sure? We were told that her husband was dead."

"Dead. But he not die."

I didn't understand. Anna finished her tea and stood to go. Mrs. Sam Lavoie stood also and began to shuffle toward the door. Anna followed and I followed Anna. When we got to the door, she turned to me.

"She kill him," she said deliberately and simply. "She kill him for the traps. My Joe see." And she was gone.

I could hardly wait for Wynn to get home so I might tell him what Anna had said. She certainly must be wrong. Surely poor Mary had not done such a thing. If she had, and Joe had seen her, he would have reported it. Something was all wrong here.

When Wynn did arrive home, he had news for me instead. Mary was now locked up in the settlement's makeshift jail. Wynn had to bring her in. She would need to be escorted out for trial and sentencing. Not only had she moved her traps onto Smith's territory, but Wynn had found her in the very act of robbing from Smith's traps as well. It was a serious offense and Mary had to answer for it.

I felt sick. "Where is she?" I asked.

"There's a little room at the back of McLain's store. He uses it for skin storage when it's not needed otherwise."

And now it was needed otherwise. It was occupied by Mary.

"Can I see her?" I asked.

Wynn looked surprised; then he answered. "Certainly. If you wish to."

I did wish to. I went the next day, taking fresh bread and stew with me. Mary took the food but did not even look at me. I spoke to her, but she ignored me completely. I could see she really didn't need my food. Mr. McLain or Nimmie had looked after her well.

I tried to talk to her. She still would not look at me.

"I want to help you," I said. "Is there anything I could get you or do for you?" She turned from me and went back to curl up with a blanket on the cot in the corner.

I came home feeling even sicker than I had before I went. I decided to discuss it with Wynn. Surely there was some other way to deal with the situation.

"Do you really have to do it this way?" I asked him.

"I'm afraid so, Elizabeth. There is no masking the evidence. I caught her red-handed. She was stealing from Smith's traps."

"But couldn't she be—be—scolded and given another chance?" I continued.

"She isn't some naughty schoolgirl. She knows the seriousness of her offense."

"But surely if she knows that you are on to her, she won't do it again," I insisted.

"Elizabeth, if I let Mary go, none of the people will have respect for the law. Besides, Crazy Mary would try it again—oh, maybe not right away, but she would try it again, sure. She has an inner drive to accumulate pelts, and she will stop at nothing to get them."

I thought of Anna and her words. I had not passed them on to Wynn yet. I remembered them now with a sick heart.

Wynn went on. "She will get a fair trial," he assured me. "They will take into consideration her mental state. She will be cared for better than she would be out on her own on the trapline."

"But it will kill her," I blurted out. "She couldn't stand to be confined. She couldn't even stay here with us!"

There was sadness in Wynn's eyes. To lock Mary up, even with tender care, would not be good for Mary's emotional state. She needed freedom. Without it, she might not be able to survive.

"There is another thing to think about, Elizabeth," said Wynn. "If I didn't handle this properly and carry out the demands of the law, Smith or someone else would handle it in his own way, according to his own laws. Mary could be killed or beaten so severely that she would be left too helpless to work her trapline or even to care for herself. Either way it could mean death."

I hadn't thought about that.

Wynn dismissed further discussion. "I was sent up north to uphold the law, Elizabeth. To the best of my ability, I intend to do just that, God helping me."

I knew Wynn would follow the dictates of the law, not his own feelings.

Mary was not sent away for trial and sentencing. Two mornings later, Nimmie found her dead on the cot in the corner, where she had died in her sleep.

29

Nimmie

MARCH HAD CRAWLED by slowly on weak and tottering limbs. I ached for spring to come dancing in with vitality and freshness. I think all the village people ached for it as well.

For some of the women of the settlement it would mean reuniting with husbands for the first time in many months. Some of the traplines were a great distance from the village, and once the men had left in the fall, they did not return again until the winter snows were melting.

The men who worked the traplines nearer home came and went, spending some time with their families and some time in the bush.

Nimmie was well again, so we resumed our Bible studies. Each time we met together, she taught me some lesson. She was a patient, beautiful person with a heart of love and an open mind to truth.

I talked to Wynn about her one night as we were stretched out before our open fire.

"I've learned to love Nimmie," I said. "She's a beautiful person. It's strange—when I first saw her, I was so disappointed. I didn't tell you that before, did I?"

Wynn shook his head, his eyes studying mine.

"I guess I didn't because I was ashamed of myself. I was prejudiced, you know. I didn't realize I was. I love the Indian people, but I had wanted someone—someone to share things with. And I—I thought— that—well that—the person needed to be like me—white. Well, I was wrong. I was wanting a white woman, and instead I found a friend, a very special friend, in Nimmie."

Wynn reached out to take my hand. I think he understood what I was trying to say.

As the days went by, Nimmie and I shared more intimately our thoughts and feelings, our understanding of Scripture.

One day Nimmie came to see me alone. It was not our Bible study day, and I was a bit surprised.

"Do you have time to talk for a while?" she asked me. Now, time was one thing I did have—in abundance. So I asked Nimmie in.

She laid aside her coat and took a chair at the kitchen table.

I pushed the kettle forward on the stove, added another stick of wood, and waited for her to begin.

"I've been thinking about that verse we studied yesterday," she started, "the one about Christ dying for the ungodly."

I nodded, remembering.

"I'm ungodly," Nimmie continued softly.

"Yes, all of us are without God," I agreed in a near whisper.

Nimmie's eyes flew open. "You too?"

"Oh, yes. Me, too."

"But—?" began Nimmie, but she didn't go on.

"The Bible says, 'All have sinned,' remember? It was one of the verses we studied a couple of weeks ago."

"I remember," said Nimmie. "I just didn't think of it at the time, I guess."

"Well, it's true. The Bible also says that 'there is none righteous, no not one.'"

Nimmie sat silently. "I remember that, too," she finally stated.

"It also says that 'while we were yet sinners,' He loved us."

"That is the part that is so hard for me to understand," Nimmie blurted out. "I can't imagine someone dying for—" Nimmie stopped again.

"Elizabeth," she said, looking full into my face, "I am a terribly wicked person."

I wanted to protest, but Nimmie went on, "You don't know me, Elizabeth. You don't know what I almost did."

She did not weep. Weeping was not the way of her people, but her head dropped in utter self-contempt and her eyes refused to look into mine.

"Do you want to tell me about it?" I finally asked, realizing that Nimmie was deeply troubled.

"I took care of Crazy Mary. I brought her all her meals and the basin to wash her hands. I bandaged her infected toe that still refused to heal from the freezing. Each time I went we spoke together. I tried to encourage her—to tell her that things would work out. But each time I went she begged me for just one thing. She pleaded with me to bring it to her. Each time, I refused. She wanted her hunting knife."

I could not understand Nimmie's words. There was silence as I puzzled over them. Why was she wicked for taking such special care of Mary? Nimmie's head came up. "I knew why she wanted her knife. She could not bear to be shut up—caged like—like a chicken."

I understood then. Crazy Mary had intended to take her own life.

"Well, I kept saying no, no. And then the other morning I couldn't stand it anymore. She was going wild in the little room, and soon she would be taken far away from her land and her people and locked in another room—forever. It would kill her. It would kill her slowly. Wouldn't it be more merciful to let her die all at once?

"And so I found her knife and tucked it in my dress and took it to her when I went to bring her breakfast. Only when I got there, Crazy Mary was—was—"

Yes, I knew. Mary, mercifully, was already gone.

My mind was whirling, my heart thumping. What could I say to the anguished Nimmie?

Did she truly realize the seriousness of her near-crime? Wynn would have needed to arrest her. *She* would have been locked up in the little room at the back of her husband's store. She would have been sent out for trial and sentencing. She would have been implicated in a terrible crime.

The horror of the whole thing washed through me, making me tremble; but Nimmie was continuing.

"I am very *unjust*," went on Nimmie. "I am a sinner. I thought before when I heard those verses that it was speaking of someone else. Now I know that it speaks of me. My heart is very heavy, Elizabeth. I could not sleep last night. I love Him, this Jesus. But I have hurt Him with my sin."

I could not have told Nimmie that what she had done was not wrong; I believed it was. It would have been a terrible thing if she had been party to Mary's suicide. But God had kept her from that. I thanked God for His intervention and mercy. I said nothing about the act that Nimmie had *almost* committed. Instead, I talked about what now must be done about it.

"Nimmie, when I realized that I was a sinner, that I could do nothing myself to atone for my sins, I did the only thing one can do—that is necessary to do. I accepted what God has provided for all of mankind—His forgiveness. His forgiveness through the death of His Son, Jesus. He died for our sins so that we need not die for our own. I don't understand that kind of love either, Nimmie. But I know that it's real, for I have felt it. When I prayed to God and asked for His forgiveness and took His Son as my Savior, that love filled my whole person. Where I had had misery and fear before, now I have peace and joy."

"And He would do that for me?"

"He wants to. He aches to. That's why He came—and died. He loves you so much, Nimmie."

Even though Nimmie's eyes remained dry, mine were filled with tears.

We bowed our heads together, and I prayed and then Nimmie prayed. Hers was a beautiful, simple prayer, beginning in faith and repentance and ending with joy and praise.

I reached over and held Nimmie for a moment when we had finished praying. Even Nimmie's eyes were wet now. We spent some time looking at God's wonderful words of assurance and promise from the Bible, and then Nimmie rushed home to share her good news with Ian.

As she left the house that day, my heart was singing. Nimmie was even more than a very special friend. She was a beloved *sister* as well.

We had no idea how quickly Nimmie's newfound faith would be tested. Less than a week after Nimmie and I had spent our time in prayer, disaster struck. The whole settlement was to suffer the consequences, but Nimmie and her husband would be hurt most of all.

It was about two o'clock in the morning when voices—loud and excited—reached our cabin. We both scrambled out of bed and hurried to the window. The whole world was lit up with an angry red glow.

"Fire!" cried Wynn before he even reached the window.

"Oh, dear God, no!" I prayed out loud.

But it was. It looked for a moment as if the whole village were going up in smoke. Wynn was dressed in the time it took me to understand the scene before me.

"Stay here, Elizabeth," he said. "I'll send people to you if they need your help. You know where all the medical supplies are kept. Get them out and ready in case they are needed."

Wynn was gone before I could even speak to him.

I dressed hurriedly, afraid I might be needed even before I could carry out Wynn's orders. The noise outside grew louder. I could hear the crackling of the flames now as well. Kip whined and moved toward the door. His instincts told him that there was danger.

"It's all right, Kip," I spoke soothingly to him. "You are safe here." I still didn't know what it was that was burning.

After I had followed all of Wynn's instructions and laid out the medical supplies, the bandages, and the burn ointments I had found, I put more wood in the fire and set a full kettle of water on to boil in case it was needed.

Smoke was in the air now, seeping through every air space into our cabin. The smell sickened me, for it meant pain and loss and even possible death. I went to the window to see if I could tell just how much of our small settlement was being taken by the fire. It was the Hudson's Bay Store that was burning. Wild flames leaped skyward. Men milled around the building, but there was really little they could do. There was no firefighting equipment in the village—only buckets and snowdrifts; and against such a fire, these had very little effect.

One cabin, close to the store, was also burning, and I prayed for the occupants' safety. I began to pick out figures then. There were men on roofs of other buildings. There were bucket brigades feeding them pails of snow. Women and children milled around or huddled helplessly in groups. The whole scene was one of despair and horror.

A noise at the door brought me from the window. Three women stood together against the night. One held a baby in her arms, and one of the others held a child by the hand.

I had seen them before at the trading post where Nimmie and I had dished out soup to the storm-chilled. I did not know them by name.

"Come in," I said. "How is Nimmie? Have you seen Nimmie?"

One lady shook her head. The others looked blank.

They pushed the little girl forward. Her face was streaked with soot and wet from tears. She had an ugly burn across her hand. I took off her coat and knelt before her.

I had no training in treating burns. I grabbed a jar of ointment and read the label. It didn't tell me as much as I needed to know. I felt I should cleanse the wound somehow, but how? I got a basin of water and warmed it to my touch. I did not want to damage the burned tissue further. With a cloth, I wiped away most of the dirt and grime, trying hard not to hurt the child. Then I generously applied the ointment and bound the wound with a clean bandage.

As soon as I had finished, the mother with the baby held him out to me. She coughed to show that the baby had a problem. She pointed out the window at the fire and coughed again. "Smoke," she said, knowing that word.

"He choked on the smoke?" I asked her.

"Smoke," she said again.

Smoke inhalation. What could I do about that? I had no idea how it was treated and, if I had known, I was almost sure I wouldn't have what was necessary to treat it anyway.

I took the baby. To put their minds at ease I had to do something. *What, God? What do they do to make breathing easier?* The only thing I had ever heard of to ease breathing was steam, and it might be the very worst thing I could do. I didn't know.

I unbundled the baby and laid him on the cot. Then I dug through Wynn's medical supply looking for something, anything, that might help the infant. I could find nothing that was labeled for smoke inhalation. I finally took some ointment that said that it was good for chest congestion and rubbed a small amount on the wee chest.

I had not finished with the small baby when the door opened again. More women and children entered our small cabin, more from fright than from injuries. A few of them did have a small burn or two but, thankfully, nothing major. The smell of smoke was on their clothing and the fear of fire in their faces.

Whenever a new group joined us, I asked the same question. "Nimmie? Have you seen Nimmie? The McLains? Are they all right?"

I got shrugs and blank looks in return.

The morning sun was pulling itself to a sitting position when Wynn came in carrying a young man who had badly burned a foot.

I was glad to see Wynn and sorry for the young man. "Nimmie?" I asked again. "What about the McLains?"

"They're fine," Wynn responded. "All three of them."

I was greatly relieved.

Then Wynn began to give instructions as to what he would need to care for the foot, and I carried them out to the best of my ability. After the young man was given some medication to dull the pain, Wynn did what he could for the ugly burn. Then he bandaged the foot lightly and, leaving the young man on our cot, went back again to help fight the fire.

Before he left he pulled me close, though he did not hold me long; there were a number of eyes fixed upon us.

"I think we'll be able to save the other homes. The fire has passed its worst. It shouldn't be long before you can start sending them home." Then he was gone.

I looked around at the still-frightened faces. "Sergeant Delaney says that the fire will soon be over," I informed them, gesturing with my hands as well, "and then you will all be able to return to your cabins. The rest of your homes are quite safe. You'll be able to go back to them."

I wasn't sure how many of them understood my words. I still knew only a few words in their tongue and none of them dealt with fire.

"But first," I said, "we'll have some tea."

It took a lot of tea that morning, and we had to take turns with the cups. Even so, it seemed to lift the spirit of gloom from the room. Some of the ladies even began to chat. It was a great relief to me.

I checked on the young man with the bad burn. He seemed to be resting as comfortably as possible under the circumstances. I asked him if he would like some tea, but he shook his head.

As the morning progressed, the fire died to a smolder of rubble, and two-by-two or in huddled little groups, the ladies and children left our cabin.

The young man had fallen asleep, whether from medication or exhaustion I did not know.

I set about doing up the dishes and tidying the small room.

By the time Wynn came, the young man had awakened and was asking me questions I could not understand nor answer. I was glad to see Wynn, for he would know what the fellow wanted.

I met Wynn at the door. After a quick look to assure myself that he was all right, I indicated the man on the cot.

"He's been trying to ask me something," I told Wynn. "I have no idea what he is saying."

Wynn crossed to the young man and knelt beside him. He spoke to him in the soft flowing sounds of his native tongue. Wynn spoke again and then, with a nod of his head, he rose and lifted the young man to his feet.

"I'm taking him home," Wynn said to me.

The young man seemed about to topple over.

"Shouldn't you—shouldn't you carry him?" I asked anxiously.

"I would," said Wynn, "gladly. But it would shame him to be carried through his village."

I looked at the proud young man. His face was twisted with pain, and still he was determined to walk rather than to be carried.

I nodded my head. "I hope he makes it," I said fervently.

"I'll see that he does," spoke Wynn softly, and they went out together.

When Wynn returned, he brought the McLains with him.

"Do you have enough food for five hungry people?" he asked me. I looked toward my stove. It was almost noon and no one had had anything to eat.

"I'll find it," I said without hesitation. But before I went to my cupboards and stove, I had to assure myself that Nimmie and Katherine were truly okay.

They clustered around our door, taking off soiled coats and kicking snow from their boots. Their faces were soot covered and streaked with tears, whether from weeping or the sting of the acrid smoke in their eyes I did not know nor ask. Their shoulders slumped with fatigue. It had been a long, hard, disheartening night. Their home was gone. Their livelihood was gone. In one night they lost their past, their present, and their future.

I crossed to them, unable to find words to express my feelings. I looked into Nimmie's eyes. My question was not voiced but she answered it. With just a quick little nod, she assured me she'd be all right.

I turned then to Katherine and put out my hand. "Are you all right?" I asked her.

Her answer was more as I would have expected. "I have no burns or outer injuries."

She was telling me that where she really hurt was on the inside. It would heal, now that she had found the secret to healing. But it would take time.

I turned back to Mr. McLain. "I'm sorry," I whispered falteringly, "truly sorry."

Mr. McLain was able to give me a crooked smile. "We're tough, Miz Delaney," he said. "Survivors. We'll bounce back."

I answered his smile and went to get them something to eat.

After we had finished our meal, we sat around the fireplace talking in quiet tones.

"What are your plans, Ian? Is there anything we can do?" asked Wynn.

Mr. McLain shrugged his shoulders. "I haven't sorted it out yet."

"You are welcome to stay here until you find other accommodations," went on Wynn.

"Katherine can have the cot," I hurried to add. "Is there somewhere we can find another bed?"

Nimmie shook her head. "There are no beds in the village," she said. "But don't worry. I can make all the bed that Ian and I need."

I looked puzzled.

"Spruce boughs and furs," explained Nimmie. "I know how to make a bed that even the richest white people of the world would envy!"

I admired Nimmie's attempt to lighten the situation and bring to us a little humor.

"It's not really *us* that I am worried about," McLain continued, his shoulders sagging in spite of his effort to keep up his spirits.

"You know what it's like this time of year," he went on, directing his conversation to Wynn. "It's been a long, hard winter. Most of the families are almost out of supplies. They were depending on the store to get them through the rest of the winter until the new growth brought fresh food again. Why, I'll wager that most of them have less than five cups of flour in the cabin. How they gonna make their bannock without flour? What about salt and tea and—?"

But Wynn stopped him.

"We'll all band together to look after them. They're hardy people. They'll make it."

There was silence for a few minutes. Mr. McLain broke it. "What about supplies for the two of you? What do you have here?"

Wynn shook his head. "Not enough for a whole village, that's for sure. We'll have to ration very carefully to get through until spring."

McLain nodded. "Right—that's a good idea," he said a little wistfully. "Don't be divying out what little you have. That way it won't do anyone any good. Someone has to stay healthy and on his feet, and seems to me you're elected, Sarge."

The full impact of our situation began to hit me. *Oh, God,* I prayed silently, *please don't let it come to the place where I have to turn hungry people away from my door. I would rather give away my last crumb of food and suffer with them.* Was McLain right? Would things become so desperate that we would be forced to withold our own in order to have the strength to minister to the community's needs? I prayed not.

"Well, I think the first thing that needs to be done is a little survey," Wynn said. "We'll go through the village family by family and find out what the situation is. I'll get you a little book, McLain, if you are up to coming with me; and you can record as we go along."

McLain nodded and rose to his feet, reaching for his heavy, soot-covered coat and his beaver hat, and prepared to follow Wynn.

Wynn turned to me then. "I would like you to do the same here, Elizabeth, as you find time. It's important to know exactly what we have to work with."

I nodded. It all seemed so serious.

After the menfolk had left, I turned to Nimmie and Katherine. "Why don't you try to get a little sleep?" I asked them. "You both really look all in."

"I'll help you with your inventory," offered Nimmie.

"No. No—it won't take me long. There really isn't that much to count. You get some rest."

Nimmie was still hesitant, but I insisted. Finally she was persuaded, and she and Katherine went to our bedroom, removed their soiled outer garments and soon were fast asleep.

I did up the dishes and straightened the small room again; and then, notebook and pencil in hand, I began to do as Wynn had suggested.

I counted everything—each cupful of flour, each tablespoon of tea. I sorted and counted every can of tinned food. I measured the salt and the sugar, the coffee, and the beans and rice. Every bit of my kitchen supply and then my storeroom was measured and recorded.

At first it seemed to me to be quite a lot; and then I began to think of the number of days until the supplies could be replenished, and I realized it was not very much. Mr. McLain was right. We were going to be awfully short of food supplies before this winter was over.

With a sinking heart, I returned to the kitchen. It would take very careful planning to make things stretch.

Now late afternoon, Wynn and Mr. McLain had been gone for a number of hours. I looked out the window nervously, willing them to return.

Nimmie came out of the bedroom looking rested. "Elizabeth," she said, "may I borrow your snowshoes?"

"Of course, but are you sure you are ready—?"

"I'm ready," she said with a soft smile. "I will even welcome the exercise and the healing of nature's breath."

"They are right outside the door," I told her. *I could use some of nature's restoring breath myself,* I noted in understanding.

Wynn and Mr. McLain returned before Nimmie. They did not have good news. The tabulation of food in the village was listed on two short pages. The Indians had come to rely more and more heavily on the trading post and did not store food ahead except for the roots and herbs they carried in and the berries they dried. By now, these too were in short supply.

The future looked even more bleak than it had before the survey. *Lord, please send an early spring.*

When it was dark and Nimmie had still not returned, I was becoming concerned. I didn't like to mention my fear because I knew Mr. McLain and Wynn already had enough on their minds. Stealthily I watched out the window. I wished I had suggested she take Kip with her.

Mr. McLain stopped what he was saying to Wynn in midsentence and turned to me. "If you are worried about Nimmie," he said, having caught me glancing out of the window again, "don't be. Nimmie is as at home in those woods as she was in her kitchen. Whether it's dark or light, Nimmie is in no danger."

I flushed slightly. "I do wish she'd come," I said rather apologetically.

Katherine came from the bedroom, also looking much better after her nap.

"I've nearly slept the day away," she confessed. "I'm sorry. I meant to be up to help you much sooner, but I just didn't wake up. You should have called me."

"I didn't have anything I needed help with," I assured her. "And, besides, you needed the sleep."

We prepared a meal. Katherine set out the plates and cutlery on the table. Because our table was small and we had only two chairs, we would fill our plates and sit about the room.

We were almost ready to eat when we heard Nimmie. I heaved a sigh of relief. When we opened the door to her, she entered the room almost hidden under spruce branches. How she had ever managed to load herself down so was beyond me. She smiled out from under the load, and Mr. McLain helped her to lay aside her bundles.

We ate together and then Nimmie disappeared again. When she returned, she had managed to get some furs from somewhere. With these at hand, she began to make a bed at one end of the room Wynn used for his office.

Wynn led our little group in prayer, and we all retired early. It had been a long, exhausting day, and there didn't seem to be anything more we could do to improve the situation at present. We would have to take our future one day at a time.

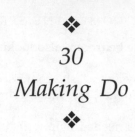

30

Making Do

❖

DURING THE NEXT few days, Wynn called for a meeting of all the people. They gathered together in front of the pile of rubble that had so recently been the source for the lifeblood of the settlement, anxious eyes surveying the pile of debris. Even the litter, as it had been poked and raked following the fire, had brought forth very little of use in the settlement.

Wynn stood before the people and spoke to them in their language. Nimmie, standing beside me with her head held high, whispered the translation.

"We meet together because we are one. We must care for one another. We have lost the trading post and the food it supplied. Now we must find our own way. It is not a new way. It has been done for many moons by our fathers. But it is a hard way. It will take us all working together.

"You have some flour and salt for bannock. You should watch your supply closely and use only a little every day. It can last for many days if you use it sparingly.

"We have the forests and the streams. They will not forsake us. They have meat for the taking. We will hunt together and share what we find.

"We have plants that can be gathered from under the snow. You know them well. We will send out groups to gather them. Those who stay behind will care for the fires.

"We have traps and snares if we run out of ammunition for our guns, so we will not starve.

"We have medicines if we become sick, so do not be afraid.

"And, most importantly, we have a God who sees us and knows that we are in need. He has promised to care for His children.

"We will live, and we will make it to the time of the flowing of the rivers, and the stirring of the new leaf upon the tree and the gathering of the wild greens."

I felt like we all should have cheered such a speech; but when Wynn had finished speaking, the people of the village filed away—silently. Yet their shoulders had lifted a little and the look of despair upon their faces had been replaced with silent acceptance and even a glimmer of hope.

Now, Wynn was hardly ever home. He organized hunting parties, carefully distributing counted shells to the sharpest marksmen. He sent out fishing parties to cut holes in the ice and spend silent, long, cold hours at the task of bringing home fish. He sent older women, bundled against the cold, into the forests with baskets to dig for edibles among the roots of trees, while the younger women were assigned neighbors' fires to tend besides their own. Children took on new responsibilities as baby tenders and firewood gatherers. All the village was called upon to work together. Even the ones who were too old and feeble to be actively engaged had a part. They stirred the pots and kept the home fires fed while others were busy with their tasks.

A previously empty cabin was repaired sufficiently for the family who had lost their home in the fire, and life in the village went on.

Some of the outlying trappers, who had seen the terrifying red glow in the sky on the night of the fire, came home to check on family. They stood with heads lowered as they realized what the disaster meant to the entire population of the village. I think they too must have been praying, in their own way, for an early spring.

Nimmie and I were alone a few days later. I knew she must be very sorrowful about losing her lovely home with all the beautiful handwork from her past. She admitted that it "made her heart sore," but she was able to smile in spite of it all.

"I still have Ian," she said with great feeling. "If I had lost him, then all would have been lost."

I thought of Wynn, and I understood what Nimmie was saying.

"I've been doing a lot of thinking," said Nimmie slowly. "Maybe this was God's punishment for my sin."

I wanted to protest, but I wasn't sure what to say.

Nimmie went on. "And then I thought, 'No, I think not.' You see, I was a sinner long before I brought the knife to Crazy Mary. I understand something now that I didn't understand before. I did not become sinful because I took in the knife, but rather I consented to take the knife because I was sinful. Do you understand me, Elizabeth?"

I nodded slowly. I did understand and I agreed.

"I have been a sinner for a long time. I just did not know about it. Oh, I knew that I had an unhappiness, a pain in my heart that twisted at times and brought me grief and shame, but I didn't know why or what it was.

"The pain is gone now. Even after the fire, I have peace. If God had been punishing me, then I wouldn't feel Him with me as I do now, as I did as I watched the fire burn away everything that had ever been mine. No, He was not punishing; but perhaps He is putting me through the testing ritual to see if I am going to be strong."

I nodded again. It seemed that Nimmie had it all sorted out. Tears filled my eyes. She was strong, our Nimmie.

"Ian and I talked long last night," Nimmie paused. "We are going to go away."

My mouth opened to protest and I reached a hand for her arm.

"We will be back," Nimmie informed me quickly. "We will be back as soon as the crows are back. We will build the trading post again as soon as wood can be hauled from the forest. And we will bring supplies back to the people."

Relieved to hear that they would be back, I still didn't understand why they felt they should go.

"Ian has much to do, to make plans for the new building," Nimmie explained. "He has to arrange for supplies to be shipped in as soon as the rivers are free of ice. We will be very busy. The time will go quickly. Ian is even going to show me the big cities that I have read about." Nimmie's face took on a glow. For a moment, I wished I could go with her; and then I quickly thought of Wynn, and any desire to leave Beaver River left me.

"Besides," said Nimmie matter-of-factly, "the supplies are low—even the supplies in *your* home. If we go soon, that will mean less people to feed and more life for the village."

"What about Katherine?"

"Ian is going to ask her what she wishes. We are sure that she will go with us."

There just seemed to be one question left to ask. "When will you go?"

"Tomorrow. Tomorrow as soon as the sun is in the sky."

Katherine did choose to go with them. They had very little to take. Mr. McLain still had his good team of sled dogs and his sled. They had no clothing to pack and no provisions except what they were given. Wynn made sure they had a good rifle and some shells. Villagers came shyly forward as the McLains prepared for travel and offered love gifts of food or clothing or traps. I knew that the people desperately needed the things they were giving away, yet so did the McLains. The gifts were not refused because it would have caused offense to the givers. They were given in love, and they were accepted in love.

At last the sled was loaded, the team harnessed, and the travelers were ready for the trail.

At the last minute, Nimmie drew me aside. I wasn't sure I would be able to talk to her without weeping.

"I have a wonderful secret," she said, her eyes shining, "and I wanted to share it with you before leaving.

"I am going to have a baby. Just think—after ten years of marriage, I am going to have a baby!"

"Oh, Nimmie," was all I could say, and I took her in my arms and cried all over her fur parka.

I was the only one in tears, for the Indian people expressed themselves in other ways. I knew their hearts were heavy, too. It was hard to see our friends go. It was hard to turn them over to the elements and the winter. I prayed that they would arrive safely. If anyone knew how to handle the rigors of the trail, it was the McLains. Nimmie had come from the forest, and Mr. McLain himself had spent many years working a trapline before becoming manager of the store. They would know what to do in all circumstances.

It would be hard for Katherine. She had not trained herself for the ways of the North. The trip would be long and difficult and very taxing. I prayed that God would help her.

And Nimmie. The little mother-to-be. The excited little mother. I prayed with all of my heart that things would go well for her and God would protect her unborn child.

I stood and watched them disappear over the whiteness of the hill outside our settlement, a final wave to us, our last glimpse of them. And then I placed a hand on Kip's furry head and started back to the cabin, the tears blurring my vision. I knew Wynn was watching me, making sure I would be all right.

31
A Watchful Eye

❖

"I SN'T THERE ANY way I can help?" I asked Wynn.

He had been working almost day and night ever since the fire in order to make sure the settlement had food. I had been doing nothing—except ache for Nimmie.

"There is, Elizabeth. A very important way," Wynn informed me. "I would like you to keep a sharp eye on all the families for sickness. I think we'll pull through this winter just fine if we don't run into some kind of epidemic. The only way I see to prevent that from happening is to detect early anyone with symptoms and try to isolate them from the rest."

"So what do you want me to do?" I questioned. I certainly wasn't a nurse, nor did I have medical knowledge of any kind.

"Just visit the homes. Go around as much as you find the time to do so. Keep your eyes and ears open for any coughs or fevers or symptoms of any kind. Note the cabin and I will take it from there."

That didn't sound too difficult.

"How is it going, Wynn? I mean *really*?" I asked him.

He looked at me, and I knew I was going to get an honest answer. "It isn't good. We are managing so far to keep food in the cabins, but the real value of a little meat boiled with a few roots leaves much to be desired. Still, we will make it if we can just keep sickness away. Everyone is cooperating well, so far. If we can keep up the morale and keep them from giving up, we'll be all right."

"Surely it won't be much longer," I said hopefully.

"Until the snow goes—no. Maybe not. But, when the snow goes, the rest of the men will be back. True, that will be more men to hunt and fish, but it will also be more mouths to feed. And it will still be several weeks after that before the forests and fields start to bear fruit."

Wynn drew me close and held me for several minutes before he left to resume his duties of another exhausting, long day.

I went to work on the dishes and cleanup. Since the fire, I no longer threw out tea leaves or coffee grounds after one use. Instead, I dried them and put them in a container to be used again. I saved any leftovers of our food as well, no matter how small the portion. It could be used in some way. Our meals were skimpy enough and were carefully portioned out. Meat had become our main staple as well, with only small servings of any tinned vegetables to complement it. Desserts were now only a dim memory. The nearest we came was to sprinkle a small amount of sugar on an occasional slice of bread. The bread was rationed as well. We allowed ourselves only one slice per day, and sometimes I cut those very sparingly, though I tried to make Wynn's a little thicker than mine—not too much different or he would notice and gently scold me.

I had been so happy for Nimmie when she told me of her coming baby. I had been longing for a baby of our own. Wynn and I had talked about it many times. Each month I had hoped with all my heart that God might decide to bless us; but now I found myself thanking God that I was not carrying a child. Our diet simply was not good enough to be nourishing a coming baby.

I'll wait, God, I prayed now. *I'll wait.*

As soon as my tasks were completed, I donned my coat and mittens and went out. We were now in April. Surely I wouldn't need heavy clothing much longer.

I visited several of the homes that morning. At each home I had to insist to the hostess, "No tea. No tea," and rub my stomach as though the tea would not agree with me. I did not want them to use any of their meager supply each time I came to call in the days ahead.

Many of these women I knew by name. They had learned to trust me, though they must have been wondering why I had nothing better to do than to wander around the settlement while everybody else was busy working. I kept close watch for anything that looked like potential trouble. At first, there was nothing more than one or two runny noses. I mentally noted them, just in case Wynn would want to check them out.

In the Arbus cabin, one of the children was coughing, a nasty sounding one that brought fear to my heart. *Please, not whooping cough,* I prayed silently and told Anna to be sure to keep him in and away from other children until Wynn saw him.

"But he get wood," said Anna. "His job."

"Not today. I will help with wood today. You keep him in by the fire."

Anna was surprised at what I said and the conviction with which I said it, but she did not argue further. I was *Mrs. Sergeant* and should be listened to.

I went for wood as I had promised. It was not an easy job. The snow was deep and the axes dull. It was hard for me to walk in snowshoes and carry wood on my back. I was not nearly as skilled as the Indian children. I had to make extra trips to get a pile as high as the others, and by the time I was finished, it was getting dark and I knew Wynn would soon be home. I had not made the full rounds of the cabins, but I would finish the rest the next day.

When Wynn returned home, I reported what I had found. "Good work," he said. "I'd better check them out."

"Why don't you wait until after you have eaten?" I suggested, "and I will go with you."

Wynn agreed and we ate our simple meal.

We walked over the crunching snow together in the moonlight, long shadows playing about us. From the cabins surrounding the little clearing, soft light flickered on the billowy banks of snow.

"It's pretty at night, isn't it?" I said to Wynn.

"But not pretty in the daytime?" Wynn prompted.

"Oh, I didn't mean that—not really. It's just—that—well, in the daytime all of the gloom and grime of the tragedy shows up, too. Some days," I went on, "I wish it would snow ten feet just to bury that terrible reminder heaped up there in the village."

"It's not a pretty sight, is it? But I thought you were very anxious for the snow to go."

"I am. I don't really mind the snow itself—it is pretty and I have enjoyed it—walking in it, looking at it. It's the wind I hate. I can't stand the wind. It just sends chills all through me. It seems so—so—vengeful somehow. I hate it!"

Wynn reached over to take my hand and pull me up against him as we continued to walk.

"I wish you could learn to appreciate the wind, Elizabeth. God made the wind, too. It has many purposes and it is part of our world. You will never be really at peace here until you have made friends with the wind. Try to understand it—to find beauty in it."

He pulled me to a stop. "Look, over there. See that snowbank? Notice the way the top peaks and drops over in a curve—the velvet softness of the purple shadow created by the glow of the moon. See how beautiful it is."

Wynn was right.

He continued to point out other wind sculptures around the clearing. I laughed.

"All right," I assured him. "I will try to find beauty in the wind."

"Its greatest beauty is its song," Wynn continued. "I still haven't had the opportunity to take you out camping under the stars, but when spring comes we'll do that. We'll camp at a spot where we can lie at night and hear the windsong in the spruce trees. It's a delightful sound."

"I'll remember that promise," I told Wynn.

We were at the first cabin. Wynn looked carefully at the throat of the child and felt for fever. There didn't seem to be any cause for alarm here, but he did give the mother a little bit of medication, telling her to give one spoonful every morning. She nodded in agreement and we went on to the next cabin.

Again we found no cause for concern. Wynn didn't even leave medicine with the family. He told me to keep an eye on the child during the next few days.

When we reached the third cabin, we could hear the coughing even before we got to the door. Wynn stopped and listened carefully.

"You're right," he said. "I don't like the sound of that at all." Whooping cough was one of the dreaded killers of the North.

"Do we have medication?" I asked Wynn, counting on the worst.

"Not nearly enough if it turns out to be whooping cough," he said quietly.

We went in then and Wynn did a thorough examination of the throat, chest, and ears of the child, with the little equipment he had.

"How long has he been coughing?" he asked Anna.

"Two," she said.

"His cough is bad, Anna. I want you to keep him in. And keep the other children away from him if you can. Wash any of his dishes in hot, hot water. Let them sit in the water and steam. Give him this medicine—once when the sun comes up, once when it is high in the sky, and once when the sun goes down. You understand?"

"Understand," said Anna.

Wynn repeated all his directions in her native tongue to be sure Anna had fully understood.

"Understand," she said again.

"Mrs. Delaney will be back tomorrow to see how he is feeling."

"Beth come," she said with satisfaction. I felt a warm glow to hear her use my given name.

"Is there any way to get more medicine?" I asked Wynn on the way home.

"Not in time. We would have to send someone out and then have him bring it back. By that time half of the town could be infected."

"What will we do?"

"We'll just have to wait, Elizabeth, and hope that we are wrong. Wait—and pray."

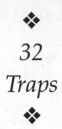

32
Traps

NOW THAT MY days were more than full, I had little time for Kip. I knew he needed his exercise, so I was forced to let him out to run on his own. I hated to do it, but he always returned home again before too much time elapsed.

One night he came in with marks on his fluffy long coat. I pulled him close and looked at him. There was a tuft of hair hanging from the corner of his lip. I pulled it out and looked at it, puzzling over what it meant.

"Looks like he's been in a little scrap," Wynn remarked as though it was of no consequence.

"Do you think so?" I asked in alarm, remembering the mean-looking Buck.

"He doesn't look much the worse for it," Wynn responded. "I'm guessing he came out top dog."

I brushed at Kip's coat. I could feel no injuries and he certainly didn't appear to be in any pain. In fact, he looked rather pleased about something.

"What will I do with him?" I asked Wynn.

"What do you mean?"

"Well, I don't have time to take him for his walks, and he can't be shut up in here all day."

"I think he will look after himself just fine."

"But what if he meets Buck? The last time, he submitted to Buck; but, if he's fighting other dogs now, he might try to fight Buck, too."

Wynn grinned. "Someone has to bring that big bully down to size."

"Oh, Wynn," I cried. "This isn't funny. He could be hurt!"

Wynn, more serious then, apologized. "I'm sorry. I didn't mean to make fun of your concern. You're right. There is the possibility of Kip getting hurt. But it's more probable that he will come out the victor. Kip didn't meet Buck's challenge last time because he knew he wasn't ready. That's a smart dog. If he does decide to take him on, it will be because he thinks he is ready. Now no one knows whether he is or not. We just have to trust Kip's instincts, that's all.

"Kip has a number of advantages over Buck. He's a little heavier. He has had better nutrition. He is younger and more agile, and I believe that he's much smarter. If it should come to a fight, I think Kip has a good chance."

Well, a good chance wasn't good enough for me. I wanted to be sure. What I really wanted was for Kip to stay out of the ring completely, but it didn't look like I was going to be able to avoid it much longer.

"You behave yourself," I warned Kip, shaking my finger at him, "or I'll—I'll tie you up."

In making the rounds of the cabins, I found a few more sniffles but no more bad coughs. Anna's small boy was not getting any worse. In fact, the medicine seemed to be working. His cough was gradually getting better. Anna beamed. None of the other children had developed the cough. I was sure that she, too, had thought of the dreaded whooping cough—she likely knew the symptoms much better than I.

The sun's rays warmed the air a bit more each day. I found myself frequently pushing back my parka and even unbuttoning my coat. The drifts were getting smaller and the wind did not have the same chill. We were now into the middle of April. *Spring must be just around the corner!* I exulted.

"How would you like a day off?" Wynn surprised me one morning. I looked up from cutting the thin slices of bread.

"I'd love it. What do you have in mind?"

"I need to make a call on a cabin about two miles from the settlement. I thought that, seeing you have been doing such a good job at being camp nurse, you might like to come along."

"I'd love to!" was my enthusiastic response.

"The snow is getting a little thin in places. We won't be using the sled much more this year." That was good news too.

"When should I be ready?" I asked Wynn.

"In about half an hour."

"I'll be waiting. Can I bring Kip for a run as well?"

"Sure. Bring Kip. Just keep him away from the sled dogs. To them, Kip is a stranger and a threat."

I was sure I wouldn't have any trouble with that. Kip was obedient and heeled whenever he was told to do so.

I hummed as I went about getting ready to go. *It's so nice to have this kind of outing! A whole day with Wynn!* The sun was shining. Soon our winter would be over and our world would change again. Nimmie would be coming back. The new trading post would be built. Our people would have proper food and supplies again. The world seemed good.

"Thank you, God," I whispered. "Thank you for seeing us through."

Wynn was soon there with the sled. Calling Kip to heel, I went out to join him. It was a wonderful day as promised. Wynn made his call and checked the man who had been reported ill in his cabin. Wynn carried wood and water in and made sure he had the necessary supplies. He gave him medicine to take for a few days and told him he would be back to see him in a couple of days. The man didn't appear to be seriously ill, just down with the flu; so we left him and started our return trip.

We were about halfway home when a terrible cry rent the stillness of the sun-filled day. I stopped in my tracks, my skin prickling.

"What was it?" I asked Wynn, who had stopped the team and drawn up beside me.

"I'd better check," he said and reached for his rifle. The piercing cry came again.

"You wait here," said Wynn. "I won't be long. It must be an animal in a trap."

I sat down, my back to the direction Wynn was taking, trying to blot out the awful sound. I watched the sled dogs. They lay on the hard-packed snow, their heads on their paws or else licking the icy snow from between their toes. They seemed oblivious to the whole thing, only appreciative of the chance to rest.

I thought of Kip then. I momentarily had forgotten about Kip. I turned to look for him now.

He was disappearing just around the clump of trees where Wynn had gone. I thought of Wynn and his rifle. What if he had to shoot and didn't know that Kip was there and Kip got in the way?

"Kip!" I cried, springing up. "Kip, get back here!"

I ran after the dog, puffing my way through the snow. It was not far. I soon found Kip and I soon found Wynn.

And then I saw it. Lying on the ground, which was covered with blood, was a small furry animal. His foot was secured in the trap, his eyes were big and pleading, and his leg—his leg—. And Wynn was swinging the butt of his rifle.

I couldn't look. I gave a little cry and turned away. Wynn's head came up quickly and he came to me.

"Elizabeth," he said, taking me into his arms and turning my head away from the awful sight, "I asked you to stay—"

"But Kip—he ran. I didn't see him until—"

Wynn held me. I started to cry and to shake. "The poor little animal," I kept sobbing. "The poor little thing."

Wynn let me cry.

"Oh, Wynn," I wept, "it's so awful."

"Yes," he agreed, "it's awful."

"You killed him?"

"I had to, Elizabeth. You saw how badly hurt he was."

"Couldn't you have let him go?"

"He was in a man's trap. And even if he had gotten away, he would have died—"

"It's terrible." I began to cry again. "Can't you stop it, Wynn? Can't you tell them not to do it anymore? You're the law; they'll listen to you."

Wynn gave me a little shake to stop my hysteria and to bring some sense to my head. "I can't stop trapping. You know I can't. Trapping is their way of life. Their livelihood. If they didn't have furs, they wouldn't have anything. I know it's cruel. I hate it, too, but it's part of life. One that we just have to accept."

I knew Wynn was right. I tried to stop crying. I thought of all the families back at the settlement. The furs for trading was the only way they had to buy their needed supplies.

I hated it, but I too would have to learn to live with it. *Yet surely, surely there must be a more humane way*, my heart told me.

I was sorry that our one day out together for so many long weeks had been spoiled. I tried to make it up to Wynn. I would not fuss further and I would not speak of it again. There wasn't any way I could prepare Wynn a special dinner, but at least I could be good company in the little time we had left. I planned a night before the fireplace, reading one of our favorite books.

When Wynn returned from settling the team, weary from the duties of the day, I told him about my plans. He grinned and lifted my face to kiss me on the nose.

"Sounds good to me."

We had just settled ourselves, and I was taking the first turn of reading aloud, while Wynn lay with his head in my lap. A commotion at the door made me jump and Wynn hollered. Fortunately, the book in his face had done no damage.

We answered our door to find one man with another man over his shoulder.

"Leg," he informed us and carried the man in and dumped him rather unceremoniously on the rug before the fire.

The injured man groaned in pain. Wynn knelt down beside him and began to feel the leg.

"It's broken," he said quietly. "We'll have to set it. At least the skin isn't broken. It's not too bad a break. No splinters or torn muscle or ligaments."

Wynn continued to feel the leg, and the man on the floor continued to groan.

"This isn't going to be nice," Wynn said to me. "Do you want to take a walk?"

"Do you need me?"

"I could use you—but I won't ask you to stay."

"I think—I think I can manage."

"Good girl." Then Wynn turned to the man who had carried the fellow in. "How did this happen?"

"Fall."

"How long ago?"

"'Bout hour."

"Let's get him on the cot."

They lifted him together and Wynn went for his medical supplies. He poured some strong-smelling stuff on a small cloth and gave it to me.

"I want you to stand here and hold this to his nose and mouth. Like this. Wait until we are ready to set the leg. Don't hold it there for too long. I'll tell you when to let him breathe it and when to move it away."

I moved in by the man, the cloth in my hand, ready to follow Wynn's instructions. I didn't watch. I was too busy with the face before me and the cloth that I held. In spite of my ministration, the man still moaned and tried to throw himself off the cot. The other man was called over to hold him. At last the ordeal was over and Wynn tied the leg securely in a makeshift splint.

"Go get one of your friends," Wynn said to the trapper, "and you can take him to his cabin."

Wynn's forehead was wet with perspiration. He brushed back the wave of hair that had fallen forward. He moved to the man on the cot and reached down to him with a gentle hand.

"It'll be all right, Strong Buck," he said assuringly. "It's all over now. They will take you to your own bed. I will give you good medicine for the pain."

The man nodded. The worst of it was over. Wynn brought the tablet and the water and he swallowed it gratefully.

The men were soon back and carefully carried their companion to his own home to be welcomed by an anxious wife.

Wynn turned back to the fire and then looked at me and smiled.

"Where is that nice, quiet evening you had arranged, Elizabeth?" he asked me.

I crossed to him and put my arms around his neck.

"Is there *anything* you can't do?" I asked him with admiration in my voice. "You deliver babies, sew up ugly cuts, set broken bones, pull infected teeth, act as doctor to the sick, feed the whole village. Is there anything that you can't do?" I repeated.

Wynn kissed me. He smiled that slow, easy smile I had learned to love.

"Now, Elizabeth," he said teasingly. "Do you think I would be so silly as to confess?"

33
Spring

THOUGH WE DID not hear from the McLains, I began to watch for them. "As soon as the river thaws," or "as soon as the logs can be brought from the forests," was not too definite a time for their return. Well, the river was running again now and the forests were losing their snow quickly. I began to watch and to hope.

"I'll be back in time to plant my garden," Nimmie had said. "We will plant a garden together."

I was anxious for that garden. I was even more anxious for Nimmie. I thought, too, of Katherine. Would she be back too? Poor Katherine! She had faced so much in life, but she had lost so much of life by her own choosing. I was so glad she seemed finally able to start picking up the pieces again.

I wondered about Nimmie's coming baby. This was not a convenient time to be on the long, difficult trail out from Edmonton. I remembered the trip well. But then Nimmie was at home with the woods and the river. She no doubt would be a better traveler than I had been. I had watched for the first bluebird when at home in Toronto. I had watched for the first song of the robin. I had waited expectantly for the sight of the first spring crocus. I had relished the day when I saw my first dainty violet. But now I was watching and waiting for Nimmie. With Nimmie's arrival, I would know that it was really spring. With the coming of Nimmie and Ian, new life would be given to the dreary, winter-weary little settlement.

Heavy parkas were put away now. Children played out again in cotton dresses and flannel shirts. Women went to the woods with baskets on their arms, hoping to find some early spring greens. Men came back from traplines and turned their attention from trapping furs to tanning the furs. Smoke still lazily drifted from the fires in the cabins, but at times they were allowed to die out. Their warmth wasn't needed through all of the days.

There was a new feeling in the settlement, a feeling of being released after a long confinement. But still, I held apart, breathless, waiting.

Was it really spring, or might another biting north wind bring in the snow again? I hardly dared to hope.

And then it happened. A man rode excitedly into camp, his horse breathing heavily. He cried out in broken English, "They come. Many wagons."

Everyone came from their cabins.

"Where? Where?"

He began to talk to them in their own language then, and I was about to explode with my question.

I ran among the people until I found Wynn.

"Is it them?" I asked him.

"It's them," he assured me, grinning. "With many wagons of supplies."

"How far away are they?"

"About five miles."

Five miles. That still seemed too far. I could hardly wait. It would seem forever. "I'll go get them some supper," I said, about to bolt off.

Wynn caught my hand. "Hold it," he said, laughing. "They won't be here for an hour or so."

At my look of disappointment, he hurried on.

"I was wondering if you'd like to go out to meet them."

"Oh, yes!" I cried.

"Grab a sweater. It might be getting cool before we get back."

I ran for the sweater, my skirts whipping about my legs. I lifted them up so that I might run faster. *They're here!* Well, they were *almost* here. They were coming.

I hurried back to Wynn. "Let's go," I said, already out of breath.

He took my arm and slowed me down. "If we have a few miles to walk, you'd better slow down. You'll never make it at that pace."

He was right. I slowed down, and the people of the village began to fall into step behind us. They came, the mothers carrying babies and the fathers hoisting young ones on their shoulders. Even the old, who needed the assistance of a walking stick, tottered on at a slower pace. The whole village was going out to meet the trader and his Indian wife.

We walked along as swiftly as Wynn would allow. I breathed deeply of the fresh tangy air. It was still cool but it smelled of growing things, I thought. Or was it just my imagination?

"Do you think spring is really here?" I asked Wynn.

"I think so."

"What signs do you go by?" I persisted.

"The river is almost ice free."

I nodded my head in assent.

"The snow is almost all gone."

I nodded again.

"It's warmer," continued Wynn. "And I've seen several flocks of Canada geese pass over."

He waited. "Do you need more?"

I swatted at my cheek. "The mosquitoes are back," I said ruefully.

"There," said Wynn. "You have one more assurance. Spring is here all right." We laughed together.

Kip frolicked on ahead of us, sniffing at rabbit dens and barking at saucy squirrels. I laughed at him.

"I think he's excited, too," I said to Wynn.

Wynn took my hand.

"This winter has been hard for you, hasn't it, Elizabeth?"

"It's been hard for everyone," I answered honestly.

"But the rest—they are used to the hardships. You haven't been. Has it—has it been too much?"

"I admit I will be very glad for a fresh carrot. And I will admit I will be glad for a piece of cake. I will even admit that spinach, which I hate, might taste good. But I am not sorry that I came with you, Wynn."

Wynn stopped me and pushed back my hair and kissed me. He looked deeply into my eyes.

"I'm glad to hear you say that, Elizabeth. I have something to say, too. Something I maybe should have said long ago, but I want to say now, with all my heart—with all my love. I'm proud of you, Elizabeth. Proud of your strength, your support, your ability to adjust to hard things. You've been my help, my support, my right arm, Elizabeth. I don't know what I ever would have done without you. You've more than proved me wrong—over and over. You belong here—with me."

Wynn kissed me again, and I brushed away happy tears and lifted my face again to his.

And then I heard the grinding of the wagon wheels. They were coming. Just over the hill was Nimmie. Just over the hill were the needed supplies—and hope. My heart gave a lurch in its happiness. I gave Wynn one more kiss with all my love wrapped up in it, and I turned to meet the oncoming wagon.

Spring had come.

WHEN BREAKS
THE DAWN

To my dear fifth sister, Joyce Ruth,
whom I had the privilege of
helping to name when she arrived
and to spoil as she grew.
I appreciate her unselfish love
and her dedication to her Lord.
To her and to her husband, Elmer Deal,
I dedicate this book with my love.

CONTENTS

1 The Homecoming   363
2 Together Again   367
3 Catching Up   372
4 Supply House   377
5 A New Day   381
6 Routine   386
7 Life Goes On   389
8 Surprises   394
9 Nonita   399
10 Summer   401
11 Another Winter   403
12 School   406
13 The Three R's   411
14 Trials and Triumphs   414
15 Another Christmas   418
16 Winter Visitor   424
17 Classes Resume   428
18 Susie   431
19 Spring Returns   436
20 Changes   444
21 Reminders   450
22 Sickness   453
23 Summer of 'Fourteen   457
24 Waiting   461
25 Temptation   466
26 Duty   469
27 Out   476
28 Calgary   480
29 Home Again   485
30 Settling In   488
31 Spring Again   494
32 The Birthday Party   496
33 Sorrow and Joy   502

1

The Homecoming

THE NEARER WE came to the rumbling wagons, the more my heart pounded. Frustrated with the wait, I wished I could just hoist my long, cumbersome skirts and break into a run, but I held my impatience in check. I wasn't sure how Wynn would feel about my impulsiveness, and I was quite sure there would be some puzzled expressions on the faces of our Indian neighbors.

They were so near and yet so far away, just dipping down over the last hills before our little village. I had missed Nimmie so much in the time she had been gone, and was anxious to see for myself that she was all right. I wanted to hug her close, to welcome her back. I wanted to talk, and talk—for hours and hours—and to hear all about the outside world and every little thing that had happened to her while she had been away from us.

I'm sure Wynn sensed my feelings. He reached for my hand and gave it a loving squeeze.

"It won't be long now," he said, trying to calm my trembling hands and heart.

I took a deep breath, gave him a quick smile and attempted to slow my stride, just a bit, but it was hard. My legs ached with the effort. I was so eager to see dear Nimmie.

Just when I thought I would burst with anticipation, I saw someone climbing down from the side of the distant wagon, and then there was Nimmie running toward me! Without another thought, I grabbed up my skirts and broke into a headlong run to meet her.

At first neither of us could talk. We just held one another, tears mingling on our faces.

Nimmie was not only my much-missed friend—she held the secrets of the outside world, the world of my family that I loved and missed so much.

By the time we had finished embracing, there was great commotion all around us. Wynn was greeting Nimmie's husband, Mr. McLain, and a crowd of people from the settlement gathered around. The wagon drivers were trying hard to hold the tired teams steady in spite of all of the confusion. Everyone seemed to be talking at once, and Nimmie and I both knew it would be useless to try to visit now. We backed up, looked at one another's face and smiled our delight, our eyes promising each other a long, long talk together as soon as it could be arranged.

But I tried one question: "Katherine?" I queried above the hum.

"She stayed," answered Nimmie. I knew that now was not the time to get more details.

Then the whole party turned toward the settlement, and in almost eerie quietness began to walk the trail that led us over the hills, through the bush, and home.

Nimmie's eyes darted back and forth over the scenery she had not seen for so long. I could sense her straining forward, eager for that first look at the familiar cabins in the small clearing. I knew her thoughts were skipping on ahead of her, but my attention was drawn back to where she had been in the recent past.

I could wait no longer.

"Did you meet my family in Calgary?" I asked, hoping with all of my heart she would be able to say yes.

She turned to me with a light in her eyes.

"They are wonderful!" she exclaimed. "Mary is so sweet; and the children—I love the children."

I swallowed the big lump suddenly welling up in my throat. How I missed Jon and Mary and their children. I hadn't realized just how much until I heard Nimmie talk about them.

"They are—well?" I struggled with the few words.

"Fine," beamed Nimmie. "But they miss you. They send their love. Little Kathleen begged to come with us so she could see her Aunt Beth. She said it has been 'almost forever' since you left."

My beloved Kathleen—I could almost feel her arms around my neck. The tears sprang again to my eyes.

"I suppose she's grown," I said wistfully.

"Mary says they've all grown a good deal in the past year," responded Nimmie, who of course wouldn't know, having just met the children.

Noticing my tears spilling onto my cheeks, Nimmie quickly changed our conversation.

"They all sent you letters," she told me briskly. "I put them right in the top crate so you could have them just as soon as we get to the settlement. I knew you would be anxious for them."

I reached over to give Nimmie a warm hug. She understood.

The horses seemed to sense rest and food just ahead and hastened their plodding strides. We had to hurry to keep up. Wynn, who had been walking next to Mr. McLain in order to snatch a few pieces of news, joined me, taking my hand to steady my footsteps.

"Are you okay?" he asked after a few silent moments.

I smiled to let him know I was, though I was sure the traces of tears still showed on my face.

"Any news from home?" he asked next.

"Nimmie said they're all fine and they sent letters." My grip on Wynn's hand tightened. "I can hardly wait to read them."

The sun was low on the horizon, making it increasingly difficult to see the trail. The Indians, with their intimate knowledge of nature and the territory, walked quickly and surely, their steps seeming never to falter. I stumbled now and then and was glad for Wynn's hand. Kip stopped his frisking about and came back to follow closely at my side.

"The McLains will need a place to spend the night, many nights perhaps, until they get themselves settled in the old Lamuir cabin," commented Wynn.

"That's a mess!" I exclaimed, horrified that he would even suggest such a place.

"It can be cleaned up and made quite livable with a little effort," Wynn maintained. "Ian has already asked if it is available." He paused for a moment and then went on slowly, "Like most women, Nimmie might prefer to be on her own."

I knew Wynn was right, at least about Nimmie preferring to be on her own. She was very independent, but oh, it would be nice to keep her with me during the rebuilding of the store.

"I'll help her clean the cabin if that's what she wants," I said rather reluctantly.

"Good," was all Wynn answered.

After we had walked a bit farther, I broke the silence again. "How long do you think it will take to rebuild the trading store?"

"It depends on the weather—how many of the men help, how things go—but Ian says he hopes to have it framed in and ready to shelter the supplies in four weeks or so. Then he will finish the living quarters as time allows."

Poor Nimmie, I groaned inwardly. She would be without a real home for some months, and with the new baby coming that would not be easy.

In the semidarkness I stole another look at Nimmie. She looked fine. She was showing now and I couldn't help but wonder when the baby was due. In my excitement about Nimmie's good news when she had shared her secret, I had not even asked the time of the expected birth. Yes, she could be due before too many weeks passed. Yet she walked with the same straight shoulders, the same confidence, as the rest of her people. I admired Nimmie.

By now it was quite dark. We were still meeting people on their way to welcome the travelers—mothers with little ones in tow, old people who could not hurry with their walking sticks, children who straggled just for the fun of it.

Finally within sight of the small settlement, we could see the dark shapes of the cabins through the gathering night. Hearing the familiar sound of barking dogs as they strained against their unwelcome tethers, I wondered fleetingly if Kip felt a bit smug about the fact that he was with the group, traveling free.

The smoke of the wood fires lingered in the air, though by now most likely every fire in the settlement would have gone out for lack of attention. The sad heap of rubble where the trading post had stood showed faintly through the darkness. I suddenly wished we had taken time to clear it away so that it might not bring returning pain to Nimmie.

I moved closer to her, hoping my presence in the darkness would be some comfort.

It must have been, too, for her voice came softly to me over the creak and grind of the wagons. "It seems like a long-ago bad dream."

Giving her arm a quick squeeze, I did not answer, for I did not know what to say.

We moved silently among the buildings so familiar to both of us as the wagons ground to a stop. The tired drivers lowered their aching bodies to the hard-packed earth, speaking to the teams as they moved forward to tether them until Mr. McLain would give the next orders. Nimmie waited to join her husband, and I spoke to her as I walked by.

"I'll light the fire and get supper ready. As soon as you are free, come to the house. You may wash and rest for a bit before we have our supper."

"Thank you," said Nimmie, her voice soft.

My heart was light as I hurried back home to my supper preparations. Nimmie was back and she looked fine. The much-needed supplies for the village were on the loaded wagons. Soon the trading post would be built again. And after the evening's supper was over and the dishes washed and cared for, Nimmie and I would at last get to have that long-coveted talk.

2

Together Again

As I RUSHED to get the fire started, my mind was busy with what I could fix for our supper. I knew the McLains had been on the trail for many days and would enjoy a full meal rather than a hastily prepared snack. The occasion merited a celebration feast, and yet my pantry was almost bare because of the scarcity of supplies. The wagons that stood in the settlement were loaded down with our future needs, so it wasn't caution that made it impossible for me to fix our guests a really fine meal, even though it was hard to break my habit of conserving during the past weeks. It was simply the fact that there was very little on my shelves to prepare.

I left my fire, the flames now devouring the wood, and began to rummage through the cupboard shelves. It seemed that each container I eagerly pulled forward and opened was almost empty. I wondered just how many more days we could have survived on the little we had left.

There was always meat. The men of the settlement, with Wynn in charge, had kept us well supplied with fresh meat. With the warmer weather, the meat had to be brought to the village daily and divided among the families, as it would not keep fresh for long. I surveyed the piece that had been brought to me for our supper. It had seemed like plenty for Wynn and me, but now, with two others to feed, it looked awfully small. It was beaver, not my favorite dish, but it was tasty enough. I tried to think of a quick way to cook it—and perhaps stretch it a bit.

I had few vegetables left. But I could make a stew of sorts. I hastened to get it into the pot and on the stove to cook. I had nothing that would make a dessert of any kind. We'd just have to do without, like Wynn and I had been doing.

Thankfully, we had plenty of wood, and the roaring flames soon had the stew simmering in the pot. I wished I had some fresh bread, but we had been rationing our dwindling flour supply. So instead I made some simple biscuits, nearly using up the last of the flour in the tin to do so. I had no shortening on hand except for rendered bear tallow. I did not enjoy the taste of it, but the biscuits would be as hard as rocks without it.

If only I had something special to celebrate this great occasion—the safe return of our friends, the coming of the food supplies. But I had nothing.

And then I remembered the one jar of blueberry preserves I had been hoarding on the top shelf for some special event. *Well, this is a special event!* I enthusiastically went for the blueberries.

Once I had my meal on to cook, the biscuits in the oven, and the table set, there was nothing more for me to do. I fidgeted about, walking the floor from the table to the stove, from the door to the window. I couldn't see anything except shadowy movements in the light from open doors and small, dirt-clouded windows in the distant settlement yard. I knew the wagons were being moved about for unloading. I knew that not all the crates and boxes would be unloaded, for there was no place to store the contents, but a few of the supplies would be organized as quickly as possible so the people of the settlement would have access to them. Tomorrow would be a busy day indeed.

I turned from the window, put more wood in the fire to be sure the pot was kept boiling, and adjusted the dishes and the tableware for the fifth or sixth time. I felt like I was missing out on all the activity in the settlement. Kip must have felt the same way, sensing there was excitement beyond our closed door, for he crossed over to it and stood whining for me to let him out.

I had no sympathy for him. "If I can't go, neither can you," I said firmly. "I'm missing it all, too."

Kip must have known from my voice that I would not let him go, for he whined once more, crossed back to his favorite place in front of the fireplace and lowered himself to the bear rug, looking at me with wide, pleading eyes.

I stirred the stew and pulled the kettle forward for hot water. I had no more tea or coffee. We had used the last of the tea for our Sunday dinner and had been out of coffee for a week or more. We would simply drink the hot water. It really wasn't so bad.

At last I heard footsteps just outside the door, and ran to open it. Nimmie entered the room with her arms full of parcels, chattering as she came in.

"I knew you'd be anxious for your letters, and Mary said I must be sure that you got these parcels right away. The men are bringing the rest."

I felt like Christmas had come with the spring! Dear Mary! I could hardly wait to see what she had sent. I reached for the parcels, prepared to begin tearing off wrappings immediately, and then checked myself. This was not just for me—it was for Wynn also. So instead of ripping away like a child, I squeezed the first parcel a bit, laid it on the nearby chair, and then took the remainder of the parcels from Nimmie and deposited them with the first.

"Wynn said to go ahead and open them," Nimmie encouraged, seeming to read my mind.

"Are you sure?" It wasn't that I doubted her word; it was just that I was so eager I was afraid to trust what I heard.

Nimmie laughed, silvery and soft. I had missed her lovely laugh. There had been so little laughter in the settlement in the past weeks. I hadn't realized just how little until I listened to Nimmie now. Tears misted my eyes. Too much joy was happening too quickly.

I brushed at my eyes with my apron and reached for the first parcel. It was just for me, filled with new yard goods, toilet articles, and some pretty lacey underthings. I ran my hands over each item, feeling its newness and enjoying the fresh scent of something unworn and unwashed.

The next bundle was prepared by the children and contained special sweet treats. There were many things there that children love, but I will admit they looked awfully good to me as well. I couldn't remember when I had eaten something just for the fun of savoring the taste. Each little gift was wrapped and identified. As I read each name, my eyes filled with tears again. There even was a lumpy-looking one from baby Elizabeth, and I knew she had had help. I was sure she had grown in the year I had been gone, but she was still a baby of only two.

The third parcel was from Mary again. It, too, was filled with treats, but of a different sort. There were spices and dried fruits, nuts and teas, vanilla, and a can of *fresh coffee*! Now the tears were really falling. I hadn't tasted some of these things since leaving Calgary. How good they would be! I couldn't express my delight, not even to Nimmie, but I was sure that she understood.

At last I picked up the packet of letters. I would wait to share them with Wynn. I fingered them, turning them over in my hands as I read the names on the envelopes. There was Mary's neat handwriting, the firm script of brother Jon, childish printing from the children and even one in the careless but expressive dash of my sister Julie! I found it hard to wait, but I laid the letters down again.

Getting control of my emotions, I turned to Nimmie. "What would you like to drink with your supper," I asked her, "fresh coffee or an exotic tea?"

Nimmie laughed again. "Well," she answered, "since I have a feeling I might have had fresh coffee and exotic tea since you have, why don't *you* choose?"

I smiled. "I will," I said and took my time deliberating. I debated first over one item and then another, like a child in a candy shop. I was about to select a lemon tea when I thought of Wynn. I was sure, that given a choice, he would pick coffee, so I laid the tea aside and went to open the coffee can. I will never forget that first burst of fragrance—it hung in the air like a promise. I savored it, looking at Nimmie to be sure I wasn't dreaming.

"We need to talk," I said, breathing in the delicious smell of the coffee as I measured it carefully into the pot.

"We will," Nimmie promised. "For as long as you want."

Just then there was a scuffle of feet on the doorstep and Wynn and Ian entered, both men carrying a large crate on their shoulders.

"The family sent rations for the starving Northerners," quipped Wynn, but his tone gave away his heartfelt appreciation for their concern.

"Oh, Wynn!" was all I could say as I looked at the crate.

The men placed it on the floor against the wall. I finally came to my senses enough to offer warm water to Ian so he could wash for supper.

"Sure smells good," Ian boomed out as he sniffed the air. "I get tired awfully fast of campfire cookin'."

"It's not much," I admitted, my cheeks flushing a bit. "I hadn't realized just how low our supplies were until I went to get our supper tonight. I don't know how much further I could have stretched the little bit of food we have left."

"Elizabeth has done a wonderful job of making do," said Wynn, genuine pride in his voice. "She has always found something to go with the meat."

I flushed even more at Wynn's praise. In fact, we both knew that sometimes there had been precious little to go with the meat.

We gathered around our small table, and Wynn led us in prayer. His voice broke a little as he expressed his gratitude to our heavenly Father for getting the wagons to the settlement in time to prevent any real hardship. I was reminded again of the heavy responsibility Wynn had carried over the past months, with the welfare of so many lives on his shoulders.

We did enjoy our simple meal together. Even the beaver meat tasted better with talk and laughter of friends. Nimmie exclaimed over the biscuits. "Bear tallow, isn't it? I've really missed it—tastes so good."

I laughed. I guess one's preferences have a lot to do with one's background.

After the meal the men announced that there were a few more things to be done in the settlement. Wynn lit the lantern and they left, leaving Nimmie and me to clear the table. Without even discussing it, we hurried through the dishes. We were both anxious for that long talk.

At last we settled ourselves. I hadn't yet read our letters, but I still wanted to wait for Wynn. For now I would relish all that Nimmie could tell me about the outside world. In some ways it seemed forever, and yet just yesterday, that I had made the trip by train, barge and wagon over the same trail Nimmie had just traveled.

I really couldn't think where to begin with all my questions. Then I remembered it was Nimmie's first trip "out," away from the settlement. "Well," I said, "what did you think of it all?"

"It was even beyond the books—the feel, the sounds, the big buildings," said Nimmie, her voice filled with excitement, her hands shaping the tall structures as she spoke. "I could not believe that such things really existed. It was all so different—so new."

I looked at Nimmie's shining eyes. I knew she had enjoyed her time out. I wished I could have been with her to show it all to her myself.

"It's wonderful, isn't it?" I spoke softly, remembering so many things, feeling that Nimmie, like me, was already missing the outside world with a hollow ache in her heart.

"Did you hate to come back?" I finally asked, hesitantly.

Nimmie's eyes widened, then softened as she spoke slowly, guardedly, "I loved seeing your world. It truly was fascinating. But as the days and weeks went by, I was so homesick for the rivers, the forests, I could hardly wait to come home."

3

Catching Up

WHEN WYNN AND Ian returned from the last of the night's duties, Wynn and I read the letters from home while Nimmie and Ian prepared floor-beds for the night.

Our letters confirmed that all of them were well. We were glad to hear that Jon's business was growing, as were his children, and Mary was busy and happy as homemaker. We also learned that after returning home to Toronto, Julie had missed the West so much she had finally persuaded Father and Mother to allow her to return to Calgary in the care of brother Jon. She was now busy giving piano and voice lessons to young Calgary students.

When it came time to retire for the night, Wynn insisted that Nimmie share my bed rather than sleep on the floor, so after we bid our tired husbands good night we went to the bedroom to prepare for bed. We did not go right to sleep but talked until late into the night. There was so much to tell one another, so many questions on my mind. I wanted to hear all about what Nimmie had seen and heard in the outside world. I wanted to know all about my family members, the cities I had left behind, the happenings in the world, the fashions that the ladies were wearing—everything that I had been missing.

Nimmie was more than glad to fill me in, though some things that she shared with me were seen through different eyes than mine and thus with a different perspective.

I laughed as I listened to Nimmie's frank appraisal of women's fashions. To her the current wearing apparel was very cumbersome and impractical and, for all that matter, not really attractive either—certainly not attractive enough to be worth fussing over.

She had learned to love my family. Though Nimmie did not pretend to totally understand the ways of "the white woman," Mary was kind and generous, and Nimmie could appreciate that characteristic in anyone.

The children in their open, candid way brought much delight to Nimmie. She was especially taken with young Elizabeth. Partly because she bore my name, partly because she was a delightful child, but mostly, admitted Nimmie, because she was still not much more than a baby and Nimmie was looking ahead to the delightful experience of having a child of her own.

I looked at Nimmie. There must have been envy in my eyes, for there certainly was envy in my heart.

"Oh, Nimmie!" I said. "I can hardly wait for your little one." I guess part of what I meant was, *I can hardly wait until it is my turn and I too have a little one, but until then I will gladly share in the joy that your little one brings you.*

Nimmie must have understood my comment for exactly what it was. She looked at me and smiled.

"Soon it will be your turn, Elizabeth. Then our time together will be spent boasting about our babies."

I smiled. I did so much hope that Nimmie was right. I wanted a child so badly.

"Did you see a doctor while you were out?" I asked.

"I really didn't want to—I didn't need to; but Ian was so insistent that I did see one to please him. Everything is just fine."

"I'm glad." I shrugged my shoulder slightly. "And I agree with Ian. I think it's wise that you saw a doctor. Why take chances with the life of your child?"

"I don't see it as 'taking chances,' " stated Nimmie matter-of-factly. "My people have been having babies without doctors for many generations."

I wanted to answer, *Yes, and look at the mortality rate*, but I bit my tongue.

"When is your baby due?" I asked instead.

"Do?" puzzled Nimmie.

"Yes, due?"

"Oh, yes, due," said Nimmie, nodding as she realized my question. "That means when will it come. Mary asked me that, too. The doctor said that it would be the fifth day of August, but I told Ian that nobody tells a baby when to 'due.' A baby decides that for himself."

Nimmie's comment brought my pillow-smothered laughter. She was right, of course. The baby would decide for himself.

Our chatter turned to other things. Just as I had been anxious to hear about the outside world, Nimmie was every bit as interested in catching up on all that had happened in the settlement in their absence. I brought her up-to-date on all of our neighbors, though there really didn't seem to be too much to tell. Our past months had been rather uneventful—and we thanked God for that. We could have had one tragedy after another, with the food supply so low. God had kept us, I realized even more as I related to Nimmie how things had gone in the time since the fire.

At last we agreed that we must get some rest. Tomorrow would be a busy day with both of us trying to get the small Lamuir cabin ready for occupancy. Reluctantly we said good night and let sleep claim us.

The next day, drippy and wet, had ushered in a storm which seemed to take perverse delight in making everything miserable for those who had so much to do in the settlement. The trails were muddy and slippery, and it was difficult just to walk about, let alone to carry goods or accomplish anything outside.

Nimmie and I made our soggy way to the little cabin. The one lone window had been broken out, and cracks in the chinking between the logs let in more than just light. Squirrels had wintered on the one small cupboard shelf, and the floor was covered with wood chips and litter. It was a dismal sight as far as I was concerned, and I was about to say so when Nimmie spoke. "This won't take long!" her tone good-natured and enthusiastic. "We'll have it cleaned up in no time."

I swallowed my protests and picked up the shovel we had brought with us.

My normal cleaning usually began with a pail of hot soapy water. That wasn't possible here in Nimmie's new dwelling. The walls were rough-hewn logs with mud chinking; the floor was hard-packed earth. Scrubbing would have only made mud puddles. Instead, we scraped and shoveled the clutter on the floor and carried it outside by the bucketful, disposing of it behind the cabin. Then Nimmie went to work mixing mud and handfuls of dried grasses. Normally she would have mixed the earth and water first, but the rain had saved her that trouble.

Her hands in mud almost to the elbow, Nimmie got right into the task. I did not envy her; it was hard enough for me to get my hands into bread dough.

When Nimmie was confident she had the right consistency, she began to carefully apply the mud pack to the gaps between the logs. She worked swiftly and skillfully, and I realized as I watched her that she had done such work before. In spite of my fastidiousness, I found myself almost wishing to try my hand at it. Somehow, Nimmie made it look like such a worthwhile skill.

"Would you like me to help?" I finally ventured, half hoping that Nimmie would agree, yet afraid she might.

"It will take me only a few minutes," responded Nimmie. "There is no use for us both to get all dirty."

I went instead to clean the squirrel nest from the shelf.

Nimmie was still working on the logs when I left to prepare a noon meal for us. I sloshed my way through the ever-deepening puddles, hating every squishy step, especially when I slipped and almost fell down.

By the time I reached our cabin my shoes were covered with the heavy gumbo and my skirt hem was soggy and splashed with mud. I surely didn't want to take it all with me into my clean house.

I could think of no way to rid myself of the mess, so reluctantly I opened the door and stepped in. I started with the messy shoes, getting my hands thoroughly mud-covered in the process. Now, how was I going to get out of the dress I was wearing? I should have thought ahead and removed my dress first.

It was too late to think of that. I wiped off my dirty hands near the already muddy hem of my dress, then attempted to lift the dripping mess over my head without dragging the mud over my face and hair. My face streaked with mud, I grumpily left the dress in a sodden heap by the door and headed for the bedroom, my wet feet leaving imprints on the wooden floor.

I felt a little better after I had washed my face and hands, put on a fresh dress and recombed my hair. I found a dry pair of shoes and went back to my kitchen to build the fire and prepare our meal.

I was glad for the heat of the fire. I hadn't noticed it till then, but the cold rain and the early spring day was chilly—and so was I. Nimmie probably would be cold when she arrived as well. And the menfolk, working out in the rain all morning, would be chilled to the bone. We would be fortunate if no one caught a dreadful cold from the ordeal. I decided to have some hot soup ready for lunch.

The men were busy now preparing to uncrate and distribute much-needed supplies which had arrived with the McLains. If only there was a building big enough to hold all of it out of the rain.

Instead, everyone would be forced to puddle through the mud around the wagons.

I had the meal ready and the room warm when Nimmie came for dinner. She was wet to the skin but did not complain. She had no other clothes unpacked so I loaned her some of mine. She was not quite as careful as I had been about leaving all her mess at the door, but then, I reminded myself, Nimmie had spent many years living in houses that didn't even have floors.

The menfolk soon joined us. They too were sopping wet but they shrugged off the need for warm, dry clothes. "We'll be just as wet in a few minutes anyway," Wynn insisted.

Wynn knew my concern for my clean house so he announced that they would take their dinner by the door. I tried to argue with him but he was adamant. Nimmie quietly took the two chairs and placed them by the door as Wynn requested, and, seeing that I was the loser on this one, I went ahead and served up their bowls of steaming soup.

In a short while they were stepping out the door into the chilling rain again. I worried, sure that pneumonia was in store for both of them.

Wynn was soon back. He stood at the open door and called to me so he wouldn't need to bring more mud into the cabin.

"Elizabeth," he said when I joined him at the door, "I hate to ask this, but I have no choice. We are going to need to bring the supply crates in here so that we can sort them out without the rain ruining the foodstuff. It's the only place in the whole settlement that is anywhere near big enough to work."

I'm sure he saw the momentary horror on my face, but I quickly recovered and nodded my head.

"You understand?" asked Wynn and I could detect the hesitancy in his voice.

"Of course," I managed to answer. "That will be fine—just fine."

Wynn looked searchingly at me, nodded his thanks, then turned to go. "We'll be back as soon as we can hitch the horses to the wagons."

I allowed myself a big sigh and went back to join Nimmie for our dinner. I would need to hurry to clean up the dinner dishes. Soon our cozy little nest would be a shambles.

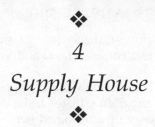

4

Supply House

EVEN THOUGH I had tried to brace myself for the intrusion into my home, I found I was totally unprepared for what happened.

The rain of course did not help matters. Everyone who came through the door brought with him mud and water that gathered on my wooden floor in dirty little puddles—which eventually got to be big puddles.

There was no use trying to clean them up. The men came in a steady stream, groaning under the weight of the crates and boxes. At first all of the supplies were stored in Wynn's office room, but soon that was filled to overflowing and the men began to stack the boxes in our living area.

I knew as well as anyone that the need for those supplies was now. I knew too that there simply was no other place in the village where they could be unpacked. It was unthinkable to try to sort and distribute it all in the rain.

By the time the last of the boxes were stacked high in our small quarters, our house no longer looked like a home. Nimmie, who had been the traffic director, of sorts, found one of their boxes, and with hammer in hand, busied herself looking for dry clothes for Ian. This reminded me that, with the boxes now all inside, Wynn, too, would be able to change into dry clothes. As Wynn shut the door for the last time and the men with the teams climbed aboard to drive off, leaving deep ruts in what had been our front path, I turned to Wynn and implored him to take the time to change his wet clothes.

He did not argue but went to the bedroom, unbuttoning his shirt as he went, not wanting to waste time. I mournfully watched the muddy tracks as they followed him out of the room.

Without comment to our two guests, I went for the mop pail and the mop.

As soon as Wynn had returned from the bedroom, looking much better and safer in dry clothes, Nimmie sent Ian in to change from his wet things.

Wynn reached for the mop. "Here, let me, Elizabeth," he offered, but I held on to it.

"You have enough to do without mopping floors," I told him. "I can't do much, but I can at least do this."

Wynn looked at the heaped-up crates and nodded his head. Ian soon joined him and the two went to work. With hammers pounding and boards squeaking their protest, the sacks, tins and cartons with their intriguing labels—flour, tea, coffee, sugar, and such—began to stack all around us.

I looked at Nimmie, hoping she would suggest we head for her temporary cabin again, but she didn't. Instead, she began sorting things into piles. I gathered my energy up and joined her.

We worked for hours, and then I looked at the clock and checked with Wynn.

"Would you like me to fix us a cup of tea?"

He straightened rather slowly, placing a hand on the small of his back, and he too looked at the clock—seven minutes to four. We had been working without a break since our noon meal.

"That would be nice, Elizabeth," he answered. "We could use that."

I went to work on it right away. I wished I had something special to go with the tea. But the cold biscuits from the night before spread with some jam Mary had sent would help to refresh us some. Our dinner soup did not stick to the ribs for long when we were working so hard.

The men did not sit and sip their tea. I feared they might burn their mouths, but they were soon back at their task.

It was shortly after five when Ian went to the door and began hammering on a tin drum. *What a strange way to celebrate the unpacking of the last crate of the day*, I thought.

Ian saw my questioning look and smiled a tired smile. "It's the dinner bell," he told me.

"The dinner bell?" My eyes traveled again to the clock.

"We told them that we'd call them when we got the supplies unpacked so they could come and get something to prepare for their suppers."

"Oh!" I nodded in understanding. Many of the Indian people probably had nothing in their homes with which to prepare a meal, except perhaps a little meat from the day before. No hunting detail would have been assigned on this day as every available back had been bent to the task of getting the crates unloaded.

As soon as Ian's call rang out, lines of hungry people began to form at our door and make their way through to hold out baskets, pails or pots to be filled with food for their evening meal.

It seemed like the rain-soaked stream would never stop—and stream it truly was. My mopped-up floor was soon a river of muddy water again.

Wynn stopped doling out supplies long enough to ask me to start a fire in the fireplace. Our door was constantly open and the room was chilly with the damp air.

Seeing the relief and gratitude in the hungry eyes of those who came, I quickly chose to ignore the muddy water that ran from their clothes and feet and thanked the Lord instead that the supplies had arrived in time. I marveled that we had actually managed to make it through the tough months of early spring without disease and death overtaking the village.

I smiled at the hollow faces and the outstretched hands, often saying a few words in their native language to welcome them to my home and to express my thankfulness that they and their families had stayed well.

It was dark now and the evening air was close to freezing. The rain clouds would keep actual frost away, but the line of people at our door—mostly women, with an occasional girl or a man holding out the container—certainly would have a cold walk home.

No one lingered. They were concerned with one thing only—to get their needs for the evening meal and to hurry home to their fires so they might prepare it for the family.

My own household needed an evening meal too. I did not as yet have my own food supplies replenished. Our boxes had been stacked in a pile at the far end of the room. There was not room for me to open them in the already crowded room, so I gave up the idea of heading for the corner with hammer in hand. The leftovers from the big pot of stew I had made the night before would have to do.

I got out the cold stew and put it on to heat. Then I set to work making another batch of bear-tallow biscuits. I nearly choked at the thought of eating them for yet another meal. I had so looked forward to having something new from the supplies—so near yet so out of reach!

The men would not stop to eat until every home in the settlement had been supplied. It was late by then. Nimmie and I had already nibbled on the biscuits. With hunger gnawing at me, I had to admit they tasted rather good. Especially when I spread them with Mary's jam.

It was almost eight o'clock when the door finally closed and the tired men straightened up and reached for a chair. I dished up our overheated stew, put out the now-cold biscuits and we gathered around the table.

Our table prayer was a little longer that night. In a reverent voice, Wynn expressed his thanks to God that the people of the village would not go to bed hungry on this night. I knew he felt it very deeply.

There was no room left on the floor for the McLains to spread their fur robes. Wynn suggested that he and Ian take the furs and blankets and go to the Lamuir cabin, and Nimmie stay with me again.

I wanted to protest. Not that I wasn't glad to share my bed with Nimmie, but I didn't like to think of Wynn, as tired as he was, sleeping on the floor in a cold cabin. The window still was not fixed. That was Ian's job as soon as he discovered where the glass had been packed. There was no wood for a fire. The mud walls were not thoroughly dry in the damp, rainy atmosphere. It would not be a nice place to spend the night.

Nimmie protested, answering us that she was quite able to sleep in the cabin, but Wynn insisted that she stay in our house; and Ian, rather reluctantly, supported him.

In ordinary circumstances, Nimmie could have slept on our cot, but even that was stacked high with sorted-out supplies.

At last the men ventured back out in the damp night, their arms filled with blankets and furs which had been bundled in slickers to protect them from the rain.

Nimmie and I were too tired to spend any more time talking. We simply stacked up dirty supper dishes and headed for the bed. I did not even stop to wash all that mud from my floor.

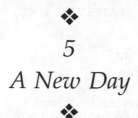

5

A New Day

❖

A SOFT STIRRING in the cabin aroused me from a deep sleep. With my wakefulness also returned a consciousness of my circumstances. It was Nimmie who shared my bed, not Wynn.

Nimmie needed all the rest the all-too-short night would afford her, I thought as I slipped cautiously out from the covers and dressed in the semidarkness. The men would soon be looking for their breakfast. I tiptoed from the room, shoes in hand, and carefully closed the door behind me.

In the soft light of the oil lamp I found Wynn back at work on the supplies. I could tell by the way he moved that he was making great effort to be quiet—which of course hampered his agility. He looked up when he heard me.

"Did I waken you? I'm sorry. I tried—"

"That's fine. I needed to be up anyway. I have so much to do and—"

My eyes traveled to the table where I had left dirty dishes the night before. They were all gone. I looked then at the floor I was dreading to clean. The mud too was gone. I glanced back at Wynn, embarrassed that he should have needed to do housework in addition to his other tasks. He was reaching for a hammer. With the loud bang, I let out a little gasp. The hammer stopped mid-swing and Wynn's eyes met mine.

"What's wrong?" he asked, the hammer still poised for the strike.

"You'll waken Nimmie and she needs—"

"Nimmie?" Wynn said cheerfully. "Nimmie was up and left for her cabin the minute I arrived, and that was almost an hour ago."

He turned his attention to his task.

I blinked. How had Nimmie wakened, dressed and left the room without me hearing her?

Wynn finished with the board and laid aside the hammer.

"I invited them for breakfast again. After that they expect to be on their own."

"So soon? Their window isn't even fixed."

"Ian's working on it right now, and Nimmie is busy doing the rest of the cleaning. They expect to move all their things out of here this morning. Then Nimmie says we should be able to have our living room back again—at least most of it."

"I'm sorry about the dishes and the floor—" I began, but Wynn stopped me in puzzlement.

"Sorry about what?"

"That you had to clean up."

"I didn't clean up."

"You didn't?"

"It looked just like this when I got here."

"Nimmie!" I said, the light finally beginning to dawn. "Nimmie must have gotten up and cleaned everything early this morning."

Wynn nodded in agreement, his attention back on what he was doing.

"And I was sleeping," I chided myself.

"I've found you some supplies," Wynn remarked, seeming not to have heard the scolding I was giving myself.

Supplies? Our supplies! I hurried over to Wynn and peered into the box he was opening.

"This is just flour, sugar, salt and such," said Wynn. "You might be more interested in those other two boxes. They came from Mary and Jon.

It seems forever since I have seen so many good things. I rejoiced as I stacked the treasures around me. Mary and Jon had thought of everything. They had even packed fresh fruit and vegetables. The Calgary newspaper piled up on the floor as I unwrapped item after item. There were even fresh eggs and butter.

I was about to crumple the newspaper out of the way. "Save that, would you please," Wynn suggested. "We'll even get to catch up on some world news, thanks to Mary's foresight." Carefully I began to smooth out each sheet of newspaper, sorry that in my eagerness I had unwrapped so hastily and carelessly.

When I turned to the kitchen, eager to get at the special breakfast I was planning with all my wonderful new supplies, Wynn was carrying armloads to our storeroom and arranging the things for our future use. Already a welcome little square of our floor was beginning to show. How I looked forward to having my house neat and orderly again.

By the time I had our sumptuous breakfast of fried eggs, jam, fresh oranges, bran muffins and oatmeal porridge ready, I heard Nimmie's and Ian's voices as they came up the path. Peering out the window, I noted it was still raining. *This day will be no more pleasant than yesterday,* I groaned.

Wynn opened the door for our guests, and I began to dish up the food for the table. On the back of my stove stood a bubbling pot of potatoes. I just couldn't wait to taste some. We had been without potatoes for weeks! I had told myself as I peeled them before breakfast that I would cook them to fry up for our noon meal. Now as I sniffed their fragrance, I knew I had been fooling myself—I'd never wait for dinner. A bit shame-faced, I put them in a dish and set them on our breakfast table.

After everyone was seated and the morning prayer said, I reached first for the bowl containing the potatoes. Yes, the oatmeal would surely taste good, the oranges would be a wonderful treat. And I could hardly wait for a bran muffin with real butter rather than dry biscuits. But the thing I wanted most was a good helping of potatoes, even if it was breakfast.

"This is silly, I know," I said, blushing, "but I just can't wait for a taste of potatoes again. I never realized how much I missed them until I saw them there this morning, all fresh and round, without wrinkles in their skins or sprouts all over them."

Ian smiled and winked at Nimmie in understanding. I sprinkled salt and pepper, dabbed on some real butter and lifted a forkful of potatoes to my mouth. They were just as good as I had expected them to be. I savored the mouthful, enjoying it to the full.

Wynn, too, bypassed the oatmeal and reached for the steaming bowl. "You're going to have potatoes, too?" I asked, surprised.

"Sure am," he laughed. "I was afraid when I smelled them cooking that you were going to make me wait for our noon meal. I was wondering how I might sneak a few from the pot without getting caught."

We all had a good laugh. Nimmie and Ian allowed us our potatoes, and they ate the oatmeal and muffins.

After breakfast Ian went for the team and wagon so their things could be taken to the cabin in a single trip. The rain had slackened, but their belongings still needed to be tucked under canvas.

With the removal of all that belonged to the McLains, and our things being put in the storage room, Wynn had more room to organize the rest of the supplies. Little by little he was getting it cleared away to the room he called his office.

I did my best to help him. He would not let me lift the heavier things, and I had to ask about most of the items I did move, to be sure that I stacked them where he would be able to find them.

By midday we had some paths through our living area, and the cot was discovered and unloaded. Kip was even able to get back to his favorite place before the fire.

I went back to the kitchen to prepare our meal, again cooking potatoes. I also cooked carrots and parsnips and turnips. It was a strange combination, but they all looked so good to me. I made up some cole slaw and informed Wynn that our dinner was ready. It wasn't until we sat down that I realized I hadn't prepared any meat. I was really tired of meat, but I wondered if Wynn would miss it. If he did he didn't mention it. Instead, he talked about how good the vegetables were.

In the afternoon Wynn finished stacking the supplies for the villagers. Almost every inch of his office floor was covered, and the stacks reached almost to the ceiling.

Then Wynn went to work at the one little window in the room. Curious, I watched to see what he was doing. He was making a shelf that extended both inside and outside at the bottom edge of the window. He didn't wait for me to ask what it was for.

"I'm making a shelf so I can distribute the supplies from here and then people won't need to enter the house to get them."

I pictured a long line of hungry, cold, damp people, standing in queue for their daily rations.

"But they can't wait out there in the rain," I protested, willing to forego the clean floors for their comfort.

"They have to wait in the rain anyway," Wynn explained. "They can't all fit in our living room at once."

Realizing he was right, I returned to my kitchen and took a few moments to pray that the rain would stop.

Ian came back, a large ledger in his hand. The Indians had been told to wait for the sound of the crude gong before lining up for more supplies. Those of the previous night had been given out at no charge, with deep thankfulness that God had seen us through. Now the books would need to be kept. Each man in the village had his winter's catch of furs, and the tally would be kept on account until the day that McLain could take in the furs to settle the accounts. First he would need to construct his new trading post.

As soon as Ian pounded on the drum with the hammer, the line began to form. Though it had not stopped raining, it had slowed down considerably. I thanked God for that.

Today there was happy chatter among the women who stood in the line. They could finally believe that the supplies were really here, enough for each day's need rather than just a fleeting dream of relief.

As Wynn distributed supplies to them, one by one, Mr. McLain busily entered the items to each one's account. Now the women were given a choice of purchase. Yesterday they all had been allotted the same items to prepare a meal.

It was getting dark before the last of the line was waited on. Wynn closed the window and turned to Ian.

"Is this going to work?" he asked him.

"Perfect," exulted Ian. "I'm glad you thought of the shelf. Nimmie will be settled by tomorrow, and she will be able to take your place. We know you can't spend all of your time dishing out store supplies."

"I'm glad to help until you are settled a bit, but I do need to get back on the trail again. There are a number of people I should check on as quickly as possible."

"We understand," Ian assured him. "Nimmie and I should be quite able to handle this from now on."

"But how about the building of the new store?" asked Wynn.

Ian pondered. It was true. He was going to be more than busy. His building skills and direction were needed on the project. Even though there were a number of men who would be happy to work for Ian, they could not proceed without supervision. Ian would need to be available every part of every day.

"We'll have to work out something," Ian was saying when I broke in hesitantly from the doorway. "I'll help Nimmie if you'll just show me what you want done."

Both of the men swung to look at me.

Wynn broke the silence. "There you are," he said to Ian with a grin.

Mr. McLain looked relieved. "You mean that?" he asked me.

"Of course. I'd be glad to."

"How about keeping the ledger?"

"The ledger?"

"Recording what is given to each family. Nimmie will tell you what to write."

"That would be fine," I stammered out. "I'm sure—sure I could handle that."

"I'm sure you could, too," said McLain confidently. "Then Nimmie could work with the people. It would be a bit easier for her, some of the people not knowing much English and you not understanding much of their language yet."

I liked his reasoning. Nimmie could wait on the customers and I could work along with her and keep the accounts. I was going to have her around after all!

In the meantime I hoped that the building project would go quickly. I was thankful for the supplies for the people. I would also be thankful to reclaim my home. I looked around at the stacked-up supplies. Our house looked so much better than it had just that morning, though Wynn's small office was not free for his use, and many things were still piled along the walls in our living quarters. Yes, I hoped with all of my heart that the building of the new trading post would go well.

6

Routine

EARLY THE NEXT morning the clouds began to break up and the heavy rain that had fallen during the night gradually diminished to a drizzle. I began to be hopeful that the rain might actually stop.

By midafternoon the sun was actually peeping out from among the clouds now and then. I got out my washtub so I could launder the wet, dirty clothes of the preceding days and get them on the line.

I worked quickly, for I knew there wasn't much time until Nimmie would arrive and clang the drum for the evening supply line.

I had just hung the last item on the line, thrown out my wash water and returned to my kitchen when I glanced out the window to see Nimmie coming up the path, dry and in her own clothing for the first time since she had returned to the settlement. Her feet were not free of the cumbersome mud, however. She looked like she was wearing brown snowshoes as she plodded along, carefully lifting one mud-packed foot after the other as she made her way up to our door.

I called for her to come in as I pushed the kettle forward onto the heat for a cup of tea before beginning our store duties. She didn't enter but called back to me from the doorway, "Could you bring me some water, please, so that I might wash my feet?"

I poured warm water into the basin, threw a towel over my arm and went to the door.

Nimmie had not bothered to wear anything on her feet. Knowing that the mud would cake as she walked, she came barefoot. It was much easier to clean feet than to clean shoes. She sat on the step and washed her feet in the basin. She refused the clean towel. "They're not clean enough for that," she protested. "Just give me an old rag." She dried her feet on a rag I found, swished out the basin and came in, shutting the door behind her.

"Isn't it great to see the sun again?" she exclaimed as she settled in a chair. I agreed as I poured our tea.

When we had emptied our teacups, we went to the storage room. Nimmie showed me how to record the items under each family's name in the ledger and then went out to call the villagers while I opened the window for our first customers.

At first it was novel and rather fun, but by the time we had measured and served, recorded and changed, argued and pleased each of our customers, I think both of us were ready to call it a day.

Wynn had gone to make some of his calls. He had no idea when he would be back so could not give me a time for the evening meal. I would have it ready and try to keep it as warm and palatable as possible, hoping that he wouldn't be too late.

Nimmie left in the semi-dusk to prepare a meal for Ian. He along with several other men had left for the woods that morning to mark out trees for felling. Nimmie did not know the hour for her evening meal either.

One thing we did know: We were both glad that it was no longer raining.

The days that followed were much like that first one. I hurried through my housework so I could accomplish what needed to be done for the day. I am sure that Nimmie did the same.

Each day the paths became a little drier, so the rutted pathway up to our door was no longer slippery with mud. I even tried to smooth out the ruts in the path, much to Nimmie's amusement.

The settlement teemed with new life and busyness. The women searched through the woods for edible spring growth for the cooking pots. Some of the men, under Ian's direction, felled trees while others cleared away the debris left from the fire at the old trading post. Stakes in the ground marked where the new post would stand, a bit larger than the first one. The living quarters at the back would be for Nimmie and Ian and the children they were anxiously looking forward to having. There would be no living quarters needed for Katherine. She had decided to go back to teaching in the Edmonton area.

Each day Wynn again took to the trail. Because the paths were free of the winter's snow, the dog team was not usable now, so Wynn's trips were even harder than normal. Swollen rivers and streams made journeys by canoes risky. With the return of the sun, the mosquitoes hatched in great numbers. The trail was not a pleasant place to be, but it was part of his job; and so without complaint, Wynn shouldered the pack with his emergency supplies and his noon lunch and left each morning at sunrise.

Nimmie and I soon established a daily routine. She would arrive promptly at three, we would have an afternoon cup of tea or coffee, and then we would bang on the drum and signal the ladies that the settlement "store" was open for business.

The sun shone on some days, the rain fell on others. Gradually a framework was taking shape in the settlement as the men worked under Ian's direction. Wynn helped when his duties did not call him elsewhere.

Wynn had found a few trappers who really had needed help, men who lived alone and did not come into the village after the winter's trapping was over. One man had been sick for over two weeks; he finally had become so weak he was unable to care for himself. Wynn traveled out to his cabin every other day to prepare food and give him medicine. Another man also had been sick, but by the time Wynn found him he was too far gone to recover. Though Wynn nursed him for several days, giving him the medicine he had available, he sorrowfully turned from being doctor to undertaker and parson, finally committing the man to the earth he had been so close to for so many years.

The mosquitoes and blackflies swooped around in droves. It was hard to remember they had been just as miserable the year before. I had to get used to them all over again.

Nimmie and I planted our gardens with seeds she had brought back. I could hardly wait for them to sprout and the tender plants to make their appearance. Nimmie was far more patient than I.

Nimmie's delivery time was drawing nearer. She didn't seem to feel anything other than anticipation, but for some reason, I felt alarm.

What if something goes wrong? What will we do if we need a doctor? For the first time I began to feel just a little thankful that I wasn't the one waiting for the arrival of a baby. I had not shared my prayers with Wynn, but for some weeks I had been praying nightly that God would see fit to grant my desire for a family—and soon. We had already been married for almost a year and it seemed like God should be answering my prayer by now.

Still, as I looked at Nimmie, daily becoming larger and heavier, I felt the shiver of fear run through me. *Perhaps it would be easier if I were facing the birth myself,* I thought, *instead of knowing that my dear friend is the one who will be going through the birth pains.* At any rate, I found myself thinking more and more about Nimmie's impending delivery time. I prayed more earnestly for her and the baby than I had ever prayed for anything in my entire life.

"Please, dear God," I pleaded daily, almost hourly, "please let everything be all right."

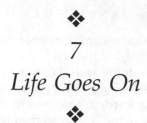

7

Life Goes On

BY NOW THE new trading post was far enough along for the supplies to be taken over and arranged inside the empty shell. Mr. McLain knew that Wynn needed his one-room office and that I was anxious to have my living quarters back.

The men again tracked through my house to load the wagons with everything that belonged to the store owner. I was relieved to see it go, and yet a little sadness tugged at me too. I had enjoyed the feeling of being needed in the little settlement.

I felt better when we decided that Nimmie and I would continue the distribution; instead of Nimmie coming to my house, now I would make the daily trek into the village.

I had not been there much in the past weeks, simply having no reason to go. Nimmie had come to my house daily, and I saw almost every woman of the village on a regular basis when they came for supplies. And our supplies for the next several months were stored in our own storage room.

Though I had not really missed the little excursions into the village, Kip had. He was restless. I tried to take him for a walk each morning as soon as I had finished my household chores, but he continued to whine at the door.

I had no time to romp with him like I used to and I was afraid to let him out on his own. I was sure he would head for the village and the other dogs, and even though he was no longer a pup, I still did not relish the prospect of a fight. I was sure one would occur if Kip were allowed to run free. I was especially determined to keep him away from Buck, the village fighter, for just as long as possible—my preference was "forever." But at least I wanted to be sure Kip was full grown so he might have some chance of holding his own. Buck was an experienced fighter and he was mean. No way did I want Kip tangling with him.

So I ran down wooded paths and trails by the river whenever I could work it into my morning schedule, just to make sure Kip's muscles got some exercise, and in the afternoons when Nimmie and I were busy as storekeepers, I kept him in.

Then even those runs were cut back.

Nimmie and I had been missing our Bible studies together, so we decided that even though we were busy, we would try to work one in each

week on Wednesdays. That meant our other duties had to be crowded
into the rest of the mornings of the week.

Both the gardens were doing well. We were proud and excited about
the growing vegetables. I could hardly wait until they would be big
enough to serve. But the garden, too, took work. Though plants grew
quickly in the summer sun, the weeds seemed to do even better. It was a
big job to keep up with them.

So the summer was a busy one, each day bringing us closer to the first
of August. From then on, I wondered if I would be able to sleep for thinking of Nimmie and the coming baby.

One afternoon as I left the house to go to the settlement for the afternoon store hours, my thoughts were busy with Nimmie and the little one
she was expecting. When I moved to the door, Kip was there by my side,
pushing against me to get out, his eyes pleading as he looked at me and
whined. It had been several days since his last run.

He looked so pitiful, his big blue eyes turned to mine.

"All right," I said, "you can come. But you've got to be good. You'll
have to lie quietly in the corner while I do my work."

Kip's tail began to wag as he recognized the consent in my voice.

We walked the short distance to the settlement together, Kip managing to get in quite a few side trips. When we reached the store, Kip obe-
diently lay down in the corner I pointed out to him and stayed there.

With the noise of the hammers and hand saws all around us, Nimmie
and I often had to raise our voices to one another to get our instructions
understood.

The customers did not need to come as often now. The women had
organized their households to the point where they had the basics, and
many of them were now taking daily trips to the woods for fresh foods.
I'm sure they welcomed the additions to their diets as joyfully as I had
done.

Nimmie urged me to leave a little early, saying she would stay for a
while in case any others came. I called Kip to heel and we started out for
our cabin.

I was not paying much attention to Kip as we walked toward home
through the late afternoon sunshine. My thoughts were again with
Nimmie. She hadn't said anything, but I thought I noticed weariness about
her eyes and slower movements than usual. Was I only imagining it?

As I walked through the settlement, the dogs barked and growled at
me, straining at their leashes. I'm sure what provoked them most was
seeing Kip invading their territory. I still respected their turf and made
sure I detoured a good distance from their tethered ground, but I did not
have the fear I once had.

Since there was now plenty of food for the village dogs, they had become round and fluffy again rather than looking mangy and shaggy as
they had through the difficult winter months. I decided there was really

no reason for their being so aggressive and nasty, so I paid little attention to them. In choosing to ignore the dogs, I tried not to antagonize them.
There was no love lost between them and me as they bared their fangs
and growled whenever they felt Kip and me getting too close.

Kip ran along beside me, heeling whenever I commanded. We were as
yet not far enough out of the village to allow him his side trips. He was
still the prettiest dog in the settlement. Wynn said he was now his full
height, though he might still put on a few pounds. He was soft and fluffy
with the beautiful silver tip to his fur. The children loved him, and even
those who had been viciously bitten by a village dog in the past had
learned that it was safe to reach out a hand to Kip. Many of the children
would wrap their arms around his neck or have a friendly tussle with
him on the floor of our cabin.

We were just reaching the last village cabin and I was about to let Kip
run free when I saw the hackles raise on his neck. It was not often that
Kip responded in this way and I hesitated, wondering what was wrong.
My first thought was that some small wild animal had strayed into the
village—perhaps a nasty smelling skunk.

And then I saw *him*. Rushing toward us was Buck, lips curled back and
teeth exposed. His hackles were up, too, and I knew that this time Kip
would take the challenge. With a flash I remembered the long-ago day
when Buck had rushed at Kip, then hardly more than an overgrown pup.
He had backed off that time in submission to the older dog. But Kip's
pose was not one of submission now. He was a full-grown dog, and he
had his pride.

Buck stopped a few feet short of Kip. I called Kip to heel again, but he
acted like he had never heard my voice before nor learned what the word
meant. He stepped sideways as though to feel out his ground and make
sure of his footing.

I watched in fascinated horror as Buck came in closer and Kip did not
back away. His own teeth bared in a snarl and I heard a rumble from
deep in his throat.

Slowly they began to circle one another, eyes blazing, throats voicing
challenges and threats; and then there was a sudden lunge forward. I
don't know which dog made the first move. I only know they met in
midair and shrieked out their rage as bodies clashed and teeth tore.

Both dogs had the protection of a heavy coat. Knowing that, they aimed
for throat, for eyes, for face, each time they came together. They struck
with lightning fury and then tumbled in the dust of the path, rolling over
and over, with grunts and snarls and sharp yips of rage or pain.

I stood rooted to the spot, wanting to stop them, wanting to run, wanting to scream for someone to do *something*! But I did nothing, only lifted
my hands to my face and prayed that it would soon be over.

Horrified, I was too dumbstruck to even cry. Would it never end? They
would break and circle and then rush at one another again, falling this

way and that, striking for each other's face or a leg in an effort to fell the opponent. I could see that Kip was bleeding. He had a gash on his cheek that was spilling blood as he rolled back and forth in the dirt.

But Kip wasn't the only one with an injury. Buck, too, was bleeding on his neck from a torn, ragged cut. Still they lashed and rolled. Over and over, their heads whipping this way and that to strike at their opponent and then jerk clear of his counter strike. *This is terrible!* I moaned.

At last, with one quick move, Kip clasped Buck's leg in his teeth and crunched down hard. The older dog screamed in pain and flipped himself forward to jerk free. Kip held firm and as Buck hurled himself away, I heard a sickening snap.

Again they struck, but it was clear that Buck's front right leg was held up and that it had been broken.

I found my voice then. I screamed for them to stop. As much as I feared and disliked Buck, I did not want to see him injured further. Nor did I want to take chances on Kip getting hurt any more. In spite of his injury, Buck still was determined to lick the younger dog. With a ferociousness I had never seen before, he struck again and another tear appeared on the side of Kip's jaw.

"Stop it!" I screamed. "Stop it, both of you! Stop it, do you hear?" But I was totally ignored.

They pulled away and circled again, Buck skillfully trying to maneuver on his three good legs. They were both panting heavily, their tongues lolling and their sides heaving.

"Stop it!" I yelled again. "Stop it! Go home, Buck. Go home. Kip, heel." But they paid no heed to my words.

It was Kip who jumped first. He aimed another blow at Buck's already torn and bleeding ear, and the big husky yelped in pain and rage.

And then it was over, as quickly as it had begun. Buck was gone, his tail tucked submissively between his legs, his one leg held aloft as he ran.

I ran to Kip and fell to my knees beside him.

"Bad dog," I scolded him, tears streaming down my face. "Bad dog. You shouldn't fight. Don't you know that you shouldn't fight? It's bad to fight. It's bad to fight unless you really have to." And suddenly I realized that Kip really had to. Buck had challenged him.

"Come on," I said, "I'll take you home."

I led him to the cabin. He heeled beautifully, just as he had been taught. I walked quickly, wanting to get him to the safety of his rug before the fireplace, where I could check and tend his wounds.

After I had closed the door securely behind us, I knelt beside him again and ran my fingers over his body. He was still trembling. His face was blood-covered from the two ragged gashes on his cheeks, but other than that he seemed to be fine.

I started to cry again as I held him. He must have wondered what was wrong with me. I trembled every bit as much as he did.

"You licked him, you crazy dog," I told him. "You licked the big bully. I didn't want you to, but you did. You licked the meanest dog in the whole village."

I straightened up and wiped my tear-streaked face. My voice became firm. "Now you won't have to fight again—ever. Do you hear?"

8
Surprises

A KISS ON the nose awoke me. I struggled to open my eyes and focus them properly. Wynn was leaning over me. He reached out and brushed back some wayward hair from my face.

"Do you know what day it is, Elizabeth?" he asked me.

It seemed like rather a foolish question to me, but I struggled to make my brain work so that I might come up with the proper answer.

"It's Friday," I said, puzzled that he had asked.

He chuckled softly and kissed me again.

"It's more than Friday, my dear. It's our first anniversary."

I jerked upright, nearly catching Wynn's chin with my head.

"Really?"

Wynn avoided my charge. "Really!" he said, laughing at me again.

Anniversaries were supposed to be special occasions—maybe a night out, dinner and candlelight. There would be no such thing here in Wynn's northland. I didn't think I could even find a candle. Candles were not necessary when only oil lamps were burned.

"Oh, Wynn," I moaned, "I forgot all about it. I don't have anything special planned."

"I do," said Wynn. "At least I hope you'll think it special. Remember that camping trip you've been begging for? The one where we will sleep out under the stars?"

I nodded, my eyes wide in anticipation.

"Well, how would you like to take that trip today?"

I squealed and threw my arms around Wynn's neck. I guess he took that for my answer.

"I have everything packed and ready to go," he said. "We can leave just as soon as we have our breakfast."

It didn't take me long to get out of bed, dressed and have breakfast on the table.

Kip sensed the excitement and whined at the door, fearful that we might go without him. I patted his head and assured him he could go.

As soon as I had cleared away the breakfast things, I gathered a few personal items I wanted to take and placed them with the packs Wynn had made. I knew Wynn was far more knowledgeable than I about what was needed on an overnight campout, but I still couldn't stop myself from asking, "Did you remember the matches? Are you sure you have all the food we'll need?"

Wynn just laughed at me and told me to trust him.

We were finally packed up and on our way, Kip frisking on ahead. Each with a backpack—Wynn's quite a bit heavier than mine—we walked for most of the morning and came to the most beautiful spot beside a small pond made by beavers damming the stream. The fir trees, thick about us, made a canopy over our heads. It looked just perfect.

"Here is where we stop," said Wynn, much to my delight.

Wynn insisted on setting up camp, and I just wandered about, taking in all of the beauty around me. Wynn cut spruce boughs for our mattress and then spread our furs and blankets to make a soft bed. It looked so inviting when he was finished that I knew I wouldn't miss our bed at home.

Wynn even fixed our meal, saying that this anniversary was my day off. I laughed and let him humor me.

We washed the dishes together in the little stream nearby and then sat with our backs against a fallen log while we watched the beavers work.

It was our first opportunity to really talk for weeks, so with our fingers intertwined, we talked softly while we watched the beaver couple. We spoke of many things, some little and foolish, others more important and part of our inner dreams and plans for the future.

I learned much about my husband on that camping trip. I had thought I already knew him well, but he shared with me so many new things— about his childhood, about his training, about his desires and goals.

I shared my thoughts and feelings with Wynn, too. I think he guessed part of my desires when I spoke about Nimmie and her coming baby with such wistfulness.

"You'd like a child, wouldn't you, Elizabeth?" more a statement than a question.

"Oh, so much," I told him. "I can hardly wait. And here we have been married for a whole year and . . ." I did not finish the sentence for fear Wynn would somehow think I was blaming him. "God knows when the time is right," I finished instead.

Wynn nodded and we talked of other things.

Wynn took me for walks and showed me flora and fauna I would never have spotted.

Our evening meal was not by candlelight, nor was it a gourmet feast at a fancy restaurant. But I wouldn't have traded it for anything in the world.

Wynn fixed it over an open fire, roasting freshly caught fish slowly until done to perfection and serving them with vegetables he had brought from our garden at home. Dessert was berries from a nearby patch, eaten from our hands as we picked them. We both laughed at our stained lips and teeth.

As the sun went down, the air became chilly and Wynn threw more sticks on the fire. Then we wrapped ourselves in a blanket and sat with our backs to a large pine tree as we watched the stars begin to appear.

The evening was astir with the night life of the wilds. Wynn identified each sound for me—the cry of the loon, the swish from the wings of the mammoth owl as it swept earthward to snatch unsuspecting prey, a mouse scurrying through the pine needles, a bull moose bellowing out a challenge.

When the wolves began their evening chorus, I shivered some and was glad for Wynn's arm about me. But not even the wolves could disturb me on this night.

Everything would have been perfect if only we could have escaped the tormenting mosquitoes. Wynn threw green branches on the fire, and we sat in the smoke to hold them at bay.

As the sun totally disappeared, more stars twinkled into view, taking their appointed position in the velvet of the night sky.

And then it was that I saw the most spectacular sight of my entire life. Suddenly the sky was alive with sweeping rainbows. Lights swished and swirled above us, sweeping across the skies in spectacular movements. Sometimes the entire sky would seem to be one giant movement of color, and then the lights would retreat as though to end a scene, then sweep back again for another curtain call.

"They are so beautiful," I whispered wonderingly over and over, finding it hard to believe that it was just the northern lights we were watching. Though I had watched them in awe many times since coming north, I had never seen such a marvelous display.

We sat on through the evening, enjoying the night even after the last lights of our great northern fireworks faded from the skies. The deep blackness around us seemed to hem us in, promising protection. The stars shone even brighter as Wynn pointed out different constellations to me.

As I sat there in the warmth of Wynn's arms, I realized there might be many anniversaries stretching before us. I prayed to God that He would make it so. But there would never be one that could outshine the one we were sharing now.

August the first. I looked at the date on my calendar with some apprehension. I had seen Nimmie the evening before and she had looked fine. She had talked about their coming baby, her eyes gleaming. "Soon," she had said, "we will know if it will be a hunter or an herb-gatherer."

I managed to laugh at Nimmie's description of her boy or girl, but inside I felt a little twinge. Part of the twinge was nothing more than envy. I was still not with child and my daily prayers had not changed. The other part of the twinge was for Nimmie and her baby. The mortality rate among the Indian people was high, and I knew how much Nimmie wanted this baby. What a terrible thing if she were to be denied.

Again the thought surfaced that I would not be nearly as worried if it were I who was soon to deliver, for the mortality rate was not nearly as high among my people. It didn't even occur to me that a baby I carried might also be in danger at delivery. I just expected that when it was my turn, all would go well.

That was what Nimmie expected, too, I suddenly realized. She wasn't even considering the possibility of something going wrong.

And so I looked at the calendar with both trepidation and anticipation. In a short time we would know. What had the city doctor said? The fifth of August. The baby was due in only five more days.

I decided to drop in on Nimmie. I would bake a batch of bread as planned, have my prayer time and then go to see her.

My quiet time was longer than usual as I pleaded with God again for Nimmie's safe delivery—of the hunter or the herb-gatherer, I didn't care. When I was finished praying, I went to check on the rising bread. While it baked I turned my attention to some mending. Some buttons had been torn from Wynn's shirt when a trapper's unprovoked lead dog had ferociously attacked him. As I sewed, I was thankful that only the shirt had been damaged in the incident. I had to mend some little tears before I could replace the buttons, and by the time I was finished I could smell the aroma of freshly baked bread.

I carefully wrapped one loaf for Nimmie. I had just said no to Kip, who looked at me pleadingly, and reached for the loaf when there was a noise at the door. It was Mrs. Sam. She had not been to my house for some weeks.

I welcomed her in. Though I would be delayed now, I could not possibly tell Mrs. Sam that I was just leaving. She would expect her usual cup of tea.

I put the bread back on the table and pulled the teakettle forward on the stove. Thankfully the water was already hot. I made the tea and we sat and sipped it and ate sugar cookies while we chatted about village life.

Mrs. Sam said the berry prospects looked good. "Many, many," she stated and I was glad for that. I hoped to pick and preserve a number of jars of berries for our winter use. That along with our good garden would make the thought of another winter not nearly so dreary.

Mrs. Sam drank slowly while I fidgeted a bit. I was polite enough to offer a second cup of tea. Then a third. After the fourth, Mrs. Sam rose from her chair and pushed her cup back into the middle of the table.

"Nimmie say, 'Come now,' " she stated simply as my eyes widened in surprise and horror. Nimmie had sent her to get me, and here we had sat sipping cup after cup of tea! I turned to grab the loaf of bread—though why, I'll never know—and hurried for the door. Mrs. Sam took her time following me.

I wanted to walk quickly—no, *run*—but Mrs. Sam kept her usual pace, which was unhurried and ambling. I wondered if it would be impolite for me to run on ahead.

"How is Nimmie?" I finally thought to ask, though I was a bit fearful of the answer.

"Good," answered Mrs. Sam.

"Is she—is she—?" I wasn't sure how to ask the question of an Indian woman with limited English. "Is she—in labor? Pain?"

"Nope."

"But she sent for me?" That wasn't like Nimmie.

"Yah."

"Was the midwife with her?"

"No more."

"No more?"

I couldn't understand it. Why would Nimmie send for me, and why would the midwife visit her and then leave? It all seemed very strange. And it was only August the first.

"Is Nimmie okay?" I asked again.

And Mrs. Sam's answer was the same as before. "Good."

"What about the baby?" I asked in exasperation.

"Her good, too."

I stopped in my tracks, trying to understand what Mrs. Sam had just said. She might have responded that way about an unborn child, but when the Indian women spoke of the unborn, they used the pronoun "him," not "her." Did that mean—surely not? But when I got my breath I asked anyway, "What do you mean, *her*?"

"Her," stated Mrs. Sam again as though it was clear enough. "Her. Girl baby."

After one wild look at Mrs. Sam I forgot to be polite any longer. I picked up my skirt and ran the rest of the way to Nimmie's cabin, causing the village dogs to nearly go mad on their tethers as I rushed.

Out of breath and trembling, I slowed down enough to rap gently on Nimmie's door; then without waiting for an answer, I pushed it open and walked in.

The small room of the cabin was filled with a strange odor, like nothing I had ever smelled before. I hurried to the bed in the corner, deciding the smell must be some herb medicine from the midwife.

And there was Nimmie, with a contented smile and a small bundle with a red, wrinkled face held possessively on her arm.

"You said—you said August the fifth," I stammered.

"No," said Nimmie shaking her head and beaming at her new baby girl. "I said *the doctor* said August the fifth. Nonita did not wait for doctor's due. She came when she was ready."

I looked back to the tiny, beautiful baby in Nimmie's arms. A prayer arose in my heart. She was here, and she was safe, and she was about the prettiest thing I had ever seen.

"A little herb-gatherer," I said with tears in my eyes. "Oh, Nimmie, she's beautiful!"

9

Nonita

I STOOD FOR many minutes looking down at Nimmie's tiny new baby girl. Her dainty curled fists lay in a relaxed position on her chubby cheeks, her dark hair slightly curled over her forehead. Her eyes were closed and just a trace of eyelash showed because of the slight puffiness due to her recent arrival. I had proclaimed her beautiful. There may be those who would have argued with me. A newborn is really not too beautiful. But she was healthy and whole, and given a few days to adjust to her new world, I knew she would look beautiful. I felt a twinge within me again—that something which told me that just at this moment, Nimmie was one of the most blessed people I knew.

I suddenly returned to reality. "When did she arrive?" I asked Nimmie.

"About an hour ago. I think the clock said 10:45."

It was now ten minutes to twelve.

"What does Ian think of having a daughter?" I asked, not because I needed to ask but because I thought Nimmie might wish to express it.

"He still doesn't know," said Nimmie, a bit of impatience in her voice.

"Doesn't *know*?" It was incredulous to me that Ian had not been informed.

"He went to the woods with the men this morning to fell some more trees for the trading post."

"But—" I began.

"He left at six," Nimmie went on.

"Didn't you know—?" I started to ask, but Nimmie interrupted.

"Yes," she said hesitantly. "I thought, but I didn't want to keep him from his work."

"Oh, Nimmie!" I said. "Don't you know Ian would have wanted to be here? The logs can wait, but your baby—"

"Yes, babies won't wait," said Nimmie. "I learned that much. I told the midwife I wanted to wait until Ian got home. He said he would be here shortly after midday. But, Nonita—well, she wouldn't wait."

I looked again at the clock. If Ian said he would be back soon after noon, he should be coming any time now. I heaved a sigh of relief and turned back to Nimmie.

"Would you like anything? Soup? Tea?"

"The midwife gave me some of her birthing herbs," she said. "I feel just fine. A little tired, but just fine."

Nonita suddenly squirmed in Nimmie's arms and screwed up her face. She began to cry, her face growing even more red. She had not yet developed the lusty cry of an older infant. Nimmie adjusted her on her arm and held her to nurse, crooning comforting words to her in her own native tongue.

The baby stopped her fussing and snuggled up against Nimmie. The deep red drained from her face. Nimmie cradled her and then began to sing her an Indian lullaby.

I discovered I was still carrying my loaf of bread, somewhat misshapen due to my run. I wanted to laugh at its ridiculous shape now, but I was afraid I might disturb Nimmie or the baby, so I crossed as quietly as I could and placed it on the table.

Nimmie's song soon ended. She looked at me, her eyes still shining.

"That is the song my mother used to sing to me. Perhaps every Indian baby has listened to that song. I will sing it to all my children as well."

"It's a pretty song," I said, crossing the room to her bedside.

"It speaks of the forests, the rivers, the moon in the sky, and promises the baby that all of nature will be her new home."

"That's nice." I touched her arm and smiled at her precious bundle.

Nimmie closed her eyes. I didn't know if she was visualizing her child in the years to come or if she was just tired.

"Nimmie, perhaps you should rest now. Would you like me to stay or to leave?"

"There's no need for you to stay, Elizabeth. Ian will soon be here. I sent for you because I was anxious for you to see Nonita. It wasn't because I did not want to be alone."

"I don't mind staying."

"I'm fine—really."

"Then I will go and let you rest."

I was about to leave when she looked up at me and smiled. "Would you like to hold Nonita before you go?"

I didn't even answer; my heart was too full and my throat too tight. I reached down for the sleeping baby as Nimmie lifted her gently toward my outstretched hands.

She was so little and so light in my arms that I felt as if I were holding only a dream, only a fairy child. She opened one squinty little eye and seemed to wink at me. It was an uncontrolled action I knew, but I laughed anyway.

"She's beautiful," I declared again, and I meant it with all of my heart.

I laid the baby on the bed beside her mother. Nimmie smiled contentedly.

"Someday, Elizabeth," she said, "it will be your turn—and then you will know the deep river of happiness flowing within me now."

10
Summer

NIMMIE WAS SOON back on her feet. Even with her new baby she still found time to work in her garden and tend the store and manage the other tasks she had been used to doing. I tried to help some, but she usually caught me at it and laughed at my concern.

"I am as strong as ever, Elizabeth," she assured me. "Where do you white women get the idea that having a child makes one weak and unable to do one's own work?"

So we went to the garden together and hoed the weeds and pulled the vegetables for use on our tables. We opened the store and cared for the customers who came for supplies. We even went to the berry patches together, with Nonita secured to Nimmie's back, and sometimes I got to carry her for short distances.

Nonita gradually lost her redness and puffiness. She did not lose her swatch of dark thick hair nor her black, black eyes, however. Ian adored her. Even Wynn seemed captured by the little one. I would gladly have babysat, but Nimmie never seemed to need anyone to care for the tiny girl.

The trading post building was coming along nicely. Rainstorms no longer delayed its progress, for there was still much to be done inside the structure. The rooms at the back were also being worked on, and Nimmie began to show her eagerness to be in and settled. This attitude was new to Nimmie, who was normally so patient and placid about everything. I suppose having the baby made her want to be in her own home rather than the makeshift cabin.

I scarcely saw Wynn these days except at night. He was usually gone before I awakened in the morning. He wanted to cover all his distant rounds before the first snowfall in a month or so.

After a morning in a berry patch or the nearby woods, the Indian ladies often came in the afternoon for their cup of tea. I was glad to resume our visits. We still didn't spend all our time talking, though I did understand many more Indian words; but there were comfortable times of sitting together just sipping tea and smiling at one another.

Kip's injuries from his fight with Buck had healed nicely. He seemed to have become a bit cocky, however, and I was sure he would never back down to any dog in the future. Whenever I went into the settlement, I left him at home or put him on the leash Wynn had provided. I did not wish a dog fight every time I went to the village, even if Kip should turn out to be the victor.

During the month of August three more babies were born in the village, but only one of them lived. There was great mourning among the people as the tiny graves were dug. I sorrowed too, thinking of the mothers and the pain they must feel.

The days became noticeably shorter, and we knew summer would not be with us forever.

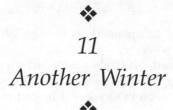

11
Another Winter

WITH THE HONKING of the Canada geese and the autumn dance of the leaves in the blustery winds, we knew fall was here. The berry patches had been stripped of all of their fruit. We had either canned the berries or else dried them in the sun.

Wynn was working a little closer to the settlement now, and I was up in time to prepare his breakfast each morning before he went to another day's work.

The welcome day arrived when Nimmie moved from the cramped cabin to her new home. I insisted on the enjoyable task of caring for Nonita while Nimmie settled in with the nesting instinct of a mother robin. When I reluctantly returned the precious little bundle, Nimmie chirped and twittered to her little nestling and Nonita smiled and gurgled back.

I often noticed the Indian men studying the sky. Even the women, as they walked to the nearby woods for their daily wood supply for their fires, glanced heavenward as though the skies held many answers to the days that lay ahead.

I wanted to keep the Indian summer forever. I was not happy about the thought of being shut in again by the swirling snow and the howling winds. I was sure Wynn was not looking forward to the difficult days of winter either, but he made no comment.

Kip's fur grew thicker and fluffier and I knew the wild animals, too, were wearing a warmer coat against the cold that was to come. I no longer heard the birds fighting over the scraps of produce left in my garden. Most of them had already migrated south.

And then one morning when I rose from my warm bed, I noticed a chill about the house, even though Wynn had already started the fire in the stove. My glance went to the window and I saw the snow gently sifting down. If I had not been dreading it so, I would have most surely thought it to be beautiful. It fell in large, soft flakes, and as it floated gently on the slight wind, it looked like fluffy down. After my time in the North, I knew better, so I did not stop to enjoy the sight. Instead, I went into Wynn's office to draw some consolation from him.

"It's snowing," I informed him as soon as I reached his door.

He looked up from the dog harness he was mending and nodded.

"It's only October," I complained, as though Wynn should know better than to let it snow so early.

"I know," he answered. "It likely won't last for long."

I knew he was trying to reassure me. I also knew that some years the snow *did* come to stay even in October. I hoped this wouldn't be one of those years.

I looked at what Wynn was doing. The dog harnesses were only used when there was snow on the ground.

He noticed my accusing gaze.

"Didn't have anything else that needed doing this morning," he explained defensively, "so I thought I might as well get an early start on this."

I nodded and changed the subject. "I'll have breakfast in a few minutes," I said, and turned back to the little kitchen area and the singing kettle.

The snow fell all that day, and the next and the next. *We won't be seeing the last of it for some time,* I groaned silently.

I was feeling close to despair when there was a knock on my door. Nimmie came in, shaking the snow from her bare head and the blankets covering Nonita.

I was surprised to see her, but I shouldn't have been. A little thing like a few inches of snow would not have kept Nimmie home.

"I have some good news," she said, even before she unwrapped the baby and removed her coat.

She didn't wait for me to ask but went on, "Remember I said that Ian had to pay a visit to the main village?"

I nodded, reaching for the squirming Nonita.

"Well, he's back. I asked him to check with the chief about us starting a school. He did, and the chief just shrugged his shoulders and said that if we wanted to teach the children letters, it was up to us, just as long as we didn't interfere with their rightful duties. We can go ahead, Elizabeth; we can start our classes! Now that winter seems to be here the children will be free to attend for a few hours each day."

We could go ahead and start our school! So the snow had brought some good. I looked out the window as my heart thanked God for the welcome news.

I turned back to Nimmie, the small Nonita still in my arms. "Oh, Nimmie!" I exclaimed, "we have so much to do to get ready! So much planning. Where will we hold it and—?"

Nimmie laughed and reclaimed her baby. "Slow down, Elizabeth," she said; "we'll get it all worked out."

I made the tea and Nimmie sat down at my table. We got pencils and paper and began to work through every part of our plan.

I would do the actual teaching. Nimmie would be my helper and interpreter as needed. We planned to pool our resources for classroom supplies. Ian could send out for some pencils and scribblers for the students' use. He had another wagon train due in soon with the winter supplies for the settlement. The carrier was leaving in two days with the additions to Ian's supply list, so our needs would have to be figured out and presented to Ian very quickly.

My mind could hardly work in the excitement. Another of my prayers had been answered: We would get our school.

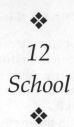

12
School

EVEN THOUGH NIMMIE and I went right to work on our plans and materials for the new school, still it was near the end of November before we held our first class.

That first early snow had not left us. Instead, it had been added to by three separate storms. Wynn now used his sled dogs for his rounds, and the snow was almost deep enough for snowshoes. Many of the village men already had left the comfort of the village and returned to their traplines.

My only consolation for the early winter was the proposed school. Even with the chief's approval, we knew our classes would have to be kept short. The children were needed to gather the family's wood supply and carry water from the river. It had not frozen over yet but would soon, and then daily a hole would have to be cut in the ice in order for them to dip out the necessary water. When the ice got too thick, the settlement families would have to simply melt the drifted snow.

I was glad we had a well with a pump. The villagers were welcome to use it, but most of them declared pumping a "bad job," as the small stream of water took a long time to fill their pail. In the summer months some of the children liked to play with the pump. They usually came together, two or three boys, and not too much of the pumped water ever found its way to the village home. Most of it remained in puddles in our yard, or soaked through the boys' clothing.

Nimmie and I planned for classes from nine to twelve. It didn't seem like much, but we thought it better to take it easy than to overdo and have parents complaining about school keeping the youngsters from their duties.

A classroom was one of our biggest problems. I knew our cabin was too small. We would be able to fit only eight at the most. We were hoping for a better attendance than that. We considered the empty Lamuir cabin Nimmie and Ian had used. It also was small, but with simple tables and benches, it might give us enough room for now. We discussed this with our husbands, and they made plans to have the tables and benches made.

We also needed a wood supply for the fireplace in the cabin. Wynn took care of that; with three or four men, he went to the nearby wood and hauled out dead, fallen logs. The logs were brought to the village and cut into proper lengths for our fireplace, then stacked up against the side of the small cabin.

We had no way to advertise our classes, so Nimmie and I walked from door to door, telling each household about our plan. Many of the people had no clocks, only the sun and their uncanny but rather accurate sense of time. Nimmie borrowed the idea of the store-hour signal, which was no longer in effect, Ian having taken over regular hours since his new building was useable. So as we went from door to door, we told them to listen for the banging of the hammer on the drum barrel, and then they would know that school was to begin.

Both Wynn and Ian supported us completely in our project. Many times as Nimmie and I worked over our lesson plans, one or the other would offer advice.

"If you want to get their attention and make them interested in learning," offered Wynn, "then you must teach them things that relate to their life. No 'c-a-t spells cat.' " (We had no cats in the village. The dogs would have torn them to shreds.)

"Use words they know: fish, canoe, river, forest, dog, moon, sun, stars, trap."

I could see what Wynn was getting at and I agreed with him, at least until we fully had introduced learning to our students. We did hope also to expand the world as they knew it.

We had few textbooks. The scribblers and pencils arrived with the winter supplies. As a surprise for Nimmie and me, Ian had also ordered a small chalkboard and a good supply of chalk with two brushes. We were thrilled with it all. When Wynn mounted the chalkboard on a wall in the cabin, it looked like a real classroom.

One further problem was lack of light. The cabin's one tiny window afforded little illumination even on the brightest of days, and much less during the dreary winter months. Ian gave us the use of two oil lamps from the store, but even they did not light up our little room very well.

But Nonita was not a problem—she was a contented baby, who still slept many hours of her life away, and Nimmie would be able to bring her to school and care for her as necessary.

Since we were beginning with words and concepts the Indian children knew, I needed teaching material. I wanted pictures to accompany the words. I had none. I was not an artist, but I set to work trying to illustrate the words on the cards I had made. "Fish" was not difficult, and my "canoe" and "sled" were recognizable, but "dog" and "deer" and "moose" required a lot of imagination.

I wasn't sure how to show the difference between the sun and the moon. Did the Indian people see the moon with a smiling face? As I labored over my drawings, I certainly recognized their inadequacies. I wasn't sure if my "art" would help or hinder my students' progress.

At last the long-awaited day arrived. Wynn promised to build our fire and have the chill out of the cabin by the time the teachers and the students arrived. I gathered the rest of my teaching tools together, bundled myself up against the cold wind, closed the door on the whining Kip, and headed for the exciting first day of school.

Nimmie was already there. The room was cozy and warm. The crude tables and chairs were the best that could be managed out of rough lumber, and I knew they held the possibility of many future slivers. Beneath our blackboard was a piece of chalk and one of our brushes. A few of my books were on a shelf along with our supply of scribblers and the pencils Wynn carefully had sharpened for us with his jackknife.

I had thought that supplies were quite limited in my schoolhouse at Pine Spring, and so they were; but here at the settlement I had even less to work with and just as great a need.

We were ready. This was our school. I took a deep breath and smiled at Nimmie, giving her the nod to "ring our bell."

I don't know if I really expected a stampede to our door. If I did, I certainly shouldn't have. I knew the Indian people better than that, and yet somehow because of my own great excitement, I guess I expected them to be excited too.

At the end of our gonging signal, we waited for our first student. No one came. The minutes ticked by, and still no one showed up.

I began to feel panicky, but Nimmie seemed perfectly at ease. She threw another log in the fireplace, then crossed over to where tiny Nonita was sleeping on a bear rug in the corner and sat down beside her on the floor.

"Do you think we should bang on it again?" I asked anxiously.

"They heard," said Nimmie.

I too was sure they had heard. One could not have lived anywhere in the village and not have heard the terrible din of the clanging barrel ringing out over the crisp morning air.

We waited.

"Why aren't they coming?" I asked Nimmie.

"They'll come," Nimmie assured me, unperturbed.

We waited some more.

Nimmie was right. At last two girls came toward the cabin. I, who had been watching out the window for any sign of activity, met them at the door. I wanted to be sure they didn't change their minds.

Three more girls, hiding giggles behind their hands, soon followed, and then another, and then four boys, grouped together as if for support. Two more girls, a single, a pair of boys. They kept straggling in until I feared that most of our morning would be taken with trying to get some kind of a roll call established.

I welcomed the children and found them each a place to sit. Nimmie repeated my words in their own native tongue. I explained to them what we would be doing at school, hoping the excitement in my voice would somehow carry over to them. Twenty-three pairs of eyes never left my face, but I saw no flicker of interest or enthusiasm. I swallowed hard and went on.

"We will be learning numbers and words and colors," I continued, trying to make it sound fascinating, but the expressions before me did not change.

Nimmie stepped forward to stand beside me. She began to speak to them in her own soft and flowing speech. I understood only a few of the words, but somehow they managed to convey to me, and to the children, a sense of wonder—an inspiration. A few eyes before me began to light.

As we worked on the roll call, other stragglers arrived. Our schoolhouse was crowded. We didn't have room to seat any more. I was exhilarated! *Wait till I tell Wynn!* I exulted. I remembered his words of caution.

"Don't be too disappointed, Elizabeth, if you have very few students. The value system of the people here varies greatly from ours. They do not see the need, or the advantage, of spending many hours trying to learn about things they will never see nor know. What good is all that learning if it will not put food in the pot, or coax the fox to the trap?"

And here we were with a full schoolhouse! Wouldn't Wynn be surprised?

About midway through the morning two women arrived, chattering as they entered and looking over the room full of children and each item in it. They discussed freely what they observed. I guess they had never been told that one does not talk without permission in a school setting. They found a place on the floor and sat down.

Later on more women joined them, singly or by twos or threes. I could hardly believe it! Our schoolroom was packed full of eager and willing learners—of all ages. We would need more room, more pencils and scribblers. I hadn't thought of teaching the women, but of course they needed it too.

Nimmie did not seem surprised. She only nodded a greeting to each one as they came and motioned them to a still-vacant spot on the floor.

I decided to concentrate on the children and let the women learn by listening and observing, so I did not put any of the adult names in my roll book.

After getting the names of the students recorded, which took a great deal of help from Nimmie, I proceeded with my first lesson. Taking my cards with the words and pictures, I held them aloft and pointed first at a picture and then at the English word. I said the word over two or three times and then Nimmie told the students to say the word with me. We went over it a number of times. *Canoe. Canoe. Canoe.* Then we went on to the next one. *Fish. Fish. Fish.* I had the class say it together and then picked out students to try it on their own. They were shy about it, hesitant to make a funny-sounding word in front of others, so I went back to having them say it together.

I took the two new words now and covered the pictures.

"What does this say?" I asked them, and Nimmie repeated my question.

No one knew. I uncovered the picture and asked the question again. They replied correctly almost in unison.

We went over the two words again and again, and still they did not seem to recognize them when the pictures were covered.

At last when I covered the picture and held one up, a small boy said, "Canoe." He was right and I was ecstatic. There was whispering in the row where the boy sat and I saw Nimmie's face crinkle with laughter.

I couldn't refrain from asking, "What did he say?"

"His classmate asked him how he knew the picture, and he said the canoe card has a small tear at one corner," explained Nimmie.

I looked down at the picture. He was right.

It set me back some, but then I realized it did prove he was observant and intelligent. Those ingredients made a scholar. I just had to find the right approach, that was all.

I switched from the word cards to colors. I was aware that the Indians know much about color. They just don't know what the white man calls them. The color lesson did not go well either. Every time I pointed to a color on an object, they thought I was asking for the name of the object, not the color.

Nimmie explained to them, and things went a bit better. After much drilling, I was quite confident a good number in the class had learned "black" and "white."

We dismissed them, telling them to hurry back to the schoolroom the next morning when they heard the bell clang. I didn't know if our admonition would avail or not. Most likely they would come when they felt ready.

The students began to file out, some looking thankful for freedom. The women still sat on the floor. It appeared they didn't intend to leave, and I thrilled with their interest in learning. I told Nimmie to express to them my happiness at seeing them at school and my promise to do my best to help them learn. Nimmie passed on my information in a flow of words, but the blank look on the women's faces did not change.

Little Deer said what all of them must have been thinking. "When tea?"

We tried our best to explain that we didn't serve tea at school, and with looks of disappointment, they got up and filed out one by one.

I felt exhausted after the first morning. Nimmie looked as fresh and relaxed as ever, and little Nonita had roused only once, nursed and gone back to sleep.

I gathered up my word cards, looked at the canoe to see if I might be able to fix the tear, abandoned the idea, and headed for home.

I honestly did not know if our first day at school had been a success or not. We certainly had a roomful of students. But if they did not learn, was it worth their time to be sitting there? I decided not to do too much bragging to Wynn as yet.

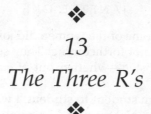

13
The Three R's

WE BANGED THE barrel the next morning and again waited for our students to return. The room was not as full as it had been the previous day, but I was not concerned. I knew that as the morning progressed more students would arrive. I didn't expect any of the ladies. They had felt cheated out of a tea party and would stay home beside their fires.

When Wynn had asked about our first day, I could not refrain from boasting some about the numbers. Wynn just nodded encouragement without comment and I wondered if he was saying silently, "Elizabeth, don't set yourself up for a heartbreak."

I'm not sure why I felt that way, except that I was getting to know the way Wynn thought. The expression in his eyes often said things he didn't put into words.

More students did straggle in as the morning went on. We went back to our two words of the day before. Everyone could now pick out the canoe once they had been given the secret of the torn corner. A few even recognized "fish"—without a tear on the card.

I went on to another word. "Dog," I said, holding high the card. Nimmie announced the Indian word for dog and then repeated it in English. There was a bit of tittering in the classroom and black eyes flashed secret messages of merriment. I turned to Nimmie.

"They think it looks more like a skinny bear," she informed me with a slight smile.

I looked back at my picture. It certainly wasn't a very good dog. I didn't dare show them my deer or moose. I went on to the moon and the sun. They seemed to have some difficulty with these concepts as well.

I tacked the cards to the wall and told them to open their scribblers, take a pencil and copy the words in their book.

They were not clumsy naturally; in fact, they were unusually dexterous, but how to hold a pencil posed a good deal of difficulty at first. Many of Wynn's carefully sharpened points were broken in the attempt.

Nimmie and I circulated among them, showing them how to hold the pencil properly and how much pressure to put on the point. I laid aside all the pencils needing to be resharpened to take home to Wynn and his jackknife.

Most of the students got "fish" and "canoe" entered in their new scribblers, though some of the attempts were hardly recognizable.

I was surprised that some of the women did join us again, even though they knew that tea was not forthcoming. They settled themselves on the floor and appeared to listen—whether out of curiosity or interest, I did not know.

As I went quietly from student to student, I was surprised by a boy of about twelve or thirteen. Not only had he printed his words, and rather neatly at that, but he had also drawn the pictures. It didn't take a teaching certificate to see that his pictures were far superior to mine. I hastened to Nimmie, excitement filling me.

"Come here," I whispered. "Look what he's done."

The "he" was Wawasee. His father was a trapper, one of those whose trapline was some miles from the village. The mother had died in childbirth two years previously. Wawasee was left each winter to care for himself and two younger sisters. Had he been alone, he undoubtedly would have been taken out to the trapline, but two small girls out there would be more bother than help. I learned from Nimmie that Wawasee spent much of his time carving wood with a dull, broken knife that had somehow come into his possession.

My heart reached out to this boy. He was dirty and unkempt, but his dark eyes glistened as he printed each word on the page and stroked in the pencil marks to skillfully create a picture. *I must talk to Wynn about Wawasee*, I determined.

At the end of the morning session we dismissed our students and instructed them to leave their pencils and scribblers on the tables as they filed out. We would ring the "bell" at the same time the next morning.

My interest in Wawasee was undoubtedly the reason I noticed that his scribbler and pencil did not stay behind. I had been so anxious to take it home to show Wynn.

I looked around to see if it had been misplaced, but I did not spot it. I gathered up each of the other scribblers and placed them back on the shelf, still glancing under tables and benches. Nimmie noticed it.

"Did you lose something?" she asked.

"Wawasee's scribbler. It isn't here."

"I'm not surprised," remarked Nimmie.

I looked at her questioningly.

"Wawasee cannot hear," she stated simply. "He lip reads some, but I was not standing where he could see me when I repeated your instructions."

"Oh, Nimmie," was all I could say.

"But even if he had been able to hear the order, I don't think Wawasee would have left his book," Nimmie went on in a quiet voice.

"Is he a . . . a . . ." I couldn't say the word *thief*. It just didn't seem to fit the child, and besides I didn't want to think of him in that way.

"Wawasee uses anything he finds to make pictures," Nimmie explained. "He draws them in the dirt, on birchbark; he scratches them on tree trunks. And you have just passed to him a scribbler and a pencil. What would you expect him to do?"

"He'll draw?"

"He'll probably have half the pages full by morning."

I stood rooted to the spot, thinking of the little Indian boy, with a full-grown man's responsibility, no hearing, and a great talent for art.

"Would you like me to go and get the scribbler?" Nimmie was asking.

I turned back to her. "No," I said, "but I would like to talk to the boy. Could you come with me? I don't know how to make him understand me."

Nimmie agreed, and we tramped our way through the softly swirling snow of another winter storm to the unkempt cabin of the boy and his two little sisters.

Nimmie opened the door and went in, and there, just as she expected to find him, was Wawasee. His concentration was totally taken with the pencil in his hand and the picture forming beneath it. He was not aware of our presence in the cabin as he sketched a moose running through the dense undergrowth, a wolf fast on its heels.

Nimmie crossed to him and laid her hand on his arm. He looked up in surprise and then alarm. Slowly he slid the scribbler off the table and hid it on his lap as if to protect it. His eyes were dark and pleading. I thought of Kip when he wanted to go someplace with me.

Nimmie smiled and some of the fear left Wawasee's eyes.

Somehow Nimmie was able to tell the boy that I wanted him to draw the pictures on the word cards for the class. In exchange for his work for me, he would be given a pencil and a scribbler all his own—one that would not need to go to school but that he could keep at home to use whenever he wished.

I knew that through lip reading and sign language, he understood all Nimmie had said, for he looked at me, back to his pencil, down at his lap, and nodded, his eyes shining with unshed tears.

14
Trials and Triumphs

AT THE END of our first week of school, we were down to thirteen students. At first I pretended they had some reason which kept them from the morning class. Nimmie knew better. She did not even seem surprised. Instead, she said with excitement, "Thirteen. Elizabeth! Thirteen. Can you believe it? We still have *thirteen* who are interested."

I wanted to argue with her. Thirteen was only about half of what we had started with.

By the end of the second week our number had dropped to five. Just five—when there was a village full of people who needed to learn to read and write. Nimmie was still not alarmed. "Five for our first year is wonderful. In the years to come the others will see the importance of knowing how to read, too."

I hoped Nimmie was right, but I will admit I was terribly disappointed.

Our remaining five included Wawasee our artist, a young lad by the name of Jim Buck, two girls—one eight, one eleven—and a young married woman who came with her nursing baby. The young mother would often get so involved in what she was learning that she would forget the child in her arms. The fussing baby eventually would bring her back to reality, and she would lift the baby to her breast and go back to her book again. I had never seen anyone so eager to learn as Brown Duck.

Kanika, our eleven-year-old, was not a quick learner, but she had a searching mind and would plod away to find the answers to the problems we assigned her.

Susie Crooked Leg, on the other hand, was a brilliant little child. She rarely had to be told a new concept twice. Eagerly she grasped all the learning the small classroom was able to give her and reached for more. I knew that if Susie could be given a chance, she could make a real contribution to her world and even beyond.

Wawasee was at a disadvantage. We had nothing in our classroom that could help a child with his handicap. He had not been born deaf but had been a bright, energetic, talkative, eight-year-old when measles left him without his hearing. We had to be sure we were directly in front of him with his eyes on our lips when we talked to him. This was not always easy to do, for Wawasee was interested only in his drawing. He drew when he should have been reading. He was not interested in numbers or letters, only shapes and colors.

I was determined that he at least should learn the fundamentals. I prompted and urged and reviewed and encouraged. Once, when he had been at school for about a week and the other students had gone on to add a number of simple words to their vocabulary, Wawasee was still struggling with the first two.

"Fish," I would say over and over, enunciating carefully for the benefit of his eyes on my lips. "Fish."

Wawasee tried the word. It sounded good.

I then put him to work printing the word over and over down his page. I even granted him the privilege of drawing a small fish to go with each of the words. After he had filled two pages with fish of various sizes and descriptions, I went to the board and with a piece of white chalk, printed in large letters F-I-S-H. After getting Wawasee's attention, I asked him for the word.

He shook his head. He did not know.

I was frustrated. I walked back to his desk and opened the scribbler to the two pages of fish. Placing a finger under Wawasee's chin, a signal we had developed to let him know we wanted him to watch our lips, I said again, "Fish. It is the same. Fish." I pointed to the board, "F-I-S-H." I pointed to his pages. "The same," but Wawasee merely shrugged his shoulders.

Lifting his eyes to my face again, I asked gently, "Do you understand?"

He looked at me evenly, as though asking me to see it his way, "Not same," he dared to say. "Yours white, mine black."

Wawasee thought in color.

I realized then that I needed a new way to relate to Wawasee. If only I had many bright books with colored pages. Perhaps then he would be interested in learning. But I did not have them, and it would be months before it would be possible to get some. In the meantime I would simply do the best I could.

One of my disappointments was that Wawasee's two younger sisters did not come to school. I asked Wawasee about them many times. At first his answer, through Nimmie's translation, was that they were not interested in drawing. When we reminded him that school was so much more than that, he looked for other answers. Each time we asked him, his reply was a little different, but it all came down to the fact that the little girls just were not interested and did not feel that classes were sufficient reason to leave the sheltered warmth of the cabin.

After the fourth week Kanika dropped out. I felt like crying. I went to their cabin after school was dismissed hoping to learn that she had been ill or needed at home. She was fine and was playing rather than doing an assigned home task. Her mother just shrugged her shoulders.

"Why you not go?" she asked the girl in English for my benefit, as though she had just realized that Kanika was at home and not at school.

Kanika barely raised her head to answer. She looked puzzled, as though she couldn't understand why she should be called upon to explain herself. It was plain to see that she just didn't feel like going, so she didn't go—that was all.

Now we had four students. Wawasee was hardly to be counted, for though we worked with him to the best of our ability, his attention was on his artwork only.

Jim Buck, Susie Crooked Leg and Brown Duck were doing well. All three were eager to learn.

Then we had another disappointment. Brown Duck's husband came home from his trapline for a few days and learned of her involvement in the classes. He could not understand her hunger for knowledge. He only knew that she was the only woman in the settlement who was leaving her work at home to go to class each morning. He could also see that skins were not getting tanned, moccasins were not getting sewn, and the cabin fire was not kept burning.

We could understand the attitude of Crying Dog, Brown Duck's husband. He saw the schooling as a waste of time for a lazy wife and he forbade Brown Duck to return to class again.

We were sorry to lose Brown Duck, but neither Nimmie nor I would have encouraged her to disobey her husband.

It was no longer reasonable to expect Nimmie to come to the schoolroom each morning when I had only three students. The students and I understood one another well enough now that we could manage. I had a little of their language, they were learning more and more words in English. I knew they should learn English, because they needed it to communicate outside their own small world; but I was sorry they were unable to have textbooks in their native tongue. They should have had the privilege of learning their own language in written form, but at this point they did not.

The weather grew colder, the winds blew more drifts of snow, tucking our little village in blankets of white. We needed snowshoes to get about. The women of the village were kept constantly busy supplying fuel for their cabin fires.

I was wrestling with a question. Was it sensible to have Wynn go to the little cabin each morning and start a fire for just the four of us? Wouldn't it make more sense to move my students over to my cabin for their lessons? But if I stayed where I was, there might be those who would return to class. I finally talked it over with Wynn.

"What should I do?" I asked him after I had thoroughly explained my predicament.

"I would like to believe that there might be those who will rejoin you, Elizabeth," he said slowly, "but to be honest, I don't suppose they will. They have had no reason to believe that education from books will benefit them. That still has to be proven to them."

"But how can we show them?" I wailed.

"We can't—not overnight. It is going to take a long time. Perhaps," he went on thoughtfully, "we are a negative example to them."

"Negative? I don't follow."

"Well, I have education. You have education. And yet we need to learn their skills to live here in their wilderness."

I began to understand what Wynn was saying. I looked out our frosted window at the swirl of the winter storm. Wynn was right. Here my teaching degree would benefit me very little unless I also knew the art of survival.

"What should I do, Wynn?" I asked again, sincerely, humbly.

He reached out and pulled me into his arms. He smiled into my eyes as he stroked back the whisp of hair forever tormenting me by curling about my cheeks and refusing to stay combed in its proper place. "You're doing a great job," he said, "and I'm proud of you for trying, for caring. You might not realize it yet, but those two pupils of yours, just those two eager learners—yes, even Wawasee too—could someday be the means of educating this entire village."

I closed my eyes and leaned hard against my husband. With all my heart I hoped he was right.

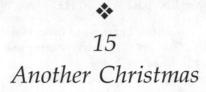

15

Another Christmas

❖

FOR SOME REASON I dreaded the coming Christmas away from family even more than I had my first one. Perhaps it was because on my first year away I was still a new bride with the excitement of creating a home for my husband. Now I was beginning to notice the loneliness of the months without family. The coming of Christmas made me feel even more homesick.

I did not go crying to Wynn. He had enough troubles of his own. Reports were coming in from the traplines about a marauding bear robbing the traps. At first Wynn found the rumors hard to believe. All the bears should have been in hibernation months earlier. Whatever would one be doing out, still foraging for food, this time of year? The reports persisted. Wynn decided he must check into them.

According to those who brought the tales to the village, the bear was mammoth. It swung deadly blows with paws the size of pine branches and was gone again before a hunter could even lift his rifle. Soon other details were added to the stories. The bear was ten feet tall, bullets would not pierce him, and when he ran he left no tracks. The people of the village were sure the bear was a spirit animal and that it had come back to avenge some wrong, hitherto undetected. So afraid had they become that when Wynn decided to go out after "the spirit bear," he could find no one willing to go with him.

I don't know if some of the Indians' superstitions affected me, or what was the true nature of my despair, but I pleaded with Wynn not to go. I was sure that if he did, I would never see him again.

Wynn tried to assure me that he would be fine and would soon be home again, but I still feared for his life. He did not let this sway his decision, however. Already two trappers had been attacked by the bear. One had lost a leg in the attack and the other was mauled badly about the head and face.

The bear had also attacked sled dogs. It had killed one outright, another had to be destroyed because of a serious injury, and a third one seemed to be slowly healing. I knew Wynn was right, that something had to be done, but how I hated to see him leave on the trail of the killer bear.

"Something is wrong," Wynn said to me. "There are too many stories for me to doubt, but why a bear should be up and about this time of year is a mystery."

With a tear-stained face I watched Wynn fill his pack with an extra large emergency supply. I had seen him pack many times during our time spent up North, and I realized he was preparing for a long time on the trail, if necessary. I was even more frightened.

After watching Wynn and the dog team disappear from view through the swirling snow, I went back to my room and cried some more. *Perhaps this Christmas I won't even have Wynn,* I mourned.

When I awoke after crying myself to sleep, I felt worse, not better. My head ached and my eyes were swollen and sore. My throat felt sore, too, and I thought I might be coming down with something dreadful. *What if Wynn comes back to a cold cabin and lifeless wife?* But, no, that was foolishness. I really was letting my imagination run away with me.

If only the cabin didn't feel so empty when Wynn was gone. I thought again of the baby I wanted so badly. I had been married for almost a year and a half, and I still had no prospects of becoming a mother. Nimmie, who already had one little one, was already expecting another. Every day that I went to the settlement, I saw young women who were with child. It was a sad reminder to me that my arms were still empty. I shivered in the stillness and then suddenly realized that I had a good reason to shiver: It was cold in the cabin. I pulled myself from the bed and went to re-build a fire.

I had prepared myself emotionally for many long, long days without Wynn. But by lunchtime the next day he was back. On the sled was tied the carcass of the largest bear I had ever seen. Though it was big, it was gaunt and empty, like it had already been skinned out and only the hide remained. One of its front paws was badly damaged, which, Wynn said, was the reason for our trouble.

"It couldn't hunt with that damaged paw and was starving slowly. It refused to go into hibernation without having the fat stored up to see it through the winter, so it stayed out to hunt. But it still had trouble finding enough to eat. Ordinarily it wouldn't have attacked dogs or men, but this bear was desperate."

I was so glad to see Wynn back that I didn't pay much attention to the bear. The Indian people did, though. They kept circling the sled, pointing at the carcass and talking in excited tones. They noticed the gaunt body, the visible ribs, the weakness of the big frame. They took it as an omen. It was not good, they said, that "brother bear" went hungry. Perhaps he was sent by the Great Spirit to warn of coming hunger for the people as well.

It was not a nice thought, and I will admit it made shivers run up and down my spine. Wynn seemed to pay no attention to the clucking tongues and shaking heads, but I do think he began to wish he had left that bear where he had shot it, instead of bringing it back to the settlement to prove to the people that it was no ghost.

Now that Wynn was safely back and the bear had been taken care of,

I again gave my attention to Christmas. Actually I tried not to think about it, but I could not help myself. I tried to keep myself busy so I wouldn't have time to think, but that didn't work either.

Two days before Christmas, Wynn came home in the morning to find the students and me poring over our books. He looked rather surprised and apologized for interrupting us. I assured him he had not troubled us and dismissed my students early.

"Aren't you even going to take a Christmas break?" Wynn inquired when the students had left for the day.

"Of course," I answered, as though Christmas were still far in the future. And then I remembered I hadn't told the students not to return the next morning, the twenty-fourth. *Well, I can't help it*, I reasoned. I just couldn't bear to spend the days alone.

Even when I worked, my thoughts kept going home. I remembered the Christmases spent with my family in Toronto. I could visualize just what preparations my mother would be making. I could see her, bending over her stove, her cheeks flushed from the warmth, her hair curling softly about her cheeks as she turned out pan after pan of delicious-smelling cookies. I could see Father as he entered the room with the fine tree, smelling as tangy as the very outdoors. Soon Julie and I, and perhaps Matthew, would enter the room with our arms full of boxes of Christmas decorations, and we would trim the tree and hang the garlands and place the wreaths in the windows and on the doors.

By this time my eyes would be filled with tears, and I'd resolve to keep my thoughts on safer ground. I honestly would try, but soon I'd be seeing the red-bowed wrappings on the gifts stacked beneath the tree. I could see myself sitting at the table in our elegant dining room, head bowed while Father said the grace. Then as he carved the turkey we would chat and laugh, just for the joy of being alive and together.

Wiping my eyes on the corner of my apron when no one was looking, I tried to gather my thoughts back to safer ground. And then I would find myself thinking of Jon and Mary and their family in Calgary. They, too, would be preparing for Christmas. I could see the house. I knew where every candle and holly wreath would be placed. I could see the children, their faces shining as they sat before the open fire listening to the familiar yet ever-new Christmas story. How I longed to be with them!

I wept. I prayed. I struggled. I felt I would never make it through this Christmas. Never in all of my life had I been so homesick.

Just hang on, I kept telling myself; *just keep yourself in hand. Soon it will be over and then you'll be all right again.* But I was beginning to wonder, to fear lest I would lose complete control, or at least make a scene. I did not want to give Wynn reason to be concerned about me. I tried even harder.

On December twenty-four we had class as usual. At noon I dismissed the children and tried to find something constructive to fill my afternoon.

I didn't have the ingredients for special baking, nor gifts to wrap in pretty Christmasy tissue paper. Mostly I puttered around in the kitchen, feeling alone and empty.

Soon it would be time for Wynn to be coming home. It would officially be Christmas Eve. I stiffened my upper lip, breathed a little prayer and hoped to be able to stay in control. One eye watched the clock, while the other watched the stew I was stirring. My ears were waiting for the sound of approaching feet.

It was then that I heard running. I knew it was not Wynn. Wynn did not approach our house at a run. Kip knew it too. He was up and over to the door before I could even turn from the stove.

The door burst open and Susie, breathless and without outdoor wraps, flung herself into the room.

"Teacher," she gasped, "Teacher, come quick! Mama needs you."

I did not wait to ask why I was needed. I grabbed my parka, flung it about me and headed for the door. I stopped only long enough to hastily tie on my snowshoes, and then I followed the running Susie. I did think briefly that I had not even stopped to push the stew to the back of the stove.

When we reached the cabin, we were both out of breath. Susie pushed open the door and after throwing aside my snowshoes I followed her in. One dim lamp was burning and the thick smoke of the open fire stung my eyes so I could hardly see. As soon as my eyes adjusted, I could see that Susie's mother was not alone. A midwife was there. I then noticed the same unusual smell I had found at Nimmie's after her baby was born.

Susie's mother moaned and tossed on her bed. The Indian midwife moved closer to her and spoke words of comfort in a sing-songy voice. Neither woman seemed to have noticed me.

"What's the matter?" I whispered to Susie.

"The baby is already here, and still she pains—bad," explained Susie in a worried tone.

"The baby?"

"Yes. There."

Susie pointed to one corner of the room. A pile of furs was lying there and, as I looked closely, I felt more than saw something stir. I looked back to Susie. Fear showed in her eyes. I reached an arm out to her and pulled her close. She did not resist me. As I held the little girl, I wondered which one of us needed the consolation, the closeness, the most. My tears nearly spilled again.

The old midwife turned to get some more of her medicine. It was the first she seemed to be aware of us. She did not look surprised.

"Not good," she said in a low voice. "Not good. Pain should go now."

I was frightened. I knew Susie felt I should be able to do something. What could I do? I knew nothing about caring for birthing mothers. Surely we wouldn't have another family of children left as orphans? Susie had already lost her father six months before in a river accident. I prayed that she wouldn't be asked to give up her mother, too.

As I looked at the frail child in my arms and thought of what the future could hold for her, my concern over myself and my homesickness suddenly left me. All my thoughts were now on this family, this mother who tossed and groaned before us. What could we do? I began to pray for the mother.

A faint whimper from the corner interrupted my talk with God. The baby was awake. With one arm still around Susie, I moved toward the corner. The little one was small, with thick black hair framing the tiny face. I reached down to lift him up. As I cuddled him close, the whimpering stopped, but Susie, who still stood close to me, had not stopped shaking.

"We need to find Mr. Delaney," I told her. "He might have gone home by now, or he might be at the store. Do you think you can find him?"

She nodded her head.

"Put on your parka and your mittens this time," I said. "It's cold out and you mustn't get chilled. I'll be here with your mother."

She followed my instructions, bundled up and then left. I was sure she was running again.

We did not wait too long before Susie was back with Wynn. He didn't stop to ask questions but went over to the Indian woman on the corner bed and began to examine her. I still clung to the baby. The little warm body in my arms seemed to give me some measure of assurance.

"Maggie," I heard Wynn speak to the Indian lady, "Maggie, do you hear me?"

The woman only groaned.

"She sleep now," said the midwife. "Get rest."

"Not get rest, yet," said Wynn. "She still has a big job left. She has a baby to deliver."

"Baby come already," the midwife informed Wynn and pointed at the baby I held in my arms.

"Maybe so," said Wynn, "but now it is time for the brother to come."

Twins! I couldn't believe it. I guess Susie couldn't either.

"What does he mean, Teacher?" she asked in a whisper.

"Your mother is going to have two babies—twins," I said to her.

"Like bear cubs?" she whispered, her eyes big.

I laughed softly.

"Like bear cubs," I told her.

By the time the second baby arrived, and the new babies and the tired mother were properly taken care of, it was no longer Christmas Eve. Wynn and I walked home arm-in-arm over the crunching snow, our breath sending little puffs before us in the cold, crisp night air. The moon shone overhead, and the northern lights played back and forth across the heavens. I wondered aloud about that night long ago, when another child was born on Christmas Eve. It always seemed like a miracle when a new life entered the world, and tonight there had been two new lives and they both seemed well and healthy. Wynn had been wrong, though; it was not a brother. The second baby, much to Susie's delight, had been a girl.

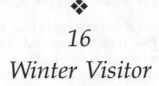

16
Winter Visitor

CHRISTMAS DAY WAS still a time of loneliness for me, but I did not feel overwhelmed with homesickness. Wynn and I spent the day before our fire. Our dinner was venison roast and vegetables, with a blueberry pie for dessert. We had planned to go for a walk along the river but the day turned out to be too cold for that.

We did exchange gifts. We didn't have much, but each of us had hidden away a few items for future giving when we had come north. With two Christmases, our anniversary and Wynn's birthday behind us, I was now at the end of my little horde. I wondered what I would do for a gift when Wynn's birthday came around again. The question nibbled at the back of my mind while I watched him unwrap the new knife which was this year's present. Perhaps I could find something to purchase from one of the Indian ladies.

My gift from Wynn brought a gasp of joy. It was two pairs of new stockings. I had mended and repaired the ones I owned numerous times, and I did so hate mended stockings. I found out later that Wynn had ordered them in from Edmonton through Ian's store with the fall supply train.

The day seemed to be rather long. There wasn't much to do except talk. We had few games to play, no music available, and the miserable weather left us no chance to leave the cabin.

While I prepared an evening snack of cold meat sandwiches and leftover pie, Wynn stretched out on the rug before the fire. By the time I returned to join him, he had fallen asleep. I knew my sleeping husband was tired. His job took so much of his time and energy. After delivering the baby last night, he had been called from our overcooked stew to see a sick child.

He had lost weight, too. I hadn't noticed it until now, but he definitely did not weigh as much as he had when we came north. I looked down at my own body. I had lost a few pounds, too, which was reasonable. We were active, walked a lot, and ate few foods that would add pounds to our frames.

I looked at my hands. They were no longer the soft hands of a pampered woman. Time had changed us—time and the northland.

I didn't know whether to waken Wynn or to let him sleep, so I just sat watching him, undecided.

Suddenly Kip arose and looked toward the door, his head cocked to one side as he listened. Was someone coming?

"No, God, please," I pleaded. "Don't let Wynn be needed again to-night."

By the time I heard the footsteps, Kip was already at the door. I could tell by his bark that whoever was coming was not someone he knew. Kip welcomed most of the settlement people with only a wagging of his tail.

Kip's barking awakened Wynn and he pushed himself up into a sitting position and looked apologetically at me.

"Sorry. I must have—" but he got no further.

There was stamping at our front door and then someone was banging on it.

Kip's barking increased, and Wynn rose to his feet and motioned him to go to his corner in silence; Kip obeyed rather reluctantly, I thought.

Wynn opened the door and a man almost fell into the room. The first thing I noticed was his clothes. He was dressed in the uniform of the Royal North West Mounted Police.

Then I noticed that he had a big bundle in his arms. He looked out from around it and his face, red with the cold of the bitter wind, broke into a sort of frozen smile.

"Sergeant Wynn Delaney?" he asked.

"Right," said Wynn and moved to relieve him of his heavy load so he would have a free hand to shake in greeting. But the man laughed softly and moved the parcel away from Wynn's outstretched hand.

"Sorry," he said, "but I have strict orders to hand this over to Elizabeth Delaney and no one else." He turned to me. "You're Mrs. Elizabeth Delaney?"

My mouth must have dropped open in astonishment. "I—I am," I stammered.

He handed me the parcel as if he was awfully glad to be rid of it. Then he brushed the snow from his parka, pulled off his mitten and reached out a hand to Wynn.

"Carl Havens of the Royal North West Mounted Police," he said evenly.

I stood with the parcel in my hands, looking wide-eyed at the young officer. How had he gotten to our small cabin in the North? What was he doing here? And where was this strange box from? Wynn was speaking, "Welcome to the North, Carl. Won't you take off your coat and tell us what this is all about? I believe Elizabeth has just brewed a fresh pot of coffee."

So it was over that fresh pot of coffee in front of our fireplace that Carl Havens filled us in on what he was doing in our area and how he happened to be our Christmas visitor.

He had been stationed in Calgary and had come to know our Julie through the small church there. When he received his new posting, and it was up North, Julie expressed a desire to send a Christmas package to her northern family. Havens checked with the Force and they gave their permission for him to act as courier. And so here was Officer Havens on his way to his posting, which was north and a little east of ours, stopping by to see us with a parcel of goodies from home!

It seemed too good to be true.

The little gifts from Jon and Mary, each of the children, and Julie in particular, should have brightened my Christmas. And I guess it did. It also made me even lonelier. I cried over everything I lifted from its wrappings. The men seemed to understand, and no one tried to talk me out of my tears.

I fixed more sandwiches. Officer Havens was famished, as though he had not eaten for days. I thought of the misery of the trail. It was hard enough traveling it in the warmth of summer. It must be nearly unbearable in the winter's cold. I wondered how the young Mountie had ever found his way to us in the snow.

"I'm traveling with guides," he said in answer to our questions. "They are camped down by the trading post. We will spend the night there and then go on in the morning. The man at the store—McLain, is it?—told me where to find you, and of course I couldn't rest until I got that parcel delivered—and right on time, too."

He smiled as I wondered just how serious the relationship was between him and Julie. He seemed like a fine young man. He'd be good for Julie.

As we had our coffee and sandwiches I plied him with questions about the family and life in Calgary. Like a fresh breath of home, it was so good to get some news of the outside world.

It was late when he said he must go. His men would be wondering where he was. They had to leave early in the morning.

Wynn invited him back for breakfast the next morning, but he declined. He would eat with his men, he said. Wynn promised to see him before he left, and then he was gone through the snow, just as he had come.

I had a strange feeling as I watched his tall figure depart into the darkness.

"Wynn," I asked, "was he really here, or have I been dreaming?"

Wynn pointed to the gifts now scattered around our small cabin.

"It looks like he was really here, Beth."

It had been a long time since Wynn had used my pet name. I blinked back tears, not sure if they were tears of joy or sorrow. I still missed my family. The gifts were nice, but they did not take the place of the ones who had sent them. I also loved my husband dearly. Yes, my choice was the same. *As long as Wynn is in the North, I will be here with him.*

He took me gently in his arms and kissed away the tear that lay on my cheek.

"It's been tough this Christmas, hasn't it?"

I nodded.

"I'm sorry you've been so lonesome," he went on.

"You noticed?"

"I noticed."

"I thought I was hiding it pretty well."

He hugged me closer. "I appreciate your trying, Beth, though I would have been more than happy to share it, to talk about it. It might have helped a bit. Sometimes I get lonesome, too. I think about home, about Mother—about the fact that I wasn't there when Dad passed away. I wish I would have been. I worry some that the same thing might happen with Mother. Every day I pray, 'Please, God, let me be there this time.' Does that sound foolish? I mean, can you understand?"

"I understand," I said as my arms tightened around him. I did understand. Wynn had family, too, that he loved deeply. It wasn't easy for him to serve in the North. But the people here needed him. It was his commitment to them that kept him with the Force, that kept him here in the small settlement. I had seen the same light of commitment in the eyes of the other young Mountie, Carl Havens. He, too, felt that being a member of the Royal North West Mounted Police was more than a job. It was a calling to serve people. Wynn's even higher calling to serve his Lord was fulfilled in his responsibilities here among the trappers and Indians.

I reached up to kiss my husband, and with the kiss was a promise—a promise of my love and support here by his side for as long as he felt that the North needed him.

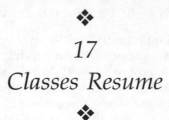

17
Classes Resume

JIM BUCK APPEARED at my door the next morning. I had not expected to start classes again for another day or two, but Jim either did not understand or pretended not to.

"Come for school," he said in answer to my puzzled look.

I did not turn him away. He came in and took his place at the table, and I brought him a few books to look at while I finished my morning tasks.

He buried himself in the books and paid no attention to me.

"What about Susie?" I asked him. "If we are having class again, shouldn't she be here, and Wawasee?"

"They come—maybe," said Jim, afraid I might change my mind.

"But they don't know about it," I continued.

"You bang bell," responded Jim, solving that dilemma.

I smiled to myself and went to "bang bell."

After a few moments Wawasee appeared. Tucked in his parka was his beloved scribbler. He proudly showed it to me, every page filled with his drawings. They were very well done, and I marveled that a child of his age, with no training or guidance, could accomplish such beautiful and skilled artwork.

I settled him at the table and assigned him to draw the illustrations on some more word cards. Then I listened to Jim's reading lesson. He was doing well.

The morning passed and Susie did not appear. I was concerned about her, and after the two boys had gone home and I had eaten my lunch and cleared the table, I decided to go over to Susie's cabin and see how things were going.

Susie's mother, Maggie, still lay on the bed in the corner along with her twins. They both looked fine, though one cried vigorously while the other slept through it all.

There was much commotion and confusion in the cabin. An elderly couple was moving in. The woman was going to care for Maggie and the babies, and as the old man also needed her care, she had brought him with her.

Susie had been sent to gather some firewood to keep the fire burning. I thought of the wood supply beside the cabin we used as our schoolhouse. Once we had stopped having classes in the schoolroom, the people of the village had taken advantage of the wood supply and helped themselves. I supposed there would be little left by now.

With two more people moving into the cabin, I wondered where they would sleep. It was already crowded with the family which presently occupied it. Besides Susie, Maggie had two small boys and now there were also the new twins.

I went over to the bedside to talk to Maggie. She still seemed weak. She smiled at me though and nodded her head at each baby. "Two," she said to me. I smiled in return.

"How are you, Maggie?" I asked her.

"Not good," she said, shaking her head; then her face brightened. "But soon."

"I'll have the sergeant drop by to see you. He might have some medicine to make you strong faster," I promised, wondering even as I said it if Wynn had any kind of tonic or vitamins.

"That good," she said. She lay for a minute and then went on, "Susie hear bell. Want to go. I need today. Now Too Many come. But Susie might go stay with other family in big village. No room here."

Maggie's face looked sorrowful at the thought.

"What do you mean?" I asked, horrified at what I thought she meant.

"No room," Maggie repeated.

I looked about me. She was right. There was no room to put another bed on the floor, yet somehow, two more would need to be squeezed in.

Without even stopping to think or to draw a breath, I said, "I have room. I'll keep her at my house; then she won't need to go to the big village, and she will be able to come and see you and help gather your wood, and—"

"That is good," agreed Maggie. "You take."

I could hardly wait for Susie to return from her wood gathering so I could tell her the good news. *She was coming to stay with me; she could continue with her classes*, I rejoiced. She would not need to leave her village or her people.

Susie received the news with quiet joy. Except for the shine in her eyes, I would not have thought she heard me.

She did not tell her mother goodbye, but I noticed their eyes exchange a glance, and I knew that both mother and daughter felt the parting. Susie would be near, so she would be able to return home each day to help in the household tasks and to visit her mother.

We started for our cabin, Susie carrying all she owned in a tiny bundle. I wondered how anyone, even a small girl, could survive with so few belongings.

As we walked silently across the clearing, the sun shone brightly from a cloudless sky, the kind of a day that lends itself to snow blindness because of the intense glare of the winter snow. I saw Susie squinting against it, and I supposed I squinted, too.

Won't Wynn be surprised when he comes home tonight, I thought. There was not a doubt in my mind but what Wynn would heartily approve of my actions. I was sure he would take in the whole village if he felt it would be for their good.

Kip welcomed Susie with generous wags of his tail. Perhaps he had missed her at class today. She placed her small bundle on the floor and threw her arms around his neck.

"I am going to live with you, Silver One," she said, calling him by his Indian name.

Kip seemed to like the arrangement. His whole body waved with his enthusiasm.

It was then I noticed a little skipping of my heart. *The cabin won't seem so empty now when Wynn is away.* It would be filled with the voice of a child.

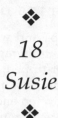

18
Susie

IT DID MAKE a difference to have Susie in our home. Where it had been quiet and empty before, it now became filled with laughter and childish games. Susie was a bright little thing who loved to chatter and laugh. Kip was her playmate. They romped together on the rug and furniture, and sometimes I was tempted to admonish them to be quiet and still. Then I would think of the house as it used to be, and how it would be again when Susie left us, and I would hold back the command.

Susie's grasp of English broadened quickly. She loved my books. When I was busy she would pore over them, trying to sound out the words. When I was free she would ask me to read to her, which didn't take too much coaxing because I loved it as much as she did.

I was careful to send her home for a portion of each day. While she was gone I worked quickly at whatever needed to be done so that when she returned I would be free to spend my time with her.

Some days I dressed warmly and went with her to the woods to help her gather the wood supply for her cabin. We always took Kip along, and he loved the romp through the snow. It was good for all of us, and we returned home with rosy cheeks and shining eyes, delighted by the things we had seen in the forest.

We didn't neglect Susie's schoolwork. In fact, I guess we advanced it. We both loved the excitement of learning. Susie shared with me many things about her people, and I told her many things about mine. She was a real help to me in understanding the ways of the Indians, and I had a wonderful chance to learn more of their language.

Though Susie would laugh at my attempts to pronounce some of the strange words, she was a good little teacher and would have me repeat the word over and over until I got it right. In my heart I hoped for the day when she would be standing in front of a classroom, teaching her own people. I was sure now that Wynn and Nimmie were right. One or two of these dear children could open the door to a new world for the entire tribe. Perhaps Susie, with her quick mind and love for laughter, would be the key to that door.

Wynn loved Susie too. At first she was shy around him. She respected the lawman, and perhaps even liked him, but she held back, a gentle smile showing only in her dark eyes.

Kip was certainly not shy. Whenever Wynn returned home, Kip met him at the door with joyous yips and wagging tail. Wynn was hardly allowed to remove his heavy winter wraps before Kip expected a tussle. Wynn would take the big, silver-tipped, furry head between his hands and press his face against the dog's fluffy coat. Then the two of them would rock back and forth, and often end up rolling on the floor.

Susie watched it all at first, her eyes round with astonishment. I'm sure she had never seen such goings-on before, not with a grown-up. Occasionally Kip would look her direction and whimper, as if inviting her to join them. Then Susie would turn away and come to me to see if I had some task I might wish her to do.

After Kip had been satisfied, Wynn would come to me. At first we weren't sure how we should conduct ourselves in Susie's presence. We felt she was probably not used to seeing an embrace and welcoming kiss among adults in the way we were accustomed. Should we, for Susie's sake, restrain ourselves? We tried that for one day. But we missed it so, we decided that Susie probably could adjust to our way of showing affection. So when Wynn came to the stove to see what was cooking, we embraced and greeted one another with a kiss just as we always had done.

At first we noticed Susie's big black eyes upon us, but as the days went by she seemed to accept it as part of the strange rituals of our household.

Wynn never failed to turn to the little girl with a question about her day. At first she was shy and hesitant, but gradually she became more open. They even shared Indian words I did not yet know. He would ask her a question in her own language and she would answer him, a twinkle in her eyes. This exchange was often followed with laughter, and I took pleasure in their private little jokes.

Susie was quick to observe. When Wynn came in and removed his winter things, he also took off his heavy boots and put on lighter, more comfortable footwear. He sat in the one big chair before the fire to remove the boots. Then he walked, stocking-footed, to our bedroom to get his slippers. Each night his little ritual was the same. Until one evening when Susie changed it.

Wynn had lowered his tired body into his chair and was tugging at the heavy boots. He sat for a moment relaxing the strained muscles, and then rose to go to the bedroom, but there was Susie, standing in front of him, his slippers in her outstretched hand.

Wynn's eyes first showed surprise, and then he beamed at her. He reached out—not for the boots but for the little girl. He pulled her to him and hugged her close. Susie did not pull back.

I wondered as I watched if this was the first time Susie had been hugged by a man. Her own father would have been a very busy trapper, often gone from the home and not accustomed to showing his love in this way, though no one could doubt that Indian fathers did love their children. Often they were seen talking and playing with them, their eyes aglow with pride and joy. I often thought as I watched, that had they been called upon to do so, I'm sure they would have given their lives for their children without a moment's hesitation.

But here was little Susie getting a warm hug. Would she understand it?

"Thank you, my girl," Wynn was saying. And then he said a few words in the Indian dialect and Susie giggled. Wynn released her and put on his slippers. Susie's eyes never left his face.

"Seeing as I didn't have to walk *all* the way to the bedroom to get my slippers, there might be time for a short story before Elizabeth calls us for supper," Wynn said with a nod toward the small stack of books.

Susie's smile grew broader and she ran for her favorite. I inobtrusively postponed supper a little. Wynn lifted Susie up onto his knee and soon both of them were completely absorbed in the story. As I watched them, tears brimmed in my eyes. This was as it should be. This was what I wanted to give to Wynn—a child, a child of his own to love and care for and cuddle. Instinctively I had known Wynn would make a good father. I had been right. I could see it clearly now in the way that he held Susie.

We were a real family now. Wynn, me and Susie. There was a family feeling in our small cabin. We had been happy together, Wynn and I, but a child was what we needed to make our life complete.

I looked at Wynn and the little girl on his knee. Their eyes were riveted to the pages of the storybook. My heart sang a little song. I loved Susie so much and I knew with certainty that she loved me in return. It was such fun to romp through the snow, to make cookies, to teach her how to embroider, to help her to make the rag doll, to . . . There were so many things we had done together in the short time since Susie had come to us. I thought ahead to all the things I still wanted to share with her.

And then a flash of insight shocked me back to reality.

I faced the fact that Susie would not be with us long. I would love to keep her. I knew Wynn would love to keep her. My heart ached as I formed the words, *But she is not truly ours*, though my mind cried out against the fact. She belonged to another family. I knew this would not change, nor would I change it if I could. Susie loved her family. Her family loved her. Ultimately she belonged with them.

I must daily remind myself of that and do nothing that would make it any harder for Susie when she returned to her own home. My deep love must protect her *from* my love. It seemed like a strange enigma, but I knew that it was true. It would be so easy to pretend Susie was mine. To take over her life. To try to make her white instead of Indian.

We would love her. We both would love her. But we—and especially I—must be conscious of who she was and preserve and keep that for her, at the same time expanding her world. It would not be easy, but I would try with all my heart.

Susie will eventually go home, I must always remember that. Perhaps by that time I would be expecting our own child. Susie would be deeply missed, but it would help to know that someone, some other little one, was on the way to fill the emptiness.

I waited for the story to end and then called them both for supper. We bowed our heads for the evening grace and Susie reached out for a hand from each of us, our custom when praying together.

I held the little hand in mine and said my own quiet prayer as Wynn prayed aloud. I prayed for Susie, our dear little girl. I would always think of her as ours. Uniquely ours. And yet not. I prayed that God would give me daily wisdom. I prayed for her salvation. I prayed for the salvation of her mother and family. Without that, Susie did not have much chance when she went back home.

My thinking changed as I sat there bowed in prayer. I saw clearly that if I wanted to affect Susie's life for good, then I had to work with her whole family. I must do more. I must reach out. I needed God's help and direction.

Wynn and I had a long talk that night after Susie went to bed. I told him how God had been speaking to me, and he held me close as I talked. I was right, he assured me. Susie's world was not our world. We had to prepare her for a return to her own, whenever that time would be.

Our days changed, though outwardly our household routine stayed the same. Susie and I spent our time together. I always went with her to gather the wood and take it to her house. While we chatted I tried to learn much more about her people. When we went to her house I spent more time talking with her mother and the little boys. I dared to try the words Susie had been teaching me. Sometimes they did not come out right and Susie would giggle, but she would correct me, and I would go on.

I even spoke to the elderly couple, often sharing bits and pieces of my faith with them. I wanted them to understand, to come to know God. They listened politely but they did not yet question me further as I hoped and prayed they would.

At the end of the day when Wynn returned home, often weary from the day's heavy demands, Kip would always meet him at the door; but now Susie was usually there too. Sometimes she jumped right in and got in on the roll on the floor. Then as Wynn took off his heavy boots, she would run to the bedroom for his slippers.

I made sure supper was not so rushed that there wasn't time for the short story from a book, as Wynn and Susie cuddled in the big chair and he read to her. As much as she loved me, I felt that this was probably her favorite time of day.

We said our table grace in her Indian language. We wanted Susie to feel it was not "the white man's God" we prayed to. He could be her God as well. And when we knelt together beside the small cot for her bedtime prayer at the end of the day, we again prayed in words Susie had learned in her cradle.

We were building together now, though Susie might have been unaware of it. We held her and loved her, cuddled and guided her, but all the time we did so it was with a consciousness that we were preparing her, and ourselves, for that inevitable day when our paths would separate and we would again walk down different trails.

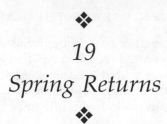

19
Spring Returns

❖

BECAUSE OF SUSIE, our days were more than filled with good things to do. I still taught class, the two village boys joining Susie each morning.

Susie was now far more outgoing and talkative than most of the settlement children. I wondered if she would find it hard to fit in with the other children again, and feared a bit for her. For this reason I began to suggest that she take some time each day to share in the village games.

She did not hesitate. She went gladly and from my observations seemed to have no difficulty at all in getting back in with her friends.

One day I had sent Susie out to play and then decided to walk to the store for a few items I needed. That would give me time to have tea with Nimmie. We still had our weekly Bible studies together, and Susie always joined us, her eyes big with wonder at the things we read and discussed. She had already decided she wanted to give her heart to this Jesus who loved her enough to die for her; and together Nimmie and I explained the gospel and what it meant to follow Him. She was such a precious child, with such a simple faith.

But now I was looking forward to just talking of women's things with Nimmie. She was already showing her pregnancy. Her two babies would not be too far apart in age. *Funny*, I thought, *here is Nimmie, married for many years without children, and now she will be a mother twice, in such a short period of time.* I smiled to myself. Perhaps that's what God had in store for me. But I did hope that I didn't have to wait as long as Nimmie had waited.

I drew near a cluster of children deeply absorbed in their play. They did not even turn to look at me as I walked by. They were seated on the snow, their eyes turned eastward, their faces intent. And then I spotted Susie. She was at the front of the group, holding up some old cue cards I had given her. She was the teacher, and they were the pupils. I stood still in astonishment. I could not believe my eyes.

"What's this one?" I heard her clear voice ask.

Many hands went up eagerly. Susie pointed to a small girl.

"Fish," said the child.

"Right," said Susie, beaming her approval. "It's *fish*."

I shook my head to clear it. How come they would not attend my school, yet here they were? Then I began to laugh softly. Hadn't Nimmie said so all the time? *Teach one, they will teach others.* Here was Susie, in play, doing something I had been unable to do.

I must be sure she has more cards, I told myself and then hurried on to Nimmie's. I could hardly wait to share this exciting news with her.

I had not done my usual chaffing and fussing about the coming of spring, and so it was rather a surprise to me when Wynn remarked one night, "I expect the ice to break in the river soon. The Indian men are expecting it to be quite a spectacle this year because of the deep freezing. They say you can watch it all from that high bluff east of the settlement. Are you interested?"

I looked at Wynn in astonishment, suddenly realizing that there truly was very little snow left around the village and that the Indian women were again out searching the nearby meadows for new growth for the cooking pots. I really had not given it much thought, my days and hours having been so taken with other things.

Susie was already jumping up and down, clapping her little hands together.

"Of course," I answered. "But why this year? Why is it any different this time?" I wondered.

"We've had colder weather. The river is frozen deeper than usual. Some of the men even fear for the fish in some areas where the water is not too deep."

I hadn't even realized that the weather had been colder than usual.

"The warm weather has come more quickly," went on Wynn. "Haven't you noticed how quickly the snow disappeared? There may be flood problems this year."

I stopped on my way to the stove, a pot in my hand. My eyes widened.

"Are we in—" I checked myself and glanced toward Susie. She was listening to every word. Wynn picked up my thought.

"There will be no danger for our village. We are high enough on the crest of this bluff, but some of the villages farther downstream might have difficulty."

I still hadn't made it to the stove with the cooking pot. "What can be done?" I asked Wynn.

"Ian and I and a couple of other men are going out tomorrow to look things over. We may ask some of them to move their belongings up onto higher ground. I hope they won't resist this. A few of the older ones might remember when the river flooded before, about twenty-six years ago. It nearly wiped out a village at that time. Those who remember might be willing to move and lead the way for the others."

Then Wynn abruptly changed his tone and the topic.

"Let's not borrow trouble," he stated philosophically. "Susie, would you like to see the ice go out of the river?"

She answered him with an Indian word, one filled with meaning of joy and anticipation. He laughed and tousled her black hair.

"Then that settles it," he said. "We'll go."

"When? When?" Susie jumped up and down in excitement.

"I'm not sure—just yet. Two men are watching the river. They will let us know when it is about to happen."

"How can they tell?" Susie echoed my own unasked question. Wynn laughed.

"Well, I'm not too sure just how they tell. All I know is that they seem to know every time. They watch carefully for certain signs. They listen to the sound of the river and the ice. They know."

"And they will tell us?" Susie wanted lots of assurance.

Wynn nodded his head.

"In time?" persisted Susie. "In time for us to get to the hill?"

Wynn smiled at her impatience.

"In plenty of time," he assured her.

I continued to the stove with my pot and put it on, almost subconsciously passing a hand over the big iron firebox to test out its hottest spot. I then put in more wood and turned back to Wynn.

"I guess I was just expecting some more snowstorms," I confessed. "I hadn't really allowed myself to hope 'spring' yet."

"I'm not saying that we won't get another snow or two," he cautioned, "but if it comes it shouldn't last long. I think spring is here to stay."

I turned to set the table and realized Susie had already put on the plates, the cups and the cutlery.

I reached a hand to her shoulder to thank her.

"Susie," I said, "how would you like to learn how to plant your own garden?"

She turned shining eyes to me. "Oh, yes!" she exclaimed. "Like Mrs. Ian?"

"Mrs. Ian" was the children's name for Nimmie.

"Like Mrs. Ian," I replied.

"She lets us taste her things sometimes," added Susie. "If we promise not to steal when she's not looking."

Yes, Nimmie would call the act exactly what it was. No soft-pedalling it by giving it some lesser name.

"Indians don't steal," went on Susie seriously, "'cause we share everything. But to be polite we should ask. And if they are not looking and we take, and hide, that means to steal."

"That's right," I agreed rather absently.

"An' white folks don't like stealers," continued Susie. She cast a furtive glance at Wynn. "They lock people up."

I knew she was identifying Wynn as the one who would do the "locking."

Wynn looked up from pulling off his boots.

"We don't lock up children," he said rather firmly.

"You don't?" Was it relief or doubt in Susie's voice?

"No, we don't," said Wynn defensively.

I knew he was often irritated at being used as the boogeyman with so many children.

Susie stood quietly for a moment and then a twinkle entered her black eyes.

"Wait 'til I tell the rest," she said. "We can do anything we want—"

But Wynn did not let her finish. Realizing even before I did that Susie was teasing him, he threw aside his heavy boot and with one off, one on, he was off after the young child. Susie ran shrieking, laughter making it hard for her to get away. There really wasn't much room to run in our little cabin anyway, so after one trip around the table Wynn had caught her. Kip could not resist becoming involved in the tussle. I stood in my little spot in front of the stove, watching all the commotion and hoping the wild howls and barking would not carry all the way to the settlement. Our neighbors would wonder what in the world was going on.

"That's enough," I finally said, and motioned Kip to his corner.

"We'd better stop," Wynn joked with Susie, "before Elizabeth sends us to a corner, too."

Susie was panting lightly from the exertion. For a few minutes she was quiet as Wynn helped her up and deposited her on the cot.

Then she turned to him, her eyes big and questioning. "It's not true, then, is it? You don't lock children away so they never see their folks again?"

"You are right, Susie. We never lock children away."

"Then what do you do if they be bad?"

"We talk to the mothers and fathers and try to get them to help their children be good. We talk to the children and tell them all the dangers of continuing to be bad. We don't want children to grow up to be bad people. It makes everyone very sad. We don't like to lock up people—not anyone. But sometimes we have to keep grown-ups who insist on being bad from hurting other people."

Susie thought about this.

She nodded her little dark head, very serious now. "You're like Jesus," she said thoughtfully.

Wynn's eyes widened. "Pardon me?"

"You're like Jesus," Susie said, more positively now that she had said the words out loud. "He doesn't like it when people be bad either. An' He doesn't like to send them away—out of heaven. But it would spoil heaven for everybody else if He let bad people in there."

Wynn said nothing, but his eyes looked misty as he reached out to tousle the little black head on his way to the bedroom for his slippers.

It was a clear, sunny day, and I had to admit as I took deep breaths of air that spring really was with us again. I eagerly looked forward to all the promises of another growing season. I loved the summer months in this beautiful land—if only there was some way to bypass the hordes of mosquitoes and blackflies. But even with them to torment me, I would cherish the summer months ahead.

The children played and the adults chatted on the bluff east of the village while we waited for the spectacular sight of the river breaking up. Ian and Wynn and the two men whom they took with them had already found that two villages would be in danger in case of flooding. They had talked with the people and urged them to leave their log cabins and move their belongings to higher ground. Some of the people had listened. Others insisted they were high enough to escape any rampaging river waters. Wynn had argued and explained as best he could, but a few had remained adamant. Finally Wynn had left them, after a promise that they would keep a man on guard to watch the river.

So now we waited on the brow of the hill, watching to see what would happen when the river threw off the heavy garments of winter and flung itself free from the icy restraints.

I smiled to myself. I felt all of us were just using this as an excuse to get away from the village and have a party on the hill. Some of us had even prepared picnic lunches for the occasion.

There was a happy hum all about me as people visited with one another. The shouts of the children rang out on the quiet of the day. They were thoroughly enjoying the outing.

It shows how short we are on entertainment, I said to myself, *when we will all walk two miles to a hill to watch river ice break up.*

And then there was a strange, eery hush. All heads turned toward the river, leaving sentences unfinished, hanging forgotten on the morning air.

I would never have believed that our quiet, placid river could react with such a wild, untamed frenzy, but as we watched she lifted her head with a defiance that both surprised and frightened me.

A low moan quickly turned into a thunderous roar, and then there was a cracking that shattered the air with its intensity. As the sound rent the stillness, huge blocks of ice were thrown many feet in the air and hurled forward. There was a shifting and grinding, and foam and angry waters began to whip the shores where the ice had been. I stared in silent amazement.

The waters and ice blocks rushed writhing and foaming as though intent on some evil, roaring out vengeful messages.

The turbulent waters rushed on to a sharp bend in the river. There they seemed to stop, struggling and lashing like some dying giant. And then a shout went up, and another followed, and soon people were milling all about me, crying out to one another in anguished tones. I could understand none of it. My eyes turned back to the river. The ice blocks were piling higher and higher, and behind them was a tumbling, twisting sea of troubled water.

I looked around me for Wynn. Then for Susie.

I spotted Susie with Kip in a group of village children. Their eyes too were turned to the bend in the river. Even as I watched, the water slowly slipped up the banks of the river and spilled out on either side, still gray and angry looking.

I saw Wynn then. He raised his hand to command the attention of the people. Slowly the group became quiet again, only the distant roaring of the river and the grinding and crunching of the ice breaking the silence.

"Women and children stay here," Wynn was calling over the noise.

I looked wildly about. Nimmie was moving quietly toward me.

"What does he mean?" I asked her, puzzled and frightened.

"The river," she said. I thought I detected fear in her voice. "It has jammed at the bend."

I turned to the river and swung quickly back to Nimmie.

I didn't have to ask my question.

"It did that one other year," Nimmie continued. "Everything in the village was lost."

"No," I almost screamed, my hands going to my face as I pictured our cozy home submerged under that icy flow.

Nimmie reached out a hand to me. It was then I realized that Susie was pressing her little body up against me. *Susie's mother is still in the cabin!* I thought wildly. She was not strong enough yet to make the pilgrimage to the bluff. With her were her twin babies, the boy and the girl, and the elderly couple who had been living with them.

My hands went down to pull Susie close. I forgot all about our cabin, Wynn's and mine, and the things in it that made it home to us. My concern was for Susie's family and the other people who might still remain in the village.

Men were running now, running toward the village. My eyes were huge as I realized that was a two-mile run. *How much time do they have?* And then I noticed that men were also running the other way—toward the jammed-up river.

"What—?" I began, and Nimmie answered, "They are going to try to break the jam."

"But how?" I stammered, and then I saw that Wynn was leading the runners toward the river.

"O God, no. Please, no," and I covered my face with my hands and sank down in a heap on the ground, pulling Susie down with me.

I began to shake uncontrollably. What could mere man do against the giant ice blocks? "O God. O God!" was all I could moan.

And then someone was patting my shoulder. I tried to pull myself together enough to respond. It was Susie. Her face too was white and her eyes wide with fear.

"We need to pray," she whispered. "We need to pray quick—before they get there. Before—" her chin was trembling. "I don't want another father killed by the ice," she continued, and I remembered hearing the story of how Susie's father had been dragged under the river's ice while trying to save his dog team and his winter's catch of furs so he could feed his family.

I pulled Susie to me. Sobs were shaking her now.

"Dear God," I implored desperately, "please, please turn them back!" Then more calmly, "Protect us, God. Protect each one of us. Protect the men who have gone to the river. Keep them safe, Lord. Be with Wynn. And be with the men who have gone to the village. May they get there in time to save the people. Amen."

I went to draw Susie to me, but she resisted. Instead, she began to pray in her own language. She implored the God who sent His Son Jesus, the same Jesus who made all things, to set free the river's waters so it would be able to continue on downstream and not be held back by the ice. She reminded God that Wynn would not lock children up—he just wanted to teach them not to be bad when they grew up, that was all. And then she told God that she loved Him, too, and would try her hardest, all her life, not to be bad, so that she'd never need to be locked up or sent away from heaven. She said "Amen" in English to close her prayer.

When Susie finished praying, I hated to open my eyes. Yet I had to see. Yes, there were the men still running down the long slope of the hill toward the river. The water was much higher and angrier now. It swirled and smashed and swung at the blocks of shifting ice. I was sure as I watched that they would never be able to do anything to free them. I prayed silently again that they would not try but would turn and run for safety before the river could sweep them away in its angry flood.

They were far enough away from us now that I could not pick out Wynn in the retreating figures. And then I saw an arm upraised and I knew it was Wynn's. He had gathered the men around and was giving them orders. It was the first I realized that many of the men were carrying their guns.

"They will fire rifle shots into the ice blocks," Nimmie was saying. And then she added, rather forlornly, I thought, "It has never worked, yet it's all there is to try."

They began to move on again. They were at the water's edge with the swirling waters all around them. As one, they lifted their rifles to their shoulders. There was deafening silence and then I heard Susie whisper, "Now, Jesus," and there was a sudden explosion. Ice flew hundreds of feet in the air, spewing out in every direction. For a few moments all was silent, and then a mighty cheer went up. The river was flowing again. It was still flooding the land beneath us, it was still raging and roaring, but there was movement downstream now. The river was free to move on.

I pulled Susie to me. She didn't appear to be one bit surprised. I held her close and rocked her back and forth, the tears, unheeded, pouring down my face.

"He did it, Susie!" I cried. "He did it."

People were beginning to move toward the village, many excited voices floating back to us on the breeze.

I stood up on shaky legs, drawing Susie up also.

"Come on, Susie," I said, hugging her to me, "let's go home now. Our village is safe. Let's go meet Wynn and we'll all go home together."

But Susie held back.

"What's the matter?" I asked her.

"You said," began Susie slowly, "you said we're s'posed to say thank you to Him."

Susie was so right, and so we did.

20
Changes

❖

AS WYNN HAD feared, the two down-river villages were flooded by the spring river waters. But because of the precautions taken in moving the people to higher ground, no lives and little property were lost. I think we all breathed easier when the flood waters finally receded and the river returned to its normal peaceful self.

As spring turned into summer, Susie's mother gained strength. She was now able to be outside at times, simply sitting in the sun. The twins were growing and becoming roly-poly and merry. Susie loved to play with them and often had one or the other in her arms or on her back. She continued to live with us, for her family's cabin was still crowded. The elderly woman, Too Many, remained to care for Maggie and the children.

Susie and I planted our garden and took great pleasure in watching the tender plants put forth their first two green leaves and then expand and grow as they drank in the summer sun. We pulled weeds and carried water when we felt that nature had not sent enough rain. The garden grew, and Susie asked nearly every day when we would have our first vegetables.

Nimmie's new baby was a healthy boy, and Ian's fatherly pride was felt all around the village. Nimmie looked pleased, too.

"Now I have both an herb-gatherer and a hunter," she told me, happiness making her face glow.

I suppose I envied Nimmie. I would have felt it even more if it had not been for Susie and the way she helped to fill my days.

I still visited her mother, Maggie, as often as I dared without making myself a real nuisance. I took her little things, chatted with her about her family, shared Susie's and my experiences, helped carry wood and water, but mostly I watched for every chance I had to tell her a little more about God and His love for her. Little by little I noticed sparks of interest in her.

Nimmie promised to help me. We prayed together for Susie's family; and Nimmie, too, made frequent calls, offering help and sharing little experiences about how God was with her each day. Nimmie watched for opportunities to assure Maggie that God was not only interested in the affairs of the white man, but that He loved Indian people, too.

We dismissed school classes the middle of June. The children were much too busy in the summer months to have time for study. I really was much too busy also. Wawasee still brought his drawings to show me and begged, with his eyes only, for another scribbler whenever he had filled the one he was working in.

Jim Buck did not come. He was being teased and bullied by the older boys in the settlement about his interest in school. I ached for Jim. He had a sharp mind that should be educated, but what would happen when school resumed? Would he be able to take the taunting and teasing of the others for the sake of learning more?

Wynn and I celebrated another anniversary. It seemed hard to believe that we had actually been married for two years. And yet, at the same time, I felt that the Elizabeth who walked the aisle of the little Calgary church on that day two years ago had been *so* young and naive. I had learned so much about life since that time.

Susie flitted through each summer day like a pretty little butterfly. She had outgrown her few dresses, and so I sewed her some more. I was careful to make them just like the dresses of the other children—no frills, no ribbons. I wanted so much to trim them up and make them feminine, like my niece Kathleen would be wearing, but for Susie's sake I did not. It wasn't that I feared Susie would not like the new attire. In fact, I was afraid she might like the frills too much and find it difficult to return to simpler clothing in the future.

But what of the future? The future looked bright. Maggie was much better, for which I was thankful, but certainly not well enough to care for herself and her family. I wondered secretly if I was also thankful for that, and hoped with all of my heart I wasn't that selfish.

Wynn took some longer trips to check on those who lived in his area of responsibility and yet were difficult to visit in the long, cold days of winter. When he went for overnight trips, I was even more thankful to have Susie with me. I didn't lie awake at nights worrying about Wynn and hearing strange noises around the house.

But just when I was feeling rather confident about the immediate future, my world came crashing down around me.

Susie had gone out to the garden to pick some lettuce for our lunch. I heard a shuffle at my door. At first I thought it must be Susie and Kip, and then I realized it was not the quick, easy movements which either the girl or the dog would be making. I turned from the tea I was brewing and looked toward the door.

It was the old woman, Too Many, who plodded in. She did not return my smile of greeting nor sit in the chair where she usually sat. Instead, she said slowly, brokenly, "Where Susie?"

I stopped and put down the teapot, fear filling my heart. Had something happened to Maggie?

I finally quieted my thudding heart enough to ask, "Is something wrong with Maggie?"

"Good," responded Too Many.

"The family?"

"Good."

I was relieved. So it wasn't some tragedy as I had feared. They probably wanted Susie to run a little errand.

"I'll send Susie down as soon as she comes in. She won't be long."

I wasn't sure how much Too Many understood. She knew very little English. I repeated the information as best as I could in her native language and with gestures, and she rose shakily to her feet and shuffled toward the door. As I watched her I wondered how the old lady could care for a sick woman, a set of twins, two lively boys and a senile elderly man.

Susie soon bounded in the door, Kip at her heels as always. Her face was flushed, her eyes shining.

"Know what?" she called to me as soon as she entered. "Soon we will have carrots. They are almost big enough now."

I looked at her, wondering if she was pulling up and replanting some of the vegetables again. She just couldn't resist seeing how big they were getting. Before I asked her, she looked at me, shaking her head.

"I didn't pull them up this time," she said. "I just scratched the dirt away from them, like this."

She showed me, with one wriggling finger, how she had taken her peek at nature's progress.

"Then I put the dirt right back again," she hastened to add.

I couldn't help but smile. I understood her impatience. I had been tempted to do the same thing myself.

"Hurry and wash, dear," I said to Susie. "Your mother wants to see you."

"Now?" asked Susie.

"Yes. I told Too Many that I would send you right away. I think you should eat first. They might have a job that will take you awhile, and you should have your dinner before you begin."

Susie ran to the basin, and I washed the lettuce and fixed our plates. It would be a hurried meal, but at least Susie wouldn't go to do her mother's bidding on an empty stomach.

We prayed together, ate our lunch, and then Susie was excused to run on home. Kip went to the door with her.

"I think you should leave Kip this time," I said. "He might just get in your way."

Both Kip and Susie looked at me with pleading eyes, but I held firm.

"You won't be long," I encouraged her.

Susie gave Kip a goodbye hug and promised him that she would be back soon. Then she skipped out the door, careful to close it behind her as she had been taught at our house, and Kip turned whining to his rug before the fireplace.

Susie was back even before I expected her. She entered the house, her small face blank. Without a word she went to her bed and began to spread out the small blanket that she had brought with her when she came.

"Why the long face?" I asked teasingly. "Are you afraid you are back so soon that I will ask you to help dry the dishes?" Susie did not especially like to dry the dishes. Washing the dishes was fun—one got to play in the warm, soapy water. Susie would gladly wash the same few dishes all afternoon.

I turned, expecting to see a smile flit across Susie's face at the teasing, but instead I saw a silent little girl carefully folding her few dresses and other garments. She was making a neat little stack in the middle of her blanket.

"What are you doing?" I asked. When there was no reply, I answered for myself. "Is your mother now able to care for the family? Is Too Many going home?"

Susie shook her head.

"We go," she said simply, much like she would have said before she came to live with us and developed such good command of the English language.

"Go?" I echoed. "Go where?"

"To big village—cross the river."

"What?" I could only stand and stare, hoping I had not heard her correctly.

"Big village. They come in wagon—get us all. Take us to new home."

"There must be some mistake," I said, wiping my wet hands on my apron as I took it off and tossed it from me.

"No," answered Susie in a resigned little voice.

I didn't wait to hear more. I started for the settlement and the cabin across the little clearing, hoping to discover that Susie was mistaken. Susie was right. There was a wagon standing in front of her house. Two men were busy loading the few cooking pots and blankets belonging to the household.

Maggie sat in her chair watching, a smile on her face.

"See," she said in her own language when she saw me, "it worked. I prayed, they come. My brothers come to get me and my family, take us home to Father's house in big village."

It was plain to see that Maggie was rejoicing in the fact of the move. *But what about Susie? What about me?* I wasn't prepared to give her up yet. And Wynn? *Wynn is away. He won't even get to tell her goodbye.* My frantic thoughts tumbled over one another. Who would bring his slippers? Who would listen to his story? I wanted to argue with Maggie but there was nothing for me to say. Instead I said, "I'll be praying for you, Maggie. For you and each of your family."

Her eyes sparkled.

"They have church in big village," she told me. "He said so." She nodded her head at one of the men who was busy carrying out the last of the cooking pots. They were almost ready to go.

"I'll go get Susie," I said numbly, and hurried away.

Susie did not cry. Perhaps it would have been better for us both if she had. She just looked at me with those dark, soulful eyes. The pain and confusion nearly broke my heart. I gathered her to me. "I'm going to miss you, Susie, so very much. I love you. Oh, I—" I couldn't go on. I knew I only was making it harder for both of us. "They are waiting," I finally managed.

Oh, why isn't Wynn here? Perhaps he could stop them—at least stall them while we sorted it all out. But Wynn was not with us, and he could have done nothing if he had been, my common sense told me.

Kip whined. I know he sensed something was not right. Susie reached out a hand to him and pulled him close, one fist buried in his deep fur coat, her other clasping tightly the little bundle of all her things. Still she did not cry. She held Kip for a moment and then turned and put her arms around my neck. She said nothing, just held me, and then she turned to the door.

She was about to close it quietly when she thought of something. She took one step back toward me, her eyes big and questioning.

"I took the dresses—was that steal?"

"No, no of course not. I made them for you."

She turned again to go, and then seemed to feel I needed to know something else.

She took a deep breath, looked into my eyes, then lowered them.

"I almost steal," she confessed. "When you gone, I almost put the book in my pack."

Her head came up and she looked at me again.

"Mr. Wynn wouldn't put children in jail. He wouldn't put me in jail. But Jesus—He would have been sad. He doesn't want stealers in heaven—so I left the book."

She turned to go.

"Susie, wait!" I cried, running to my little stack of books. I chose the three Susie loved the best.

"I want you to take these," I said as I hastened to shove them into an open corner of her little pack. "I want you to keep on reading. To think of us as you read the stories. To remember all the good times we had here."

Her eyes looked misty then. I thought the tears might spill over, but they didn't. "I remember," she nodded.

She was gone then, the door closing softly behind her. Then it opened again, just a crack and a small dark head leaned back into the room.

"I forgot thanks," she said humbly, and the door closed again.

I stood looking at the door. It didn't reopen. Kip whimpered and brushed against me. He wanted to go with Susie, and for one moment I was tempted to open the door and send him, to send the Silver One to take care of her, but reason kept me from doing so.

And then I let the hot tears stream down my face. She was gone. Just like that, our little Susie. Gone with her own people, back to her own world. Would she have a chance to be all the things I had dreamed for her? Would she ever be able to stand in front of a classroom? Would she be properly cared for? Would she have a chance to grow in her Christian faith? All these questions and more pounded in my brain, but all I could manage as I cried for Susie was, "She won't even get to eat her carrots!"

21
Reminders

THE SILENCE ROARED all around me, deafening in its finality. Day after day I tried to adjust to being without Susie. Wynn eventually returned. He understood how I felt and held me as I cried. I believe he shed a few tears too over the loss of the little girl.

"We knew we'd have to give her up," he reminded me and himself.

I sniffed noisily. "Yes, give her up, but not so much 'up.' "

Wynn looked at me questioningly.

"I thought Susie would go back to her home here," I maintained. "I never dreamed that Maggie would move her away where we'll probably never see her again. I thought—I thought she'd just return home and she could still visit now and then, and I'd see her about the village, and she'd still come to school, and we'd work in the garden together, and—"

Wynn stopped me.

"We all thought that," he affirmed. "No one knew that Maggie had close family in the other village." He waited for a moment and then went on. "This is better for Maggie and her family. You know that, Elizabeth? They can be properly cared for now. Perhaps Maggie can regain her strength. Too Many tried hard, but she was an old woman. She had too much to do and too little strength to do it. I don't think they ate well. I—"

But this time I stopped Wynn.

"I know all that. I'm not sorry for Maggie—or—or for her family. It is best for her—and I've prayed—many times, for what was best. For Susie, too, I—I want what's best. I'm not crying about that. I'm crying about me," and the tears gushed out again.

At last Wynn got me comforted to the point where I could function, but I missed Susie dreadfully.

When the house was silent beyond my endurance, I fled to the garden. It was growing well. Susie would have been proud of her little patch. In spite of the attacks of mosquitoes and blackflies, I worked at pulling all the weeds. Then when I could stand the flies no more, I returned to the sanctuary of my quiet house.

Kip missed Susie, too. He seemed to be watching and listening constantly, his head cocked to one side, his ears thrust forward and straining. But Susie did not come.

Now the leaves went tumbling on the wind, wild geese honking as they passed overhead. I took in all of the produce from our garden. I gathered the produce from Susie's garden as well, sharing her vegetables with the people I knew to be her special friends. The men of the village prepared to leave for the traplines at the first fall of snow. I clanged the big bell and classes began again. This time five students came. The new interest was due to Susie's summer class sessions of play, I was sure.

We fell into a routine, and I was thankful for all the activities which filled my days. Still I thought about Susie. I thought about Maggie. Had I done enough? Said enough? Did Susie know how a Christian was to live out her faith? Did Maggie really understand about God's plan of salvation? Had I made it plain that it was for her, too? Had I really done what I could have, *should have*, done? Nagging thoughts picked away at me. I prayed and prayed for the family.

And then one day as I was praying, God spoke to my heart.

"Do you think I am unaware of where they are?" He seemed to gently say. "Do you think I have deserted them? Don't you think that I care, that my love is certainly as strong as yours? And don't you know that I, through my Holy Spirit, can go on talking to them, even in your absence?"

I felt humbled. Of course I knew all that. Maggie's salvation did not depend upon me. Susie's nurture did not depend on me. It had depended on God all along. Where they lived really had nothing to do with it. Now I committed them totally to God and let the guilt and fear slip from my shoulders.

I was still lonely, but the pain around my heart had eased. I visited Nimmie and some of the other women a little oftener to help fill the hours. Many of them began to drop in for tea again. Even though the fall days seemed to trudge along slowly, the calendar showed that our world was indeed continuing on.

In the midst of one of our first winter flurries, two Indian men on horseback approached our small cabin. Kip had alerted me, and I watched them as they came. One of the men dropped down from his horse, handed the reins to the other, and walked up our path to the door.

He bumped at the door rather than knocking, which sent Kip into a frenzy that I stopped by commanding him to go quietly to his corner. When I opened the door, the man reached into his leather jacket and withdrew a folded sheet of paper. He said not a word, just handed it to me, turned on his heel and went back to swing onto the back of his horse. Mystified, I watched them ride away.

The cold wind blew snow into the cabin as I stood there with the door open. Kip whined and I was jerked back to the paper I held in my hand.

I closed the door and went to the table, looking at the unfamiliar thing I held. I finally found my senses and spread it out on the table. It was a letter, just a simple letter written on a sheet torn from a child's work scribbler. There was no salutation at the top. It began with the message. I flipped it over and looked at the back side. It was signed "Susie."

My heart began to beat faster as I read. Susie's printing had improved;

she had not forgotten what she had been taught. Hungrily I searched each word, each line.

"How are you. I am good. My mother is good two. We have a church here. I go. My mother gos two. We like it. We have a school here. Many boys and girls go. The teacher is nice, but not as nice as you. My mother feels better she says to say thank you. She didn't know before to say that. I miss you and Kip and Mr. Wynn. Did my garden grow okay. Susie."

I read the letter three times before I let the tears fall. She was fine! Our Susie was fine! She was in school, and in church, too. A little voice within me seemed to say, "See, I am caring for her," and I bowed my head in thankfulness to acknowledge that care.

Though the winter storm seemed to intensify, rattling the windows in its fury, it could not bother me. I felt warm and content. God was taking good care of our Susie.

22
Sickness

CHRISTMAS CAME, a cold stormy day, and Wynn and I stayed indoors beside the fireplace, hoping he wouldn't be called out for some emergency. He wasn't, and we were thankful.

The next day was just as cold but this time Wynn was called upon. An elderly man, trying to gather wood in the storm, had fallen, breaking his hip. There was nothing much Wynn could do except give him something for the pain and try to make him as comfortable as possible.

Wynn talked to the family about trying to get the man out to the Edmonton hospital, but they would not even consider it. I fought my way through the storm with a pail of hot soup, which they seemed to appreciate.

Since I was out and already in the settlement, I decided to call on Nimmie. She was busy with her two little ones. Nonita, a cheerful little girl with an angel face that broke easily into a grin, was walking and trying to converse now.

Ian junior, whom they called Sonny, was not as cheerful nor as chubby. He had been a fussy baby from the first and did not seem to gain weight as he should. He was crying now as I was welcomed into Nimmie's home. Nimmie did most of her work with the baby cradled on her back or held in her arms.

Nimmie's face brightened when she saw me. "Whatever are you doing out in this weather, Elizabeth?" she wanted to know.

"I came to bring some soup to the LeMores, so I decided as long as I was out I would stop by."

"I'm so glad you did," said Nimmie. "I needed someone to talk to." She smiled a bit ruefully and passed me the fussing Sonny.

"He has been so cranky. I think he must be cutting teeth. Nonita gave us no trouble. Even when she cut her teeth. She was such a contented baby, but sometimes I just don't know what to do with this one."

I walked the floor, patting his back and bouncing him up and down. He looked exhausted, but he couldn't seem to settle down to sleep. Nonita wanted her share of attention and ran to get her favorite book to show me the pictures. She jabbered as she pointed and I tried to reply as I walked back and forth across the wooden floor.

I had just gotten the baby to sleep when Nimmie said tea was ready. I didn't dare try to lay the baby down for fear he would waken, so I held him up against me and drank my tea with him in my arms.

Nimmie looked pale. I asked if she was feeling ill, and she just smiled a weak smile.

"Again?" I said in astonishment.

She only nodded her head.

Little Nonita tried to crawl up onto her mother's lap and Nimmie slid back her chair so she could lift the girl.

"I love my babies," Nimmie said, "and I am glad that another one is on the way, only this time I have been feeling so sick. I hope it passes soon. It is hard for me to care for the two of them when I feel as I do. Especially with the baby so fussy."

I felt sorry for Nimmie. I would have offered to take the baby home with me for a few days had Nimmie not been nursing him. "I could take Nonita if that would help," I offered.

"She's no trouble," Nimmie answered, cuddling the little girl she held.

"I'll come over and give you a hand here," I decided.

And so through the wintry months of January and February, I trudged off to Nimmie's almost every day where I helped with laundry, dishes and baby care.

On many days Nimmie was forced to stay in bed. She usually took the baby Sonny with her; cuddled up against her, he seemed to rest better. While they slept I did Nimmie's work and played with Nonita. What a little dear she was, and I found myself eager to get to Nimmie's each day just so I could spend time with the child.

At our supper table I shared with Wynn all of the funny things she said and did that day. We laughed about them together.

Being with Nimmie's babies did not lessen my ache for a child of my own but, rather, increased it. Each day I would petition God's throne for the child I still did not have. My heart grew heavier and heavier. It seemed I had been praying for a baby forever, and God still had not heard my prayer.

The first of March ushered in a terrible storm. The blizzard raged around us and Wynn did not leave the cabin. One could not see even a few feet in front of one's face.

I worried about Nimmie. Wynn reminded me that Ian senior would not be needed to tend the store on such a day, and he would be home to help Nimmie with the children. Although I knew Wynn was right, yet I missed my daily trip over to Nimmie's. Would Nonita be wondering where Aunt Beth was?

The storm continued for four days. I was sure we would be buried alive by the snow before it ended. What about those who had to get their wood supply daily? What would they be doing to keep warm? Wynn was concerned, too, and in spite of the weather he decided to see how people in the village were faring.

I hated to see him go. It was so nasty out and I feared he might lose his way in the storm. He took Kip, fastening a leash to his collar. He also took his rifle; he might have to fire some shots in the air, and I would need to reply with his lighter gun if he should get confused in his directions by the storm.

It seemed forever before Wynn was back. The news from the village was not good. Many people lay huddled together under all the furs and blankets they owned. Two elderly women had already died from exposure. In some cabins they had not been able to keep the fires going, and without fires there was no food, so those who were not well were getting even weaker.

Wynn said he was going to hitch up his dog team to haul wood to the homes where it was needed and asked me if I would take my largest pot and make up some stew or soup to be taken to the hungry.

I hastened to comply, my fears for Wynn's safety uppermost in my mind. It was risky working out in such weather. We both knew it, but under the circumstances it was the only thing that could be done.

It wasn't long until I heard Wynn and the complaining dogs outside our cabin. I knew Wynn was taking from our winter's wood supply to build fires in some of the other homes. If only the Indian people could be convinced to bring in a wood supply each fall and stack it by their doors. To them that was unnecessary work. The wood was always right there in the nearby thicket, they reasoned. I added some more sticks to my own fire so the stew would cook more quickly.

I bundled up and went with Wynn. It took me awhile to convince him I should, but at last he conceded. We carried the stew pot between us.

Wynn was right. Some of the people were desperate. While Wynn got the fire going in each cabin, I dished out some of the stew into a pot in the home and put it over the fire to keep hot. As soon as the chill was off the cabin, the people would crawl from under their blankets and sit around the fire to eat.

As we moved from cabin to cabin, we were thankful for each one in which the people had been able to care for themselves. When our rounds were over, Wynn took me back home and then he set off again. He still had the two bodies to care for. As usual in our northern winters, they couldn't be buried properly till spring.

The storm finally ended and I breathed a sigh of relief, but it wasn't to be for long. With many people in a weakened condition, sickness hit the village. For many days and nights, Wynn worked almost around the clock. He gave out all the medicine he had and sent a runner out with an emergency call for more.

I made soup and stew, kettle by kettle, and we carried it to those who could not manage by themselves. We spoon-fed those too weak to eat alone. The homes were a nightmare of offensive odors, for there were no sanitation facilities and it was too cold, and the people too weak, to go outdoors.

I had to stop, pray and steel myself before entering many of the cabins. It was impossible to clean them up, though we did try, but illness soon had them in the same condition again. I was often glad for the mask Wynn insisted I wear over my mouth and nose. Though it did not shut out all the smell, it helped enough that I could function without getting sick.

The few who remained healthy helped us care for the sick. I don't know what we would have done without Ian, our faithful standby. He was always there, carrying wood and water and bringing food supplies from his store. And then Nimmie and her family became sick as well, and Ian was needed at home.

I called on Nimmie often. She was so sick I feared we would lose her. She did miscarry the baby she was carrying, but she fought tenaciously for her own life. Both the children were sick. I worried about the weak and sickly little Sonny. Surely his frail little body would not stand this additional illness.

But, strangely, it was darling little Nonita we lost. I would have cried for days had I not been needed so desperately. As it was I could only ache. *Poor Nimmie's little herb-gatherer, her little sunshine, is gone.*

When the sickness was finally conquered, the village had lost nine of its members. The rest of us were so exhausted, so empty, that we could hardly mourn. The bodies were all wrapped and placed in a shed belonging to the trading post—all except little Nonita. Ian spent many hours fashioning a tiny casket for her to rest in. Again, we would need to wait for spring before the burying could take place.

With heavy hearts we tried to strengthen one another. Nimmie valiantly braved her daily chores, but there was an emptiness in the cabin. She had looked forward to a family of three children, but she now had only one. Little Nonita's laughter and chatter was only a memory. I think Nimmie was glad even for Sonny's fussing. It gave her a good excuse to constantly hold him. Nimmie greatly needed her arms full during those difficult days.

23
Summer of 'Fourteen

WHEN SPRING CAME that year, I greeted the new life like old friends—tiny leaves, the flights of birds. I began to make plans for my garden.

Our classes of the year had been interrupted by the storm and then by the sickness. We missed nearly three months that should have been spent on the books. So we continued our studies a little longer than we normally would have. The village people agreed to it, I believe, out of gratitude to me. I tried not to take advantage of their goodwill and promised I would dismiss the children as soon as I saw that they were needed at home.

And so it was mid-July before we closed our school for the summer. I was ready for the break, too. With classes each morning, helping Nimmie and her little ones each afternoon in January and February, caring for the sick villagers for many weeks following that, and then trying to catch up with the schoolwork we had missed, I was exhausted. No wonder I was not expecting a baby, I told myself. My body was just too tired. In spite of my reasoning, my lack of motherhood still weighed heavily upon me.

I tried hard not to let my feelings show, but it wasn't easy, especially when I walked through the village and saw so many women who were with child. Why was it that I seemed to be the only one in the settlement who could not conceive?

One beautiful warm summer day, I decided I would fix a picnic lunch and take Kip for a long walk on the riverbank. Wynn was out on patrol and I was restless and lonely. I had just made up my sandwiches when there was a light rap on my door. Nimmie entered, her eyes shining, her cheeks flushed. She hadn't looked that well or that happy for months.

"Guess what," she said excitedly, but didn't give me any time for a guess, "we're going to have another baby!"

I was happy for Nimmie, really I was, but at the same time my own heart felt a pang of disappointment. Here it was again! I was called on to share the happiness of another when she was given the very thing I longed for so desperately.

I managed a smile and gave Nimmie a hug. I set aside my sandwiches and went to fix us some tea.

"I can't stay," stated Nimmie. "I left Sonny with Ian. The little rascal will be pulling things off the shelves. He's starting to walk now and is into everything. But I just couldn't wait to tell you. I know you grieved for Nonita almost as much as I did. It was so hard to lose her, Elizabeth. I thought I just wouldn't be able to bear it. And now God is sending me another child! I can hardly wait. This baby won't take Nonita's place, but it will fill a big emptiness in my heart."

It was the first Nimmie had really talked to me about losing Nonita. I knew that her heart ached, that she grieved. But she tried so hard to be brave. And now, as she said, the emptiness was about to be filled.

My emptiness remained. I turned so that Nimmie would not spot my brimming eyes and trembling lips.

"Are you sure you can't stay for tea?" I finally managed.

"I've got to get back."

She crossed the room to give me another hug, and I smiled and told her how happy I was for her, and then she was gone.

I didn't go for the picnic and walk after all. Instead, when Nimmie left I went to my bedroom. I cried for a long time before I was able to focus my thoughts and form words into prayer. My soul was still heavy when I finally pulled myself from the bed and went to wash my puffy face.

I took Kip then and went to the garden. I had just weeded the few weeds left in the garden, but I searched on my knees for any strays and pulled them with a vengeance.

When I returned to the house I still had not recovered from the heavy feeling in my heart. I prepared the same old supper meal I had been preparing for an eternity, it seemed. The same old blackflies and mosquitoes managed to find their way through any tiny chink in the cabin to plague me. The sunny day had turned cloudy and threatened rain. Wynn was late for supper and the meal sat at the back of the stove getting dry and disgusting. I was fighting hard to keep my emotions under control.

When Wynn did get home and stopped to rough-house with Kip and then came to greet me, I was rather distant and unresponsive.

"Something wrong?" he asked me, and I struck out at the first thing that came to my mind.

"How come the dog comes first?"

Wynn looked puzzled. "What do you mean?" he asked me. "When has the dog ever come first?"

"Now! Always! You always greet him before you kiss me."

It was a very silly thing to say. It had never even occurred to me before, but in my present state it loomed like a thundercloud.

Wynn took a moment to answer. Then he said, very softly and not accusingly at all, "That's because I can't get past him until I do. He's always right there at the door—"

I cut in, "And I'm not—is that what you're saying? The dog thinks more of you than I do?"

There was pain in Wynn's eyes but he was not to be baited.

"I'm sorry to be late, Elizabeth. I know it makes things hard for you."

I whirled around. "Do you think I care for a moment how hard and dry these old potatoes and carrots get? Or how cold and—and?" I dissolved in tears, turned from Wynn and ran to the bedroom.

I heard Wynn dishing up his own supper. I heard Kip coaxing for a sample of his food and Wynn telling him not to beg at the table. I heard Kip lower his body to his rug in front of the fire. Then I heard Wynn clear the table and quietly wash up the dishes. Still he did not come to me. Instead he took Kip for a walk.

They returned and I heard the complaint of the overstuffed chair as Wynn lowered himself into it. I heard his boots drop softly to the floor, one, two, and I knew Wynn hoped to be home for the night.

He'll come for his slippers now, I thought, and I turned my face to the wall and buried my head in my arms.

Wynn did come to the bedroom, but he did not bother with his slippers. Instead, he took me in his arms and held me close. He made no comment and asked no questions; he just held me and let me cry.

At last I was all cried out. Wynn kissed my tear-stained face.

"Want to talk about it?"

"It was silly," I murmured into his shoulder. "I really don't care if Kip—"

"No, not that. About what's *really* bothering you."

I played for time.

"The supper?" I questioned.

"Elizabeth," said Wynn, "I'm sorry about the dog; I'm sorry I was late for supper. But I don't think that is the real problem here. Something has been bothering you for days. I was hoping you would choose to share it with me, but you haven't. Can we talk about it?"

So it had shown.

"I guess the winter was rather tough—"

Wynn waited for me to go on but I didn't. Finally he prompted me.

"Are you saying you need a break?"

"Sort of . . . I—"

The silence between us seemed endless. Then Wynn spoke slowly, deliberately, "I can understand that, Elizabeth. I will see what I can do."

I jerked upright. "About what?" I demanded.

"About getting you out—back to Calgary for a—"

"I don't want to go back to Calgary. Whatever made you think—?"

"Well, Toronto then."

"Wynn, I don't want to go out—anywhere. That's not the problem."

"It's not?"

Poor Wynn. I had him totally confused. I looked at his anxious face, shaking my head slowly back and forth.

"Then what is the problem?" he asked.

"A baby."

"A baby? You mean you are going to have a baby?"

"No!" I cried, and began weeping again. *"That's* the problem. I want a baby—so much—we have been married for three years, and I still—" I broke off the sentence and threw myself into his arms, weeping uncontrollably.

We spent a long time talking and praying together that night. Wynn wanted a family, too. He had prayed about it many times. He was sure I would make a great mother, and every time he watched me with a child he felt sorrow that it was not our child I was holding.

"I still think you should get out for a bit," he told me. "You need to get to a doctor in the city. Who knows—I'll see what I can do."

"Wynn," I said, "I don't want to travel out with just anyone, not if you can't go too."

"I wouldn't send you with just anyone," said Wynn. "It might take a while to make the arrangements, but I'll work on it. Now and then Mounted Police personnel go through the area, or nearby. I'll see what I can find out."

My heart was really not that much lighter, but it did help to have shared my pain with Wynn. He'd be working on it. Perhaps the answer was near at hand.

24
Waiting

❖

IT SEEMED TO me that fall came awfully early that year, but perhaps this was because I knew I would not be going out to Calgary yet.
Winter could come quickly to the land and stay for a long time, and Wynn
and I had already decided that once there was a chance of my being
caught in a winter storm when trying to get back to the settlement, I
would not go. Now I would wait for spring and another year.

Heaviness hung about me as I gathered my garden vegetables and
started the school classes again.

There were seven students now who were quite faithful. Wawasee still
came—so that he could draw, but he now brought the younger members
of the family, too. Jim Buck, my star pupil, rarely missed. Even teasing
by the other boys did not keep him away. Two girls and a boy joined
them. It really did seem like a school. They were learning well, and I was
proud of them. As we got into the routine again, my despondency began
to lift. My concern now was lack of material to take the youngsters further. I had to devise and make-do. Wawasee's drawing skills were a big
help to me.

I thought of Susie. I still missed her. News from her village told us that
she and her family were doing well. Her mother was feeling much better
and was able to care for her own family. I was pleased for them.

The arrival of Ian's fall supply train created great excitement and anticipation, especially for Wynn and me. It meant letters and news from
the outside world.

The news this year was not all good. The world was at war. This was
hard for us to believe, tucked away as we were in our isolation. We pored
over all the outdated papers that had been sent to us and tried to fit together the broken pieces of the world-affairs puzzle.

The war was across the great ocean and shouldn't have involved us,
yet in one sense it did, for mankind cannot suffer anywhere without it
bringing sorrow to other hearts. But the war was ours in another sense,
too. Great Britain had joined the fight, and so would Canada if her troops
were needed.

I thought of my young brother Matthew and prayed the war would
end quickly. He was almost old enough to join, and I feared he might
consider it if the fighting continued.

Most of the personal news was good. Julie was to be married—no, not the young officer with the Force; he had only been a friend. A young Calgary minister had won her hand and heart. Page after page was filled with her detailed description and her love and admiration for him. I was disappointed that I would miss Julie's special occasion but I was so happy for her.

Jon and Mary's family were all well and happy and growing steadily. Kathleen wrote a letter all by herself, telling me of her interests at school and her new cat, Bubbles. William, now a teenager, was a sports man, his favorite being football. Sarah, too, had grown up, proving to be quite a little seamstress under Mary's skilled tutelage. She was also studying the violin. "Baby Elizabeth" was almost old enough to begin school, and was constantly reminding the family that she was not a baby anymore.

Wynn's mother had not been well. I saw the worry mirrored in Wynn's eyes as he read the paragraph. However, Mary was quick to add, she did seem to be much better than she had been.

The wagon trains with the winter supplies and the mail had hardly been unloaded when winter sailed in from the Northwest. We all settled in, knowing that life would not be easy for the next several months. The men left for the traplines, the women took up their sewing, and the children played as they could between their duties of carrying wood and water. My students were not exempt. They too had responsibilities that must be attended to as soon as morning class was over. Therefore I never assigned homework of any kind. Our few hours together in the morning would be all the studying they would have.

Christmas, for a change, was a beautiful day. The temperature was cold, but the wind was not blowing and the sky was clear. We decided to go for a walk in the snow. Kip blocked the door, his tail wagging furiously as soon as he sensed that something out of the ordinary was happening. He wanted to be sure he would not be left behind.

I did not pack a lunch. We had no way to keep it from freezing, and on such a chilly day a frozen sandwich would not be too enjoyable.

We bundled up against the cold and laced on our snowshoes. I'm sure every member of our small village would have thought us extremely foolish to be setting off through the deep snow when we did not even need fuel or water.

It was a beautiful walk. We saw several deer and admired their gracefulness. We did not need the meat, so they were in no danger from us. The beaver pond was almost totally iced over except for a small hole they somehow kept open. We did not see the beavers but it was obvious they had been around recently. Some young poplars were newly cut and the strange tracks, with the dragging tail, were clear in the fresh snow.

We could tell it was getting chillier by the time we returned to the cabin. The warmth from the fires felt good as we removed our heavy outer things. I fixed us some hot chocolate and sandwiches. Then we curled up on the rug before the fire and read to one another.

It was an enjoyable Christmas Day. Then I thought of the pleasure of having a little one sitting between us, but I pushed the thought aside. I would not let it spoil our time together. I'd try to be patient as I waited. It wouldn't be long until spring and then Wynn could start trying to make arrangements for me to see a doctor in the city.

One blustery March afternoon I welcomed Little Deer in for tea. She had not been over for some time, and when I saw her I understood why. She was large with child. Though she did not say so, restlessness and boredom with the waiting had driven her from her cabin. We talked in her native dialect—fortunately for me, fairly simple in structure. Now and then I still needed to search for a word, but I could converse quite freely with the women.

"How soon—your baby?" I asked her.

"Soon now—too long already," was her answer.

She sipped her tea.

"How many now?" I asked.

She held up her fingers, like a child. "This makes five—two gone, two stay, and this."

I understood. She had lost two children, had two at home and this would make three.

"I'm happy for you," I said, smiling.

She looked a bit doubtful. "You like babies?" she asked.

"I love babies," I was quick to respond.

"Then why you not have some?" The question was abrupt, direct, and Little Deer's black eyes searched my face.

Panicked, I stammered and searched for words. How could I answer her? What were the Indian words to tell her that God had not seen fit to bless me with a child—yet? That I needed to see the city doctor to find out what was wrong. What should I do? I was still trying to sort it all out when Little Deer spoke again.

"When we do not have a baby, we go to Big Woman for good medicine. It make baby come."

My eyes must have opened wide and my mouth dropped open. Did the Indian people really have medicine to help with a pregnancy?

"Does—does it really work?" I asked, forgetting myself and switching to English, then having to repeat it in Little Deer's language.

"Good," she said with emphasis. "It work good. You get the medicine, pay Big Woman, you have a baby. Like that." She gave a little wave of her hand to show just how easy it really was.

My head was spinning. Surely—surely, there wouldn't be any harm in paying Big Woman for a little medicine. If it didn't work I wouldn't be any worse off than I was now. It was likely some special herb. The Indian people knew of many good herbs to help all kinds of things. I would ask Nimmie.

Now I was anxious for Little Deer to finish her tea and depart for home. I wanted to rush right down to Nimmie's to find out about Big Woman's special medicine. When I finally was able to get to the trading post, I tried hard not to be too eager. Very casually, I thought, I led the conversation around to the herbs of the Indian people, of which Nimmie was very knowledgeable. Then I said, as though it was of no special import, "Little Deer was in for tea this afternoon, and she said that Big Woman even has a medicine to help women conceive."

I waited, my heart thumping. Nimmie made no response.

"Is it true?" I prompted her.

"Partly," said Nimmie.

"What do you mean, partly?"

"There's a little ceremony that goes with it."

"What kind of a ceremony?"

"It's a little song, or chant."

"Do you know the words?"

"I don't think anyone but Big Woman knows the words."

I wanted to ask more, but just then Sonny pulled the dish of cookies onto the floor before either of us could make a grab for it. Nimmie sat him in the corner and was cleaning up the mess when a strange look came over her face.

"What is it?" I asked, worried that she might have hurt herself in some way.

She straightened slowly.

"They have been coming and going since noon. I think that it is time, Elizabeth."

I didn't stop to ask her more but ran through the side door into the store. Ian went to get the midwife, and I ran back to assist Nimmie into bed.

"I'll take Sonny home with me," I assured her. "Just as soon as Ian and the midwife get here."

She was one of the two in the village. When she arrived with Ian, I recognized her at once as Big Woman. She took over with a great deal of authority and assurance. I watched her as she set about making Nimmie comfortable. While she worked she talked to Nimmie in a soothing sing-songy voice. Was this what Nimmie meant by a chant? Her old face, lined with wrinkles, seemed to be void of all expression.

I bundled up the small Sonny and bid Nimmie goodbye. I hoped it would not be long until we heard good news. I thought Nimmie was probably hoping for another little herb-gatherer, though she had not said.

We had finished our supper when Ian came for Sonny, his face broad with a grin.

"Another boy," he beamed. "Alexander." And I wondered if Nimmie shared his great joy. Then I decided that she certainly would. She would welcome whom God chose to send.

How I envied Nimmie with her new son. There hadn't been a chance to ask her if she had ever tried any of Big Woman's medicine in her long years of waiting for a child. I wanted to ask her, yet I was hesitant.

Something about the whole idea troubled me. Yet what harm could it possibly do?

25
Temptation

THROUGH THE FOLLOWING days I continued to think about Big Woman and her medicine. Wouldn't it be wonderful if I could find help right here in the village and not need to travel way to Calgary, leaving Wynn behind? I wanted to talk to Wynn about it, but something I couldn't identify always held me back. It seemed so reasonable to go to see Big Woman. Yet something made me uneasy whenever I made up my mind to go.

I visited Nimmie and her new baby frequently. He was a lovely, healthy boy and seemed to have grown each time I went to see him. Alexander was a contented baby with a chubby little face and dimples. His dark eyes watched your face and his small fists knotted themselves at the front of your gown. I loved him, almost like he was my own.

I held him and thought of the sweet little Nonita and my heart ached. Was it possible that in the days ahead fever again might strike the village and this one, too, would be taken? *Does Nimmie ever think these thoughts?* I wondered. *Maybe I should be glad that I've never had a child.* I didn't think I could stand to have one and then lose it. I couldn't imagine anything harder to bear.

But Nimmie made no reference to fear. Daily she thanked God for her new baby and for the fact that Sonny was healthier than before. He still was small for his age and seemingly fragile, but he was active, and he was not the fussy baby he had been.

I never did find the courage to ask Nimmie if she had been to see Big Woman. It seemed too private a thing for me to ask.

I did ask Nimmie what she thought of Big Woman as a midwife.

"I have told Ian that I would prefer Kantook, but if she is busy, Big Woman is fine."

I later found out that when Ian had gone looking for Kantook, she was already busy delivering Little Deer's child, a boy, too. So two new braves were added to the village that evening.

Nimmie's answer had not really told me what I had wanted to know, so I pried a little further.

"In what way is Kantook better?"

"I didn't say she was better," said Nimmie.

"Then what did you mean?"

"I really don't know how to explain it to you," said Nimmie. "I guess one could say that Big Woman is the 'old,' Kantook is the 'new.'"

It sounded reasonable enough, but I still didn't know what Nimmie meant by it.

With the coming of spring, I knew Wynn would be searching for a way to get me out to Calgary. If I was really serious about seeing Big Woman, I would need to do something quickly.

I thought of just getting up my nerve and going on my own, without even mentioning the fact to Wynn. Then if Big Woman's medicine did not work, I would be the only disappointed one. A nagging little voice inside told me that would not be right. Wynn should know what I was planning. I broached the subject one night after we had retired. I found it easier to express myself in the dark, when Wynn could not study my face.

"Little Deer was over for tea one day a while back," I began, "and happened to mention that there is a woman in the village who has special herbs to help one to—to—" I faltered some. I wasn't sure just how to go on. "For those who do not have children," I finally said.

Wynn made no reply, though I knew he was carefully listening to every word I said.

"She said she has helped women here in the village."

"Who is it—this woman?" asked Wynn.

"She's one of the midwives."

Before I could even name her, Wynn said, "Big Woman?"

"Yes. You knew about it?"

"No, but I'm not surprised."

"What do you mean?"

"Big Woman will promise anything for a little money."

I was a bit put out with Wynn. Didn't he think a baby was worth a little money?

"City doctors want money, too," I reminded him.

"But they're not witch doctors," Wynn stated simply.

"Big Woman is a witch doctor?" I was astounded.

"Hadn't you heard? She practices all kinds of witchcraft when she has opportunity. We try to discourage it, but we can't control it altogether."

I sank back against my pillow. In my desperation I had nearly consulted a witch doctor. I had rationalized that a little chant could do no harm. Yet I knew with all my heart that any kind of witchcraft or sorcery was wrong. No wonder I had felt uneasy! And then, much to my dismay, I realized that in the days and weeks I had considered going to see Big Woman, I had not once prayed about it, asking God what He would direct me to do.

If I had prayed, if I had just prayed, I would have known. Yet even in my ignorance and my own waywardness, God had protected me from going.

I humbly closed my eyes and offered up a contrite prayer. I would not try to take matters in my own hands from now on. I would leave it to God. And if I was to go out to see a proper doctor, I would trust Wynn to make the arrangements.

And then I poured out the whole story to Wynn, telling him about my desperation, my temptation, my holding back, and now my deep thankfulness for being kept from perhaps bringing into our home a child who had been conceived through witchcraft.

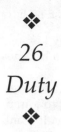

26
Duty

SPRING WAS SLOW in coming. Just when I was beginning to hope, another storm would strike. The sun made no visible headway on the hip-deep snowdrifts, and the icicles on the eave troughs grew and grew.

I suppose I was more anxious for spring than ever, once the idea of going "out" had taken root. I also was looking forward to seeing family and friends again. So I chafed with each new flurry that came our way.

One afternoon, just as another swirl of snow began to cover our little settlement, Wynn returned to our cabin, his face set in a grim expression. I knew something serious had happened. He did not bother to play with Kip, but pushed him aside and came to me.

He kissed me first and then spoke, his voice grave. "I have just gotten word, Elizabeth, that someone has been trading illegal liquor to our Indians. I don't know who it is or where he is working, or if there is more than one. But I have to go check it out."

He kissed me again and released me to go and pack his gear. I followed him, not knowing what to say or to do. He was preparing much more carefully than usual.

"How long will you be gone?" I asked him, able at last to find my voice.

"I have no idea. I wish I could say it will take only a day or two, but the truth is, I have no idea how long it might take."

"Are you taking some men with you?"

"No, I will be going alone."

"But why? You might need help. The man, or men, might be dangerous."

"That's true. That's why I am going alone. This isn't the kind of thing that you can ask others to share. It's the law that is needed here."

His words frightened me and brought a chill to my heart. His trail gear caused me further fear. Never had I seen Wynn take such pains. He made his list and double- and triple-checked it, making sure he had everything. The amount of ammunition also frightened me. Did he think he might need it? Were whiskey runners really that dangerous? Yes, I had heard enough stories from others to know that indeed they might be.

"What can I do?" I asked him helplessly. "Will you want to eat before you go?"

Wynn gave me a rather absent-minded smile. "Great idea," he said; "something hot would be good."

I left him and went back to my kitchen. The fire was burning well and it did not take me long to have a hot meal for Wynn and a pot of strong tea.

When he came from his office, I was ready. He noticed just the one plate on the table. "Aren't you going to join me?" he asked.

"No, I—I'm really not hungry. It's only three o'clock."

"How about a cup of tea then?"

"It's stronger than I like it."

"You could water it down some."

I shook my head. I just didn't feel like putting something into my churning stomach.

Wynn studied my face, but said nothing more.

"Is there anything I should do while you're gone?" I asked, feeling helpless and lonely already.

"Just take good care of yourself! I have left word with Ian to keep a close eye on you. If anything is needed, you be sure to let him know."

Wynn finished his meal all too quickly and was pushing away from the table.

"I'm going for the team," he told me. "I will load up here. You might watch Kip. I don't want him slipping out the door and tangling with the sled dogs."

I nodded and mechanically began to clear the table.

Wynn was not gone long. I could hear the yipping and complaining of the dog team as they made their way to our cabin. I wondered if they were thinking the same thing that I was—that this was a strange time of the day to be taking to the trail. I had thought of asking Wynn to wait until morning but I checked myself. If Wynn had not felt it was important to leave immediately, he would have decided to sleep at home and strike out on the trail early the next day.

It did not take Wynn long to pack. I helped only by carrying some of the gear to the door of the cabin. Wynn himself had to arrange and pack the sled. He would want to know exactly where everything was located.

I determined not to cry as I said goodbye, but it was difficult. I reminded myself over and over that Wynn had gone on dangerous missions before and always returned.

We prayed together before he left as we always did, each of us imploring God to protect the other. Then our door was closed and I heard Wynn's voice commanding his dogs to be on their way.

I did not go to the door or a window. I did not want to see the snow flurries blot him from my vision. Instead, I went to the bedroom to spend some more time in prayer.

I will confess that I did shed a few tears as I prayed, but when I came out of my bedroom it was with renewed peace of mind and a determination to use, rather than waste, the days that Wynn would be gone.

The first thing I did was to get out the stew pot. I had heard that one of the elderly couples in the village had not been well. I would take them something nourishing.

By the time I returned from my trip to the invalids, it was already dark. I was glad for the warmth of the cabin as I entered and for Kip who met me at the door. I tried to play with him in the same manner Wynn always did, but it just wasn't quite right, and Kip backed away from me with a puzzled look in his eyes.

I fixed a plate of stew for myself and took it and my tea to the chair before the fire. I wasn't hungry. I ended up scraping my stew into Kip's dish for him to finish.

If only there was some way of knowing how long it would take Wynn to locate and apprehend the criminal. I did hope and pray there wasn't more than one of them.

I mended a pair of Wynn's socks and a tear in one of my slips and then turned to a well-read book. I had read it so often I was sure I could have recited it by memory, but I couldn't concentrate. I decided to go to bed early. Maybe the night would pass quickly.

It didn't. I lay awake listening to the storm. The wind was stronger now. I pictured Wynn out in the open somewhere, trying to get some sleep in the cold, wintry night.

Kip was restless, too. He kept moving from his fireplace rug to my bed, and then back again. I was about ready to get up and shut the bedroom door to keep him in one place, and then I realized he would only sit outside my door and whine and that would be even worse.

The night finally did come to an end, but the new day was not much better. After I dismissed my morning class, I went to visit Nimmie to help her with her little ones. She really didn't need my help that much. She had everything well under control, but she humored me by finding small jobs for me to do.

I trudged home through more flakes. Would it never stop snowing?

Kip met me at the door, excited about my homecoming. I fixed some supper and gave Kip his evening meal and wondered how in the world I would fill the long evening ahead.

It seemed forever that I went through a similar daily routine, but the calendar on the wall told me it was just six days.

Ian was the one to bring the news. When I saw him coming toward the cabin, his long strides eating up the snow-covered ground, my heart filled with fear. Did he have bad news? He walked so purposefully.

But when I opened the door, Ian was smiling. "An Indian trapper just stopped at the Post and said that Wynn is on the way in. I thought you'd like to know."

I thanked Ian, my glad heart rejoicing. He was finally coming home!

"Did he say how long it will be?" I asked.

"Should be here in a couple of hours. He's bringing a prisoner, so he sent word for me to have the cell ready."

A prisoner! Then Wynn had found his man.

Ian turned to go and I went to prepare a meal. Suddenly I felt very hungry and I was sure Wynn would be hungry, too.

It was a little more than a couple of hours before I heard a dog team enter the settlement. I could tell by the strange yip of his lead dog, Flash, that it was Wynn's team. I looked out the window. I had to scratch a spot in the frosted pane in order to see.

I could just make out Wynn's tall form in front of the Post. After commanding the team to lie down, he was ushering a man into the building. I knew he would care for the team before he came to the house, so there would still be a wait.

I could hardly contain myself. It had been so long, and I was so glad to see him safely home again. I wanted to throw on my parka and run down to the settlement to join him. But I knew Wynn would have things to attend to before he would be free to come home for his supper and a much-deserved rest.

I don't suppose it really took Wynn all that long to do what had to be done, but it felt like a lifetime to me. Then at last I saw Kip leave his place by the fire and press his nose hard against the door, and I knew Wynn was on the way.

This time I did not wait by the stove, letting Kip get first greeting. I ran to the door and threw it open and even before Wynn could step inside I was in his arms.

He looked very weary, his face drawn from exhaustion. I did not hold him at the door long, but pulled him inside. I helped him remove his heavy mittens and parka, the whole time telling him how relieved I was to have him home again. Kip kept telling him that, too, with joyful little yips and great tail wagging.

It wasn't until Wynn crossed to his chair to remove his heavy boots that I noticed the limp.

"What happened?" I asked in alarm.

"I'm fine," he replied. "Nothing to worry about."

"But you're limping."

"A little."

"Is it your foot or your leg?"

"Leg."

"Wynn," I said, exasperated, "what happened?"

"How about having some supper, and then I'll tell you all about it?" said Wynn. "I'm absolutely starved."

I hurried to the stove to dish up our meal. I would not ask Wynn for more until he had eaten.

I never did hear "all" about Wynn's experiences. What I did hear was enough to give me chills.

Wynn started his hunt by going to the cabin of a trapper who was reported to have purchased liquor from the trafficker. Wynn found a very sober Indian, his head in his hands. Empty bottles were strewn about his cabin. There were signs that he had been sick from the alcohol. "Gone," he groaned out to Wynn. "All gone. All my winter's furs, all gone." He had traded some of the furs for the whiskey, and then when he was too intoxicated to defend himself the lawless trader had slipped away with the rest of them.

Wynn had gone on, following the fresh trail. He found another trapper in much the same condition. Wynn pressed on. Soon he found a third. This man was still out from the liquor, and Wynn knew the trail was getting hot. However, he could not leave the Indian until he was sure he was sober enough to care for himself. The weather was still cold enough that one could freeze to death if left unattended.

This delayed Wynn and he had to really push his team when he got back on the trail.

The next cabin made Wynn realize just what kind of a man he was looking for. The trapper had apparently refused to trade his furs for the whiskey. Wynn found him dead from a gunshot wound through the heart, and the cabin was stripped of furs.

Now Wynn knew he was up against not only a thief but a murderer as well. He knew also that the man would stop at nothing. It was imperative that Wynn get to him before more lives were lost.

Wynn pushed the dog team for most of the night to close the gap between himself and the man. The storm had finally broken, and the moon gave enough light for Wynn to see his way.

Near morning he stopped for some rest, more for the dogs than himself, and then he was on his way again.

He overtook the man about noon the next day. He had stopped for a meal and had built himself a little fire for a hot cup of tea. Wynn approached cautiously, leaving his team fanned out in the snow over the hill away from the man.

When Wynn got in close to the man's camp, he called to him. He told him who he was and that he was coming in to get him.

The outlaw called back, "You've got me, Sarge. I know when I'm licked. But at least let me have a cup of tea to thaw me out a bit before you run me on in."

Wynn stepped out into the open and approached the man slowly. He was almost into the camp when the man swung around with a hand gun and took a shot at Wynn, just missing as Wynn dived into the snow.

From his concealed position behind a bank of snow, Wynn watched the outlaw. Wynn was afraid to take his attention off him for fear he would make a run for it. But the man preferred to stay close to his fire, confident that a Mountie would not shoot to kill if there was another way.

The sun went down and the moon came out, big and bright. The man fired at Wynn just often enough to hold him at bay. All night long they lay on the snow, challenging one another, but the trader had the advantage of a small fire.

In the morning, before the sun returned to the sky, Wynn could sense that the trader had plans for some new deception. Wynn decided that he must move first and so he did. He worked himself around slowly in the cover of the snowbanks and spruce trees until he was no longer in front of the man, but to his left side.

Wynn could tell that the man was preparing for travel. Knowing that time was against him, he made a dash for the camp, hoping to catch the man off guard.

The plan worked. The surprise rush gave Wynn just enough time to shoot the gun from the man's hand as he swung around to meet him. There was a price to pay, though, for as the trader's gun went off the bullet caught Wynn in the right leg, causing a painful flesh wound.

Wynn didn't say too much about what happened after that, but somehow he managed to get the bootlegger in cuffs and extract from him the locations of the trappers he had dealt with.

There were two others besides the ones Wynn had already seen, and with the illegal trader leading the way, Wynn traveled to those cabins to check on the men. At the first cabin they discovered a very angry Indian man who himself had been tramping the woods looking for the trader. Wynn assured him that justice would be done, and sent him to recruit the help of another nearby trapper to transport all the stolen furs back to the village where they would duly be returned to the rightful owners.

Then Wynn and the arrested man went on to the last victim. It was as Wynn feared. The trapper, in his drunken condition, had been unable to keep his fire going and had frozen to death in the sub-zero weather.

Wynn tied this body, too, on his sled and, with the two dead men and the outlaw in handcuffs, he headed back to the village.

Now the prisoner was in the security of the Post jail. Wynn told me he would spend the night at home and then set out to bring the man to Edmonton.

I protested. He was in no condition to travel again so soon, I told him, but Wynn waved aside my concern.

"Elizabeth," he said, "that man is deadly. Never in my years of law enforcement have I met a man as cold and calculated. He would stop at nothing."

I was sure Wynn was right and that only increased my fear.

Wynn did allow me to nurse the angry red wound in his leg. I was afraid it would become infected, but Wynn poured on medicine that made him wince with the pain and assured me it would heal just fine. He did, however, take more of the disinfectant with him when he left the next morning. I didn't know if that was a good or a bad sign.

My greatest fear was for Wynn's safety. The outlaw had already proved that he had no regard for human life. What was to stop him, in his desperation, from attempting to kill the man who was taking him in? Surely he would do everything in his power to avoid being tried for the crimes he had committed. Wynn, with little sleep and an injured leg, was at a disadvantage.

I spent a restless day and a sleepless night, praying for Wynn's protection. I was glad when morning finally came and I could crawl from my bed and try to find something to occupy my hands and mind. I was more than eager to bang the school bell that morning, and called the children a bit early to class. Their presence would help fill the emptiness of the cabin.

I was mentally prepared for many sleepless nights and worry-filled days, but, much to my relief, Wynn was back that next evening. He had met two members of the Force who had been sent out from Edmonton to help with the manhunt.

I was grateful to have Wynn back home again and glad that he had not had to travel all the way to Edmonton on his bad leg. He had been told by the man in charge of the mission to rest for several days, and he took his advice—at least for a few days. Then he was up and about, anxious to have more to do than catching up on his paper work. Soon he was back out among the villagers again, his limp barely noticeable.

27
Out

THE TWO TRAPPERS who had picked up the stolen furs had brought them in to Ian's trading post, and Wynn oversaw the sorting of whose furs were whose. I couldn't see how the men could tell one fur from another and asked Wynn about it.

"Oh, they know their own furs all right, no problem there," said Wynn. "Little marks or nicks or coloring. They can identify them all."

The furs of the dead trappers were traded in at the Post for the families of the men. Wynn told me that Ian had given them more than a fair price.

All the village men returned from their traplines, and then I knew that spring really had returned.

We finished up our classes, and I started to work on my garden. I was glad to have my hands back in the soil and to watch things begin to grow. A few of the other women in the village had seen the advantages of a garden, and Nimmie and I had been happy to help them get their own started.

I was just settling in to another quiet summer day when Wynn came back to the house.

"Are you all packed?" he grinned, and I looked at him questioningly.

I knew Wynn was still trying to find a way for me to travel out of Edmonton, and then to Calgary. For several reasons, I was anxious and chafing to go, and yet at his words now, a strange little reluctance raised its head.

"What do you mean?" I asked him.

"I heard of a party going out, so I sent a runner to ask them if they could drop by this way."

I didn't say anything.

"If they come, they should be here sometime tomorrow. I expect that they will spend the night here and then move on early Thursday morning," continued Wynn.

Thursday morning. Excitement and doubt filled me at the same time. Could I really leave Wynn for several weeks with no means of communication between us?

Wynn pulled me close. "I'm going to miss you, Elizabeth," he said, taking for granted that I would be going.

I sniffed. "Who is it?" I asked, almost hoping it would be someone whom I could refuse to travel with.

"A couple from the Force. I didn't discover their names."

Members of the Force! I could hardly refuse to go with them, if they would have me.

"Are you sure they'll be willing to take along a woman—?"

"I think they will. Most of us try hard to accommodate one another. We need to help each other in any way we can. I'll send along a small tent for your use. They won't mind setting it up for you."

I sighed. "Then I guess I'd better get ready," I said reluctantly.

"I guess you had," replied Wynn, and he kissed me on the nose and then went back to his work.

I was suddenly in a frenzy. I hauled out my wardrobe and realized that I didn't have a thing decent to wear. Whatever would I do? I had no time to make anything and no material to do so, even if there had been the time.

I hope no one sees me before I have a chance to get to a store and make some purchases, I thought frantically.

Yet I wasn't as concerned about my own preparations as I was about Wynn. I did his laundry, although I had done it all just a few days before. I baked some fresh bread and some cookies and a cake. I made up some stew and sealed it in jars so that he could heat it as needed.

In a fever pitch, I worked all afternoon and the next day until in the afternoon I heard the sound of many barking dogs in the village.

I rushed to the window and looked down toward the settlement and found that the visitors had come. The men traveled in a wagon with a pair of tired-looking horses, thin and ill-kempt from the long winter.

I could see even from my vantage that they wore the stripes of the Mounties. I saw Ian's hand raise and point in the direction of our cabin, and then the wagon rolled on toward me.

I had no hay to offer them for their horses but told them they were welcome to let them graze on the tall grass out back of our cabin, provided they kept them well away from my garden. The shorter one grinned at my comment and went to care for the horses.

I invited them in to have a cup of coffee and some fresh bread and they seemed to like the idea. They were still at the table when Wynn came in. He had heard they had arrived and hurried home to have a chance to visit with them and to catch up on any pertinent news.

"So what takes you out?" he asked them. "New orders?"

"No," said the taller one known as Hank Lovess. "The war."

"They haven't settled it then?" was Wynn's response. "I was hoping by now it would be over and done with."

"Guess that's what we'd all hoped, but 'fraid it ain't so," said the shorter one, Ted James. "From the reports we been gettin' it might be lastin' awhile yet."

"So you're joining up?"

"Gonna do what we can," said James.

Again I thought of Matthew. If this horrid war continued, would he go? A chill gripped my heart.

The men talked on, but I went outside to the clothesline to get Wynn's things so I could iron them. I didn't want to hear about the war anyway.

Wynn took the two men for a tour around the village while I prepared supper. I was relieved to have them out from under foot, and then I remembered that I would be "under foot" for them for the next several days. I wondered how they felt about that.

Just as Wynn had supposed, the men stayed overnight. They declined our offer to sleep on the floor in the cabin and spread their bed rolls out under the tall pine trees. Perhaps they knew Wynn and I needed this time alone. There was so much to say to one another and yet words were so inadequate. We talked on until late into the night, yet I can't remember one thing of importance that was said.

Morning came all too early. The men were anxious to get on the way, and I was determined not to be any more of a nuisance than was necessary. Wynn held me for a long time before we went to join the men, yet it wasn't nearly long enough. *When will I see him again?* my heart wailed as my eyes searched his face one last time. He was sending a letter to Headquarters asking that when members of the Force next traveled back our way, I would be contacted and given opportunity to travel with them. That might be in a few days' time, or several months—I did not know.

The trip out was not too difficult—probably because I was better prepared and knew what to expect. I was busy counting off the days until we would be in Edmonton.

The men were not talkative. They did not even converse with one another. I guess they were both used to silence.

I tried to help out where I could, but even the cooking they did better than I, being more used to the trail and open fires.

The nearer we got to Edmonton, the more my blood began to race. I was going "out." How different would the world be from the one that I had left behind? How much change would there be in my family? *How much change will they see in me?* I wondered as I looked down at my faded, patched dress and rough hands.

When we reached Edmonton, the men arranged for my stay in a hotel, purchased my train ticket to Calgary and told me how and when to be at the train the next morning. I thanked them for their kindness, and then with a lump in my throat, I wished them well in the war they were going to fight on behalf of myself and the rest of Canada. They had been good to me, these young gentlemen. They had not fussed nor pampered me, but they had been kind and patient. I assured them that my prayers would follow them.

I was on my own then. *On my own in a big city—I wonder if I still know how to act?*

I asked for help from the man behind the desk and set out, embarrassed about my attire, to find the nearest dress shop.

After doing enough shopping to at least get me to Calgary in a somewhat presentable state, I went back to my room.

What *plush accommodations*! I exulted. A soft carpet covered the floor, and lacy curtains, overhung by thick draperies, graced the window. The room was as large as our kitchen-living quarters, and then some. I hardly knew what to do with all that room to myself.

I went into the bathroom and gasped in amazement at what at one time I had taken simply for granted. It had been years since I had seen such luxury. I crossed to the tub, my fingers caressing the smooth white surface. The towels were so soft they felt like Kip's thick fur, and the room smelled as fresh as a pine forest.

I ran the water, pouring in a generous supply of bubbly soap and then submerged myself in the warm, soapy water. It felt so good! I stretched out lazily. *What a treat to get all of me in the tub at the same time!*

I don't know how long I spent in the tub. I only know that by the time I reluctantly crawled from it, my fingers were all wrinkled and the water was quite cold.

I wrapped myself in my worn old robe, thinking ahead to the soft fluffy one I had left behind at Mary's. It would be good to see my fashionable clothes again. The soft things, the dainty things, the pretty colors, the frills and foibles. I could hardly wait. I had missed them.

I dressed in my simple new gown. It really was quite becoming. I carefully did my hair up in a way I hadn't combed it for ages. When I was done I surveyed myself in the mirror and was pleasantly surprised at how good I looked.

Then I looked down at my hands and saw the stains and callouses from working in the garden, peeling vegetables, washing clothes on the scrub board, and I hid my hands behind me. I was no longer the cared-for and manicured girl who had left Calgary for the wilderness a few years earlier. I hoped no one would look at my hands. And then I noticed my arms. They had a number of telltale little welts on them, each indicating a spot where a mosquito or blackfly had visited me. I knew my face and neck bore the same spots, and my confidence began to quickly wane.

Then I straightened up to my full height, reminding myself that I wasn't "out" to set the fashion world to buzzing. I was here to see my doctor—to get some answers, to get some help. And, just as quickly as possible, I would be rejoining my husband in the North where I belonged.

With those thoughts to bolster my courage, I left my room and went down to the front desk to ask the attendant where I might find the dining room.

28
Calgary

❖

THE NEXT MORNING as the train left the Edmonton depot bound for Calgary, I was almost giddy with excitement. I would soon be seeing my family again! I would be back to the city life I had once known. And, more importantly, I hoped to get some help from my doctor.

The train had not changed. It was still ponderously slow and stopped at every little siding to waste some more precious time. I could hardly bear the agony of it all.

At long last we came to Lacombe, and I strained to see if I could catch a glimpse of faces that I might know. Though the streets of the little town were busy, I did not see anyone whom I had known while a teacher there.

At long last we were on our way again, chugging south, the tracks clicking as we made our slow progress.

Again it was stop and go, stop and go. The sun swung around toward the west, hot as it came in the window. I wished for a seat on the other side of the aisle, but the train was filled with passengers. I shifted farther away from the window and tried to keep from looking out to determine just how far along the tracks we were.

It was no use; I was soon crowding the window again, straining to see out and to guess the distance left to Calgary.

We finally reached the city, and I held my excitement at bay while the train pulled into the depot and with a giant sigh, shuddered to a halt. I remembered well the first time I had entered Calgary. The city had changed much since then, but I had changed even more. The young, stylish schoolteacher from the East no longer existed. In her place was an older, wiser and, I hoped, more sensitive woman.

Jon's entire family was there to meet me. I had called them from the Edmonton hotel the evening before, telling them I would be arriving by train. They were almost as excited as I was. How the children had grown! I couldn't believe how tall William was—and how mature-looking for a mere boy. He was a teenager now and hoped everyone would realize it.

Sarah, too, had shot up and looked like a young lady rather than a child. She was now eleven and carried herself with an air of grace.

But I suppose that it was Kathleen who had changed the most. From the dear little child of four who had met me at the station and become my constant companion, she was now a young nine-year-old girl, poised and proper. I fell in love with her all over again, though I found it difficult not to wish the little girl back again.

Baby Elizabeth, who had been only a few months old when I arrived in Calgary the summer of 1910, was now ready to start school in the fall.

Mary had the same bright smile, the same beautiful reddish hair, the same flashing eyes I remembered so well. Jon had not changed much either, although I noticed a few white hairs in his carefully trimmed sideburns.

I looked around for Julie. I guess Mary could read my mind.

"Julie is out of town. Her husband is taking some services at Lethbridge and Julie went with him. We phoned her last night and she was so excited she could hardly stand it. She was going to hop the train and come right on up, but he will be finished tomorrow and then they will both be home."

I understood, but it would be hard to wait.

I hadn't remembered that Jon and Mary's beautiful home was so big. Nor so lovely. I wandered around, running my hand affectionately over furniture and fancies. I had almost forgotten that such things made up a house—at least some of them.

Dinner was delicious. We had dishes that I had not tasted for years. Wonderful Stacy had prepared all my favorite things—stuffed chicken breasts, whipped potatoes, creamed broccoli, corn on the cob, and for dessert her famous chocolate mousse. I ate until I felt ashamed of myself.

All the time I was enjoying Mary's home and Stacy's dinner, I thought of Wynn. *If only he were with me—this would be sheer heaven!* But Wynn was far away in his northland. A little ache tugged at my heart.

Back in my old room and after soaking in a luxurious bath, I reclaimed one of my lacy, silk nightgowns. Feeling much the pampered lady, I climbed into bed, smiling to myself in the darkness. The bed was so soft and smelled so good that I had visions of the best sleep I'd had for years. But it didn't work that way. I had become used to a harder mattress. I tossed and turned but sleep did not come. Around three o'clock, in desperation, I threw my pillow on the carpeted floor, took a blanket with me and lay down to sleep.

I felt foolish curled up on the carpet and fervently hoped I would waken in the morning before I was discovered. I was soon asleep.

The next day was busy. I got out all my stored dresses and admired their beauty as I pressed them ready for use. I had forgotten I had so many pretty things. I did need to do some shopping, however, so in the afternoon I took the streetcar downtown.

I had felt sophisticated and proper when I left Mary's house, but I hadn't been on the streets for long until I realized that my beautiful gowns were now dreadfully out of style. The farther I went, the more evident it became. I certainly didn't have the funds for a complete new wardrobe, yet it was plain to see that the dresses of today were far different from mine; I stood out on the streets as one who had been clothed from missionary barrels supplied by the castoffs of the rich.

In embarrassment, I headed home.

I was hardly in the door when I told Mary, "My dresses are dreadfully out-of-date. What will I do? I had no idea that the styles have changed so much."

Then I looked more carefully at Mary. If I had been observant, I would have noticed yesterday that she, too, dressed in the newer fashions.

"Oh, my," said Mary noticing my discomfiture, "I should have thought to tell you, Elizabeth, but you always had such pretty things."

"Well, they might be pretty, but they definitely aren't in vogue. I don't want to buy a new wardrobe for the few days I will be in the city, and I don't have the money for that even if I did wish to. But I will need something else. Most of the dresses on the street were much shorter, and not as frilly, more—more tailored looking. And my hat—it was all wrong, too."

"Why don't we see what we can do?" offered Mary. "If you don't mind them being cut, I'm sure we can find ways to change your dresses and make them quite acceptable."

"They are no good to me as they are. If you can fix them, even two or three of them, I can make do."

We chose three dresses that seemed to lend themselves to change and then dear Mary set out to alter them. They turned out quite well, and I felt that now I could walk the city streets without too much embarrassment. Jon and Mary added a little surprise. They asked if they could take me shopping for a new suit and hat, with shoes and bag to match. I hesitated at first, but when Mary expressed her love and deep desire to do this, I consented, and gave them both a big hug.

Julie finally arrived, running quickly up the front walk. She was bubbly. She was beautiful. She was in love. And she was noticeably pregnant. My breath caught in a little gasp.

"I wouldn't let Mary tell you," she enthused. "I just had to tell you myself. Oh, Beth, I never knew just how happy one could be."

I hugged her close. I was happy for her, too, and no one there knew that the tears on my cheeks were more than just shared joy for Julie.

We had a lot of catching up to do. Her eyes shining with love, she proudly introduced her young husband. I remembered that Julie had once swooned over Wynn and had asked me if the Force had any more like him. Well, Reverend Thomas Conway was not another Wynn. He was much shorter and slender in build. He had rust-colored hair, with a carefully trimmed little mustache to match. He had laughing deep blue eyes and a kind smile. He looked like just what Julie needed, and I liked him immediately.

Julie insisted on sharing her wardrobe for the time I would be in Calgary and brought over three dresses that fit me just fine. Actually, she couldn't wear these particular ones in her condition anyway, she assured me. With six dresses, a suit and proper shoes, hat and bag, I felt quite confident to face the world.

I smiled to myself as I hung up the garments. *Imagine the Beth of old wearing hand-me-downs, made-overs and garments of charity!*

We called Toronto on Jon's telephone and I had a long talk with Mother and Dad, their voices bringing back so many memories. They were alone now. With the older girls married and scattered, me up north, Julie out west and, as I had feared, Matthew gone to war, there were just the two of them.

Mother was worried about Matthew and I'm afraid I was no comfort to her. I was worried about him, too. I thought about this young brother, a man now, who wished to serve his country, and a little prayer went up even as my chest constricted. *Why did he have to go?* I asked myself. But I knew. He went for the same reason so many other young men were going. Their country needed them.

After the first few days of flurry and bustle had passed, I decided I was now ready to phone the doctor and make my appointment.

Mary immediately became concerned when I told her that my real reason for making the trip was to consult a doctor. But when I hastened to explain that, no, I had not been ill, not more than an occasional cold or flu the entire time I had been in the North, she relaxed. I was having a checkup at my husband's request, I informed her, and she agreed that it was a good idea and Wynn was right to desire it.

The doctor visits and tests were soon behind me and the day came for my final consultation. With anticipation and fear I went to see him.

He was a balding, elderly man, his understanding eyes almost hidden behind bushy eyebrows and dark-rimmed glasses. He motioned for me to be seated and cleared his throat.

I nervously twisted the handkerchief I carried, my eyes studying his face for some clue. I wanted so much to hear good news.

"Well, Mrs. Delaney," he said, clearing his throat again, "all the tests are in now, and"—he hesitated for what seemed like forever and then went on—"I find no reason for you to not conceive."

I exhaled and let my body relax.

"That's good news," I said in almost a whisper.

The doctor looked over the glasses. "That depends on how you look at it," he said. "If we don't find a problem, then we cannot do anything to correct it." He cleared his throat again.

He waited for my reaction, wondering if I had understood what he had just said.

I understood what he was saying. *There is nothing he can do for me. I might as well not have come.* It really made no difference. No difference at all.

The good doctor continued talking, explaining things I did not understand, but then I was not really listening. I had already heard all I needed to know. Now I just wanted to get out of his office.

I went for a long walk before catching the streetcar home. I don't really know where I went, I just walked, not paying much attention to where I was going or what was around me.

I came to the river, and as I stood gazing down on it my mind began to clear of its fog. Perhaps the river reminded me of the wilderness. It was the only thing in the city that looked like home.

I lowered myself to the grassy bank in the shade of the poplar trees and let the tears flow. I wanted Wynn. With all my heart I wanted Wynn. No one else really understood how I felt. I cried for quite a while before I got myself in hand. Then I blew my nose, dipped cool water for my face and went in search of a streetcar.

Mary and I had a long talk that night. I told her all about my problem, my aches, my longing. She understood as well as another could understand. She promised that she too would pray that my desire would be granted. I appreciated her love and understanding and encouragement, but I still felt empty.

Besides, I felt threatened by this strange world I had come back to. All the talk of the war, the daily news of more conflicts, the lists of those killed or missing in action filled the papers and caused an atmosphere of constant fear. I didn't feel comfortable with this new world. My northern isolation had protected me from all this.

I got in touch with Headquarters for any information on when I might be able to return to the North. The man with the deep bass voice told me that there was nothing he knew of in the immediate future, but that he had my number and strict orders to contact me as soon as something came up.

I thanked him and hung up the phone. I did pray, with all my heart, that it would be soon.

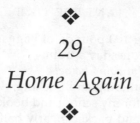

29

Home Again

THREE WEEKS, AND still I had not heard from the Force Headquarters. At night I thought I could not stay for one more day. The days
were a little better. I found many ways to fill them. I went for walks with
Kathleen, inspected Sarah's sewing, took shopping trips with Julie and
had long talks with Mary.

My greatest joy was the Sundays. I enjoyed more than I can tell being
back in a church service. I guess that was when I missed Wynn the most.
I kept thinking how much he would appreciate the services, too.

In spite of my loneliness for Wynn, I was glad to be home again. I even
took a trip to Lacombe and spent some time with Mother Delaney and
Phillip and his family. I was relieved to find Wynn's mother doing much
better. Wynn would be glad for the news.

While I was in the area I visited Anna and had coffee and some of her
delicious Swedish baking. We drove by the school and I saw they had
added another room onto the little teacherage. I was so glad to see that
school was continuing.

As I visited I was often reminded of why I was "out." Repeatedly, inquiries were made about my "family" and though the questioners were
asking out of interest, I found the remarks deeply painful.

In spite of the delights of the city, I chafed inwardly. I was lonesome
for Wynn. I even felt a little homesick for the North. I was beginning to
understand how Nimmie had felt. It seemed that I had been out for such
a long time. Surely there must be someone from the Force heading north.
What if they had forgotten me? What if someone had already left and
now I must wait for many weeks more? Should I phone them again or
would they think me a nuisance?

I longed for Wynn. I longed for Nimmie and her babies, for the Indian
women who came for tea, for the sound of the wind in the pines and the
smell of wood smoke in the air.

I longed for Kip, pressing his cool nose into my hand, coaxing me to
stroke the softness of his beautiful coat.

I was homesick. I was miserable. And no matter how hard I tried to be
agreeable and enthusiastic about all that folks were doing for me, the ache
never left me.

At long last, two men were being dispatched to a post near our area,
and they would accommodate me in their travels. I had three days to get

ready. I could take along 100 pounds of baggage, no more, and should be ready to leave on Wednesday's train.

I was beside myself. *I'm going home!*

The time was spent gathering and packing, weighing and repacking. I wanted to take supplies for my school and books were so heavy. I sorted and pondered, resorted and packed nearly half a dozen times.

When it came time for me to dress for the train trip to Edmonton, I again had trouble deciding, *What should I wear?* The new suit would be ideal for train travel, but would not be of use to me in the North. Yet to wear one of the simple dresses I had purchased to take north with me would look absurd.

Mary solved my dilemma. "Why don't you wear the suit, hat and shoes, and when you get to the hotel in Edmonton, just send them all on back to us in this little case?"

I did.

I dreaded all the goodbyes, but I was so anxious to be on my way that I did not linger over them. I held my little Kathleen longer than the other children, perhaps. It was hard to leave her again, knowing that the next time I saw her, she might be a young lady. Then it was all over and we were on the train, moving ever so slowly toward Edmonton and the river that would take us on the first leg of our journey north.

I tried to relax, but every nerve seemed to be straining forward. The time would never end.

The days on the trail were no better. I joyfully greeted each familiar landmark. It was the thick cloud of mosquitoes that first welcomed me back to the northland. I swatted at them and smiled to myself. I would soon be home.

The men were kind. One of them was a little too kind, I thought, and took every opportunity to offer his extended hand, or assist me up or down or wherever. I avoided him as much as possible.

At last we left the river, too, loaded the waiting wagon and started up the trail that would lead to the Post.

We camped for the last time, the men setting up my tent before building the evening fire. I was walking about, studying the clear night sky and wondering how on earth I could endure another day on the trail before I would see Wynn when a figure moved toward me in the semi-darkness. I would have recognized the stride anywhere, and with a glad cry I ran to meet him.

Wynn had heard we were coming and had come to meet us. We held one another tightly while the tears coursed down my face. Oh, how I had missed him! I would never be able to tell him just how much. For now I was content to be held closely. For the first time in weeks the little gnawing pain was gone from my heart.

Proper manners demanded that Wynn greet the other Mounties and spend some time catching up on the outside news. I wanted him all to myself but I held myself in check. There would be many days ahead for us to catch up on everything.

The next day as we walked along behind the wagon, Wynn and I talked about all the things that had happened to each of us while we had been apart, except I said nothing about the doctor's report. I was afraid it might bring tears with the telling, so I wanted to be in the privacy of our own home before I reported to Wynn. He, wisely, did not ask. Instead, we talked about the family, the villagers, the war, and what we had seen and done during the weeks apart.

Many people from the settlement came out to meet us. I was deeply touched that they should care so much. I greeted them by name and was pleased to discover I had not forgotten the difficult Indian language I had picked up over the years.

We trudged on the last mile together. A warmth and close-knit feeling seemed to hang in the air all about me. As we neared the settlement the smell of the wood smoke hung in the air. I sniffed deeply. I had missed it. In the distance I could hear the gentle roll of the river, and nearer at hand the soft whispering of the wind in the pines. I put my hand in Wynn's.

"You wouldn't believe," I murmured, "how wonderful it is to be home."

Wynn squeezed my hand and pulled me closer to him. I could see by the shine in his eyes that he was just as happy as I.

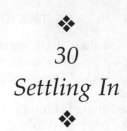

30
Settling In

THE LITTLE CABIN we called home looked tiny and simple after being in Mary's lovely home. But I looked around at the bear-skin rug before the fire, the shelves that held my dishes and supplies, the table where we sat to partake of venison stew and biscuits, the home-made pillows on the cot, and I felt at home again.

The first day was a busy one. Though I was tired from the trip, I could not rest until I was sure that everything was spotless and orderly.

As soon as the sun was up I ran down the little path leading to my garden. Wynn had kept it weedless while I had been away. I couldn't believe how much it had grown. The rabbits had been raiding again. I could see where they had nibbled off many of the plants.

My next errand was to get Kip. Wynn had left him in the care of Jim Buck. He seemed as pleased to see me as I was to see him. I thanked Jim, and Kip and I ran the short distance home together.

During the morning Wawasee came, bringing his most recent drawings for me to see. I smiled my approval, and spoke very slowly in his native tongue so he could follow me by lip-reading.

"I like your pictures, Wawasee. I brought you a picture book from the city. You must come back to look at it as soon as I get unpacked. In the morning—in the morning I should have it for you."

He beamed and I knew by his shining eyes that he would be back in the morning.

In the afternoon several ladies came for tea. They did not all come together but in twos and threes. I would no sooner clear away the cups from one group than another would be at my door. I was soon caught up on all the village news.

I had seen Nimmie briefly the night before, but I was longing for a good chat with her. My first day was too busy to arrange for that chat. I still needed to unpack my things so the book would be there as promised when Wawasee came the next morning.

I cooked Wynn a special supper that night. It wasn't stuffed chicken breasts and creamed broccoli, but I took special pains with what I had on hand.

I settled back into the routine of village living with a light heart, except for the news from the doctor that I shared with Wynn.

I continued to argue with God. Didn't Hannah receive the child she had prayed for? Weren't there numerous women in the world who had children which they did not really want nor care for? Did the whole thing seem reasonable? Why shouldn't those who would love and protect the child be the ones to give birth? Why not me? Why should I be denied?

I tried to push the thoughts from me, but daily they nagged at me, eventually making me nervous and listless. I lost weight. I did not sleep well. I found no answers.

I had been home for two weeks. I felt again the peacefulness of the little settlement, but I had been wrong about one thing. I had thought that in leaving behind the newspapers, the radio and the war-talk, I could shut out the fact of the war. With Matthew somewhere in the fighting, that was impossible. My thoughts and prayers often were of him and the other sons who had gone to fight. I thought of the parents, the wives, the sweethearts whom these men had left behind and I prayed for them also. Especially did I pray for my own mother and father as they waited out the long, long days for Matthew's safe return.

It was beginning to look like fall again. The sun spent fewer hours in the sky, the leaves turned to yellow-gold on the poplars, the birds gathered in the trees, calling to one another. Our garden was full-grown and tasty. It would soon need to be gathered into our storage room. We started our school again.

One day Wynn came to the cabin in the early afternoon. I looked up from the bread I was kneading. He had not planned to be back until the supper hour, so I knew something had happened to change his plans.

"Remember the young woman who had the baby boy about ten days ago?" he asked.

I nodded. The couple was new in the village and I did not know them well.

"She's not well. I've just been over to take her some medicine again. Do you think you could check on her in a short while? Maybe take her something to eat? Her husband is away, and she is all alone."

I promised Wynn I would go just as soon as I prepared the food.

The young couple had built a new cabin on the edge of the settlement, and I hurried there with my soup and bread. There was no response to my knock on the door, and then I remembered that she likely did not know what a knock meant. I opened the door and went in.

On the corner bed I found the woman, weak with fever. Her forehead was very hot. A tiny baby lay against her, sleeping contentedly. I checked the water pail and found that it had just been refilled. Probably Wynn had done that when he had looked in. I didn't know whether to try to get her fever down first or to feed her some nourishment. I decided to sponge bathe her.

I spoke to her in her own language, and I could see a response in her eyes.

"How long have you been sick?" I asked her.

"Not know—many days have gone."

"Where is your husband?"

"In big village."

"Do you know when he will be back?"

"Not know."

She didn't seem to cool much with the bathing, so I gave up and began to spoon some of the soup into her mouth. She was able to swallow the food, for which I was thankful. I then gave her a piece of bread and she fed that to herself.

It was then that the baby stirred and began to whimper. I reached down and picked him up so I could comfort him and check his condition.

There was nothing wrong with him except that he was in desperate need of changing. I took care of that and cradled him for a moment before I placed him back beside his mother so he could nurse.

He did not appear to be suffering even though his mother was ill. He looked filled-out and healthy.

"I will go now," I said to the young woman, and left her to see if I could find Wynn.

Wynn was not hard to find. He was checking a winter supply list with Ian. Medicines were number one on his list.

"How is she?" he asked as soon as I entered.

I frowned, concerned. "Not good, Wynn. She is so hot. I'm afraid she is very ill. Do you think you should send for her husband? She says he is at the big village."

"I've sent for him. It'll be three days at best before he gets here, and if he is hard to locate, perhaps many more."

"I don't think she should be left there alone, Wynn. Is there a way that she could be moved to our place so I could care for her properly?"

Wynn thought about it.

"That will be a big job, Elizabeth—and what about your school?"

"We'd have to cancel classes for a few days, but that wouldn't hurt. It's more important to try to get her well."

"I think we could find a way to get her there."

"I'll go get the cot ready."

It was not long until the woman and her baby had been bedded on the cot in our living quarters. Most of the time she slept, restlessly tossing about in her fever. I bathed her often, trying to get the fever down. I was afraid that in her tossing she might injure the baby, so I had Wynn bring in a crate and we made him a comfortable bed.

For the next four days all my time was spent caring for the mother and baby. I would just begin to think there was some improvement, and then she would get worse again. At times she could not even nurse her child. I had Wynn bring some canned milk from the store and we fixed a makeshift bottle to supplement his feeding. On the fifth day the worried-looking husband came to our door. He crossed quickly to the side of his wife's bed without even exchanging greetings with me. She was a bit better, and I was glad she recognized him. He went to the crate and picked up his young son. He seemed pleased that the child fared well. It was only then that he turned to me and spoke, "I take them home now," he said.

I wanted to protest. The woman was not fit to be moved, but I knew better than to argue. I just nodded my head in agreement.

He left for some help and was soon back with two other men to carry the woman on a blanket and pole stretcher to their own cabin. The baby was crying as they left. He was hungry and the woman no longer had much milk.

I worried about them. For the first few days I would drop by to check on them. The husband always greeted me at the door and said that mother and baby were "good." He was caring for them. From the smells coming from the cabin I knew that he was doing some cooking and was feeding her. He seemed to be responsible. I would have to leave the matter with him.

One day as I walked to the store I met Big Woman coming from the new cabin. She was carrying a strange-looking leather pouch. I had not seen her with it before.

She gave me a toothless grin, her face softening in wrinkles.

"She get better now," she said. "I make strong medicine."

I didn't know what she had done. Probably one of the chants that Nimmie had spoken of, and it had likely cost the young brave much of his hard-earned money. I felt sorry for the family.

When the days passed and there was no news of the family, I dared to hope that things had improved. Wynn still visited the cabin. He continued to give the medicine he had on hand, but that did not seem to stem the fever either.

One dark evening as we sat before our fire expecting the night to bring the winter's first snowfall, there was a shuffling at our door. Kip ran to welcome whoever it was, with Wynn close behind him.

It was the young man. In his arms he carried the baby boy. He nodded solemnly to Wynn and crossed the room until he was standing before the cot where I sat.

"You take. Keep," he said, holding the baby out to me. "She gone now. I go trap."

He placed the baby in my arms which had raised automatically to receive him, and then spun on his heels and was gone.

I stood staring after him, not knowing what he meant or what I was to do.

The door closed softly and Wynn was beside me.

"What did he mean?" I asked, my voice full of wonder.

"He lost his wife," said Wynn.

"But the baby?"

"He has to go to his trapline. He wants you to keep the baby."

Tears began to trickle down my face. I cried for the young father. His eyes were filled with pain as he handed me his child. I cried for the mother who had fought so hard but had died so young. I cried for the baby who had been left motherless at such an early age. And I cried for me, tears of joy, because I now held a baby in my arms, a baby to love and care for. I held him close and thanked God for answering my prayers.

We named the wee baby Samuel. It seemed fitting. Hannah had named her baby Samuel after God had answered her prayer. The name meant "asked of God," and every time I said the name I was reminded again of the miracle of Samuel coming to us.

He had lost weight since I had last seen him. I knew that his poor sick mother had not been able to feed him properly. I was not alarmed. He seemed healthy, and I was sure he would gain rapidly when given proper nourishment.

My days were so full that I scarcely had time to have my morning classes. For the first few days I often sat and sewed while the children studied, as Samuel had very little to wear. My pieces of soft yard goods were finally being put to use.

At first Kip seemed a little jealous of all of the attention the little one was getting, but then he too seemed to decide that this little bundle must be pretty special. He took to guarding the cradle, fashioned lovingly by Wynn out of packing crates. Kip did not allow even the ladies who came for tea to go near the baby until I commanded him to let them.

At first Samuel had a great deal of catching up to do. He slept and ate, making up for the time when he had not been properly fed. He soon rounded out and as he regained his strength, he also became more aware of his surroundings.

It wasn't long until he was smiling and cooing like any normal baby. He was so easy to love. He made our little cabin a place that was alive and warm.

When winter came, I scarcely noticed the storms. I was too involved with my baby. Kip did not get his exercise as faithfully. I was much too busy and Samuel could not go out on the colder days.

Nimmie provided me with a cradle board to fasten Indian-fashion on my back with Samuel held securely in place, so when I did take him out for fresh air, it was not difficult for me to carry him.

Christmas was the best one we had ever had. Wynn and I spent many evenings making toys for Samuel. We could hardly wait for Christmas morning to arrive. Samuel rewarded our efforts with squeals and chuckles, and we felt that we had discovered what Christmas was really meant to be.

That Christmas our prayer time was thoughtful and filled with devotion. It meant even more to us now to read that God gave His Son—*His Son*—to bring eternal life to the world.

We had been so busy enjoying Samuel that I had not thought about his age. Suddenly one day it hit me: I did not know his birthday. I was anxious to ask Wynn. The Indian people in our village paid little attention to the day of their birth. To know the season of the year seemed to be close enough. "I was born at the time of the coming of the geese," or "I was born at the time of the heavy snow," but not, "I was born on May 15" or "on November 21."

When Wynn came in that night and headed right for the cradle and a squealing, arm-waving Samuel, I expressed my concern.

"We don't know Samuel's birthday," I said. "That might be important some day, when he registers for school or—"

"That's easy to find," said Wynn. "I keep a record of all of the births and deaths in the settlement."

We went to Wynn's office together, Kip trailing along behind. Wynn passed Samuel rather reluctantly to me while he got out a thick record book. He ran his finger down a column and came to, "infant boy born to Little Fawn and Joe Henry Running Deer, August 15, 1915."

"That's a strange name," I said.

"Whose?"

"The father's."

"They often combine English and Indian names."

"Yes, but not with two like that. A middle name. Henry. Joe Henry."

"Ian said a white trapper by the name of Joe Henry used to live near the big village. He said that the Indians thought highly of the man, and several of the young men were named after him."

As I looked again at the page and Wynn's recorded announcement of the birth of our small Samuel, another little pain went through me. Again I felt sorrow for the young man and woman whose home had been struck by such tragedy.

I carried the baby back to the living quarters while Wynn put the record book safely away.

"We'll try to make it up to you, Samuel," I whispered. "We'll care for you and love you, and when you are older we'll tell you all about your mother and father. They loved you, too, you know."

I kissed his soft, dark cheek and laid him back in his cradle so I could get supper on. He didn't stay there for long. Wynn was soon back and giving him horsey rides on his bootless foot.

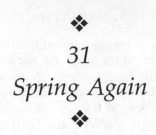

31
Spring Again

❖

NEVER HAD THE trees looked so green or the breeze sung so softly. With spring, the birds returned, and I held Samuel up to the window so he could see their bright feathers and hear their twittery songs.

He was crawling now and pulling himself up to stand on two rather shaky legs. He no longer fit his cradle, so Wynn again went to the packing crates for more lumber to make a bigger bed. It hardly fit in the small room, and we were tempted to move the cot out. Instead, we squeezed things in as best as we could—there was very little room for walking around.

The men came back with their winter furs, most of them having had a good year. The pelts were plentiful, thick, and brought good prices. I shut my eyes against the vision of the small helpless animals caught in the cruel traps and thought instead of the better food and clothing that the winter's catch would bring to the families in the village.

I watched, without really admitting it to myself, for Joe Henry Running Deer. I thought he might come to see his son, but he did not. I did not even see him in the village. Wynn thought of it, too, I guess, for he remarked one night that it appeared Joe had returned to the big village and that the cabin was now going to be used by another young man and his new bride. It was an unwritten law in the village that when a cabin was not occupied, it could be used by someone else who needed it.

I took Samuel out more and more as the weather warmed. He loved the out-of-doors. We took long walks with him riding in his special carrier on my back. We went to the river, down forest paths, to the village—all over our home area. And as we went I talked to Samuel, in English and in his own language. Wynn and I both encouraged him to try new words in each tongue.

In the evenings I read to him or showed him picture books. I sang him little songs. First I sang to him the songs my mother had sung to me when I was a child, and then I had Nimmie teach me the songs she sang to her little ones so Samuel would know them, too.

We visited Nimmie and her children often. Samuel loved other children. He would smile with delight whenever he saw Nimmie's boys. They loved him, too, and they had a wonderful time sharing toys on the floor while Nimmie and I sipped our tea and watched them with eyes of love and pride.

We sent word out to our family and friends, telling them of our son. I suppose I did boast a bit, but probably no more than most new mothers. Back with our infrequent mail came parcels and well-wishes. Now Samuel not only had handmade toys but commercial ones as well.

When it came time for the spring planting, I set Samuel on a fur rug while I worked in my garden. He played in the soil, letting it trickle through his fingers. I watched him carefully for a time, to see if he would try its taste. He didn't, so I left him happily playing and went on with my work.

When I checked on him only a few minutes later, he had not only tasted the dirt but he seemed to enjoy it. His chin was covered with mud from the mixture of dirt and dribble. He grinned at me happily as though to say, "Don't get alarmed. No baby has died from eating dirt yet."

I picked him up, wiped him off, scolded him as a matter of course, and placed his rug on the grass instead.

We closed the little school for the summer and I had more time to spend with Samuel. He was taking a few faltering steps now. Wynn and I spent our evenings together coaxing him to walk between us. He seemed to sense he was doing something pretty special, and he would squeal to be sure he had our full attention each time he took a step.

Much of my time was taken with sewing new garments. Samuel outgrew his things so quickly. I wondered how Hannah ever managed to get by with one small new coat a year. I smiled as I thought of the mother-love that must have gone into that one new coat.

One thing plagued me. Samuel was growing up so quickly, and I would have no pictures of him as a baby. I knew that in years to come the pictures would be very special—not just to Wynn and me but to Samuel himself. I tried to think of ways to get the use of a camera, but I could come up with no good solution. And then I thought of Wawasee. Samuel and I went to see him, and I explained to the young boy what I wanted and promised him all the scribblers he needed if he would draw several pictures of the baby for me.

Wawasee seemed to think this was a strange request. He was used to drawing wild animals and birds, or dog teams, or men fishing. But he didn't argue. He set to work sketching Samuel. At first he seemed a bit awkward and the pictures did not turn out well, but as he worked he began to get the feel for it. Soon he was producing very good likenesses of the baby.

He came often after that and spent hours sketching the little boy, sleeping in his bed, playing with his toys, burying his face in Kip's thick fur, feeding himself his mashed vegetables. All of the pictures caught the spirit of the baby Samuel. As I looked at them, I knew I had a treasure far beyond what a mere camera could have given me.

32
The Birthday Party

SAMUEL'S FIRST BIRTHDAY was drawing near. I was busy trying to come up with ideas that would make it a special occasion, but I
hadn't made much headway. I decided to discuss it with Wynn. I waited
until after Samuel had been tucked in for the night and was sound asleep.

"Samuel will be one on Saturday," I informed Wynn.

"I remember," he said. "I've already picked out his gift."

My eyes widened. "You have? What?"

"Not telling," Wynn said with a grin. "You'll just have to wait and see."

"Wynn," I pleaded, "that's mean."

But Wynn only laughed.

"Well, you've already got your gift. I've seen you sewing on that stuffed
horse for days," he said.

"Shhh," I cautioned, casting an apprehensive eye at the bed in the corner, and Wynn laughed harder.

"I would like to make his birthday really special," I went on.

"For Samuel—or for you?" Wynn said, his eyes twinkling.

"For all of us," I stated, a bit annoyed at Wynn's teasing.

"I'm sure the day will be special, just because we are together. But what
would you like to do?" Wynn asked, becoming more serious.

"That's the problem. I still haven't thought of anything."

"Then might I give you my suggestion? I think it might be fun to pack
a lunch and take our son on his first trip into the wilderness. We could
spend the whole day—take Kip, our birthday dinner and make a whole
day of it."

I loved the idea and began at once to think of the things I would need
to prepare for the backpack birthday dinner.

Saturday dawned fair and bright. I went early to the kitchen and began my preparations for the dinner we would carry with us. Wynn had
already left the cabin but would be back soon for breakfast.

Samuel awoke and pulled himself up in his bed, his face crinkled up
to cry until he saw me nearby. Then he began his chattering to tell me
that he was hungry and ready for another day.

I went to him and lifted him up, kissing him on the cheek.

"Today is your first birthday," I informed him, but he didn't seem too
excited about it. "We are going to take a long walk in the woods, Daddy

and Kip and you and me. We'll see all kinds of things that you should know about. Beaver dams, animal tracks, different trees and birds, and Daddy will tell you all about them."

Samuel was interested only in what was for breakfast.

I dressed the baby and went back to the kitchen just as Wynn arrived. He had his hand tucked inside his tunic and a funny grin on his face. "Is it time for birthday gifts yet?" he asked and I laughed at him. He was even worse than I was.

"Okay," I agreed, my eyes on Samuel, "but you have to wait until I get mine."

I went to the bedroom and brought the small calico horse I had made, entering the room with it hidden behind my back, and then while Samuel sat with a bewildered look on his face, Wynn and I sang "Happy Birthday to You."

"You first," said Wynn, and I pulled the toy horse out from behind my back and kissed Samuel as I presented it to him. He reached for it with a smile on his face and stuck one small hoof into his mouth.

"No," I told him. "It's not to eat. You're not that hungry, are you?"

"I hope he doesn't do that with my gift," said Wynn and I was even more curious.

"Well, give it to him and we'll see," I urged.

Wynn pulled his hand from his tunic and there was the fluffiest, smallest, brightest-eyed little huskie pup I had ever seen.

"Wynn!" I squealed, "how did you keep him so quiet?"

"It wasn't easy."

I reached for the puppy but Samuel beat me to it. I do think that Samuel would have put the puppy into his mouth as well if he had had opportunity, but after holding the puppy close so that Samuel could feel its softness, Wynn took him back and placed him on the floor.

He sat there, blinking his big blue eyes and looking at this strange new place. Kip joined the act then. He had been watching the whole procedure, his head cocked to one side, but now he came forward to sniff at the puppy and see if it really was a dog.

The puppy immediately turned to Kip, rejoicing to see one of its own kind and greeted Kip with such exuberance that Kip backed off and eventually retreated, the puppy tumbling along after him.

We laughed together at the sight.

I turned to Wynn. "How are we ever going to fit another body in this house? We already have three people and a dog."

"He's quite capable of living outside," said Wynn. "He doesn't need to be in the house at all. Every boy needs a dog of his own."

I shook my head. I was sure Wynn already knew that I would never be able to put that puppy outside alone. He would be sharing the fireside rug with Kip.

We had our breakfast then and together prepared for our journey.

I don't know when I ever enjoyed a day so much. Samuel seemed to understand that this great outdoors—this wilderness—was a part of himself. He studied it all with big, black, serious eyes, pointing his finger and chattering about the things that caught his attention.

Both Wynn and I were pleased at the small child's response.

"He's a sharp little fellow, isn't he, Wynn?" I couldn't resist asking.

Wynn agreed.

We ate our birthday dinner on a blanket spread out on the soft floor of the forest, cushioned by years of pine needles. Wynn gave Samuel a large pine cone to play with while I arranged the picnic lunch. As usual, it went to his mouth.

We traveled on to the beaver dam and let Samuel watch the beavers at work, telling him the native word for the small energetic animal. We even pretended that he tried to say the word after us but, to be honest, I think it was just more of his baby gibberish.

We took Samuel down to the pond's edge and Wynn held him so he could splash his hand back and forth in the cool water. His eyes brightened and he splashed so hard that even Wynn was getting wet.

When we took him from the pond he coaxed to go back, pointing and complaining as he was carried away.

The sun was in the west and beginning its descent when we turned toward home. We had not gone far when I noticed that Samuel, on his father's back, was sound asleep, his little dark head nodding with each step Wynn took.

"We've played the poor little fellow out," I said sympathetically.

Wynn chuckled. "I think he's enjoyed every minute of it."

"I think so too. I'm so glad you thought of it, Wynn. It was fun, wasn't it?"

Wynn reached for my hand and we walked home together. Kip ran on ahead, searching out rabbit burrows, or squirrel hide-outs. Samuel slept on. Perhaps his dreams were of wilderness things. He looked contented and healthy.

"We must get home to feed his puppy," I said, and Wynn tightened his grip on my hand.

Two nights later we were sitting by the open fire, Wynn working on some records, I doing some hand sewing and Samuel sleeping in his nearby bed, when there was a sound at our door. Kip rose quickly with a sharp bark, upsetting the puppy who slept beside him.

"Hush, Kip," I commanded, afraid that the barking might waken the baby.

Wynn got up and went to the door, expecting, as I was, someone with a problem.

It was young Joe Henry Running Deer who stood on the doorstep.

It took me awhile to recognize him, but when I did a slow smile crossed my face. He had come to see his son. I was sure he would be pleased to see we had taken good care of him.

Wynn greeted him and motioned him in. He came, rather hesitantly, urging a woman ahead of him. She looked young, hardly more than a girl, and very shy. I wondered if it was his sister.

He did not come farther into the room, did not ask to see his child, but instead pushed the girl forward a bit more and spoke in broken English, "New woman now. I come for son."

The blood drained from my face. I hoped I had misunderstood him. I looked at Wynn. His face was white, too, and I looked back at the young man again, about to ask him what in the world he was talking about. Wynn said something to him and the man answered, but I didn't hear or understand what either of them was saying.

"What is he saying?" I demanded of Wynn. "Why is he here?"

"Stay calm, Elizabeth," Wynn told me. But I couldn't stay calm.

"Wynn," I demanded, "what did he say?"

Wynn turned to me then, his eyes filled with anguish. "He has come for his child. He wants him back, Elizabeth."

I wanted to scream, to protest, but my throat would let no words come. I looked imploringly at Wynn, begging him with my eyes to get the two of them out of our cabin.

Wynn was still talking softly to the young man. I couldn't hear his words, but surely he was explaining the situation. *Samuel is our baby now! We will not give him up.* Joe Henry and his young bride could have many more children of their own.

I looked at the crib. Samuel was stirring. The noise in the cabin must have disturbed him. I jumped to my feet and rushed to his bed, ready to take him in my arms and shield him. He was still sleeping. I looked up again. Wynn was easing our visitors from the cabin. *Soon this whole nightmare will be over—it has to be!* Wynn closed the door, standing for a few moments with his head leaning against it. There was a droop to his shoulders I had never seen before. I wanted to cross to him, to tell him that it was all right now, but my legs wouldn't work. I sat back down slowly on the cot, and Wynn straightened his shoulders and turned to me.

"We should have been prepared for this, Elizabeth," he said sorrowfully. "We should have known."

"It's all right now," I told him. "I'm sure he understands. After all, it's been almost a year since he gave him to us. He can't just walk in and—"

"Elizabeth," cut in Wynn, "it's his child."

"He gave him to us."

"Not—not the way we thought." Wynn sounded very tired.

"But he's gone now."

"He'll be back."

I was on my feet then, terror bringing the strength back to my legs. "What do you mean? What are you saying?" I demanded. "You sent him away, didn't you?"

There was a defeated look on Wynn's face. "I sent him away, yes, so that we'd have a little time, a little time to think, a little time to prepare ourselves."

"What did you tell him?"

"I don't know. Something—something about the baby being asleep and we didn't want him to lose his dream or something. I'm really not sure. I just said the first thing that came to my mind."

Wynn shrugged his shoulders.

"And he's coming back?" I said in an empty voice.

"In the morning," said Wynn.

"Well, we won't let him go."

"There's no way to stop it, Elizabeth. He wants his baby."

"We'll go to court; we'll fight it."

"And only delay the agony. We wouldn't stand a chance."

I started to cry then—deep, agonizing sobs that shook my whole body. Wynn moved to comfort me, to hold me in his arms, and then I realized that Wynn was weeping, too. I don't suppose anything would have brought me to my senses more quickly. Knowing of Wynn's deep pain brought me out of myself. Wynn needed me. We needed each other. We were losing our baby. In the morning Samuel would be gone and there was nothing we could do about it.

For a moment I hated the young man. How could he do such a thing? And then, I dared to go a step further. I became very angry at God. Why was He letting such a thing happen? I tried to push the anger from me, knowing that it wasn't right, but it would not go away. I clung to Wynn and cried some more.

There was very little sleep for us that night. We talked, we prayed, I cried, but we did not rid ourselves of the deep pain within us.

I arose quietly about three o'clock to go out and check on Samuel. I crept quietly so that I would not waken Wynn, but when I entered the room, Wynn was already there, bending over the small boy, watching him sleep in the semidarkness, the open fire sending shivery little shadows over his face.

I went to Wynn's side and wordlessly took his hand. Again the tears fell. *We loved him so. We had thought him ours. We had planned his future.*

I went to make some coffee. We drank it together silently, our eyes on the baby. Kip seemed to understand that something was wrong. He came to me and pressed his muzzle into my hand, whimpering deep in his throat.

"We need to talk," said Wynn.

I nodded.

"They'll be here in a few hours."

Still I said nothing.

"What do you want to send with him?"

I couldn't name the things one by one—all the things Wynn and I had made for Samuel. I knew I would send all of them. I wanted him to have familiar things. Besides, they only would be hurtful reminders left with us.

"I'll pack his things," I managed through numb lips, and got up to do so.

I guess I cried over everything I packed. The little clothes, the blankets, the Christmas toys, the gifts that had come. I emptied the drawer where I had kept his things, and then I reached for the little calico horse and wept some more.

"Why, God? Why?" my heart kept crying, but there was no answer.

When I had all of his things packed and my tears under control, I rejoined Wynn by the fire.

"What about the puppy?" I asked Wynn. "We haven't even picked out a name for him yet."

"Samuel should name him. If Joe wants him, he can go."

"And if he doesn't?"

"Jim Buck has always wanted a dog. He can take him if his parents say it's okay."

The sky was beginning to lighten. I knew that Joe and his new wife would soon come. They were traveling to the big village and would want to leave early. I thought I should invite them for breakfast, but I could not bring myself to do so. I went to the bedroom and dressed. Wynn was already in his uniform.

I came out and walked to the crib again, looking down at the sleeping Samuel. "Wynn," I said, "I don't think I want to be here when they come."

Wynn nodded his head in understanding.

"I was wondering," he said slowly, "if you'd like me to take Samuel to them, so they won't need to come here?"

I hesitated, thinking over Wynn's suggestion.

"I—I think so," I agreed.

"Then we'd better get him up and get him fed and ready."

Wynn got the baby up and dressed him while I fixed his morning porridge, and then we gave him his breakfast. We had prayer together, asking God to go with our Samuel, wherever his path led—to keep him, and protect him, and most of all to give him opportunity to know Him as we had planned that he should.

Samuel seemed to think it was just another morning. He squealed at his puppy, chewed on his little horse and grabbed handfuls of Kip's fur. We gathered all his things then and Wynn took the small baby in his arms and the bundle on his back, the puppy tucked within his tunic as he had brought him home such a short time ago, and set off for the village after I had given Samuel one last squeeze.

I wondered as I watched them go with the tears streaming down my cheeks if life would ever again have meaning for me.

33
Sorrow and Joy

THE NEXT WEEKS were the worst days of my life. I wandered in an empty world, void of feeling except for pain. The house was empty, the bed in the corner—which I had insisted remain where it was—was empty, but worst of all, my life was empty as well.

At times I tried to pray but God seemed far away. I knew it wasn't God's fault. He hadn't moved. I had. I no longer felt close to Him. I couldn't understand how He could have let this happen.

I didn't even feel close to Wynn. He quietly went about his daily tasks. I tended to mine. He tried to communicate, to hold me, to get me to talk it out, but I resisted, putting him off with one flimsy excuse or another.

I lost weight, which was not surprising. I wasn't eating. I still couldn't sleep. I just lay in bed at night, wondering what was happening to Samuel.

Nimmie came to see me, and brought her children. Where before I would have enjoyed their play and their laughter, now it was only a cruel reminder; and when Nimmie invited me to her house, I found reasons to stay at home.

There was nothing to do at home. No sewing, little washing, no reason to make special food or plan special childish games. Jim Buck came to see me, wondering when we would be starting classes again; but I put him off with some evasive answer and told him that I would bang on the drum when I was ready for classes to resume.

I took in my garden and stored the vegetables—not because I found pleasure in it, but because it was something to do. Almost daily I went for long walks with Kip. I didn't enjoy the walking, but it got me away from the village and I would not need to try to act civil to other people.

I knew Wynn was worried about me, but I really couldn't make myself care.

When winter's snow swept in, burying all the uncleanness of the village beneath a blanket of white, I watched without comment. *It would be nice*, I thought, *to be able to bury one's feelings as completely.*

But God had not forgotten me. Day by day snatches of scripture verses began to chip away at the coldness of my heart. Little phrases and promises began to come to my mind. There were those who prayed, I know, and perhaps it was in response to them that the Lord kept working with me. It was also because I was His child and He loved me.

One day as I looked at the snow lying cold and clean on the village paths, I thought of the verse, "Wash me, and I shall be whiter than snow." For some reason I got a look at my heart as the words flashed before me. In the past I had been washed, I had been cleansed. I had then bowed before my Maker with a guilt-free conscience because of the washing, cleansing power of His blood. I didn't feel clean now. I felt defiled. Dirty. Angry and bitter. I knew that if I bowed before Him now, it could be only with a head hung down in shame.

"But it's your fault, God," I condemned Him. "Look at the pain you caused me."

"He was wounded for our transgressions, he was bruised for our iniquities," whispered in my mind.

"I know, I know," I admitted reluctantly. "You did send your Son to die for me. It did cause you pain. I've said I'm sorry. I've asked for forgiveness for my sin, but this is something different. As your child I thought you would shield me, care for me—but here I am. I'm all alone and I'm hurting, Lord—because you—"

"For the Lord your God is a merciful God; he will not forsake you or destroy you," came the scripture verse.

"But I feel forsaken, Lord. I feel empty and—"

"Call on me, and I will answer you, and show you great and mighty things, which you do not know."

"Could you, Lord? Could you really help me? Could you lift this burden from my heart and make life meaningful again?"

"For you shall go out with joy, and be led out with peace; the mountains and the hills shall break forth into singing before you, and all the trees of the field shall clap their hands."

That was what I needed, what I longed for. Perhaps it wasn't the absence of Samuel that was making my life so miserable, but the absence of the presence of God. *I must find that joy again. I must.* I took my Bible and went to my bedroom. I would spend as long on my knees as necessary to find and restore the peace with Him that I had known.

I had to go right back to the beginning and work my way through God's plan for mankind. I knew that in order to have peace with God one must meet His conditions. The first thing I had to do was to confess my sin. In this case it was my bitterness and resentment. I was angry with God because I had not borne a child. I was angry with God for taking from me the children I had learned to love, first Susie and then baby Samuel. I had no right to blame God. He couldn't be held accountable for Susie's family's decision to move, or for Joe Henry's choice to come for his son. And how did I know but that those actions might not be for the best? What I *did* know was that God was in charge of my life. He was my sovereign God. He knew what was good for me, and I needed to understand that in His great love for me, He would comfort and sustain me through this devastating loss. *He will give me what is best*, I determined.

I cried out in repentance, and all of the bitterness began to melt from my soul. I then went on to tell God that I accepted His plan for my life, whatever it was, even if it meant I would be childless, and I would stop fighting against it and leave things in His hands. I no longer wanted to be miserable or to bring misery to others. I thought of Wynn and the pain I had caused him. I asked the Lord to forgive me, and vowed to ask Wynn to forgive me also.

I prayed for Samuel. I prayed also for Joe Henry Running Deer, that he would be a good and wise father. That somehow Joe might be given opportunity to know the Lord so that he could introduce Samuel, and any more sons and daughters that he might be blessed with, to the Savior.

I prayed for the young girl who was now Samuel's mother. I prayed that God would help her in her motherhood. That she would be loving and kind, patient and caring, and that she would grow to love Samuel as I had loved him.

I talked to God about many things, keeping nothing back, and by the time I rose from my knees I felt clean and at peace again.

I knew there still would be days ahead when I might wish for a child. I would take those days as they came, asking God to help me through them, but I was sure that I would not chafe and be impatient and insistent. With God's help I would look for the joy in life that He would choose to give me. It was foolish to go through life pouting and complaining and making myself miserable when I already had so much to be thankful for. I would make each day an experience with the Lord. I would find many things to thank Him for. I started out by thanking Him for Wynn.

Wynn knew as soon as he came in our door that something had happened. I shared my experience with him that night. We spent some time talking it over and praying together. It was good to feel whole and close again. "I shouldn't have acted as I did," I admitted. "I will treasure the memories of the days spent with Samuel. They will always be special to me."

We removed the crib from the living quarters. We no longer needed those kinds of painful reminders. We had pleasant memories now, and we found that we could share them together. "Remember when?" one of us would say, and we would both laugh at the incident.

We cherished the pictures Wawasee had made. Many of them I mounted and hung in our bedroom. Each day as I looked at them, I thanked God again for giving us those precious months of parenting Samuel.

Wynn entered the cabin with a strange-looking document in his hands. "What's that?" I asked.

"A new posting," was his reply.

"A new posting—how did you get that?"

"A special runner just brought it."

"Can't we just stay on here?" I asked, frowning as I thought of all of our friends in the village.

"The Force feels that it is not wise to leave a man for too long in one area."

"Why?"

"There is the chance of becoming too attached to certain friends, or making enemies."

"So where is it? Still in the North?" I asked, coming closer to get a look at the paper.

"It is, but it really doesn't matter," Wynn said rather absently. "I'm not going to take it."

"You're not?" I was surprised. Wynn usually did not question his orders. "How do you get out of it?"

"Request it. Under the circumstances, I think they will be reasonable."

Wynn took the paper to his office and then came back out. He kissed me and turned to go. "We'll talk about it later," he said.

I did a lot of thinking after he had gone. Somehow I knew it was because of me that Wynn was thinking of questioning the order. I looked down at myself. I was still skinny, but I was eating better now. I was sure that in no time I would be up to the proper weight again. I was sleeping fine now, too, and I had resumed classes and was having ladies in for tea and getting out to the village. I was enjoying life again, and I was wise enough to know that when we left this village, I would be lonesome for the friends we had made. And the thought of leaving dear Nimmie brought a special pang of sorrow.

But I was no longer afraid, nor was I bitter. I was now willing to walk in God's path for my life. With Him it did not matter where one lived or the circumstances of the living. Wherever one was located, there could still be peace and joy.

I did not bring up the matter of the letter. We had settled before our fire that evening when Wynn spoke.

"You wondered about that new posting," he said, lowering the book he was reading. "It was to Smoke Lake."

"Where's Smoke Lake?"

"North and west of us."

"Bigger or smaller?" I asked.

"A little bigger, I guess."

"What's it like?"

"It's even more primitive than it is here."

There was silence for several minutes.

"You've decided not to take it because of me, right?"

Wynn hedged. "Well, not because I think you couldn't handle it, only because I don't think it would be fair to you."

"Why?"

"As I said, it's even more difficult and secluded than it is here."

"What will you do then?"

Wynn had laid aside his book and was giving me his complete attention. "I will ask for a post back in civilization. If not Calgary or Edmonton, at least a fair-sized town where you can live similar to the way you are used to living, Elizabeth. The North has been hard on you. You've been asked to give so much, and you've always been willing, but it's time now—"

I did not let Wynn finish. "You know," I said, "it was good for me to make that trip to Calgary. I found out that stores and sidewalks and even bathrooms aren't necessary for life after all."

"You're saying that you don't want to go back?" Wynn asked incredulously.

"No, I'm not saying that. I could enjoy living back there, too. But I don't need it to be happy. I can be happy here just as well. Don't you see, Wynn, the important thing is being with you."

"But I'd be with you."

"In body maybe, but your heart would still be in the North. I wouldn't want that, Wynn, and I don't think either of us would be happy under those circumstances."

There was silence again.

"So just what are you saying?" Wynn finally asked.

I stood up and walked to the fire. I threw on another log and watched the sparks fly upward, reminding me of the multitude of stars in the clear northern sky over our cabin.

"I'm saying, let's take that posting, now, while we are young and healthy and want to do it. There will be plenty of time for city living in the years ahead. The people need us, Wynn. There are lots of men and their wives who are willing to take the city postings. We're needed here." I hesitated for a moment. "Who knows what exciting things might be just over the next hill?"

Wynn stood to his feet and took me in his arms. He looked deeply into my eyes. "You're sure?" he asked me.

"Perfectly sure."

And I was. With Wynn's arms about me and God's peace in my heart, I had no reason to doubt or fear anything the future might hold.

WHEN HOPE
SPRINGS NEW

Dedicated with love and respect
to my youngest sister,
Sharon Violet Fehr,
another proof of the old saying,
"last but not least."
I appreciate her faith
and her dedication.
This comes with love—
to her, to her husband Richard,
and to Shawna, Eric and Amy.

CONTENTS

1 Uprooted   511
2 Smoke Lake   515
3 A New Home   518
4 Getting Settled   522
5 Lonely Days   526
6 Blueberry Pie   530
7 Winter   532
8 Neighbors   536
9 Spring   539
10 Planting the Seed   543
11 Introductions   547
12 Summer   552
13 Panic   556
14 Reversal   562
15 Aftermath   566
16 Difficulties   571
17 Counting the Days   576
18 The Gift   581
19 Misunderstanding   585
20 Relief   590
21 Reunion   594
22 Starting Over   597
23 Adjustments   601
24 Change   607
25 Leaving   614
26 Athabasca Landing   618
27 Involvement   625
28 Service   630
29 Winter   633
30 Sunday Dinners   638
31 Answers   645

1

Uprooted

"IS IT much farther?"

I felt like a small child asking again, but I really could not help myself. My whole being seemed to be in a state of agitation as we topped each hill, and the settlement was still not in view.

Wynn smiled understandingly. "Not too far," he comforted.

He had been saying that for quite a while now.

"How many hills?" I asked, hoping to pin him down to an answer that I could understand.

Now he didn't just smile, he chuckled. "You sound like a kid asking— 'How many sleeps?'" he teased me.

Yes, I did sound like a kid. We had been on the trail for what already seemed forever. My common sense reminded me that it really hadn't been that long—four days, to be exact—but it felt like weeks.

Wynn reached out and squeezed my hand. "Why don't you ride for a while again?" he asked me. "You've walked enough now. You'll tire yourself out. I'll see what I can find out from the guide."

He signalled the driver of the lumbering team to stop and helped me up to a semicomfortable position on a makeshift seat. We resumed forward motion as he moved on down the line of wagons to seek out the guide of our small, slow-moving expedition.

He wasn't gone long, and then, without even slowing the wagon, he swung himself up beside me.

"You'll be happy to know that we should be there in about forty-five minutes," he said. Giving my shoulders a hug, he hopped down and was gone again.

Forty-five minutes! Well, I would manage somehow, but that still seemed like a long time.

During our four days of travel I had acquired aching bones, a sunburned nose, and a multitude of mosquito and blackfly bites. But it wasn't these irritations that had me troubled the most.

I realized that my agitation, that hollow, knotted spot in the center of my stomach, was all due to my fear of the unknown. I had not been nearly as frightened when I had come with Wynn to our first Northern outpost. Then I had been a new bride, eager to share the adventures of my Mountie husband.

I was still eager to share the adventures with Wynn, but this move was different. I had learned to know and love the Indian people at Beaver River. I had left behind not only the known but the loved. Now I had to start all over again.

I don't believe I was afraid that I would not be able to make new friends. What worried me was how well I would be able to get along without my *old* friends. I was going to miss Nimmie so much. Surely there was not another person like her in all of the Northland. I would even miss Evening Star and Mrs. Sam and Little Dear and Anna. I would miss Wawasee and Jim Buck and my other students. I would miss the familiar Indian trappers, the simple homes I had visited so often, the curling woodsmoke, even the snarling dogs. Tears welled up in my eyes and slid down my cheek again. *I must stop this*, I chided myself, as I had done so many times already on the trail. *I will have myself sick before I even arrive.*

I pushed my thoughts back to safer ground, making myself wonder what our new home at Smoke Lake would be like. Well, I would not need to wonder for long. Wynn had said forty-five minutes, and the minutes were ticking by, even though slowly, with each rotation of the squeaky wheels.

Home again, I exulted inwardly, *after these days and nights on the trail!* I was looking forward to a nice hot bath and a chance to sleep in a real bed. Mosquito netting on the windows and a door to close for some privacy would seem like a luxury after this trip—with its heat, rain, and wind, by turn; with its steep hills, flat marshland, dusty trails and soggy gumbo. Well, it would not be long now.

I looked at the sky. Perhaps we had had our last rain shower four hills back. The sky above me was perfectly clear. *Surely it can't cloud over and drench us again in just forty-five minutes of time—probably thirty-five by now.* Even as I reasoned with myself, I wasn't completely convinced of our safety against another storm. Some of them had seemed to come upon us with incredible swiftness. I fervently hoped we would arrive at the new settlement in dry clothes. I hardly had anything left fit to wear. I was anxious to get out my washtubs and scrub up the wet and soiled things we had been stashing away in the wagon. They would be ruined if I didn't get at them soon.

The driver stopped to rest the team, and I climbed down from the wagon again. At least when I was walking, my anticipation was being channeled into something. I debated whether I should walk ahead of the team where I felt the risk of being run over at any minute, behind the team, where I would be forced to swallow trail dust, or off to the side where the walking was even more difficult. I decided to follow the team. I would lag far enough behind to let the dust settle a bit.

While I waited for the team to resume, I strolled to the side of the trail and looked around for signs of berries. I hoped there would be some in our area. Many of my canning jars were empty, and I did want to fill them again before another winter.

The area did not look promising.

There's lots of land around here, I assured myself. *There could be many good berry patches.*

Kip came bounding up. In contrast to me, he thoroughly enjoyed the trip and all the new things there were to investigate. I had hardly seen him all day. He ran this way and that, ahead and behind, only coming back occasionally to check and make sure I was still traveling with the wagons.

I patted his head and was rewarded with generous waves of his curly tail. He licked my hand, then wheeled and was gone again before I even had time to speak to him.

Wynn dropped back, bringing with him a canteen of water.

"Need a drink?" he asked, and I suddenly realized I was thirsty. I smiled my thanks and lifted the canteen to my lips. The water was tepid, not like the refreshing water from our cabin well. Still, it was wet and it did help my thirst.

"We will soon be there," Wynn informed me. "I think it would be good to slip the leash on Kip. The village dogs might be running loose."

"He's gone again," I answered, alarmed. "He was here just a minute ago and then he ran off."

"Don't worry," Wynn assured me; "he won't be far away."

He was right. At the sound of Wynn's whistle, Kip came bounding through the underbrush at the side of the trail. His coat was dirty and tangled with briers and leaves, his tongue was lolling out the side of his mouth from his run, but he looked contented, perhaps even smug, about his new adventures.

I couldn't help but envy him. There was no concern showing in his eyes, like I must surely have been showing in mine.

Wynn slipped the leash on Kip and handed it to me. "I'm expected to be up at the front of the wagons when we enter the village," he stated simply. "Would you like to walk with me?"

I hesitated, not knowing what I wanted to do. I would like Wynn's support; still, I hated to walk into that new village like I was on display. I disliked the thought of all of those staring eyes.

"I think I'll just stay back here with Kip," I mumbled. "He won't fuss as much if he isn't in the center of the commotion."

Wynn nodded. I think he might have guessed my real reason.

The wagons up ahead had paused on the brow of the hill. I knew without even asking that just down that hill lay our new settlement—our new home. I wanted to see it, yet I held back in fear. How could one be so torn up inside, wanting to run to see what lay before, yet holding back from looking, all at the same time?

Without comment, Wynn reached forward and took my hand, then bowed his head and addressed our Father simply, "Our Father in heaven, we come to this new assignment not knowing what is ahead. Only You know the needs of these people. Help us to meet those needs. Help us to be caring, compassionate and kind. Help Elizabeth with all the new adjustments. Give her fellowship and friendships. Give her a ministry to the people, and keep us close to one another and to You. Amen."

I should have felt much better after Wynn's prayer, and I guess I did, but it was also another reminder of all the new things and experiences lying ahead.

I smiled at Wynn to assure him that I was fine. The wagons were moving again. We turned to follow, Wynn crossing the ground in long strides that would soon carry him out in front where he was expected to be.

I hesitated, holding in check the impatient Kip. The dust could settle some before I followed. There would be much commotion in the village at the coming of the new law enforcer. Everyone would be out to check him over. I was in no hurry to be thrust into the center of the staring throng.

2
Smoke Lake

THERE IT WAS—our new village stretching out before us on the floor of the forested valley. Wynn was right. It was larger than Beaver River. It was also more primitive and scattered in appearance. Wynn was right again. Yet it did not seem to be properly named. In the hazy stillness of the summer afternoon, not one of the many village homes had smoke ascending from the chimney.

I stood and let my eyes wander over the small, roughly constructed houses. Which one was ours, the one we would call home? In Beaver River our cabin had been set apart from the settlement. I let my eyes travel to the west, then the east, then the north and south. I could find no cabin located on the outskirts of the little village.

I found myself searching then for the sign of a garden. Surely someone in the village must wish to plant. But no, I could find nothing that looked like a cultivated area.

Even from this distance the small cabin homes looked shoddy and ill-kept. Compared to our homes in Beaver River, these looked like shacks. The large building in the center, which I assumed was the trading post, also looked hurriedly slapped together and run-down. Disappointment welled up within me.

For a moment I wished I could turn around and head back to the village I knew and loved. There I would be welcomed with softly curling woodsmoke. I would find a well-constructed, well-stocked trading post. I would discover my comfortable cabin at the outskirts of the village. I would be welcomed by neighbors and friends with gardens and berry patches.

Kip did not share my longings. He pulled forward on the leash and reminded me with a whine that I was to follow the wagons down the dusty, winding hill.

I broke from my reverie and started my descent. Already I could hear the village dogs as they set up their frenzied barking to announce the coming of strangers. Wynn's crated dog sled team, which rode the second wagon, responded to the howls. What a noise they all made!

Amid the din caused by the dogs, there were a few shouts and hellos, and arms were lifted in greeting. The first wagon was already rolling to a stop, boiling dust whirling in around it.

I pulled back on Kip's leash. I wanted some of the excitement to die down before I entered the village.

I saw a larger rock at the side of the trail in the shade of the tall pine trees. I led Kip to it and sat down to watch the milling around in the village below us. Kip whined and strained at the leash until I commanded him to be quiet and to lie down. He obeyed, rather reluctantly, and I turned my eyes back to the scene below.

It was several minutes before the wagons moved forward again. They stopped before a very small cabin with a sagging roofline, and I saw Wynn signal the men to begin unloading our crates and boxes.

Surely there must be some mistake! I thought. *That cabin isn't large enough to house Wynn's office, let alone our household too.*

Then a new thought passed through my mind. *No, we couldn't possibly be expected to live in that. It must be that our cabin is not ready, and we need to make do with temporary quarters.*

The unloading continued, and I saw Wynn look toward our hill. I knew he was searching for me, wondering what was taking me so long. I lifted my arm to let him know I was fine and coming to join him, and Kip and I started down the hill again.

I had not avoided the curious eyes. The people of the village stood in groups all around me as I entered with Kip straining forward on the leash. I knew they considered the white woman a strange spectacle. My skin was different, my hair was different, my dress was different—even my dog, leashed and fluffy, was different.

I smiled and softly greeted them in the Indian tongue. I was thankful that at least I knew their language.

No one answered my words or smiled in return. They continued to stare, moving back slightly from the path that led me to the small cabin.

Relieved, at last I reached my husband and hoped to be able to divert some of the staring eyes. I wished for a door to duck through, but there was only one in the very small cabin, where men were busy moving in and out, carrying crates and boxes.

"Well," said Wynn in a tired-sounding voice, "we are here." Then his tone turned teasing. "I thought for a minute that you got lost."

"I was in no hurry," I explained, and Wynn smiled, remembering the "hurry" I had been in throughout the morning.

"It isn't much, is it?" he said then, nodding his head at the cabin.

I tried to sound cheerful. "It'll do for now," I responded.

"What do you mean, for now? This is it, Elizabeth. This is our new home."

"It is?" I know that shock registered in my voice.

"It is. I'm sorry, Elizabeth. I had expected something better than this—even for here."

I had expected something better than this, too. Never had I thought that anyone lived in such crowded, miserable quarters. I'm sure my face turned pale, in spite of my healthy tan and my sunburned nose.

I recovered as quickly as I could, gulped away the tears in the back of my throat, and tried to speak. My voice sounded strange, forced. "We'll manage," was all I could say.

"Why don't you find a spot in the shade somewhere until the men are done unloading?" Wynn suggested, and I nodded dumbly and moved Kip around the cabin.

Indian cabins were all around us. There was no place to go where I wouldn't be subject to staring eyes. I wasn't ready for that yet. I wished I could go into the house to get away from it all, but I would only be in the way. Goodness knows, there was little room in there as it was.

With new determination I lifted my chin, took Kip's leash well in hand and started down the trail that led in a winding, circuitous route out of the village.

It took several minutes to walk far enough to be clear of the shabby little cabins. Kip whimpered and complained as I hurried him along. He wished to stop and investigate his new surroundings and make the acquaintance of the many thin, rough-coated dogs that strained against their tethers.

I hurried Kip right on by.

When we finally reached the woods beyond the village, I slowed my pace. I took a deep breath of the fresh summer air. It was tangy with the smell of pine trees and scented flowers. A small stream trickled nearby, and I followed the path that led along the bank.

We had not gone far when we came to a small lake. I looked out across it, enjoying its beauty, its tranquillity. I cannot explain what that little lake did for my spirits at that moment.

Here was a hallowed spot in the middle of all the squalor, the disappointment, of the little village. Here was someplace where I could go to refresh my soul. I eased myself down on the grass beside the waters and let my frustration and loneliness drain from me.

Surely, God is in this place. The words formed in my mind without any conscious effort. As I repeated them again, a quiet peacefulness settled upon me.

"Surely, God is in this place." I spoke the words aloud. It was true. It was a promise. It was enough.

3

A New Home

THE SUN WAS dipping behind the western horizon and the evening was beginning to cool when I retraced my steps down the path and into the village. The familiar scent of woodsmoke greeted me, and I breathed it in deeply. Maybe life in this new village wouldn't be so different after all.

For one panic-stricken moment I feared I might not be able to find the shabby little cabin that was to be our new home amid all the other shabby little cabins. But Kip led me right to it. Actually, I think I would have found it without difficulty, even by myself. There simply was no other cabin in the village with so much activity. One wagon still stood in front of our little building, boxes and crates piled high in the wagon box. I wondered why Wynn had not instructed the men to unload all the things.

I entered the door with caution, not sure just what I would find. In among boxes and empty crates, I found Wynn working alone and trying to sort some order out of the chaos. He looked up as I entered, relief showing in his eyes.

"I was a little worried about you," he said. "I wondered where you had gone, but one of the children said you took the path out of the village. If you hadn't come back soon, I would have been out looking for you."

"I'm sorry," I quickly apologized. "I didn't mean to alarm you. I just thought it would take some time until things were settled down so I could get in the cabin."

Wynn was quick to reassure me. "Well, I felt better knowing that you had Kip, and also knowing that you have a good sense of direction in the woods now. I was quite sure you wouldn't take yourself too far to find your way back again."

"I found a lake," I informed him with some excitement.

Wynn's head lifted from his hammering on the crate.

"I found a lake," I repeated. "It isn't very big, but it is lovely."

Wynn seemed to realize that the little lake was important to me.

"You'll have to show it to me," he stated with a brief smile.

"I will," I promised, "just as soon as we get settled."

I moved forward then, slipping Kip's leash so he was free to explore his new home. There wasn't much to explore. He would have it covered in two or three minutes. For me, it might take a little longer.

"I see there is still a lot to be unloaded," I remarked as I moved forward.

"I don't know what we'll do with it," responded Wynn doubtfully.

"What do you mean, 'do with it'?" I asked him.

"There's no storage available, and it will never fit in here. We might just have to throw a tarp over it and leave it on the wagon."

My eyes traveled over the cabin. Wynn was right. It was already very crowded. There was a blackened cookstove, a handmade table, two wooden chairs, a fireplace, a sagging bed in the corner, and a few rough wooden shelves. That was it.

Above me were dusty, weathered rafters. My first sight from the hill had been right. The roof did sag. I hoped it would not come crashing down upon us with the first heavy snowstorm.

My eyes turned then to the floor. It was hardpacked earth. Imagine! Not even rough boards to cover the dirt.

I had never lived in a dwelling with an earthen floor before. I wondered how I would manage living in one now. *At least it won't need washing*, I thought ruefully. I closed my eyes tightly as a shudder passed through me.

"We will soon need the lamp," Wynn was saying. "Do you remember what crate it was packed in?"

His words jolted me back to my senses. I tried to think. Yes, it was the big crate, the one with our bedding. I moved forward to point it out.

Wynn soon had the crate open and I joined him to remove the contents.

"I'll get this crate out of our way and make some more room," offered Wynn. "Perhaps with it out of the center of things, there will be enough room for you to make us some supper."

I looked toward the stove. Already a brisk fire was heating the room. The cooking surface was much smaller than I was used to. It looked like it would hold only the kettle and one pot at a time. I went over to check the kettle for water. It was already filled. A pail of water stood on the nearby shelf. It too had been filled with fresh water. *Dear Wynn*, I noted mentally. He was so thoughtful. I turned to find that food supplies had already been arranged on the two shelves provided. Our dishes were stacked on the small table.

"I don't know where you are going to find room to store things," said Wynn. "Those two shelves won't hold much."

Wynn was right. I looked around. There didn't seem to be any wall space left to build more shelves either.

"Some things can be hung up," I said, noticing a few nails in the walls.

With Wynn working to empty some boxes and clear some space, and me busy with our first meal, we began to feel that this small, poorly built cabin was going to be home.

When I had our supper ready, Wynn laid aside his hammer and went outside to wash in the basin he had set on a stump by the door. Soon he was back, his sleeves still pushed up and his hairline wet from rinsing his face. He looked tired—and he hadn't even begun to unpack his office supplies or medicines.

"Where is your office?" I asked him after we had bowed in prayer together.

"There isn't one," he answered simply.

"Nothing?"

"Nope."

"What did the last Mountie do?"

"He was alone, so he just stacked things up by the wall, I guess."

"Oh," was all the answer I could manage.

"You're the first white woman to live in this village, Elizabeth," Wynn went on.

"I am?" Suddenly I felt a heavy responsibility. As the first one here, I had much to uphold. The people of the village would undoubtedly judge the whole white race by what they found in me. It was scary, in a way.

Would I be found worthy? Would I be able to contribute to their way of life, or would I appear to threaten it? Would I fit in where no white woman had been before? Would the Indian women feel free to come and sip tea, or would they see me a strange creature with odd ways who should be shunned and avoided?

I did not have the answer to any of those questions. I looked at the small space around me. I knew without even visiting the other homes that this one was much like theirs. I smiled. I was beginning to feel some comfort in my strange, new home. If I lived like they lived, then surely it would not be as difficult for me to cross the barriers. If my floor was dirt, if my stove was small, if my bed stood in the corner of the same room, then wouldn't the Indian women find it easier to accept me as one of them?

Wynn must have noticed my smile. He lifted his head and looked at me, the question showing in his eyes.

"Well," I said, "I might be white, but my home will be no different. Perhaps that will make it easier to become one of them."

Wynn nodded. "Maybe so," he said slowly, "but I am sorry, Elizabeth, that it has to be so . . . so . . . uncomfortable for you."

I shrugged my shoulders. "Uncomfortable, yes. But it certainly isn't impossible, is it? I mean, with so many people living this way, I guess one must be able to do it and survive."

Wynn still looked doubtful. I was sure he was sorry he had agreed to bring me here.

"Look at it this way," I said, attempting to make my voice light. "Think of the little time that it will take to keep house. Why, I'll be able to loaf away hour after hour out by that little lake."

Wynn appreciated my effort, I know he did, but he still wasn't quite ready to respond.

During the days that lay ahead, I would have to show him, bit by bit, that I was able to handle living in such a poor little cabin as a home. It would take time. First I would have to thoroughly convince myself.

A deep thankfulness swept through me that this was my second experience, not my first, in Wynn's wilderness. If I had faced such conditions when originally coming to the Northland, I was sure I would not have been able to accept it as readily. Now, bit by bit, I had been seasoned to the rigors of the North. I felt that I might even be ready to endure such stark barrenness. After all, it would not be for long. Wynn himself had said that the Force never left a man for too long in one location—perhaps not more than three or four years.

I looked about me. Three or four years seemed like an awfully long time.

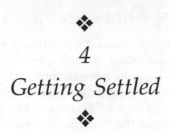

4
Getting Settled

❖

THE NEXT FEW days were busy with unpacking, sorting and repacking anything not absolutely essential. There was no way that all our material goods, few as they were, would fit in our tiny cabin.

It was very difficult for me to decide what I could live without. I had thought I was already down to the basics in the two rooms, plus storeroom, plus office, that we had occupied at Beaver River. Looking about me now, our Beaver River cabin seemed like a large, spacious home in comparison.

Now I began to wish that Kip had been raised as an outside dog. He seemed to be underfoot no matter where I stepped.

I carefully sorted my pots and dishes, keeping only a minimum. If we should ever have company, I would need to wash plates and cutlery before I could serve them, but it was the only way I could make things fit. I allowed only one extra of each item, and packed all the serving dishes. I would dish up our meals directly from the stove. Two pots and a frying pan were hung on nails on the already crowded wall. I did not even have room to put up my pictures of Samuel, so carefully drawn by Wawasee. With a heavy heart, I packed them away in one of the crates to be stored.

My washtubs, brooms, dustpan, scrubboard, and anything else that would hang, were also on the wall. Back at Beaver River many of these things had hung on the outside of our cabin. Here, according to the trader who ran the post, everything had to be hung on the inside. The people of the village understood that anything outside was community property. Only they often forgot to bring the items back to the spot from which they had originally borrowed them.

I wondered about the possibility of adding on a room or two, but I didn't say anything to Wynn. He was busy enough trying to sort through his new responsibilities and figure out where to keep his much-needed supplies.

I had not realized how much I had enjoyed the ready water supply of our Beaver River well until we reached this new village. There was no handy well with a pump here. All our water had to be carried from the stream which was almost a quarter of a mile from the settlement. One soon learned to conserve. I found that one kettleful would do many jobs before it was thrown out to settle the dust on our path.

The other problem concerned the fact that there was no outbuilding. In Beaver River Wynn quickly had a building constructed for more privacy and convenience for me as his new bride. Here, there did not seem to be materials, labor, nor time for that construction. I had to quickly learn the "rule" of the villagers so I would know which paths were used by the women and children, and which paths to avoid. There were no signs with directional arrows—this was an unwritten understanding of village life.

When I felt I had packed away everything I could possibly do without, Wynn placed all the full boxes back on one of the wagons and carefully covered them with a canvas tarp to keep out the rain or snow. Then he tied heavy ropes backward and forward, over and under the wagon, to keep out other things. I hated those crisscrossed ropes. They seemed to speak of a way of life that was foreign and objectionable to me.

Wynn still had not found a place to keep his medical supplies, so he had to stack them in our cabin. Already every available space seemed to be filled with our few belongings. The extra blankets and our clothing were in boxes under our bed. Boxes of canned foods were stacked beneath the table. When we sat to eat a meal, we had to turn sideways in our chairs since our feet would not fit beneath our table.

There was room in the middle of our floor for the one bearskin rug. It helped to hide some of the earthen floor. I placed a few cushions on our bed. Seeing we had no couch of any kind, I felt it would be nice to have some extra back support, but in the days that followed I tired quickly of shifting the cushions each time we went to bed. I began to wish I had packed them away, too. But they did add a note of color and cheeriness to our drab surroundings, I decided.

More than a week had gone by before I visited the village trading post. There was no use buying anything more, since I couldn't find room even for what we had on hand. I went to the store more to make the acquaintance of the trader and the villagers than anything. I had been outside my own cabin very little in the few days I had been in the settlement. It was now time to meet the people and make some new friends.

English would do me no good in Smoke Lake. None of the people understood it. Even the trader in the store knew only a few English words. He spoke the Indian dialect like a native, which he actually was in part, though his mother tongue was French. I was thankful I had at least a working knowledge of the Indian tongue.

I met two women from the village as I walked to the trading post, and I smiled and greeted them in their own language. But they avoided eye contact and passed on, looking almost frightened. It was easy to see it would take some time for me, the white woman of the lawman, to be accepted. I would need to be patient.

I entered the store by its one low door and looked around. The interior was dark and smelled strongly of furs and tobacco smoke—not a pleasant smell at the best of times, and in the close, suffocating little building, it was nearly unbearable. I held my breath against it and looked about. I did need eggs and lard, if they were to be had. In the clutter of the small store, I saw nothing that looked like egg crates or lard pails, but then not everything was visible, I reminded myself.

The trader eyed me shrewdly, squinting against the smoke wafting up from his hand-rolled cigarette and into his eyes. He spoke to me, but I did not understand a word of it.

"I'm sorry," I said in English, forgetting for a moment, "I don't understand."

He gave me a quizzical look and shrugged his shoulders.

I remembered then, and I switched over to the Indian tongue. He answered me in the native dialect, though his words were accented much differently than mine.

At least we can understand one another, I sighed in relief.

"I need eggs," I announced carefully, using the rather unfamiliar Indian words.

"No eggs," he informed me with an accompanying shake of the head.

"I also need some lard."

"No lard," he stated.

"Oh, my," I said in English. "What am I going to do now?"

"What you say?" he asked in the Indian dialect.

I looked at him apologetically and tried to explain that I had been speaking to myself.

"When in here," he informed me coldly in our mutual language, "best you speak to me—not you."

I had the feeling that I wasn't going to care too much for this surly man with his unkempt appearance and piercing eyes.

"You need coffee?" he asked me.

"No," I said, "no coffee. I have coffee now, thank you."

"You need flour?"

"No. No, I have flour."

"Sugar? Beans? Salt?"

I shook my head at each of the items as he listed them.

"Then why you come here?" he threw at me.

"I came for eggs and lard," I reminded him, just a bit annoyed.

"Don't got. Here we get eggs from bird nest, lard from animal. Not need eggs and lard in store."

I nodded again and headed for the door without even wishing him a good morning. Not surprising, he did not wish me a good morning either.

I was glad to again be in the fresh air. I breathed deeply of the scent of pine. Even the lazy smoke from the cabin fires could not disguise it.

I didn't wish to go back to my small, confined cabin. Nothing there needed my further attention. My small house had been put in order, the pair of white curtains hung in the one small window, the rug spread upon the floor, the rest of the homey things packed away and stored on the wagon, and it would be hours before the bread dough would be ready for the oven. I was looking for companionship.

All around me people were busy with work and play. In front of the cabins women were weaving or sewing. Children played in the dirt or carried armloads of wood from the forest to the fires. Old men sat together in silent comradery. Young women chattered gayly as they spread pounded meat out to dry in the sun. But as soon as I approached, all fell silent. Eyes turned to the ground, tongues became hushed. My smile and my words in their language were totally ignored. They were not going to even give me a chance to get to know them.

In frustration and despair, I finally turned my steps toward our small cabin. If only I had Nimmie. If only there were an Anna or a Mrs. Sam to drop in for tea. I sighed deeply. I already could feel the loneliness of a long, silent winter closing in about me.

Kip met me at the door. His coat had now been restored to its usual fluffiness after the tangled mess it had become on the days spent on the trail. With washtub and brush I again had him looking like the house dog he had come to be. In comparison with the dogs of the village, he looked like he came from a different species entirely. I gave his head a pat, glad for his eager eyes and his waving tail.

At least here was a friendly face. I slipped on his leash and led him down the path that wove out of the village and along the stream to the quiet little lake. It might be that Kip would be the only companion I would have for the next few weeks—until I had somehow managed to break through the reserve of these villagers.

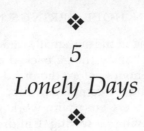

5

Lonely Days

❖

OUR EXCURSIONS TO the small lake became almost a daily ritual for Kip and me. It was a beautiful walk and a lovely spot. No one seemed to resent us using the trail and sitting on the lakeshore or strolling through the pines, but no one seemed to pay much attention to us anyway. I still was unable to get the women to even acknowledge my presence. It was a very difficult time for me.

Wynn and I discussed it often at our supper table.

"Though these Indians are from the same tribe as our Beaver River Indians, they have not been exposed to the white man in the same way," he reminded me. "In coming to this remote village, it is as though we stepped back in time. We live with a very primitive people, Elizabeth."

Wynn sympathized with my need for friendship, but cautioned me to be patient and let the people have time to come to know and accept me. I secretly wondered just how long my patience would need to endure. I seemed to be getting nowhere.

Fall came with dry winds rustling the party-dressed leaves on the poplar trees and the birds twittering and instructing one another concerning their coming flight south. I loved the fall, but the thought of the coming winter, with no friends to help me see it through, concerned me. I needed to take action but I didn't know what to do.

Then one day I had an idea. I was passing down the path to again walk to the lake when I noticed two women enter the village with baskets of berries. So there *were* berries around! I did want some for the winter ahead. I also saw it as an opportunity to "build a bridge." Hadn't it been berries that had brought me my first friends at Beaver River? I hurried home to find some kind of container.

I left Kip behind in the cabin. I didn't want him to interfere in any way with my attempt to make friends. With a light step and heart, I went to find some village women.

I did not need to go far. Just down the trail from our cabin, two Indian women sat in the afternoon sun sewing buckskin moccasins. I approached them with my cooking pot extended and a smile on my lips.

As usual they stopped their chatter and lowered their eyes, but I was not to be discouraged so easily.

I greeted them with the proper Indian greeting. They did not return it as was the custom. I waited for a moment and when there was no response I raised the question.

"I want to pick berries," I informed them with my limited vocabulary.

Still no response. They continued their work, seeming nervous at my presence, but they did not look up nor acknowledge me.

"Where can I find berries?" I tried to keep my voice friendly in spite of how I was beginning to feel, but it wavered some.

One of the women grunted, and they both picked up their work and went into the cabin.

I could have cried. How was I ever going to make friends in this strange new village? I was about to turn around and go home again when I spotted two younger women, their babies on their backs, stirring a blackened pot over an open fire. Perhaps the younger ones would be less hostile, I decided, and headed for them.

They too dropped their eyes and ceased speaking when I came near, though their eyes did lift occasionally to steal little glances at me.

I greeted them, but did not wait for their response. I hastened right on. "I want to pick berries and I not know where they are. Can you tell me, please?"

For a moment there was silence and then they exchanged brief looks. One of them shrugged slightly, but the other pointed to the west and said simply, "There." It wasn't much, and it certainly didn't locate a patch for me, but it was the first word that had been spoken to me since I had entered their village. I smiled my thanks and started west.

I tramped around through the woods for the rest of the afternoon and still did not find a berry patch.

That night at our evening meal I told Wynn about my adventure of the day. He looked concerned, feeling my hurt at being rejected by this village, but we both acknowledged that it was a start—a small start.

"I've seen a patch or two as I've made my rounds," Wynn informed me. "Let's see if I can remember just where it was. Guess I didn't pay enough attention because I knew all your canning jars were packed away—even if we did get them out and fill them, we'd have no place to store them. If we put them back on the wagon, they'd just freeze with our first cold spell."

"Even if I just get a few for now, so that we can have some fresh and a pie or two," I said, realizing that Wynn was right about preserving, "it would be nice for a change."

Wynn nodded and took pencil and paper to draw me a crude little map.

The next morning I took Kip and my cooking pot, a sandwich for my lunch, and with Wynn's map in hand I set out to find a berry patch.

It took a bit of looking but I finally found a patch big enough to fill my pot, and I settled down to the picking, humming to myself as the pot slowly filled.

I let Kip run while I picked. He took little ventures into the woods, chasing rabbits and worrying the squirrels, but he returned often to keep check on me.

Midday I stopped for my sandwich. I wished I had a cup of tea to go with it. I was not far from the stream, so I left my pot and strolled to the stream for a drink. The water was cool and refreshing. I splashed a little on my face and washed the blue stain from my hands.

Kip lapped at the water, wading out in it just far enough to reach it with his tongue without bending too much. The flowing water licked at his legs and swirled around his nose as he thrust it into the stream.

I picked up a short stick and played a game of chase-the-stick with Kip for a few minutes. By the time our game was over, Kip was dripping wet from chasing the stick out into the middle of the stream. I forgot to keep my distance, and when Kip left the stream he shook water all over my skirt. I laughed at myself and ran back toward the berry patch and my nearly full pot.

Kip ran on ahead of me, still shaking wetness as he ran. He seemed to know exactly where we were going and led me directly toward my cooking pot with its berries. He reached it first—or would have reached it had he not suddenly stopped dead still, his hackles bristling and his throat rumbling.

His eyes were fastened on the spot where I had left my berries, and my eyes lifted from Kip to search out the pot as well.

There, feasting undeservedly from my hard-earned berries, was a skunk. I held my breath, not daring to stir.

The skunk seemed undisturbed. I wanted him to stay that way. I had no desire at all to tangle with him. I put a hand down to restrain Kip, but I wasn't fast enough.

Kip knew the berries were mine. He also knew that the skunk was an imposter. With his throat sending out warnings, he sprang forward to chase the skunk from the berry container.

It all happened so quickly I hardly had time to think. There was a flash as Kip left my side, the instant flag of the skunk's tail, a brief skirmish, and then Kip was screaming in rage and pain and rolling his head around in the debris on the forest floor as a sickening and powerful smell rolled over us.

I looked up from Kip just in time to see the last of the skunk disappearing through the underbrush.

I hurried Kip back to the stream. I didn't even need to throw in the stick for him to seek out the water. He plunged his whole head into its depths, burying himself in the coolness. His eyes stinging and his nose smarting, again and again he thrust his head into the stream.

It did nothing for the odor. It seemed to just grow worse and worse. I looked down at my skirt, then sniffed of my hands. Though I had not been sprayed directly by the skunk, I seemed to smell almost as bad as Kip. What in the world would I ever do now?

After Kip had received all the help he could get from the flowing stream, we went back to the berry patch to reclaim our pot.

I was tempted to leave it just where it sat. I knew from the concentration of the smell in the area that just to walk through the bushes and over the ground would cover my shoes and skirts with more of the offensive odor. Yet I couldn't afford to leave the cooking pot behind. I had only one other with which to cook.

I found a long stick and stretched as far as I could to hook the pot and lift it to me. It slipped from the pole mid-air and clattered to the ground. Try as I might I could not get the handle hooked again. I finally gave up and, hoisting my skirt the best I could, waded through the short bushes and reclaimed my pot. As I had anticipated, it reeked!

I emptied out the rest of the berries, nearly crying as I watched them fall into a small pile on the ground, and headed once again for the stream. I used sand to scrub and scour my pot, but even so some of the smell seemed to cling to it. Whatever would I do? I needed that cooking pot.

At last we started for home.

"Kip, you stink!" I informed him as I slipped his leash back on, and then smiled in spite of myself—the pot calling the kettle black. I was sure I was just as offensive as the dog. And my cooking pot wasn't much better.

I wondered just how in the world I would be able to get back into the village without causing chaos.

"Well, at least they won't be able to ignore me," I said to Kip with a grin. But I really wasn't that amused by it all. We were in a terrible fix, and well I knew it. How in the world, and when in the world, would we ever be free of the odor?

6
Blueberry Pie

THE ODOR PRECEDED us into the village. I heard children shouting the Indian word for skunk and then saw them run toward their cabins even before I came into the settlement. The women, too, left what they
were doing and went indoors.

With a red face and a hurried step, I hastened toward my own cabin
with the smelly Kip tightly in tow.

When we reached the cabin I tethered Kip outside and put my pot
beside the door. Then I leaned down and removed my shoes, stepped just
inside the door and removed my heavy skirt, reaching around the door
to toss it back out onto the path. After that I removed the rest of my
clothes and scrubbed with soap and water until I had my skin red and
chafed. Still I smelled like a skunk!

I was forced to put clean garments on a still odorous body; then with
a tub of hot sudsy water I attacked my clothes. I washed them as best as
I could and hung them on my outside line. I could still smell them. I next
took Kip and scrubbed him in the water. His wet fur seemed to smell
worse, not better.

I saw many curious looks directed my way. Little clusters of Indian
children stared without reservation, and the women gathered in whispery little groups, trying not to be as obvious as the children, but not suc-
ceeding very well.

I clamped my jaw and scrubbed harder on Kip. He whined and tried
to pull away from me, but I scolded him mildly and scrubbed on. After
all, he was the one who had gotten us into the mess!

In spite of all my efforts, when Wynn returned that night he was greeted
by the strong smell of skunk.

"What do I do about it?" I moaned.

"Not much that you can do," Wynn answered.

"You mean nothing will help it?"

"Only time, as far as I know," responded Wynn.

I moaned again. "Time" always seemed so slow when you needed it
to pass quickly.

"You could try filling the pot with dirt and burying your clothes,"
Wynn said. "Some seem to think that the earth takes some of the odor
away."

"Kip is the worst," I insisted.

"Bury him, too, if you like," said Wynn, but he smiled to let me know he was teasing.

I did bury my clothes. I also buried the pot. The Indians watched me, hiding their eyes and their comments behind work-stained hands.

I did not leave my clothes buried for long. I could not take the chance of the moist ground causing rot. The clothing I had was scarce enough at best and to lose an outfit simply would not do, even if I did reek each time I wore it. I dug it up carefully and washed it with soap and water again and hung it on the line.

The soil *did* seem to help my cooking pot. I scoured it thoroughly again and set it out in the sun.

Kip didn't seemed to mind being left outside—except at night. Then he would whine to come in. His whining wasn't as objectionable as his barking. He seemed to bark at every night sound. Wynn and I had supposed that we were used to the sound of barking dogs, but we found that Kip kept awakening us night after night with his fussing.

Undaunted, I was still determined to have a blueberry pie, so the next week I took Kip and again headed for the west and some berry patches. This time I did not remove Kip's leash when we got to the patch. Instead, I tied him to a small sapling and went about picking the berries to fill my pot.

Kip fussed and whined the whole time. To make it up to him, when I had picked my container full, I took him to the stream and let him loose so he could play in the water. We had a lively game of chase-the-stick. When I felt that he had had enough exercise, I slipped on his leash again, picked up my full pot of berries and headed for home.

The Indian people watched me enter the village again. I smiled and spoke to those who were near the path, but they turned their backs and pretended not to notice me. I tried not to let it bother me, but it did.

"Well, anyway," I said to Kip, who seemed to be the only one willing to listen to me, "I have my berries for pie."

When Wynn arrived home that night he was welcomed by a new aroma. The smell was nearly gone from Kip, my garments, and the cooking pot. Instead, the wonderful smell of fresh blueberry pie wafted throughout the cabin. I was pleased with myself. I had found the patch, I had persevered, I had baked my pie.

"Great!" said Wynn with an appreciative pat on my arm as he pushed back from the table after a second helping. His short, emphatic comment was enough to make it all worthwhile.

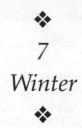

7
Winter

MORE DETERMINED THAN even my pursuit of berries was my search for new friends. Daily I took Kip for his walks, and each time I met or passed the Indian ladies I smiled and called out a greeting to them. They still chose to ignore me but even that did not stop me.

I made up my mind then to concentrate on the children. I was sure the children would be more responsive—after all, the children at Beaver River had learned to love both Kip and me.

I chose the paths where I heard children playing and smiled warmly and greeted them in their own tongue whenever I was near enough to be heard.

They lifted their heads and stared at me, but they refused to answer any of my questions. They did not even respond to the wild tail-wagging of Kip. They looked at us until their curiosity was satisfied, and then they either turned back to their play or else ran off, leaving us standing looking after them.

I even tried a little friendly "blackmail." I took some of my most colorful and fascinating books and held them out to them, showing them the pretty pictures as I let the pages flip slowly by. They stared at the strange new thing, but they did not draw closer or reach for it. In disappointment, I took my books and went back to my lonely cabin.

I stopped sharing my experiences with Wynn. It only pained him to hear of my loneliness. Instead I asked him all about his day. For the most part it was simply routine. He inspected boundaries, checked on trappers, distributed a small amount of medicine, settled a few local disputes, pulled a few teeth, delivered a few babies and bandaged ever so many knife wounds, axe cuts, accidentally fish-hooked fingers and sprained ankles.

I went to the trading post only when it was absolutely necessary. I did not feel comfortable with the dark-eyed trader, who watched me so closely as I looked around his crowded quarters trying to find the item I wanted.

He never moved from his spot behind his makeshift counter to assist me in any way. Squinting his eyes, puffing on his ever-present cigarette, he scowled at me as though I were an intruder rather than a customer.

Matches—or rather the lack of them—one day drove me from the safe confines of my cabin to the trading post. Wynn had asked me to get them, as our supply was low, and he would not be back from his patrol in time to visit the store.

I certainly couldn't tell Wynn I'd rather not go to the post simply because I did not like the man, so I said nothing. Midmorning, I freshened up, closed the door on Kip and ventured forth.

On the path I again met women from the village. I smiled and nodded, giving the customary greeting. They would not look at me anyway.

I found the trading post the same as always, dark, stale and clouded with cigarette smoke. The trader stood behind his little barrier and scowled as two Indian women made their selections. I did not merit even a nod from any of them.

I stood back, patiently waiting until the women had finished their business and left by the low door. Then I quickly purchased the matches and left the store.

As I ducked out the door I heard voices just around the corner. The two Indian ladies were chatting. Surprised they had not already left the area, I stopped short. I knew they were right there on the path. I would need to pass by them. Would they answer me if I stopped and greeted them? I took a deep breath and determined to try it. And then some of their discussion reached me.

"Why she go there?"

"Don't know."

"Who?" A third woman must have joined them.

"The pale-faced one with the dog child."

The "dog child"? Why would they say that? Pale face, I could understand. It did not bother me to be referred to in such a way. But dog child? What did they ever mean by that?

And then I remembered Kip. The Indian women saw me often with Kip. They saw Kip fluffed and brushed. They had watched me bathe him and dry him with an old towel. They had seen me take him with me while others left their dogs tethered at home. They saw Kip enter our small cabin, while their dogs spent the days and nights, rain or shine, out-of-doors. They knew me to be a married woman, but they had never seen children at our home. The conclusion was that I had substituted a dog for the child I did not have.

Had I? Could the Indian women actually think that Kip, as much as I loved him, could take the place of the child I longed for? Never! If only they knew, I thought. If only they could understand my pain.

I turned and went around the trading post in the opposite direction so I would not need to confront the Indian women. It was a long detour, but I needed the long walk. I had to have time to think, to sort things out, to recover from the hurt.

I walked briskly while the tears streamed down my cheeks, praying as I walked. I had never thought it possible to be so lonely, so shut off from one's world.

At length I was able to get a firm hold on my emotions. I decided I would not engage in self-pity even though the days ahead did look bleak.

I have my Lord, I told myself. *He has promised to be with me even to the end of the world.* For a few moments I felt that I must indeed be very near to the end of the world, my world, but I jacked up my courage and lifted my chin a little higher. God had promised He would never leave me nor forsake me. That held true on a city street, in a rural teacherage, or in a remote part of the North.

Besides, I had Wynn. Though his job took him away during the day and often into the night, still it was a comfort to know that he would be back and that he loved me and understood my needs and my longings.

And I had my "dog child." I smiled to myself. Kip might not be the companion I desired, but at least he was *someone*. I could talk to him, walk with him, and appreciate the fact that I was not entirely alone. Yes, I was thankful for Kip. It seemed he might be the only friend I would have in this settlement.

When I reached home, Kip met me at the door. His tongue teased at my hand and his curly tail waved a welcome flag. I patted his soft head.

"You won't understand a word of this," I said softly, "but in the village they think that you are my pampered 'child.' Well, you're not the child that I wanted, but at least you are a friend. Thanks for that. It looks like it might be just you and me here." I stopped to brush away some unbidden tears. "So—somehow we've got to make it on our own. It's not going to be easy—but I think we can do it."

Kip looked into my face and whined. He seemed to sense that I was troubled.

Then I made conscious effort to push the hurt from me so that I would be able to have a cheerful face for Wynn's return. I did not want him to be burdened with the pain I was feeling.

When Wynn entered our cabin I nodded toward the new supply of matches.

"Good," he said. "I was hoping you wouldn't forget. My supply pack is getting low, and I have a feeling that winter might be arriving any day now."

Wynn was right. In just two days' time, a north wind blew in a storm. It came howling around us with the wrath of the Indians' storm gods. In a few short hours, our settlement was covered with ten inches of snow.

From then on we lived with the cold and the wind. Each day more snow seemed to add to our discomfort. I kept busier now, and I guess that it was good for me. Bundled against the elements, I was constantly working just to keep our water supplied, our fires fed, and our clothes clean.

Kip and I still found time for walks—by the frozen stream to the frozen lake over frozen ground. I took the snowshoes and he plunged ahead breaking trail. We always came home refreshed from our outing and ready to stretch out before the open fire and let its warmth thaw our frost-stung bodies.

At night, when the supper was cleared away and Wynn sat at the crowded little table to do reports, I pestered him with all of the details of his day. He never rebuked me for my chatter—indeed, he encouraged it. Perhaps he knew he was the only one I had to talk to. At any rate, I enjoyed hearing each detail and felt that at least in a secondhand way I was getting acquainted with some of the area residents through Wynn.

Christmas came and went. I determined that I would not be lonely—well, lonely maybe, but not homesick. Homesickness was a miserable feeling and profited nothing.

And so, by taking one day at a time, I was managing to get through the long winter days. With the spring would come new activities. I would find some way to have a small garden and Kip and I would continue our exploration of the countryside. Perhaps I would even be able to take a trip or two with Wynn. Until then I would be patient, keep myself as busy as possible, and endeavor to keep my spirits up. As I had it figured, there would be only three more such years—at the most.

8
Neighbors

❖

OUR INDIAN NEIGHBORS enjoyed much more social life than the people in Beaver River had. Though we were never asked to participate, we often heard the beating of the drums as one ceremony or another was conducted. Toward the east end of the settlement there was a long, low building known as the council house where most of the ceremonies took place. The rest of them were held in the village "open."

At first the strange drumbeats and the rising and falling chants wafting over the night stillness seemed eery. The sounds reminded me that we were the outsiders here. We were in the midst of a different culture from our own. To us, the chants and drumbeats were distracting noise, but to the Indians these symbolized their religion, their very being. They believed in the "magic" and supernatural power of the chants and dances.

As far as we knew, the Indians in this remote yet rather large village had never seen a Christian missionary nor been introduced to his God. The old ways were never questioned and were held to with strict rigidity. The rain fell or the killing frost descended in accordance with the pleasure of the spirits, so it behooved the people to do all in their power to keep those gods happy with age-old ritual and age-old worship.

The drumbeating and the dancing were performed to welcome the spring rain, to strengthen the spring calves of the moose and deer, to make quick and strong the trap, to thicken the pelts, to send the schools of fish, to make healthy the newborn, to safeguard the hunter, to protect the women, to give an easy "departure" to the elderly, and on and on.

It was no wonder, as the Indians felt obligated to perform all the rituals, that it seemed as if the drums were always beating, the rhythm of dancing feet always thrumming on the ground, the drone of chanting voices always rippling out over the frosty night air.

A death was a very important event to the villagers. Day and night they beat their drums and chanted as mourners wailed before their gods, impressing them with the fact that the soul departed would be greatly missed here on earth and thus should be equally welcomed into the new land.

The higher one was in the tribal caste system, the longer they would beat the drums. When the next-in-line as chieftain, the chief's eldest son, died in a drowning accident, the drumbeat continued for a total of seven days. For the chief himself, it would be just seven days plus one.

By the time the seven days had passed, my whole body was protesting. Kip and I took to the woods whenever we could, but even many miles from the village the drumming could still be heard in the cool, clear fall air.

When the ceremony finally did cease, I felt I had suddenly gone deaf. The world seemed a little shaky without the vibration of the shuffling feet. It was two days before I felt normal again.

The tribe had many superstitions and they held to them rigidly. It was not unusual to see a woman suddenly drop what she was carrying and run shrieking to her cabin to shut herself in behind closed doors because she had seen something "taboo."

Children, too, were very conscious of tribal customs and teachings. You could see them watching the sky, the woods, the ground for "signs" to live by.

So I should not have been surprised when word filtered back to me of the Indian women's fear that association with the "pale-faced" woman might somehow bring down the wrath of the gods. There didn't seem to be any consensus as to why the spirits might object, but the elders informed the younger, and the younger warned their children, and the villagers, with one accord, were afraid to test the conviction.

I could think of nothing I could do to break the barrier—except wait. Surely if I continued to live among them, greet them in a friendly manner and not push in where I was not invited, in time they would see and understand that I did not invoke the anger of their gods.

The Indian people of this tribe had a strange conception concerning the rule of the Mountie. To them he represented the enforcement of the law. Law was closely tied to payment for sins committed. The gods frowned upon wrongdoing and reacted with a vengeance when one stepped out of line. Therefore, in some strange, invisible way, the white lawman might have some connections with the super powers. They treated Wynn with both deference and fear.

As Wynn's wife, I was suspect. Perhaps I had been brought to the village for the sole purpose of spying on the villagers, and as such I would report any misdeed to Wynn the moment he returned at the end of the day. Therefore no one wished to take any chances by having communication with the "pale-face."

The fact that I had no children and was often seen walking a dog made me even more suspect, and set me even further apart from the women of the village. I did wish I could do something about my circumstances, but I had no idea how I might break through the superstitions.

When I eventually had come to understand the reason for the shunning, I believe it did help my peace of mind. At least I did not feel rejected on a personal level. I prayed about it and left the entire matter in God's hands, in the meantime asking Him for patience and understanding.

I had to recognize also that my position as a white woman contrasted greatly with that of the Indian women. In their culture the women did most of the manual labor. The men hunted for the food, trapped the animals for fur and went to war if necessary. The woman, a laborer, was also in total subjection to the man, and her very posture showed her position. Never was she to stand before a man in the same way that another man would. Always her eyes were to be downcast and her attitude one of humility and respect.

Though very deeply committed to their religion, the Indian tribe was also dedicated to fun. They loved their ceremonies simply because they brought pleasure to an otherwise rather drab and difficult life. They celebrated births and weddings with gay abandon. They loved sporting events as well, wrestling and running and hunting, and the young men were very serious in their desire to better their opponents.

The young women loved the contests too. They stayed apart in shy, clustering groups, hiding their downcast dark eyes discretely behind slim, brown hands, but they never missed a thing. And though the young braves pretended that their skills were displayed for the eyes of the other men only, no one was fooled for a moment.

Many a marriage took place soon after one of their sporting events, with the winner making his intentions known to some young maiden of his choice by presenting her with gifts. If she accepted the gifts, it was understood that she accepted his proposal too.

The Indians were great practical jokers as well—particularly the young men, though the children too enjoyed playing pranks on one another. A young brave seemed to enjoy nothing better than to "bring down" another young fellow in the eyes of many witnesses. The laughter and teasing made the unfortunate hide his scarlet face in embarrassment. However, he usually got even at some future time when the prankster was least expecting it.

So we lived with our new neighbors—together, yet apart; inhabiting the same village, but feeling ourselves to be of another time and another world. It was so different from Beaver River, where we had been not only neighbors but true friends, sharing totally in the village life. Daily I prayed that somehow the reserve might be broken; that we would be seen as more than a "law-enforcer" and his "spying" wife; that the Indians might realize we had come as friends as well.

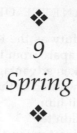

9
Spring

WE DARED TO hope that spring was on the way when the sun began to spend more time in the sky and the days began to grow longer and warmer.

For Wynn, the winter had been uneventful. There were no major epidemics within the village, no disasters, and very few troublesome incidents.

For this we were truly thankful, for we weren't sure what the response of the people would have been if some calamity had fallen on the tribe soon after our arrival. Perhaps with their superstitious leanings they would have felt that the disaster had come because of us.

On one of the first warm days, Wynn suggested that I might like to go on an outing with him. I wholeheartedly agreed. It seemed forever since I had been beyond the exercise trails where I walked Kip.

I bundled up, for the temperature was still cool, and put the leash on Kip until we got beyond the settlement. The trip would not be long, so Wynn decided to dispense with the sled dogs. That way we could walk together and enjoy the signs of spring.

"If you want to pack a lunch, we'll celebrate the departure of another long winter," Wynn had said, so I prepared a picnic. Like the Indians, I was ready to celebrate almost anything.

There was enough winter snow left for us to lace on our snowshoes.

Kip was excited. He could sense this was a special outing when we were being joined by Wynn.

Wynn walked slower than his normal pace in order to accommodate me. I still had not become truly adept on snowshoes. Besides, I wished to enjoy every minute of the day. As we walked, I was full of my usual questions about everything from squirrels to ferns. Wynn pointed out trappers' boundaries and told me the names of some of our neighbors.

"Do you think they'll ever accept us?" I asked him. "I mean, as part of them, not as the 'Force'?"

"I don't know, Elizabeth. They don't seem to know much about the white man here. They don't have anything to base their trust on, as yet."

"But wasn't there a Mountie here before us?"

"Yes . . ." Wynn hesitated. "That might be some of the problem."

I looked at Wynn, concern showing in my eyes. "You mean they had a 'bad' officer?"

"No, not bad. He did his duty as the King's representative honestly enough. But he held himself apart from the people. From what I have heard, he might have even taken advantage of their belief that he might be . . . ah . . . different. If they wanted to think he was in cahoots with the spirits, then that was fine with him."

"Oh, Wynn! Surely he wouldn't—"

"Oh, he didn't foster it, I don't mean that, but he didn't mind if the Indian people thought him a little different—a little above them."

"But why?"

"It's hard to say. Some men just like having authority. He was a loner and didn't like to be bothered. One way to keep the villagers at a distance was to keep them believing that there was a 'great gulf' between them and the lawman, so to speak."

"I think that's terrible!" I blurted out. "And now we, who would like to befriend them and help them, have to bear the brunt of it all."

"We'll just have to keep chipping away at it. I think I am feeling a little less tension on the part of some of the men."

"I'm glad *someone* is making headway." I shook my head. "I sure haven't. This has been about the longest winter I ever remember—at least since the one when I had both the measles and the chicken pox as a child."

Wynn chuckled and hugged me.

We trudged on for a few moments in silence, both busy with our own thoughts. The brightness made me squint against the morning glare, and the snow squeaked with a delightful, clean sound as our snowshoes made crisscross tracks across the unbroken whiteness.

A bush rabbit streaked across the hill in front of us, and Kip was off on the chase. I could have told him not to bother. There was no way he was going to catch that rabbit. But I said nothing. Let him have his fun!

"You didn't tell me where we are going," I commented to Wynn.

"Oh, didn't I? There's a trapper out here who was burned when some of his clothing caught on fire—he fell asleep too close to his campfire coals. I thought I'd better check him out to see if he needs any attention."

"Was he badly burned?"

"I don't think so, but best not to take chances with infection. Some of these wounds aren't cleansed too carefully. An infection could give him more trouble than the original burn."

We found the cabin with no difficulty. I sat on a tree stump and waited while Wynn went to check on the man. When he came out, he said the injury fortunately wasn't deep, and the man had seemed to care for it properly. The burn was on his left leg, from his knee nearly down to the ankle. Wynn left him some medicated ointment and promised to stop by to see him in a couple days.

We retraced our steps to the brow of a hill and sat down on a log to eat our sandwiches. How good they tasted in the fresh air, especially after our exercise of the morning.

The sun climbed into the sky and sent down such warm rays that we both removed our heavy jackets.

"Do you think it is *really* spring?" I asked with great longing.

"Why not?" responded Wynn. "It's that time of year."

"I'm always afraid to hope for fear it will storm again," I confided.

"It might," Wynn replied, "but even that won't keep spring from coming. Slow it down a bit maybe, but spring will still come."

It was a good thought. Springtime and harvest, God had promised, will always come to the earth.

I breathed more deeply.

"I'm glad," I responded happily. "Glad that winter is almost over. Glad that I won't have to melt snow for water. I'd rather carry it by the pail from the stream. I'm glad that I'll be able to let the fires go out for part of the day. And I'm especially glad that I will be able to hang the laundry outside again—all of it. I am so tired of dodging under shirts and dresses and of having to move socks from bedpost to chair to bedpost." I sighed a deep sigh. "I really will be glad to see spring."

Wynn reached out and stroked my hair.

I broke the silent moment by turning to him. "Wynn, we haven't found a garden spot yet."

He smiled his slow, easy smile.

"No—guess we haven't."

"Well, we need to pick one."

"Guess there is plenty of time. You won't be planting for a few days yet, Elizabeth."

"I know, but we need to find a good one before—"

"There is all of the woods and all of the meadow. You can take your pick," he answered. "From what I hear, you'll be the only one in the whole area in need of one."

"It's a shame," I said, "that's what it is. All this beautiful soil—just going to waste."

Wynn looked around us at the heavy stand of trees. Under the snow we knew that grasses and plants grew in abundance.

"Well, not exactly to waste. All the forest creatures seem to feed very well."

"You know what I mean. It could be supplying nourishment for the people of the settlement."

"I guess it's doing that, too," said Wynn. "LaMeche tells me that they eat very well from the land."

At the name of the trader my back straightened somewhat. I still didn't feel comfortable with the man.

"Wynn," I asked, "do you know anything about him?"

"Who?"

"LaMeche. He seems so strange. So . . . so . . . sullen." I thought that my choice of word may be a compliment to the man, but I didn't want to do him an injustice.

"Louis LaMeche? Not much. His father was French and his mother Indian. His father moved into the area east of here about forty years ago and staked out a claim. He did well as a trapper until an epidemic hit. Both of the parents and all of the children were ill, though LaMeche seemed to make out the best. LeMeche was nine or so at the time. He struck out on his own to find help for his family. He got lost and it took him several days to find his way to a cabin. Even then he stumbled across it accidentally. By the time help got back to his cabin all his family were dead."

It was a dreadful story. My original assessment of the man needed altering. No wonder he was withdrawn and—and sullen. What an awful experience for a young boy to endure.

"What did he do then?" I found myself asking.

"Some of the local trappers got together and scraped up enough money to send him 'out.' Supposedly he had an aunt or someone near Winnipeg. He stayed for a few years, but he didn't like it, so he ended up coming back. He started the post about ten years ago. Been here ever since."

"Who told you all this?" I asked Wynn, wondering if LaMeche himself had shared it.

"It's in the files. It's not marked confidential—still, I don't think it's for common knowledge. Just thought that it might help you to understand the man a bit."

It certainly did. Now I was ashamed of myself for the way I had felt about Mr. LaMeche.

Wynn stood to his feet. "We'd better be getting on home," he stated. "I need to write up the report on Red Fox."

I stood too. I didn't want to return to the village. I disliked even more the thought of returning to the small cabin. I was so thankful that it would soon be spring again and I could enjoy more and more of the outdoors.

"Thanks for taking me along," I smiled at Wynn with deep appreciation. "I needed that."

Wynn reached out and took my hand.

"I needed it, too," he said. "I wish I could include you more often, Elizabeth. You're great company."

"Why, thank you, Sergeant Delaney," I teased. "Now that spring is here, I'll see if I can fit you into my crowded calendar again some time."

Wynn gave me a wink and a smile, and we headed for home.

10

Planting the Seed

"I THINK IT'S time."

I had been waiting for those words from Wynn for *ages*! When he spoke them now I could hardly refrain from cheering. Instead I smothered my enthusiasm by nearly smothering Wynn.

He laughed as I hugged him. "If you don't leave me a little breath!" he gasped, "I won't be able to help you."

Then he hugged me in return before I quickly pulled away and began scurrying around in preparation.

It was gardening time! That meant the long winter was over. That meant I could again be outside more. That meant our poor diet could be supplemented with fresh vegetables. I could hardly wait!

"Have you picked a spot?" Wynn asked me.

"Sort of. It has to be in the open. We have no way to clear trees and, anyway, it seems that it would grow much better out where it could get plenty of sun."

Wynn nodded in agreement.

"There's that small clearing to the south of the village, but the children use it a lot. Then there is the little meadow to the west. Kip and I go there often. It is pretty, but I'm afraid it might be a little low and wet."

Wynn was following every word I spoke.

"Then there is a large meadow to the east, but the men run their horses in there. The lake has some nice areas around it, but I don't think the deer and moose would leave it alone."

I stopped for a quick breath.

"So—I have decided that the best spot I've seen so far is that little clearing down at the stream. The water forks there and leaves a little island right out in the middle. You have to get to it by the use of those steppingstones, though when the water is high they are under water and you have to go upstream a ways and use a fallen log. Have you seen it? It looks like a cabin might have stood there at one time."

I was almost out of breath by the time I finished, but I was rewarded by a wide grin from Wynn.

"Good scouting, Elizabeth." He gave me a playful pat on the bottom. "Your eyes are as sharp as an Indian's. Good choice. Lead the way."

So carrying my basket of beloved seed, and Wynn with a shovel over his shoulder, and Kip bounding along beside us to oversee the project, we started that spring Saturday morning by heading down the winding path leading to the small stream.

There were many curious eyes following our passing, you can be sure. *They must be wondering whom we are planning to bury, seeing Wynn with his shovel,* I thought, and I couldn't help but be amused.

When we reached the place I had selected, Wynn went right to work. It wasn't easy digging. The ground was heavy with wild grasses and plants. I had been right. A cabin had stood there at one time. We found bits and pieces of the debris as Wynn dug.

I helped to shake the dirt from the clods as Wynn turned them over. The soil was rich and promising, and it felt so good to allow it to sift through my fingers. Already I was tasting carrots and potatoes.

"Oh, oh!" Wynn exclaimed as he turned over a shovelful of ground with some strange objects intertwined in it.

"What is it?" I asked, wondering why he stopped to study the items.

Wynn turned them over with one hand, looking at each one carefully.

"We might have done it again, Elizabeth," he said. "These are some objects used by a medicine man."

I couldn't follow Wynn's reasoning. I shook my head in perplexity. "So?"

"I don't know how this cabin burned, or who this fellow was, but I've a feeling that we should find out before we go any further," went on Wynn.

"Are you saying that . . . that . . . ?"

"I'm saying that this spot might be another of their taboos."

"Oh—h!" escaped my lips in a soft, pleading whisper. Surely I hadn't done something more to separate us from the village people.

"What should we do?" I asked Wynn, my face draining of its color.

"I'm not sure. Guess I'll go see LaMeche. We've already disturbed the place. I'd better see how much fuss it might cause."

"Should I go with you?" I asked in a nervous voice, thinking that after all it was my fault and I should be there to shoulder the blame and excuse Wynn.

"No. No need for that. You can wait here. I shouldn't be long."

So saying, Wynn thrust his shovel into the soil and started up the path to the village.

I sat down in the grass, my eyes on the shovelful of evidence, nervous and agitated. I don't know what I expected might happen, but I was afraid that *something* might. Would the Indians burn down our cabin in order to avenge the disturbance of their beloved medicine man?

I decided to move farther away. I found a fallen log a few feet away in the shade of a small clump of poplar trees growing on the little island, and settled myself on it.

The minutes seemed to drag by, but in reality it wasn't long until Wynn was back. I stood to my feet when I saw him coming, but when he arrived he motioned me back to the seat on the log and sat down beside me.

"It was a medicine man who lived in the cabin, all right—but he wasn't a popular one with the villagers. In fact, he moved in from another area and took over the position of the local witch doctor by force—or by stronger 'medicine.' There almost was a local war over it. He brought several of his followers with him, and they settled over toward that large meadow." Wynn pointed off to the meadow.

"An epidemic of some kind hit the outside camp," he went on. "The villagers said it was due to the 'medicine' of the rightful, resident chief, who was also the village witch doctor. They said that the gods were showing who really was the man who should have power in the village.

"The intruding medicine man also got sick and died with the fever. Some daring young braves, in an act of defiance and revenge, rode out and burned his cabin, with his body in it. Those of his people who survived the disease hurriedly moved on. Then the villagers had a great victory celebration. Since that time, no one has ever visited the island. We were right—it is taboo."

"Oh, dear," was all I could say.

"Look at it this way, Elizabeth," Wynn said with a grin, "you'll never need to fear having raiders in your garden."

"Oh, Wynn!" I exclaimed, horrified that he should joke about it.

Wynn stood to his feet, still laughing at his comment, walked over to reclaim his shovel, and thrust it deeply into the earth, turning over another shovelful of the rich soil and a few more Indian relics.

"What are you doing?" I gasped.

"I'm digging you a garden."

"But—"

"Any harm we are going to do has already been done. We might as well enjoy the garden spot."

"Are you sure?" I was still hesitant.

"I'm sure. The Indians leave this spot alone because they are afraid of it—not because they hold it sacred."

I thought about that. Certainly I was not afraid of this bit of ground, even if a medicine man had lived upon it. It was, after all, God's creation and God's bit of land. If He chose to grant me a good garden here, then I would accept it as from His hand. I went to join Wynn.

We spent the rest of the morning preparing the soil. Often we felt hidden eyes watching us from among the trees at the other side of the stream. We tried not to let it bother us and went right on with our digging. "See," I wanted to shout to them, "there is no curse on this ground. The power of the medicine man does not compare to the power of the One True God who created this soil and planted these grasses." But I said nothing. I prayed that time might prove it to the people.

In the meantime, I truly was sorry we inadvertently had placed another barrier between the people and ourselves. We so much wanted to help them, to live with them, to be their friends, but we could not because of all of their religious taboos.

By the time the soil was tilled, the sun was high in the sky. I fell to my knees as Wynn dug little trenches for me to place the seeds. I rejoiced as each seed dropped in and I patted the rich, brown soil over them. I could hardly wait for them to grow.

Wynn broke into my reverie.

"I had thought that we would need to build a makeshift fence. That is the customary sign to the villagers that this spot has ownership and should not be disturbed, but I guess it won't be needed out here, under the circumstances."

"Oh, Wynn," I moaned. "I do hope I haven't gotten you into any trouble."

"We didn't do it intentionally, Elizabeth," Wynn said, straightening and placing a hand on his back. It had been hard work. "Who knows, God might use it for good."

"Oh, I hope so." It was almost a prayer.

"I've been thinking," Wynn went on, "maybe I should move the sled dogs out here. It would save me paying rent for that little space from LaMeche and would give them so much more room. Right now I have to have their tethers so short they hardly have room to move around. I could stake them all around your garden. There's plenty of room and it would keep the animals from raiding."

It sounded like a good idea to me. I wasn't opposed at all to sharing my island with Wynn's dogs.

"Don't forget to leave me lots of clearance for my path," I warned him. "I don't trust some of your dogs."

Wynn laughed, then went on. "There's only one problem."

"What?"

"Kip."

"Kip? How is he a problem?" I puzzled.

"You couldn't let him run free when you come to the garden. He'd get himself into a fight every time."

I knew Wynn was right.

"I'll just have to keep him leashed, too, when we are here," I said. "He can get his exercise elsewhere."

I patted the soil over the last seeds and stood up. Our garden was done. Now I just had to wait and watch. Mother Nature, God's "force," would do the rest.

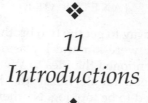

11
Introductions

❖

WITH THE WARM days of spring, the mosquitoes came in droves, and the blackflies too began to hatch and torment us. I draped cloth down the back of my neck whenever I went to the stream for water, to work in my garden or to exercise Kip. Even so I was bitten unmercifully every time I left the small cabin.

Those little creatures weren't enough to keep me in, however. I was out as much as I could dream up reasons to be. I had been confined in the few feet of cabin space long enough over the dreary winter.

I even found reasons to go to the store. Now that I knew something about the trader, I tried to be more patient and understanding. I will admit it was difficult. He was still sour and unfriendly. He snapped when spoken to, and blew his cigarette smoke in my face whenever I came near his counter to settle my account. I tried not to let it bother me, but sometimes it was hard to keep my smile in place.

I still spoke to the Indian women each time I had contact with them. I don't know if it was just wishful thinking, but I was beginning to feel that they didn't turn from me quite as quickly as they had at first. Perhaps they were getting used to my imposing myself upon them.

The little children could not be accused of being friendly toward me, but they didn't scatter quite as quickly either. Sometimes they didn't even run, just stared for a moment and then returned to their play.

I could hardly call it a triumph, but with the sun overhead and my garden sending up little spikes of promise, I couldn't help but feel a happiness in my heart.

Wynn had moved his dogs to the island and whenever I went to weed, I also carried food scraps I had gathered to feed his dogs. They were beginning to welcome me with little yips of anticipation, and I enjoyed being wanted—even by sled dogs. I found that some of them enjoyed petting, and I ventured close enough to do that. They really weren't such a bad lot after all, if you took them one by one.

My favorite was Flash, the lead dog, a full-blooded brother of Kip. Though Flash was not as pretty as Kip, he certainly was an impressive dog. His shoulders were thick-set, his legs muscled and strong, his face intelligent, and his eyes deep blue and trusting. I petted Flash more than any of the others and we soon became close friends.

I wished there were a way to get the two brother dogs together. Surely they would realize they were kin and lay aside all challenges for supremacy, but when I mentioned the idea to Wynn, he laughed.

"Don't you believe it for a minute, Elizabeth," he warned me. "Kip and Flash are both determined to be top dog. Neither of them would give an inch. You'd have the worst fight on your hands you've ever seen."

Well, I had seen enough dog fights since coming to the North that I certainly didn't want to see a "worse" one, so I kept Kip well away from his brother.

I felt a bit guilty about making friends with Wynn's dogs. I wasn't sure how a sled dog was to be treated. I knew that many of the trappers handled theirs with a heavy hand and no mercy or love whatever. I knew Wynn did not treat his dogs in that manner, but just how *did* he handle his dogs? Could I spoil them with my petting and pampering? I decided I had better check with Wynn.

One night at our evening meal, I raised the subject.

"When I go out to the garden, I take food scraps to your dogs."

I watched for Wynn's reaction. No frown appeared.

I went on. "They really aren't so bad."

"'Course not," said Wynn. "I don't know why you were afraid of them in the first place."

"Well, I didn't know them really. I still don't know all of their names."

I wanted to ask Wynn if I would spoil them by petting them, but Wynn stood to his feet.

"How about if I take you out and introduce you?" said Wynn. "If you leave the dishes, we still have time before dark."

Wynn knew I seldom left unwashed dishes, but this time I agreed.

"Okay," I nodded. "You've got yourself a date. I've been aching to show you how quickly the garden is growing. You just wouldn't believe it! Medicine man or no, I still think we picked the best spot in the whole region for our garden."

Wynn chuckled and picked up his plate and cup and carried it to the dishpan. I followed behind him and in next to no time our table was cleared, and I was ready to go.

I had thought that the dogs welcomed me when I came to the island, and so they did; but you should have heard the din when they saw Wynn! Each dog clammered for his attention, and he made the rounds, ruffling fluffy fur and petting bodies that wiggled from head to tail as they squirmed in their eagerness to get some of the loving. I stood amazed. I would never worry about spoiling Wynn's sled dogs again.

"This is Flash," Wynn said, burying his face against the thick fur of the dog's coat as he murmured strange sounds that only he and the dog understood.

I knew Flash.

"He's the best lead dog in the whole north country," Wynn went on.

"I'd put him up against any other—any day. He sleeps right beside me when we are on the trail. I never tether him. Nothing would get near me without Flash warning me."

I didn't know that before. I was comforted to know that Wynn had Flash on "guard duty." I felt a new appreciation for the team leader. I reached down and patted his massive head.

We moved on.

"This is Peewee," said Wynn, "the only dog in the bunch that Flash has not whipped into submission. He hasn't needed to. Peewee has never questioned his authority. Peewee is small, but all heart and willpower. He'd never give up while he had an ounce of energy left."

Wynn knelt down and took the dog's head in his hands. The dog whined, deep devotion written all over him.

"Peewee would do anything I asked of him," said Wynn, "or die trying. Great little dog, aren't you, Peewee?"

I felt a lump in my throat as I looked at the small animal. In my mind's eye I had visions of this little fellow valiantly struggling to pull his share of the load. He was smaller than the usual sled dogs, but if Wynn could boast of him in this manner, then I knew he was worthy to be harnessed next to the great Flash.

"This is Tip. How are you, Tippy?" Wynn ruffled the dog's fur and played with her ears. "She loves to be praised, hates to be scolded. Temperamental, just like any woman—make that *many* women." Wynn stopped long enough to laugh at his own remark and stroke Tip's dark brown fur.

"Here's Keenoo. He's a half brother of Flash. Notice some of the same markings. He's the heaviest dog of the team. I count on him when I have a heavy load. Boy, can he pull! Might even be able to outpull Flash—though I've never tested it. But Flash is the more intelligent of the two. In spite of his size, Keenoo hates to fight. Uncommon for his breed."

Wynn stopped to pet the dog, who pushed up against him, thrusting his nose deeply into Wynn's hand.

"And this is Franco. I wouldn't get too close to him. He's the least friendly of the lot. He'll let me pet him if I don't overdo it, but he doesn't take to others very quickly."

Franco growled deeply within his throat as his eyes held my face, then he turned to Wynn and his tail waved, ever so slightly.

Wynn patted and talked to him, just as he had each dog, and then we moved on again.

"Why do you keep him?" I asked, concerned about the difference in that last dog's temperament.

"He's a good worker," said Wynn, "and he's never been a problem. He's the quickest to pick a fight and Flash has to straighten him out every so often, but he settles down and does his job when he has to."

I turned to get another look at Franco, and found his sharp eyes still upon me. It was a bit unnerving. I wondered if he was jealous of me being with Wynn.

"He sure seems to have a chip on his shoulder," I commented.

"That's a good way to describe him," Wynn laughed. "He certainly does seem to have a chip on his shoulder."

There were two more dogs to go. They whined and pulled at their tethers, anxious for Wynn to get to them.

"This is Morley. He's sort of ordinary, I guess, but he works well and he tries hard, don't you, Morley? He has unusually sensitive ears. Morley is usually the first one to alert me if something or someone is in the area. Sometimes he is too quick. He growls over a mouse visiting a grass clump fifty feet away."

I knew Wynn was purposely exaggerating, but we both laughed.

"Hard to get your sleep sometimes, with Morley near you on the trail," went on Wynn, "but once or twice I've been thankful for his keen sense of hearing."

Wynn stopped to pamper Morley.

"And last of all, this is Revva, the other female. I'm thinking of using her to raise me some pups. With her as a mother and Flash to father them, I think I could get some top-notch sled dogs. Look at her intelligent eyes and her broad head. See the thick shoulders and deep chest. She has a great deal of stamina on the trail—something very important for a sled dog. I hate to lose her from the team, but I think she would be of even more value to me raising puppies."

Wynn leaned down to run a hand over Revva's silky side. She pushed up against him, begging for more attention. I leaned to pet her, too. She licked at my hand, letting me know she welcomed my caresses.

"So now you know them all," Wynn said, still stroking Revva as he spoke. "The only one you shouldn't get too close to is Franco. Leave him alone—at least for the present."

I nodded. I certainly would not be pushing Franco, yet deep inside me was a desire to win the friendship even of that unfriendly dog. I would take it slow and easy, but I knew I would try.

"I've already been petting Flash and Peewee and Revva," I admitted, rather hesitantly.

"Good," said Wynn. "They like lots of love and attention."

I let out my breath. So I hadn't done anything wrong in babying his dogs. Dogs, like people, needed lots of assurance that they were loved and appreciated. Wynn knew that. He treated them that way as well.

I leaned over to give Revva one last pat. The sun had left us. The twilight seeped in around us, cloaking us in a comfortable garment of softness. The evening sounds began to fill the air. Off in the forest a bull moose called out a challenge, or a love call, I did not know which. A screech owl sounded an alarm to our right. In the distance a wolf lifted its nose skyward and poured out his melancholy into a long, penetrating, lonely call. Revva shivered beneath my hand.

"She's not afraid of a wolf, is she?" I asked Wynn. I knew that I shivered even yet whenever I heard one of them.

"No," said Wynn. "I don't think it's fear. She is too closely related to that wolf out there to be afraid of him. Perhaps it's just the 'wild' in her that is responding."

I stroked the dog. She whimpered, but did not move away from my hand.

"Are you lonesome, girl?" I asked her quietly. "Would you like to be free to roam with your own kind? Is that a lover you hear calling you out there?"

Revva licked my hand and wagged her tail, pushing her body up against me.

"Just checking," I said. "But I'm glad to know you'd rather stay with us."

I gave her one final pat and rose to go with Wynn.

12
Summer

WE WERE ALREADY enjoying some early vegetables from our garden. Wynn had been right. Due to the dog team being tethered in the area, we were not bothered by raiding rabbits or rodents. The vegetables were free to grow in the hot, summer sun, unhampered by marauders.

When the summer became unusually hot and dry, even the pesky mosquitoes thinned out some. It was just too dry for them to do much hatching.

About three times a week I went to the garden with my water pail and spent most of the morning watering my plants. It was hard but rewarding work. Between the water that I poured on them, the warmth of the sun, and my words of encouragement, they prospered.

I longed to share my garden as soon as some of the plants were big enough to use. I took a few vegetables to Louis LaMeche, the trader, first. He accepted them with a scowl and no thank you.

I then decided to share some of my carrots with the Indian women. I was sure that once they tasted them they would want more. It was hard to find a woman I could approach close enough even to offer my produce. When they saw me coming they either walked the other way or else went into their cabins.

At last I found a young woman who was unable to avoid me. I handed her the small cluster of freshly pulled carrots, explaining that they added much flavor to the stew. She took them and walked away. I watched in anticipation, but as soon as she thought I would no longer be looking, she threw them in the bush by the path and wiped her hand on her skirt. With a pang, I realized I still had a long way to go to make friends here.

We desperately needed rain. Wynn was beginning to get concerned. The forest was getting too dry. Animals were being driven out into the open areas looking for food. The forest floor was brittle underfoot. Our small stream was only about half its usual size.

I didn't know enough about this part of the country to have intelligent concern, but I could see the worried lines crease Wynn's brow as he looked to the west in the hope of spotting rain clouds, and I knew that the lack of rain was a real issue.

I could see the Indian people looking to the skies as well. I even heard them talking in low, frightened voices as I went by. Then I began to notice renewed glances my way and nodding of heads, and I knew that the lack of rain and the pale-faced woman were somehow connected in their thinking. Then I *did* get worried.

One day as I walked the path to the garden I heard the words, "Bad omen," and saw the thrust of the chin my way as I went by. I knew that they were speaking of me.

I wanted to eavesdrop further, but I forced myself to keep on walking. All the time I was in the garden, I prayed. I hardly knew what to say in my prayers. The facts were all so scattered as far as I was concerned, but I prayed on, trusting that my God knew far more about the circumstances than I did.

"Lord," I said, "I really don't understand what is going on here. The people of the village are so steeped in their pagan belief. I don't know how to help them, God, but I don't want to be guilty of driving them even further from You.

"It's all tied up in this garden spot and the fact that we planted here. Now I'm afraid they think the rain is not falling as a punishment to me, and that all of them, and the animals of the forest, will have to suffer because of it.

"I don't want that, Lord. I don't know what to do about it. We do need rain. Wynn is worried about it. Lord, I don't even know what to ask You for, but if you could turn my mistake into something good, I would be so thankful.

"Certainly, the reasonable thing to me would seem to be for You to send rain. That would water the ground, replenish the food supply for the animals and fill our stream again. It should help our problem with the villagers, too. Then they might understand that I really had nothing to do with the drought.

"But I leave it in Your hands, God. Help me to be patient and to do things Your way. I can't untangle this myself. Thank You, Lord, for hearing me. Amen."

I guess I expected to see a "cloud the size of a man's hand" when I lifted my eyes heavenward, but there was none. I scanned the sky in each direction, but it remained brassy bright with sun. I had prayed for patience; I knew I was going to need it in the days ahead.

Then a strange peace came to my soul. I didn't know what or how, but I had the assurance that God had heard my prayer and was going to act on my behalf.

I left the garden and hurried home. I didn't want to get soaked on the way, I guess. When I got to our cabin, I wrestled with the empty rain barrel until I had it properly positioned under the crude downspout on our roof. We hadn't had water in that barrel since early spring. In fact, it had dried out to such an extent that I wasn't sure if it even would hold water. Still, I positioned it, feeling as I did so the many pairs of curious eyes upon me.

"I do hope that Wynn took his slicker with him," I said to Kip who was idly watching my activity. "He could be soaking wet by the time he gets home."

Kip yawned and laid his head on his paws. It was clear he was unimpressed.

"You just wait," I told him. "You'll see."

I might have spoken softly to the dog before me, but in my heart I knew that the words were really directed toward the women who peeked through the overhanging branches, slyly watching to see what the crazy "pale face" was doing now.

Wynn came home several hours later as dry as he had left that morning. It hadn't rained a drop.

"What's with the water barrel?" he asked me, and I felt my face flushing. There was little use trying to be evasive so I decided to tell Wynn exactly what had happened.

"I can't explain it," I said honestly, "but when I was praying this morning, asking God to help break the barrier among the people, I felt strongly that He was going to answer my prayer."

Wynn's eyes held mine. He did not question me.

"Wynn," I went on, "are you aware that they are blaming me and my garden for the fact that it hasn't rained?"

"I've heard little snatches of rumors," said Wynn.

Surprised that he had kept it to himself, I asked, "Why didn't you tell me?"

"What good would that have done? It would only have upset you. There is nothing that can be done about it anyway."

I knew Wynn was right. I could do nothing. I would only have fretted about it.

"But go on," prompted Wynn. "You were telling me about your answer to prayer."

"Well, I just felt so sure—so at peace, that I . . . I . . . I think that God is going to do something about it. I feel sure that He will send rain."

Wynn smiled and whispered, "Well, praise God." Then he looked back at the rickety barrel. "I'm not sure how much that poor old barrel will hold, no matter how much it rains, Elizabeth."

"I don't really care," I stated, "I just . . . I just . . . well, I wanted to let Him know that I believed Him, that's all."

There were a few moments of silence as Wynn and I looked deeply into one another's eyes. Then he stepped forward and laid a hand on my arm.

"Get some old rags, Elizabeth, and I'll get the tar, and we'll stuff those holes the best we can," said Wynn.

With a grin I went to do his bidding.

We worked together on the barrel. Some of the cracks were quite wide. We weren't really sure if it would hold water even when we were finished with it. All the time we worked, we could sense the villagers watching us.

When we had done our best, we positioned it once more below the spout, making sure that the plank nailed along the roof was slanted correctly to send the water toward the barrel, and then we went in to have our supper.

All night long I expected to hear rain. Even in my sleep, one ear was attuned. No rain fell. In the morning I was sure I would waken to clouded skys, but the sun shone brightly into the one small window.

Kip and I left the village by our usual path. I greeted women and children along the way. They passed me by with downcast eyes and reproachful looks. I prayed inwardly and looked to the sky, hoping to see that one little cloud. The sky was cloudless, the sun already glaring.

"I don't understand, Lord," I whispered.

"Be patient," came back the inward reply.

"Lord, give me the patience!" I cried. "I have never been patient. You know that."

"Then trust Me," said the inner voice. "You have always been able to trust."

"Lord, I trust You. I trust You completely." I knew as I said the words that they came from an honest heart. I did trust Him! I did! I might not understand His workings, but I did trust His ways.

13
Panic

ALL THAT DAY I watched for the rain. Nothing happened. There was not a cloud in the arch of blue above us.

That night, I again lay awake for the first part of the night. There was not a hint that a wind was arising to bring in a storm. At last, sheer fatigue called me to sleep.

The next morning, the sun was already up, sending shivery heat waves back from the earth. It promised to be even hotter than the day before. Cracks were showing in the ground where the thirsty soil had long since lost all its moisture.

I took Kip and went to the garden. I talked to God on the way there. "Lord," I explained. "This pail in my hand does not mean that I don't trust You. I know that You are going to answer my prayer. Bringing rain seems like the logical way for You to do it, Lord—but it might not be. Now, in the meantime, I have my garden that You have blessed with growth. I think You expect me to do my part, so I will continue to water it, Lord, until You tell me not to."

I tied Kip to a sapling well away from the other dogs, and proceeded to scoop water from the decreasing stream to give a drink to the thirsty plants.

Even with my careful ministrations, it was apparent that the plants were also suffering from the drought. Water as I might, I could not do for them what just one good rain sent down from God's heaven could do.

I saw the drooping plants and I knew they were crying not just for drops of moisture but for a good soaking of the earth.

Carrying the water was back-breaking work. I stood to rest and looked heavenward again. The western sky was clear and bright. The southern sky was a haze so dazzling I could not even look upon it without squinting my eyes.

I turned to the north. Another cloudless sky. And then, by habit, I looked eastward.

There was a strange cloud in the east. My heart gave a little skip. Would our rain come from the east instead of the west or north as usual?

I smiled to myself. Wasn't that just like the Lord, to do something out of the ordinary so that there would be no doubt as to its coming from Him?

I looked closer at the cloud. It was raising up in strange, billowy puffs of brown and gray. It seemed to be originating from the land, not the sky. I couldn't understand it.

I continued my watering until my back was so sore I could do no more.

I soaked and soaked the earth, pouring on bucketful after bucketful. Kip whimpered at me, to let me know that he thought that I was really going to extreme.

"I know," I told him. "It is getting late but they are so thirsty. They seem to just be begging for more. I'll come—soon." And I continued to pour on more water.

By the time I left the garden, much of the eastern sky was under the strange cloud. Kip whined at me and pulled against his leash. He was in a hurry to get home.

There were people everywhere I looked when I entered the village and always they stood studying the eastern sky, pointing and exclaiming excitedly to one another. They shook their heads and chattered nervously, but when they spotted me they hurried away, giving me the path totally to myself.

I was almost to our cabin when I heard children calling to one another. "Fire!" they screamed at one another. "Fire come!"

I looked to the east again and the truth of the words hit me. Fire! Of course it was.

Panic seized me. I had no firsthand knowledge about a forest fire, but if the little I had heard was true, we were all in mortal danger.

I shoved Kip into the cabin and pulled the door shut behind him. Then lifting my skirt, I headed for the trading post on the run.

"Oh, dear God," I prayed, "if only Wynn were here. He'd know what to do."

But Wynn wasn't in the village. As far as I knew he was many miles to the west. He had left the day before on a trip that would take him three or four days. He had carried plenty of provisions just in case he was held beyond that third or fourth day. I knew that Wynn would not be home in time to tell us what to do.

When I reached the store, the trader was already outside, surrounded by many nervous and chattering villagers. They all seemed to talk at once and he tried to hush them and keep them under control, but I could tell that he was just as concerned as the rest of us.

When he saw me he nodded his head toward the door of his store, and I understood him to mean that he wished to speak to me privately.

As soon as he broke away from the people, he came in. I met him at his counter, my agitation showing in my breathless question, "This is bad trouble?" My nervousness made my limited grasp of the Indian dialect all the more difficult, but I knew even without his answer that he thought it was serious.

"Coming this way?" I asked next.

"It is," was all he said.

"How much time?"

"Hard to say. If wind starts to blow, it could travel fast. If it rain—" He shrugged.

Rain! I latched onto the word. Rain! Of course. Why hadn't I thought of that? God was using the fire to get everyone's attention before He sent the rain. I smiled and turned to Mr. LaMeche.

"Rain stop fire?"

He looked at me with questioning eyes. I knew he must think me a little mad. He did answer me though. "Good rain—yes. If it come soon."

"Good," I answered, and started to move around him to go out the door.

"Mrs. Delaney," he stopped me, "if rain does not come soon—very soon—then whole village be burned. We cannot stop forest fire. We have nothing to fight with. We can only run—or fry like chickens."

I stopped long enough to let his words sink in, then asked slowly, "Run where?"

"I do not know," he responded and his shoulders sagged.

I wanted to tell him not to worry, to be patient and trust in God, but I didn't know how to say the words in either Indian or French, so I just smiled again and went on out the door.

I looked to the west. Surely the rain clouds would have to be showing by now. There wasn't much time left. But the sky was still clear. The smell of smoke was heavy in the air, and I was smart enough to know that the smell was not coming from the cooking fires.

All around me people were milling about, concern and fright showing in their faces.

There were few men in the village. They had all left four days before to attend a feast and rain dance at another village two days' ride away. Now we had only those who were ill, or old, or too young to participate in manly affairs. It was not a comforting thought.

I looked at the nervous women. Crying children clung to the skirts of some of them. Older children gathered in groups, pointing at the sky and chattering in alarm.

I knew the fire was much closer by now. I decided to run to the open meadow where I could get a better look.

It was even worse than I had feared. The whole eastern sky seemed to be one boiling smoke cloud. You could hear the crackling of the flames, and the snap as large pine trees split wide open with the intensity of the heat. Bits of debris were carried sunward, and the wind, which had seemed to come from nowhere, carried them forward to plant new fires, leading the way for the giant flames leaping behind them.

I looked once more at the sky. There was no rain.

"Father," I prayed, my voice breaking, "I don't understand this, but I do trust You. What do I do now?"

When I lifted my head I caught sight of two empty wagons Wynn had left beside the small clearing. In the corral nearby, their eyes rolling in fright and their nostrils flaring as they snorted at the unwelcome smell of smoke, tramped the horses that had pulled those wagons. Grasping my skirts in my hand, I ran toward the trading post.

Without waiting for Mr. LaMeche to say anything, I flung an order his way. "Put harness on horses and hook to wagons. I find drivers." I didn't even wait to see if he would follow through with it but turned and ran on.

A group of frightened women stood by the path. "Get ready to go," I called to them. "Gather everything you can and put it on your backs, and then go to lake," I said, gesturing to emphasize my words.

They stared at me. I knew they had understood my Indian words—that was not the reason they were hesitant. It was because of who I was that they questioned me. The thought made me angry. "Go!" I flung at them. "Do what I say!"

In the panic of the moment, they acted on my words and scattered to do my bidding.

I ran toward a group of huddling young boys and picked out the two I considered to be the most likely to be able to handle horses.

"You and you," I said, pulling them forward, "run to corrals and help trader harness horses. When they are hitched to wagons, drive through village and gather up all who cannot walk; then go to lake."

They just looked at me, their eyes large with fear and hesitation.

"Go!" I said, giving them a little push in the right direction. They started hesitantly toward the corral.

"Run! Quickly!" I called to them, and they ran.

I turned to the rest of the boys. "Tell everyone in village to grab what they can and run to lake. Hurry! We do not have time. Everyone! Those who cannot run go in wagons. Run!"

They scattered and I could hear them yelling the warnings and commands as they ran.

Soon the whole village was alive with activity, people hurrying to the lake with hastily gathered packs on their backs. Mothers bundled up children and sent them running ahead; then they picked up younger ones and ran after them.

I watched for only a moment and then turned to hurry to the corrals. Already LaMeche had the teams harnessed and hitched to the two wagons. The two young boys were each given a team to drive.

It was not an easy task, especially for ones so young with no driving experience. The boys looked as frightened as the horses who plunged and jumped, champing on the bits as they tossed their heads at the sound of the coming fire.

"Go quickly through village," I called to one of them above the roar and crackle. "Get everyone who cannot walk."

Mr. LaMeche looked at me. He was trying to hold the heads of the extra team of horses. They wanted to bolt and he was hard put to hold them in check.

I picked up the slack reins and took a firm hold of the team. I had never handled horses before and this was a poor time to be choosing to learn, but I could see no other option.

"Go with him," I called to LaMeche. "Get what you can from trading post, then see if everyone has left."

He did not let go of the horses but stood questioning my command.

"Go!" I screamed. "We not have time."

He went then and the horses reared the moment he let go of their heads. For a moment I feared I would not be able to hold them. They pitched wildly, tearing at the reins in my hands. I brought a rein slapping down across the sorrel's flank, and it seemed to be enough to bring the horses to their senses.

Running behind them, I managed somehow to get them to the spot where our cabin stood. I will never know how I managed, except that God was with me, for somehow I was able to get that pitching team hooked to that wagon. I thought of our few belongings in the cabin and wondered how I would be able to both control the team and collect our few necessities.

I was still wondering when a young Indian woman appeared.

"I hold!" she cried. "You get pots to cook."

"No," I called back. "Don't wait. Drive them to lake. Take wagon right out in water. Do you understand? Drive out far in lake."

She nodded and then, wildly plunging, the team was gone, the woman calling to the horses and urging them on. The wagon was heavy but the horses left the village at a gallop, weaving in and out among the cabins and their surrounding trees.

I did not stand to watch them leave. Kip was still in the cabin. I rushed to the door and threw it wide for him.

"Run!" I screamed at him. "Run to the lake." But Kip stood whining, refusing to leave without me.

I waited only long enough to hurriedly grab around me for anything that my hands touched. As I pulled things off the wall or from the cupboards, I threw them onto the blankets on our bed. Then wrapping it all up together in one large backpack, I heaved it over my shoulder, and Kip and I started for the lake as fast as we could.

The air was heavy now with the smell of smoke. I could hardly breath from the intensity of it.

I came to the stream and stumbled across. My throat was parched and my chest burning with each breath. I was afraid I would not make it. Just behind me I could hear the crackling of the fire.

I turned once to look back. Already the fire had reached the village. I saw the red flames leap up higher as they fed their hunger on the village homes.

"Oh, God!" I cried. "May everyone be at the lake. Please God, may they be at the lake."

And then my cry changed, "Help me to make it, God. Help me to make it."

I cast aside the cumbersome bundle that I was carrying so that I might run faster. All the necessities for our living were in that bundle, but I did not hesitate in mourning. I did not have time. I picked up my skirts, heavy with the wetness of wading through the stream and ran on.

Someone's hands reached to me from the darkness. A voice coached me on as I ran, and then I felt the merciful coolness of the lake waters. I sank down on my knees, the blackness engulfing me. My last thought was, "Thank You. I made it."

14
Reversal

SOMEONE WAS POURING water over my head. The water was cold. I shivered and fought to right myself. I was in the lake. All around me were people. They should have been milling and wailing, but they were not. There was a deathly silence.

Ahead of me I could see the three wagons. They all stood in water almost up to the wagon box, and at the head of each team someone stood holding the horses' heads. They still snorted and tossed their heads, their frightened eyes reflecting the firelight behind us.

I could see our belongings still under the tarp, piled high on one of the wagons. Another was stacked with articles I could not make out through the smoke and darkness, and the third held silent people. Now and then someone would slip from the wagon to dip under the coolness of the water and then climb slowly back onto the wagon bed again. Nearby, people used cooking pots or pails to dip water and slosh it over themselves or one another.

It wasn't until I wondered about this that I realized how hot it was. It was a strange sensation. The water was so cold—the air so burning. I dipped my head underwater again and reached up to squeeze some of the water from my tumbling hair.

Behind us was the roar and crackle of the flames. I didn't want to turn and look at the village, but I couldn't help myself. I turned slowly but a hand on my arm stopped me.

"Should not look," said a familiar voice and I realized that Mr. LaMeche, the trader, was beside me.

I could not stop my backward glance.

The flames had claimed the whole village and were moving rapidly toward the stream. It was the only obstacle now between the fire and the lake. Already my face seemed to be blistering from the heat, and the fire was almost a half mile off.

I looked back to LaMeche.

"We be safe?" I asked him.

"Who can know," he replied. "But if we are not, not be safe anywhere."

The lake was our only hope. The water should keep us from severe burns, but would there still be air for us to breathe?

I dipped under again.

"Did we get everyone?" I asked LaMeche.

"I think so," was his reply.

"Thank God!" I cried and the warm tears ran down my face to mix with the cold lake water.

Next to me a child was crying. I moved in the semidarkness. The mother was exhausted from holding the little one.

"Here," I said, "let me hold him for you."

She gave up the child and I took my hand and thoroughly soaked his hair and face. He squirmed his displeasure but I held him firmly.

"It is coming closer," I heard a frightened little girl say, and I looked up at the flames.

I passed the child to LaMeche and reached out to help an elderly woman. For a moment she lost her footing after dipping into the lake, and she struggled in the chilling waters. She murmured as her balance was restored and I turned back to LaMeche.

"Will the stream stop it?" I asked, but in my heart I already knew the answer.

"No," he answered. "The wind blows too hard, the stream is too dry. The fire will jump like it was not there."

I began to pray again. There still was no rain, though I could not see the sky for the billowing smoke all around us.

I looked for Kip. In my concern for the people, I had forgotten him. He was near me, treading water, only his nose and eyes showing above the surface.

Then I noticed that Kip was not the only animal in the lake. Here and there were other dogs and woodland creatures who had been driven from their homes by the flames. A fox paddled not more than five feet away, and showing just beyond him were the horns of a buck. Rabbits, reluctant to take to the water, ran panicky along the shoreline.

I thought then of Wynn's dog team. They were tethered on the little island! If the stream did not stop the raging flames, they would all be burned alive! I started to weep, and to get control of myself again, I ducked my head back under the water and held it there until I had to gasp for air.

The flames were almost on the banks of the stream when a strange thing happened. I think we all saw it, and yet none of us who watched could really believe our eyes.

One moment the fire was being driven directly toward us, the wind sending sparks and burning bits of charred branches sailing through the air, and then the next, the wind completely changed direction, and the flames were being driven back the other way, turning again to the area that had already been consumed.

We watched in unbelief. Could it possibly be so? Would it change again in another moment? Did we dare to hope? Did we dare?

Even as we watched, the fire lost some of its ferocity. There was nothing more to feed upon. Though the flames still sent up sparks from the burning trees and logs of the village homes, yet it burned more slowly now, and more importantly, the lethal fumes and the stifling air were blown away from us and the wind brought in fresh air for our bursting lungs.

It was then that I heard the barking of dogs. Wynn's team was still alive! They complained about their lot, but they were still alive.

I breathed another prayer of thankfulness and then looked about me.

"How much longer to stay here?" I asked LaMeche.

"Not safe yet," he answered. "Soon maybe."

I decided to wait for LaMeche to give the order to leave the lake. I had had enough of commanding to last me a lifetime.

It was the animals who left the water first. The things of the forest quietly slipped from the water and bounded off to find themselves new homes.

In the distance the fire still crackled, but the heat was not as intense now. I looked at the villagers in the water. I knew they were as anxious as I was to leave the cold water. My legs cramped and my body numb, I wondered if I would ever be warm again. Except for my face. It felt brittle from the heat. I was sure that my skin was parched and my lips cracked.

The village dogs left the water next. Several of them had been freed by thoughtful people as they fled before the fire. Those who had not would no longer be alive. I shuddered as I thought of them.

The horses began to snort and to plunge again and it was apparent that we needed to get them moved from the lake. LaMeche passed the child back to me.

"I will take out wagons now," he said, and moved forward, the water coming up past his waist.

As soon as LaMeche started toward the wagons, the people took it as a signal to leave the water. They would be in the way if they stayed where they were.

With one accord we waded toward the shore. The night air felt warm compared to the coldness of the water. I shivered. We had no way of drying ourselves—and we were hungry. No one had eaten for many hours, but we likely did not even have a way to start a fire.

With that ironic thought I looked to where our village had been. *Imagine*, I thought, *in the face of all that and I'm longing for a fire!*

We gathered in soppy, shivering little clumps. Here and there a child cried or a dog on the loose decided to challenge another. The fights that broke out here and there did not even turn heads. We had far more serious things to think about.

In the eery light from the still-burning fire, people began to search out the belongings they had dropped by the lakeshore.

LaMeche came back from tethering the horses. The wagons were left standing on the sands of the lakeshore, the teams tied away from the company of people. They were still skitterish because of the heavy smell of smoke and the crackle of dying flames. They snorted and jumped and kicked, so LaMeche tied them securely in a nearby stand of poplars.

Someone produced some matches and got little fires burning here and there. Around them huddled wet women and children. A few blankets and furs were spread out and children were stripped of their wet clothing and put down to sleep. As many as could be covered huddled under each blanket.

Elderly men and those who were ill were also bedded. The rest of us sat around the fires, still too stunned to even talk.

I had no blanket and I was unable to get near enough to the fire. I was thinking that we needed more fires when a voice spoke to me through the darkness.

"You have no blanket?" LaMeche asked me.

I shook my head. "I dropped it by stream. I had everything wrapped in our blankets but it was very heavy."

LaMeche nodded. "All blanket and furs from post cover old folk," he said, and there was apology in his tone.

I smiled, though I'm afraid it was a wobbly one.

"I am all right," I said. "I am warm now."

LaMeche left me and soon many small fires were dotting the lakeshore. At each of the campfires Indian people huddled for warmth. Gradually they had lost their looks of terror and a few even talked together in quiet voices.

As the night wore on, we took turns, without discussion, adding sticks to the fire. Beyond the stream the forest fire died away. Only here and there flames still flickered and sparks periodically flew heavenward.

The wind slackened and the stars came out. Somewhere an owl hooted. I heard a splash in the lake behind me and guessed that a fish had jumped. Nature seemed to be striving to return to normal again.

I still shivered. My wet clothes did not help. I turned one side and then another to the fire and hoped I could dry out a bit.

Here and there people curled up on the sand beside the fires and attempted to get some sleep. I told myself that I should walk through the camp to see how everyone was faring. If Wynn were present, he would do that. I didn't seem to be able to move. Totally exhausted, I shivered again and wished for morning.

From somewhere LaMeche produced a coffee pot and coffee. I will never be able to find the words to express what it was like to sit before the fire, smelling coffee brew on that horrible night. Somehow it seemed to be a promise that the world would one day be normal again. The trader had also found a couple of battered tin cups. I clutched the cup closely in chilled hands and drank of the dark, hot liquid. I knew that with the help of the coffee I would somehow make it through this nightmare until the morning came again.

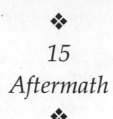

15
Aftermath

❖

WHEN THE DAWN began to break, I hated to leave the warmth of the fire. My clothing was still wet and I felt chilled in spite of sitting near the small fire for most of the night. Yet, when the camp began to stir, I knew I, too, would need to get on my feet.

I was stiff and aching in all of my bones. My limp skirt hung about me like some old rag. Underneath it, my inner garments were still wet and chafed uncomfortably at my sensitive skin when I moved. My shoes were squishy and waterlogged. I wished I would have had the presence of mind to remove them the night before. They would have had a better chance of drying sitting by the open fire.

All around me people were stirring. Babies cried, children called to one another, and women moaned in anguished cries as they looked toward what had been their village homes.

As the sun made an appearance we could see the smoke still curling here and there as the fires smoldered in spots. The blackened, desolate area that had been our village was not visible to us because of the trees that still stood between us and the settlement. Perhaps it was a mercy of God that it was hidden from us. I don't think any of us were ready for it.

Now it was a new day—with many challenges facing us. Here were almost two hundred people with no homes, no clothing except what they wore on their backs, and no food to fill their empty stomachs.

I walked back and forth before the small campfire. I hurt so bad I thought I would never feel comfortable again. I worked my arms and legs and rubbed at my back—all the time thinking and praying. I could not have said where my thoughts ended and my prayers began—they seemed to be one and the same.

"Lord," I said, "we need food. I don't know where we are going to get it. But You know. Show me how to care for these people. Give me wisdom—and, Lord, give me help. I can't do it on my own."

I had no sooner come to the end of the sentence when a voice spoke behind me. "Yours, I think so."

I jumped and whirled around. LeMeche stood with my big bundle supported on his back.

"You found it!" I cried with joy.

"Yes. Lucky for you, you drop it on this side of stream. It is safe."

"Yes," I said, reaching to take it from him. "Yes, I remember. I just crossed stream and could not run anymore with it."

A twinkle appeared in his eyes. I had never seen this man show even the hint of a smile before.

"A surprise you could run at all," he joked. "You must bring everything but iron bed."

The pack passed from his hands to mine, and I could hardly lift it.

"Oh, yes," I said, attempting to laugh. "You are right. What do I have here?"

I set my bundle of blankets on the ground and spread it open. I had grabbed the cooking pots. I faintly remembered doing so. I had several items of clothing. I must have stripped all the pegs on the wall, for scattered throughout the clothes I found kitchen items. Cups and plates and cutlery clattered to the ground. I had the dustpan—but no broom. A hammer—but no nails. A frying pan. A coffee pot—but no coffee. Tea—but no teapot. The picture of Wynn and me on our wedding day. A stubby pencil, some writing paper and two of my picture books. No food. No shoes. And three heavy sticks of wood for the fire.

I turned each item over as I looked at it. Why did I select as I did? Or did I select at all? I must have grabbed whatever was closest to me.

I looked at the sticks of wood, wondering how I had managed to pick them up. Then I laughed at myself and threw them on the fire. Perhaps they would make our morning coffee—that is, if I could find some coffee.

"We need food," I said absently. Mr. LaMeche was still standing nearby.

"Yes," he answered me.

I looked up from where I was still sorting through the things I had carried from our home. I would change into dry clothes now if I could find a private place to do so.

"How are the people?" I asked.

"Good. Some lips crack, faces swell from the heat, but good."

"Did . . . everyone . . . ?" I hated to ask that question, but I had to know.

"I have each family check. No one not here."

What a relief that was! It was bad enough thinking about the dogs. Wynn's dogs! I had to go to the island and check on the team.

I rose to my feet. There were so many things to be done—so precious little to do it with. I looked about me for Kip. He was playing nearby with some village children. It was hard to believe there could still be play and laughter after what we had just gone through. I shook my head to try to get my thoughts in order.

"I must go," I said to the trader. "I must go to the island and see Wynn's dogs—and garden. Must check my garden."

"Go," he answered. "It safe to go there—but don't cross stream. The fire still burn, though you cannot always see it. It burns deep down, underfoot."

I nodded in understanding and hurried away.

I didn't bother with the steppingstones. I didn't bother with the walking log. My shoes were already wet. I lifted my skirts and waded the shallow stream.

As soon as I approached the island, I could hear the dogs barking. They saw me coming and yipped out their welcome. I looked around me, counting out each one in turn. All seven dogs were present, but three were not barking. Three of them lay on the ground rather than straining on their tethers. I hurried forward.

Flash seemed fine. I ran my hand over his back. Not three feet from him lay pieces of debris from the fire, carried over to the island on the wind.

I went to Peewee. He, too, seemed okay, though he whined as he pressed close to me, his eyes running, as if they had been injured.

Tip was laying on her side, still breathing, though it seemed to be with great difficulty. Her sides heaved with every breath. I didn't know what to do for her. I patted the curly hair and moved on, my eyes streaming with tears.

Keenoo was also down. I knelt beside him and passed a hand over his still form. It was stiff and motionless and I knew that Keenoo was dead.

Franco, too, was unable to stand. I could see his eyes flutter open and then close again. His lip curled back as he sensed my presence. Even near death, Franco would not welcome a stranger's hand. I didn't know if I should go near him, so I left him without a touch.

These three dogs had been staked at the south side of the island, the closest to the ravaging flames. Though the fire itself had not touched them, it seemed as if it had done its evil work.

Morley and Revva both appeared fine.

Though the dogs were tethered so they could all reach the stream when they were thirsty, I knew they must be hungry, yet I had nothing to give them.

"I'll be back," I promised them. "I'll be back with some food."

Wynn had left an Indian boy responsible for feeding his team, but their food supply had been back in the village, and it too was gone now.

I went to my garden. It was limp and parched. The heat of the flames must have nearly cooked it. And yet I was amazed that there seemed to be life in many of the plants. They were able to hold up their heads. Then I remembered the thorough watering of the day before. I had soaked them, and soaked them, even though I had not understood why at the time. But God knew. He had prompted me to water my vegetables.

I looked at them with thanksgiving. They would be more important than ever now. The whole village needed to be fed. Yet, what would one small garden do among so many?

"Trust Me," again came the words.

I turned and went back to the camp beside the lake, formulating some plans as I walked. Food was our first need, so food would be our first matter of business. When we had been without supplies at Beaver River,

Wynn had organized the total village into responsible groups. I would do that now. A hunting party, a fishing party, an herb-gathering party; each member of the village who was old enough to carry a responsibility would be assigned a detail.

LaMeche was at the fire. I was glad to see him, for I was going to need his help.

He had made coffee again and I thanked him as I accepted the cup. My stomach cried for something to go with it.

I set my cup down and dug through the bundle of my belongings, coming up with the pencil and a sheet of paper.

"We need to do things," I stated, and LaMeche nodded his head.

"Do we have any food?"

LaMeche nodded at the one wagon. It was heaped high with miscellaneous items that he had hurriedly pulled from his store.

"What is there?" I asked him.

"Flour, salt, sugar, coffee, tea, cornmeal, baking powder. Most needed things, I think. Not sure. Like you, I just grab quick."

I was thankful that we had at least "grabbed quick." We could have been left with nothing at all.

"We must take it all out of wagon and see it," I said.

"Now?" he questioned.

It seemed like the proper time. At least the people would realize there was some action.

"Yes," I said. "Now. Find boys and put them to work. They can put it all in piles on ground."

We found boys who were more than willing to do our bidding, and I turned back to my list.

"Do we have guns or bullets?" I asked.

"I think I grab bullets. Gun—maybe not."

"Knives to hunt, knives to cook?"

"I check," he agreed.

"Fishhooks or nets to catch fish?"

He nodded his head. It did not mean that he had the items; it just meant that he would see if he could find them.

"We now divide people into groups," I said, "with one person to lead each group. They make fire and shelter. We send someone to hunt and someone to fish. Women go to woods for herbs and roots. Children and older ones carry wood."

LaMeche looked at me, his eyes getting larger with each instruction, his head nodding agreement to everything I said. When I stopped talking he reached for the paper where I had been hurriedly scribbling down our plan. "I will do," he said and took the sheet from me. Then he saw it was written in English and handed it back to me.

"I will help," I assured him.

"You count food supplies," he countered.

That sounded like a good idea. I headed back to my fire and my heaped-

up blanket pack and rummaged for another piece of paper. Then I went to
the wagon where the boys were unloading and sorting.

LaMeche had been right. We had a good supply of tea, coffee, and
cornmeal, a fair supply of flour, salt, sugar and baking powder. There
were several tins of canned food, some crackers, and a few spices.

There were also matches, shells, a few hunting knives, three fishhooks,
a length of fishing line, four axes, and some tins of something.

I reached for one of the tins. It was not labeled and the lid did not want
to come off, so I gave up. I told the boys they had done good work and
then went on to find LaMeche.

He had rounded up several of the younger children to help him tell
the people what he wanted. All along the shore, various ones were laying out for inspection the belongings they had managed to rescue from
the fire.

LaMeche and I walked down the line, taking stock.

I was relieved to see a number of pots. There were more knives and
fishing supplies, and some had even carried their grinding stones with
them to the lake. Many of the women had managed to save containers
and baskets with food items. It would not last for long, but it would help
with a few meals. There were a number of blankets and skins. Though
not enough to go around, still they would help to at least protect the
children and the older folk from the chilly night air.

We took our census, assigned our areas for family fires, and called for
volunteers for the work details.

It was not a problem to get those willing to fish. Several young boys
joyfully took the lines and fishhooks and scampered to the lake. A number of young women volunteered to go into the forest for herbs and greens
for the cooking pots.

There were those willing to go to the forest for wild game, but what
good were bullets without a gun? Our search had turned up none. We
didn't even have a bow and arrow in the whole camp.

"We send some boys to trap—to snare something," I said, gesturing
with my hands. It didn't seem possible they would be able to provide
meat for so many people in such a way, but there was nothing else we
could do.

The whole camp bustled with activity. The empty, despairing faces
began to come alive again, and calls and laughter of children rang out
along the shoreline. Suddenly we were no longer in the midst of a tragedy but an adventure.

LaMeche and I portioned out basic food for the day for each of the
campsites. The women came with their containers for the food staples.
Young girls ran laughing to the stream for water, pails in hand, or headed
for the woods to bring back plenty of wood for the fires.

Our spirits began to lift somewhat, though we knew the days ahead
would be difficult and uncertain.

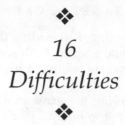

16
Difficulties

We LIMITED OURSELVES to two meals per day. We were all so hungry that our breakfast, a thin cornmeal gruel and coffee, was gladly welcomed. Each cooking pot fed a small, family-sized group. At my fire I had ten people of various sizes and ages. There was a young widow with two small children, two teenage girls who had been orphaned, a middle-aged widow who was alone, an elderly couple who had no family members to care for them, and LaMeche and I.

Midmorning the boys returned from the lake with four fish. Though they were proud of their achievement, I knew four fish would not go far among all the people. I smiled when I thought of how many the "two fishes" had fed. *Well, the Lord will need to perform another miracle if we all are to eat today*, I thought.

The snaring had produced nothing. The boys who had tried came home discouraged and ashamed. I assured them they would be more successful the next time, but I did wonder knowing that snaring takes great skill, untold patience, and perhaps a good measure of luck.

We kept the fires going and the pots boiling. I divided the fish among the families who had elderly or sick to feed. I pulled vegetables from my garden and put some of them in my pot. At least we would have vegetable stew for our evening meal.

I walked the line of fires, a handful of vegetables ready to hand out where they seemed to be especially needed. I wanted to be sure that everyone had something to eat. For many it was only gruel again.

I was feeling a bit downcast. *If only someone, somewhere had a gun!* I wished. When the men came back they, of course, would have guns, and Wynn would bring a gun with him upon his return. But we needed a gun *now*. It might be three or four days until any of them returned, and with our limited amount of cornmeal and flour, we had to have meat. With so many to feed, the basic foods would last a very short time.

I was so deep in thought I scarcely noticed the barking of the dogs, which was a constant thing anyway. And then I realized this sounded different somehow, and I looked in the direction from which it was coming.

Others in the village must have sensed the difference, too, for I saw women lift their heads, and children stop in their play, and boys hesitate mid-stride—all looking toward the approaching sound.

And then the most unusual sight met our eyes. The village dogs had formed a pack and were hunting, Kip leading the chase. Stumbling along in front of them, his eyes wild and his flesh seared by the fire of the day before, limped a bull moose. He bellowed his rage and headed straight for the safety of the lake.

I jumped to my feet, waving my arms in a foolish display of excitement. "Stop him!" I cried. "Stop him!"

Of course there was no way we could stop him. As I watched him lope nearer to the water's edge, I saw the hopes of a meat supply for the next few days disappear with his coming swim.

But just as he neared the water, he stumbled and fell, no longer able to continue. The dogs were fast upon him, and just as fast upon the dogs was LaMeche. He seemed to be everywhere, dragging off animals and pushing them aside, eventually striking a fatal blow to the suffering moose with a blunt club.

Boys ran to help him and claimed their dogs and pulled them aside. With great excitement the people crowded around, exclaiming over the meat that nearly had fallen right into our cooking pots.

The moose was skinned and dressed and portions of meat were handed out to hungry families. I added some chunks of meat to my own cooking pot and sniffed deeply as the fragrance began to waft upward from two dozen fires.

The remainder of the meat was tied and hoisted high in a tree to protect it for the next day's meal.

I remembered Wynn's sled dogs. I still had not taken them any food except for a small amount of cornmeal mush. I picked up scraps and bones now, and hurried off to feed them while my stew cooked.

We were all fed to satisfaction that night. By now we were dry, our stomachs were full, and we were fairly comfortable. The families had constructed crude shelters of pine boughs and skins. Some of them even had bits of canvas to stretch across small areas.

I had been too busy to prepare a shelter, but I wasn't concerned. I would sleep by the fire again if need be. At least I was dry now, and I had a blanket to keep me warm.

I had just washed my dishes in the lake water and set them out to dry when I heard a strange sound. I looked skyward. It had sounded like distant thunder.

To the west, storm clouds had gathered. The storm was moving our way and looked dark and ominous. I pushed back my wayward hair and studied the sky.

"I know we need rain, Lord," I whispered, "but now doesn't seem like a good time."

I looked around me at the makeshift dwellings. Few of them would keep out water.

I was still standing, wondering what to do, when LaMeche joined me.

"Rain now come," he commented, and I nodded.

"Where you sleep?" he asked, and I broke from my deep thoughts and pointed toward the fire.

"No," he said, shaking his head, "not tonight."

He looked around deep in thought. When his eyes rested on the wagons, he stopped and studied them.

"What is under canvas?" he asked me.

I looked at him with wide eyes and open mouth. I had not even stopped to think about what was under that canvas.

"Supplies," I said. "Blankets, clothes, dishes and pots. Lots of things we need! There are impractical things we cannot use but—"

"Can we take canvas?" he interrupted.

I was surprised that the trader was more interested in the canvas than the contents of the crates.

"Yes," I nodded vigorously. "Take it."

He was gone, rounding up three boys as he went. Soon I saw them throwing ropes off the wagon and freeing the canvas covering it. Two wagons were then lined up side by side about eight or nine feet apart and the canvas was stretched from the one to the other, forming a shelter of sorts. Then with axes in hand, the four headed for the pines.

I turned back to replenish the fire and check on my "family" members. The wind was up now, bringing with it the smell of rain. Thunder rumbled across the heavens and flashes of lightning streaked the sky. I hastened to get everything I could under some kind of cover.

Soon LaMeche was at my side again. With him came sprinkles of rain.

"It is ready," he stated, motioning toward the wagons.

A shelter had been made—the three sides protected by pine branches and the top sealed off by the canvas. It looked wonderful.

"Good!" I exclaimed. "Help me get everyone under."

"It is for you," he argued.

I looked toward the poor, makeshift shelter that held the elderly couple. It would do little for them in a storm. Then I looked at the two sleeping babies, and the two girls and two women who huddled around them, their scant blankets insufficient to cover their frames. "Please," I said to the impatient trader.

With a shrug of his shoulders he followed my bidding.

We got all ten moved just in time. We had no sooner set up under the canvas than the rain began to fall heavier. The rain we had prayed for had come.

There was no room under the canvas for another sleeper, so I wrapped a bearskin rug around me and went back to the fire.

LaMeche was there, smoking his cigarette. I wondered where he had found the "fixing." It was the first time I had seen him smoking since the fire.

He scowled at me and turned back to the sputtering flames. I said nothing but reached for a stick of wood.

"No," he stopped me. "No use. Very soon now it will go out because of rain. No use to waste wood. We need it more later."

I listened to what he said, wanting to protest, but I knew he was right. We could not keep a fire going in the rain. Already there was only a small flame, fighting to stay alive, and then as I watched, it too sputtered and died.

So, I would have to manage without even the small comfort of the open fire. I shivered in my bearskin. My feet were sopping wet again, and my dragging skirt seemed to be soaking up the rainwater like a sponge. Soon I would be completely soaked.

I lifted the skirt out of the puddle and tucked it more tightly around me. LaMeche still stared ahead saying nothing.

I deplored the silence. I disliked the black look. I hated being so cut off from another human being.

I tried for conversation.

"I am glad for all your help today," I said. "I don't know what I do without you."

There was no reply.

Boldly I spoke again, softly, because I didn't know how this man might respond.

"When I get up in morning and look at all people—and I know Sergeant Delaney not here to care for them, I don't know what to do." I waited for a moment and then went on slowly, "I pray . . . I pray a lot. I ask God what to do—but I . . . I ask for something more. I ask Him for help."

I looked directly at the sullen man.

"He answer me," I whispered. "He send you."

I watched his face only long enough to see the muscles twitching in his jaw, and then I dropped my gaze.

We both sat in silence now, the heavy rain falling in sheets around us. I stole another glance toward LaMeche. He no longer had his dark, angry expression. He pulled on his cigarette, sending up little puffs of smoke around him, making him squint his eyes.

I could hardly see his face through the storm, but I noticed little rivers sliding down his cheeks and I wondered if it was all from the rain. I still said nothing.

He brushed a hand across his face.

"You are stubborn woman," he said, but there was no malice in the words.

"I know," I admitted quietly.

"You saved village, you know?"

"Not true, I only—"

He broke in, "No one else think. We all run around in circles, and then it be too late to run."

I did not know what to say, so I remained silent.

"Now you sit in rain while everyone else sleeps."

I looked around me at the crude dwellings. I was sure not too many of our number were really comfortable where they were. Very few, I guessed, were getting much sleep this night.

But perhaps LaMeche thought—"I not ungrateful for what you do for me," I tried to explain. "Shelter very nice—best one. I not think to arrange wagons and—"

"But someone else need it more?"

"Yes. Yes. Old folks and—"

A chuckle stopped me. I looked up in surprise. I could no longer see his face through the rain and darkness, so I could not read there what might be making him laugh so unexpectedly.

"Women!" he said, "They are strange creatures. They want most—but they accept least."

"I beg your pardon?" I asked, not understanding him.

"You. You trim window with fancy curtains, you brush dog like he was toy, you fluff up hair like going to party, and then—this. When there is nothing, you give away little you have to people stronger than you, and you go without."

He laughed again.

I was afraid I was being mocked. Then his words came softly through the rain, "I had forgotten. It was way of my mother also."

"I'm sorry—about your mother," I whispered.

There were a few moments of silence; then he spoke again.

"She Indian," he said. "She not fuss with curtains or hairdos. But she like pretty things. She make beaded vests and moccasins with beautiful designs. She hunt wild flowers just to study them. She point out to us rainbow, sunset." He stopped again. "But she was fighter, too. She last to give up when fever took us. She nursed others when she could only crawl. She gave me last medicine when she need it more." He hesitated again. "She Indian," he said, "but she much like you."

I blinked the tears from my eyes. It was the nicest compliment I had ever been paid, and it brought a big lump to my throat.

"Thank you," I whispered in English, just before the thunder cracked and a fresh outburst of rain came sweeping down upon us.

The night was cold and wet, the fire was out, we sat and shivered in our bearskins that offered us little protection, but somehow a new warmth was stealing through me.

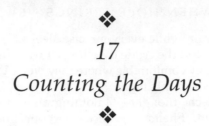

17
Counting the Days

❖

UNCOMFORTABLE IN THEIR soggy beds, people began to rise earlier than usual. A steady rain still fell the next morning. Wet and miserable, they crawled from a cold bed to a cold day. Children cried and women hushed them in quiet tones, as miserable as their offspring. I was glad I hadn't bothered to change my clothing.

A few of the women made attempts to get a fire going. The wet wood smoked and sizzled but produced no flame. There would be no hot gruel, no hot coffee or tea to warm up cold bodies.

I fed my group leftover cold stew from the night before and prayed that the rain would soon cease.

LaMeche asked my permission to use a team and the remaining wagon. I didn't ask what he had in mind but nodded agreement. I was surprised he assumed that I had the authority to respond one way or the other.

He gathered some of the older boys, and they set off toward what had been our village. I wondered briefly about their mission but was too busy serving stew to ask.

In about an hour's time they were back. By their cargo and sooted hands and clothing, it was evident they had been rummaging through the ashes of the village. Three small, blackened cookstoves were on the wagon, plus a number of sooted pots and hand tools. My smoke-darkened washtub and scrubboard also were on board. They also had a small amount of charcoaled lumber that had not burned completely in the fire.

With my hammer and the trader's nails, they began to construct a shelter of sorts. There was not enough lumber to fill in the sides, but at least an overhang was provided. Then skins were thrown over the lumber and two of the stoves were moved under the canopy.

It was not long until a fire was going in each of them. The children were sent to the woods to bring back sticks to feed it, and the women excitedly moved their cooking pots onto the stoves.

We had to take turns in the shelter. It seemed to take most of the day to get one round of meals cared for. Many of the children wanted to huddle around the crude kitchen trying to catch a little of the warmth from the fires, and the cooks had to constantly be chasing them out from underfoot.

What a day of misery! We never did see the sun, and there was no way to dry any of the bedding for the coming night.

Even the beds under the tarp and the two wagons got wet. The ground was so waterlogged that it ran in under the pine branches and soaked the bedding of those inside.

But no one could accuse the storm of being partial—it treated all alike. No one was exempt from the cold and wetness.

Again we sat huddled in our bits of furs or skins or blankets. Like protective hens, mothers tried to crowd all their children under their outstretched arms. The older folk and the sickly were invited to take turns near the cooking stoves. LaMeche took on the task of feeding the fires.

There was no sleep for me that night either. I was too miserable. I stirred around the campsite trying to check on others. It was more comfortable to keep moving than to sit still anyway.

Wynn should be back tomorrow or the next day, I kept promising myself. That was the hope that kept me going. When Wynn arrived, I was sure he would put things to right.

Toward morning the rain began to lessen—not quitting entirely, but it did slow down. I took my turn at the woodstoves to get a hot meal for my "family." I made a big pot of cornmeal, and while it cooked I also cooked my meat and vegetables for the supper stew. I thought it would save time and space to have all my cooking done at one time.

Silver Star, the young widow, came to join me.

"I work now," she said. "You rest."

I thought as I listened to her soft voice that she should have been called Silver Tongue rather than Silver Star. Her voice was soft and musical like a gently flowing brook or a trilling songbird.

"If you watch pot I go feed sled dogs," I said, smiling at her.

She nodded and I turned the stirring stick over to her and left the enclosure.

LaMeche was busy slicing up meat portions for the day's supper meal. I asked him for some of his scraps and started out for the small island.

I was reminded that I had not been back to see the dogs since the day the moose had been killed. I had sent some of the boys across with some food scraps for them and had promised myself I would check on them later. I had forgotten. I chided myself for not taking better care of the team. I should have done something for Tip and Franco. I had been so busy caring for the people that the dogs had slipped my mind. *Well*, I told myself, *I have no idea what I could have done for them anyway*. Still I felt that I had failed Wynn in this. I knew how important a good team was to him.

When I reached the stream, I could not believe my eyes. The steppingstones could not even be seen and the fallen log that stretched from bank to bank was under water as well. *How will I ever get across?* I despaired.

I looked down at my clothes. They were already wet. My shoes sloshed with every step I took. I decided I couldn't be much worse, so without even hoisting my skirt, I waded into the swiftly flowing little stream.

Unprepared for the strength of the current against the sweep of my heavy clothing, I stumbled, hardly able to keep my balance against it. I finally righted myself and made it to the other shore.

The dogs were glad to see me. I think they wanted companionship just as much as food. They pressed against me, leaving the meat scraps momentarily untouched as they licked my hands and waved their whole bodies.

Someone had removed Keenoo. I had told LaMeche about the dog, and I surmised he had been the one. Another post was vacant also. I saw the leash dangling from the stake where the dog had been tethered. I had to look around the circle and review the dogs in my mind before I knew which one was missing. Tip, too, must have succumbed to the smokey fumes from the fire.

Franco was on his feet, but he looked weak and wobbly. He breathed with a raspy sound, and I wondered how badly his lungs had been damaged. Perhaps he would never be able to pull the sled again.

I fed them all, gave pats where they were welcomed and talked to each dog in turn, and then I pulled some vegetables from my garden and started back to the campsite. I did not want the stream to get any deeper or swifter before I made my way back across, and the rain and runoff were still feeding it.

When I got back to the lakeshore, Silver Star had already served the cornmeal. She and Small Woman, the other widow, were washing up the dishes in the lake. They smiled when I came near.

"You eat now?" invited Small Woman as she handed me the bowl she had just washed.

I smiled my thank you and went to dish up my cornmeal. It was hot. That was about all one could credit it with. Though not tasty, it was filling and, under the circumstances, we were thankful to have it.

Kinook, the older of the teenage girls, brought me a tin cup filled with coffee. She smiled shyly as she handed it to me, and ducked her face to avoid eye contact.

"You bring me joy," I said in her native tongue. There were no words for thank you.

Her face flushed. She turned from me, but not before stealing one little glimpse of my face.

"Kinnea and I find dry sticks," she said, and was gone.

By noon there was a break in the clouds, and in midafternoon the sun came out. Its brightness and warmth soon had the earth and the people steaming. *Perhaps*, I thought with great longing, *perhaps we will sleep tonight*.

We spread our blankets and furs on bushes and branches all around us. Everything that could be spared off our backs was hung out to dry.

The pine branches were stripped away from the dwellings to allow the sun total access into the shelters in hopes that the ground would be dry enough to sleep on by nightfall.

The children rallied to assist in the tasks. Boys picked up the crude poles with their lines and hooks and hurried to the lakeshore. Girls scrambled into the woods looking for dry fire material. Young women left their young in the care of older ones and went into the pine forest for dry branches for bedding foundation.

Even the younger children became more cheerful, stopping their fussing and resuming their play. Many of them had been totally stripped of their clothing and were running naked in the summer sun.

The elderly moved or were assisted to places in the sun where they could benefit from the warmth of the rays. They sat steaming in the afternoon brightness as the clothing they wore began to dry out.

The Indian women and children were all walking shoeless, and I decided that it was the smart thing to do. However, I still had on my stockings. They were torn and mud-stained, but there was no privacy for me to remove them. Even as I looked down at them and noted their deplorable condition, I realized that now they were the only pair I had.

I constantly watched the trails for any sign of Wynn. Oh, how I longed for him! Even though our situation was still grim, I felt that things would all work out someway when Wynn returned.

Even as I watched to the west, I saw many of the Indian women looking to the northeast. Undoubtedly they were longing for the return of their husbands with the same intensity as I waited for mine.

But another day ended and Wynn had not come. With a heavy heart I again prepared the beds under the canvas top.

The Indian wives went about their evening preparations, their eyes just as heavy as mine. They too longed for their mates.

I sat down before our private fireside. The big stoves had done their work well, but with the rainclouds passing on, we were now able to have our fires again. I was lonely. I was weary. Every bone in my body seemed to ache. I was afraid—afraid that LaMeche and I would not be able to get this group of people through another day. Our meat supply was gone. We had no gun. It seemed unlikely that God would drive another injured buck into our camp. But most of all, I needed sleep. It had been many nights since I had a good rest. I was exhausted.

I was on the verge of frustrated tears when a voice spoke softly beside me. "You sleep now."

It was Silver Star.

"There not room," I answered and was quick to hurry on. "But it's all right. I have dry blankets now. Sleep here by fire."

"No, you must sleep good. You go to wagons. I sit by fire."

"But your babies?"

"They will sleep—all night. They sleep good. You go sleep by them."

I was too weary to argue.

"You take my blanket," I told her and passed it to her. She did not object but took the blanket and wrapped herself in it. Then she sat down beside the fire.

I worried about her as I crawled carefully into the vacated spot under the tarp, careful not to awaken her sleeping children or the other occupants of the enclosed area. I hated to think of her all alone in the stillness of the night. But I was too weary to fight sleep anymore.

Just as I was dozing off I remembered LaMeche. He had no place to sleep either. He, too, would be sitting by the fire. Silver Star would have company. Good company. Perhaps he would make them coffee and they would chat about the day's events together. I was content. I let sleep claim me.

18
The Gift

E XCITED VOICES AND many tramping feet awakened me. For a moment the haze of sleep kept me from focusing on where I was and what was going on around me, and then I remembered the devastating fire. We were all homeless and we were waiting for the men to return.

Like a bolt I was out of bed. *The voices!* They were men's voices. Perhaps Wynn was back. I crawled carefully from my bed and peered out into the dawning new day.

All around me men were meeting with their families, and the reunions turned into excited talk. Wives were weeping and clinging to their husbands, trying to answer questions that seemed to have no answers.

I emerged slowly, made an attempt to smooth down my messy hair and looked about the campsite for a glimpse of Wynn. He was nowhere to be seen. Tears stung my eyes. I turned to crawl back to my warm bed when a male voice called to me.

"White woman!" he shouted. I froze in my tracks. Slowly and reluctantly I turned to face him, and I'm sure my face was even whiter than normal.

I did not speak. The man before me was the village chief, and one, especially a woman, did not address him. That much I knew about tribal ethics.

He approached me, his face void of expression. I did not know what he intended to do. Perhaps he had decided that it was due to the ill-placed garden that the curse of the forest fire had come upon them.

I stood where I was, as custom demanded—with my eyes lowered.

I did not look up even when I saw the pair of brightly beaded moccasins standing not three feet from me.

Oh, dear God, I prayed silently. *Bring Wynn back quickly. Surely he will respect the white man's law—and the lawman—even if he does blame the lawman's wife.*

The chief reached a long, buckskinned arm toward me. I shuddered. I had seen it done before. To sentence the condemned the chief placed a hand on the head of the accused and pronounced his judgment.

But the hand did not travel to my forehead. Instead, it rested lightly on my shoulder.

"You do good," the strong voice declared loudly enough for the whole tribe to hear. A shiver ran all through me. I scarcely could believe my own ears.

"You do good," he stated again. "You save women and children—our wise old ones and our sick."

I shut my eyes and breathed a prayer of thanks.

The brown hand dropped from my shoulder. I waited but he did not move away.

"What you want?" he asked me.

I was confused. I didn't understand what he meant.

My eyes lifted involuntarily to study his face. "What great chief mean?" I stammered in his native tongue.

"Horses? Furs? I give it you."

And then I understood. The pride of this man would not allow him to be indebted to anyone. In his thinking, my saving the village had incurred a large debt. He must pay that debt or be shamed in the eyes of the people. I stammered for words, trying to find some way to tell him I did not see him as indebted to me.

"Oh, no. No, please," I struggled, but he went on naming amounts of horses or furs, seeming to think that his price still was not satisfactory.

His oldest wife slipped up beside him and spoke to him in a quiet voice. He looked at her, his face becoming grim. He answered her as though questioning what she had said, but she lowered her eyes and determinedly shook her head.

He looked defeated, but he squared his shoulders and called to his youngest wife. She slowly moved to his side. In her arms she held her baby boy, her eyes never leaving his tiny face. She clung to him as if her life depended upon it, but even as I watched she straightened her shoulders and her chin came up. She stood beside the chief with the proud look of her people.

The chief spoke to me again.

"I give you best I have. I give you boy child."

I gasped as I looked from the proud man to the timid wife who held the small child in her arms. He was a beautiful baby. I longed to hold him—to cuddle him. With all my heart I wanted to embrace him. The very thing I wanted more than anything else in the world was being offered! I sent up a quick prayer and stepped back a pace.

"Give him," commanded the chief, and the young woman stepped forward and held the baby out to me.

For a moment I held him close, the tears beginning to slide down my face. His somber black eyes studied me closely and then a chubby hand reached up and brushed carelessly at my cheek. I could feel the silence of the onlookers, all eyes on me. The minutes ticked by as I enjoyed the warmth of the baby in my arms. Then I took a deep breath, willed away my tears and lifted my eyes to the chief.

"White woman has glad heart because of gift. He is beautiful boy child. It give me joy to hold him."

I looked up then, directly into the eyes of the chief. I breathed deeply and took a step forward.

"Now I give chief a gift."

I did not flinch as I faced him. His eyes in his brown, comely face gave no indication of his emotions.

"I give you boy child."

With the words I passed the baby back to his father.

"The debt is paid," I said simply. "You owe me no more."

Then lowering my eyes with the proper respect, I stepped back as a sign to the chief that he could dismiss me if that was his pleasure.

I heard his guttural exclamation, a sign that the little ceremony was now over and had ended satisfactorily. I turned, my eyes still downcast, and made my way back to the shelter under the wagons.

I was glad I was alone. I buried my head in the blankets and cried until I could cry no more. In my arms there was still the warmth of the baby I had just held. Oh, if the chief only knew what he had just offered me! *Oh, if only Wynn would come!*

And then as quickly as I began my sobbing, I brought it to an end. There was a lot of work to be done. I took myself in hand and crept down to the lake to splash cold water on my face. Then I went in search of LaMeche. With the men now back in camp, I decided it would be wise for a man to be organizing things.

I found him sitting on a rock smoking a cigarette. He pushed the stub into the ground when I joined him and then placed the remaining butt in his shirt pocket.

"You look for me?"

I flushed some. I wasn't sure just how to approach the subject.

"Yes, I . . . I'm not sure—men—now back, I not need to . . . to tell what to do."

He nodded in agreement.

"But we need meat," I went on. LaMeche nodded.

"And they have guns."

"Yes," he said. "I give them shells—tell them to go hunt."

I heaved a sigh and smiled slightly as he nodded.

I turned to go but he stopped me with his words.

"You like papoose?"

"Oh, yes," I admitted before I could even stop myself.

"Then why you not keep? Chief would keep his word. Would not take boy back."

Tears stung my eyes again. "It not right. A child belongs with parents. You see his mother? Too big price for anyone to pay—to give up child."

"I see," he said, and I felt he really did. "Then why not ask for horses? Or furs?" he questioned.

"But they don't owe me anything. I do what Wynn do if he be here. Not for pay."

"You think not?"

"Of course!"

"There is nothing you ask in return?"

"No, nothing," I shook my head, and then I stopped and my eyes filled with tears in spite of my effort to stop them. "Only . . . only to be a friend—one of them. A friend. I . . . I . . ." I could not go on.

"It has been hard for you, this past year?"

My lips were trembling so I didn't trust my voice. I nodded my head, wiping the tears from my face with an unsteady hand.

"You shame us," he said softly. "You give—but not to get. From now on, it will take whole village to hold your friends. You will see."

19
Misunderstanding

IT WAS HARD to get to sleep that night. All the Indian men were now back in the camp, and it should have been a great relief to me. But for some reason they still seemed to expect me to be in charge.

Around each family fire were a number of additional people to feed.

The men did take the bullets LaMeche provided and went out on a hunting expedition. The result was two small deer, five squirrels, three rabbits and four grouse for our supper. It hardly stretched to all the cooking pots. I again added some of my vegetables to my stew pot. It improved the taste, added nutrition and made the meat go further. Many of the Indian families ate the meat with a sort of flat bread cooked over the coals.

The returning villagers made more to feed, more to sleep and less room to move. I knew I did not want to sleep out by the campfire, but there was no room for even one more body in our shelter under the wagon.

Again Silver Star came to my aid. She approached me quietly as I added a few sticks to the fire. Her soft voice sounded like the rippling of water. "The children sleep. I watch fire—you sleep now."

I argued with her but she insisted. LaMeche, coming to the fire with an armload of freshly chopped wood, overheard our words and joined Silver Star's urging.

"You must sleep," he said. "You work hard."

"But Silver Star work right with me all day," I continued.

"But I sleep better at fire than you," she maintained.

"She is right," said LaMeche, "you need some privacy."

I chuckled inwardly at his words. How strange that sleeping under a canvas with two children, two teenagers, a widow, and an elderly couple could be described as "private."

"I stay here with her," continued LaMeche, and I noticed Silver Star shyly dip her head. I smiled. Silver Star was an attractive young woman, and LaMeche certainly could do with the mellowing that a woman and children would bring to his life.

I stopped protesting and went toward the wagon.

The Indian men were not tired. They talked and laughed and visited in the shadows of the dancing campfires. Much of their conversation reached me where I lay in the darkness, clasping the few blankets close to my fully clothed body. Even in the press of many bodies, it was still cold. I shivered and moved closer to Kinook.

I was so tired I wanted only sleep. I closed my eyes, trying to shut out the sound of the voices. They went on and on, calling to one another across the distance of campfires. Then someone decided that since the families had been spared from the fires, they should celebrate with a dance of thanksgiving, or the spirits might think their kindness had gone unnoticed. A few drums which had been saved from the fire were brought out and the beating began. These were enough to make the very earth pulsate with the vibration as the tempo picked up. I felt as if I were trying to sleep with my head on the throbbing heart of Mother Nature. The very ground seemed to rumble with the beating drums and the dancing feet.

Many of the women and children joined the men. Kinook and Kinnea were the first two to leave our shelter. Silently they crawled out, taking their blankets with them to wrap themselves against the chill of the night.

Small Woman left next, not nearly as quiet in her departure. Though she was small of stature, she was not light of foot. She tripped over the elderly Shinnoo, whose heavy snore was interrupted in mid-release and replaced by an angry growl.

Small Woman did not even stop to apologize. She hastened away in the shadows as Shinnoo rolled back over and was soon snoring again.

My whole being cried for sleep, but the beating drums and thumping feet would not allow it. As the night wore on, instead of tiring, the drummers and dancers seemed to get more frenzied. Shouts and laughter often mingled with the chants, and I lay shivering in my blankets, praying that there was no "fire water" in the camp.

It was almost morning before the dancing ceased. Kinnea and Kinook crept again into their places between the sleepers. Small Woman carelessly pushed aside bodies so she could reclaim her spot under the canvas. Soon her snores were joining those of Shinnoo. They made quite a duet. As her voice rose, his snore fell; then his gained volume, while hers decreased. Up and down, up and down, like I was in a rocking boat.

It was to the rise and fall of the snoring that I finally succumbed to sleep.

When morning came, far too early, I hated to crawl out from beneath my canvas security. The sun was already streaking across the eastern horizon. I thought of all the hungry people around my campfire and forced myself to pull free of the blankets.

Silver Star was already stirring a big, boiling pot of cornmeal at the fire. LaMeche was nowhere to be seen. All around were sleeping bodies. The revelers of the night before had not even crawled off to their crude shelters. Men, women and children lay huddled together on the ground against the cold of the night.

Most of the campfires had been neglected and allowed to burn out. Only a few women stirred cooking pots. I knew those who lay strewn around on the shore would be hungry when they awakened. I skirted around them, careful to avoid disturbing them, and after a walk and a wash in the chilly lake water, I went to my own campfire.

Silver Star smiled shyly at me as she continued to stir the pot.

"Did you get sleep?" I asked her, covering a yawn and wondering if she, too, had been in on the festivities.

She shook her head. "About as much as night owl in bush," she said. Turning back to her kettle of hot cornmeal, she asked, "You eat now?"

Since we did not have enough dishes to feed everyone at the same time, we took turns. Usually everyone was fed before I took my turn, but now with the others still sleeping and much to be done, I nodded to Silver Star.

"We both eat," I told her, and realized I was hungry. "Where's LaMeche? We should feed him, too."

"He borrowed horse and gun and went out."

He must have realized that we would have very little help from the men who had expended all their energies in the night of revelry. I hoped he would have some luck—we were going to need lots of meat.

As I looked around at the sleeping villagers, a heaviness pressed in upon me. *If only Wynn would come.* It was so hard to be responsible for all of them. I didn't want the task. I had not asked for it, yet it had somehow fallen on my shoulders.

I heaved a heavy sigh and turned back to the fire. Silver Star was holding out a dish of the hot gruel. I was hungry, but my stomach had no appetite for tasteless cornmeal again. I took it with a rather reluctant hand and began to spoon it slowly to my mouth. How long would we have to live like this? *Dear Lord, help us,* I prayed. And then I remembered I hadn't even thanked the Father for my breakfast. I looked at it. Could I be thankful? Yes, of course. We could be in this situation with nothing—nothing at all. I was thankful God had allowed us the time to get a few supplies from the trading post. At least we weren't starving. I bowed my head and prayed again.

The children were the first to come looking for food. Because their parents still slept, Silver Star and I were kept busy trying to fill hungry tummies. We cooked cornmeal, served breakfast, washed dishes, cooked cornmeal, served breakfast, washed dishes—over and over again.

I could hear Wynn's dog team over on the little island protesting that they had not been fed, but I had nothing to feed them. It was after the noon hour and still LaMeche had not returned. Very few of the Indian men had aroused. Those who had stirred looked for something to eat, and when they found nothing, returned to their blankets.

The women, too, were still not up. I began to worry that if they slept all day, they would be ready to dance again all night. I even considered awakening them and assigning them tasks in the hopes they would be tired at nightfall. But I was not quite brave enough to do that.

By the slant of the sun it was around two o'clock when the chief crawled from his blankets. Because none of his three wives were stirring a pot at his own fire, he came to ours. I sensed tenseness from Silver Star. She lowered her eyes and shifted her slender body uneasily.

The chief began the conversation with a grunt. I assumed that that was his way of announcing he was now ready to eat. I shifted nervously as well, but actually I was tired and put out with the whole lot of them.

Why should a few carry the whole load? And why should it be the women? Why couldn't he get his braves off the ground and out on the trail for a buck?

I lowered my eyes as I was expected to do, but did not move forward to get a dish of food for the chief. Since Silver Star considered this "my fire," she did not offer the chief food either.

When neither of us moved forward, the chief took a seat on a log and grunted again.

Still I did not move. I stood quietly, my eyes studying the unkempt toes of my only pair of shoes.

"Hungry now," the chief stated in a rather unnecessarily loud voice.

I raised my eyes just a fraction. "Chief honors our fire," I said and took a deep breath, "but Chief not know he is at wrong fire. Camp is broken up into campfires, and this humble place not where great Chief eats. His cooking pots at fire near tall pine trees, a fitting place for chief to eat."

I stopped and waited to see what would happen. Silver Star had stopped her stirring, and I could almost feel her holding her breath. The chief looked at me with wonder in his eyes, then grunted again and stood up. He was going to leave our fire without a word. I breathed again.

Then he stopped and turned, one finger pointed to the pot of simmering vegetables.

"What in pot?" he asked me.

"Vegetables. Vegetables from my garden on island."

He sniffed. Then stepped closer and sniffed again. He looked directly at me, and this time I did not lower my eyes. I had expressed enough submission to his authority. He was at my fire, he was questioning me, I was the wife of the lawman, not under his rule. I stood straight and kept my eyes level with his.

"You grow there?"

"Yes."

"I am told island did not burn."

"It did not."

The chief studied me more closely, his dark, sharp eyes sending messages I did not understand.

"You make strong medicine," he said.

"It not medicine," I corrected him with a shake of my head. "It is food."

"Make strong medicine," he repeated, "to make food grow on cursed island and to make fire turn and run."

And then he was gone, his stiff, straight back sending out signals even in his departure, that he was the chief of his people.

I turned back to Silver Star. She resumed stirring the cooking pot.

"What chief mean?" I asked her in a low voice.

It was not a mystery to Silver Star. She looked at me shyly and then explained, "Chief Crow Calls Loud says you have great power to make food to grow where evil curse had been. When one makes good to come from evil, then one has more power than evil that was there before."

"But—but—" I stammered. "I have no powers—none."

"Then why plants grow? Why Great One lead you from fire? Why you have wisdom to know what to do?"

"I . . . do not . . . Is this what all village thinks?"

Silver Star just dipped her head again, as though in the presence of one greater than she. I was confused and ashamed. How could these people be so—so superstitious as to believe I was some—some sorceress or something? I was greatly disturbed.

Oh, God, I prayed, *please send Wynn back soon.*

The chief had roused one of his wives, who had in turn wakened some of his children. She turned to the pots, and the children scattered to find wood for the fire. I watched the proceedings, shivering uneasily over the awesome position they had bestowed upon me. Suddenly a new thought came to me. I squared my shoulders, swallowed a couple of times, brushed at the wrinkles in my dirty skirt and headed for the chief's fire.

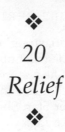

20
Relief

CHIEF CROW CALLS LOUD was sitting on a big rock next to his family's firepit, his back to his middle wife who was coaxing a small flame to life. I cleared my throat so he would know I wished an audience with him. When he grunted in return, I dared to lift my eyes and begin to speak.

"Great chief gives honor to welcome me to speak to him." I hesitated, searching for the right words.

"I come to Chief Crow Calls Loud to speak of garden. I know my garden is planted on island where none dared to go because of evil spell. I have no power over such evil. I am woman—white woman—who knows little about Indians' spells, and I am not strong against them. But I know Great God of all heaven and earth—same God who made all things and rules over all people." He stared impassively at me, and I breathed a prayer for wisdom.

"He is One who gives knowledge and power," I continued. "In His name I come to Chief. This mighty people of Chief in need because fire took village. We need much food for many people. We need skilled braves to hunt deer and elk and moose." He was watching me very carefully now. He seemed to be interested in spite of himself. I said, "We need many hands to gather pine boughs to build shelters. If rains come again, people will not be warm and dry. We must build now.

"We need young maidens to gather long marsh grasses to weave baskets, and nets to catch fish. Young men who know ways of fish brothers must drag nets so fish will fill our pots to cook.

"We need children to gather sticks from forest to keep fires under pots.

"We must all work together to care for village," I concluded a bit breathlessly. It had been a longer speech than I had intended to deliver, but the chief was kind enough to give me his total attention. When I was finished he nodded his head. He stood silently for several minutes and then spoke, "What does Golden-Haired Woman want from chief?"

"Someone to tell people what must be done."

"You tell."

"No longer. I tell the people when only women and children, sick and elderly in camp. Now men have returned. Chief is back. Not fitting for woman to still give orders."

He thought about that. Then he nodded again.

"You tell me," he said. "I give orders."

"First you must choose best hunters to find meat for pots to cook," I began, concerned that I would need to go over the whole thing again.

The chief called his oldest son. The young man had not stirred since his wild dancing of the night before. I had thought that nothing would waken him, but as the sharp command rang out from his father, he was on his feet.

"Much to do," the chief told him sternly. Then he began to talk so swiftly in his native tongue that I was able to catch only a few words here and there.

The son listened in rapt attention. I gathered as the chief talked that he had relayed my total message. He slowed down near the end and I could follow the conversation again.

"When all done," he concluded, "ask Golden-Haired One if she need more."

I took a deep breath and stepped back a pace. I hadn't expected to be so successful. Even now the eldest son was awakening other men and giving them assignments. Some seemed groggy and displeased with the assignment, but no one questioned him.

The chief then called to his oldest wife and gave her the job of organizing the women for their tasks.

He called the youngest wife and put her to work rounding up the children for the duties of carrying wood for the fires.

In a few minutes the whole scene had changed. From a people sleeping all over the lakeshore in the sun, everyone was now busy with some assigned task. It was unbelievable.

The chief turned back to me. "More?" he asked.

"No." I stammered. "No—no more now. Chief brings me joy, and I . . . I . . ." How did one say "thank you for your cooperation" in the Indian tongue? I searched my mind quickly but came up with no word. "People will eat and be happy," I finished lamely.

I lowered my gaze for my dismissal and stepped away from his family campfire.

When I returned to my own fire, Silver Star looked at me with wonder. She said nothing but busied herself adding fuel to the fire.

LaMeche, who had returned from his hunt, was eating some vegetable stew, and his eyes looked at me with amusement.

"What you say to get great chief to dance to your drum?" he asked me, smiling.

I ignored his teasing. "I tell him we need hands of everyone if we are to eat," I answered simply.

He grinned.

"You have magic powers," he stated.

I spun around and looked at him, my eyes snapping. But I tried to hold my voice steady.

"I have no magic," I informed him quietly. "Magic not needed when work is done." I repeated, "Not magic—*work*," with great emphasis.

He threw back his head and laughed.

I gave him one cold look that only made him laugh harder.

"I think Chief wise. Better not to get you angry. You are worse than injured bear." And he laughed again.

I could not be angry for long. His laughter was what I needed to forget the heavy burdens of the last few days.

"You laugh," I told him. "You not laugh when you hear what I give you to do."

LaMeche and Silver Star exchanged glances and he groaned.

"No, no!" he exclaimed. "I have done my duty, is that not so, Silver Star?"

Silver Star avoided meeting his eyes again, but she smiled ever so slightly.

"What have you done?" I asked LaMeche.

"I brought meat for your pot to cook."

"You did?" I was excited now. The teasing could wait. "What did you get?"

"One fat porcupine, two rabbits—and one moose."

"You did not—you tease now."

"No, no. I do not tease. Ask Silver Star. She already has meat in pot."

I bent over it to sniff. He was right.

I smiled at him. "Then you do work. We can eat tonight. And I feed dogs. Sled team asks for food all day."

"Do they ask now?" inquired LaMeche.

I listened. I could not hear the dogs.

LaMeche smiled again. "I feed them," he said. "Who can stand noise of hungry dogs?"

I nodded my thanks to LaMeche, fearful that my voice might catch if I tried to speak.

The sun was just hanging low in the western sky when Chief Crow Calls Loud's middle wife came to see me.

"My husband say he want talk with you."

I was apprehensive. What did this mean? Only men were asked to the chief's council. Reluctantly I followed her to the chief's campfire. He did not stand to welcome me but motioned me toward a seat beside him on furs spread on the ground.

I sat down and waited for him to speak.

"It is done. All you say," he informed me. "Hunters find meat. Two deer, one bear. Women carry pine branches, make warm shelters. Tomorrow nets will be finished to catch fish. Fires burn. People warm and full."

He waited and I knew he wanted me to respond.

"It is good," I said.

He solemnly nodded his head.

Then I went on, "Tomorrow men must hunt again. Women must finish nets and young men must fish. We need more baskets. More mats."

He nodded and without further talk I was dismissed. I was returning to my own campfire when I heard a commotion off to the side. Someone was entering the camp from the west-side trail, hurrying toward us.

And then across the distance I recognized Wynn! With a joyous cry I raced toward him.

"Elizabeth!" he exclaimed as he threw his arms around me. "Oh, thank God you're safe," he cried, pulling me close while I held him and wept on his scarlet tunic.

He brushed back the hair that curled around my face. In the absence of a comb I had run my fingers through it and braided it like the Indian people, but the little curls insisted on coming loose.

"I was so frightened when I came back to the village," he whispered in my hair. "I didn't know what had become of you."

I stifled my sobs and tried to speak. "I'm fine. Now that you're here, I'm fine."

"Oh, my darling," he said and pulled me close again.

We did not talk for many minutes and then Wynn pulled back and studied me carefully.

"Has it been hard for you—being here with all these people who—who mistrust you?"

For a moment I was stunned. In the days since the fire I had not stopped to think about the way my situation had changed. Only a short time ago the village people would not even speak to me. As Wynn said, they considered me an outsider, an impostor—but now? Now the chief called me to council. Now all the village did my bidding. Now they wanted to attribute to me magical powers.

I began to laugh. Wynn must have thought the strain of it all was more than I could bear. He looked at me intently, his eyes anxious.

"I'm fine," I assured him. "Fine, and so glad you are back. I missed you so much. There was no one to take charge."

Wynn looked around at the family firepits, the shelters, the meat hung in the trees, the fishnet that was taking shape, the newly formed baskets.

"It looks very well organized to me," he commented.

"I'll tell you all about it later," I promised. "Right now I just want to hear that you'll never leave me again."

I knew Wynn couldn't promise me that, and he knew that I knew it—still, I was glad he held me close for a moment before we turned to the fire and the cookpot to get his supper. He looked at the size of the stew that was simmering. Then he looked back at me.

"It looks like you are cooking for an army," he said.

"Not an army. Just our 'family.' It's grown a bit since you left, and they will soon all be coming for their supper, so you'd better hurry and eat. We'll need to wash that dish you are using about four times before we get them all fed."

Then I laughed and kissed Wynn on his stubbled cheek.

"You were gone so long, I was worried," I told him. "Thank God you are finally back."

21
Reunion

AFTER THE EVENING meal was served to all our little group and the dishes washed and set out to dry, Wynn and I sat around the fire with LaMeche and visited while Silver Star put her children to bed. I had not been watching her, so I did not notice she went to a pine-bough shelter instead of the make-shift shelter between the wagons.

I knew our crowded quarters would not house Wynn now too, but he and LaMeche were talking so I wasn't able to make plans.

Wynn wanted to know all the circumstances of the fire, and LaMeche explained it all in great detail, using all his Indian vocabulary plus his French heritage of gestures. He made such a heroine out of me that I blushed with embarrassment.

LaMeche told Wynn how I had organized the women and children to care for themselves and one another after the fire, and then when the chief and the men came back, I again had gotten things going.

Wynn's eyes were big with wonder. It was so uncharacteristic of me and such a reversal of my previous contact with the Indians that he could scarcely believe it. Now that I thought about it, I found it hard to believe myself.

"They think she has great 'magic' powers," went on LaMeche.

"Magic?" said Wynn. "Why magic?"

"Because her garden grows in forbidden place—the fire stops when it comes to the spot of her garden and turns and runs. She gets all people out of village, and she keeps them in camp. Even Chief thinks she has magic!"

Wynn looked at me as if to ask me whether that was true. I could only shrug my shoulders, feeling uncomfortable.

"I did nothing to make them think that," I protested quietly in English to him. "I only—oh, Wynn! It's so mixed up and ridiculous. What are we going to do now?"

Wynn smiled. "From outcast to goddess, all in a few days. That's quite a switch, Elizabeth," he responded, also in English.

"I don't think it's funny," I protested. "I wish you wouldn't tease. Don't you see the awkward situation? I don't want to be tied in with their superstitious worship."

Wynn reached for my hand. He could see it troubled me deeply.

"We'll explain," he said confidently. "I'll talk to the chief tomorrow."

And then he couldn't resist adding, "—if you'll be so kind as to get me an audience."

I swatted at him, but he managed to avoid my playful blow.

The talk turned serious then. Wynn turned to LaMeche. "How much did you lose?" he asked him in his language.

The eyes of the trader darkened. He shrugged his shoulders and answered carelessly, "Only everything."

"You saved nothing?"

"Only what will be eaten by the people before many days are gone."

"None of your furs?"

"Just a few furs and blankets that people use," LaMeche answered.

I had not stopped to think about the unselfishness of the trader. He had held nothing back from the people. Everything he had left in the world he had placed at their disposal.

"I will see if anything can be done for you," Wynn promised.

"And you?" asked LaMeche.

"Me?" said Wynn.

"You lost much, too."

Wynn shook his head. He reached for my hand. "I lost very little," he said, "now that I know that Elizabeth is safe."

I squeezed his hand tightly.

"I am sorry," Wynn went on, "about all my medicine. I hope we won't need it before a new supply can get here."

"And how you plan to get more?" asked the trader.

"I will see the chief tomorrow and ask his help in sending a runner out to Athabasca. From there I will send word to Headquarters, and they will do what is necessary."

LaMeche nodded. "How long?" he asked.

"I'm not sure. It depends on weather and availability of material and men."

It was such a relief for me to hear Wynn making the plans and arrangements. I settled back, relaxed, and let his words wash over me. The fire flickered and its warmth spilled over me, making me drowsier and drowsier as I listened to the hum of voices. My head dropped to my knees and I pulled my blanket more closely around me.

"What will you do?" Wynn asked the trader.

"I will build again. It will be hard to make start. I have no money. I might have to return to traplines for a few years, but I will work, and I will build." I could hear the smile in his voice as he continued, "Not magic," he said, "but work."

I was sure Wynn would not understand all the significance of his statement.

"What do the people have left?" Wynn was asking.

"Enough," said LaMeche. "They have survived on less."

Then there was only silence until LaMeche said softly, "You must take her to bed. She has had little sleep for many nights. Last night when she might have slept, the braves danced and drummed all night. She will be sick."

I felt Wynn's hands upon my arms. "Beth," he whispered. "Beth, it's bedtime. Come on, let's get you some sleep."

"We can't go to bed," I mumbled. "No room."

"Plenty room," responded LaMeche. "I move all the Indians out of your shelter today. They have own place now."

I hadn't known that.

Wynn bade LaMeche good night and helped me to my feet. I was hardly aware of being led as we zigzagged our way through the camp and over to the wagon shelter.

I was so tired that I couldn't even undress, even if we had privacy. Wynn bundled me close in the blankets and then removed his boots and lay down beside me.

I remember his arm drawing me close, and my whisper, "Thank God you are home," and then I was gone, relaxing in the comforting arms of Wynn and sleep.

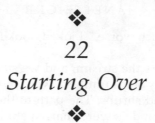

22
Starting Over

NO ONE WAKENED me the next morning, and I slept much later than I intended. I was embarrassed when I finally did get up and found the camp a bustle of activity. Silver Star and Small Woman had fed all of our family, and the two girls had carried enough wood for the day. Chief Crow Calls Loud had already sent each of the camp workers to his or her assigned task.

When Silver Star informed me that Wynn had gone to see his dog team, I did not even wait to eat some breakfast but hurried over to the small island to join him.

I found him bending over Franco. The dog was quite steady on his feet but he still breathed heavily, like an old man with asthma. Wynn's fingers traveled over the dog's chest and rib cage, seeking out the extent of the damage.

I knelt beside him, my eyes asking questions.

"'Morning, Elizabeth," he said, his serious face breaking into a smile.

"How bad is it?" I asked.

"Pretty bad. It's a wonder we didn't lose them all when you see how close that fire came."

"I forgot to tell you about Tip and Keenoo," I said softly. I knew how much Wynn's dog team meant to him.

"LaMeche told me."

The other dogs were all clamoring for some attention, so I left Wynn and went to pet them, starting first with Flash and then proceeding around the circle. Wynn soon joined me.

"Will Franco still be able to pull?" I asked him.

"I don't think so," said Wynn, "but we'll give him a few weeks and see what happens."

I led Wynn by the hand to admire my garden. He could hardly believe the plants had survived the heat of the fire. I told him about my extensive watering the day before, and he just smiled and shook his head.

"Have you been back to the village, Elizabeth?" he asked me.

"No. There really hasn't been time—and I didn't think I wanted to see it," I admitted.

Wynn looked down at my shoes. "There's something I would like you to see—but it will make a sooty mess of your shoes."

"They couldn't be much worse," I joked, looking at the mud-smeared, rain-stained boots.

Wynn helped me cross the stream, and we started for the settlement.

We hadn't gone many steps until we were in the charcoal remains of what had been trees and shrubs. The path to the village was no longer distinguishable. All around us were charred stumps and fallen trees that had not completely burned. It was an awful sight.

"What happened to LaMeche?" Wynn asked me.

The words struck terror to my heart. "Did something happen—"

"No, no." Wynn was quick to explain, "I just mean he's changed. He's different somehow. Remember how you used to dread talking to him because of his sullen—"

"He *is* different. Oh, Wynn, I don't know what we would have done without him. He has been so much help. I guess the fire did it." I was thoughtful for a moment. "I guess the fire changed a lot of things."

"Well, some changes I don't like, but LaMeche—I rather like that change," responded Wynn.

"Me, too," I agreed. "He smiles and even laughs. Why, he even teases—mercilessly." I smiled to myself, remembering how I had gotten angry with his teasing, but maybe it helped me to keep my sanity in the process.

"You know what I think?" I went on. "I don't think he was ever as mean and morose as he tried to appear. I think it was all a cover-up. Look at him. He's given everything he had left to the people, without a murmur. No one could reform that much, that quickly, unless they were already like that underneath."

Wynn laughed. "Maybe you're right," he said. "Maybe LaMeche was just trying to act tough."

We came then to what had been the village. It was a sorry sight. Bits and pieces of logs stood crisscrossed where homes had been. True, they had been crude dwellings, but they had been homes nonetheless. Here and there an iron object raised its head through the debris, defying even the fire.

I wanted to shut my eyes to it all, but I couldn't. I studied it carefully as we walked along, trying to picture in my mind what had been there before. I could see the cabin, could picture which dogs were staked out in front, which women busied themselves around the door, to turn from their work as I passed by. I could picture the children playing in the yard, their eyes big with wonder or fright at the strange white woman.

And now, these same women washed their dishes in the lake beside me, the children ran to me for orders, others cooked over my fire or shared from my stew. How things had changed!

"Look here," commented Wynn and I jerked back to the present. We were standing before what had been our cabin. Part of the framework of one wall remained, looking like it would topple over with the first breath of wind but still supporting a few feet of roofline. The plank that had been nailed to the roof at a slant to form a crude water channel still swept along the length of it, charred and burned but still visible.

Then my eyes traveled to follow Wynn's pointing finger. There in front of us stood my "promise" barrel, overflowing with rainwater. I could not believe my eyes. Here and there the protruding rags showed where we had worked on it. The tar discolored much of the outside, but it was holding water!

Tears sprang to my eyes and I could not speak. I felt Wynn's arm slip around me and draw me close. I looked at him with wet eyes and noticed that his eyes were glistening, too.

"Oh, Wynn," I finally managed, "He kept His promise. Right in the middle of the fire."

"He always keeps His promises, Elizabeth," Wynn reminded me.

Then I looked around at the remains of the village. "But it is so different than the way I expected."

Wynn's arm tightened about me. We both stood in silence.

We turned from the barrel and began to look at the scarred wreckage of our cabin to see if there was anything salvageable.

Wynn pulled out the metal teakettle. "Do you suppose it will still hold water?"

"Let's take it and see," I answered.

The metal frame of our bed was there, but it was twisted beyond further use. There were a few containers and crocks, most of them no longer usable. But a few things looked like they would merit scrubbing up.

After we had finished poking around, we headed back to camp. I remembered that I hadn't eaten breakfast and was hungry. I also knew there was much work to do in the camp and, like I had told the chief, everyone needed to work together. Even though I was glad to have Wynn back to shoulder the main responsibilities, I still had tasks that I needed to attend to.

"I must get back," I told Wynn. "Poor Silver Star has been doing all my work this morning."

"Speaking of Silver Star," said Wynn with a twinkle in his eyes, "am I imagining things, or do I see her casting little glances in the direction of our trader?"

"I hope so," I enthused. "Wouldn't that be wonderful?"

"If the trader thinks so!"

"I hope he does. Wouldn't it be wonderful for him to have a wife and family? Oh, Wynn, I hope it works out!"

"Have you turned Cupid?" Wynn asked me with a sly grin.

"No, I have not," I retorted. "Honestly, I have had nothing to do with it. But," I admitted more slowly, "if I thought I could influence it, I might try."

Wynn laughed and helped me over the fallen log across the stream.

We walked on in comfortable silence. As we neared the camp, Wynn said, "I'm to have a chat with the chief this morning. I had to have some time first to review the damage and formulate our needs. I expect to send a runner out as quickly as I can get organized. Will you have time to make out a list of things you'll be needing?"

"I'll take time."

Wynn still looked pensive. "I still haven't figured out just how to do this," he admitted. "Nobody can just remember the whole list—and it will hardly do to try to scratch it on birch bark."

"What do you mean?" I asked.

"I don't have anything for writing a letter or making a list," said Wynn.

I smiled slowly. "You know," I said, "there is just no way that my head would have worked well enough to think ahead to grabbing pencil and paper—yet that is exactly what I did."

"You what?"

"I have a stub of a pencil and sheets of paper. When I ran into our cabin, I just grabbed at random, not even thinking—I even got some sticks of firewood," I laughed. "I thought it strange when I saw the pencil and paper, but I guess there was a good reason for it after all."

"I guess there was," said Wynn, giving me another hug.

After talking for several hours with Chief Crow Calls Loud, Wynn spent the rest of the day organizing the needs of the village and making out his list on the paper I had saved from the fire. It wasn't very official look- ing but it sufficed. When he had finished his task, every sheet of the paper had been covered with the essential supply list.

Early the next morning three braves and LaMeche left on the best horses for the settlement of Athabasca Landing. Wynn had given them instruc- tions as to whom to see when they got there. The braves seemed excited about this new venture but tried not to let it show. LaMeche did not appear to enjoy the thought of returning to "civilization," but he went without question. I saw Silver Star looking shyly from downcast eyes for one last glimpse of him before they had disappeared from our sight. We had many days to wait before the men and the needed materials could possibly get to our campsite.

23
Adjustments

WYNN NOW HAD great cooperation from the chief on running the affairs of the camp. Though the chief had not been openly hostile in the past, he had been at times withdrawn and rather arrogant. It was much easier to work together with him in his present frame of mind.

The women chatted and laughed as they did their laundry in the lake water or carried their water supply from the swiftly flowing stream. Now that their men were back, the experience of "camping out" was not a difficult one for them—except on the days and nights when it rained. Even with reinforcements to the pine shelters, there was no way to keep all the water out, so people walked around drippy, wet, cold and rather miserable. I feared an epidemic of colds or fever, but they seemed to stay healthy.

Wynn found more canvas in our supply wagon that he draped around our shelter. We *almost* had privacy, a great relief to me. I was able to change my filthy clothes and take a bath of sorts. I did as the Indian women and washed my hair in the lake water. It was cold, and I had no soap of any kind, so it was not a very satisfactory job. But it did wash some of the woodsmoke smell from my hair.

The Indian women now shyly included me in their chatter, even coming to my campfire for a cup of tea.

The children, too, smiled and even waved occasionally when they went by the campsite on their way to gather wood. It helped, I am sure, to have the two orphans, Kinook and Kinnea, at our campfire.

I wondered about the two young girls. I had been told that they had lived alone since the death of their mother, having lost their father several years previously. Now that their cabin was gone, would the settlement people rebuild it for them? Would they be forced to find refuge with another crowded family? Or would they be married off early—too early, in my opinion—to one or another of the village men as a second or third wife?

I wished to keep them with Wynn and me. But remembering our small, one-room cabin and expecting our new home to closely resemble it, I realized there was no way we could crowd them in. I hadn't yet had opportunity to speak to Wynn about them, but I promised myself that at my first chance, I would do so.

Some of the women found a berry patch to the northwest of us where the fire had not burned, and we all set off one morning with newly woven baskets.

Our spirits were high on this bright, clear, late-summer day in spite of our meager existence. The chatter of the women and the giggling of the young girls swirled around me as I walked slowly, enjoying the outing.

Silver Star dropped back to walk beside me. She had left her two young children in the care of the elderly woman who shared our campfire.

We walked in silence for some time and then she spoke, softly, "Has sergeant heard from the braves?"

"No," I replied, "not yet."

Her eyes looked sad.

"Is Silver Star worried?" I asked gently.

She only nodded her head slightly, lowering her eyes. But not before I could see the concern in them.

"You worry about one of the braves?" I asked her.

She shook her head.

"Then you worry about the trader?"

Her eyelashes fluttered and her face flushed slightly. She said nothing.

"He will be fine," I assured her. "He has lived in outside world before. He knows all about it."

"Silver Star knows that," she whispered.

"Then why do you fear?" I asked her.

Suddenly I knew the answer. She was afraid LaMeche might not come back—that he might decide to stay in the outside world where the way of life was so much easier than facing forest fires, disease, and famine far from any help.

"He will come," I comforted, hoping with all my heart that I spoke the truth.

Silver Star dared to look at me, her face still anxious, yet hope shining in her eyes.

We reached the berry patch and all set to work filling our containers. The berries were small and scarce because of our lack of summer rains, yet they tasted delicious and were a real treat after our days on a limited diet. I sneaked a few every now and then as I picked. The others did, too—I could tell by the blue stains on tongues and teeth.

There would be no way to make a pie or can what was left over, but we would enjoy them fresh and perhaps even have a few left to dry in the sun.

We cleaned the patch before we left it, though we had not even filled our containers. We would need to do more scouting in the area to look for additional patches if we wanted further picking.

We silently started for home, walking single file or two-by-two. Again Silver Star walked at my side, but she offered no conversation as we walked and, respecting her silence, I did not talk either.

Nanawana, the youngest wife of the chief, walked just ahead of us, her sleeping son strapped to her back. I couldn't help but watch the child as she walked.

What a darling baby! my heart cried. His black hair and eyes, his pudgy, dimpled cheeks, his tightly clenched fist near his mouth just in case he needed something to suck on reminded me of Samuel.

A tear came unbidden, and Silver Star saw me wipe it away. She looked at the baby, his little head nodding with each step of his mother, and I knew she understood my empty arms.

I was glad when we reached the village and I again was too busy to think about anything other than the tasks at hand.

The days did not change much. Our biggest task was to keep everyone fed. My little garden was nearly depleted. There would be nothing to store for our winter use.

Without admitting it to one another, we soon began to watch the southeastern horizon for a glimpse of the returning men. If we were to have decent homes constructed before the winter set in, we must begin immediately. Every day counted.

Wynn said nothing to me of his concern, but I saw his eyes shift often to the southeast. I knew he was willing the return of those he had sent out.

About sunset of the twelfth day, we had just finished washing the dishes for the last time after our evening meal. A shout went up from someone in the camp.

All eyes quickly lifted toward the southeast where three horses appeared, the riders answering with upraised hands. *Three*—but there should have been four! I quickly stole a glance at Silver Star. Her head was lowered, concealing her face. I knew she was quite aware that one of the men was missing.

How could he? I accused LaMeche silently, knowing that Silver Star's heart would be broken. *How could he do this to her?*

But when the three reached the village and were greeted by the villagers circling around them, it was not LaMeche who was missing. He pushed his way through the crowd and approached our campfire.

I smiled my welcome, more relieved than I dared show, and looked around for Silver Star. She was not there. Sometime during the commotion, she had slipped quietly away.

I saw LaMeche glancing around as well, and I guessed that he, too, was looking for her, though he did not ask. Instead, he picked up a cup and asked for some coffee.

"There is still hot soup, too," I informed him. He welcomed a bowl and sat down at the fire.

"How was your trip?" I asked.

"Good to be home," was his answer.

I knew his report would be given in full to Wynn, so I did not ask further questions.

"It is good to have you home," I said instead.

He sipped slowly from the steaming cup. "Things have gone well?" he asked.

"Yes," I said with some hesitation, thinking of the days of rain and the difficulties of wet clothes and blankets. "As well as one could hope."

Wynn joined us then, and LaMeche stood to his feet, extending a hand. Then he reached into his pocket and produced a bulky envelope. Wynn accepted it, sat down on a log, and slit open the envelope to review the contents. He was silent as he read. When he folded the official letter and returned it to the envelope, I could stand it no longer.

"Well?" I questioned.

"The supplies will be coming just as soon as they can get them through," he said with some relief. "They will also send in some men to help with the rebuilding."

I heaved a big sigh. It was such a weight off our shoulders to know that there would be help coming to furnish the villagers with adequate shelters before the coming of winter.

"How was your trip?" Wynn asked LaMeche.

LaMeche just hunched his shoulders.

I thought he was going to refuse to talk about it, but he surprised me. When he had finished his soup, refilled his coffee cup, rolled himself a cigarette and settled back on his log with his back to a tree, he began to tell all about his trip out, the braves he traveled with, the people he met, where they stayed, the reaction of the three young men to the things they saw. Then he told of the "fire water" that the three braves had somehow obtained, how they managed to drink themselves into a stupor that eventually ended up in a fight resulting in one of the braves being locked behind bars for a two-month period.

Try as he might to reason and barter, LaMeche was not able to get the young man released from jail. At last he gave up and was forced to return home without him.

I knew the young man by appearance only, but he was cocky and swaggering even around the camp. It was not hard for me to picture him getting himself into trouble when he reached a place where he was not closely supervised.

"Why did the chief send him?" I asked Wynn later when we were alone. Wynn shook his head.

"Perhaps he thought he needed a lesson—I don't know."

"Have you talked to the chief?" I asked.

"LaMeche went to report to him. If the chief wants me, he will send for me."

Wynn was right. In a few minutes the chief's son came asking Wynn's presence at his fire.

I stirred up the coals and added a few more sticks to our own fire, still wondering about Silver Star.

I did not wonder for long. She was soon back, her eyes heavy. I was about to break the news about LaMeche's return, but she spoke first.

"Silver Star might need to leave your campfire," she said solemnly.

"What do you mean?" I asked quickly.

"Grey Wolf leaves me gifts."

My head jerked up. Leaving gifts was the way that an Indian man proposed to a desired maiden.

But Grey Wolf? He was loud and cantankerous. He already had one wife and was known to beat her with a good deal of regularity. I held my breath, not knowing what to say.

It was clear from Silver Star's face that she did not like the idea. And then I realized that Silver Star *did* care about the trader and had been hoping LaMeche might make his move before Grey Wolf would demand his answer.

"But—but—" I stammered, "can't you wait?"

"He says he has waited long enough. He looks at me with anger in his eyes."

"Can't you just say no?"

Silver Star lifted herself from her squatting position, her eyes met mine and she spoke softly, yet forcefully. "I am widow, with two small children. I am burden to village people. If someone wish to marry me and care for my needs, it is my duty to accept."

"But—but *Grey Wolf?*" I said, hating the thought. Silver Star lowered her eyes again and squatted down by the fire. Her head and slim shoulders drooped in resignation. She made a pitiful picture. I was reaching to place a hand on her shoulder when a voice behind us spoke forcefully, cutting the stillness of the dark night.

"Never," he spat out, and a curse followed. "Never would I let him take you."

It was LaMeche. He had returned in time to hear at least a part of our conversation. Silver Star gave a startled gasp and involuntarily her hand went out toward LaMeche, but she quickly recovered her poise and dropped her gaze and let her hand fall.

Silence fell and seemed to linger. No one was doing or saying anything. Why didn't LaMeche continue? He just stood there, looking angry and upset, his eyes still on the trembling Silver Star.

I took a breath and moved back a step. I wanted to shake them both. I wanted to make them talk to each other.

"And how can she stop him?" I dared ask rather pointedly.

LaMeche did not look at me. His eyes were still full of Silver Star. They softened, and she glanced up at him, with love and hope in her gem-black eyes.

"By her accept *my* gifts," he said gently, and Silver Star lowered her flashing eyes again. Then she was gone, slipping away quietly into the darkness of the night.

I looked at LaMeche. He nodded at me, his face still serious, and then he, too, was swallowed up by the darkness of the night.

When I reached our fire the next morning Silver Star was already there, stirring the boiling pot with flushed cheeks. I wasn't sure if the new flush was due to the heat or to whatever was causing the sparkle in her eyes.

She was wearing a new skirt as well—one with bright colors that circled the fullness, standing out among all of the worn, faded skirts worn by the rest of us. She had a silver chain with turquoise stones about her neck, glistening in the morning sun.

I asked no questions, though I suppose that keeping silent right then was one of the hardest things I had ever done in all my life. It was obvious that someone had "gifted" Silver Star and that she had indeed accepted what he had given. I was nearly sure I knew the giver.

I did not wait long for confirmation. LaMeche and Wynn soon came for the morning meal. I saw Wynn's questioning eyes fall on the attractive young widow, and then I quickly switched my glance to LaMeche. He attempted to be very casual as he took his place, but I saw him look at Silver Star and his face relaxed. He smiled slightly, and then their eyes met and a promise passed between them. I knew our settlement would soon be celebrating a wedding.

As I passed by Silver Star to get the steaming pot from the open-fire spit, I reached out to give her hand a little squeeze. She understood my message and returned the pressure slightly. I had wet eyes as I served the men their morning coffee.

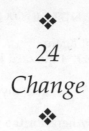

24
Change

"ELIZABETH, DO YOU have a few minutes?"

Wynn's voice made me turn from spreading the few newly washed clothes on the low-hanging bushes. I looked at him, nodded my head, and smiled.

"What is it?" I asked.

"I thought we might take a walk away from the camp and talk for a few minutes," he invited.

I was puzzled. Wynn usually did not ask me to forsake my morning tasks, just to talk.

"Certainly," I responded, sensing that something would be different about this talk. I felt a little knot of apprehension within me, but I tried not to let it show.

We were joined by Kip who spotted us heading down the path that led around the lake. I put a hand out to stroke his heavy coat. He had not been washed or brushed for several days, and he was dirty and matted like most of the village dogs. He was in good spirits, though. Life in the rough seemed to agree with him.

I decided I would not question Wynn until he was ready to speak. Instead, I chatted about Silver Star and LaMeche, sharing with Wynn that they would be married just as soon as LeMeche could build a permanent shelter.

Wynn smiled, knowing how pleased I was about the coming wedding.

We walked to a small knoll overlooking the lake, and Wynn indicated that we should sit down on the grass-covered bank. I lowered myself to the ground and hoped he would not make me wait much longer.

"Is something wrong?" I asked, unable to stand it a minute more when Wynn appeared to be settling himself in for a few moments of silence.

"No. Nothing is wrong," he said quickly, turning to me. "I'm sorry if I alarmed you."

I breathed more easily.

"I just wanted to discuss with you the letter I got from headquarters. I haven't had opportunity, with all that keeps you busy." He reached over and took my hand. "Don't you think that you could slow down a bit now?" he asked me.

"I'm fine," I assured him. "I like being busy. It makes the days go faster."

Wynn smiled but was silent again.

"But what about your letter?" I quizzed him.

"They have new orders for us."

"New? What do you mean?" I asked, my face lifting quickly to study Wynn's eyes.

"They don't want us to stay here for the winter."

"I don't understand—"

"They feel they will not be able to get a proper building up for us in time for winter."

"But you said they were coming soon to build," I reminded him.

"Yes, they are. But the native people must be provided for first. They have no other place to go."

It was becoming more and more confusing to me. I shook my head to clear the fog. Wynn's grip on my hand tightened.

"Let me start at the beginning," he said.

I nodded my head in assent and he began.

"The Force has promised to not only send in the required materials, but also to send in some government-paid men to build new cabins for the people of the village. They also will send in a man to take my place for the winter months. He will be single and will be quite able to spend the entire winter in tight quarters."

I couldn't help but smile, remembering the cabin where Wynn and I had spent the past winter. *How could one have "tighter quarters" than that?* I wondered. But Wynn was continuing.

"He will carry on the law enforcement necessary while the village is being rebuilt.

"They have also taken my suggestion of compensating LaMeche to some measure," he explained. "The trading post will be the first building to be constructed because of its importance to everyone. They plan to partition off a very small room in the trading post for the officer to use as a sleeping quarter. This later will be turned back over to the trader, or used as a temporary lock-up room if LaMeche and the Force reach an agreement. Just like we had at Beaver River."

I remembered the little room in the McLain's store. It had been the place where Crazy Mary had been kept until her untimely death.

"When everyone else has been properly sheltered, they will turn their attention to building a new cabin for the Mountie."

"Then we can come back?" I quickly cut in. I suddenly realized how much I wanted to stay now that things had changed with the villagers.

"They didn't state that for sure," Wynn said honestly. "They did say that it would be considered."

That didn't sound too promising as far as I was concerned. I chafed under such hedging, but I said nothing to Wynn. There was little that he could do about it.

"When do we go?" I asked, with little enthusiasm.

"We are to go back with the wagons that bring in the supplies."

That would not be long then. We expected the wagons and supplies in any day now.

"And where are we to go?" I asked. Then with sudden hopefulness, I continued, "Can we go back to Beaver River?"

Wynn smiled but shook his head. "I'm sorry, but no Beaver River. It would have been nice, though, wouldn't it?"

"Oh, yes," I said, sighing.

"We are to go to Athabasca Landing."

"To do what?"

"I will work in the office there, supervising the two younger men who will be on patrol in the area. You will . . . I guess you can just be a . . . lady of leisure."

"I don't think I will like that," I said soberly.

"Who knows," said Wynn, in an effort to cheer me, "maybe you will learn to like it."

I stubbornly shook my head. I could not see myself enjoying having nothing to do but make the beds and cook the meals. It would be as bad as the last winter when I had nothing to do and nowhere to go. I had hated it. It had been all that I could do to keep my outlook cheerful so that I wouldn't be a drag on Wynn.

"It will be quite different there than it is here at the village," Wynn went on, knowing where my thoughts were leading me. "It is already a fair-sized settlement. You will find many new neighbors—both white and Indian. It will give you a nice break from roughing it."

I still wasn't sure I was going to like the new arrangement, but I knew Wynn needed my support. When I thought about it, I wasn't sure if Wynn would welcome the new life either. He wasn't particularly fond of paper work, yet he would be stuck with it for the winter while younger men did the patrolling and contacted the Indians. I tried to look a bit more enthusiastic and turned to Wynn with a slow smile.

"Guess we can stand it for a few months," I said, and he pulled me close.

Kip came bounding up to us and nearly pushed me over with his exuberance. I laughed and fought my way upright again, shoving Kip away and playfully rubbing his ear.

"Take it easy," I told him, "we won't go without you—" then I looked quickly at Wynn, my concern in my voice, "will we?"

"We'll take Kip," Wynn assured me.

"What about the rest of the team?" I asked him, hoping that Wynn would not be asked to give up his well-trained dog team.

"I plan to take them."

"You are still short two or three dogs, aren't you?" I reminded him.

"That's one of my reasons for taking them. I hope that soon I will have a batch of Revva's pups old enough to start training."

I was excited about seeing Revva's litter when it first arrived. I wanted to help train them right from puppyhood onward. I knew that was the way Wynn preferred to train his dogs. Living in Athabasca, I was sure I would have lots of spare time to help him.

I stood to my feet and looked out over the little lake. In the distance I could hear the calls of the children in the camp. A loon cried—a lonely, wilderness-sounding cry. I knew I would miss it.

"What did LaMeche say?" I asked Wynn.

Wynn stood beside me, his arm around my waist. "About what?" he asked me.

"About all this?"

"I haven't talked to him—and I don't expect that they told him anything about it when they gave him the letter with the new orders."

"Then he doesn't know?"

"I wanted to talk to you before I talked to anyone else," Wynn informed me.

I smiled at him. "Thank you," I said softly. "I'm glad I was first."

He took my hand then and we started back to the campsite. I knew I would see it differently in the days that lay ahead. Each time I looked around me, I would be thinking, "I will leave this soon." It would make a difference. Undoubtedly the tears would fall at times.

"Wynn," I said as we walked, "there is something that I have wished to speak to you about. I am concerned about Kinnea and Kinook. What will happen to them? Will they be given a cabin of their own again? What if they aren't? I'm really concerned about them, Wynn."

"I am, too," returned Wynn. "I hear that Chief Crow Calls Loud has been looking at Kinook."

I stopped in my tracks and stared at Wynn. "No!" I said. "Surely not?"

"She could be in worse circumstances," Wynn assured me.

"But the fourth wife? Who would ever want such a position? She would be the servant of all the rest of them."

"Until she bore her first child, maybe."

"A child? She is still a child herself. Wynn, that's unthinkable! Can't you do something?"

"Our laws do not govern their marriages, Elizabeth. You know that."

"Can't we take her with us," I blurted out. "Both of them. Can't we get some kind of custody and—"

"Do you think they'd be happy?" Wynn asked softly.

I started to say that of course they would, but even before the words formed I knew it was wrong. The two girls would be happy only in their own village, with their own people.

It seemed a hopeless situation. I swallowed the lump in my throat and took Wynn's hand again. In my heart I prayed for wisdom and God's help as I walked. Surely there was something that could be done—some way to make arrangements for them. I prayed that the Lord would work on their behalf.

The next evening Wynn invited me to go with him to care for the dog team. I went readily enough, but inwardly I suspected that he might have other reasons for asking for my company.

I was right. As soon as we passed from earshot of the village people, Wynn took my hand and slowed my stride. We never felt free to talk for very long in front of the Indians when we wanted a private conversation. We both knew they could not understand our English, yet we couldn't bring ourselves to discuss a private matter in front of them.

"I had a long talk with LaMeche," Wynn informed me.

I turned to Wynn in my eagerness, forgetting to take a forward step, nearly tripping over my own feet.

"Why don't we sit down for a minute?" Wynn asked me, nodding toward a shaded spot near the path.

We took our seat and Wynn idly picked a blade of tall grass, broke a piece of it and put it in his mouth. I could almost taste it, cool and sweet.

"LaMeche was excited to hear that he will get help in rebuilding and restocking his post," said Wynn. "He can hardly wait for the supplies to get here—but I've this strange notion that it might have more to do with Silver Star than with the trading post." Wynn smiled.

"He is quite willing to share a small room with the Mountie who comes to relieve us." Wynn continued. "Later he will let the Force have the room for a temporary cell as they had hoped.

"After the two of us had discussed this for a while," said Wynn, taking both my hands in his, "he started asking me some questions about you—about how a white woman in these circumstances could have the inner strength and the wisdom to save the whole village from certain destruction."

I was watching Wynn's face carefully, my mind racing ahead to what he might be telling me.

"I explained to him that without God's inspiration and help, you probably would not have been able to do what you did. He looked so interested and so—so *wistful* at the same time that I went on to explain to him about our faith in Jesus Christ.

"'I wish I had a faith like that,' was his comment. I could hardly believe my ears—" Wynn's voice was full of deep emotion as he talked. "The people here have never showed the slightest bit of interest in Jesus or in our faith when I've talked about it in the past. I told LaMeche that he *could* have a faith like that. I told him that Jesus had died for him—that he could repent of his sin, receive the Lord Jesus as his Savior, and be born into God's family."

I'm sure my eyes were as full of wonder and joy as Wynn's when he said, "And you know what, Elizabeth? LaMeche did just that! We prayed together on a log out there in the woods, and he is now a Christian!"

The tears rolled down my cheeks as I thanked the Lord for this one small light in the spiritual darkness of Smoke Lake. "Oh, Lord," I prayed, "help him to be strong and to grow and to convince others here to follow his example."

"LaMeche said something else that I think will make you very happy," Wynn went on, and then hesitated, driving me mad with curiosity.

"Silver Star had already spoken to him. It seems that she has gotten quite attached to the two orphan girls."

I held my breath.

"Silver Star has asked LaMeche if he would mind if they took them. Kinook will soon be of marriageable age, but Kinnea would have two or more years to be on her own yet. It seems that Silver Star has been as worried about them as you have."

I bowed my head in another prayer of thanks. Then I asked God to also bless Silver Star for her love and concern. I would have no apprehension about leaving the two young girls in the care of Silver Star and her new husband.

"Oh, Wynn," I said, "that's a real answer to prayer. I never even thought of Silver Star taking them. That'll be perfect! They already love her and her little ones."

"But there is something else, too," Wynn went on, "and I think that it will make you equally as happy."

"What?" I prompted, wondering what in the world could make me as happy as that last bit of news.

"I dared to have a talk with the chief."

"And?"

"And he heard me out—very patiently. I told him of my concern. And I dared to tell him of the concern of the white woman—you. And he nodded solemnly and then passed a decree that no man in the village shall take gifts to Kinook until the frost comes a year from now."

"Oh, Wynn," I cried, "did he really? Did he really say that?"

"He did. And he made sure that every male in the village knows about it, too."

A new, more sobering thought struck me. *Did the chief pass his law to save the young girl for himself?* I didn't like to think of it.

"Why?" I asked Wynn. "Why do you think he did that? Was it to protect her for himself? She is very pretty, Wynn."

"If he wanted her for himself," said Wynn, "there would be nothing stopping him from taking her right now."

"I know, but maybe even he realizes she is still too young."

"Then give him a little credit—even if he does want her for his fourth wife, at least he is willing to give her a little time to grow up. Let's be thankful for that, Elizabeth."

Then Wynn continued, "I am more inclined, however, to think that the chief might want Kinook for a wife for his oldest son. He didn't say so directly—but I caught him looking in the young brave's direction as we talked. I wouldn't be surprised if the boy has let his wishes be known to his father."

I pictured the young brave. Come to think of it, I had seen him strutting past our campfire on more than one occasion. I was sure that Kinook, though she kept her eyes properly lowered, had seen him, too. I smiled.

"That would be nice—sometime in the future," I murmured.

"In the future," repeated Wynn. "For now let's be glad that she will be allowed to grow up."

Wynn was right. For now Kinook would have a home where she was loved and cared for. At least she would not need to be a child bride. A year was not long, but perhaps by then she would be ready to receive gifts from the young Indian brave.

Wynn told me he would send for a French translation of the New Testament for LaMeche.

"Oh, Wynn, wouldn't it be wonderful if there was a group of believers here when we return?"

Wynn smiled at my certain "when" and gave me a hug.

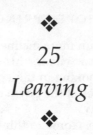

25
Leaving

THE DAY THE loaded wagons and team of builders pulled laboriously into the camp was one of surprises in more than one way. I never would have guessed that the people would react so strangely. The Indian men strutted about, putting on a show of great bravery in the face of possible danger at the hands of the strange white men. Women fearfully held their ground with lowered eyes and bated breath—you could see them wishing to be able to take to the woods for protection. In fact, a few of them did just that. Many of the little children ran and hid themselves, wild with fright at the sight of all the strange-looking newcomers.

The chief, too, forced a brave front and stalked out to meet the men, but it was clear he feared placing his life in danger by doing so.

Wynn and LaMeche took charge and told the crew where to leave the wagons and tether the tired horses. Then Wynn supervised the setting up of the canvas tents and welcomed the trail-weary men to our fire for coffee to wash the dust from their parched throats.

There were nine of them in the party. All but three would be staying. The Mountie who was to take our place looked very young to me, and I wondered if it was his first posting and if he would be able to handle things if a crisis were to develop.

It is none of my business, I reminded myself. The Force must know their own men, and certainly all of them had to start someplace.

And then lovely young Kinook walked by our fire, her tall back straight, her dark hair swinging free, her head supporting a container of fresh water. And I saw the Mountie look after her, his eyes full of wonder as he nearly forgot to swallow the hot coffee in his mouth. I smiled to myself, realizing just how young he really was.

I greeted the supply wagons with mixed emotions. I knew it was best for the settlement that work begin as quickly as possible on the building of the post and the cabins. I knew there was much to be done before the coming of the winter snows. I knew also that LaMeche was anxious to have a home so he might take Silver Star to be his wife. But in spite of all those things, I also realized that in just a few days' time I would be asked to leave with those same departing wagons, and I dreaded that thought— even if our circumstances here were primitive.

The men spent the evening hours in counsel with Chief Crow Calls

Loud. He had to be consulted about his wishes for the site of the new settlement. He also, out of respect for his position, was informed about the new trading post, introduced to the young Mountie who would represent the law, and informed that Wynn and I would be leaving.

Wynn was surprised at the chief's reaction to that news. He expressed first surprise and then displeasure, asking if it was possible to revoke the decision.

"The home for Golden-Haired One can be built first," he insisted. "The chief and the people wish her to stay."

"It seems that you made quite an impression on our chief," Wynn told me with a grin. "He doesn't want to lose you."

I flushed slightly, very surprised at the turn of events. Had the villagers really been so fearful of the evil connected with the site of the impinging witch doctor that the chief was seeing in my departure a possibility that the powers could be reestablished? It was all very strange.

Silver Star stayed close to me the next day. I was glad to have her nearby. But we had very little time to talk in private.

When we went to the lake to wash the evening dishes for the last time, we were finally alone.

"I want to tell you how much—how full of joy I am to know Kinook and Kinnea will be in your home," I said to Silver Star as I swished sand around in a pot to scour the sides.

Silver Star kept her eyes lowered.

"They are like sisters to me," she said softly.

"And to me," I said, a tear rolling down each of my cheeks.

"I will miss you," I continued. "I am sorry we cannot go to your wedding."

She nodded silently.

"I hope much joy will share your path," I continued.

She looked at me then. "I will make him happy if it is in my power to do so; in that I will find joy."

Yes, I thought, that is the secret. Silver Star's love caused her to think only of the way that she could bring happiness to the man she loved. She asked nothing except that she be successful at that. Then she too would find her happiness.

Silver Star pushed aside the pot on which she was working. She looked at me and there was no shyness in her now. She regarded me evenly, her eyes not lowering as they met mine. "You will be back when summer comes again?" she asked me.

"That is what I want," I answered honestly.

"I, too, have much hope," she said in her soft, flowing voice. "Louis told me about his prayer, and I ask him to tell me more about it. I want to give honor to Louis' Great Spirit."

"Oh, Silver Star," was all I could manage right then. I wanted to hug her, but since that was not the Indian way, I squeezed her arm instead.

"Someday He be your Great Spirit too. I pray for you every day," I promised her.

"I see you pray after time of fire, like talk to a real person," Silver Star told me with wonder in her voice.

Then she said, "I wish to plant your garden. Louis has promised to help. I know not the way of the seed, but he has planted before. You will need your garden when you return."

I was deeply touched. I reached out to take Silver Star's hand. She returned my brief squeeze ever so gently.

"That would please me," I said. "I will bring you seeds."

Such a small thing—yet it brought me so much joy. When I returned—if I returned, I reminded myself—I would be coming not to a village where hostility and isolation awaited me; I would be coming back to dear friends—friends who thought of me while I was gone. Friends who welcomed me back. Friends who cared for my garden. Friends who would be ready to be introduced to the God I knew and loved. I swallowed away the tears in the back of my throat and smiled at Silver Star.

It was a sad parting the next morning at sunup. I wanted to take Silver Star and her dear babies in my arms and hold them before I bid them good-bye, but that was not the way of this people. I looked tenderly at beautiful Kinook and longed to hold her, too. Then I turned to her younger sister, Kinnea. She would be just as beautiful as her pretty sister one day soon.

I said my good-byes in the proper way, all the while aching inside. Would it really help the pain to be able to embrace them? I supposed if I could put my arms around them, I would also cry. But even crying might bring some relief.

Just as we were ready to step up into the wagon, LaMeche came. He held out his hand to Wynn and shook it firmly. Then he extended his hand to me. I took it, saying nothing but feeling so much. This hostile man whom I once feared had turned out to be my friend, my burden-sharer—and now a fellow believer!

He must have read my thoughts—or else shared them, for without a word, he stepped closer to me and gave me a generous, brotherly embrace. My breath caught in my throat and just as I expected, tears began to flow.

I was busy wiping them away when a voice from behind made me turn around. It was the chief, dressed in beaded buckskins and flowing feathers, his entourage trailing behind him. All three wives, his children, his councilors stood in their respective positions.

He approached slowly, his arms extended toward me. In his hands he held a beautiful silver fox fur.

"The chief gives gift to Golden-Haired One as token that village is her home, and we will wait for her return when meadows again bring forth their blossoms," he said.

I was deeply touched. In my confusion, I almost forgot to lower my gaze. Just in time I caught myself and dipped my head respectfully; then I stepped forward and without looking up, extended my hands.

"Great chief and his people honor me," I said in an unsteady voice. "I, too, will watch for time of meadow flowers and my return to village of my people."

Then I stepped back and Wynn helped me to climb aboard the lumbering wagon where our few belongings were piled in behind us.

The driver shouted a command to the horses, and the slow wheels started to grind forward. We were on our way.

I dared not look back. Even if it had not been a native custom to never look back when one took to the trail, I could not have done so. The tears were freely falling down my cheeks. I did not want to see the strange little campsite beside the lake. I did not want to look at those who stood there, those villagers who were now my friends—including one who was now part of our spiritual family and another who was very close to God's kingdom. I did not want to see the little area off to the side on the small island where my garden, now almost bare, had provided many meals for our fellow survivors. Nor did I want to see the charred remains of what once had been the village.

I forced myself to look ahead, to gaze at the winding trail, the rutted roadway that would lead us over the next hill, and many, many, more hills before we reached the small settlement of Athabasca Landing.

What awaits us there? I wondered. Surely it could not be better than what we now left behind.

Then I brought my thoughts under control. Did not the same God still have His hand upon me for good? In my sorrow over having to leave friends, had I forgotten that He was still traveling with me? I wiped the tears and blew my nose. Surely, if He had something better than all of this for me, it must be good indeed.

26

Athabasca Landing

As WAS MY custom, I walked and rode interchangeably, partly for my own comfort and partly so I would be company for Kip.

Most of our time on the trail we had decent weather, although the mosquitoes and blackflies were hard to endure. It rained most of one day, which did not totally stop our progress, though it certainly did slow us down. I think I was as glad as the horses to stop that night.

Wynn pitched our tent under the shelter of the tall spruce and pine trees, and it looked as if we had a good chance to stay comparatively dry for the night. But in the night a strong wind came up and uprooted a tree. As it fell, one of its branches caught our tent and ripped a large tear all along the right side.

I was so thankful the tree itself hadn't fallen on us that I couldn't complain over a little rain. We did have to get up and dress and try to keep dry by wrapping the remaining piece of canvas around ourselves.

The next day it was sunny again, and as we traveled Wynn stitched the tent the best he could. The patch wasn't very attractive, but it did manage to give us some privacy on the rest of the journey.

I had given up even thinking about Athabasca Landing when we dipped over a sharp hill, and there stretched out beneath us was the shimmery ribbon of the river and the little town tucked on its south shores.

What a relief! Even in my weariness, my heart beat extra fast with excitement.

We had to cross the river by ferry. It was a large, flat barge that took one wagon at a time, horses and all. The horses were distrustful of the conveyance and snorted and plunged about, rocking our boat and causing me to nearly panic, lest they upset us midstream. It was all the drivers could do to hold the horses in check.

When at last, wagon by wagon, we docked on the other side, we set out, Wynn reading the map to our driver so he could find our new location.

It was a small settlement, but to my delight it looked quite civilized. There were shops and places of business, and even some small churches and a *school! I might enjoy my winter here after all!* I exulted.

Wynn first stopped to report to the North West Mounted Police Office and after a few minutes, came out with a large key in his hand and the directions to what would be our new home.

Pulling to a stop in front of it, I decided it was not a grand place by any means, but it was adequate. Coming from the small cabin of our past winter, to us it looked more than comfortable.

It was made of lumber and painted white, with a bit of black trim, and the windows, real windows, looked so large to me I wondered where I would ever find enough curtain material to cover them.

We entered the attached porch and passed through to a compact kitchen with its own small cupboard, a cookstove, table and chairs. Not only did it have a floor, but it also had linoleum covering the boards.

Off the kitchen was a family sitting room with a large stone fireplace and a couch and chair. A small writing table was tucked up against one wall.

Off the sitting room were *two* bedrooms! We used the largest one for our own use and set the other aside for storage or a guest room, whichever was needed. Both rooms held beds, and though the mattresses were rather lumpy, I told myself I would be spoiled in no time by such luxury.

A neat little picket fence surrounded the property and in back were three small buildings—one for storage, one for wood supply, and the third for the outside toilet.

Near the door was a well with a pump. I thought of my trips to the stream with my bucket and marveled at all the comforts of the modern world.

After exploring our new surroundings, Wynn and the driver began to unload our wagon. We had very little to unload. We did have the things we had decided were unnecessary for survival when we moved into the tiny cabin at Smoke Lake. In the crates were some of my most treasured possessions, and I was thankful to God they had been preserved for me. If it had not been for their being crated and stored on the wagon, I was sure I no longer would have my books or the pictures of baby Samuel.

With the few things I had managed to grab before the fire, we had precious little. *But "things" don't seem nearly as important since the fire*, I thought as I looked at Wynn.

The Force had given Wynn an allowance to help purchase items we had lost in the fire. This helped greatly in establishing our new home. Wynn turned the money over to me, and I spent several days searching through the little shops, trying to find the best bargains. I had to stretch the money a long way to make us presentable again.

One of my first purchases was an old treadle sewing machine. It did not work very well, but it did manage to make a seam. With its use, and many hours of work, I was able to sew quite a number of things to help our dollars stretch.

All my dresses, my undergarments, all the curtains, towels, tea towels, cushions, potholders, and countless other articles were sewn on that old machine.

After three weeks of searching for materials and sewing from morn-

ing to night, I finally felt that Wynn and I were really "at home." I had
hardly taken the time to look beyond our doors.

Another one of my first tasks was to write lengthy letters to all our
family members. It was such a long time since we had been able to write
to them. Now we were where mail could be sent out and brought in with
regularity, and I was anxious to let them know where and how we were.

The first Sunday we were in the town, I had nothing fit to wear to a
berry patch, let alone church. Under the circumstances, Wynn suggested
that we have our own worship at home as we had been doing for a number of years. I agreed, though I was anxious to attend worship services
again.

The next Sunday I had a dress ready, new shoes purchased and an
inexpensive hat I had found in one of the downtown stores. I was not
fancy, but I felt presentable. But after walking the several blocks to the
little mission, we found a note posted on the door that due to a death in
the family, the parson had left town and would be gone for the following week as well. Deeply disappointed, we returned home and had our
own time of worship again.

There was no use returning the third Sunday as we already knew the
parson would still be away, so we fixed a picnic lunch and walked to the
river where we watched the water traffic, had our lunch and then our
worship time together.

Now with the fourth Sunday soon approaching, I was looking forward
with all of my heart to getting together with those who shared like-faith
to sing praises to the Lord and worship Him with a body of believers.
And besides, I had an appropriate dress, hat and gloves just waiting to
be worn to church!

I cleaned and pressed Wynn's scarlet tunic and polished my new shoes
until they shone. I had put new lace on the plain hat and added a little
bunch of velvet violets. It looked quite attractive when I had finished. I
dug my best lace handkerchief out of the mothballs along with my woolen
shawl, aired them both thoroughly to get rid of the smell, and felt that I
was finally ready for the day of worship.

It was a cool day when we set off once more for the little church. I was
as nervous and excited as a young girl being courted for the first time.
Anxious and frightened about meeting my new neighbors, I wondered if
I would still know how to act in public.

About thirty-five people gathered together for worship. Most of them
were elderly women and women with young children. A few men were
sprinkled among them. *Rather a morose and quiet lot*, I thought as I looked
around me. *I wonder if there are any couples our age in the town.*

The church had an old upright piano that sat in one corner, but no one
played to accompany the singing. My hands ached to try it. It had been
so long since I had had opportunity to sit at a keyboard. I wondered if I
would still be able to read the music.

The singing did not go well. The preacher himself was unable to stay on tune and the others were not sure what to sing either. It pained me to hear the dear old songs so abused.

We all stood for the reading of the Scriptures. I gloried in taking part in the congregational reading of the Word.

The parson's sermon was about "choices." "Ye cannot love God and mammon," he reminded us. "A choice has to be made." He expounded on the theme for fifty-five minutes, citing several examples—all on the "mammon" side of the issue that he had encountered in his lifetime.

I knew the preacher spoke with conviction. I knew the Word was true. I knew it was a lesson every Christian must learn and practice. But my heart felt a little heavy as I walked down the steps of the church that first day back to worship after so many years of worshiping alone in the wilderness. I had so hoped for a note of joy. I wanted to praise. I wanted to worship. I wanted to fellowship. I felt I had not been allowed to really do any of those things. I would have to wait for another whole week for joint communion. My steps were a little slower going home, but I said nothing to Wynn.

Just as we reached the gate to our little abode, he reached out and took my hand.

"After we have our dinner," he said, "would you mind if we took our Bible and went out alone somewhere for our own little praise service again? Guess we've done it for such a long time I have the feeling that the day won't be complete unless we do."

I wanted to hug him. I did so need to worship.

After we had read the Scriptures and had our time of praise and prayer, remembering especially LaMeche and his newly discovered faith and Silver Star as she searched for truth, we still lingered on the banks of the Athabasca River. There was very little traffic on this day, though I knew on some occasions it was teeming with life and activity. Perhaps it too was taking the day off.

I sat dreamily, my thoughts wandering through many things.

"Wynn," I questioned him, "do you think the rest of the Indians at Smoke Lake will be open to the gospel?"

"I would like to think so. They certainly have changed a lot since the fire. They will be watching those two very closely. And I can't believe the new attitude of the chief. He might be very open to some changes."

"But he is so superstitious," I said. "I'm afraid he would just try to make God a part of his pagan worship someway."

"That's a danger, of course."

"How does one get them to understand that it is not like that? It isn't a bunch of mumbo-jumbo—of appeasing one deity who is the stronger to get him to take your side against the less strong?"

"I don't know."

I was silent for a few minutes, thinking over the incident when the chief called me to his fire to commend me.

"I was frightened," I admitted. "After the fire, the chief seemed to get this strange notion that I had some kind of special power. He . . . he acted so . . . so different than he had toward me before that."

"LaMeche told me about it."

"Did he also tell you that the chief presented me with a gift?"

"You mean the silver fox?"

"No, another one before you came back."

"You didn't show it to me that I remember," Wynn said, looking puzzled.

"I didn't show it to you because . . . because I couldn't keep it," I stammered.

"But that is an afront to a chief—"

"I know," I said with great feeling, "and I was afraid—afraid to give it back and yet I knew I couldn't keep it," I admitted.

"What did he do when you gave it back?"

"Well, you see, you had told me about the Indian custom of giving gifts—of how the chief gave a gift to honor a person, and that if the person didn't accept the gift, it would disgrace the chief. So I knew it might make a problem to return the gift, yet I didn't know—well, what to do about it."

"I don't follow," said Wynn. "You have totally lost me. The chief gave you a gift. You knew he would be offended if you gave it back—and yet you did."

"Well, not at first. At first I accepted it and thanked him for his kindness. I even told him that it gave me joy—and it did."

Wynn shook his head. He reached out and took my hand, giving me his lopsided grin. "My dear Elizabeth," he said, "you are talking strange riddles."

"No—" I insisted, "no riddles."

"So what was the chief's gift?"

I bit my lip to keep it from trembling. Even now, thinking about the gift brought tears to my eyes. Slowly I lifted my eyes to Wynn's. "It was his youngest son," I answered. "Nanawana's baby boy."

Wynn took my hand and squeezed it. He was silent for many minutes. When he spoke his voice was soft with emotion. "What did you do?"

I still didn't look up. "I took him, like I said. I held him for a few minutes."

Then my eyes went to Wynn's. "Oh, Wynn! he was so precious. He looked at me with those big black eyes. He didn't even look frightened. Then he sort of squirmed in my arms and smiled right at me. I could see Nanawana holding her breath in anguish. I knew how much she loved her son and what a hard thing the chief was asking of her.

"I told the chief that his gift pleased me greatly, and then I said that I wished in return to give the great chief a gift, and I . . . I gave him back his son."

"What can I say, Elizabeth," said Wynn, turning my hand over in his much larger ones. "I had no idea anything like this had happened. I'm sure it made you relive our loss of Samuel. I'm sorry, truly sorry."

I blinked away my tears.

"No wonder the chief holds you in such high esteem," Wynn went on.

"Esteem, I think I can handle," I said soberly. "Reverence—no."

"Meaning?"

"Meaning it frightened me when comments were made alluding to some strange power on my part. I don't want them to mix me up in their paganistic worship. They attribute everything to some power—good or evil. And it seems to me that good is equated with strength. Whoever wins is the one they follow."

"Yes," agreed Wynn, "they are still a very superstitious people. They have been isolated from civilization and from the truth of Christianity. Most other villages have had missionaries, trappers, extensive contact with other people, but this little village at Smoke Lake seems to have been left behind by the rest of the world."

"I pray there will be some way to reach them. Some way to make them understand the true God—on His terms."

"Perhaps—" mused Wynn, "—perhaps God has used you to open a door for spiritual understanding."

My eyes grew wide. It was hard to believe that I could have had a part in such a glorious venture. And then I dropped my gaze again.

"I may have spoiled it," I admitted.

"Spoiled it? In what way? You said the chief accepted the gift back without offense."

"He did. But I . . . when I found that the chief thought I . . . well, that I had power of some kind, well, I decided to take advantage of it. Not for myself, but for all the people. You see, everyone—that is, all of the men except LaMeche—were just lying around camp doing nothing. And after the men came back, then the women didn't want to do anything either. It was pure chaos, with no one hunting or fishing or getting the meals for their groups or anything. Then when the chief sort of set me up, with authority, I decided to go ahead and make him listen to me. I didn't mean to take advantage of him—not at the time. But when I got to thinking about it later, that's exactly what I did.

"I went to him and told him that we had to get organized, that everyone had to work. And strangely enough, he listened and then did what I said."

I sat quietly, waiting for Wynn to say something. He said nothing.

I looked up, my lip trembling again. "I've been feeling guilty ever since I realized how it must have seemed to him," I confessed. "By going to him as I did, I as good as claimed to be what he thought me to be—someone with special powers. He never would have listened to an ordinary woman, you know that."

"And it's been bothering you?"

"Very much," I admitted, my voice faltering. "That's why I've been so touchy when anyone teased me about it. You see, I had hoped too that maybe now the villagers and the chief would be open to the salvation message. But I might have spoiled that. By taking the power and authority that didn't belong to me, I might have ruined any chance for the people to listen."

"Did you tell the chief you had special power?"

"Of course not!"

"What did you tell him?"

"I told him that I was just a woman—that I came in the name of the true God—that I—" I stopped short, struggling with emotion, and then went on. "But don't you see? That is what frightens me. I didn't mean it in that way, but I think the chief misunderstood. He seemed to think of me as . . . as some kind of sorceress or something, representing some new god. Oh, Wynn, it was like I was just a—a new witch doctor with another group or something. It frightens me. How can we make him understand the truth when he seems to have it so mixed up? And I'm the one who mixed him up," I finished lamely.

Wynn passed me his handkerchief and sat quietly for several minutes while I wiped away tears. When he felt I was under control, he spoke again.

"We'll pray, Elizabeth. You didn't mean to deceive him. You tried to explain the truth to him. When we speak the truth and someone misunderstands us, I don't believe God holds us responsible for his misinterpretation. We can't work within his mind. At least, by appearances, the chief is at a point where he has recognized another power—another god. Now someone—maybe LaMeche—needs to explain to him just who that God is and how one worships Him. You might have opened that door after all."

27

Involvement

THE PASTOR CAME to call on us, welcoming us to his church and expressing his desire for us to be an active part of the fellowship.

"It has not been easy," he stated, "getting enough willing workers to make the church function as it ought."

"What might we do to help?" asked Wynn on behalf of both of us.

The pastor's eyes showed surprise. It had been awhile since he had had a volunteer.

He cleared his throat, seeming to find it difficult to know just where to start. "We need Sunday school teachers in the worst way," he stated. "We have some junior boys, five of them, and no teacher. Right now I fear they will stop coming if something isn't done. Two of them already have."

Wynn thought quietly, nodding his head at the pastor's words.

"We need other teachers in the children's department as well. There is only one teacher for all of the primaries. She has fourteen, from grades one through four. They're a real handful. She's threatening to quit."

"I would love to teach some of them," I quickly responded.

"And I would consider that group of boys," said Wynn.

The pastor's face relaxed. Then a broad smile began to spread across it.

"My wife will be so relieved," he said. "She's the teacher of the primaries now. It has been such a handful for her. She's not as young as she once was, you know. She raised five of her own, but it's not as easy for her to handle young ones now as it used to be."

There was silence while the pastor wiped his brow.

"I noticed you have a piano," I said cautiously.

The man smiled. "A piano, yes, but no pianist. It would boost the singing so much if we had someone to play." Then he grinned, a twinkle in his eye. "As you could undoubtedly tell, I'm not much of a song leader. I'm afraid the Lord neglected to give me that gift."

He laughed, and I found myself liking the man who tried so hard to do all he could.

I stole a glance at Wynn, wondering just how he would respond to my announcement.

"My husband has a lovely singing voice," I said, "and he knows almost all of the hymns."

The preacher looked from me to Wynn. Wynn showed no signs of embarrassment or resentment.

"Would you consider—" The pastor let the words hang.

"If you feel it would be of service, I would try it," said Wynn, very simply.

"Oh, my, I would appreciate that," the man said sincerely.

Then Wynn cleared his throat and looked at me with his special grin. "And while we are announcing the talents of one another," he said, "I might inform you that my wife is a pianist."

Pastor Kelly looked at me. Now his eyes were very wide. His mouth hung open. He pulled out his handkerchief again, but this time he wiped at the corners of his eyes.

"Would you?" he asked sincerely.

"I would be happy to," I assured him.

He blew his nose rather loudly, put his handkerchief away and fumbled for words. "You folks can't appreciate what this means to me—and to Martha. We sort of struggled along here—and it's been tough going. We served in larger parishes before, but we felt the Lord wanted us to give some of our years of service to a mission. I . . . think perhaps we did it backward. We should have spent our years in a mission first and then gone to a larger parish.

"Anyway, it has been hard for us. Especially for Martha. Wait until she hears the news. You see, we've been praying for some time now—"

He stopped and cleared his throat. Then he looked up with glistening eyes. "Well," he said, "one should not be so surprised when God answers. Just thankful. Just thankful."

My own eyes felt a little misty, so I decided it was time to serve the tea and cake.

After the good parson had left us, Wynn and I reviewed our commitments of the past hour. It would be so good to be involved in the life of the church again, we both decided. We had missed it.

"I need to go over to the church and get in a little practice on that piano," I said. "It has been so long since I have played that I'm sure I'm quite rusty."

"Bring a hymnbook home with you if you can," Wynn said, "and we'll pick out the Sunday hymns together."

"I'm going to love teaching children again," I mused, thinking about the small minds and their interest in the Bible stories. It had been several years since I'd had the privilege.

Wynn just smiled. "Well, since you're so enthusiastic, I might give you my junior boys and I'll take your little people," he said laughingly. "Do you know what junior boys can be like?"

"I do. And I'm sure you will make out just fine."

"You heard the pastor. Some of them have already dropped out. I'm guessing the rest of them are looking for an excuse too."

"Don't forget," I reminded Wynn. "They have never had a man for a teacher. I'm sure you'll win them over in no time—just wait and see."

"I hope you're right, Elizabeth, but I wouldn't count on junior boys being quickly 'won over' by anyone."

I patted Wynn's shoulder. "Just wait," I said with total confidence. "You'll see."

The truth was I could hardly wait to start teaching, and deep down under his banter, I was sure Wynn felt the same way.

I had a caller the next morning. When I answered the door, a small, carefully dressed lady stood on the step. I smiled a welcome and opened the door.

"Mrs. Delaney," she said, "I do hope this isn't an imposition. I'm Martha Kelly and I wanted to bring the Sunday school material for you and your husband."

"Oh, yes. It's so nice to meet you, Mrs. Kelly," I said, extending my hand. "Please come in."

I led Mrs. Kelly to our small but cozy sitting room and took her coat. She retrieved the bundle she had brought with her and lifted out a small package.

"I brought you a bit of baking," she said rather shyly, "as a welcome to our church and little town."

It had been so long since anyone had welcomed me in such a way. I was delighted. I expressed my thanks to Mrs. Kelly and excused myself to put on the teakettle.

She showed me the Sunday school material and explained how the classes would be divided and where my room would be found and then we chatted about other things.

She was a delightful lady! It would be so nice to have a friend—a warm and understanding friend.

I went to the church the next day to practice the piano. I knew I would be rusty and fumbling. The first few tries were frustrating, but I was surprised at how quickly it all came back to me. Soon I was enjoying the sound of the hymns of praise.

The piano was understandably out of tune, but it was not horribly so. I decided that Wynn would have no problem leading the singing to its accompaniment.

The pastor came out of his study just as I was about to leave the church. I apologized for disturbing him. I realized, too late, that I should have checked before I began to play.

"It was not a disturbance," he assured me. "It was a ministry. I needed that music to lift my soul. I am sure my Sunday sermon will be the better for it."

I asked about taking home a hymnal for Wynn and me to pick the hymns. He assured me I was most welcome.

I asked for the theme of his Sunday sermon, and he said he planned to speak on the surety of God's promises. I could hardly wait for Sunday.

I was beginning to settle into our new little community. After I had done all of my sewing and arranged our small house, I could not find enough to do to fill my days. The hours until Wynn came home often weighed on me. I was sure there were things I could be doing to serve this small community if I could just discover what they were.

I still had not become very acquainted with neighbors. In fact, where our house stood we had few neighbors. To our right was a large vacant lot and beyond it was the property belonging to the North West Mounted Police. Their small office was located there as well as storage sheds, wagon yards and barns.

Wynn was so close that he could come home for his noon meal, which helped to fill my day. It was a great pleasure for me to be able to see so much of my husband after his being gone all day and sometimes many days at a time.

Wynn settled into the routine of office work. I knew it was a very different life than he was used to, and I am sure he sometimes chafed under the load of paper work, but he did not complain. He seemed to like the two young men who served under him, and that certainly helped his circumstances.

The two-month sentence of the young brave from the village expired and Wynn had his horse, which also had been kept in custody, brought to him. Wynn also saw to it that he had provisions for the long ride home. I sent a letter for LaMeche to read to Silver Star. Then Wynn escorted the boy a day's ride out of town to make sure he wouldn't come into possession of illegal whiskey again; and bidding him good-bye and a safe journey, he sent him on his way.

When I asked Wynn if he felt the young man had learned a lesson, he smiled.

"I think he has learned several lessons, Elizabeth," he said: "how to play blackjack, how to chew tobacco, how to curse in English, and who knows what else."

I cringed at Wynn's words. Though he spoke partly in jest, I knew there was truth in it.

As for me, I was getting acquainted with the shopkeepers in the town, though I still knew few of them by name. Most of the shopkeepers were men, but there was a woman working in the drygoods store and one in the bakeshop.

Our home was small but adequate, our town was scattered but interesting, our church was struggling but growing, and though we both missed the life with the Indian people, we settled in to enjoy this one winter set apart.

We talked about and prayed often for the village we had left in the fall. We hoped with all our heart that the building was going well, that the young Mountie was able to care for the needs of the people, and that the Force would see fit to return us to the posting in the spring. We also prayed that the gospel witness in that town would take root and grow.

Mail from the South arrived. Wynn brought the letters home to me when he came for lunch one day. There were four of them: one from Mary, one from Julie, one from my mother, and one from Mother Delaney.

There was both good news and bad news. The war was finally over and Matthew had returned home safely. I thanked God fervently. Matthew was now busy learning the business to take over from Father.

Julie's baby boy had arrived. He had been a healthy baby until he was five months old, at which time he had contracted measles with complications and he had gone home to God. Julie had been heartbroken, but God had been with her and her husband. They were now expecting a second child.

My tears fell uncontrollably as I thought of my dear, light-hearted sister and her deep sorrow. I thanked God her letter held no bitterness, only love for her young preacher husband and faith in her mighty God.

Jon and Mary's family were keeping well, though Elizabeth, their climber, had suffered a broken arm in a fall from a ladder left beside the house. The arm had healed nicely, and they hoped she had learned a lesson.

Mother Delaney had had two more hospital stays, one resulting in gall-bladder surgery. Now she was feeling much better. Phillip and Lydia's family were all well and growing.

I read each letter over many times before I laid them aside. It was the next best thing to a good visit with those we loved.

28
Service

I WAS EXCITED with my new Sunday school class—even more excited than I was about the opportunity to again play the piano. I was given a class of six energetic seven- and eight-year-olds. Four of them were girls and two were boys.

One of the boys, a real handful, had been raised by a man who had lost his wife in childbirth. He had chosen, in his bitterness, not to remarry. I'm afraid his wrath affected his growing son. It was a neighbor lady who somehow managed to get Willie to Sunday school. The father had no room in his life for God, but the woman's son was the only friend of the young boy and so the two came to Sunday school together.

They could not have been more different. Stephen Williams was a quiet, small-framed boy with a lisp and questioning blue eyes. He had learned not to speak unless spoken to. I think it had to do with being ridiculed by other children rather than because of good manners.

Willie Schultz, on the other hand, was big for his age, loud and cantankerous, never stopped talking, and had a quick and fiery temper to go with his shock of unruly reddish hair.

They seemed such an unlikely pair to be "best friends," but it was evident to me from the first Sunday that they considered themselves just that.

They insisted on sitting together, sharing a book, that they be separated from "the girls," and that they be allowed to communicate whenever they wished.

I, on the other hand, insisted that they sit across the room from one another, each have his own book, be intermingled with the girls and be quiet unless I asked them to speak.

For a few moments it seemed as if I would be the loser. They looked glumly at one another, threatening to "never come again," Willie's rage showing in his eyes, but as the lesson went on they got involved and forgot to continue their protest.

Thankfully, all four of my girls were quite well behaved. I learned that one, called Mary, was the daughter of the lady in the bakeshop. She was a bit on the tubby side—*she must have free hand in sampling the goods*, I decided.

Molly and Polly were twins, daughters of the town's blacksmith, and Sue Marie was the daughter of the man who worked on the ferry boat. I later learned that Sue Marie and her family had lived in many places, her father shifting from job to job. For this reason Sue Marie had had very little education. She would just be starting classes at one school and they would be on the road again, often to places where there was no school. Sunday school was a new experience for Sue Marie as well, and it was because of the kindnesses of Mrs. Kelly to the family that Sue Marie was allowed to attend.

So I looked at my Sunday school class as a great challenge. Here were six students who needed to know the truths from God's Word. For some of them, this might well be their only opportunity. I prayed for the help of the Lord.

Wynn began his class with a group of four reluctant and withdrawn boys. The first Sunday he was discouraged with their actions and their response, but much to his surprise all four were back the following Sunday.

He took them on a backpacking trip the next Saturday. Over the open fire they cooked the fish they had caught, and Wynn taught them some of the skills of survival in the wilderness. The next Sunday there were six boys in his class, and the following Sunday he had eight, all eager to get in on the activities if not to learn, and pressing for his attention.

Wynn followed the backpacking trip with canoeing and hiking. One Saturday was even spent showing how to properly start training a puppy. The puppy belonged to Jock MacGregor, and all the boys then clamored for a dog of their own so they too could get involved. I knew that when Revva's litter arrived, we would have more trainers than we had puppies.

Wynn enjoyed his "boys" and they took to dropping by our house in the evenings or on Saturday and Sunday afternoon. I often felt like I was running a restaurant for hungry youngsters, but it was fun and I never objected.

My class, too, felt welcome at our house. We spent some Saturdays baking cookies or making candy. Even the boys took part, though they were much better at eating than baking. We went for nature walks together. I promised them that when the snow was deep enough, I would teach them how to walk with snowshoes, and they were all eager to try.

With the activity of our classes and the dropping in of our students, my days were soon full. It was like having a great big family of our own.

Not all of our "family" listened well to our instructions. Willie, though he never missed Sunday school and came to the house oftener than any of my other students, still seemed to carry a chip on his shoulder. He was often belligerent and unyielding, and sometimes flew into a rage if things didn't go his way.

I tried to understand him and his needs, but I also had to be quite firm. In spite of the fact that Willie was a boy who needed lots of love and attention, I felt he also needed strong discipline to help him grow up to be of use to himself and society.

Wynn had two boys who were also a problem. One was from a home with no resident father. His father had gone away, leaving the home and the family, and no one seemed to know where. The second one was the youngest of a brood of twelve, very needy and excessively transient. They stayed in one place only long enough to completely wear out their welcome and then moved on.

Only two of the twelve were not still living at home, though many of them were of an age to be considered adults. They stayed with the family group, clinging to one another—not out of love, however. Continual inner strife often resulted in horrible fights, with fists, or knives or anything they could get their hands on. That family was Wynn's greatest source of distress. The police force probably answered more calls to that one ramshackled home than to any other area under their patrol.

Wynn feared the young boy would grow up to follow the same wayward path as the rest of his kin. So he tried to spend time with the boy and encourage him in any way he could. The boy's name was Henry Mayers, but the kids at school all called him "Rabid," a nickname he seemed quite pleased with.

Because of all the time we were spending with our Sunday school classes, Wynn and I found that we were not getting much time to ourselves or to becoming acquainted with other people our age. We discussed it and decided we would have to set aside one night a week, informing our students we were unavailable that night. We would use that time to cultivate friendships of our own.

It didn't work out too well. There always seemed to be one child or another standing at our door with a problem to solve or a joy to share. We finally decided we would save Sunday dinner for inviting couples or families in, and the rest of the time we would be available to our class members.

I had two mothers approach me about giving piano lessons to their children, and, with the permission of the kind pastor, we used the church piano. I began by teaching three lessons a week. More mothers were soon calling and the lessons increased to eleven per week. There would have been more, but I felt that was all I could handle.

Our lives were busy, our days so full, that it caught me quite by surprise when it started snowing. Winter was with us again, and I hadn't even had time to anticipate or dread its coming.

29
Winter

THIS WAS A very different winter than I had been used to. Instead of hauling wood and melting water to keep my fire going and wash my laundry, I was teaching piano lessons to prim little girls and baking cookies for hungry boys.

My physical labor was much easier, but my days were much busier. I couldn't believe how full our life was. I was seeing less of Wynn now than when we lived at one of the villages. Even our Sundays were full, the day of the week we had previously guarded jealously for one another.

Revva's puppies arrived—five of them—but I was much too busy to help in their training. Besides, all Wynn's Sunday school boys were clamoring to help him and I knew it was important to them.

We took on the enjoyable task of taking turns having all the families of our students in for Sunday dinner. A few found some nice way to decline our invitation, but most of them accepted, and I was kept busy preparing meals both affordable and tasty.

The students each were given a written invitation to carry home with them, inviting his or her family to our house for dinner two weeks hence. The next Sunday they were to carry back the reply. We could have asked the parents ourselves, but we wanted the students to feel part of the process. They took such delight in carrying the envelope home.

When it was Willie's turn to carry home his invitation, he looked at me with angry eyes. As it turned out, he was not angry with me.

"Why bother?" he fumed. "My old man wouldn't come."

"Perhaps you should take home the invitation and let him decide," I coaxed Willie.

"Won't do no good. He's so ugly mean. He'll just get mad and take a swing at me."

I couldn't believe one so young could be so disrespectful and mistrustful of his father.

"I'll deliver the invitation myself if you'd rather," I told Willie.

He shoved the invitation deep into his pocket. "Might swing at you, too," he growled.

I let the matter drop and went on with the class.

I decided Willie might need a little help in encouraging his father, so I did not wait for the next Sunday when Willie would bring back his reply to the invitation. Instead, I dressed in my best on Tuesday morning and headed for the small local hotel that Willie's father owned.

When I entered the building I approached the man at the desk, pleased that I would not have to ask for Mr. Schultz. His swatch of reddish hair told me where Willie got his, and a brisk, friendly mustache twitched as though in amusement when he talked. His name was pinned to the front of his striped vest, G. W. Schultz.

I smiled warmly.

"Mr. Schultz," I said, extending my hand. "I am Mrs. Delaney. It is a pleasure to make your acquaintance."

He took my hand and shook it thoroughly, murmuring something about the pleasure being all his.

"I am here to invite you to my house for dinner a Sunday from next," I continued. "I assume that you have already received a written invitation, but I wanted to make it a personal invitation as well."

"That is most kind," said Mr. Schultz.

"We will be dining at one o'clock and you are most welcome to come a few minutes before that time if you wish. However, we don't get home until around twelve-thirty from our morning church service."

"That sounds lovely," said Mr. Schultz, giving me a big smile, his mustache twitching.

He certainly seems friendly enough, I thought to myself. *Why do people paint him as such an ogre?*

I got even more daring.

"It would be delightful to have you join us for the morning service if you are free."

"I just might do that," said Mr. Schultz.

I felt ecstatic. Never had I been received so graciously.

"We will count on that then," I said, and gave the man one of my nicest smiles.

"Certainly. And I thank you for your kindness. I shall look forward to the Sunday after next."

I turned to go and then turned back again, with what I hoped was a winning smile, "Mr. Schultz," I said rather teasingly, yet meaningfully, "you don't have to wait for two weeks to attend our church, you know. You would be most welcome anytime—even next Sunday."

He twirled his long reddish mustache. "Mrs. Delaney," he said, "I have never had a more pleasant invitation."

I flushed slightly and fumbled with the doorknob. Just as I was about to make my exit, he spoke again.

"Mrs. Delaney," he said, "please don't take offense, but are you a widow, ma'am?"

I turned back, my face warming under his gaze.

"No . . . no . . . of course not."

"Then might I ask just why you are asking a bachelor like myself to dinner?"

"The invitation explained that, I—"

"What invitation?"

"Why the one your son—"

"My son? I have no son. As I said, I am a bachelor, Mrs. Delaney."

My gloved hand flew to my face.

"But Willie, my Sunday school pupil—"

The man began to laugh. His roar shook the building. I saw nothing funny about the situation. He didn't even explain it really, just pointed to a door, and said, "In there. That's who you wish to see—my brother."

It was a bad start all around. By the time I knocked on the door, I was already flustered and embarrassed. When he answered the knock, I opened the door and stepped in.

The room was an office. The desk in front of the man was piled high with accounts and books. He didn't even look up but growled at me, "Yeah?"

I cleared my throat to begin.

"Excuse me, sir."

His head jerked up at the sound of my voice. He scowled at me as though I had some nerve to come interrupting his work.

He had the same shock of reddish hair, the same bushy mustache, only his did not twitch with amusement. It bristled with indignation. His eyes pinned me to the spot.

I wanted to get out of there. The only way I could see to do so was to speak my piece quickly and then retreat.

I wanted no misunderstandings. I started by clarifying my position.

"I am Mrs. Delaney," I said in what I hoped was an even voice. "My husband is the new commander at the North West Mounted Police Post. I am Willie's Sunday school teacher. I understand you are Willie's father?"

There was silence for a few moments. I began to think he wasn't even going to answer me; then he threw down the pencil he was working with and gave me a withering look.

"So what's he done now?"

"Done? Why, nothing. I . . . I . . ."

He glared at me.

"If he hasn't done anything, what are you doing here?"

"I came to personally follow up the invitation I sent home with your son last Sunday."

He stood to his feet. He was a tall man, stockily built. I could see why a child would find him intimidating.

"What invitation?" he snapped. "One to your little Sunday school class?" he actually sneered as he asked the question. "Now look here, Miss Whatever your name is"— he left his chair and came around his desk where he could stand glowering down on me— "they asked for my kid to go to that there church. I'm not for it, but I didn't think it could do no harm; besides, it gets him out of my hair for a few hours. Sunday morning is the only time I get to sleep. Now you got the kid; what more do you want?"

I was angry. I was frightened. I was trembling with inner rage. How could this overgrown child be acting so foolishly? *It must run in the family!* I fumed. First his—his humorous brother allowed me to make a complete fool of myself, and now he had the nerve to stand over me as though shaking a finger at a naughty school child, all because I happened to care about his son!

I stepped back, not to get away from him, but so I could get a good look at his angry red face and his snapping eyes.

"Excuse me, Mr. Schultz," I said. "I think you have a few things confused here. In the first place, I am not inviting you into my Sunday school class. I do not allow spoiled, cantankerous children to take a part. And second, I was here to invite you to our home for Sunday dinner, not because I feel that your presence will be particularly enjoyable but because I happen to care about your son.

"No, Mr. Schultz, Willie has not 'done something,' but he will someday if you don't give him more of your time and love. He needs a parent—now! We at the church love him and are trying to help him to grow up to be a God-fearing, law-abiding citizen, but we can't do it alone. Willie is already hostile—and he's not going to reform unless *you* do."

The face before me was changing. There was first a look of such anger that I thought he might strike me, and then there was a look of absolute unbelief. I was sure no one, at least no one in his right mind, had ever addressed him the way I had. I still wasn't through.

"And finally, Mr. Schultz," I said, "I am willing to guess that Willie had a mother who was an upright, decent woman, and it would bring her great pain if her son did not grow up to be a decent man."

I stopped and took a breath. My words were beginning to catch up with me and in shame and embarrassment I mumbled to a halt. My face flushed, and tears that I had stubbornly refused threatened to appear. I lowered my face.

"I'm sorry," I stammered. "I apologize for my outburst. I had no reason to act in such a rude manner. It's inexcusable. Forgive me, please."

I stepped around the big man who had not moved out of my way and reached with a trembling hand for the doorknob. I needed to escape.

I hesitated just long enough to say in not much more than a whisper, "The invitation still stands. A week from Sunday." I opened the door and hurried out of the office.

I would have fled to the street, but as I passed the desk where the other Mr. Schultz still worked a crossword puzzle, he looked up with a twitching mustache and twinkling eyes and said, "Bully for you."

I gave him a stony look and continued out, fighting hard to preserve some dignity.

As I reached the door, he called after me. "By the way, does my invitation still stand, too?"

Without answering him, I pulled the door open, closed it securely behind me, and kept right on going. I could hear his uproarious laughter following me.

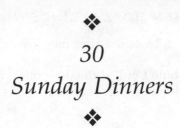

30
Sunday Dinners

THE NEXT SATURDAY I was at the church rehearsing with some of the junior girls for a part in the Sunday school Christmas program. Suddenly the door burst open and Willie came flying in. Without even waiting to remove his hat or take a breath, he rushed at me, his hand outstretched.

He couldn't speak, he was too out of breath. He just poked the strange piece of paper at me and urged me to take it.

I reached out and took it while he waited, breathless as I opened it on the spot.

It was a simple note, expressing only that on behalf of his son Willie and himself, Mr. Schultz would be happy to accept my invitation for Sunday dinner. I gasped and Willie looked at me with a grin on his face, his red hair flopping across his forehead.

"Why, Willie," I said, giving him a hug, "that is wonderful!"

"Told ya, he'd come," panted the boy.

"I'm so pleased," I said honestly.

"Gotta show Stephen," Willie said and was gone again.

I stood watching him, wondering what had changed the mind of the senior Schultz. Surely Willie's uncle was not playing another trick on me. No, I told myself, even he wouldn't be that heartless.

I turned back to my girls. Even our song seemed to go better, and when I left the church I walked through the lightly falling snow with a lighter step.

Maybe, just maybe, something had jolted the father to make him realize that he had a son who needed him.

Our Sunday with the Schultzes went very well. Mr. Schultz did not join us at church like I had hoped, but he and Willie arrived promptly at one o'clock.

To my relief Wynn and Mr. Schultz visited very easily and he proved to be an intelligent and even agreeable man.

Nothing was said about my visit to the hotel or my outburst. Nor was anything said about the brother who enjoyed his teasing. I wondered if Willie's father even knew of that part of the incident.

I served the dinner, letting Willie help me in the kitchen. He was pleased to pour his own milk and put on the rolls, butter and pickles. I glanced at Mr. Schultz once or twice to see if he might object to his son doing "woman's work," but he seemed to not even notice.

It turned out that Mr. Schultz was very interested in the work of the Force. He asked several questions and Wynn was happy to answer them. They chatted amicably until I announced the meal was ready.

Mr. Schultz acted cordial enough at the table, evidencing fine table manners, even when Wynn said the table grace. The talk was light and friendly and after coffee and dessert, which I let Willie help serve, they visited a bit more; then he thanked me politely and left.

I took a big breath after I closed the door. Before I tackled the dirty dishes I turned to Wynn. "Well," I asked, "what do you think?"

"Pleasant enough man. Certainly nobody's fool," Wynn responded.

"Except where Willie is concerned," I murmured. "I'm afraid the man knows very little about the needs of a growing boy."

I turned to the dishes then, musing as I washed them. Wynn came to take a towel for drying them.

"If I help with the dishes, Mrs. Delaney," he proposed, "will you promise to go for a walk with me?"

"Is that a request or an order, Sergeant?" I teased back.

"A request," Wynn stated. "If you turn down my request, then it becomes an order."

We laughed together and hurried with the dishes so we could get our walk in.

We took Kip with us. He bounded ahead, loving his freedom to run. He did not enjoy being confined to our fenced-in yard even if there was plenty of room.

It was a lovely winter afternoon and the fresh, crisp snow crunched underfoot as we walked.

"Just think," I remarked to Wynn. "In just three weeks it will be Christmas again."

"Are you looking forward to it?" he asked.

"I am," I admitted. "I really am. It will seem more like Christmas this year. There will be the Christmas program for the Sunday school, the church service, a tree, decorations, even a turkey for dinner. I think I will really enjoy having an old-fashioned, honest-to-goodness Christmas again."

"I'm looking forward to it, too," stated Wynn. "I'm tired of giving you new stockings."

We both laughed heartily and walked on through the downy falling snow.

Sue Marie and her family were the last students we would have in for dinner before Christmas. After Christmas we would begin asking Wynn's class members. Already we had asked each other what we would do when it came time to ask the family of Henry "Rabid" Myers. We pushed the problem into the future, vowing to cross that bridge when the time came.

Sue Marie accepted our invitation, but her family did not come with her. I was sorry we were not going to have the opportunity to meet them but promised myself that after Christmas I would at least try to get to know her mother.

With solemn, sober face, Sue Marie sat quietly and sedately in a chair while I got the meal on the table. Wynn tried to entertain her, but she only shook her head yes or no to his questions.

At the table she ate very little, though her eyes took in everything. She looked uncomfortable and shy. The apple pie she did like, and even accepted a second piece.

I didn't want to shoo her off home as soon as we had finished, so I suggested she might want to look at some books while I washed the dishes. She took the books and studied the pictures, but she didn't attempt to read them. I wondered if Sue Marie could read at all.

After I had finished with the dishes, I went in and sat down beside the little girl.

"Would you like to hear the story?" I asked. She seemed hesitant, but finally nodded her head. I was surprised at her reluctance. She had not been so shy the many times that she had been in our home with the other children. I picked up the book and began to read. Before long she was totally engrossed in the story.

We read book after book together and then she looked at the clock.

"I've got to go," she said. "Mommy said to be home by three."

I found her coat and mittens and helped her on with her boots.

She turned at the door and said politely, "Thank you for the good dinner, Miz Delaney."

"You are most welcome," I answered her. "I'm so glad you came."

She turned then to pat Kip who had bounded up to get some attention. Kip always made sure he got in on the party when the children came to the house.

Then she turned soberly to me. "Did I be good enough, Miz Delaney?" she asked, her eyes big and questioning.

"Why, you were just fine," I said kneeling beside her and putting an arm around her.

"Good," she said seriously. "'Cause Mamma said if she heard that I don't be good, I'd get one awful spanking when I get home."

"When I see your mamma," I told her, "I'll tell her what a well-behaved little girl she has."

She broke into a big grin, and then she was gone, tripping through the winter afternoon.

The church was packed for the Sunday school Christmas program. I was responsible for all the singing and had rehearsed with the children for several Saturdays prior to the big event.

Most of our numbers were done as a group, but the twins were singing "Away in a Manger," and Willie, who I discovered had a lovely boy-ish tenor, sang a solo, "O Little Town of Bethlehem." Though I hoped his father would come to hear him, I didn't hazard another trip to the hotel with an invitation.

Pastor Kelly's face beamed as he welcomed the large group to the little church. From my spot at the piano, I looked over the crowd, too, spot-ting many parents of our students. Much to my amazement, not only was Willie's father there, but his uncle as well. The latter caught my eye and twitched his mustache in amusement before I quickly turned away.

We had only one calamity—apart from a few little mishaps, that is. When Ralph Conners, one of the shepherds from Wynn's class, turned to leave the stage, his foot caught Joseph's robe and toppled him right over before he could free his foot. Joseph's crook, Mrs. Belasky's cane, tumbled to the floor with a loud clatter, and Joey's mother's towel that he wore as a turban toppled off his head.

Joseph picked himself up, mumbling threats under his breath, plunked his headpiece haphazardly on his head partly covering one eye, and went on with his speech. The audience tittered a bit, but the play went on.

I enjoyed the evening. It was wonderful to be part of the Christmas celebration again.

As we had planned, after Christmas we started on our invitations to Wynn's class members. We didn't get quite the enthusiastic response we had gotten from my younger children. Still, we were pleased at the num-ber of families who accepted our invitation to Sunday dinner.

The last family belonged to Henry "Rabid" Myers. Again we discussed what we should do. I took a deep breath.

"Well," I said, "the Lord Jesus loves Henry too. We invited the fami-lies of all the others—I guess that means Henry's family, too."

"That means twelve people, Elizabeth."

I nodded.

"Twelve big people."

I sighed.

"Twelve, big, mean people," teased Wynn.

"Oh, Wynn," I wailed, "don't make it any worse than it is. I'm scared enough already."

"You don't have to do it," reminded Wynn.

"I think we should."

"Okay. Then I'll give you all the help I can."

So the invitation went out to the entire Myers family, and I held my breath wondering what would happen.

Henry brought the answer the following Sunday. It was not on paper—it was by word of mouth. They said, "Sure."

Oh, my, I thought. *Oh, my.*

And then I reminded myself I had served nearly that many day after day around an open fire at the camp. I had had only vegetables and wild meat to do it with too. Why did "civilization" make things seem so much more difficult? I began planning my dinner.

I was determined to have plenty to eat—it might not be fancy, but there would be enough. I could not imagine anything more embarrassing than to have all those hearty appetites and not enough food. I dug out my largest kettle, had Wynn bring home some even bigger ones from the Force supply room and cooked in great quantities.

I had planned for twelve, the ten children who were reportedly still living at home and two parents, but when they arrived there were only ten. They all looked rather young so I assumed that the father and mother had not been able to make it.

"I'm sorry your father and mother were unable to come," I said to the girl who stood closest to me.

"Ma's been dead and gone fer years," she informed me with no seeming emotion. "Pa wasn't feeling up to it—"

"Got hisself too drunk last night," cut in one of the boys. "Can't even walk this mornin'."

He laughed, obviously thinking it a great joke.

"Sure smells good," said one of the others.

With a bit of doing, we got them all around the table. Wynn had warned me that we might have some trouble holding them back while we said the blessing, so I had planned ahead. I didn't put the food on the table. But my strategy didn't work too well. They looked around the table the moment they were seated, and then one fellow cried out, "Lizzie, get on up and make yerself useful. Food's not on yet."

We did manage to have prayer, and then all dug in. Now and then during the meal someone would say some snapping remark to one of the other ones. I was afraid at one point that a fight might break out over who was to get the first dibs on a third serving of potatoes, but they got it worked out someway and the meal went on.

When they had finished they got up, wiped their mouths on already dirty sleeves and headed for the door. There was nothing said about the meal, except for one girl who stopped momentarily and said, "Pa's sure gonna be some mad he missed it." Then with a chuckle among themselves, they left us.

Henry stood at the door for just a moment, looking ill at ease and confused and then he hurried after them.

I washed all the dirty dishes, scrubbed at the mammoth pots and tidied up the kitchen. There wasn't too much food left to put away—hardly enough to make a meal for Wynn and me the next day.

Wynn was taking apart our makeshift extension to the table as I finished the last of the kitchen chores. I took my leftover vegetables and meat to the shelf in the porch that acted as my cold storage.

Well, at least I have an extra pumpkin pie, I told myself. With a total of only twelve rather than fourteen for dinner, I had cut only three of the four. We would enjoy the pumpkin pie the next day.

I placed the dishes of leftover food on the shelf, my mind still on that tasty pie. In fact, I was tempted to cut just a sliver and have it with coffee. I figured I had earned it after serving so many and doing all those dirty dishes.

I looked about in unbelief. My pie was nowhere to be seen. And then the truth hit me like a blow.

"Wynn," I cried out, "those Myers have stolen my pie!"

Three days later the word came through the police office. The Myers had left town. A number of small items that had belonged to neighbors and businesses seemed to have left town along with them.

My heart ached for Henry. What chance was the boy to have? I prayed earnestly for him. At first he might have attended Wynn's class because he heard about the hikes and the canoe trips and the fishing, but I had hoped that he now came out of respect for Wynn. He knew that Wynn cared about him—perhaps the first person in his life who truly did.

Two nights later we were reading on one of those rare quiet evenings at home when there was a knock on our door. Wynn went to answer it and much to his amazement, Henry stood outside, shivering in the frigid night air.

Wynn hurried him in and I busied myself finding the boy something to eat. We asked no questions, but after Henry had eaten, he picked up his thin coat, mumbled his thanks, and headed for our door.

"Where are you going?" Wynn asked.

He hesitated to answer. Wynn decided to take another approach.

"I understood all your family had left town. Did they come back?"

He just shook his head.

"How did you get back then?" Wynn asked him.

He looked down uncomfortably and picked at the sleeve of his coat. "I didn't go," he finally offered. "When they said that they were goin', I ran out an' hid. They called around for a while an' then they just gave up an' left without me."

"So you are alone?"

He nodded.

"Where are you staying?"

"I was gonna stay in the house, but today some guys came an' boarded it all up, an' I can't get in."

"So you have no place?"

"I'll make out," he said, suddenly taking on a tough stance.

Wynn looked at me across the head of the young boy and I nodded in agreement.

"Tell you what," Wynn said, "we have that extra bedroom with no one in it. Why don't you just stay here?"

Henry looked too frightened to even talk.

"'Course," said Wynn, "we'd expect you to work for your board. You'd need to carry wood and haul water. We'd also expect you to go to school every day."

The boy still said nothing.

"In return, you'd get your clothes and your meals. Mrs. Delaney is a pretty good cook. Is it a deal?" asked Wynn.

Henry shuffled his feet. I had the feeling he was trying hard to keep a smile from appearing.

"Guess so," he answered.

"Might as well take your coat off and pull up to the fire then. Maybe we could talk Mrs. Delaney into making some popcorn."

The grin finally came in spite of Henry's reluctance.

31
Answers

A<small>T</small> FIRST IT seemed strange to have a young boy in the house. There were many things to do. Wynn had to report the whereabouts of the child and seek temporary legal custody so we could keep him.

I had to shop for clothes and make arrangements at the local school for consultation to determine the grade in which he should be placed. His attendance had been so sporadic before that they had not even attempted to place him.

I worked with him in the evenings to help him catch up to his age group, but even though he was bright enough and we worked hard, I knew it would be some time before he was where he should have been.

He loved Kip and coaxed to have the dog share his room. As Kip was used to being in the house in the cold winter, I gave in rather readily. I did insist that Kip's place be on the rug beside the bed rather than on the bed, and when we checked the room at night after the two had retired, Henry always slept with one hand resting on the dog, his fingers curled in the heavy fur.

He was quick to learn his assigned tasks and thankfully proved not to be lazy. He carried wood and water with no prompting from me, and even looked for additional jobs to do, knowing that it would bring our praise.

The calendar was quickly using up the winter months, and I looked forward to spring with mixed emotions. I knew it could mean we would be returning to the village. I longed to go. I missed our Indian friends. I had been praying daily that God would somehow open the door so we could return and help to share the good news of Christ's coming to earth to live and die for mankind. *How can they believe on Him in whom they have not heard*, I kept asking myself? How could they know that the evil they feared could be overcome through acceptance of God's great plan of salvation?

And yet when I thought about going back to the Indian people, I also thought of my Sunday school class. They, too, needed to know about Christ and His love. I thought about Willie's father who had lived in deep bitterness for so many years and now appeared to be slowly moving out of his self-exile. I thought about Wynn's boys and their need of making that personal commitment to the Lord Jesus. If we went, would there be anyone to teach them?

But more than all that, I thought about Henry, our little deserted waif. Who would care for Henry?

Wynn and I talked about it many times, but with no conclusion. We kept putting it off. I don't think either of us wanted to face the thought of giving up the boy. It was so much easier to push the decision off into the future.

At last, one mid-April day when the spring sun was pouring its warmth upon the hillsides, causing little rivulets to run trickling toward the groaning Athabasca River as it tried to free itself from her winter ice, we knew we needed to face squarely the question: What about Henry?

"He's trying so hard and he has come so far," I maintained.

Wynn agreed, though we both knew Henry still had many things to work through.

"I'm afraid if he faces another change right now, he might regress," I continued.

"Do you suppose Stephen's folks would take him?" proposed Wynn.

"They are a fine young couple, but I'm not sure they can handle their own," I stated quite honestly. "I feel that the girls are totally undisciplined. Henry still needs a very strong hand, and Stephen's father doesn't get involved at all, and his mother is not able to follow through."

"You're right," Wynn agreed. "That is exactly the way I see them."

"What about the Kellys?" I asked.

"Do you think that would be fair? After all, they are not young anymore. They are looking forward to retirement—not raising another family."

"I suppose it would be an imposition," I reluctantly agreed.

"I wonder if Phillip and Lydia would take him?" pondered Wynn.

"Don't forget they have added another two young ones to their own family in the last few years," I reminded him. "Lydia might have all that she can handle." I paused for a moment and then said thoughtfully, "Do you suppose Jon and Mary might be willing—?"

"I don't think Henry would like city life at all. He wouldn't fit in there. The school system—William and his friends? It would be a very difficult adjustment."

"Wynn," I said, "couldn't we take him with us to the village?"

"What about his education?"

"I could get the books and teach him."

"Yes, I suppose you could. But do you really think it would be the best for him? I mean, he wouldn't know the language, wouldn't fit in with the other boys. I think he needs more support than that, Elizabeth. And you know how much I need to be gone. You'd have so much of the care of him."

We both were quiet as we thought about it. It didn't seem like the Indian village was the right place for the boy.

"I'm afraid I just don't have the answer," admitted Wynn. "We'll have to keep praying."

We both agonized over Henry. It was so important that he have love and grounding in order to be taught the truths of the Gospel and make his own decision to follow the Lord.

And yet, our Indian people were important, too. They needed someone to take the Gospel to them—and they needed it now.

I tried to leave it all with the Lord. "Cast your burden upon the Lord," the Scripture said, and I cast it—and then I pulled it back—and then I cast it again. I was miserable with my worrying, and then one day in my quiet prayer time I became honest, totally honest before God.

"Lord," I said, "I am sick of worrying about Henry. Now I know that I am not the only person that You can minister through. I give Henry over to You, Lord. If You ask us to leave him with someone else, then I am going to trust You that his needs will be met and that You will care for him—physically and spiritually.

"Help me to truly release him to You, knowing that You love and care for him. And help me not to take this burden of Henry's care back on my own shoulders again.

"Amen."

I finally found release. And strangely enough, instead of Henry seeming less important to me, as I had feared might happen, I loved him even more deeply. Still I did not fret about what would happen when the new orders came from the Police Headquarters.

It was a Wednesday. Henry had come home from school, had his snack of cookies and milk, hurried through his chores with Kip fast on his heels, and then come to me with pleading in his eyes.

"Can I go over to the police office to play with the puppies and then walk home with Sergeant Wynn?" he asked me.

I wanted to correct him by saying, "May I," but I bit my tongue. Henry had so many things to learn that I must show patience.

He had developed a deep devotion for Wynn, and I knew it was good for him. I looked at the clock. I didn't want Henry getting in Wynn's way, but I knew he would be more than willing to play with the puppies until Wynn was ready to come home.

"I suppose you may," I told the eager Henry.

"Can I take Kip?" he asked next.

"Very well, take Kip. He needs a bit of a run. Make sure you keep him out of trouble. The sergeant won't take kindly to a dog fight in the street."

"I will," promised Henry, and he was off on a run, Kip bounding along ahead of him.

Henry had not been gone long when he was home again. He was all out of breath from his run, and his cheeks were flushed with excitement.

"Sergeant Wynn says to tell you that he will be another twenty minutes or so," he said, gasping for breath. "And he also said to tell you that we will have a guest for supper. A real live Indian. I saw him myself."

My excitement matched Henry's. Which one of our friends would be coming for supper? Was he from Beaver River or Smoke Lake? I could hardly wait to find out as I placed another plate on the table and checked to see if I would have enough meat and potatoes.

"I'm going back to walk home with them," said Henry, and he was off on a run again.

The time seemed to drag as I waited for Wynn and his guest to come for supper. I looked at the clock and then the road, over and over again.

When they finally did come, it was a stranger Wynn brought with him.

"Elizabeth," he said, "I want you to meet Pastor Walking Horse. He is from the village south of Smoke Lake. He has been out taking his training to become a minister to his own people."

My heart gave a flip.

"A pleasure to meet you, Mrs. Delaney," said the young man, and then he switched to the Indian tongue. "It gives me great joy to be a guest at your table."

Oh, it was so good to hear the flowing language again! I took his hand and shook it as the white man greets a friend, but my heart was crying out to him in the words of the Indian.

I welcome you to my fire, the words formed in my mind. *My heart is glad for your presence. You make my joy increase as flowers after winter snows, and my soul sings like ripples of a brook with gladness.*

Henry was excited about sitting at the table with a real Indian. Wynn had told him much about the wisdom and the knowledge of the people in their own environment, and Henry had developed a healthy respect for them.

He listened now with Wynn and me as the young man explained how he had become acquainted in a personal way with the God of the Bible, and had cast aside all of the superstitious teachings of his forefathers in order to follow Him.

His desire now, he said, was to teach his people, and so he had gone out to take training and was ready to go back and challenge his people with the truth.

"My heart aches within me," he said sorrowfully, "because when I left my village to go to the white man's school, my chief said I would no longer be welcomed back, so I must go to another settlement to start my work."

"Ours," I said at once. "Ours. They are wonderful people, and they are ready, I'm sure. We have been praying and praying for someone to go to them. You are the answer to our prayers."

The man was almost as excited about this news as I was.

We talked on and on about the village and the people. Henry was finally scooted off to bed. He obeyed, but he went reluctantly. He hated to miss one word of the conversation.

We talked until long into the night, and by the time we were finished and had prayed together, Pastor Walking Horse was convinced that Smoke Lake was the place where the Lord was leading him, especially with LaMeche already a believer. He would try to be ready to leave as soon as the road was fit to travel.

Two days later Wynn came home from the office with a telegram in his hands. The Force had sent his new orders.

Much to the surprise of both of us, we were told we would be staying on at Athabasca Landing for the present time. The young Mountie at Smoke Lake would continue there at his post.

It came as a surprise to me, and yet it shouldn't have. I committed Henry to the Lord because I thought He would need me to care for the Indians. God had answered by preparing and sending a qualified young minister to the Indians and leaving Henry with me. I smiled. *One should never try to outguess the Lord*, I reminded myself.

"Well," I said to Wynn, "I guess God took care of it all in His own way. We wouldn't have needed to fret about it at all."

Wynn smiled and then kissed me.

"Do you mind, Elizabeth?" he asked.

I thought about that. I would miss our people. I had been counting on going back—expecting to go back. But when I thought about it, I could answer honestly, "No, not really. It does seem best to stay for the present, doesn't it? The church needs us here. The Sunday school children need us. Then there is Henry. I expect great things from that boy someday, Wynn."

In a reflective moment I went on to answer Wynn's question.

"No, I don't mind. I guess I am quite content with God's direction in this."

I thought again about the village people.

"I will write a letter to Louis LaMeche and Silver Star," I said, "and send it with Pastor Walking Horse. I will tell Silver Star that she can have my garden. I will give them both our love and best wishes. Can I send her a few things—and Kinnea and Kinook, too?" I asked.

"I'm sure the pastor would be willing to take a few small gifts," said Wynn.

"You know," I pondered, "I might even write a short note to Chief Crow Calls Loud. Just a short note of introduction, telling him that he might be very interested in what Pastor Walking Horse has to say."

Wynn smiled again.

"So you will manage to run the village even from a distance, will you?" he teased.

I brushed aside his remark with a wave of my hand.

"Run it? No. But I certainly will continue to pray for those in it."

Then I turned to my cupboards.

"But right now I'd better get busy," I said, and there was love and joy in my voice. "I've a young boy due home from school in a few minutes, and he's always half-starved."